An Inspector Morse Omnibus

The other Inspector Morse mysteries

An Inspector Morse Omnibus

The Dead of Jericho
Service of all the Dead
The Silent World of Nicholas Quinn

Colin Dexter

M
MACMILLAN
LONDON

First published in Great Britain 1991 by
MACMILLAN LONDON LIMITED
4 Little Essex Street London WC2R 3LF
and Basingstoke

Reprinted 1990

Associated companies in Auckland, Delhi, Dublin, Gaborone, Hamburg,
Harare, Hong Kong, Johannesburg, Kuala Lumpur, Lagos, Manzini,
Melbourne, Mexico City, Nairobi, New York, Singapore and Tokyo

ISBN 0-333-54917-1

A CIP catalogue record for this book is available from the British Library

Typeset by Matrix, 21 Russell Street, London WC2

Printed by Billings Bookplan Ltd, Worcester

CONTENTS

For
Patricia and Joan,
kindly denizens of Jericho.

The Dead of Jericho

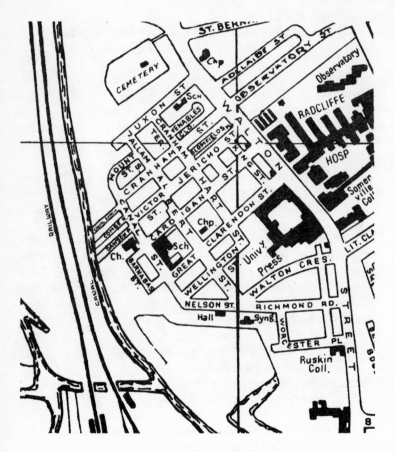

Street Plan of Jericho

Prologue

And I wonder how they should have been together
T. S. Eliot, *La Figlia che Piange*

Not remarkably beautiful, he thought. Not, that is to say, if one could ever measure the beauty of a woman on some objective scale: *sub specie aeternae pulchritudinis*, as it were. Yet several times already, in the hour or so that followed the brisk, perfunctory 'hullos' of their introduction, their eyes had met across the room – and held. And it was after his third glass of slightly superior red plonk that he managed to break away from the small circle of semi-acquaintances with whom he'd so far been standing.

Easy.

Mrs Murdoch, a large, forcefully optimistic woman in her late forties, was now pleasantly but firmly directing her guests towards the food set out on tables at the far end of the large lounge, and the man took his opportunity as she passed by.

'Lovely party!'

'Glad you could come. You must mix round a bit, though. Have you met – ?'

'I'll mix. I promise I will – have no fears!'

'I've told lots of people about you.'

The man nodded without apparent enthusiasm and looked at her plain, large-featured face. 'You're looking very fit.'

'Fit as a fiddle.'

'How about the boys? They must be' (he'd forgotten *what* they must be) 'er getting on a bit now.'

'Michael eighteen. Edward seventeen.'

'Amazing! Doing their exams soon, I suppose?'

'Michael's got his A levels next month.' ('Do please go along and help yourself, Rowena.')

'Clear-minded and confident, is he?'

'Confidence is a much over-rated quality – don't you agree?'

'Perhaps you're right,' replied the man, who had never previously considered the proposition. (But had he noticed a flash of unease in Mrs Murdoch's eyes?) 'What's he studying?'

'Biology. French. Economics.' ('That's right. Please do go along and help yourselves.')

'Interesting!' replied the man, debating what possible motives could have influenced the lad towards such a curiously uncomplementary combination of disciplines. 'And Edward, what's – ?'

He heard himself speak the words but his hostess had drifted away to goad some of her guests towards the food, and he found himself alone. The people he had joined earlier were now poised, plates in their hands, over the assortment of cold meats, savouries, and salads, spearing breasts of curried chicken and spooning up the cole slaw. For two minutes he stood facing the nearest wall, appearing earnestly to assess an amateurishly executed water-colour. Then he made his move. She was standing at the back of the queue and he took his place behind her.

'Looks good, doesn't it?' he ventured. Not a particularly striking or original start. But a start; and a sufficient one.

'Hungry?' she asked, turning towards him.

Was he hungry? At such close quarters she looked more attractive than ever, with her wide hazel eyes, clear skin, and lips already curved in a smile. *Was* he hungry?

'I'm a bit hungry,' he said.

'You probably eat too much.' She splayed her right hand lightly over the front of his white shirt, a shirt he had himself carefully washed and ironed for the party. The fingers were slim and sinewy, the long nails carefully manicured and crimsoned.

'Not too bad, am I?' He liked the way things were going, and his voice sounded almost schoolboyish.

She tilted her head to one side in a mock-serious assessment of whatever qualities she might approve in him. 'Not too bad,' she said, pouting her lips provocatively.

He watched her as she bent her body over the buffet table, watched the curve of her slim bottom as she leant far across to fork a few slices of beetroot – and suddenly felt (as he often felt) a little lost, a little hopeless. She was talking to the man just in front of her now, a man in his mid-twenties, tall, fair-haired, deeply-tanned, with hardly an ounce of superfluous flesh on his frame. And the older man shook his head and smiled ruefully. It had been a nice thought, but now he let it drift away. He was fifty, and age was just about beginning, so he told himself, to cure his heart of tenderness. Just about.

There were chairs set under the far end of the table, with a few square feet of empty surface on the white table-cloth; and he decided to sit and eat in peace. It would save him the indigestion he almost invariably suffered if he sat in an armchair and ate in the cramped and squatting postures that the other guests were happily adopting. He refilled his glass yet again, pulled out a chair, and started to eat.

'I think you're the only sensible man in the room,' she said, standing beside him a minute later.

'I get indigestion,' he said flatly, not bothering to look up at her. It was no good pretending. He might just as well be himself – a bit paunchy, more than a bit balding, on the cemetery side of the semi-century, with one or two unsightly hairs beginning to sprout in his ears. No! It was no use pretending. Go away, my pretty one! Go away and take your fill of flirting from that lecherous young Adonis over there!

'Mind if I join you?'

He looked up at her in her cream-coloured, narrow-waisted summer dress, and pulled out the chair next to him.

'I thought I'd lost you for the evening,' he said after a while.

She lifted her glass of wine to her lips and then circled the third finger of her left hand smoothly round the inner rim at the point from which she had sipped. 'Didn't you want to lose me?' she said softly, her moist lips close to his ear.

'No. I wanted to keep you all to myself. But then I'm a selfish beggar.' His voice was bantering, good humoured; but his clear blue eyes remained cold and appraising.

'You might have rescued me,' she whispered. 'That blond-headed bore across there – Oh, I'm sorry. He's not – ?'

'No. He's no friend of mine.'

'Nor mine. In fact, I don't really know anyone here.' Her voice had become serious, and for a few minutes they ate in silence.

'There's a few of 'em here wouldn't mind getting to know *you*,' he said finally.

'Mm?' She seemed relaxed again, and smiled. 'Perhaps you're right. But they're all such bores – did you know that?'

'I'm a bit of a bore myself,' the man said.

'I don't believe you.'

'Well, let's say I'm just the same as all the others.'

'What's that supposed to mean?' There were traces in her flat 'a's of some north country accent. Lancashire, perhaps?

'You want me to tell you?'

'Uh uh.'

Their eyes held momentarily, as they had done earlier; and then the man looked down at his virtually untouched plate of food. 'I find you very attractive,' he said quietly. 'That's all.'

She made no reply, and they got on with their eating, thinking their own thoughts. Silently.

'Not bad, eh?' said the man, wiping his mouth with an orange-coloured paper napkin, and reaching across for one of the wine bottles. 'What can I get you now, madame? There's er fresh fruit salad; there's cream gâteau; there's some sort of caramel whatnot – '

But as he made to rise she laid her hand on the sleeve of his jacket. 'Let's just sit here and talk a minute. I never seem to be able to eat and talk at the same time – like others can.'

Indeed, it appeared that most of the other guests were remarkably proficient at such simultaneous skills, for, as the man became suddenly aware, the large room was filled with the chatter and clatter of thirty or so other guests.

'Drop more wine?' he asked.

'Haven't I had enough?'

'As soon as you've had enough, it's time to have a little drop more.'

She laughed sweetly at him. 'Is that original?'

'I read it on the back of a match-box.'

She laughed again, and for a little while they drank their wine.

'You know what you just said about – about – '

'Finding you attractive?'

She nodded.

'What about it?'

'Why did you say it?'

The man shrugged in what he trusted was a casual manner. 'No call for any great surprise, is there? I expect hundreds of fellers have told you the same, haven't they? It's not your fault. The Almighty just happened to fashion you wondrously fair – that's all. Why not accept it? It's just the same with me: I happen to be blessed with the most brilliant brain in Oxford. I can't help that either, can I?'

'You're not answering my question.'

'No? I thought – '

'When you said you found me attractive, it wasn't just *what* you said. It was – it was the way you said it.'

'Which was?'

'I don't know. Sort of – well sort of nice, somehow, and sort of sad at the same time.'

'You shouldn't say "sort of" all the time.'

'I was trying to tell you something that wasn't easy to put into words, that's all. But I'll shut up if you want me to.'

He shook his head slowly. 'I dunno. You see where honesty gets you? I tell you I find you attractive. You know why? Because it does me good to look at you, and to sit next to you like this. And shall I tell you something else? I reckon you're getting more attractive all the time. Must be the wine.' His glass was empty again and he reached over for a bottle.

'Trouble with most men is that "attractive" just means one thing, doesn't it? Slip in between the sheets. Ta very much! Cheerio!'

'Nothing much wrong with that, is there?'

'Of course there isn't! But there *can* be more to it all than that, can't there?'

'I dunno. I'm no expert on that sort of thing. Wish I were!'

'But you can like a woman for what she *is*, can't you – as well as what she looks like?' She turned her head towards him, the dark hair piled high on top, and her eyes shone with an almost fierce tenderness.

'Will you just tell me – ?' He found himself swallowing hard in the middle of whatever he was going to say and he got no further. She had slipped her right hand under the table and he felt the long soft fingers slowly curling and entwining themselves with his own.

'Can you just pass that wine across a sec, old chap?' It was one of the older guests, red-faced, pot-bellied, and jovial. 'Sorry to barge in and all that, but a chap needs his booze, eh?'

Their hands had sprung guiltily apart and remained so, for

the other guests were now returning to the tables to make their choice of dessert.

'Do you think we'd better mix in again?' he asked, without conviction. 'We shall be causing a bit of comment if we're not careful.'

'That worry you?'

The man appeared to give his earnest attention to this question for a good many seconds; and then his face relaxed into a boyish grin. 'Do you know,' he said, 'I don't give a bugger. Why the hell shouldn't we sit together all night? Just tell me that, my girl! It's what *I* want. And if it's what *you* –'

'Which it is – as you know! So why not stop pretending, and go and get me some of that gâteau? And *here*!' She gulped down the rest of her wine. 'You can fill this up while you're at it – right to the top.'

After finishing their gâteaux, and after twice refusing the offer of coffee, he asked her to tell him something about herself. And she told him.

She'd been born in Rochdale, had been a hardworking and clever girl at school, and had won a place at Lady Margaret Hall to read modern languages. With a good second-class honours degree behind her, she had left Oxford and worked as the (sole) foreign sales rep of a smallish publishing company at Croydon, a company started from scratch a few years previously by two bright and reasonably ambitious brothers and dealing with text books in English as a foreign language. Just before she'd joined the company an increasing number of contracts had been coming in from overseas, and the need for some more effective liaison with foreign customers was becoming ever more apparent. Hence the appointment. Pretty good job, and not bad money either – especially for someone without the slightest experience in business matters. It had involved a good deal of necessary (and occasionally unnecessary) travel with the elder of the two brothers (Charles, the senior partner), and she had stayed in the job for eight years, enjoying it enormously. Business had boomed, the pay-roll had increased from ten to over twenty, new premises were built, new machinery purchased; and during this time, amid rumours of expenses fiddles and tax avoidance, the workforce had witnessed the arrival of the inevitable Rolls Royce, first a black one, then a light-blue one; and, for a favoured few, there was a spanking little beauty of a yacht moored somewhere up at Reading. Her own salary was each year – sometimes twice a year – increased, and when three years ago she had finally left the company she had amassed a nice little nest-egg of savings, certainly enough for her to envisage a reasonably affluent independence for several years to come. Why had she left? Difficult to say, really. Eight years was quite a long time, and even the most enjoyable job becomes a little less challenging, a little more – more familiar (was that the word?) as the years pass by, with colleagues seeming to grow more predictable and more . . . Oh! It didn't much matter *what* they grew! It was far simpler than that: she'd just wanted a change – that was all. So she'd had a change. At Oxford she'd read French and Italian, and through her work with the company she'd become comprehensively fluent in German. So? So she'd joined the staff of a very large (eighteen hundred!) comprehensive school in the east end of London – teaching German. The school was far rougher than she could have imagined. The boys were doubtless good enough at heart, but were blatantly and impertinently obscene, not infrequently (she suspected) exposing themselves on the back rows of their classes. But it was the girls who had been the real trouble, seeing in their new teacher a rival intruder, likely enough to snatch away the coveted affections of the boys and the male staff alike. The staff? Oh, some of them had tried things on a bit with her, especially the married ones; but they weren't a bad lot, really. They'd certainly been given a Herculean task in trying to cure, or at least to curb, the pervasive truancy, the mindless vandalism, and the sheer bloody-mindedness of those truculent adolescents to whom all notions of integrity, scholarship, or even the meanest of the middle-class virtues were equally foreign and repugnant. Well, she'd stuck it out for four terms; and looking back she wished she'd stuck it longer. The boys and girls in her own form had clubbed together generously to buy her an utterly *hideous* set of wine glasses; and those glasses were the most precious present she'd ever had! She'd cried when they made the presentation – all of them staying behind after final assembly, with one of the boys making a stupidly incompetent, facetious, *wonderful* little speech. Most of the girls had cried a bit, too, and even one or two of the inveterate exposers had been reduced to words of awkward farewell that were sad, and mildly grateful, and quite unbearably moving. Oh dear! Then? Well, she'd tried one or two other things and, finally – two years ago that is – she'd come back to Oxford, advertised for private pupils, got rather more offers than she could cope with, bought a small house – and well, there she was! There she was at the party.

She'd missed something out though – the man knew that. He remembered, albeit vaguely, how Mrs Murdoch had introduced her to him; remembered clearly the third finger on her left hand as she'd wiped the inside of her wine glass. Had she missed out a few other facts as well? But he said nothing. Just sat there, half bemused and more than half besotted.

It was just after midnight. The Murdoch boys had gone to bed and several of the guests had already taken their leave. Most of those who remained were drinking their second or third cups of coffee, but no one came up to interrupt the oddly assorted pair who still sat amidst the wreckage of the trifles and the flans.

'What about you?' she asked. 'You've managed to get me to do all the talking.'

'I'm not half as interesting as you are. I'm not! I just want to keep sitting here – next to you, that's all.'

He'd drunk a prodigious amount of wine, and his voice (as she noticed) was at last becoming slurred. 'Nesht to you, thas aw,' would be the more accurate phonetic equivalents of his last few words; and yet the woman felt a curiously compelling attraction towards this mellowing drunkard, whose hand now sought her own once more and who lightly traced his fingertips across her palm.

The phone rang at twenty minutes past one.

Mrs Murdoch placed her hand tactfully on his shoulder and spoke very quietly. 'Call for you.' Her keen eyes had noticed everything, of course; and she was amused and – yes! – quite pleased that things were turning out so sweetly for the pair of them. Pity to interrupt. But, after all, he'd mentioned to her that he might be called away.

He picked up the receiver in the hallway. 'What? . . . Lewis? What the hell do you have to . . . ? Oh! . . . Oh! . . . All right.' He looked at his wrist-watch. 'Yes! Yes! I *said* so, didn't I?' He banged down the receiver and walked back into the lounge.

She sat just as he had left her, her eyes questioning him as he stood there. 'Anything wrong?'

'No, not really. It's just that I've got to be off, I'm afraid. I'm sorry – '

'But you've got time to see me home, haven't you? *Please!*'

'I'm sorry, I can't. You see, I'm on er on call tonight and – '

'Are you a doctor or something?'

'Policeman.'

'Oh, God!'

'I'm sorry – '

'You keep *saying* that!'

'Don't let's finish up like this,' he said quietly.

'No. That would be silly, wouldn't it? I'm sorry, too – for getting cross, I mean. It's just that . . . ' She looked up at him, her eyes now dull with disappointment. 'Perhaps the fates – '

'Nonsense! There's no such bloody thing!'

'Don't you believe in – ?'

'Can we meet again?'

She took a diary from her handbag, tore out a page from the back, and quickly wrote: 9 Canal Reach.

'The car's here,' said Mrs Murdoch.

The man nodded and turned as if to go. But he had to ask it. 'You're married, aren't you?'

'Yes, but – '

'One of the brothers in the company?'

Was it surprise? Or was it suspicion that flashed momentarily in her eyes before she answered him. 'No, it wasn't. I was married long before that. In fact, I was silly enough to get married when I was nineteen, but – '

A rather thick-set man walked into the lounge and came diffidently over to them. 'Ready, sir?'

'Yes.' He turned to look at her for the last time, wanting to tell her something, but unable to find the words.

'You've got my address?' she whispered.

He nodded. 'I don't know your name, though.'

'Anne. Anne Scott.'

He smiled – almost happily.

'What's *your* name?'

'They call me Morse,' said the policeman.

Morse fastened his safety-belt as the police car crossed the Banbury Road roundabout and accelerated down the hill towards Kidlington.

'Where do you say you're dragging me to, Lewis?'

'Woodstock Crescent, sir. Chap's knifed his missus in one of the houses there. No trouble, though. He came into the station a few minutes after he'd killed her.'

'Doesn't surprise you, Lewis, does it? In the great majority of murder cases the identity of the accused is apparent virtually from the start. You realise that? In about 40 per cent of such cases he's arrested, almost immediately, at or very near the scene of the crime – usually, and mercifully for the likes of you, Lewis, because he hasn't made the slightest effort to escape. Now – let me get it right – in about 50 per cent of cases the victim and the accused have had some prior relationship with each other, often a very close relationship.'

'Interesting, sir,' said Lewis as he turned off left just opposite the Thames Valley Police HQ. 'You been giving another one of your lectures?'

'It was all in the paper this morning,' said Morse, surprised to find how soberly he'd spoken.

The car made its way through a maze of darkened side streets until Morse saw the flashing blue lights of an ambulance outside a mean-looking house in Woodstock Crescent. He slowly unfastened his seat-belt and climbed out. 'By the way, Lewis, do you know where Canal Reach is?'

'I think so, yes, sir. It's down in Oxford. Down in Jericho.'

BOOK ONE

Chapter One

A certain man went down from Jerusalem to Jericho
St Luke x. 30

Oxford's main tourist attractions are reasonably proximate to one another and there are guide books a-plenty, translated into many languages. Thus it is that the day visitor may climb back into his luxury coach after viewing the fine University buildings clustered between The High and the Radcliffe Camera with the gratifying feeling that it has all been a compact, interesting visit to yet another of England's most beautiful cities. It is all very splendid: it is all a bit tiring. And so it is fortunate that the neighbouring Cornmarket can offer to the visitor its string of snack bars, coffee bars and burger bars in which to rest his feet and browse through his recently purchased literature about those other colleges and ecclesiastical edifices, their dates and their benefactors, which thus far have fallen outside his rather arbitrary circumambulations. But perhaps by noon he's had enough, and quits such culture for the Westgate shopping complex, only a pedestrian precinct away, and built on the old site of St Ebbe's, where the city fathers found the answer to their inner-city obsolescence in the full-scale flattening of the ancient streets of houses, and their replacement by the concrete giants of supermarket stores and municipal offices. *Solitudinem faciunt: architecturam appellant.*
But further delights there are round other corners – even as the guide books say. From Cornmarket, for example, the visitor may turn left past the Randolph into the curving sweep of the Regency houses in Beaumont Street, and visit the Ashmolean there and walk round Worcester College gardens. From here he may turn

15

northwards and find himself walking along the lower stretches of Walton Street into an area which has, thus far, escaped the vandals who sit on the City's planning committees. Here, imperceptibly at first, but soon quite unmistakably, the University has been left behind, and even the vast building on the left which houses the Oxford University Press, its lawned quadrangle glimpsed through the high wrought-iron gates, looks bleakly out of place and rather lonely, like some dowager duchess at a discotheque. The occasional visitor may pursue his way even further, past the red and blue lettering of the Phoenix cinema on his left and the blackened-grey walls of the Radcliffe Infirmary on his right; yet much more probably he will now decide to veer again towards the city centre, and in so doing turn his back upon an area of Oxford where gradual renewal, sensitive to the needs of its community, seems finally to have won its battle with the bulldozers.

This area is called Jericho, a largely residential district, stretching down from the western side of Walton Street to the banks of the canal, and consisting for the most part of mid-nineteenth century, two-storey, terraced houses. Here, in the criss-cross grid of streets with names like 'Wellington' and 'Nelson' and the other mighty heroes, are the dwellings built for those who worked on the wharves or on the railway, at the University Press or at Lucy's iron foundry in Juxon Street. But the visitor to the City Museum in St Aldates will find no *Guide to Jericho* along the shelves; and even by the oldest of its own inhabitants, the provenance of that charming and mysterious name of 'Jericho' is variously – and dubiously – traced. Some claim that in the early days the whistle of a passing train from the lines across the canal could make the walls come tumbling down; others would point darkly to the synagogue in Richmond Road and talk of sharp and profitable dealings in the former Jewish quarter; yet others lift their eyes to read the legend on a local inn: 'Tarry ye at Jericho until your beards be grown'. But the majority of the area's inhabitants would just look blankly at their interlocutors, as if they had been asked such obviously unanswerable questions as why it was that men were born, or why they should live or die, and fall in love with booze or women.

It was on Wednesday, October 3rd, almost exactly six months after Mrs Murdoch's party in North Oxford, that Detective Chief Inspector Morse of the Thames Valley Police was driving from

Kidlington to Oxford. He turned down into Woodstock Road, turned right into Bainton Road, and then straight down into Walton Street. As he drove the Jaguar carefully through the narrow street, with cars parked either side, he noticed that *Sex in the Suburbs* was on at the Phoenix; but almost simultaneously the bold white lettering of a street sign caught his eye and any thoughts of an hour or two of technicolour titillation were forgotten: the sign read 'Jericho Street'. He'd thought of Anne Scott occasionally – of course he had! – but the prospect of a complicated liaison with a married woman had not, in the comparatively sober light of morning, carried quite the same appeal it had the night before; and he had not pursued the affair. But he was thinking of her now . . .

That morning, in Kidlington, his lecture on Homicide Procedures to a group of earnest, newly-fledged detectives (Constable Walters amongst them) had been received with a polite lack of enthusiasm, and Morse knew that he had been far from good. How glad he was to have the afternoon free! Furthermore, for the first time in many months he had every reason to be in the precincts of Jericho. As a member of the Oxford Book Association he had recently received advanced notice of a talk (Oct. 3rd, 8 p.m.) by Dame Helen Gardner on *The New Oxford Book of English Verse*; and the prospect of hearing that distinguished Oxford academic was quite sufficient in itself to stir an idle Morse to his first attendance of the year. But, in addition, the Association's committee had appealed to all members for any old books that might be finished with, because before Dame Helen's talk a sale of secondhand books had been arranged in aid of the Association's languishing funds. The previous night, therefore, Morse had decimated his shelves, selecting those thirty or so paperbacks which now lay in a cardboard box in the boot of the Jaguar. All books were to be delivered to the Clarendon Press Institute in Walton Street (where the Association held its meetings) between 3 p.m. and 5 p.m. that day. It was now twenty-five minutes past three.

For very good reasons, however, the delivery of Morse's offerings was temporarily postponed. Just before the OUP building, Morse turned right and drove slowly down Great Clarendon Street, crossed a couple of intersections, and noticed Canal Street on his right. Surely she must live somewhere very close?

It had been raining intermittently all day, and heavy spots were spattering his windscreen as he turned into the deserted street and looked around for parking space. Difficult, though. Double yellow lines on one side of the street, with a row of notices on the other – a series of white P's set against their blue backgrounds: 'Resident Permit Holders Only'. True, there was a gap or two here and there; but with a stubborn law-abiding streak within him – and with the added risk of a hefty parking fine – Morse drove on slowly round the maze of streets. Finally, beneath the towering Italianate campanile of St Barnabas' Church, he found an empty space in a stretch of road by the canal, marked off with boxed white lines: 'Waiting limited to 2 hours. Return prohibited within 1 hour'. Morse backed carefully into the space and looked around him. Through an opened gate he glimpsed the blues, browns, and reds of a string of house-boats moored alongside the canal, whilst three unspecified ducks, long-necked and black against the late-afternoon sky, flapped away noisily towards a more northerly stretch of water. He got out of the car and stood in the rain awhile, looking up at the dirtyish yellow tower that dominated the streets. A quick look inside, perhaps? But the door was locked, and Morse was reading the notice explaining that the regrettable cause of it all was adolescent vandalism when he heard the voice behind him.

'Is this your car?'

A young, very wet traffic warden, the yellow band round her hat extremely new, was standing beside the Jaguar, trying bravely to write down something on a bedrenched page of her notebook.

'All right, aren't I?' mumbled Morse defensively, as he walked down the shallow steps of the church towards her.

'You're over the white line and you'll have to back it up a bit. You've plenty of room.'

Morse dutifully manoeuvred the Jaguar until it stood more neatly within its white box, and then wound down the window. 'Better?'

'You ought to lock your doors if you're going to stay here – two hours, remember. A lot of cars get stolen, you know.'

'Yes, I always lock – '

'It wasn't locked just now!'

'I was only seeing if . . . '

But the young lady had walked on, apparently unwilling to

discuss her edicts further, and was writing out a sodden ticket for one of the hapless non-permit holders just a little way up the street when Morse called out to her.

'Canal Reach? Do you know it?'

She pointed back up to Canal Street. 'Round the corner. Third on the left.'

In Canal Street itself, two parking tickets, folded in cellophane containers, and stuck beneath the windscreen wipers, bore witness to the conscientious young warden's devotion to her duties; and just across the road, on the corner of Victor Street, Morse thought he saw a similar ticket on the windscreen of an incongruously large, light-blue Rolls Royce. But his attention was no longer focused on the problems of parking. A sign to his left announced 'Canal Reach'; and he stopped and wondered. Wondered why exactly he was there and what (if anything) he had to say to her . . .

The short, narrow street, with five terraced houses on either side, was rendered inaccessible to motor traffic by three concrete bollards across the entrance, and was sealed off at its far end by the gates of a boat-builder's yard, now standing open. Bicycles were propped beside three of the ten front doors, but there was little other sign of human habitation. Although it was now beginning to grow dark, no light shone behind any of the net-curtained windows, and the little street seemed drab and uninviting. These were doubtless some of the cheaper houses built for those who once had worked on the canal: two up, two down – and that was all. The first house on the left was number 1, and Morse walked down the narrow pavement, past number 3, past number 5, past number 7 – and there he was, standing in front of the last house and feeling strangely nervous and undecided. Instinctively he patted the pocket of his raincoat for a packet of cigarettes, but found he must have left them in the car. Behind him, a car splashed its way along Canal Street, its side-lights already switched on.

Morse knocked, but there was no answer. Just as well, perhaps? Yet he knocked again, a little louder this time, and stood back to look at the house. The door was painted a rust-red colour, and to its right was the one downstairs window, its crimson curtains drawn across; and just above it, the window of the first floor bedroom where – Just a minute! There *was* a light. There was a light *here*. It seemed to Morse that the bedroom door must be open, for he could see a dull glow of light coming from somewhere: coming from the other room across the landing, perhaps? Still he stood there in the drizzling rain and waited, noting as he did so the attractive brickwork of the terrace, with the red stretchers alternating in mottled effect with the grey-blue contrast of the headers.

But no one answered at the rust-red door.

Forget it? It was stupid, anyway. He'd swallowed rather too much beer at lunch time, and the slight wave of eroticism which invariably washed over him after such mild excess had no doubt been responsible for his drive through Jericho that day . . . And then he thought he heard a noise from within the house. She *was* there. He knocked again, very loudly now, and after waiting half a minute he tried the door. It was open.

'Hello? Anyone there?' The street door led directly into the surprisingly large downstairs room, carpeted and neatly decorated, and the camera in Morse's mind clicked and clicked again as he looked keenly around.

'Hello? Anne? *Anne?*'

A staircase faced him at the far left-hand corner of the room, and at the foot of the stairs he saw an expensive-looking, light-brown leather jacket, lined with sheep's wool, folded over upon itself, and flecked with recent rain.

But even leaning slightly forward and straining his ears to the utmost, Morse could hear nothing. It was strange, certainly, her leaving the door unlocked like that. But then he'd just done exactly the same with his own car, had he not? He closed the door quietly behind him and stepped out on to the wet pavement. The house immediately opposite to him was number 10, and he was reflecting vaguely on the vagaries of those responsible for the numbering of street houses when he thought he saw the slightest twitch of the curtains behind its upper-storey window. Perhaps he was mistaken, though . . . Turning once more, he looked back at the house he had come to visit, and his thoughts lingered longingly on the woman he would never see again . . .

It was many seconds later that he noticed the change: the light on the upstairs floor of number 9 was now *switched off* – and the blood began to tingle in his veins.

Chapter Two

Towards the door we never opened
T. S. Eliot, *Four Quartets*

She seemed on nodding terms with all the great, and by any
standards the visit of Dame Helen, emeritus Merton Professor
of English Literature, to the Oxford Book Association was an
immense success. She wore her learning lightly, yet the depths
of scholarship and sensitivity became immediately apparent to
the large audience, as with an assurance springing from an
infinite familiarity she ranged from Dante down to T. S. Eliot.
The texture of the applause which greeted the end of her lecture
was tight and electric, the crackling clapping of hands seeming
to constitute a continuous crepitation of noise, the palms smiting
each other as fast as the wings of a humming bird. Even Morse,
whose applause more usually resembled the perfunctory flapping
of a large crow in slow flight, was caught up in the spontaneous
appreciation, and he earnestly resolved that he would make an
immediate attempt to come to terms with the complexities of the
Four Quartets. He ought, he knew, to come along more often to
talks such as this; keep his mind sharp and fresh – a mind so often
dulled these days by cigarettes and alcohol. Surely that's what life
was all about? Opening doors; opening doors and peering through
them – perhaps even finding the rose gardens there . . . What
were those few lines that Dame Helen had just quoted? Once he
had committed them to memory, but until tonight they had been
almost forgotten:

> Footfalls echo in the memory
> Down the passage which we did not take
> Towards the door we never opened.

That was writing for you! Christ, ah!

Morse recognised no one at the bar and took his beer over
to the corner. He would have a couple of pints and get home
reasonably early.

The siren of a police car (or was it an ambulance?) whined
past outside in Walton Street, reminding him tantalisingly of the

opening of one of the Chopin nocturnes. An accident somewhere, no doubt: shaken, white-faced witnesses and passengers; words slowly recorded in constables' notebooks; the white doors of the open ambulance with the glutinous gouts of dark blood on the upholstery. Ugh! How Morse hated traffic accidents!

'You look lonely. Mind if I join you?' She was a tall, slim, attractive woman in her early thirties.

'Delighted!' said a delighted Morse.

'Good, wasn't she?'

'Excellent!'

For several minutes they chatted happily about the Dame, and Morse, watching her large, vivacious eyes, found himself hoping she might not go away.

'I'm afraid I don't know you,' he said.

She smiled bewitchingly. 'I know you, though. You're Inspector Morse.'

'How – ?'

'It's all right. I'm Annabel, the chairman's wife.'

'Oh!' The monosyllable was weighted flat with disappointment.

Another siren wailed its way outside on Walton Street, and Morse found himself trying to decide in which direction it was travelling. Difficult to tell though . . .

A few minutes later the bearded chairman pushed his way through from the crowded bar to join them. 'Ready for another drink, Inspector?'

'No – no. Let me get you one. My pleasure. What will you have – ?'

'You're not getting anything, Inspector. I would have bought you a drink earlier but I had to take our distinguished speaker back to Eynsham.'

When the chairman came back with the drinks, he turned immediately to Morse. 'Bit of a traffic jam outside. Some sort of trouble down in Jericho, it seems. Police cars, ambulance, people stopping to see what's up. Still, you must know all about that sort of thing, Inspector.'

But Morse was listening no longer. He got to his feet, mumbling something about perhaps being needed; and leaving his replenished pint completely ungulped walked swiftly out of the Clarendon Press Institute.

Turning left into Richmond Road, he noticed with a curiously disengaged mind how the street lights, set on alternate sides at intervals of thirty yards, bent their heads over the street like guardsmen at a catafalque, and how the houses not directly illuminated by the hard white glow assumed a huddled, almost cowering appearance, as if somehow they feared the night. His throat was dry and suddenly he felt like running. Yet with a sense of the inevitable, he knew that he was already far too late; guessed, with a heavy heart, that probably he'd always been too late. As he turned into Canal Street – where the keen wind at the intersection tugged at his thinning hair – there, about one hundred yards ahead of him, there, beneath the looming, ominous bulk of St Barnabas' great tower, was an ambulance, its blue light flashing in the dark, and two white police cars pulled over on to the pavement. Some three or four deep, a ring of local residents circled the entrance to the street, where a tall, uniformed policeman stood guard against the central bollard.

'I'm afraid you can't – ' But then he recognised Morse. 'Sorry, sir, I didn't – '

'Who's looking after things?' asked Morse quietly.

'Chief Inspector Bell, sir.'

Morse nodded, his eyes lowered, his thoughts as tangled as his hair. He walked along Canal Reach, tapped lightly on the door of number 9, and entered.

The room seemed strangely familiar to him: the settee immediately on the right, the electric fire along the righthand wall; then the TV set on its octagonal mahogany table, with the two armchairs facing it; on the left the heavy-looking sideboard with the plates upon it, gleaming white with cherry-coloured rings around their sides; and then the back door immediately facing him, just to the right of the stairs and exactly as he had seen it earlier that very day. All these details flashed across Morse's mind in a fraction of a second and the two sets of photographs seemed to fit perfectly. Or almost so. But before he had time to analyse his recollections, Morse was aware of a very considerable addition to the room in the form of a bulky, plain-clothes man whom Morse thought he vaguely remembered seeing very recently.

'Bell's here?'

'In there, sir.' The man pointed to the back door, and Morse felt the old familiar sensation of the blood draining down to his shoulders. 'In there?' he asked feebly.

'Leads to the kitchen.'

Of course it did, Morse saw that now. And doubtless there would be a small bathroom and WC behind that, where the rear of the small house had been progressively extended down into the garden plot at the rear, like so many homes he knew. He shook his head weakly and wondered what to do or say. Oh, God! What *was* he to do?

'Do you want to go in, sir?'

'No – o. No. I just happened to be around here – er, at the Clarendon Institute, actually. Talk, you know. We er we've just had a talk and I just happened . . . '

'Nothing we can do, I'm afraid, sir.'

'Is she – is she dead?'

'Been dead a long time. The doc's in there now and he'll probably – '

'How did she die?'

'Hanged herself. Stood on a – '

'How did you hear about it?'

'Phone call – anonymous one, sir. That's about the only thing that's at all odd if you ask me. You couldn't have seen her from the back unless – '

'She leave a note?'

'Not found one yet. Haven't looked much upstairs, though.'

What do you do, Morse? What do you *do*?

'Was – er – was the front door open?'

The constable (Morse remembered him now – Detective Constable Walters) looked interested. 'Funny you should ask that, sir, because it *was* open. We just walked straight in – same as anybody else could've done.'

'Was that door locked?' asked Morse, pointing to the kitchen.

'No. We thought it was though, first of all. As you can see, sir, it's sagging on its hinges and what with the damp and all that it must have stuck even more. A real push, it needed!'

He took a step towards the door as though about to illustrate the aforesaid exertion, but Morse gestured him to stop. 'Have you moved anything in here?'

'Not a thing, sir – well, except the key that was on the middle of the door-mat there.'

Morse looked up sharply. 'Key?'

'Yes, sir. Newish-looking sort of key. Looked as if someone

had just pushed it through the letter box. It was the first thing we saw, really.'

Morse turned to go, and on the light-green Marley tiles beside the front door saw a few spots of brownish rain-water. But the gentleman's black umbrella he'd seen there earlier had gone.

'Have you moved anything here, constable?'

'You just asked me that, sir.'

'Oh yes. I – I was just thinking er – well, you know, just thinking.'

'Sure you don't want to have a word with Chief Inspector Bell, sir?'

'No. As I say, I just happened . . . ' Morse's words trailed off into feeble mumblings as he opened the door on to the street and stood there hesitantly over the door-sill. 'You haven't been upstairs yet, you say?'

'Well, not really, sir. You know, we just looked in – '

'Were there any lights on?'

'No, sir. Black as night up there, it was. There's two rooms leading off the little landing . . . '

Morse nodded. He could visualise the first-floor geography of the house as well as if he'd stayed there – as he might well have stayed there once, not all that long ago; might well have made love in one of the rooms up there himself in the arms of a woman who was now stretched out on the cold, tiled floor of the kitchen. Dead, dead, dead. And – oh Christ! – she'd hanged herself, they said. A warm, attractive, living, loving woman – and she'd hanged herself. Why? Why? Why? For Christ's sake, *why*?

As he stood in the middle of the narrow street, Morse was conscious that his brain had virtually seized up, barely capable for the moment of putting two consecutive thoughts together. Lights were blazing behind all the windows except for those of number 10, immediately opposite, against which darkened house there stood an ancient bicycle, with a low saddle and upright handle-bars, firmly chained to the sagging drainpipe. Three slow paces and Morse stood beside it, where he turned and looked up again at the front bedroom of number 9. No light, just as the constable had said. No light at all . . . Suddenly, Morse found himself sniffing slightly. Fish? He heard a disturbance in the canal behind the Reach as some mallard splashed down into the water. And then he turned and sniffed specifically at the cycle. Fish! Yes, quite certainly it was fish. Someone had brought some fish home from somewhere.

Morse was conscious of many eyes upon him as he edged his way through the little crowd conversing quietly with one another about the excitement of the night. He turned right to retrace his steps and spotted the telephone kiosk – empty. For no apparent reason he pulled open the stiff door and stepped inside. The floor was littered with waste paper and cigarette stubs, but the instrument itself appeared unvandalised. Picking up the receiver, he heard the buzzing tone, and was quietly replacing it when he noticed that the blue telephone directory was lying open on the little shelf to his right. His eyes were no longer as keen as they once had been, and the light was poor; but the bold black print stood out clearly along the top of the pages: Plumeridge – Pollard – Pollard – Popper. And then – he saw the big capitals in the middle of the right-hand page: POLICE. And under the Police entries he could just make out the familiar details, including one that caught and held his eye: Oxford Central, St Aldates, Oxford 49881. And there was something else, too – or was he imagining it? He sniffed closely at the open pages, and again the blood was tingling across his shoulders. He was right – he knew it! *There was the smell of fish.*

Morse walked away from Jericho then, across Walton Street, across Woodstock Road, and thence into Banbury Road and up to his bachelor apartment in North Oxford, where he slumped into an armchair and sat unmoving for almost an hour. He then selected the Barenboim recording of the Mozart Piano Concerto number 21, switched on the gramophone to 'play', and sought to switch his mind away from all terrestrial troubles as the etherial Andante opened. Sometimes, this way, he almost managed to forget.

But not tonight.

Chapter Three

We saw a knotted pendulum, a noose: and a strangled
woman swinging there

Sophocles, *Oedipus Rex*

When Constable Walters closed the door, his eyes were puzzled,
and the slight frown on his forehead was perpetuated for several
minutes as he recalled the strange things that Morse had asked
him. He'd heard of Morse many times, of course, albeit Morse
worked up at the Thames Valley HQ in Kidlington whilst he
himself was attached to the City force in St Aldates. Indeed,
that very morning he'd heard Morse giving a lecture: just a
little disappointing that had been, though. People said what an
eccentric, irascible old sod he could be; they also said that he'd
solved more murders than anyone else for many leagues around,
and that the gods had blessed him with a brain that worked as
swiftly and as cleanly as the lightning.

'Chief Inspector Morse was here a few minutes ago.'

Bell, a tall, black-haired man, looked across at Walters with
a mixture of suspicion and distaste. 'What the 'ell did he want?'

'Nothing really, sir. He just asked – '

'What the 'ell was he *doing* here?'

'Said he'd been to some do at the Clarendon Institute or
something. I suppose he must have heard about it.'

Bell's somewhat dour features relaxed into a hint of a grin,
but he said nothing.

'Do you know him well, sir?'

'Morse? Ye-es, I suppose you could say that. We've worked
together once or twice.'

'They say he's an odd sort of chap.'

'Bloody odd!' Bell shook his head slowly from side to side.

'They say he's clever, though.'

'Clever?' The tone of voice suggested that Bell was not firmly
convinced of the allegation; but he was an honest man. 'Cleverest
bugger I've ever met. I'm not saying he's always right, though –
God, no! But he usually seems to be able to see things, I don't
know, half a dozen moves ahead of most of us.'

'Perhaps he's a good chess player.'

'Morse? He's never pushed a pawn in his life! Spends most of his free time in the pubs – or listening to his beloved Wagner.'

'He never got married, did he?'

'Too lazy and selfish to be a family man, I reckon. But – ' Bell stopped and his eyes suddenly looked sharp. 'Perhaps you'd like to tell me, would you, Walters, exactly what this sudden interest in Morse is all about?'

As well as he could remember them, Walters repeated the questions that Morse had asked him; and Bell listened in silence, his face showing no outward sign of interest or surprise. The fact of the front door being open was certainly a bit unusual, he realised that; and there was, of course, the question of who it was who'd rung the police and how it was that he (or she?) had come to find the grim little tragedy enacted in the kitchen behind him. Still, these were early hours yet, and many things would soon be clear. And what if they weren't? It could hardly matter very much either way, for everything was so pathetically simple. She'd made a neatly womanish job of fashioning a noose from strands of household twine, fastened the end to a ceiling-hook, fixed deep into the joist above to support a clothes-rack; then stood on a cheap-looking plastic-covered stool – and hanged herself, immediately behind the kitchen door. It wasn't all that uncommon. Bell had read the reports some dozens of times: 'Death due to asphyxia caused by hanging. Verdict: suicide.' And he was an experienced enough officer – a good enough one, too – to know exactly what had happened here. No note, this time; but sometimes there was, and sometimes there wasn't. Anyway, he'd not yet had the opportunity of searching the other rooms at all thoroughly; and there was every chance, especially in that back bedroom, that he'd find something to help explain it all. Just the one thing that was really worrying – just the one thing; and he was going to keep that to himself for the present. He'd said nothing to Walters about it, nothing to the police surgeon, nothing to the ambulance men – and, for the last hour, as things were slowly straightened out inside the kitchen, nothing much to himself, either. But it was very strange: how in heaven's name does a woman stand on a flimsy kitchen stool and then, at that terrible, irrevocable second of decision, kick it away from under her so that it lands, still standing four-square and upright, about two yards (well, 1.72 metres, according to his own careful measurement) from the suspended woman's left foot, itself dangling no more than a few inches above the white and orange floor-tiles? And that's where it *had* been, for it was Bell himself who had exerted his bulk against the sticking door, and there had been no stool immediately behind it: only a body, swaying slightly under the glaring light of the neon strip that stretched across the ceiling. A fluke, perhaps? Not that it affected matters unduly, though, since Bell was utterly convinced in his own mind (and the post mortem held the next morning was to corroborate his conviction) that Ms Anne Scott had died of asphyxiation caused by hanging. 'The police', as the *Oxford Mail* was soon to report, 'do not suspect foul play.'

'C'mon,' said Bell, as he walked over to the narrow, carpeted stairs. 'Don't touch anything until I tell you, right? Let's just hope we find a note or something in one of the rooms. It'd pull the threads together all nice and tidy like, wouldn't it?'

Bell himself, however, was to find no suicide note in the house that evening, nor any other note in any other place on any other evening. Yet there was at least one note which Anne Scott had written on the night before she died – a note which had been duly delivered and received . . .

From number 10 Canal Reach, George Jackson continued to watch the house opposite. He was now 66 years old, a sparely built man, short in stature, with a sharp-featured face, and rheumy, faded-blue eyes. For forty-two years he had worked at Lucy's iron foundry in neighbouring Juxon Street and then, three years since, with the foundry's order books half empty and with little prospect of any boom in the general economy, he had accepted a moderately generous redundancy settlement, and come to live in the Reach. He had a few local acquaintances – mostly one or two of his former work-mates; but no real friends. To many he appeared to exude an excessive meanness of soul, creating (as he did) the impression of being perpetually preoccupied with his own rather squalid self-interest. But he was not a particularly unpopular man, if only because he was good with his hands and had undertaken a good many little odd-jobs for his Jericho neighbours; and if the charges he made were distinctly on the steep side, nevertheless he was punctual, passably expeditious, and quite certainly satisfactory in his workmanship.

He was a fisherman, too.

Although he seldom drank much, Jackson stood at the back of his darkened front room that evening with a half-bottle of Teacher's whisky on the cupboard beside him and a tiny, grimy glass in his right hand. He had seen the police arrive: first two of them; then a doctor-looking man with a bag; then two other policemen; and after them a middle-aged man wearing a raincoat, a man with windswept, thinning hair, who was almost certainly a policeman, too, since he'd been admitted readily enough through the front door of the house opposite. *A man Jackson had seen before.* He'd seen him that very afternoon, and he felt more than a little puzzled . . . After that there'd been the ambulance men; then a good deal of activity with the lights throughout the house flicking on and off, and on and off again. And still he watched, slowly sipping the unwatered whisky and feeling far more relaxed, far less anxious than he'd felt a few hours earlier. Had anyone seen him? – that was his one big worry. But even that was now receding, and in any case he'd fabricated a neat enough little lie to cover himself.

It was 3 a.m. before the police finally left, and although the whisky bottle had long since been drained Jackson maintained his static vigil, his slow-moving mind mulling over many things. He felt hungry, and on a plate in the kitchen behind him lay the fish he'd caught that morning. But when at last he could see no further point in staying where he was, the two rainbow trout remained untouched and he climbed the stairs to the front bedroom, where he pulled the flimsy floral-patterned curtains, jerking them into an ill-fitting overlap across the window, before kneeling down by his bed, putting his hand beneath it, and sliding out a large pile of glossy, pornographic magazines. Then he slipped his hand still further beneath the bed – and drew out something else.

Earlier that same evening, in a posh-addressed and well-appointed bungalow on the outskirts of Abingdon, Mrs Celia Richards at last heard the crunch of gravel as the car drove up to the double garage. He was very late, and the chicken casserole had long been ready.

'Hello, darling. Sorry I'm so late. God! What a foul evening!'
'You might have let me know you were going to be – '
'Sorry, darling. Just said so, didn't I?' He sat down opposite her, reached to his pocket and pulled out a packet of cigarettes.

'You're not going to smoke just before we eat, surely?'

'All right.' He pushed a cigarette carefully back into its packet and stood up. 'Time for a quick drink though, isn't there, darling? I'll get them. What's yours? The usual?'

Celia suddenly felt a little more relaxed and – yes! – almost happy to see him again; felt a little guilty, too, for she had already drunk a couple of jumbo gins herself.

'You sit down, Charles, and have that cigarette. I'll get the drinks.' She forced herself to smile at him, fetched another gin for herself, a whisky for her husband, and then sat down once more.

'You see Conrad today?'

Charles Richards looked preoccupied and tired as he repeated the word absently: 'Conrad?'

'Isn't it the duty of your dear little brother Conrad, as co-partner in your dear little company – ?'

'*Conrad!* Sorry, yes, darling. I'm a bit whacked, that's all. Conrad's fine, yes. Sends his love, as always. Enjoyed his trip, he said. But the meeting finished at lunch time – well, the formal part of it – and then I had some er some rather delicate business to see to. That Swedish contract – you remember me telling you about it?'

Celia nodded vaguely over her gin and said nothing. Her momentary euphoria was already dissipated, and with a blank look of resignation she sank back into her armchair, an attractive, smartly-dressed, and wealthy woman on whom the walls were slowly closing in. She knew, with virtual certainty, that Charles had been unfaithful to her in the past: it was an instinctive feeling – utterly inexplicable – but she felt she almost always *knew*. Had he been with another woman today? Dear God, could she be wrong about it all? Suddenly she felt almost physically sick with worry again: so many worries, and none greater than her awareness that she herself was quite certainly the cause of some of Charles's orgiastic escapades. Sex meant virtually nothing to her – never had – and for various reasons the pair of them had never seriously considered having children. Probably too late now, anyway, with her thirty-eighth birthday shortly coming up . . .

Charles had finished his whisky and she went out to the kitchen to serve the evening meal. But before she took the casserole out of the oven she saw the gentleman's black umbrella, opened and resting tentatively on two fragile points, in the broad passage-way that led to the rear door. The place for that (Charles could be so very fussy about some things!) was in the back of the Rolls – just as the place for her own little red one was in the back of the Mini. She furled the umbrella, walked quietly through into the double garage, flicked on the lights, opened a rear door of the Rolls, and placed the umbrella along the top of the back seats. Then she looked around quickly in the front of the car, sliding her hands down the sides of the beige leather upholstery, and looking into the two glove-compartments – both unlocked. Nothing. Not even the slightest trace of any scented lady lingering there.

It was almost half-past eight when they finished their meal – a meal during which Celia had spoken not a single word. Yet so many, many thoughts were racing madly round and round her mind. Thoughts that gradually centred specifically around one person: around Conrad Richards, her brother-in-law.

It was three quarters of an hour later that someone had rung the Police in St Aldates and told them to go to Jericho.

Chapter Four

I lay me down and slumber
And every morn revive.
Whose is the night-long breathing
That keeps a man alive?
A. E. Housman, *More Poems*

At exactly the same time that Bell and Walters were climbing the stairs in Canal Reach, Edward Murdoch, the younger of the two Murdoch brothers, was leaning back against his pillow with the light from his bedside table-lamp focused on the book he held in his hand: *The Short Stories of Franz Kafka*. Edward's prowess in German was not as yet distinguished and his interest in the language (until so recently) was only minimal; but during the previous summer term a spark of belated enthusiasm

had been kindled – kindled by Ms Anne Scott. Earlier in the
evening he had been planning the essay he had to write on
Das Urteil, but he needed (he knew) to look more closely at
the text itself before committing himself to print; and now he
had just finished re-reading the fifteen pages which comprised
that short story. His eyes lingered on the last brief paragraph
– so extraordinarily vivid and memorable as now he saw it: *In
diesem Augenblick ging uber die Brucke ein geradezu unendlicher
Verkehr*. In his mind the familiar words slipped fairly easily from
German into English: 'In this moment there went across the
bridge a' (he had difficulty over that *geradezu* in its context
and omitted it) 'a continuous flow of traffic'. Phew! That was
while the hero (hero?) of the story was hanging by his faltering
fingertips from the parapet, determined upon and destined for
his death by suicide, whilst the rest of the world, unknowing
and uncaring, passed him by, driving straight on across – Ah,
yes! That was the point of *geradezu*, surely? He pencilled a
note in the margin and closed the slim, orange volume, a cheap
white envelope (its brief note still inside) serving to mark the
notes at the back of the text. He put the book down on the
table beside him, pressed the light-switch off, lay on his back,
and allowed his thoughts to hover in the magic circle of the
night . . .

It was Anne Scott who dominated and monopolised those
thoughts. His elder brother, Michael, had told him one or two
stories about her, but surely *he*'d been exaggerating and roman-
ticising everything? It was often difficult to believe what Michael
said, and in this particular case quite out of the question until –
until last week, that was. And for the hundredth encore Edward
Murdoch re-enacted in his mind those few erotic moments . . .

The door had been locked the previous Wednesday afternoon,
and that was most unusual. With no bell to ring, he had at first
tapped gently in a pusillanimous attempt to make her hear. Then
he had rapped more sharply with his knuckles against the upper
panel and, with a child-like surge of relief, he was aware of a
stirring of activity within. A minute later he heard the scrape of
the key in the lock and the noisy twang as the key was turned –
and then he saw her there.

'Edward! Come in! Oh dear, I must have overslept for hours.'
Her hair, usually piled up high on the top of her head, was resting

on her shoulders, and she wore a long, loose-fitting dressing-gown, its alternating stripes of black, beige, brown, and white reminding Edward vaguely of the dress of some Egyptian queen. But it was her face that he noticed: radiant, smiling – and somehow almost *expectant*, as if she was so pleased to see him. Him! She fussed for a further second or two with her hair before standing back to let him in.

'Come upstairs, Edward. I shan't be a minute.' She laid her hand lightly on his arm and shepherdessed him up the stairs and into the back bedroom (the 'study', as she called it) where side by side they invariably sat at the roll-top desk while Edward ploughed his wobbling furrows through the fields of German literature. She came into the study with him now and, as she bent forward to turn on the electric fire, the front of her dressing-gown gaped wantonly open awhile, and he could see that she was naked beneath it. His thoughts clambered over one another in erotic confusion and the back of his mouth was like the desert as she left him there and walked across the little landing to the front bedroom.

She had been gone for two or three minutes when he heard her.

'Edward? *Edward?*'

Her bedroom door was half open, and the boy stood beside it, hesitant and gauche, until she spoke again.

'Come *in*! I'm not going to *bite* you, am I?'

She was standing, with her back towards him, at the foot of a large double-bed, folding a light-grey skirt round her waist, and for some inconsequential reason Edward was always to remember the inordinately large safety-pin fixed vertically at its hem. With her hands at her waist, tucking, fastening, buckling, he was also to remember her, in those few moments, for a far more obvious cause: above the skirt her body was completely bare, and as she turned her head towards him, he could see the swelling of her breast.

'Be a darling and nip down to the kitchen, will you, Edward? You'll find a bra on the clothes-rack – I washed it out last night. Bring it up, will you?'

As he walked down the stairs like some somnambulant zombie, Edward heard her voice again. 'The black one!' And when he returned to her room she turned fully towards him still naked above the waist, and smiled gratefully at him as he stood there, his eyes seemingly mesmerised as he stared at her.

'Haven't you seen a woman's body before? Now you be a good boy and run along – I'll join you when I've done my hair.'

Somehow he had struggled through that next three-quarters of an hour, fighting to wrench his thoughts away from her, and seeking with all his powers to come to grips with Kafka's tale *Das Urteil*; and he could still recall how movingly she'd dwelt upon that final, awesome, terrifying sentence . . .

He turned over on to his right side and his thoughts moved forward to the present, to the day that even now was dying as the clock ticked on to midnight. It had been a huge disappointment, of course, to find the note. The first of the household to arise, he had boiled the kettle, made himself two slices of toast, and listened to the 7 a.m. news bulletin on Radio 4. At about twenty-past seven the clatter of the front letter box told him that *The Times* had been pushed through; and when he went to fetch it he'd seen the small white envelope, face upwards, lying in the middle of the door-mat. It was unusually early for the mail to have been delivered, and in any case he could see immediately that the envelope bore no stamp. Picking it up he found that it was addressed to himself; and sticking an awkward forefinger under the sealed flap he opened it and read the few words written on the flimsy sheet inside.

And now, as he turned over once again, his mind wandered back to those words, and he eased himself up on his arm, pressed the switch on the bedside lamp, slid the envelope out of the text book, and read that brief message once more:

Dear Edward,
I'm sorry but I shan't be able to see you for our usual lesson today. Keep reading Kafka – you'll discover what a great man he was. Good luck!
    Yours,
    Anne (Scott)

He had never called her 'Anne' – always 'Miss Scott', and always slightly over-emphasising the 'Miss', since he was not at all in favour of the 'Ms' phenomenon; and even if he had been he would have felt self-conscious about pronouncing that ugly, muzzy monosyllable. Should he be bold next week – and call her 'Anne'? Next week . . . Had he been slightly brighter he might have been puzzled by that 'today', perhaps. Had he been slightly older than his seventeen years, he might, too, have marked the ominous note in that strangely final-sounding valediction. He might even have wondered whether she was thinking of going away somewhere: going away – perhaps for ever. As it was, he turned off the light and soon sank into a not-unpleasing slumber.

Morse awoke at 7.15 a.m. the following morning feeling taut and unrefreshed; and half an hour later, in front of the shaving-mirror, he said 'Bugger!' to himself. His car, he suddenly remembered, was still standing in the court of the Clarendon Institute, and he had to get out to Banbury by 9 a.m. There were two possibilities: he could either catch a bus down into Oxford; or he could ring Sergeant Lewis.

He rang Sergeant Lewis.

To Morse's annoyance, he found that a sticker had been obstinately glued to the Jaguar's windscreen, completely obscuring the driver's view. It was an official notice, subscribed by the Publisher of the Oxford University Press:

This is private property and you have no right to leave your vehicle here. Please remove it immediately. Note has been taken of your vehicle's registration number, and the Delegacy of the Press will not hesitate to initiate proceedings for trespass against you should you again park your vehicle within the confines of this property without official authorisation.

It was Lewis, of course, who had to scrape it off, whilst Morse asked vaguely, though only once, if he could do anything to help. Yet even now Morse's mind was tossing as ceaselessly as the sea, and it was at this very moment that there occurred to him an extraordinarily interesting idea.

Chapter Five

The mass of men lead lives of quiet desperation
Henry Thoreau

Detective Constable Walters had been impressed by Bell's professionalism after the finding of Anne Scott. The whole grisly gamut of procedures had been handled with a quiet and practised authority, from the initial handling of the swinging corpse through to the post-mortem and inquest arrangements. And Walters admired professionalism.

Upstairs in the two small bedrooms of 9 Canal Reach, Bell had shown (as it seemed to Walters) an enviable competence in sifting the relevant from the irrelevant and in making a few immediate decisions. The bed in the front room had not, it appeared, been slept in during the previous night, and after a quick look through the drawers of the dressing table and the wardrobe Bell had concluded that there was nothing there to detain him further. In the back room, however, he had stayed much longer. In the two bottom right-hand drawers of the roll-top desk they had found piles of letters in a state of moderate – though far from chaotic – confusion. At a recent stage, it appeared, Anne Scott had made an effort to sort some of the letters into vaguely definable categories and to tie them into separate bundles, since the bank statements from the previous two and a half years, conjoined with her mortgage receipts and electricity bills, were neatly stacked together and fastened with stout household twine, rather too thick for its modest purpose.

'Recognise that, Walters?' Bell had asked quietly, flicking his finger under the knot.

Two or three loops of the twine, also knotted, were to be seen loose amongst the scores and scores of envelopes, as though perhaps Ms Scott had recently been searching through the pre-tied bundles for some specific letters. Almost an hour had been spent on these two drawers, but Bell had finally left everything where it was. It was under the cover of the roll-top desk that he had found the only three items that held his attention: a recently dated letter headed from a Burnley address and subscribed 'Mum'; an address book; and a desk diary for the current year. Bell had looked through the address book with considerable care, but had finally laid it back on the desk without comment. The desk diary, however, he had handed to Walters.

'Should be helpful, my son!'

He had pointed to the entry for Tuesday, 2 October: 'Summertown Bridge Club 8 p.m.'; and then to the single entry for the following day, Wednesday, 3 October – the day that Anne Scott had died. The entry read: 'E.M. 2.30'.

When Walters reported to Bell on the Friday morning of the same week, he felt he'd done a good job. And so did Bell, for the picture was now pretty clear.

Anne Scott had been the only child of the Revd Thomas Enoch Scott, a minister in the Baptist Church (deceased some three and a half years previously) and Mrs Grace Emily Scott, presently living in Burnley. At the time of Anne's birth and throughout her childhood, the family had lived in Rochdale, where young Anne had been a pupil at Rochdale Grammar School, and where she had shown considerable academic prowess, culminating in her gaining a place at Lady Margaret Hall to read Modern Languages. Then the cream had turned sour. At Oxford, Anne had met a fellow undergraduate, a Mr John Westerby, had fallen in love with him, fallen into bed with him, and apparently forgotten to exercise any of her contraceptual options. The Revd Thomas, mortified by his beloved child's unforgivable lapse, had refused to have anything whatsoever to do with the affair, and had dogmatically maintained to the end his determination never to see his daughter again; never to recognise the existence of any child conceived in such fathoms of fornication. Anne had attended the funeral service when her father's faithful soul had solemnly been ushered into the joyous company of the saints, and she had been corresponding regularly with her mother since that time, occasionally travelling up to Lancashire to see her. Anne and John had been married at a registry office, she 19, he 20; and then, almost immediately it seemed, they had left Oxford at the beginning of one long summer vac – no one knowing where they went – and when Anne returned some three and a half months later she told her few friends that she and John had separated. The gap of the lost months could be filled in only with guesswork, but Walters suggested (and Bell agreed) that the time was probably

spent touting some back-street abortionist, followed by miserable
weeks of squabble and regret, and finally by a mutual acceptance of their incompatibility as marriage partners. After that,
Anne's career had been easy to trace and (in Walters' view) un-
exceptional to record. John Westerby was more of a mystery,
though. A Barnardo boy who had made good (or at least started
to make good) he had not finished his degree in Geography, and
after the break-up of his marriage had lived in a succession of
dingy digs in the Cowley Road area, carrying on a variety of jobs
ranging from secondhand car salesman to insurance agent. He
was well-liked by his landladies, popular enough with the girls,
generous with his money; but also somewhat withdrawn, a little
unpredictable, and – according to two former employers whom
Walters had interviewed – almost totally lacking in drive or ambition. Anyway, that was all hearsay now, for John Westerby, too,
was dead. He had been killed just over a year ago in a car crash
on the Oxford-Bicester road – one of those accidents where it
was difficult to apportion blame, although the inquest findings
revealed that the quantity of beer in Westerby's belly placed him
just beyond the limits of statutory sobriety. Unlike the young male
driver of the other car, he had not been wearing his safety-belt –
and his head had gone straight through the windscreen. *Finis.*
'Type it all up,' said Bell. 'Nobody'll read it – but get it
typed. There's not much else we can do.'
Bell had a busy day ahead of him. Two more burglaries overnight, one a wholesale clear-out in North Oxford; an appearance
before the magistrates' court in half an hour's time; lunch with
the Chairman of Oxford United to discuss the recurring hooli-
ganism of the club's ill-christened 'supporters'; and a good deal
of unfinished business from the past week. No, he could hardly
feel justified in allowing young Walters to worry much more about
what might have happened many years ago to a woman who had
just put herself out of whatever misery she was in. Anyway, Bell
had a secret respect for suicides . . . But he couldn't just leave
things where they were, he knew that. There was the inquest to
think about. *Why* had she done it? – that would be the question
nagging away in the minds behind those saddened, tense, and
self-recriminating faces. Oh dear! It was always the same old
questions. Was there anything that was worrying her? Anything
at all? Health troubles? Money troubles? Sex troubles? Family

troubles? Any bloody troubles? And the answer to most of these questions was always the same, too: it was 'yes', 'yes', 'yes', and so they all said 'no', 'no', 'no', because it seemed so much the kinder way. Bell shook his head sadly at his own thoughts. The real mystery to him was why so many of them thought fit to soldier on . . . He got up and lifted his overcoat from the hook behind the door.

'Any luck with "E.M."?'

'No, sir,' said Walters, with obvious disappointment. That Anne Scott had taken in several private pupils each week had been made perfectly clear to him, but there seemed to have been an *ad hoc* acceptance of fees in cash for the tutorials rendered. Certainly there was no formal record of names and receipts of monies, and doubtless the tax-man was far from well informed about the scope of Anne's activities. The neighbours had spoken of various visitors, usually young, usually with books, and almost always with bicycles. But such visits appeared to have been some- what spasmodic, and none of the neighbours could promise to recognise any of the callers again, let alone recall their names. Pity! Walters was slowly coming to terms with the sheer volume of work associated with even the most mundane enquiries; beginning, too, to appreciate the impossibility of following up every little clue. Yet, all the same, he would have been much gratified to have come up with a name (if it was a name) for those tantalising initials.

He found Bell looking at him with a half-smile on his lips.

'Forget it, Walters! It was probably the electricity man! And just let me tell you one thing, my lad. That woman committed suicide – you can take the word of a man who's been finding 'em like that for the last twenty years. There is no way, *no way*, in which that suicide could have been rigged – have you got that? So. What are we left with? *Why* she did it, all right? Well, we may learn a few things at the inquest, but I doubt we're ever going to know for cer- tain. It's usually cumulative, you know. A bit of disappointment and worry over this and that, and you sort of get a general feeling of depression about life that you just can't shake off, and some- times you feel why the hell should you try to shake it off anyway.' Bell shrugged on his coat and stood holding the door-handle. 'And don't you go running around with the idea that life's some wonder- fully sacred thing, my lad – because it ain't. There's thousands of unborn kids lying around in abortion clinics, and every second

– *every second*, so they tell me – some poor little sod somewhere round the globe gets its merciful release from hunger. There's floods and earthquakes and disease and plane crashes and car crashes and people killed in wars and shot in prisons and – Agh! Just don't feel too surprised, that's all, if you come across one or two people who find life's a bit too much for 'em, all right? This woman of yours probably put her bank balance on some horse at ten-to-one and it came past the post at twenty-to-six!'

Walters didn't see the joke, although he took the general drift of Bell's philosophy. Would Morse though (he wondered) not have been slightly more anxious to probe more deeply?

'You're not too worried about that chair in the – ?'

The telephone rang on the desk, and whilst the outside call was switched through, Bell put his hand over the mouthpiece.

'I'm not worried about *anything*. But if *you* are, you go and do something about it. And find me one or two people for the inquest, lad, while you're about it.'

At that point, as Walters walked out into the bright, cold air of St Aldates, he had not the remotest notion of the extraordinary sequence of events which was soon to unfold itself.

Chapter Six

The fatal key,
Sad instrument of all our woe
Milton, *Paradise Lost*

Walters returned to Canal Reach at 2 p.m. the same day. It was the brief conversation with Morse that had given him the idea, and over a pint and a pork pie he had decided on his first move. Although he had already spoken to most of the residents in the Reach, he now knocked once again at the door of number 7, the house immediately adjacent to number 9.

'I just wondered whether Ms Scott ever left a key with you, Mrs Purvis,' he asked of the little, grey-haired widow who stood in the slit of the hall – here leading directly to the staircase.

'Well, as a matter of fact she did, yes. Left it about a year ago, she did. I always keeps it in me little pot on the – Just a minute, me dear.'

Mrs Purvis retreated through one of the doors that led off the hall to the downstairs rooms, and returned with a key which Walters took from her and examined with interest.

'Did she ever ask you for it?'

'No, she didn't. But I know she were locked out once, poor soul, and it's always just as well to have a fall-back, isn't it? I remember once . . . ' Walters nodded understandingly as the old girl recalled some bygone incident from the unremarkable history of the Purvis household.

'Do you remember how many keys you had when you came here?'

'Just the two, me dear.'

Was Walters imagining things, or did Mrs Purvis seem rather more nervous than when he had interviewed her the day before? Imagining things, he decided, as he took his leave of her and walked along Canal Street to Great Clarendon Street where, turning left, he could see the sandstone, temple-like church of St Paul's, its fluted columns supporting the classical portico, facing him at the far end on the other side of Walton Street. Yes, he'd been right, and he felt pleased with himself for remembering. There it was, the corner shop he'd been looking for, only twenty-odd yards up the street on the left: *A. Grimes, Locksmith.*

The proprietor himself, surrounded by a comprehensive array of keys, locks, and burglar-alarm devices, sat behind a yellow-painted counter sorting out into various boxes a selection of metal and plastic numerals such as are used for the numbering of street houses. Putting a large, white '9' into its appropriate box, he extended a dirt-ingrained hand as Walters introduced himself.

'You cut quite a lot of extra keys, I suppose?'

Grimes nodded cautiously, pushing his horn-rimmed glasses slightly further up his porous-looking nose. 'Steady old line, that sort of thing, officer. People are forever losin' 'em.'

Walters held out the three keys now in his possession: the one (that found on the cupboard-top just inside Anne Scott's lounge) a dull, chocolate-brown in colour; the other two of newish, light-grey gun metal, neither of them looking as if it had often performed its potential function.

'You think you cut those two?' asked Walters, nodding to the newer keys.

'Could've done, I suppose.' The locksmith hesitated a moment. 'From Canal Reach, officer? Number 9, perhaps?'

'Perhaps.'

'Well, I did then.'

'You've got a record of doing the job?'

The man's eyes were guarded. 'Very doubtful, I should think, after all this time. It must have been eighteen months, coupla years ago. She locked herself out one day and came in to ask for help. So I went down there and opened up for her – and I suggested that she had a couple more keys cut.'

'A couple, you say?'

'That's it.'

'I suppose most of the people round here have two to start with, don't they?'

'Most of 'em.'

'So she finished up with four,' said Walters slowly.

'Let's say that one time or another she had four different keys in her possession. Wouldn't that be slightly more accurate, officer?'

Walters was beginning to dislike the man. 'Nothing else you can tell me?'

'Should there be?'

'No, I'm sure there shouldn't.'

But as Walters was half-way through the door, the locksmith decided that there might be a little more to tell after all. 'I shouldn't be surprised if somebody else in the Reach knows something about those keys.'

'Really. Who – ?'

But the locksmith had no further need of words. His right hand selected one of the numerals from the boxes in front of him, his left hand another. Then, like an international judge at a skating championship, he held his arms just above his head, and the number thus signalled was 10.

Walters walked thoughtfully back to Canal Reach and let himself into number 9 with the key that Mrs Purvis had kept for her neighbour. It slipped easily into the socket and the tongue of the lock sprang across with a smooth but solid twang. He walked through into the kitchen, every detail of death now removed, and looked out on to the narrow back garden, where he noticed that the wall fronting the canal had recently (very recently, surely?) been repaired, with thirty or so new rosy-red bricks and half a dozen coping stones – all most professionally pointed. Then he went upstairs into the front bedroom and looked around quietly, keeping as far as he could from the line of the curtainless window. The bed was just as he had seen it before, neatly made, with the edge of the purple quilt running uniformly parallel about three inches from the floor. Would Morse have noticed anything here, he wondered? Then he suddenly stepped boldly right in front of the window – and saw what he was half expecting to see. The floral curtains of the bedroom across in number 10 had moved, albeit very slightly, and Walters felt quite sure that the room in which he stood was under a steady and proximate surveillance. He smiled to himself as he looked more closely at the houses opposite – brick-built, slate-roofed, sash-windowed, with square chimneys surmounted by stumpy, yellow pots. No tunnel-backs to the houses, and so the bicycles had to be left outside: like the bicycle just opposite. Yes . . . perhaps it was high time to pay a brief call at number 10, one of only two houses in the Reach at which he'd received no answer to his knocks the day before.

The door was opened almost immediately. 'Yes?'

'I'm a police officer, Mr er – ?'

'Jackson. Mr Jackson.'

'Mind if I come in for a minute or two, Mr Jackson?'

Here the ground floor of the house had (as at number 9) been converted into one large, single room, but in comparison it seemed crowded and dingy, with fishing paraphernalia – rods, baskets, keep-nets, boxes of hooks, and dirty-sided buckets – providing the bulk of the untidy clutter. Removing a copy of The Angler's Times, Walters sat down in a grubby, creaking armchair and asked Jackson what he knew about the woman who had lived opposite for the past two years.

'Not much really. Nice woman – always pleasant – but I never knew her personally, like.'

'Did she ever leave her key with you?'

Was there a glimmer of fright in those small, suspicious eyes? Walters wasn't sure, but he felt a little surprised at the man's hesitant reaction; even more surprised at his reply.

'As a matter of fact she did, yes. I do a few little jobs, you know – round about, like – and I did one or two things for Miss Scott.'

'She used to let you have a key for that?'

'Well, you see, she wasn't always in in the afternoons – and with me, well, not in much in the mornings, like – so I'd let meself in if – '

'Was it you who did the brick-work?'

There was no fright this time – Walters was sure of that – and perhaps he'd been wrong earlier. After all, most of the public get a little flustered when the police start questioning them.

'You saw that?' Jackson's ratty-featured face was creased with pleasure. 'Neat little job, wasn't it?'

'When did you do that?'

'This week – Monday and Tuesday afternoons it was – not a big job – about four or five hours, that's all.'

'You finished Tuesday afternoon?'

'That's right – you can ask Mrs Purvis if you don't believe me. She was out the back when I was just finishing off, and I remember her saying what a nice and neat little job it was, like. You ask her!' The man's small eyes were steady and almost confident now.

'You've still got the key?'

Jackson shook his head. 'Miss Scott asked me to give it back to her when I'd finished and – '

'You gave it back to her, then?'

'Well, not exactly, no. She was there on the Tuesday afternoon and while she paid me, like, it must have slipped me memory – and hers, as well. But I remembered on the Wednesday, see. I'd been fishing in the morning and I got back about – oh, I don't know – some time in the afternoon, so I nipped over and – '

'You did?' Walters felt strangely excited.

' – just stuck it through the letter box.'

'Oh.' It was all as simple and straightforward as that, then; and Walters suspected he'd been getting far too sophistical about the key business. Could Jackson clear up one or two other things, as well, perhaps? 'Was the door unlocked, do you remember?'

Jackson closed his eyes for a few moments, inclining his head as though pondering some mighty problem. 'I didn't try it, I don't think. As I say, I just stuck – '

'What time was that, do you say?'

'I – I can't remember. Let's see, I must have slipped across there about – it must have been about half-past . . . No, I just can't seem to remember. When you're out fishing, you know, you lose all track of time, really.' Then Jackson looked up with a more obvious flash of intelligence in his eyes. 'Perhaps one or two of the neighbours might have seen me, though? Might be worth asking round, mightn't it?'

'You mean people here tend to er to pry on what all the others are doing?' Walters had chosen his words carefully, and he could see that his point had registered.

'Only a tiny little street, isn't it? It's difficult not to – '

'What I meant was, Mr Jackson, that perhaps – perhaps *you* might have seen someone – someone else – going over to number 9 when you got back from your fishing.'

'Trouble is,' Jackson hesitated, 'one day seems just like any other when you're getting on a bit like I am.'

'It was only two days ago, you know.'

'Ye-es. And I think you're right. I can't be sure of the time and all that, like – but there *was* someone. It was just after I'd nipped over, I think – and – yes! I'm pretty sure it was. I'd just been up to the shop for a few things – and then I saw someone go in there. Huh! I reckon I'd have forgotten all about it if – '

'This person just walked in?'

'That's it. And then a few minutes later walked out.'

Phew! Things had taken an oddly interesting turn, and Walters pressed on eagerly. 'Would you recognise him – it was a *man*, you say?'

Jackson nodded. 'I didn't know him – never seen him before.'

'What was he like?'

'Middle-age, sort of – raincoat he had on, I remember – no hat – getting a bit bald, I reckon.'

'And you say you'd never seen him before?'

'No.'

Walters was getting very puzzled, and he needed time to think about this new evidence. In a few seconds, however, his puzzlement was to be overtaken by an astonished perplexity, for Jackson proceeded to add a gloss on that categorically spoken 'no'.

'I reckon I seen him later, though.'

'You *what*?'

'I reckon I seen him later, I said. He went in there again while *you* was there, officer. About quarter-past ten, I should think it was. You must have seen him because you let him in yourself, if me memory serves me right. Must have been a copper, I should think, wasn't he?'

After Walters had left, Jackson sat in his back kitchen drinking a cup of tea and feeling that the interview had been more than satisfactory. He hadn't been at all sure about whether he should have mentioned that last bit, but now he felt progressively happier that he had in fact done so. His plan was being laid very carefully, but just a little riskily; and the more he could divert suspicion on to others, the better it would be. How glad he was he'd kept that key! At one point he'd almost chucked it into the canal – and that would have been a mistake, perhaps. As it was he'd just 'stuck it through the letter box' – exactly the words he'd used to the constable. And it was the truth, too! Telling the truth could be surprisingly valuable. Sometimes.

Chapter Seven

I say, 'Banish bridge'; let's find some pleasanter
way of being miserable together

Don Herold

The recently formed Summertown Bridge Club had advertised itself (twice already in *The Oxford Times* and intermittently in the windows of the local newsagents) as the heaven-sent answer to those hundreds of residents in North Oxford who had played the game in the past with infinite enjoyment but with rather less than infinite finesse, and who were now a little reluctant to join one of the city's more prestigious clubs, where conversation invariably hinged on trump-coups and squeezes, where county players could always be expected round the tables, and where even the poorest performer appeared to have the enviable facility of remembering all the fifty-two cards at a time. The club was housed in Middle

Way, a road of eminently desirable residences which runs parallel to the Banbury Road and to the west of it, linking Squitchey
Lane with South Parade. Specifically, it was housed at a large
white-walled residence, with light-blue doors and shutters, some
half-way down that road, where lived the chairman of the club
(who also single-handedly fulfilled the functions of its secretary,
treasurer, hostess, and general organiser), a gay and rather gaudy
widow of some sixty-five summers who went by the incongruously
youthful name of Gwendola Briggs and who greeted Detective
Constable Walters effusively under the mistaken impression that
she had a new – and quite handsome – recruit to a clientèle that was
predominantly (much too predominantly!) female. Never mind,
though! A duly identified Walters was anxious, it seemed, to talk
about the club, and Gwendola, as publicity agent, was more than
glad to talk about it. Ms Scott ('She wore a ring, though,') had
been a member for about six months. She was quite a promising,
serious-minded player ('You can never play bridge flippantly, you
know, constable'), and her bidding was improving all the time.
What a tragedy it all was! After a few years (who knows?) she
might have developed into a very good player indeed. It was her
actual *playing* of the cards that sometimes wasn't quite as sharp
as . . . Still, that was neither here nor there, now, was it? As
she'd said, it was *such* a tragedy. Dear, oh dear! Who would
ever have thought it? Such a *surprise*. No. She'd no idea at all
of what the trouble could have been. Tuesday was always their
night, and poor Anne ('Poor Anne!') had hardly ever missed.
They started at about 8 p.m. and very often played through until
way past midnight – sometimes (the chairman almost smiled) until
3 or 4 a.m. Sixteen to twenty of them, usually, although one quite
disastrous night they'd only had nine. ('*Nine*, constable!') Anne
had moved round the tables a bit, but (Gwendola was almost
certain) she must have been playing the last rubber with Mrs
Raven ('The Ravens of Squitchey Lane, d'you know them?'),
old Mr Parkes ('Poor Mr Parkes!') from Woodstock Road, and
young Miss Edgeley ('Such a scatter-brain!') from Summertown
House.

Walters took down the addresses and walked across the paved
patio towards the front gate with the strong impression that the
ageing Gwendola was far more concerned about the re-filling of
an empty seat at a green-baize table than about the tragic death of

an obviously enthusiastic and faithful member of the club. Perhaps even such modest stakes as tuppence a hundred tended to make you mean deep down in the soul; perhaps with all those slams and penalty points and why-didn't-you-play-so-and-so, a bridge club was hardly the happiest breeding-ground for any real compassion and kindliness. Walters was glad he didn't play.

It was not a good start, for Miss Catharine Edgeley was away from home. The young, attractive brunette who shared the flat informed Walters that Cathy had left Oxford that same morning after receiving a telegram from Nottingham: her mother was seriously ill. Declining the offer of a cup of tea, Walters asked only a few perfunctory questions.

'Where does Miss Edgeley work?'

'She's an undergraduate at Brasenose.'

'Do they have women there?'

'They've always had women at Brasenose, haven't they?' said the brunette slowly.

But Walters missed the second joke of the day, and drove down to Squitchey Lane, where he received from Mrs Raven an inordinately long and totally unhelpful account of the bridge evening; and thence to Woodstock Road, where he received from Mr Parkes an extremely brief but also totally unhelpful account of the same proceedings. So that was that.

As it happened Walters had been unusually unlucky that day. But life can sometimes be a cussed business, and even a policeman with a considerably greater endowment of nous than Walters possessed must hope for a few lucky breaks here and there. And, indeed, Walters was no one's fool. As he lay beside his young wife in Kidlington that night, there were several points that now appeared clear to him. Bell was quite right – there was no doubt about it: the Scott woman had hanged herself, albeit for reasons as yet unapparent. But there were several fishy (fishy?) aspects about the affair. The bridge evening (evening?) had finally finished at about 2.45 a.m., and almost certainly Anne Scott had gone home shortly after that. *How*, though? Got a lift with someone? In a taxi? On a bicycle? (He'd forgotten to put the point to the garish Gwendola.) And then something had gone sadly wrong. Time of death could not be firmly established, but the medical report suggested she had been dead at least ten hours

before the police arrived, and that meant . . . But Walters wasn't
quite sure what it meant. Then again there was the business of
the front door being left open. Why? Had she forgotten to lock
it? Unlikely, surely. Had someone else unlocked it, then? If so,
the key on the inside must first have been removed. Wasn't that
much more likely, though? He himself always took the key out
of his own front door and placed it by the telephone on the hall
table. Come to think of it, he wasn't quite sure why he did it.
Just habit, perhaps. Three keys . . . three keys . . . and *one* of
them must have opened that door. And if it wasn't Anne Scott
herself and if it wasn't Mrs Purvis . . . Jackson! What if Jackson
had gone in, unlocking the door with his own key, called out for
Ms Scott, heard no reply, and so walked through – into the kitchen!
Jackson would know all about that sticking door because he'd been
through it at least twice on each of the two previous days. And
what if . . . what if he'd . . . Yes! The chair must have been in
the way and he would almost certainly have knocked it over as he
pushed the door inwards . . . would probably have picked it up
and placed it by the kitchen table before turning round and – Phew!
That would explain it all, wouldn't it? Well, most of it. Yet why,
if that had happened, hadn't Jackson phoned the police immediately? There was a phone *there*, in number 9. Had Jackson felt
guilty about something? Had there been something – money,
perhaps? – in the kitchen that his greedy soul had coveted? It
must have been *something* like that. Then, of course, there was
that other mystery: Morse! For it *must* have been Morse whom
Jackson had seen there that day. What on earth was *he* doing there
earlier in the afternoon? Was he taking German lessons? Walters
thought back to those oddly tentative, yet oddly searching questions that Morse had asked that night. 'Is she – is *she* dead?'
Morse had asked him. Just a minute! How on earth . . . ? Had one
of the policemen outside mentioned who it was they'd found? But
no one could have done, for there was no one else who knew . . .
Suddenly Walters shot bolt upright, jumped out of bed, slipped
downstairs, and with fingers all thumbs, riffled through the telephone directory until he came to the M's. Rubbing his eyes with
disbelief he stared again and again at the entry he'd been looking
for: 'Morse, E., 45 The Flats, Banbury Road'. Morse! 'E.M.'! Was
it *Morse* who'd been expected that afternoon? Steady on, though!
There were a thousand and one other people with those initials –

of course there were. But Morse *had* been there that afternoon –
Walters was now quite sure in his own mind of that. It all fitted.
Those questions he'd asked about doors and locks and lights – yes,
he'd been there, all right. Now if Morse had a key and if *he*, not
Jackson, had found his way through into the kitchen . . . Why
hadn't he reported it, then? Money wouldn't fit into the picture
now, but what if somehow Morse had . . . what if Morse was
frightened he might compromise himself in some strange way if he
reported things immediately? He'd rung later, of course – that
would have been his duty as a police officer . . . Walters returned
to bed but could not sleep. He was conscious of his eye-balls dart-
ing about in their sockets, and it was in vain that he tried to focus
them on some imaginary point about six inches in front of his nose.
Only in the early hours did he finally drift off into a disturbed
sleep, and the most disturbing thought of all was what, if anything,
he was to say to Chief Inspector Bell in the morning.

Chapter Eight

For he who lives more lives than one
More deaths than one must die
Oscar Wilde, *The Ballad of Reading Gaol*

It was not only Walters who slept uneasily that night, although for
Charles Richards the causes of his long and restless wakefulness
were far more anguished. The undertow of it all was what he
saw as the imminent break-up of his marriage, and all because
of that one careless, amateurish error on his own part. Why, oh
why – an old campaigner like he! – when Celia had seen that
long, blonde, curling hair on the back of his dark brown Jaeger
cardigan, hadn't he shrugged her question off, quite casually
and uncaringly, instead of trying (as he had) to fabricate that
laboured, unconvincing explanation? He remembered – kept on
remembering – how Celia's face, for all its fortitude, had reflected
then her sense of anger and of jealousy, her sense of betrayal
and agonised inadequacy. And that hurt him – hurt him much

more deeply than he could have imagined. In the distant past she might have guessed; in the recent past she must, so surely, have suspected; but now she *knew* – of that there now was little doubt.

And as he lay awake, he wondered how on earth he could ever cope with the qualms of his embering conscience. He could eat no breakfast when he got up the next morning, and after a cup of tea and a cigarette he experienced, as he sat alone at the kitchen table, a sense of helplessness that frightened him. His head ached and the print of *The Times* jumped giddily across his vision as he tried to distract his thoughts with events of some more cosmic implication. But other facts were facts as well: he was losing his hair, losing his teeth, losing whatever integrity he'd ever had as a civilised human being – and now he was losing his wife as well. He was drinking too heavily, smoking too addictively, fornicating far too frequently . . . Oh God, how he hated himself occasionally!

Saturday mornings were hardly the most productive periods in the company's activities, but there was always correspondence, occasionally an important phone call, and usually a few enquiries at the desk outside; and he had established the practice of going in himself, of requiring his personal secretary to join him, and of expecting his brother Conrad to put in a brief appearance, too, so that before adjourning for a midday drink together they could have the opportunity of discussing present progress and future plans.

On that Saturday morning, as often when he had no longer-ranging business commitments, Charles drove the five-minute journey to the centre of Abingdon in the Mini. The rain which had persisted through the previous few days had now cleared up, and the sky was a pale and cloudless blue. Not an umbrella day. Once seated in his office he called in his secretary and told her that he didn't wish to be disturbed unless it were absolutely necessary: he had, he said, some most important papers to consider.

For half an hour he sat there and did nothing, his chin resting on his left hand as he smoked one cigarette after another. *That* could be a start, though! He vowed earnestly that as soon as he'd finished his present packet (Glory be! – it was still almost full) he would pack up the wretched, dirty habit, thereby deferring, at a stroke, the horrid threats to heart and lungs, with the additional sweet benefits of less expense and (as he'd read) a greater sexual potency in bed. Yes! For a moment, as he lit another cigarette, he almost regretted that there were so many left. By lunch time they'd be gone though, and that would be the time for his monumental sacrifice – yes, after he'd had a drink with Conrad. If Conrad were coming in that morning . . . He sank into further fathoms of self-pitying gloom and recrimination . . . He had tried so hard over the years. He had reformed and vowed to turn from his sinful ways as frequently as a regular recidivist at revivalist meetings, and the thought of some healing stream that could abound and bring, as it were, some water to the parched and withering roots of life was like the balm of hope and grace. Yet (he knew it) such hope was like the dew that dries so early with the morning sun. So often had his inner nature robbed him of his robe of honour that now he'd come to accept his weaknesses as quite incurable. So he safeguarded those weaknesses, eschewing all unnecessary risks, foregoing those earlier, casual liaisons, avoiding where he could the thickets of emotional involvement, playing the odds with infinitely greater caution, and almost persuading himself sometimes that in his own curious fashion he was even becoming a fraction more faithful to Celia. And one thing he knew: he would do anything not to hurt Celia. Well, almost anything.

At ten-fifteen he rang his brother Conrad – Conrad, eighteen months younger than himself, not quite so paunchy, far more civilised, far more kindly, and by some genetic quirk a little greyer at the temples. The two of them had always been good friends, and their business association had invariably been co-operative and mutually profitable. On many occasions in the past Charles had needed to unbosom himself to his brother about some delicate and potentially damaging relationship, and on those occasions Conrad had always shown the same urbanity and understanding.

'You thinking of putting in an appearance today, Conrad? It's after ten, you know.'

'Twenty past, actually, and I'm catching the London train at eleven. Surprised you'd forgotten, Charles. After all, it was you who arranged the visit, wasn't it?'

'Of course, yes! Sorry! I must be getting senile.'

'We're all getting a little older day by day, old boy.'

'Conrad – er – I want you to do me a favour, if you will.'

'Yes?'

'It'll be the last one, I promise you.'

'Can I have that in writing?'

'I almost think you can, yes.'

'Something wrong?'

'Everything's wrong. But I can sort it out, I think – if you can help me. You see, I'd – I'd like an alibi for yesterday afternoon.'

'That's the *second* time this week!' (Was there an unwonted note of tetchiness in Conrad's voice?)

'I know. As I say, though, I promise it won't – '

'Where were we?'

'Er – shall we say we had a meeting with some prospective – '

'Whereabouts?'

'Er – High Wycombe, shall we say?'

'High Wycombe it shall be.'

'The Swedish contract, let's say.'

'Did I drive you there?'

'Er – yes. I – er – we – er – finished about six.'

'About six, I see.'

'This is all just in case, if you see what I mean. I'm sure Celia wouldn't want to go into details, but – '

'Understood, old boy. You can put your mind at rest.'

'Christ, I wish I could!'

'Look, Charles, I must fly. The train's – '

'Yes, of course. Have a good day! And, Conrad – thanks! Thanks a million!'

Charles put down the phone, but almost immediately it rang, and his secretary informed him that there was a call on the outside line: personal and urgent.

'Hello? Charles Richards here. Can I help you?'

'*Charles!*' The voice was caressing and sensual. 'No need to sound quite so formal, darling.'

'I told you not to ring – ' The irritation in his voice was obvious and genuine, but she interrupted him with easy unconcern.

'You're on your own, darling – I know that. Your secretary said so.'

Charles inhaled deeply. 'What do you want?'

'I want *you*, darling.'

'Look – '

'I just wanted to tell you that I had a call from Keith this morning. He's got to stay in South Africa until a week tomorrow. A week tomorrow! So I just wondered whether to put the electric blanket on for half-past one or two o'clock, darling. That's all.'

'Look, Jenny. I – I can't see you today – you know that. It's impossible on Saturdays. I'm sorry, but – '

'Never *mind*, darling! Don't sound so *cross* about it. We can make it tomorrow. I was just hoping – '

'Look!'

'For God's sake stop saying "look"!'

'I'm sorry; but I can't see you again next week, Jenny. It's getting too risky. Yesterday – '

'What the hell *is* this?'

Charles felt a rising tide of despair engulfing him as he thought of her long, blonde, curling hair and the slope of her naked shoulders. 'Look, Jenny,' he said more softly, 'I can't explain now but – '

'Explain? What the hell is there to *explain*?'

'I can't tell you now.' He ground the words into the mouthpiece.

'When shall I see you then?' Her voice sounded brusque and indifferent now.

'I'll get in touch. Not next week, though. I just can't – '

But the line was suddenly dead.

As Charles sat back breathing heavily in his black-leather swivel chair, he was conscious of a hard, constricting pain between his shoulder-blades, and he reached into a drawer for the *Opas* tablets. But the box was empty.

That day *The Oxford Mail* carried a page-two account (albeit a brief and belated one) of the death of Anne Scott at 9 Canal Reach, Jericho; and at various times in the day the account was noticed and read by some tens of thousands of people in the Oxford area, including the Murdoch family, George Jackson, Elsie Purvis, Conrad Richards, Gwendola Briggs, Detective Constable Walters and Chief Inspector Morse. It was quite by chance that Charles Richards himself was also destined to read it. After three double Scotches at the *The White Swan*, he had returned home to find the Rolls gone and a note from Celia saying that she had gone shopping in Oxford. 'Back about five – pork-pie in the frig.' And when she had returned home, she'd brought a copy of *The Oxford Mail* with her, throwing it down casually on the coffee table as Charles sat watching the football round-up.

The paper was folded over at page two.

Chapter Nine

Suicide is the worst form of murder, because
it leaves no opportunity for repentance
                                    John Collins

The inquest on Ms Anne Scott was one of a string of such
melancholy functions for the Coroner's Court on the Tuesday
of the following week. Bell had spent the weekend arranging
the massive security measures which had surrounded the visit to
Oxfordshire of one of the Chinese heads of state; and apart from
exhorting Walters to 'stop bloody worriting' he took no further
part in the brief proceedings. He had already been informed of
the one new – and quite unexpected – piece of evidence that had
come to light, but he had betrayed little surprise about it; indeed,
felt none.

Walters took the stand to present a full statement about the
finding of the body (including the one or two rather odd features of that scene), and about his own subsequent enquiries.
The Coroner had only two questions to ask, which he did in a
mournful, disinterested monotone; and Walters, feeling considerably less nervous than he'd expected to be, was ready with his
firm, unequivocal replies.

'In your opinion, officer, is it true to say that the jury can
rule out any suspicion of foul play in the death of Ms Scott?'

'It is, sir.'

'Is there any doubt in your own mind that she met her death
by her own hand?'

'No, sir.'

The hump-backed surgeon was the only other witness to be
called, and he (as ever) delighted all those anxious to get away
from the court by racing through the technical jargon of his medical
report with the exhilarating rapidity of an Ashkenazy laying into
Liszt. To those with acute hearing and micro-chip mentalities it
was further revealed that the woman had probably died between
7 and 9.30 a.m. on the day she was found – that is, she had been
dead for approximately eleven hours before being cut down; that
her frame was well nourished and that her bodily organs were all
perfectly sound; that she was 8–10 weeks pregnant at the time of

death. The word 'pregnant' lingered for a while on the air of the still court-room as if it had been acoustically italicised. But then it was gone, and Bell as he stared down at the wooden flooring silently moved his feet a centimetre or two towards him.

Only one question from the Coroner this time.

'Is there any doubt in your own mind that this woman met her death by her own hand?'

'That is for the jury to decide, sir.'

At this point Bell permitted himself a saddened smile. The surgeon had answered the same question in the same court-room in the same way for the last twenty years. Only once, when the present Coroner had just begun his term of office, had this guarded comment been queried, and on that occasion the surgeon had deigned to add an equally guarded gloss, at a some-what decelerated tempo: 'My job, sir, is to certify death where it has occurred and to ascertain, where possible, the physical causes of that death.' That was all. Bell was sometimes surprised that the old boy ever had the temerity to certify death in the first place; and, to be fair, the surgeon himself had grown increasingly reluctant to do so over the past few years. But, at least, that was his province, and he refused to trespass into territory beyond it. As a scientist, he had a profound distrust of all such intangible notions as 'responsibility', 'motive', and 'guilt'; and as a man he had little or no respect for the work of the police force. There was only one policeman he'd ever met for whom he had a slight degree of admiration, and that was Morse. And the only reason for such minimal approbation was that Morse had once told him over a few pints of beer that he in turn had a most profound contempt for the timid twaddle produced by pathologists.

The jury duly recorded a verdict of 'death by suicide', and the small band of variously interested parties filed out of the court-room. Officially, the case of Ms Anne Scott was filed and finished with.

On the evening of the day of the inquest, Morse telephoned the hump-backed surgeon.

'You fancy a drink in an hour or so, Max?'

'No.'

'What's up? You stopped boozing or something?'

'I've started boozing at home. Far cheaper.'

'No licensing hours, either.'

'That's another reason.'

'When do you start?'

'Same time as you, Morse – just before breakfast.'

'Did this Scott woman commit suicide, Max?'

'Oh God! Not you as well!'

'*Did* she commit suicide?'

'I look at the injuries, Morse – you know that, and in this case the injuries were firm and fatal. All right? Who it is who commits the injuries is no concern of mine.'

'Did she commit *suicide*, Max? It's important for me to have your opinion.'

There was a long hesitation on the other end of the line, and the answer obviously cost the surgeon dearly. The answer was 'yes'.

A little later that evening, Detective Constable Walters, in the course of his variegated duties, was seated by the bedside of a young girl in the Intensive Care Unit of the John Radcliffe Two. She had swallowed two bottles of pills without quite succeeding in cutting the thread – sometimes so fragile, sometimes so tough – that holds us all to life.

'It's getting dreadful, all this drugs business,' said the sister as Walters was leaving. 'I don't know! We're getting them in all the time. Another one besides her today.' She pointed to a closed white door a little further down the corridor, and Walters nodded with a surface understanding but with no real sympathy: he had quite enough to cope with as it was. In fact, as he walked along the polished corridor he passed within two feet of the door that the Sister had pointed out to him. And, if Walters had only known, he was at that very second within those same two feet of finding out the truth of what was later to be called The Case of the Jericho Killings.

BOOK TWO

Chapter Ten

There's not a note of mine that's worth the noting
Much Ado About Nothing Act II, scene iii

On Saturday, 13th October, four days following the inquest on Anne Scott, a man knocked on the door of 2 Canal Reach, and told the heavily pregnant, nervous-looking young woman who answered the door that he was writing an article for the Bodleian archives on the socio-economic development of Jericho during the latter half of the nineteenth century. Not surprisingly, he elicited little information likely to further his researches, and was soon knocking at number 4: this time with no answer. At number 6 he was brusquely told to 'bugger off' by a middle-aged giant of a man, heavily tattooed from wrists to muscular shoulders, who supposed the caller to be some peripatetic proselytiser. But at number 8, the slim, pale-faced, bespectacled young man who opened the door proved a gushing fount of information on the history of the area, and very soon the researcher was filling his amateurish-looking, red-covered Cash Book with rapid notes and dates: 'Key decade 1821–31 – see monograph Eliza M. Hawtrey (? 1954) Bodleian – if they'd ever let me in – variable roof lines, brick built, sash-windowed – I went down to Jericho and fell among thieves – artisan dwellings – there was a young fellow from Spain – Lucy's Iron Works 1825 – who enjoyed a tart – OUP to its pres. site 1826 – now and again – Canal: Oxford-Banbury-Coventry-Midlands, compl. 1790 – not just now and again but – St Paul's begun 1835 – now and again and – St Barnabas 1869 – again and again and again'.

'Marvellous, marvellous!' said the researcher as the young

man at last showed the first welcome signs of flagging. 'Most interesting and – and so valuable. You're a local historian, I suppose?'

'Not really, no. I work on the line up at Cowley.'

With further profuse expressions of gratitude for a lengthy addendum on the construction of the railway, the researcher finally saw the door to number 8 close – and he breathed a sigh of relief. Most of the other residents in the Reach would now have seen him, and his purpose was progressing nicely. No answer from number 10; no bicycle there, either. Over the narrow – ridiculously narrow – street, and no answer from number 9, either, in spite of three fairly rigorous bouts of knocking, during the third of which he had surreptitiously tried the door-knob. Locked. At number 7 he introduced himself with a most ingratiating smile, and Mrs Purvis, on hearing of his projected monograph for the Royal Architectural Society on the lay-out of the two-up, two-down, dwellings of the mid-Victorian era, duly invited him into her home. Ten minutes later he was seated in the little scullery at the back of the house drinking a cup of tea (as Mrs Purvis was to tell her married daughter the next day) proving to be 'such a charming, well-educated sort of person'.

'I see you grow your own vegetables,' said Morse, getting to his feet and looking out onto the narrow garden plot beyond the dark-green doors of what looked like an outside lavatory-cum-coal-shed. 'Very sensible, too! Do you know, I bought a caulie up in Summertown the other day and it cost me . . . '

Willingly, it appeared, Mrs Purvis would have spent the rest of the day discussing the price of vegetables, and Morse had no difficulty in pressing home his advantage.

'What's your soil like here, Mrs Purvis? Sort of clayey, is it? Or,' – Morse hunted around in his mind for some other vaguely impressive epithet – 'alkaline, perhaps?'

'I don't *really* know too much about that sort of thing.'

'I could tell you if . . . '

They were soon standing in the garden, where Morse scooped up a handful of soil from a former potato furrow and let it trickle slowly through his fingers. His eyes missed nothing. The wall between number 7 and number 9 was a lowish red-brick affair, flaked into lighter patches by the tooth of countless frosts; and beyond that wall . . . Morse could see it all now. What, in Mrs

Purvis's house, had been the original low-ceilinged scullery had there been converted into a higher, longer extension, with the line of the slates carried forward, albeit at a shallower angle, to roof it. Beyond that, and shielding the plot from the boat-building sheds which fronted the canal, was a wall some eight feet high – a wall (as Morse could see) which had recently been repaired at one point.

Interesting . . . Tonight, perhaps?

It says something for Morse that he proceeded to knock (though very gently) on the doors of numbers 5, 3, and 1 of the Reach, and he was fortunate to the extent that the first two were either at that moment empty or tenanted by the slightly hard-of-hearing. At number 1 he satisfied his talent for improvisation by asking the very old man who answered the door if a Mr – Mr er – Green lived anywhere about; and was somewhat taken aback to see an arthritic finger pointing firmly across to number 8 – the abode of the polymath from the car-line at Cowley.

'Haven't I seen you somewhere afore, mister?' asked the old man, peering closely at him.

A rather flustered Morse confessed that he'd often been in the district doing a bit of local research ('For the library, you know'), and stayed talking long enough to learn that the old boy spent a couple of hours across at *The Printer's Devil* every evening. 'Eight o'clock to ten o'clock, mister. Reg'lar as clockwork – like me bowels.'

If it was going to be tonight, it had better be between 8 and 10 p.m., then. Why not? Easy!

Morse was more honest (well, a little more honest) with the locksmith – the same locksmith whom Walters had visited and questioned a week earlier. Introducing himself as a chief inspector of police, Morse stated (which was quite true) that he had to get into number 9 Canal Reach again, and (which, of course, was quite untrue) that he'd left his key at the police station. It was a bit of a nuisance, he knew, but could . . . ? Mr Grimes, however, was unable to oblige: there wasn't a single key in the shop that could fit the front door of number 9. He could always open the lock himself, though; could open *any* door. Did Morse want him to . . . ? No! That was the last thing Morse wanted.

'Look,' said Morse. 'I know I can trust you. You see, we've had some outside information about the trouble there – you remember? – the suicide. The big thing is that we don't want the neighbours to be worried or suspicious at all. And the truth is that my incompetent sergeant has er temporarily misplaced both the keys – '

'You mean *three* keys, don't you, inspector?'

The locksmith proceeded to give an account of his earlier visit from Walters, and Morse listened and learned – and wondered.

'I didn't tell him about the back door key, though,' continued the locksmith. 'It didn't seem important, if you follow me, and he didn't ask me, anyway.'

Two minutes and one £5 note later, Morse left the shop with a key which (he was assured) would fit the back door lock of number 9: Grimes himself had fitted the lock some six months earlier and could remember exactly which type it was. 'Keep all this quiet, won't you?' Morse had said, but he'd found no kindred spirit in the locksmith. And how foolish and risky it all was! Yet so much of Morse's life was exactly that, and now, at least, his mind was urgently engaged. It made him feel strangely content. He walked up Great Clarendon Street and saw (as Walters had seen) St Paul's now facing him at the top of Walton Street. 'Begun 1835,' he said to himself. Even his memory was sharpening up again.

Chapter Eleven

He can't write, nor rade writing from his cradle,
please your honour; but he can make his mark equal
to another, sir

Maria Edgeworth, *Love and Law*

It was the same morning, the morning of Saturday, 13th October, that Charles Richards had received the letter at his home address. The postage stamp (first class) corner of the cover had been doubly cancelled – the first postmark clearly showing 'Oxford, 8 Oct.', with the second, superimposed mark blurred and illegible. Nor was the reason for the delayed delivery difficult to see, for the original address was printed as 61 (instead of 261) Oxford Avenue, Abingdon, Nr. Oxford, and someone (doubtless the householder at number 61) had been aware of the mistake, had re-addressed the envelope correctly, and had put the letter back in the pillar box. The clean, white envelope (with 'Private' printed across the top-left of the cover) was neatly sealed with Sellotape, with the name and address written in capital letters by what seemed a far from educated hand. 'Abingdon' was mis-spelt (the 'g' omitted), and each of the lines gradually veered from the horizontal towards the bottom of the envelope, as if the correspondent were not particularly practised in any protracted activity with the pen. Inside the cover was another envelope, of the same brand, folded across the middle, the name 'Charles Richards' printed on it in capitals, with the words 'Strictly Personal' written immediately above. Richards slit this second envelope with rather more care than he had done the first, and took out the single sheet of good quality paper. There was no address, no signature, and no date:

Dear Mister Richards
Its about Missis Scott who died, I now all about you and her but does Missis Richards. I now ALL about it, I hope you beleive me because if you dont I am going to tell her everything, You dont want that. I am not going to tell her if you agree, You are rich and what is a thousand pounds. If you agree I will not bother to rite again, I keep all promisses beleive that. The police dont now anything and I have never said what I now. Here is what you do, You go down to Walton Street in Jericho and turn left into Walton Well Road and then strate on over the little Canal brige and then over the railway brige and you come to a parking area where you cant go much further, then turn round and face Port Medow and you will see a row of willow trees, the fifth from the left has got a big hole in it about five feet from the ground. So put the money there and drive away, I will be watching all the time. I will give you a ring soon and that will be only once. I hope you will not try anything funny. Please remember your wife.

Although the writing was crudely printed, with several words written out in individual, unjoined characters, the message was surprisingly coherent – and disturbing. Yet as Charles Richards read it, his mind seemed curiously detached: it was almost as if the writing had been submitted to him as a piece of English prose that had to be corrected and commented upon – its message secondary and of comparatively little significance. He read the letter through a second time, and then a third, and then a fourth;

but if a hidden observer had recorded the conflicting emotions of puzzlement, anger, and even anxiety, that played upon his face, there was never the slightest hint of panic or despair. For Charles Richards was a clever and resourceful man, and he now re-folded the letter, replaced it in its envelope and put it, together with the outer cover, inside his wallet.

Five minutes later he waited for a few seconds by Celia's bedside as she sat up, drew a cardigan round her shoulders, and took the breakfast tray of orange juice, tea, and toast. He kissed her lightly on the forehead, told her that he had to go into Oxford, that he'd take the Mini, and that he'd certainly be home for lunch about one. Was there anything he could get her from the shops? He'd perhaps have to nip into Oxford again in the evening, too.

Celia Richards heard him go, a great burden of anxiety weighing on her mind. How could a man so treacherous seem so kind? It had been an extraordinary coincidence that the first copy of *The Oxford Mail* she'd read for months had contained that account of Anne Scott's death, and she felt quite sure that Charles had read the article, too. Had he been responsible for that terrible thing? She couldn't really know and, to be truthful, she didn't care much either. What she *did* know was that their life together just couldn't go on as it had been. Putting things off was merely aggravating that almost intolerable burden, and she would put it off no longer. He'd said he'd be in for lunch; and after lunch . . . Yes! She would tell him *then*. Tell him all she knew; tell him the truth. It was the only way – the only way for *her*. Conrad had counselled against it, but Conrad would understand. Conrad always understood . . . She munched the tasteless toast and drank the luke-warm tea. Oxford . . . He'd always insisted how important it was for him to put in a few hours at the office on Saturday mornings. So why Oxford? With Anne Scott dead, what could possibly be dragging him to Oxford?

In the Intensive Care Unit at the JR2, Doctor Philips walked from the side of the youth lying motionless beneath the startlingly white sheets, and pulled out the chart from the slot at the foot of the bed: temperature still high, pulse still rather disturbingly variable.

'Bloody fool!' he mumbled to the nurse who stood beside him.

'Will he be all right?' she asked.

Philips shrugged his shoulders. 'Doubt it. Once you start on that sort of stuff . . . '

'Do we know what stuff it was?'

'Can't be sure, really. Cocaine, I shouldn't wonder, though. High temperature, dilatation of the pupils, sweating, goose-flesh, hypertension – all the usual symptoms. Took it intravenously, too, by the look of things. Which doesn't help, of course.'

'Will he get over *this*, I mean?'

'If he does it'll be thanks to you, nurse – no one else.'

Nurse Warrener felt pleased with the compliment, and just a little more hopeful than she had been. She thought she could perhaps get to like Michael Murdoch. He was only a boy really: well, nineteen according to the records – exactly the same age as she was – and a prospective undergraduate at Lonsdale College. What a tragedy it would be if his life were now to be completely ruined! She thought of Michael's mother, too – a brisk, energetic-looking woman who seemed on the face of it to be taking things none too badly, but who (as Nurse Warrener rightly suspected) was hiding behind that competent, no-nonsense mien the ghost of some distraught despair.

Chapter Twelve

Sophocles lived through a cycle of events spatially narrow, no doubt, in the scale of national and global history, but without parallel in intensity of action and emotion

From the Introduction to *Sophocles,*
The Theban Plays, Penguin Classics

The gates of the boat-yard were open as Morse moved swiftly along Canal Reach that night, no lights showing in the fronts of either 9 or 10. It was just before 9 p.m., and the Jaguar stood on double yellow lines outside *The Printer's Devil*, into which Morse had slipped a quarter of an hour earlier, not only to establish some spurious *raison d'être* for his presence in the area, but also to down a couple of double Scotches. Once inside the yard, he turned immediately to his left and felt his way along the brick wall, treading cautiously amid the petrol drums, the wooden spars, and the assorted, derelict débris of old canal barges. There was no one about, and the boatman's hut just ahead of him was securely padlocked. The only noise was a single splash of some water-bird behind the low bulk of the house-boat moored alongside the canal, and the moon had drifted darkly behind the scudding clouds.

With the level of the wharf a foot or so higher than the street behind it, the wall was not going to pose such a problem as Morse had feared, and standing on one of the petrol drums, he peered cautiously over the recently repaired section of the wall. No lights shone in the back rooms of numbers 9, 7 or 5. He hoisted himself up and, keeping his body as close to the top of the wall as he could, dropped down on the other side, feeling a sharp spasm of pain as his right foot crushed a small, terracotta flower pot beneath. The noise startled him, and his heart pounded as he stood for several minutes beside the deep shadow of the wall. But nothing moved; no lights came on; and he stepped silently along to the back door, let himself in, stood inside the kitchen, and waited until his eyes could slowly accustom themselves to the darkness. The door immediately to his right would lead, he guessed, to a small bathroom and WC; to his left, the door at the other side of the kitchen would lead (he knew) directly into the lounge. And lifting the latch of the latter, he pulled it open, the bottom of the lower panel scraping raspingly along the floor. Inside the lounge, he felt on familiar territory, and taking a torch from his raincoat pocket he carefully shielded the light with his left hand as he made his way up to the back bedroom. He had already decided that it would be far too risky to venture into the front bedroom, let alone switch on any lights; and so he spent the next half hour by torchlight looking through the drawers of the desk in what had clearly been the woman's study, feeling like some scrawny bird of prey that is left with the offal after the depredations of the jackals and hyenas. Finally he pocketed one book, shone his torch timorously around the room, and nodded with sad approval as the light picked out the black spines of a whole shelf of Penguin Classical Authors, correctly ordered in alphabetical sequence through from Aeschylus to Xenophon. One little gap, though, wasn't there? And Morse frowned slightly as he shone the torch more closely. Yes, a gap between Seneca's *Tragedies* and Suetonius' *Lives of the Caesars*. What could that be? Sophocles, perhaps? Yes, almost certainly Sophocles. So what? So bloody what? Morse shrugged his shoulders, pulled the door to behind him, and stepped carefully down the narrow, squeaking stairs.

Standing motionless for a few seconds in the lounge, he was suddenly aware how very cold the house was, and his mind momentarily settled on the household's heating arrangements. No central heating system, that was clear. No night-storage heaters, either, by the look of things; and the only heating appliance so far encountered was that small electric fire upstairs. A coal fire, perhaps? Surely there'd be a grate here somewhere. His torch still turned off, Morse stepped across the carpeted floor – and there it was in the far wall, surrounded by the lightish-coloured tiles of the fixture. Yes, he remembered it now; and bending down he felt with his right hand along the iron grill. Something there. He switched the torch on right up against the back of the grate, and then slowly allowed the beam to illuminate whatever there was to be seen. It wasn't much: the blackened, curled remains of what had probably been a sheet of notepaper, the flimsy fragments floating down and disintegrating as his delicate fingers touched them. But even as they did so, the torch-light picked out a small piece of something white in the ash-pan below, and Morse pulled away the front and gently picked it out. It seemed to be part of the heading of an official letter, printed in small black capitals, and even now Morse could quite easily make out the letters: ICH. Then he found another tiny piece; and although the flames had obviously curled across it, leaving the surface a smoky brown, it seemed clear to him that it was probably part of the same line of print. KAT, was it? Or RAT, more likely? He inserted the pieces between two pages of the book he had pocketed from upstairs, and his mind was already bounding down improbable avenues. Many of the books and papers he'd looked through upstairs were linked in some way with German literature, and he remembered from his schooldays that '*Ich rat*' meant 'I judged' or 'I thought'. Something like that anyway. He could always look it up later,

of course, although it promptly occurred to him that he would
hardly be overmuch enlightened if his memory proved to have
been reliable. And then as he stood in that cold, dark room beside
the fire-less grate another thought occurred to him: what an idiot –
what a stupid idiot – he was! It was that first, cowardly evasion of
the truth that had caused it all – all because he didn't want it to be
known that he'd been floating around in Jericho looking for some
necessary sex one afternoon. Suddenly, he felt a little frightened,
too . . .

He locked the back door behind him, walked down the strip
of garden, and looked for a place in the wall where he could
get something of a foot-hold in order to scale what, from this
side, appeared a most formidable precipice. What if he couldn't
manage . . . But then Morse saw it. At the foot of the wall was
a wooden board, about one foot square, on which someone had
recently been mixing small quantities of cement, and beside it a
bricklayer's trowel. The shudder that passed through Morse at
that moment was not of fear – but of excitement. With his crisis
of confidence now passed, his brain was sweetly clear once more.
Spontaneously it told him, too, of a dustbin somewhere nearby;
and he found it almost immediately, moved it against the wall,
and standing on it clambered to the top. Easy! He breathed a
great sigh of relief as he landed safely inside the boat-yard, where
the gates were still open, and whence he made his exit without
further alarum.

As he walked into Canal Reach, keeping tightly to his right,
a hand clamped upon his shoulder with an iron grip, and a voice
whispered harshly in his ear: 'Just keep walking, mister!'

At about the same time that Morse was entering the house in
Canal Reach, a Mini-Clubman turned down into the northern
stretch of the Woodstock Road, having travelled into Oxford
from Abingdon via the western Ring Road. The car kept closely
into the bus-lane, crawling along at about 10 m.p.h. past the
large, elegant houses, set back on higher ground behind the
tall hedges that masked their wide fronts and provided a quiet
privacy for their owners. The driver pulled the car completely
over on to the pavement beside a telephone kiosk on his left,
turned off the lights, got out, entered the kiosk, and picked
up the receiver. The dialling tone told him that the phone

was probably in working order, and keeping the instrument to his ear he turned round and looked up and down the road. No one was in sight. He stepped out and, as if searching his pockets for some coinage, carefully examined the surrounds of the kiosk. The stone wall behind it was luxuriantly clad with thick ivy, and he pushed his hands against it, seeming to be satisfied that all was well. He got back into the Mini and drove along the road for about fifty yards, before stopping again and taking note of the name of the road that stretched quite steeply off on his left. He then drove the short distance down to Squitchey Lane, turned left, left at the Banbury Road, left into Sunderland Avenue, and finally left again into the Woodstock Road. For the moment there was no traffic and he drove slowly once more along the self-same stretch of road. Then, nodding to himself with apparent satisfaction, he accelerated away.

The plan was laid.

Michael Murdoch opened his eyes at about ten minutes to ten that evening to find the same pretty face looking down at him. He noticed with remarkable vividness the strong white teeth, a gold filling somewhere towards the extremity of her smile, and he heard her speak.

'Feeling better?'

Momentarily he was feeling nothing, not even a sense of puzzlement, and in a dry-throated whisper he managed to answer 'Yes'. But as he lay back and closed his eyes again, his head was drifting off in a giddying whirl and the body it had left behind seemed slowly to be slipping from the sloping bed. He felt a cold, restraining hand on his drenched forehead, and immediately he was back inside his skull once more, with a giant, brown rat that sat at the entrance of his right ear, twitching its nose and ever edging menacingly forward, its long tail insinuating itself centimetre by centimetre into the gaping orifice, and the long white slits of teeth drawing nearer and nearer to a vast and convoluted dome of pale-white matter that even now he recognised: it was his own matter, his own flesh, *his own brain*.

He heard himself shriek out in terror.

* * *

Miss Catharine Edgeley returned to Oxford that night. Her mother had died of a brain tumour; her mother was now buried. And there was little room in Miss Edgeley's mind that night for any thoughts of the last time she had played bridge in North Oxford. Indeed, she had no knowledge at that time that Anne Scott, too, was dead.

Chapter Thirteen

Sit Pax in Valle Tamesis
Motto of The Thames Valley Police Authority

Morse's mind was curiously detached as he 'kept walking', eyes frozen forward, along the short length of Canal Reach. With Teutonic recollections the order of the night, he recalled that in Germany the situation might have been regarded as serious but not hopeless, in Austria, hopeless but not serious. Or was it the other way round? To his astonishment, however, he found himself being firmly manipulated towards a police car, parked just round the corner, its gaily-coloured emblem illuminated by the orange glare of a street lamp. And as he reached the car and turned about, he found himself looking slightly upwards into the face of a rather frightened-looking young man.

'*You*, sir!' It was Detective Constable Walters who was the first to speak, and Morse's shoulders sagged with a combination of relief and exasperation.

'Are you in the habit of arresting your superior officers, constable?'

A flustered Walters followed the Jaguar up to Morse's North-Oxford flat, where over a few whiskies the two of them sat and talked until way after midnight. On his own side, Morse came almost completely clean, omitting only any mention of his bribing of the Jericho locksmith. For his part, Walters admitted to his own anxiety about Morse's behaviour, recounted in detail his own investigations, and revealed that after working late in St Aldates that night he had been on his way to return the few items taken from Canal Reach when he had seen the yellow glow flitting about the dark and silent rooms. Throughout Walters' somewhat discontinuous narrative, Morse remained silent, attentive, and seemingly impassive. When Walters had mentioned the strange discoveries of the chair in the kitchen and the key on the door-mat, Morse had nodded non-committally, as though the incidents were either of little moment or perfectly explicable. Only during Walters' account of his visit to the Summertown Bridge Club had Morse's eyes appeared to harden to a deeper blue.

'You're in a tricky position, young fellow,' said Morse finally. 'You find a superior officer snooping around in an empty house – a house in which he'd poked his nose the day the dead woman was found – an officer who had no more right to be there than a fourth-grade burglar – so what do you do, Walters?'

'I just don't know, sir.'

'I'll tell you what you *ought* to have done.' The sudden sharp edge on Morse's voice made Walters look up anxiously. 'If you had any nous at all you would have asked me how I *got in*. Not really good enough, was it?'

Walters opened his mouth to say something but Morse con-tinued. 'How long have you been in the Force?'

'Eighteen months altogether, but only three – '

'You've got a lot to learn.'

'I'm learning all the time, sir.'

Morse grinned at the young man. 'Well, you've got something else to learn, and that's exactly what your duty has got to be now. And in case you don't know, I'll tell you. It's your duty to report everything that's happened tonight to Chief Inspector Bell, agreed?'

Walters nodded. The point had been worrying him sorely, and he felt glad that Morse had made things so easy for him. Again he was about to say something, but again he was interrupted.

'But not just yet, understand? I'll see the Assistant Chief Constable first and explain the whole position. You see, Walters, there's something a bit odd about this business; something that needs an older and a wiser head than yours.'

He poured another liberal dose of whisky into Walters' glass, another into his own, and spent the next half hour asking Walters about his training, his prospects and his ambition; and Walters responded fully and eagerly to such sympathetic interest. At half-past midnight he felt the profound wish that he could work with

this man; and at a quarter to one, when about to depart, he was
only too happy to leave with Morse the items he had originally
set out to deposit in the house on Canal Reach.

'How *did* you get in there, sir?' he asked on the doorstep.
'Did you have a key or – '

'When you've been around as long as I have, constable, you'll
find you don't need a key to get through most doors. You see,
the lock on the back door there is a Yale, and with a Yale the
bevel's always facing you when you're on the outside. So if you
take a credit card and slip it in, you'll find it's just strong enough
and just flexible enough to – '

'I know, sir. I've seen it done on the telly.'

'Oh.'

'And er the lock on the back door there *isn't* a Yale, is
it? Goodnight, sir. And thanks for the whisky.'

Morse spent the next hour or so looking through the two
Letts' diaries now in his possession, the one (for the current year)
just handed to him by Walters, the other (for the previous year)
taken a few hours earlier from Canal Reach. If Walters could be
trusted, no letters of even minimal significance had been found
in the drawers of the desk; and so the diaries were probably
as near as anyone could ever come to unlocking the secret life
of the late Anne Scott. Not that the entries seemed to Morse
particularly promising. Times, mostly: times of trains; times of
social events; times of pupils' lessons – yes, that was doubtless
the meaning of those scores of initials scattered throughout the
pages, several of them recurring at regular (often weekly) intervals over months, and in a few cases over a year or more. The
'E.M.' entry on the Wednesday she'd died held his attention
for a while – as he knew it must have held the attention of
Walters and of Bell. But, like them, he could only think of
one person with those same initials: himself. And he had never
quite forgiven his parents for christening their only offspring as
they had.

Morse slept soundly, and woke late next morning, his brain
clear and keen. The images and impressions of all he had learned
had flashed across his mind but once, yet already the hooks and
eyes of his memories were beginning to combine in strange and
varied patterns.

Almost all of them wrong.

Chapter Fourteen

Chaos preceded Cosmos, and it is into Chaos without
form and void that we have plunged
John Livingston Lowes, *The Road to Xanadu*

Mrs Gwendola Briggs was very soon aware of the different nature
of the beast when, on the following Monday, Morse, after a rather
skimped day's work at the Thames Valley HQ, finally found time
to pursue his unofficial and part-time course of enquiries. This man
(it seemed to Gwendola) was quite unnecessarily objectionable
and bullying in the series of questions he bombarded her with.
Who was there that night? Where had they sat? What were
the topics of conversation? Had anyone cancelled? Had anyone
turned up at the last minute? Were the bridge-pads still there?
Exactly what time had they finished? Where were the cars parked?
How many cars? It was all quite flustering for her, and quite
unlike the vague and pleasant questions that the big and gentle
constable had asked her. *This* man irritated her, making her feel
almost guilty about not quite being able to remember things. Yet
it was surprising (as she later confessed to herself) how much he'd
compelled her to remember; and as Morse prepared to take his
leave, holding the list of the names and addresses of those who
had attended the bridge evening, he felt adequately satisfied. With
the losing pair of each rubber (as he had learned) staying at the
same table, and the winning pair moving along, it seemed more
than likely that Anne had spoken with everyone there, at least
for some intermittent minutes.

'Oh, yes. There *was* something else a little unusual about that
night, Inspector. You see, it was our first anniversary, and we had
a break about eleven to celebrate. You know, a couple of glasses
of sherry to mark the occasion – drink to our future success and – '
Gwendola suddenly broke off, conscious of her tactlessness. But
Morse refused to rescue her.

'I'm sorry. I didn't mean to – Oh dear! What a tragedy it all is!'

'Did you meet last week, Mrs Briggs?'

'Yes, we did. We meet every – '

'You didn't feel that because of the er tragedy that – '

'Life must go on, mustn't it, Inspector?'

Morse's sour expression seemed to suggest that there was probably little justification for such continuance in the case of this mean-minded little woman, doubtless ever dreaming of over-tricks and gleefully doubling the dubious contracts of the recently initiated. But he made no answer as his eyes skimmed down the list she had given him. 'Mrs Murdoch'! Was that the same one? The same Mrs Murdoch who had invited him to the party when he and Anne . . . ? Surely it was! His thoughts floated back to that first – no, that only – evening when he and Anne had met; the evening when but for the cussedness of human affairs he – Augh! Forget it! *Should* he forget it, though? Had there been *something* he had learned that evening that he should, and must, remember? Already he had tried to dredge up what he could, but the simple truth was that he'd drunk too much on that occasion. Come to think of it, though, there was that bit of research he'd heard of only the previous week. Some team of educational psychologists in Oxford was suggesting that if you'd revised whilst you were drunk, and turned up sober for the next day's examinations, you'd be lucky to remember anything at all. Likewise, if you'd revised in a comparatively sober state of mind and then turned up drunk, you'd hardly stand much chance of self-distinction. But (and this was the point) if you'd revised whilst drunk, and maintained a similar degree of inebriation during the examination itself, then all was likely to be well. Interesting. Yes . . . Morse felt sure there *was* something he'd heard from Anne that night. Something. Almost he had it as he stood there on the doorstep; but it slipped away and left him frustrated and irritated. The sooner he got drunk, the better!

As he finally took his leave, he realised how less than gracious he'd been to the chairman of the Summertown Bridge Club.

When the door opened, Morse recognised one of the Murdoch boys he'd seen at the party, and his memory struggled for the name.

'Michael, is it?'

'No. I'm Ted.'

'Oh, yes. Is your mother in, Ted?'

'No. She's gone down to the hospital. It's Michael.'

'Road accident?' What made Morse suggest such a possible

cause of hospitalisation, he could not have said; but he noticed the boy's quite inexplicable unease.

'No. He's – he's been on drugs.'

'Oh dear! Bad, is he?'

The boy swallowed. 'Pretty bad, yes.'

Things were beginning to stir a little in Morse's mind now. Yes. This was the *younger* brother he was talking to, by quite a few inches the taller of the two and slightly darker in complexion, due to sit his A-level examinations – which year had Mrs Murdoch said that was? Then it hit him. E.M. . . . . Edward Murdoch! Wednesday afternoons. *And* (it flooded back) for the latter part of the previous year and for the present year up until June, the initials M.M., too, had appeared regularly in the diaries: Michael Murdoch.

Morse took the plunge. 'Weren't you due for a lesson with Ms Scott the day she committed suicide?' His eyes left the boy's face not for the flutter of an eye-lash as he asked the brutal question; but, in turn, the boy's brown eyes were unblinking as a chameleon's.

'Yes, I was.'

'Did you go?'

'No. She told me the previous week that she – wouldn't be able to see me.'

'I see.' Morse had noticed the hesitation, and a wayward fancy crossed his mind. 'Did you like her?' he asked simply.

'Yes, I did.' The voice, like the eyes, was firm – and oddly gentle.

Morse was tempted to pursue the theme, but switched instead to something different.

'A-levels this year?'

The boy nodded. 'German, French, and Latin.'

'You confident?'

'Not really.'

'Shouldn't worry too much about that,' said Morse in an objectionably avuncular tone. 'Over-rated quality confidence is.' (Weren't those the words of Mrs Murdoch, though? Yes, the memories of the night were stronger now.) 'Hard work – that's the secret. Put your foot through the telly, or something.' Morse heard himself drooling on tediously, and saw the boy looking at him with a hint of contempt in those honest eyes.

'I was working when you called, actually, Inspector.'

'Jolly good! Well, I er I mustn't interrupt you any longer, must I?' He turned to leave. 'By the way, did Ms Scott ever say anything to you about her – well, her private life?'

'Is that what you wanted to see Mum about?'

'Partly, yes.'

'She never said anything to me about it.' The boy's words were almost aggressive, and Morse felt puzzled.

'What about your brother? Did he ever say anything?'

'Say anything about what?'

'Forget it, lad! Just tell your mother I called, will you? And that I'll be calling again, all right?' For a few seconds his harsh blue eyes fixed Edward's, and then he turned around and walked away.

It says little for Morse's thoroughness that Miss Catharine Edgeley (next on his list and living so close to the Murdochs) was to be the last of the bridge party destined to be interviewed. Yes, she realised now, there *was* something that might be valuable for him to know: Anne had asked her to drop a note through the Murdochs' letter box, a note in a white, sealed envelope, addressed to Edward Murdoch.

'Why didn't you give it to Mrs Murdoch?'

'I'm not sure, really. I think, yes, I think she left just a bit before the others. Perhaps her table had finished and if she wasn't in line for any of the prizes . . . I forget. Anyway, Anne wrote – '

'She wrote it *there*?'

'Yes, she wrote it on the sideboard. I remember that. She had a silver Parker – '

'Did she seem worried?'

'I don't *think* so, no. A bit flushed, perhaps – but we'd all had a few drinks and – '

'What were you all talking about? Try to remember, please!'

Catharine shook her pretty head. 'I can't. I'm sorry, Inspector, but – '

'Think!' pleaded Morse.

And so she tried to think: think what people normally spoke about – the weather, work, inflation, gossip, children . . . And slowly she began to form a hazy recollection about an interlude. It was about children, surely . . . Yes, they were talking at one stage about children: something to do with the Oxfam appeal for the Cambodian refugees, was it? Or Korean? Somewhere in that part of the world, anyway.

Morse groaned inwardly as she tried to give some sort of coherence to thoughts so inchoate and so confused. But she'd told him about the note, and that was something.

Unfortunately, the item of far greater importance she'd just imparted was completely lost on Morse. At least for the moment.

Chapter Fifteen

Well, time cures hearts of tenderness, and now I can let her go
Thomas Hardy, *Wessex Heights*

Over breakfast on Tuesday morning, Morse read his one item of mail with mild, half-engaged interest. It was the Oxford Book Association's monthly newsletter, giving a full account of Dame Helen's memorable speech, discussing the possibility of a Christmas Book Fair, reporting the latest deliberations of the committee, and then – Morse stopped and stared very hard. *It was with deep regret that we heard of the death of Anne Scott. Anne had served on the committee only since the beginning of this year, but her good humour, constructive suggestions, and invariable willingness to help even in the most routine and humdrum chores – all these will be sadly missed. The chairman represented the Association at Anne's funeral.* Well, that was news to Morse. Perhaps – no, almost certainly – he would have seen Anne at that last meeting if things had turned out differently. And if only he'd been a regular member, he would have seen her often. If only! He sighed and knew that life was full of 'if only's for everyone. Then he turned the page and the capital letters of the corrigendum jumped out at him. 'The next meeting NOTE THE CHANGE PLEASE will be on Friday, 19th October, when the speaker (this as previously advertised) will be MR CHARLES RICHARDS. His subject *Triumphs and Tribulations of the Small Publisher* will be of particular interest to many of our members and we look forward to a large attendance. Mr Richards apologises for the late notification of the change which is necessitated because of business commitments.' Morse made a brief note in his diary: there was nothing else doing that evening. He might go. On the whole, he thought not, though.

When the phone rang at 10.30 a.m. the same morning, Charles Richards was in his office. Normally the call would have filtered from the outer office through his secretary, but she was now sitting opposite him taking down short-hand (interspersed, Richards noticed, with rather too many pieces of long-hand to give him much real confidence in her stenographic skills). He picked up the phone himself.

'Richards here. Can I help you?'

A rather faint, working-class voice replied that he (it was a 'he', surely?) was sure as 'ow Mister Charles Richards *could* 'elp; and at the first mention of his wife, Richards clamped his hand over the mouthpiece, told his secretary to leave him for a few minutes, waited for the door to close, and then spoke slowly and firmly into the phone.

'I don't know who you are and I don't *want* to know, you blackmailing rat! I believe what you said in your letter and I've made arrangements to get the money – exactly *one quarter* of what you asked for, do you understand me?'

There was no reply.

'There's no chance of my agreeing to the arrangements you made – absolutely none. So listen carefully. Tomorrow night – got that? – tomorrow night I shall be driving slowly down the Woodstock Road – from the roundabout at the top – at half-past eight. Exactly half-past eight. I shall be driving a light-blue Rolls Royce, and I shall stop just inside a road called Field House Drive – two words: "Field House". It's just above Squitchey Lane. I shall get out there and I shall be carrying a brown carrier bag. Then I shall walk up to the telephone kiosk about fifty yards north of Field House Drive, go into the kiosk, and then come out again and put the carrier bag behind the kiosk, just inside the ivy there. *Behind* the kiosk – got that? – not inside it. It will be absolutely safe, you can take my word on that. I shall then walk straight back to the car and drive back up the Woodstock Road. Do you understand all that?'

Still no reply.

'There'll be no funny business on my part, and there'd better be none on yours! You can pick up your money – it's yours. But there'll not be a penny more – you can take that as final. Absolutely final. And if you *do* try anything else like this again, I'll kill you, do you hear that? I'll kill you with my own hands, you snivelling swine!'

Throughout this monologue, Richards had been continuously aware of the harsh, wheezy breathing of the man on the other end of the line, and now he waited for whatever reply might be forthcoming. But there was none.

'Have you got it all straight?'

Finally, he heard the tight voice again. 'You'll be glad you done this, Mister Richards. So will Missis Richards.' With that, the line was dead.

Charles Richards put away the sheet of paper from which he had been reading, and immediately called in his secretary once more.

'Sorry about that. Where were we . . . ?' He sounded completely at ease, but his heart was banging hard against his rib-cage as he dictated the next letter.

Mr Parkes was old, and would soon die. For the last few years he had been drinking heavily, but he had no regrets about that. Looking back over his life, however, he felt it had been largely wasted. Even his twenty years as headmaster of a primary school in Essex seemed to him now a period of little real achievement. A great addict from his early boyhood of all types of puzzles – mathematical problems, crosswords, chess, bridge – he had never found his proper niche. And as he sat drinking another bottle of Diet lager he regretted for the millionth time that no academic body had ever offered him a grant to set his mind to Etruscan or Linear C. He could have cracked those stubborn codes by now! Oh yes!

He had stopped thinking about Anne Scott several days ago.

Mrs Raven was discussing with her husband the final stages of their long-drawn-out (but now at last successful) campaign to adopt a baby. Both of them had been much surprised at the countless provisos and caveats surrounding such an innocent and benevolent-sounding process: the forms in duplicate and triplicate; the statements of incomes, job prospects, religious persuasions, and family history; oaths and solemn undertakings that the prospective parents would 'make no attempt whatsoever to discover the names, dwellings, situations, or any other relevant details of the former parent(s), neither to seek to ascertain' – etc., etc., etc. Oh dear! Mrs Raven had felt almost guilty about everything, especially since it was she herself, according to the gynaecologist, who was thwarting her husband's frequent and frenetic attempts to propagate the Raven species. Still, things were nearly ready now, and she was so looking forward to getting the baby. She'd have to stay at home much more, of course. No more badminton evenings for a while; no more bridge parties.

She had stopped thinking about Anne Scott several days ago.

Catharine Edgeley was busy writing an essay on the irony to be found in Jane Austen's novels, and she was enjoying her work. There was little room in her mind for a dead woman whom she had met only twice, and of whom she could form only the vaguest visual recollection. She'd rather liked the policeman, though. Quite dishy, really – well, he *would* have been when he was fifteen or twenty years younger.

Gwendola Briggs sat reading *Bridge Monthly*: one or two pretty problems, she thought. She re-read an article on a new American bidding system, and felt happy. Only just over half-an-hour and the bridge players would be arriving. She'd almost forgotten Anne Scott now, though not that 'cocky and conceited officer' as she'd described Morse to her new and rather nice neighbour – a neighbour whom she'd promptly enrolled in the bridge-club's membership. So *fortunate*! Otherwise, they might have been one short.

Mrs Murdoch was another person that evening for whom Anne Scott was little more than a tragic but bearable memory. At a quarter-to-seven she received a telephone call from the JR2, and heard from a junior and inexperienced houseman (the young doctor had tried so hard to find some euphemistic guise for 'nearly poked his eyes out') that her son Michael had attempted to do . . . to do some damage to his sight. The houseman heard

THE DEAD OF JERICHO

the poor woman's moan of anguish, heard the strangled 'No!' – and wondered what else he could bring himself to say.

Charles Richards was not thinking of Anne Scott when he rang the secretary of the Oxford Book Association at nine o'clock to say that unfortunately he wouldn't be able to get to the pre-talk dinner which had been arranged for him in the Ruskin Room at the Clarendon Institute on Friday. He was very sorry, but he hoped it might save the Association a few pennies? He'd arrive at ten minutes to eight – if that was all right? The secretary said it was, and mumbled 'Bloody chap!' to himself as he replaced the phone.

It was only as he sat in a lonely corner of his local that evening that Morse's mind reverted to the death of Anne Scott. Again and again he came so near to cornering that single piece of information – something seen? something heard? – that was still so tantalisingly eluding him. After his fourth pint, he wondered if he ever *would* remember it, for he knew from long and loving addiction that his brain was never so keen as after beer.

Only Mrs Scott, now back in her semi-detached house in Burnley, grieved ever for her daughter and could not be comforted, her eyes once more brimming with tears as she struggled to understand what could have happened and – most bitter thought of all – how she herself could surely have helped if only she had known. If only . . . if only . . .

Chapter Sixteen

The lads for the girls and the lads for the liquor are there
A. E. Housman, *A Shropshire Lad*

After declining the Master of Lonsdale's invitation to lunch, Morse walked from The Mitre along The High up to Carfax. He had turned right into Cornmarket and was crossing over the road towards Woolworths when he thought he recognised someone walking about fifteen yards ahead of him – someone carrying a brown brief-case, and dressed in grey flannels and a check-patterned sports coat, who joined the bus queue for Banbury Road; and as the boy turned Morse could see the black tie, with its diagonal red stripes, of Magdalen College School. Games afternoon, perhaps? Morse immediately stopped outside the nearest shop, and divided his attention between watching the boy and examining the brown shoes (left foot only) that rested on the 'Reduced' racks. Edward Murdoch himself seemed restless. He consulted his wrist-watch every thirty seconds or so, punctuating this impatience with a craning-forward to read the numbers on the buses as they wheeled round Carfax into Cornmarket. Five minutes later, he felt inside his sports jacket for his wallet, picked up his brief-case, left the queue, and disappeared into a tiny side street between a jeweller's shop and Woolworths. There, pulling off his tie and sticking it in his pocket, he walked down the steps of the entrance to The Corn Dolly. It was just after ten minutes to one.

The bar to his right was crowded with about forty or fifty men, most of them appearing to be in their early twenties and almost all of them dressed in denims and dark-coloured anoraks. But clearly Edward was no stranger here. He walked through a wide porch-way into the rear bar – a more sedate area with upholstered wall-seats and low tables where a few older men sat eating sausages and chips.

'A pint of bitter, please.'

Whether it was his upper-class accent, or the politeness of his request, or his somewhat youthful features, that caused the barmaid to glance at him – it made no difference. She pulled his pint, and the boy sauntered back to the main bar. Here, to his left, was a small dais, about one foot high and measuring some three yards by five, its dullish brown linoleum looking as if a group of Alpine mountaineers had walked across it in their crampons. Only a few chairs were set about the room, and clearly the clientèle here was not the kind to sit quietly and discuss the *Nichomachean Ethics* of Aristotle. And even had any wished to do so, such conversation would have been drowned instantly by the deafening blare of the juke-box. Edward sat on the edge of the dais, sipped his Worthington 'E', stared down at the red-and-black patterned carpet – and waited. Most of the other men pulled fitfully and heavily upon their cigarettes, the smoke curling slowly to a ceiling already stained a deep tobacco-brown. These men were waiting, too.

Suddenly the blue and yellow spotlights were switched on, the juke-box switched off, and a buxom girl in a black cloak, who had hitherto been seated sipping gin in some dim alcove, stepped out on to the miniature stage. Like iron filings drawn towards a powerful magnet, fifty young men who a moment before had been lounging at the bar were now formed into a solid phalanx around the three sides of the dais.

At that second only one man in the room had his eyes on the large blackboard affixed to the white-washed wall behind the dais – a blackboard whereon the management proudly proclaimed the programme for the week: go-go dancing every lunch time; live pop groups each evening; with 'Bar snacks always available' written in brackets at the bottom as an afterthought. But now a softer, more sensuous music filled the semi-subterranean vaults, and the girl billed as the 'Fabulous Fiona' was already unfastening the clasp at the top of her cloak. All eyes (without exception now) were riveted upon her as amateurishly but amiably enough she pranced about the floor, exhibiting a sequence of sequined garments, slowly divested and progressively piled on top of the cloak beneath the blackboard, until at last she was down to her panties and bra. A roar of approval greeted the doffing of this latter garment; but the former, its sequins glittering in the kaleidoscopic lights, remained staunchly in place, in spite of several quite unequivocal calls for its removal. She was a daring girl. With the palms of her hands supporting her weighty breasts, she paraded herself under the noses of several of the more proximate voyeurs – like a maiden holding up a pair of giant bowls in a ten-pin bowling alley. Then the record stopped, the synthetic smile was switched off, and with the cloak now covering all once more, the fabled girl retired to her alcove where she joined two bearded men whose functions in the proceedings had not been immediately apparent.

Most of the audience drifted back to the bar; some of them left; and one of them resumed his seat on the dais. In five minutes the girl would be repeating her routine, Edward was aware of that – as he was also aware of someone who had just sat down beside him.

'Fancy another pint?' asked Morse.

Edward looked as guilty as someone just accused of stealing from a supermarket; but he nodded: 'Yes, please.' Morse was a little surprised at this; and as he stood waiting for two further pints he wondered if the boy would take his chance to get away. Somehow, though, he knew he wouldn't. He just managed to beat the second lunge of bodies to the dais, where he managed a considerably closer view of a now more sinuously synchronised Fiona. The beer, too, was beginning to encourage a rather more positive reaction amongst the ringside viewers, for this time there was even a smattering of applause as she finally turned away to find her cloak.

'Do you come here often?' asked the boy.

'Not *every* lunch time,' Morse said lightly. 'What about you?'

'I've been once or twice before.'

'Shouldn't you be at school?'

'I've got the afternoon off. What about you?'

Morse was beginning to like the boy. 'Me? I do what I want to do every afternoon: watch the girls, drink a pint or two – anything. You see, I'm over eighteen, like you, lad. You *are* over eighteen, aren't you? For those who *aren't*, you know, "the girls and pints are out of order" – if you see what I mean. It's an anagram. "Striplings" – that's the answer. You interested in crosswords?'

But Edward ignored the question. 'Why did you follow me here?'

'I wanted to know why you lied to me, that's all – '

'*Lied?*'

' – about the note Ms Scott left for you.'

The boy took a deep breath. 'Hadn't we better sit somewhere else?'

For a start he was evasive; truculent even. But he had little chance against Morse. In some strange way (the boy felt) Morse's eyes were looking straight into his thoughts, alerted immediately to the slightest deviation from the truth. It was almost as if the man had known this truth before he'd asked, and was doing little more than note the lies. So, in the finish, he told Morse everything about Anne Scott: told him about his brother's boasts; about that week before she died when he'd seen her semi-naked and lusted after her; about the note he'd found on the door-mat; even about his own thoughts, so adolescently confused and troublous. And, progressively, he found himself liking Morse; found himself taking to a man who seemed humane and understanding – a man who listened carefully and who seemed so ready to forgive. Perhaps he was almost like a father . . . and Edward had never known his own.

Two things surprised Morse about his time with Edward Murdoch. The first was to discover what a pleasant and engaging lad he was, and to realise that others must have found this, too: his mother, his friends, his teachers – including Ms Anne Scott . . . The second cause of Morse's surprise was a more immediately personal one: during the energetic gyrations of the fair Fiona, he had felt not the slightest twinge of mild eroticism – and what would Freud have made of that? On second thoughts, however, he didn't much care; he'd come round to the view that Freud would have been a far more valuable citizen if he'd stuck to his research on local anaesthetics. Yet it was a bit worrying, all the same. As a boy, the apogee of any voyeuristic thrill had been the static nude, demurely sitting sideways on, and found about two-thirds of the way through the barber's copy of *Lilliput*. But now? The nudes were everywhere: on calendars, on posters, in fashion adverts, in newspapers – even on the telly. And the truth seemed to be that the naked female body was losing its magic. Understandable, yes; but for Morse, most disappointing. After all, he was only just past his fiftieth birthday.

The boy had gone now, and Morse debated whether he should stay on for Act V of the stripper's scheduled stint. But even the anticipation had now grown as cold as the experienced reality. And he left.

Chapter Seventeen

Go on; I'll follow thee
Hamlet, Act I, scene iv

At eight-thirty that evening, George Jackson was crouching behind a hedge, his bicycle lying a few yards away in the dark undergrowth. He had carefully reconnoitred the area, and chosen a large house standing well back from the western side of the Woodstock Road. No lights had shown in the front of the house on his two previous visits, and there were none tonight. No dogs, either. The hedge was high and thick, but where it reached the adjoining property it grew more thin and bedraggled. Ideal – affording a perfect view of the entrance to Field House Drive about thirty yards to the right and the telephone kiosk about twenty yards to the left, both illuminated adequately by the street lamp immediately opposite. Occasionally a solitary person strolled by. Once a young couple, their arms round each other's waists. A few cyclists, and an intermittent flow of traffic either way.

The light-blue Rolls Royce appeared from the direction of the A40 roundabout, travelling slowly along the bus lane. Jackson could see the driver fairly clearly, and he felt the pulses jumping in his wrists as he moved slightly forward and watched intently. The Rolls was doing no more than ten miles-per-hour as it passed the kiosk and covered the short distance to Field House Drive, its left blinker startlingly bright as it turned into the Drive and stopped – still almost completely visible. The driver got out, slammed the door to, and locked it. With the car keys still in his hand, he walked to the boot of the car, unlocked it, peered inside, and closed and re-locked it, without removing anything. Then he disappeared (though for no more than a few seconds) from Jackson's view, and must obviously have opened something on the obscured near-side of the car, for almost immediately another door was closed with an aristocratically engineered 'clunk'. The man was in full view again now, and this time he carried a brown carrier bag in his right hand. He appeared quite calm, glancing neither to his left nor right in curiosity or apprehension.

As he came directly opposite, Jackson could see him plainly beneath the street lamp: a thick-set man of medium height, about forty to forty-five, his thick, dark hair going grey at the temples. He was dressed in an expensive dark-blue suit, and looked exactly as Jackson thought he would – fortunate and prosperous. Not for a second did the staring eyes behind the hedge leave the man as he walked up to the kiosk, went inside, lifted the receiver, came out again, thrust a hand in his pocket as if to find loose change, and then re-entered the kiosk as a grey-haired woman went slowly by with her white-haired terrier. Jackson's body suddenly felt numb with panic as the man in the kiosk appeared to be speaking into the telephone receiver. Was he ringing the police? But, just as suddenly, all was normal again. The man came out of the kiosk, thrust the carrier bag swiftly into the ivy behind it, and then walked back to the Rolls, fingering his car keys as he did so. The Rolls turned in a slow and dignified sweep and, with a momentary flash from the polished silver of the bonnet's grill, accelerated away and disappeared towards the northern roundabout. The road was as still as the grave.

Jackson was now in a dilemma which his limited mental capacities had not foreseen. Was he to leave his vantage-point immediately, grab the bag, and cycle off as fast as he could down the nearest back streets into Jericho? Or was he to wait, take things coolly, saunter over the road when he could convince himself the coast was completely clear, and then cycle sedately down the well-lit reaches of the lower part of Woodstock Road as if nothing were amiss? He decided to wait. Five minutes; ten minutes; fifteen minutes. And still he waited. Suddenly a light flashed on in the front room of the house behind him, and he crouched down further as a young woman pulled the curtains across the window. He had to move. Feeling his way carefully along the inner side of the hedge, he reached the gate and walked down the grassy slope to the pavement. Cold sweat stood out on his brow, and he felt a prickling sensation along his shoulders as he crossed the road and walked the few yards to the kiosk. No one was in sight, and no car passed as he put his hand behind the kiosk and found the bag at once. He recrossed the road, put the bag inside the fishing-basket secured to the rack on his cycle, and rode down towards Jericho. Below South Parade the traffic was busier, and Jackson felt his confidence growing. He turned round as two youngsters behind him zoomed nearer on their L-plated motor-bikes, and saw them almost force off the road a middle-aged don – gown billowing out behind him, his left hand clutching a pile of books. But they were soon gone, searing through the streets and leaving a wake of comforting silence behind them. At The Horse and Jockey Jackson turned right and rode down Observatory Street; then straight over Walton Street and down into the familiar grid of the roads in Jericho. Outside 10 Canal Reach he padlocked the rear wheel of his cycle to the drain-pipe, unfastened the fishing-basket, and took out his door key. It had been more nerve-racking than he'd expected; easier, though, in a way. He looked up the Reach briefly before letting himself in. A few youngsters were fooling about outside The Printer's Devil, one of them jerking the front wheel of his cycle high into the air as he circled slowly round; two women pushed their way through the door marked 'Saloon'; a man was trying to back his car into a narrow space. Quite a bit of activity, really. But none of them had noticed *him* – Jackson was confident of that. And what if someone *had*?

Jackson was quite right in believing that none of the people he had noticed so casually had noticed him, in turn. Yet *someone* had noticed him; someone whom Jackson could not possibly have seen; someone bending low behind one of the cars parked outside The Printer's Devil, getting his hands very dirty as he fiddled with the greasy chain of his bicycle – a chain that had been, and still was, in perfect working order. The gown this person had been wearing, together with the pile of books he had been carrying, were now stowed away in the basket fixed to the front of the new, folding bicycle which he held upright on the pavement as he watched the door of 10 Canal Reach close.

Chapter Eighteen

An experienced, industrious, ambitious, and often quite picturesque liar
Mark Twain, *Private History of a Campaign that Failed*

The Chairman of the Oxford Book Association was relieved to see the Rolls Royce edge slowly through the narrow entrance to the Clarendon Institute car park. It was six minutes to eight, and he was having an anxious evening all round. Only about fifteen members had so far turned up, and already two of the committee were hastily removing many of the chairs in the large upstairs hall reserved for the meeting. Friday was never a good night, he knew that, and the late change of date could hardly have helped; but it was embarrassing, for everyone, to have an attendance as meagre as this.

Morse counted twenty-five in the audience when he tip-toed into the back row at five-past eight. After listening to *The Archers* he had felt restless, and the thought that he might be able to have a word with the chairman of the OBA about Anne Scott had finally tilted the balance in favour of 'Charles Richards: *Triumphs and Tribulations of the Small Publisher*'. It took only a few minutes for Morse to feel glad he had made the effort to attend. It was not (in Morse's eyes) that this thickishly set man, of medium height, had a particularly forceful presence – although, to be fair, his expensively-cut dark-blue suit lent a certain air of elegance and rank. It was his *manner* of speaking that was impressive. In his quietly spoken, witty, tolerant, self-deprecatory way, Richards spoke of his early days as a schoolmaster, his life-long interest in books, the embryonic idea of starting up for himself as a small publisher, his first, fairly disastrous months, his ladling of luck as time went by, with a few minor coups here and there, and finally the expansion of his company and the recent move to Abingdon. In his peroration he quoted Kipling (much to Morse's delight), and exhorted his listeners to treat that poet's 'twin impostors' with the same degree of amused – or saddened – cynicism.

He'd been good – there was no doubt of that – possessing as he did that rare gift of speaking to an audience in an individual-ised, personal sort of way, as if he were somehow interested in each of them. Afterwards there were a lot of questions, as if the audience, in its turn, was directly interested in the man who had thus addressed them. Too many questions, for Morse's liking. It was already half-past nine, and he hadn't drunk a pint all day.

'One more question – we really must make this the last, I'm afraid,' said the chairman.

'You said you were a schoolmaster, Mr Richards,' said a woman in the front row. 'Were you a *good* schoolmaster?'

Richards got to his feet and smiled disarmingly. 'I was rather hoping no one would ask me that. The answer is "no", madam. I was *not* a roaring success as a schoolmaster, I'm afraid. The trouble was, I'm sorry to say, that I just wasn't any good at keeping discipline. In fact, my lessons sounded rather like those recordings on the radio of Mrs Thatcher addressing the House of Commons.'

It was a good note on which to end, and the excellent im-pression the speaker had made was finally sealed and approved. The audience laughed and applauded – all the audience except one, that was, and that one man was Morse. He sat, the sole occupant of the back row, frowning fiercely, for the suspicion was slowly crossing his mind that this man was talking a load of bogus humbug.

At the bar downstairs, the chairman greeted Morse and said how glad he was to see him again. 'You've not met our speaker before, have you? Charles Richards – Chief Inspector Morse.'

The two men shook hands.

'I enjoyed your talk – ' began Morse.

'I'm glad about that.'

' – except for the last bit.'

'Really? Why – ?'

'I just don't believe you were a lousy schoolmaster, that's all,' said Morse simply.

Richards shrugged his shoulders. 'Well, let's put it this way: I soon realised I wasn't really cut out for the job. But why did you mention that?'

Morse wasn't quite sure. Yet the truth was that Richards had just held a non-captive audience for an hour and a half with ridiculous ease – an audience that had listened to this virtually unknown man with a progressively deeper interest, respect, and enthusiasm. What could the same man have done with the receptive, enquiring minds of a class of young schoolboys?

'I think you were an excellent schoolmaster, and if I were a headmaster now, I'd appoint you tomorrow.'

'I may have exaggerated a bit,' conceded Richards. 'It's always tempting to play for a laugh, though, isn't it?'

Morse nodded. That was one way of putting it, he supposed. The other way was that this man could be a formidable two-faced liar. 'You've not been here – near Oxford – very long?'

'Three months. You couldn't have been listening very carefully, Inspector – '

'You knew Anne Scott, didn't you?'

'Anne?' Richards' voice was very gentle. 'Yes, I knew Anne all right. She used to work for us. You know, of course, that she's – dead.'

The chairman apologised for butting in, but he wished to introduce Richards to the other committee members.

'You won't perhaps know . . . ?' Morse heard the chairman say.

'No, I'm afraid I don't get over to Oxford much. In fact . . . '

Morse drifted away to drink his beer alone, feeling suddenly bored. But boredom was the last thing that Morse should have felt at that moment. Already, had he known it, he had heard enough to put him on the right track, and, indeed, even now his mind was beginning to stir in the depths, like the opening keys of *Das Rheingold* in the mysterious world of the shadowy waters.

When Richards took his leave, just on ten o'clock, Morse insinuated himself into a small group gathered round the bar, and lost no time in asking the bearded chairman about Anne Scott.

'Poor old Anne! She wasn't with us long, of course, but she was a jolly good committee member. Full of ideas, she was. You see, one of our big problems is getting some sort of balance between the literary side of things – you know, authors, and so on – and the technical side – publishing, printing, that sort of thing. We're naturally a bit biased towards the literary side, but an awful lot of our members are more interested in the purely technical, business side – and it was Anne, actually, who suggested we should try to get Charles Richards. She used to work for him once and she – well, we left it to her. She fixed it all up. I thought he was good, didn't you?'

Morse nodded his agreement. 'Very good, yes.' But his mind was racing twenty furlongs ahead of his words.

'Pity we didn't get a decent turn-out. Still, it was their loss. Perhaps with the change of date and everything . . . '

Morse let him go on, then drained his beer, and stood silently at the corner of the bar with a replenished pint. His mind, which had been so obtuse up until this point in the case, was now extraordinarily clear – and he felt excited.

It was then that he heard the whine of the police and ambulance sirens. *Déjà écouté.* How long was it since Charles Richards had left? Quarter of an hour, or so? Oh God! What a fool he'd been not to have woken up earlier! The light-blue Rolls Royce he'd seen outside The Printer's Devil that day when he'd tried to call on Anne, the parking ticket on the windscreen; the reminder of that incident the following morning (that had *almost* clicked!), with the notice pasted on the Jaguar's windscreen in the car park of the Clarendon Institute; the recollection (only now!) of what it was that Anne had told him . . . All these thoughts now shifted into

focus, all projecting the same clear picture of Charles Richards –
that fluently accomplished liar he'd been listening to less than an
hour ago. It was *Charles Richards* who had visited 9 Canal Reach
the day Anne Scott had died, for when Morse had parked in the
comparatively empty yard of the Clarendon Institute more than a
couple of hours ago he had reversed the Jaguar into a space next
to a large and elegantly opulent Rolls. A light-blue Rolls.

Morse pushed a 5p piece into the pay-phone in the foyer and
asked for Bell. But Bell wasn't in, and the desk sergeant didn't
know exactly where he was. He knew where Bell was making for
though: there'd been a murder and –

'You got the address, sergeant?'

'Just a minute, sir. I've got it here . . . it was somewhere down
in Jericho . . . one of those little roads just off Canal Street, if I
remember . . . '

But Morse had put down the phone several words ago.

'Don't tell me you've had another meeting at the Clarendon
Institute, sir,' said Walters.

Morse ignored the question. 'What's the trouble?'

'Jackson, sir. He's dead. Been pretty badly knocked about.'
He pointed a thumb towards the ceiling. 'Want to see him?'

'Bell here yet?'

'On his way. He's been over to Banbury for something, but he
knows about it. We got in touch with him as soon as we heard.'

'Heard?'

'Another anonymous phone call.'

'When was that?'

'About a quarter-past nine.'

'You sure of that?' Morse sounded more than a little puzzled.

'It'll be booked in – the exact time, I mean. But the message
was pretty vague and . . . '

'Nobody took much notice, you mean?'

'It wasn't that, sir. But you can't expect them to follow up
everything – you know, just like that. I mean . . . '

'You mean they're all bloody incompetent,' snapped Morse.
'Forget it!'

Morse ascended the mean, narrow, little flight of stairs
and stood on the miniature landing outside the front bedroom.
Jackson's body lay across the rumpled bed-clothes, his left leg

dangling over the side, his bruised and bleeding head turned towards the door. The floor of the small room at the side of the single bed was strewn with magazines.

'I've not really had a good look around, sir,' ventured Walters. 'I thought I'd better wait for the inspector. Not much we could have done for him, is there?'

Morse shook his head slowly. The man's head lay in a large sticky-looking stain of dark red blood, and to Morse George Jackson appeared very, very dead indeed.

'I'll tell you exactly when he died, if you like,' volunteered Morse. But before he could fill in the dead man's timetable, the door below was opened and slammed, and Bell himself was lumbering up the stairs. His greeting was predictable.

'What the 'ell are you doing here, Morse?'

For the next hour the biggest difficulty was for the three policemen, the two fingerprint men, and the photographer to keep out of one another's way in the rooms of the tiny house. Indeed, when the hump-backed police surgeon arrived, he flatly refused to look at the corpse unless everyone else cleared out and went downstairs; and when he finally descended from his splendid isolation, his findings appeared to have done little to tone down his tetchiness.

'Between half-past seven and nine, at a guess,' he replied to Bell's inevitable question.

Walters looked quizzically at Morse, who sat reading one of the glossy 'porno' magazines he had brought from upstairs.

'You still sex-mad, I see, Morse,' said the surgeon.

'I don't seem to be able to shake it off, Max.' Morse turned over a page. 'And you don't improve much, either, do you? You've been examining all our bloody corpses for donkey's years, and you still refuse to tell us when they died.'

'When do *you* think he died?' From his tone the surgeon seemed far more at ease than at any time since he'd entered.

'Me? What's it matter what I think? But if you want me to try to be a *fraction* more precise than you, Max, I'd say – mm – I'd say between a quarter-past seven and a quarter-to eight.'

The surgeon allowed himself a lop-sided grin. 'Want a bet, Morse?'

'You can't loose with your bloody bets, can you? What's your bet? He died sometime *tonight* – is that it?'

'I think – *think*, mind you, Morse – that he might well have died a little later than you're suggesting; though why anyone should take an atom of notice of your ideas, God only knows. What really astounds me is that with your profound ignorance of pathology and its kindred sciences you have the effrontery to have any ideas *at all*.'

'What's your bet, Max?' asked Morse in the mildest tones.

The surgeon mused. 'Off the record, this is – agreed? I'll say between er – No! You only allowed yourself half an hour, didn't you? So, I'll do the same. I'll say between a quarter-past *eight* and a quarter-to *nine*. Exactly one hour later than you.'

'How much?'

'A tenner?'

The two men shook hands on it, and the surgeon left.

'Very interesting!' mumbled Bell, but Morse appeared to have resumed his reading. In fact, however, Morse's mind was peculiarly active as he turned the pages of the lurid and crudely explicit magazine. After all, he was at least contemplating one of the few clues furnished at the scene of the crime: mags (pornographic); mags (piscatorial); fingerprints (Jackson's); body (Jackson's) – and little else of much importance. A bare, stark murder. No obvious motive; no murder weapon; a crudely commonplace scene; well, that was what Bell would be thinking. With Morse it was quite different. He was confident he knew the solution even before the problem had been posed, and his cursory look round Jackson's bedroom had done little more than to corroborate his convictions: he knew the time of the murder, the weapon of the murder, the motive of the murder – even the name of the murderer. Poor old Bell!

Morse was still thinking, ten minutes later, that he had probably missed the boat in life and should have been a very highly paid and inordinately successful writer of really erotic pornography – when Walters came back into the room and reported to Bell.

Jackson, it appeared, had been seen around in Jericho that evening: at half-past five he had called in the corner grocery store for a small loaf of brown bread; at a quarter-to seven he had gone across to Mrs Purvis's to try to normalise the flushing functions of her recently installed water closet; at about five-past eight –

'*What*?' cried Morse.

' – at about five-past eight, Jackson went across to The Printer's Devil and bought a couple of pints of – '

'*Nonsense!*'

'But he *did*, sir! He was *there*! He played the fruit-machine for about ten minutes and finally left about twenty-past eight.'

Morse's body sank limply into the uncomfortable armchair. Had he got it all wrong? *All* of it? For if Jackson was blowing the froth off his second pint and feeding 10p's into the slot after eight o'clock, then without the slimmest shadow of doubt it could assuredly *not* have been Charles Richards who murdered George Alfred Jackson, late resident of 10 Canal Reach, Jericho, Oxford.

'Better have that tenner ready, Morse!' said Bell.

Chapter Nineteen

Alibi: (L. 'alibi', elsewhere); the plea in a criminal charge of having been elsewhere at the material time
Oxford English Dictionary

In the current telephone directory, neither Richards (C.) nor Richards Publishing Company (or whatever) of Abingdon was listed, and Morse realised he would have saved himself the bother of looking if he had remembered Richards' recent arrival in Oxfordshire. But the supervisor of Telephone Enquiries was able, after finally convincing herself of Morse's *bona fides*, to give him two numbers: those of Richards, C., 261 Oxford Avenue, Abingdon, and of Richards Press, 14 White Swan Lane, Abingdon. Morse tried the latter first, and heard a recorded female voice inform him that in gratitude for his esteemed enquiry the answering machine was about to be activated. He tried the other number. Success.

'I was just on my way to the office, Inspector, but I don't suppose you've rung up about a printing contract, have you?'

'No, sir. I just wondered if you'd heard about the trouble in Jericho last night.'

'Trouble? You don't mean my vast audience rioted after my little talk?'

'A man was murdered in Jericho last night.'

'Yes?' (Had Charles Richards' tone inserted the question-mark? The line was very crackly.)

'Pardon?'

'I didn't say anything, Inspector.'

'His name was Jackson – George Jackson, and I think you may have known him, sir.'

'I'm afraid you're mistaken, Inspector. I don't know any Jackson in Jericho. In fact, I don't think I know *anyone* in Jericho.'

'You used to, though.'

'Pardon, Inspector?' (Surely the line wasn't all *that* bad?)

'You knew Anne Scott – you told me so.'

'What's that got to do with this?'

'Jackson lived in the house immediately opposite her.'

'Really?'

'You didn't know where she lived?'

'No, I didn't. You tell me she lived in Jericho but – well, to be truthful, I thought Jericho was somewhere near Jerusalem until . . . ' Charles Richards hesitated.

'Until what?'

'Until I heard of Anne's – suicide.'

'You were, shall we say, pretty friendly with her once?'

'Yes, I was.'

'Too friendly, perhaps?'

'Yes, you could say that,' said Richards quietly.

'You never visited her in Jericho?'

'No, I did not!'

'But she got in touch with you?'

'She wrote – yes. She wrote on behalf of the Book Association, asking me if I'd talk about – well, you know that. I said I would – that's all.'

'She must have known you were coming to Abingdon.'

'We're beating about the bush, aren't we, Inspector? Look, I was very much in love with her once, and we – we nearly went off together, if you must know. But it didn't work out like that. Anne left the company – and then things settled down a bit.'

'A *bit*?'

'We wrote to each other.'

'Not purely casual, chatty letters, though?'

Again Richards hesitated and Morse heard the intake of breath at the other end. 'I loved the girl, Inspector.'

'And she loved you in return.'

'For a long time, yes.'

'You've no idea why she killed herself?'

'No, I haven't.'

'Do you remember where you were on the afternoon of the day she died?'

'Yes, I do. I read about her death in *The Oxford Mail* and – '

'Where were you, sir?'

'Look, Inspector, I don't want to tell you that. But, please believe me, if it really – '

'Another girl friend?'

'It could have been, couldn't it? But I'm – '

'You deny your car was parked in Jericho at the bottom of Victor Street that afternoon?'

'I certainly do!'

'And what if I told you I could prove that it was?'

'You'd be making one almighty mistake, Inspector.'

'Mm.' It was Morse's turn to hesitate now. 'Well, let's forget that for the minute, sir. But it's my official duty, I'm afraid, to ask you about er about this person you saw that afternoon. You see – '

'All right, Inspector. But you must promise me on your honour that this whole thing won't go an inch further if – '

'I promise that, sir.'

Morse rang the girl immediately, and she sounded a honey – although a progressively angrier honey. She was reluctant to answer any of Morse's questions for a start, but she slowly capitulated. Yes, if he must know, she'd been in bed with Charles Richards. How long for? Well, she'd *tell* him how long for. From about eleven-thirty in the morning to after five in the afternoon. All the bloody time! So there! As he put down the phone Morse wondered what she was like, this girl. She sounded sensuous and passionate, and he thought perhaps that it might be in the long-term interests of justice as well as to his own short-term benefit if he kept a note of her address and telephone number. Yes. Mrs Jennifer Hills who lived at Radley – just between Oxford and Abingdon: Jennifer Hills . . . yet another part of the new picture that was gradually forming in his mind. It was rather like the painting by numbers he'd seen in the toy shops: some areas were numbered for green, some for orange, some for blue, some for red, some for yellow – and, suddenly, there it was! The picture of something you'd little chance of guessing if you hadn't known: 'Sunset over Galway Bay', perhaps – or 'Donald Duck and Goofy'.

If Morse had but known it, Jennifer Hills was thinking along very similar lines. Her husband, Keith, a representative for the Gulf Petroleum Company, was still away in South Africa, and she herself, long-legged, lonely, randy and ready enough this featureless Saturday morning, had liked the sound of the chief inspector's voice. Sort of educated – but sort of close, too, and confidential – if only she could have explained it. Perhaps he might call and give her some 'inter-' something. Interrogation, that was it! And possibly some inter-something-else as well . . . How silly she'd been to get so cross with him! It was all Charles Richards' fault! She'd heard nothing from him since that exasperating phone call, and instinct told her to keep well away – at least for the time being. Yes . . . it might be nice, though, if the inspector called, and she found herself willing the phone to ring again.

But it didn't.

Chapter Twenty

Certum est quia impossibile est
Tertullian, *De Carne Christi*

'You were quite right, you know,' conceded Bell, when Morse looked into his office in the middle of that Saturday afternoon. 'Jackson had been bashed about the head quite a bit, it seems, but nothing all *that* serious. Certainly not serious enough to give him his ticket. The real trouble was the edge of that head-post on the bed – just like you said, Morse. Someone must have tried to shake his teeth out and cracked his skull against the upright.'

'You make it sound like a football match.'

'Boxing match, more like.'

'Blood all over the other fellow?'

'Pretty certainly, I'd think. Wouldn't you?'

Morse nodded. 'Accidental, perhaps?'

'Accidentally bloody deliberate, Morse – and don't you forget it.'

Morse nodded again. As soon as the surgeon had mentioned 'a squarish sharp-edged weapon', it had merely corroborated the suspicion he'd originally formed when he'd examined the bed-post, only about a foot from Jackson's head. To his naked eye, at the time, there had been nothing to confirm the suspicion, but he was as happy as the rest of them to rely upon the refinements of forensic tests. The weapon was settled then, and Morse felt he ought to put his colleague on the right lines about motive, too.

'Whoever killed him was pretty obviously looking for something, don't you think, Bell? And not just the address of some deaf-and-dumb nymphomaniac, or the results of the latest pike-angling competition.'

'You think he found what he was looking for?'

'I dunno,' said Morse.

'Well, I'll tell you one thing. We've been over the house with a nit-comb, and – nothing! Nothing that's going to help us. Fishing tackle galore, tools, drills, saws – you name it, he's got it in the do-it-yourself line. So what, though? He goes fishing most days, and he does a few handyman jobs round the streets. Good luck to him!'

'Did you find a trowel?' asked Morse quietly.

'Trowel? What's that got to – '

'He mended the Scott woman's wall – did you know that?'

Bell looked up sharply. 'Yes, as a matter of fact, I did. And if I may say so, Morse, I'm beginning to wonder – '

'What about bird watching?'

'What the 'ell's – '

'There was a pair of binoculars in the bedroom, you knew that.'

'All right. He went fishing, and he occasionally had a look at the kingfishers.'

'Why keep 'em in the bedroom, though?'

'You tell *me*!'

'I reckon he used to have a look at the bird across the way every now and then.'

'You mean, he – '

'No curtains, were there?'

'The dirty little sod!'

'Come off it! I'd have done the same myself.'

'Funny, isn't it? The way you just happened to be in Jericho. Both times, too.'

'Coincidence. Life's full of coincidences.'

'Do you appreciate, Morse, what the statistical chances are of you – '

'Phooey! Let me tell you something, Bell. *Statistically*, a woman should have her first baby at the age of nineteen, did you know that? But she shouldn't really start copulating before the age of twenty-six!'

Bell let it go, and his shoulders sagged as he sat at his desk. 'It's going to be one helluva job getting to the bottom of this latest business, you know. Nothing to go on, really. No one saw anybody go into the house – no one! It's that bloody boat-yard, you see. All of 'em there just get used to seeing people drifting in and out all the time. Augh! I don't know!'

'You interviewed the people who saw Jackson in the pub that night?'

'Most of 'em. The landlord sets his clock about five minutes fast, but you can take it from me that Jackson was there until about twenty-past eight.'

Morse pursed his lips. Charles Richards certainly seemed to have provided himself with a Kruger-rand alibi, for *he* – Morse himself – had been sitting in the audience *listening* to the beggar, from about five-past eight to way gone half-past nine. It was absolutely and literally impossible for Richards to have murdered Jackson! Shouldn't he accept that indisputable fact? But Morse enjoyed standing face-to-face with the impossible, and his brain kept telling him he could – and must – begin to undermine that impregnable-looking alibi. It was the second telephone call that worried him: someone had been anxious for the police to have a very definite idea indeed of the time when Jackson had died – a time that put Charles Richards completely in the clear. And who was it who had made that call? It couldn't, quite definitely, have been Jackson this time. But, just a minute. *Could* it just conceivably have been Jackson? What if . . . ?

Bell's thoughts had clearly been following along a parallel track. 'Who do you think phoned us about it, Morse? Do you think it was the same person who rang us about the Scott woman?'

'I don't think so, somehow.'

'Morse! Have you got *any* ideas about this whole business?'

Morse sat silently for a while, and then decided to tell Bell everything he knew, starting with the evening when he'd met Anne Scott, and finishing with his telephone call to Jennifer Hills. He even told Bell about the illicit fiver handed over to the Jericho locksmith. And, in fact (could the two men but have realised it) several of the colours in the pattern were already painted in, although the general picture seemed obstinately determined not to reveal itself.

'If you can help me in any way,' said Bell quietly, 'I'll be grateful – you know that, don't you.'

'Yes, I know that, my old friend,' said Morse. 'And I'll tell you what I'll do. I'll try to *think* a bit more. Because there's something, *somewhere*, that we're all missing. God knows what it is, though – *I* don't.'

Chapter Twenty-one

'I have already chose my officer'
Othello Act I, scene i

Sunday-working was nothing particularly unusual for Bell, but as he sat in his office the following afternoon he knew that he would have been more gainfully employed if he had stayed at home to rake the autumn leaves from his neglected lawn. Reports were still filtering through to him, but there seemed little prospect of any immediate break in the case. After the initial spurt of blood and splurge of publicity, the murder of George Jackson was stirring no ripples of any cosmic concern. Apart from a few far-flung cousins, the man had left behind him neither any immediate family nor any traceable wake of affection. To those who had known him vaguely, he had been a mean and unloved little man, and to the police the manner of his death had hardly risen to the heights of inglorious wickedness. Yet several facts were fairly clear to Bell. Someone had managed to get into number 10 between half-past eight and nine that Friday evening, had probably argued with Jackson in a comparatively pacific way, then threatened and physically intimidated the man, and finally – accidentally or deliberately – cracked his thinly-boned skull against the bed-post in his bedroom. The evidence strongly suggested, too, that Jackson's visitor had been looking for something specific, since the contents of all the drawers and cupboards in the house had been methodically and neatly examined; only in the bedroom were there the signs of frenetic haste and agitation. But of the identity of this visitor, or of the object of his quest, the police as yet had no real ideas at all. No one in the Reach or in the neighbouring streets appeared either to have seen or heard anything or anyone suspicious, and the truth was that only the sudden and disastrous blowing of a TV valve would have caused the majority of Jackson's fellow-citizens to look out into the darkened streets that evening: for from 8.30 to 10.30 p.m., viewing all over Britain was monopolised by the Miss World Competition. Poor Jackson, alas, had missed the final adjudication, and faced instead the final judgement.

Walters called in at the office in mid-afternoon, after yet another fruitless search for the smallest nugget of gold. He was fairly sure in his own mind that they were trying to drive a motorway through a cul-de-sac, and that the solution to Jackson's murder was never going to be discovered in isolation from the death of Ms Scott. He told Bell so, too, but the answer he received was callous and unkind.

'You don't need to be a bloody genius to come to that conclusion, lad.'

Bell was weary and dejected, Walters could see that, and there seemed little point in staying. But there was one further point he thought he might mention:

'Did you know, sir, that there wasn't a single book in Jackson's house?'

'Wasn't there?' said Bell absently.

* * *

Mr Parkes felt happy that Sunday afternoon. One of the social workers from the Ferry Centre had brought a cake for him, and there were tears of gratitude in his old eyes as he asked the young lady inside and poured two glasses of dry sherry. It had been several years since anyone had remembered his birthday. After his visitor had left, he poured himself a second glass and savoured his little happiness. How had she known it was his birthday? And suddenly something clicked – birthdays! That's what they'd been talking about when Gwendola had laid on her little treat with the sherry. Talk of the Bridge Club's anniversary must have led on to birthdays, he was sure of it now – although it seemed a trivial remembrance. Yet the police had asked him to let them know if he could recall anything about that night, and he rang up St Aldates immediately.

'Ah, I see,' said Bell. 'Yes, that's very interesting. Birthdays, eh?'

The old man elaborated as far as he could, and Bell thanked him with a fair show of simulated gratitude. It was good of the old boy to ring up, really. Birthdays! He made a note of the call and put the sheet of paper in his tray: Walters could stick it with the rest of the stuff.

In fact, the note just written was to be the final contribution of Chief Inspector Bell to the riddle of the Jericho Killings.

Morse had been a little surprised when earlier in the week, after seeking an interview with his Assistant Chief Commissioner, he learned that the ACC, in turn, would welcome a little chat with Morse, and that 'a cup of tea at my little place up at Beckley' would make a pleasant rendezvous. At four-thirty, therefore, on that sunny October afternoon, the two men sat on a weedless lawn overlooking the broad, green sweep of Otmoor, and Morse recounted to his senior officer the irregularities and improprieties of his own investigations over the previous fortnight. The ACC was silent for a long time, and the answer, when it finally came from those rather bloated lips, was unexpected.

'I want you to take over the case, Morse. You're quite good at that sort of thing; Bell isn't.'

'But I didn't come to ask – '

'It's what you've got.'

'Well, I'm sorry, sir, but I can't accept the case. It's just not fair to belittle Bell – '

'Belittle?' The ACC smiled curiously, and Morse knew he'd missed a point somewhere. 'Don't worry about Bell! I'll ring him and put things straight myself.'

'But I just – '

'Shut your mouth a minute, Morse, will you?' (That maddening smile again!) 'You see, you've done me a good turn in a way. I know you didn't apply for the vacant super's post, but I was er thinking of recommending you, actually. On second thoughts, though, I don't think I shall bother. The job's going to involve an awful lot of public relations – very important these days, Morse! – and er I just don't think you're cut out for that sort of thing. Do you?'

'Well, I don't know, really.'

'Anyway, Bell applied – and he's senior to you anyway, isn't he?'

'Only just,' mumbled Morse.

'He's a good man. Not the greatest intellect in the Force – but neither are you, Morse. So I can work things very sweetly for you, can't I? I can let Bell know he's got promotion and tell him to drop this Jericho business straightaway.'

'I'd rather think things over, sir, if you don't mind.'

'No sense, old chap. We made the appointment yesterday, actually.'

'Oh.' Morse felt a twinge of envy and regret; but all that public relations stuff would have bored him to death, he knew that.

The ACC interrupted his thoughts. 'You know, Morse, you don't go about things in the right way, do you? With your ability you could have been sitting in my chair, and earning a sight more – '

'I've got a private income, sir – and a private harem.'

'I thought your father was a taxi driver?'

Morse stood up. 'That's right, sir. He used to drive the Aga Khan.'

'You got any of your private harem to spare?'

'Sorry, sir. I need 'em all.'

'You'll need Lewis, too, I suppose?'

For the first time that afternoon Morse looked happy.

BOOK THREE

Chapter Twenty-two

Those milk-paps
That through the window-bars bore at men's eyes
Timon of Athens Act IV, scene iii

Even if, in his boyhood, Sergeant Lewis's parents had been twinly blessed with privilege and wealth, it seems unlikely that their son would have won a scholarship to Winchester. As it was – after leaving school at fifteen – Lewis had worked his way up through a series of day-release courses and demanding sessions at night schools to a fair level of competence in several technical skills. At the age of twenty he had joined the police force and had never really regretted his decision. Promoted to the rank of sergeant ten years ago, he was as sensibly aware of his potential as of his limitations. It was six years ago that he had first come within Morse's orbit, and in retrospect he felt honoured to have been associated with that great man. In retrospect, let it be repeated. During the many, many hours he had spent in Morse's company on the several murder cases that had fallen within their sphere of duty, there had been frequent occasions when Lewis had wished him in hell. But there were infinitely worthwhile compensations – were there not? – in being linked with a man of Morse's almost mythical methodology. For all his superior's irascibility, crudity, and self-indulgence, Lewis had taken enormous pride – yes, *pride* – in his friendship with the man whom almost all the other members of the Thames Valley Constabulary had now come to regard as a towering, if somewhat eccentric, genius. And in the minds of many the phenomenon of Morse was directly associated with *himself* – yes, with *Lewis*! They spoke of Morse and Lewis almost in the same vein as they spoke of Gilbert and Sullivan, or Moody and Sanky, or Lennon and McCartney. Thus far, however, in the case of the Jericho killings, Lewis's sole contribution had been to drive his chief down to the Clarendon Institute car park about a fortnight ago. And why, oh why (as Lewis had then wondered) hadn't the idle beggar taken a bus? Surely that would have been far, far quicker.

It was, therefore, with a lovely amalgam of treasured reminiscence and of personal satisfaction that Lewis listened to Morse's voice on the phone at 7.30 a.m. the following morning.

'Yes, sir?'

'I want your help, Lewis.'

'How do you mean, sir? I can't help much today. I'm running this road-safety campaign in the schools and – '

'Forget it! I've had a word with Strange. As I say, I need your help.'

Suddenly the uplands of Lewis's life were burnished with the autumn sun. *He* was needed.

'I'll be glad, sir – you know that. When do you want me?'

'I'm in my office. Just get your bloody slippers off and get the car out!'

For the first time for many months, Lewis felt preternaturally happy; and his Welsh wife, cooking the eggs and bacon, could sense it all.

'I know 'oo that was – I can see it from your face, boy. Inspector Morse. Am I right?'

Lewis said nothing, but his face was settled and content, and his wife was happy for him. He was a good man, and his own happiness was a source of hers, too. She was almost glad to see him bolt his breakfast down and go: he had that look about him.

Lewis saw the stubs of filter-tipped cigarettes in the ash-tray when he knocked and entered the office at ten-past eight. He knew that it was Morse's habit either to smoke at an extravagantly compulsive rate or not at all, and mentally he calculated that the chief must have been sitting there since about six-thirty. Morse himself, showing no sign of pleasure or gratitude that Lewis had effected such an early appearance, got down to business immediately.

'Listen, Lewis. If I left my car on a double yellow line in

North Oxford and a traffic warden copped me, what'd happen?'

'You'd get a ticket.'

'Oh, for Christ's sake, man! I know that. What's the *procedure*?'

'Well, as I say, you'd get a ticket under your wipers, and then after finishing work the warden would have to put the duplicates – '

'The what?'

'The duplicates, sir. The warden sticks the top copy on the windscreen, but there are two carbons as well. The first goes to the Fixed Penalty Office, and the second goes to the Magistrates' Clerk.'

'How do you come to know all this?'

'I'm surprised *you* don't, sir.'

Morse nodded vaguely. 'What if I wanted to pay the fine straightaway? Could I take the money – or sign a cheque – and, well, just pay it?'

'Oh, yes. Not at the Penalty Office, though. You'd have to take it to the Magistrates' Office.'

'But if the warden hadn't taken the carbon in – '

'Wouldn't matter. You'd take your ticket in, pay your fine – and then things would get matched up later.'

'They'd have a record of all that, would they? I mean, what the fine was for, who paid it, and so on?'

'Of course they would. On the ticket there'd be the details of the date, the time, the street, the registration number, as well as the actual offence – double yellows or whatever it was. And there'd be a record of who paid the fine, and when it was paid.'

Morse was impressed. 'You know, Lewis, I never realised how many bits and pieces a traffic warden had in that little bag of hers.'

'A lot of them are men.'

'Don't treat me like an idiot, Lewis!'

'Well, you don't seem to know much about . . . '

But Morse wasn't listening: he needed just a little confirmation, that was all, and again he nodded to himself – this time more firmly. 'Lewis, I've got your first little job all lined up.'

* * *

In fact, Lewis's 'first little job' took rather longer than expected, and it was just before noon when he returned and handed Morse a written statement of his findings:

Parking fine made out on Wed. 3rd Oct. for Rolls Royce, Reg. LMK 306V, parked on corner of Victor St. and Canal St. at 3.25 p.m. in area reserved for resident permit holders only. Fine paid by cheque on Friday 5th Oct. and the Lloyds a/c of Mr C. Richards, 216 Oxford Avenue, Abingdon, duly debited.

'Well, well, well!' Morse beamed hugely, wondered whether the last word was mis-spelt, reached for the phone, and announcing himself rather proudly by his full official title asked if he could speak to Mr Charles Richards. But the attractive-sounding voice (secretary, no doubt) informed him that Mr Richards had just gone off to lunch. Could Morse perhaps try again – in the morning?

'The *morning*?' squeaked Morse. 'Doesn't he work in the afternoons?'

'Mr Richards works very hard, Inspector' (the voice was somewhat sourer) 'and I think er I think he has a meeting this afternoon.'

'Oh, I see,' said Morse. 'Well, that's obviously much more important than co-operating with the police, isn't it?'

'I could *try* to get hold of him.'

'Yes, you could – and I rather hope you *will*,' said Morse quietly. He gave the girl his telephone number and said a sweet 'goodbye'.

The phone rang ten minutes later.

'Inspector Morse? Charles Richards here. Sorry I wasn't in when you called. Can I help you?'

'Yes, you can, sir. There are one or two things I'd like to talk to you about.'

'Really? Well, fire away. No time like the present.'

'I'd rather *see* you about things, if you don't mind, sir. Never quite the same over the phone, is it?'

'I don't see why not.'

Nor did Morse. 'One or two rather – delicate matters, sir. Better if we meet, I think.'

'As you wish.' Richards' voice sounded indifferent.

'Tomorrow?'

'Why not?'

'About ten o'clock?'

'Fine.'

'Any parking space outside your office?' Morse asked the question innocently enough, it seemed.

'I'll make sure there's a space, Inspector. Damned difficult parking a car these days, isn't it?' His voice sounded equally innocent.

Outside the inn the legend was printed 'Tarry ye at Jericho until your beards be grown'. Inside the inn, Joe Morley hoisted his vast-bellied frame on to the high stool at the corner of the public bar, and the landlord was already pulling a pint of draught Guinness.

'Evenin', Joe.'

'Evenin'.'

'Bit of excitement, we hear, down your criminal neck of the woods.'

Joe wiped the creamy froth from his thick lips. 'Poor old George, you mean?'

'You knew him pretty well, didn't you?'

'Nobody knew George very well. He were a loner, were George. Bloody good fisherman, though.'

'Bird watcher as well, wasn't he?'

'Was he?'

The landlord polished another glass and leaned forward. 'Used to watch the birds, Joe – and not just the feathered variety. Used to watch that woman opposite as killed herself – with a pair of bloody binoculars!'

' 'Ow do you know?'

'Mrs Purvis was tellin' old Len – you know old Len as comes in sometimes. No curtains in the bedroom, either!'

'Very nice, too, I should think.'

The landlord leaned forward again. 'Do you want to know summat else? George weren't doin' too badly with all the odd jobs he used to do, neither. Two hundred and fifty quid he put in the post office last Thursday – some OAP bonds or something.'

' 'Ow do you know?'

'You know old Alf as comes in. Well, his missus was talkin'

to, you know, that woman, whatsername, who works in the post office and – '

A group of youths came in, and the landlord reached up for two sets of darts and handed them over. 'The usual, lads?'

The middle-aged man who had been sitting silently at one of the tables moved over to allow the dartboard area to be cleared. He was beginning to feel very hungry indeed, for Morse had insisted (when he'd divided the Jericho pubs into two lists) that the early evening was the best time for pub gossip. 'Just *listen*, if you like,' Morse had said. 'I'll bet most of 'em there will be talking about Jackson.' And Lewis's hearing was good.

Morse himself, however, had heard nothing whatsoever about Jackson: it seemed that darts, football, and the price of beer had resumed their customary conversational priorities. Life went on as before – except for Anne Scott and George Jackson.

When, considerably over-beered, Morse looked back in his office at 9 p.m., he found an interesting report awaiting him. He had insisted that the fingerprint men should go and have another look round 10 Canal Reach; and they had found something new. Two prints – two fairly clear ones, too. And they weren't Jackson's.

Morse felt he'd had a pretty good day.

Chapter Twenty-three

And he made him a coat of many colours
Genesis, xxxvii. 3

Morse allowed himself half an hour along the A34 from Kidlington; and it was ample, for he spotted White Swan Lane as soon as he approached the town centre. *Richards Brothers, Publishing & Printing*, marked only by a brass plate to the right of the front door, was a converted nineteenth-century red-brick house, set back about ten yards from the street, with four parking lots marked out in white paint on the recently tarmacadamed front. One of the spaces was vacant, and as Morse pulled the Jaguar into it he was aware that someone standing by the first-floor window had been observing his arrival. A notice inside the open front door directed him up the wide, elegant staircase where the frosted-glass panel in the door to his right repeated the information on the plate downstairs, with the addendum *Please Walk In*.

A woman looked up from behind a desk littered with papers. A very attractive woman, too, thought Morse – though considerably older than she'd sounded on the phone.

'Inspector Morse, isn't it?' she asked without enthusiasm. 'Mr Richards is expecting you.'

She walked across to a door (CHARLES RICHARDS, MANAGER, in white plastic capitals), knocked quietly, and ushered Morse past her into the carpeted office, where he heard the door click firmly to behind him.

Richards himself got up from his swivel-chair, shook hands, and beckoned Morse to take the seat opposite him.

'Good to see you again, Inspector.'

But Morse ignored the pleasantry. 'You lied to me, sir, about your visit to Jericho on Wednesday, 3rd October, and I want to know why.'

Richards looked across the desk with what seemed genuine surprise. 'But I *didn't* lie to you. As I told you – '

'So if your car picked up a parking ticket that afternoon, someone *else* must have taken it to Oxford – is that right?'

'I – I suppose so, yes. But – '

'And if you paid the fine a couple of days later, someone must have pinched your cheque book and forged your signature? Is that it, sir?'

'You mean – you mean the cheque . . . ' Richards' voice trailed off rather miserably, and Morse pounced again.

'Of course, I fully realise that it must have been someone else, because you yourself, sir, were not in Oxford that afternoon – I checked that. The young lady – '

Richards leaned over the desk in some agitation, and waved his right hand from side to side as though wiping the last three words from a blackboard with some invisible rubber. 'Could we forget that, please?' he said earnestly. 'I – I don't want to get anyone else involved in this mess.'

'I'm afraid someone else already *is* involved, sir. As far as I'm concerned, you've got a water-tight alibi yourself – and all

I want to know is who it was who drove your car to Jericho that afternoon.'

'Inspector!' Richards sighed deeply and contemplated the carpet. 'I should have had more sense than to lie to you in the first place – especially over that wretched parking ticket. Though goodness knows how . . . ' He shook his head as if in disbelief. 'You must have some sharp-eyed policemen in the force these days.'

But Morse was too involved to look unduly smug, and Richards continued, his shoulders sagging as he breathed out heavily.

'Let me tell you the truth, Inspector. Anne Scott worked for me for several years, as you know. She was a very attractive girl – in her personality as well as in physical looks – and when we went away on trips together – well, I don't need to spell it all out, do I? I was happily married – in a vague sort of way, if you know what I mean – but I fell for Anne in a big way, and when we were away we used to book into hotels as man and wife. Not that it was all that often, really – I suppose about five or six times a year. She never made any great demands on me, and there was never really a time when we seriously thought of, you know, my getting a divorce and all that.'

'Did your wife know about it?'

'No, I honestly don't think she did.'

'So?'

'Well, I suppose like most people we – we perhaps began to feel after a while that it wasn't all quite so marvellously exciting as it had been; and when Anne decided it would be better if she left – well, I didn't object too strongly. In fact, to tell you the truth, I remember feeling a huge sense of relief. Huh! Odd, isn't it, really?'

'But you wrote to each other.'

Richards nodded. 'Not all that often – but we kept in touch, yes. Then last summer, when I moved up here, we suddenly found we were pretty near each other again, and she wrote and told me she could usually be free at least one afternoon a week and I – I found the temptation altogether too alluring, Inspector. I went to see her – several times.'

'You had a key?'

'Key? Er, no. I didn't have a key.'

'Was the door unlocked on the afternoon we're talking about?'

'Unlocked? Er, yes. It must have been, mustn't it? Otherwise – '

'Tell me what you did *then*, sir. Try to remember *exactly* what you did.'

Richards appeared to be reading the runes off the carpet once more. 'She wasn't in – well, that's what I thought. I called out, you know, sort of quietly – called her name, that is . . .'

'Go on!'

'Well, the place seemed so quiet and I thought she must have gone out for a few minutes, so – I went upstairs.'

'Upstairs?'

Richards smiled sadly, and then looked squarely into Morse's eyes. 'That's right. Upstairs.'

'Which room did you go in?'

'She had a little study in the back bedroom – Look! You know all this anyway, don't you?'

'I know virtually everything,' said Morse simply.

'Well, we normally had a little drink in there – a drop of wine or something – before we – we went to bed.'

'Wasn't that a bit risky – in broad daylight?'

There was puzzlement and unease in Richards' eyes for a moment now, and Morse pondered many things as he waited (far too long) for the answer.

'It's always risky, isn't it?'

'Not if you pull the curtains, surely?'

'Ah, I see what you mean!' Richards seemed suddenly relaxed again. 'Funny, isn't it, that she hadn't got round to putting any curtains up there?'

(One up to Richards!)

'What happened then, sir?'

'Nothing. After about twenty, twenty-five minutes or so, I began to get a bit anxious. It must have been about half-past three by then, and I felt something – something odd must have happened. I just left, that's all.'

'You didn't look into the kitchen?'

'I'd never been into the kitchen.'

'Had it started raining when you left, sir?'

'*Started*? I think it had been raining all the afternoon – well, drizzling fairly heavily. I know it was raining when I got there because I left my umbrella just inside the front door.'

'Just on the right of the door as you go in, you mean?'

'I can't be sure, Inspector, but – but wasn't it on the *left*, just *behind* the door? I may be wrong, though.'

'No, no, you're quite right, sir. You must forgive me. I was just testing you out, that's all. You see, somebody else saw the umbrella that afternoon – somebody who'd poked his nose into that house during the time you were there, sir.'

Richards looked down at his desk and fiddled nervously with a yellow ruler. 'Yes, I know that.'

'So, you see, I just had to satisfy myself it *was* you, sir. I wasn't sure even a minute ago about that; but I am now. As I say, your car was seen there, your black umbrella just behind the door, your dark-blue mackintosh over the banisters, and the light in the study. It wouldn't have been much good lying to me, sir.'

'No. Once I knew you'd found out about the car, I realised I might as well come clean. I was a fool not to – '

'You're *still* a fool!' snapped Morse.

'*What?*' Richards' head jerked up and his mouth gaped open.

'You're still lying to me, sir – you know you are. You see, the truth is that you weren't in Jericho at all that afternoon!'

'But – but don't be silly, Inspector! What I've just told you – '

Morse got to his feet. 'I shall be very glad if you can show me that mackintosh you were wearing, sir, because whoever it was who was in Anne Scott's house that afternoon, he was quite certainly *not* wearing a blue mackintosh!'

'I – I may have been mistaken – '

'You've got a dark blue mackintosh?'

'Yes, as a matter of fact, I have.'

'Excellent!' Morse appeared very pleased with himself as he picked up his own light-fawn raincoat from the arm of the chair. 'Have you also got a dark-grey duffle-coat, sir? Because that's the sort of coat that was seen on the banister in Anne Scott's house. And it was wet: somebody'd just come into the house out of the rain, and you told me – unless I misunderstood you, sir? – that there was no one else in the house.'

'Sit down a minute!' said Richards. He rested his chin on the palms of his hands and squeezed his temples with the ends of his fingers.

'You've been lying from the beginning,' said Morse. 'I knew that all along. Now – '

'But I *haven't* been lying!'

Suddenly Morse's blood surged upwards from his shoulders to the back of his neck as he heard the quiet voice behind him.

'Yes you have, Charles! You've been lying all your life. You've lied to me for years about everything – we both know it. The odd thing is that now you're lying to try to *save* me! But it's no good, is it?' The woman who had been seated behind the table in the office outside now walked into the room and sat on the edge of the desk. She turned to Morse: 'I'm Celia Richards, the wife of that so-called "husband" behind the desk there. He told me – but he'd no option really – that you were coming here today, and he didn't want Josephine, his normal secretary – and for all I know yet another of his conquests,' she added bitterly, 'he didn't want her to know about the police, and so he got *me* to sit out there. You needn't worry: it was all perfectly amicable. We had it all worked out. He'd told me you'd be asking about Jericho, and we decided that he'd try to bluff his way through. But if he didn't quite manage it – you did *pretty* well, you know, Charles! – then I agreed to come in. You see, Inspector, he left the intercom on all the time you've been speaking, and I've listened to every word that's been said. But it's no good any longer – is it, Charles?'

Richards said nothing: he looked an utterly defeated man.

'Have you got a cigarette, Inspector?' asked Celia as she unfolded her elegant legs and walked over to stand behind the desk. 'My turn, I think, Charles.'

Richards got up and stood rather awkwardly beside her as she took her seat on the executive chair, and drew deeply on one of Morse's cigarettes.

'I don't want to dwell on the point unduly, Inspector, but poor Charles here isn't the only accomplished liar in the room, is he? I think, if I may say so, that it was a pretty cheap and underhand little trick of *yours* to go on about those coats like you did. Mackintoshes and duffle-coats, my foot! You see, Inspector, it was *me* who went to see Anne Scott that afternoon, and I was wearing a brown leather-jacket lined with sheep-wool. It's in the cupboard next door, by the way.' For a moment her voice was vibrant with vindictiveness: 'Would you like to see it, Inspector Morse?'

Chapter Twenty-four

Some falsehood mingles with all truth
Longfellow, *The Golden Legend*

As he drove back to Oxford that lunch time, Morse thought about Celia Richards. She had told her tale with a courageous honesty and Morse had no doubt whatsoever that it was true. During her husband's earlier liaisons with Anne Scott, Celia had no shred of evidence to corroborate her suspicions, although there had been (she knew) much whispered rumour in the company. She *could* have been mistaken – or so she'd told herself repeatedly; and when Anne left she had felt gradually more reassured. At the very least, whatever there might have been between the pair of them had gone for good now – surely! Until, that is, that terrible day only a few weeks earlier when, with Charles confined to bed with 'flu, she had gone into the office to see Conrad, Charles's younger brother and co-partner, who worked on the floor above him. On Charles's desk, beneath a heavy, glass paper-weight, lay a letter, a letter written in a hand that was known to her, a letter marked 'Strictly Personal and Private'. And even at that very moment she had known, deep inside herself, the hurtful, heart-piercing truth of it all, and she had taken the letter and opened it in her car outside. It was immediately clear that Charles had already seen Anne Scott several times since the move to Abingdon, and the letter begged him to go to see her again – quickly, urgently. Anne was in some desperate sort of trouble and he, Charles, was the only person she could turn to. Money was involved – and this was stated quite explicitly; but above all she had to *see* him again. She had kept (she claimed) all the letters he had written to her, and suggested that if he didn't do as she wished she might have (as far as Celia could recall the exact words) 'to do something off her own bat which would hurt him'. She hated herself for doing it, but if threats were the only way, then threats it had to be. Celia had destroyed the letter – and taken her decision immediately: she herself would go to visit her husband's former lover. And she had done so. On Wednesday, 3rd October, Charles said he had a meeting and had taken the Mini to work, telling her not to expect him

home before about 6.30 p.m. The Rolls had been almost impossible to park – even the double yellow lines were taken up; but
finally she had found a space and had walked up Canal Reach,
up to number 9, where she found the door unlocked. ('Yes,
Inspector, I'm absolutely sure. I had no key – and how else
could I have got in?') Inside, there was no one. She had shouted.
No one. Upstairs she had found the study immediately, and
within a few minutes found, too, a pile of letters tied together
in one of the drawers – all written to Anne by Charles. Somehow, up until that point, she had felt an aggression and a purpose which had swamped all fears of discovery. But now she felt
suddenly frightened – and then, oh God! the next two minutes
were an unbearable nightmare. For someone had come in; had
shouted Anne's name; had even stood at the foot of the stairs!
Never in the whole of her life had she felt so petrified with
fear!

And then, it was all over. Whoever it was, had gone as suddenly as he had come; and after a little wait she herself, too,
had gone. The parking ticket seemed an utter triviality, and she
had paid the fine the next day – by a cheque drawn on her own
account. (' "C" for "Celia", Inspector!') So, that was that, and
she had burned all the letters without reading a single word. It
was only later, when she read of Anne's suicide, that the terrible
truth hit her: *she* had been in the house where Anne was hanging
dead and as yet undiscovered. She became so fluttery with panic
that she just *had* to speak to someone. At first she thought she
would unbosom herself to her brother-in-law, Conrad – always a
kind and loyal friend to her. But she'd realised that in the end
there could be only one answer: to tell her husband everything.
Which she had done. And it was *Charles* who had insisted that *he*
should, and would, shoulder whatever troubles his own ridiculous
escapades had brought upon her. It all seemed (Celia confessed)
too stupid and melodramatic now: their amateurish attempts at
collusion; those lies of Charles; and then his pathetic attempts
to tip-toe a way through the mine-field of Morse's explosive
questions.

Throughout Celia's story, Richards himself had sat silently;
and after she had finished, Celia herself lapsed into a similar,
almost abject, silence. How the pair would react – how they
did react – after his departure, Morse could only guess. They

had refused his offer of a drink at The White Swan, and Morse himself stoically decided that he would wait for a pint until he got back to Kidlington. For a couple of minutes he was held up along Oxford Avenue by temporary traffic lights along a short stretch of road repairs, and by chance he found himself noticing the number of the house on the gate-post to his left: 204. He remembered that he must be very close indeed to the Richards' residence, and as he passed he looked carefully at number 216 – set back some thirty yards, with a gravelled path leading up to the garage. Not all that palatial? Certainly there were other properties a-plenty nearby that could more appropriately have housed a successful businessman and his wife; and it suddenly occurred to Morse that perhaps Charles Richards was not quite so affluent as he might wish others to believe. It was a thought, certainly, but Morse could see little point in pursuing it. In fact, however, it would have repaid him handsomely at that point to have turned the Jaguar round immediately and visited the Abingdon branch of Lloyds Bank to try to seek some confidential insight into the accounts of Mr and Mrs Charles Richards, although not (it must be said) for the reason he had just considered. For the moment a mystery had been cleared up, and that, for a morning's work, seemed fair enough. He drove steadily on, passing a turning on his right which was sign-posted 'Radley'. Wasn't that where Jennifer Something, Charles Richards' latest bedfellow, was dispensing her grace and favours? It was; but even that little loose end was now safely tucked away – if Celia Richards was telling the truth . . .

At that point a cloud of doubt no bigger than a man's hand was forming on Morse's mental horizon; but again he kept straight ahead.

Back in Charles Richards' office, Celia stood by the window staring down at the parking area for many minutes after Morse had left – just as she had stood staring down when he had arrived and parked the Jaguar in the carefully guarded space. Finally she turned round and broke the prolonged silence between them.

'He's a clever man – you realise that, don't you?'

'I'm not sure.'

'Do you think – ?'

'Forget it!' He stood up. 'Feel like a drink?'

'Yes.' She turned round again and stared down at the street. She'd told only one big lie, but she'd felt almost sure that Morse had spotted it. Perhaps she was mistaken, though. Perhaps he wasn't quite as clever as she'd thought.

Chapter Twenty-five

The life of a man without letters is death
Cicero

In the light of a bright October morning the streets assumed a different aspect, and the terraced houses seemed less squeezed and mean. Along the pavements the women talked and polished the door fixtures, visited the corner shops and in general reasserted, with the men-folk now at work, their quiet and natural birthright. A sense of community was evident once more and the sunlight had brought back the colour of things.

Yes, Sergeant Lewis had spent an enjoyable and reasonably profitable morning in Jericho, and after lunch he reported to Morse's office in the Thames Valley Police HQ buildings in Kidlington. Discreet enquiries had produced a few further items of information about Jackson. Odd jobs had brought him a considerable supplement to his pension, and such jobs had hardly been fitful and minor. Indeed, it was quite clear that the man was far from being a pauper. The house had been his own, he had almost £1,500 in the Post Office Savings Bank, a very recent acquisition of £250 in Retirement Bonds, and (as Lewis guessed) perhaps some £1,000 of fishing equipment. Yet his business dealings with the Jericho traders had been marked by a grudging frugality, and the occasional granting of credit. But it seemed that he always met his debts in the end, and he was up to date with the Walton Tackle Shop on his instalments of £7.50 for a carbon-fibre fishing rod. He had no immediate relatives, and the assumption had to be that Jackson was the last of an inglorious line. But Lewis had met no real ill-feeling against the man: just plain indifference. And somehow it seemed almost sadder that way.

Morse listened with interest, and in turn recounted his own rather more dramatic news.

'Did you get a statement from her?' asked Lewis.

'Statement?'

'Well, we shall need one, shan't we?'

So it was that Lewis rang the number Morse gave him, discovered that Mrs Celia Richards was at home, and arranged to meet her that same afternoon. It seemed to Lewis an unnecessary duplication of mileage, but he forbore to make the point. As for Morse, his interest in the Richards' clan appeared to be waning, and at 3.40 p.m. he found himself entering 10 Canal Reach – though he couldn't have told anyone exactly why.

The blood-stained sheets had been removed from the bedroom in which Jackson had died, but the blankets were still there, neatly folded at the foot of the bare, striped mattress. On the floor the magazines had been stacked in their two categories, and Morse sat down on the bed and picked up some of the pornographic ones once more, flipping through the lewd and lurid photographs. One or two pages had an accompanying text in what looked to him like Swedish or Danish, but most of the magazines had abdicated the requirement of venturing into the suburbs of literature to enhance their visual impact. The angling magazines remained untouched.

Downstairs, the kitchen boasted few of the latest gadgets, and the tiny larder was ill-stocked. Some copies of *The Sun* lay under the grimy sink, and the crockery and cutlery used by Jackson for his last meagre meal on earth still stood on the dingy, yellow rack on the draining-board. Nothing, really.

In the front room, similarly, there seemed little of interest. A small brass model of a cannon from the Boer War era was the only object on the dusty mantelpiece, and the sole adornment to the faded green wallpaper was a calendar from of one of the Angling Associations, still turned to the month of September. A small transistor radio stood on a pile of oddments on the cupboard, and Morse turned on the switch. But the batteries appeared to have run out. There were one or two things in the pile which Morse had vaguely noted on his previous visit, but now he looked at them again: an out-of-date mail-order catalogue; a current pension-book; an unopened gas bill; an old copy of *The Oxford Journal*; an illustrated guide to 'Fish of the British Isles'; two leaflets entitled *On The Move*; a slim box containing

two white handkerchiefs; a circular – Suddenly Morse stopped
and turned back to the leaflets. Yes. He remembered reading
about the successful TV series *On The Move*, catering as it did
for those viewers who were illiterate – or virtually so. Would
illiteracy account for the lack of reading material in the Jackson
household? Many a pornographic pose, but hardly a line of pornographic prose? What a different set-up across the way at number 9,
where Anne Scott had surrounded herself with books galore! That
long line of Penguin Classics, for example – many of them showing the tell-tale white furrows down their black spines: Homer,
Plato, Thucydides, Aeschylus, Sophocles, Horace, Livy, Virgil
. . . If poor old Jackson could only have seen . . . He *had* seen
though: he'd almost certainly seen more than he should have
done, both of the house itself and of the woman who regularly
unbuttoned her blouse at the bedroom window.

Morse went upstairs to the front bedroom once more, took the
binoculars that hung behind the door, and focused them upon the
boudoir opposite. Phew! It was almost like being inside the actual
room! He walked into the tiny back bedroom and looked out in
the fading light along the narrow strip of garden to the shed at
the far end, about thirty yards away. He focused the binoculars
again, but finding the dirty panes hardly conducive to adequate
delineation he took the catch off the window and pushed up the
stiff, squeaky frame. Then he saw something, and his blood raced.
He put the binoculars to his eyes once more – and he was sure of
it: *someone was looking around in Jackson's shed*. Morse hurriedly
made his way downstairs, put the key quietly into the kitchen door,
took a deep breath, flicked open the lock, and rushed out.

Unfortunately, however, his right shin collided with the dustbin standing just beside the coalhouse, and he suppressed a yowl
of pain as the lid fell clangingly onto the concrete and rolled
round like an expiring spinning-top. It was more than sufficient
warning, and Morse had the feeling that his quarry had probably
been alerted in any case by the opening of the window upstairs.
A quick glimpse of a man disappearing over the low wall that
separated number 10 from the bank of the canal, and that was
all. The garden was suddenly still again in the gathering darkness.
If Lewis had been there, Morse would have felt more stomach for
the chase. But, alone, he felt useless, and just a little scared.

The hut was a junk-house. Fishing gear crowded every square

inch that was not already taken up by gardening tools, and it seemed impossible to take out anything without either moving everything else or sending precariously balanced items clattering to the floor. Against the left-hand wall Morse noticed seven fishing rods, the nearest one a shiny and sophisticated affair – doubtless the latest acquisition from the tackle shop. But his attention was not held by the rods, for it was perfectly clear to see where the intruder had been concentrating his search. The large wicker-work fisherman's basket lay open on the top of a bag of compost, its contents scattered around: hooks, tins of bait, floats, weights, pliers, reels, lengths of line, knives . . . Morse looked around him helplessly. Who was it who had been so anxious to search the basket, and why? It was seldom that Morse had no inkling whatsoever of the answers to the questions that he posed himself, but such was the case now.

Before leaving Canal Reach, he walked across to number 9, unlocked the door, and turned on the wall switch immediately to his left. But clearly the electricity had been disconnected, and he decided that his nerves were in no fit state to look around the empty, darkened house. On the mat he saw a cheap brown envelope, with the name and address of Anne Scott typed behind the cellophane window. A bill, no doubt, that probably wouldn't be settled for a few months yet – if at all. Morse picked it up and put it in his jacket pocket.

He drove along Canal Street and found himself facing the green gates of Lucy's Iron Works, where he turned right and followed Juxon Street up to the top. As he waited to turn left into the main thoroughfare of Walton Street, his eyes casually noticed the signs and plaques on the new buildings there: The Residents' Welfare Club; The Jericho Testing Laboratories; Welsh & Cohen, Dentists . . . Yet still nothing clicked in his mind.

Lewis was already back from Abingdon. He had seen Celia Richards alone at the house, and Morse glanced cursorily through her statement.

'Get it typed, Lewis. There are three "r"s in "corroborate", and it's an "e" in the middle of "desperate". And make sure you've got the address right.'

Lewis said nothing. Spelling, as he knew, was not his strongest suit.

'How much exactly did that new rod of Jackson's cost?' asked Morse suddenly.

'I didn't ask, sir. These modern ones are very light, sort of hollow – but they're very strong, I think.'

'I asked you how much it cost – not what a bloody miracle it was!'

Lewis had often seen Morse in this mood before – snappy and irritable. It usually meant the chief was cross with himself about something; usually, too, it meant that it wasn't going to be long before his mind leaped prodigiously into the dark and hit, as often as not, upon some strange and startling truth.

Later that same evening Conrad Richards drove his brother Charles to Gatwick Airport. The plane was subject to no delay, either technical or operational, and at 9.30 p.m. Charles Richards took his seat in a British Airways DC 10 – bound for Madrid.

Chapter Twenty-six

Some clues are of the 'hidden' variety, where the letters of the word are in front of the solver in the right order
D. S. Macnutt, *Ximenes on the Art of the Crossword*

The next morning, two box files, the one red and the other green, lay on the desk at Kidlington, marked 'Anne Scott' and 'George Jackson' respectively. They remained unopened as Morse sat contemplating the task before him. He felt it most unlikely that he was going to discover many more significant pieces to the puzzle posed by the deaths of two persons separated only by a few yards in a mean little street in Jericho. That the two deaths were connected, however, he had no doubt at all; and the fact that the precise connection was still eluding him augured ill for the cheerful Lewis who entered the office at 8.45 a.m.

'What's the programme today, then, sir?'

Morse pointed to the box files. 'It'll probably not do us any harm to find out what sort of a cock-up Bell and his boys made of things.'

Lewis nodded, and sat down opposite the chief. 'Which one do we start with?'

Morse appeared to ponder the simple question earnestly as he stared out at the fleet of police vehicles in the yard.

'Pardon?'

'I said, which one do we start with, sir?'

'How the bloody hell do I know, man? Use a bit of initiative, for Christ's sake!'

Lewis pulled the red file towards him, and began his slow and industrious survey of the documents in the Scott case. Morse, too, after what seemed an inordinately prolonged survey of the Fords and BMWs, reluctantly reached for the green file and dumped the meagre pile of papers on to his blotting-pad.

For half an hour neither of them spoke.

'Why do you think she killed herself?' asked Morse suddenly.

'Expecting a baby, wasn't she.'

'Bit thin, don't you reckon? It's not difficult to get rid of babies these days. Like shelling peas.'

'It'd still upset a lot of people.'

'Do you think she knew she was pregnant?'

'She'd have a jolly good idea – between ten to twelve weeks gone, it says here.'

'Mm.'

'Well, I know my missus did, sir.'

'Did she?'

'She wasn't exactly sure, of course, until she went to the, you know, the ante-natal clinic.'

'What do they do there?'

'I'm not sure, really. They take a urine specimen or something, and then the laboratory boys sort of squirt something – '

But Morse was listening no longer. His face was alight with an inner glow, and he whistled softly before jumping to his feet and shaking Lewis vigorously by the shoulders.

'You-are-a-bloody-genius, my son!'

'Really?' replied an uncomprehending Lewis.

'Find it! It's there somewhere. That plastic envelope with a couple of bits of burnt paper in it!'

Lewis looked at the evidence, the 'ICH' and the 'RAT', and he wondered what cosmic discovery he had inadvertently stumbled upon.

'I passed the place yesterday, Lewis! Yesterday! And still I be-have like a moron with a vacuum between the ears! Don't you see? It's part of a letterheading: the JerICHo Testing LaboRATories! Ring 'em quick, Lewis, and offer to take 'em a specimen in!'

'I don't quite see – '

'They *tested* her, don't you understand? And then they wrote and – '

'But we *knew* she was having a baby. And so did she, like as not.'

'Ye-es.' For a few seconds Morse's excitement seemed on the wane, and he sat down once again. 'But if they wrote to her the day before she– Lewis! Ring up the Post Office and ask 'em what time they deliver the mail in Jericho. You see, if – '

'It'll be about quarter-to-eight – eightish.'

'You think?' asked Morse, rather weakly.

'I'll ring if you want, sir, but – '

'Ten to twelve weeks! How long has Charles Richards been in Abingdon?'

'I don't think there's anything about that here – '

'Three months, Lewis! I'm sure of it. Just ring him up, will you, and ask – '

'If you'd come off the boil a minute, sir, I might have a chance, mightn't I? You want me to ring up these three – '

'Yes. Straightaway!'

'Which one shall I ring first?'

'Use a bit of bl – ' But Morse stopped in mid-sentence and smiled beatifically. 'Whichever, my dear Lewis, seems to you the most appropriate. And even if you ring 'em up in some cock-eyed order, I don't think it'll matter a monkey's!'

He was still smiling sweetly as Lewis reached for the phone. The old brain was really working again, he knew that, and he reached happily for the documents once more. It was the start he'd been waiting for.

Within half an hour, Lewis's trio of tasks had been completed. Anne Scott had called at the Jericho Testing Laboratories on the afternoon of Monday, 1st October, to ask if there was any news and she had been told that as soon as the report was through a letter would be in the post – which it had been on Tuesday, 2nd October: pregnancy was confirmed. The Jericho post was delivered somewhat variably, but during the week in question almost all letters would have been delivered by 8.30 a.m.. Only with the Richards' query had Lewis experienced any difficulty. No reply from Charles's private residence; and at the business number, a long delay before the call was transferred to Conrad Richards, the junior partner, who informed Lewis that the company had indeed moved to Abingdon about three months ago: to be exact, twelve weeks and four days.

Morse had sat silently during the phone calls, occasionally nodding with quiet satisfaction. But his attention to the documents in front of him was now half-hearted, and it was Lewis who finally picked up the small pink slip of rough paper which had fallen to the floor.

'Yours or mine, sir?'

Morse looked at the brief note. ' "Birthdays", Lewis. It seems that one of the old codgers at the bridge evening remembers they were talking about birthdays.'

'Sounds pretty harmless, sir.' Lewis resumed his study of his documents, although a few seconds later he noticed that Morse was sitting as still as the dead, the smoke from a forgotten cigarette drifting in curling wisps before those unblinking, unseeing eyes.

Later the same morning, Conrad Richards dialled a number in Spain.

'That you, Charles? *Buenas* something or other! *Cómo está?*'

'Fine, fine. Everything OK with you?'

'The police rang this morning. Wanted to know how long we'd been in Abingdon.'

'Was that all?'

'Yes.'

'I see,' said Charles Richards slowly. 'Celia all right?'

'Fine, yes. She's gone over to Cambridge to see Betty. She'll probably stay overnight, I should think. I tried to persuade her, anyway.'

'That's good news.'

'Look, Charles. We've had an enquiry from one of the Oxford examination boards. They want five hundred copies of some classical text that's gone out of print. No problem over royalties or copyright or anything. What do you think?'

The brothers talked for several minutes about VAT and profit margins, and finally the decision was left with Conrad.

A few minutes later Charles Richards walked out into the bright air of the Calle de Alcalá and, entering the Café León, he ordered himself a Cuba Libre. On the whole, things seemed to be working out satisfactorily.

All the way, Celia Richards' mind was churning over the events of the past two weeks, and she was conscious of driving with insufficient attention. At Bedford she had incurred the honking displeasure of a motorist she had not noticed quite legitimately overtaking her on the inside in the one-way system through the centre; and on the short stretch of the A1 she had almost overshot the St Neots' turn, where the squealing of her Mini's brakes had frightened her and left her heart thumping madly. What a terrible mess her life had suddenly become!
  In the early days at Croydon, when she had first met the Richards brothers, she had almost immediately fallen for Charles . . . Charles with his charm and vivacity, his sense of enjoyment, his forceful masculinity. Yet, even then, before they agreed to marry, she was conscious of other sides to his nature: a potential broodiness; a weakness for false flattery; a slightly nasty, hard streak in his business dealings; the suspicion – yes, even then – that his eye would linger far too long on the lovely limbs and the curving breasts of other women. But for several years they had been as happy as most couples: probably more so. Social events had brought her into an interesting circle of friends, and on more than one occasion other men had shown more interest in her own young and attractive body than their wives would have wished. Just a few times she had been *fractionally* disloyal to her marriage vows, but never once had she entertained the idea of any compromising entanglement. But Charles? He had been unfaithful, she knew that now: knew it for certain, because at long last – when there was no longer any hope of screening his impulsive affairs with his fond, if wayward, affection towards her – he had told her so . . . And then there was Conrad. Poor, faithful, lovely Conrad! If only she'd been willing to get to know him better when, in the early days, his own love for her had blazed as brightly as that of Charles . . . But he'd never had the sparkle or the drive of his elder brother, and he'd never really had a chance. A bit ineffectual, a bit passive – a bit 'wet', as she'd once described him to Charles. Oh dear! As things had turned out, he'd always been wonderful to her. No one

could have been more kind to her, more thoughtful, more willing
to forget himself; and she thought again now of that mild and self-
effacing smile that reflected a dry, fulfilled contentment in the
happiness of others . . . What would it have been like if she'd
married Conrad? Not that he'd ever asked her, of course: he was
far too shy and diffident to have joined the lists with Charles.
Physically he and Charles looked very similar, but that was only
on the surface. Underneath – well, there was no electric current
in Conrad . . . or so she'd thought until so very recently.

In Cambridge she turned into the Huntingdon Road and drove
out to Girton village, where her sister lived.

When Betty brought a glass of sherry into the lounge, she
found her sister in tears – a series of jerky sobs that stretched
her full and pretty mouth to its furthest extent.

'You can tell me about it later, Celia, if you want to. But I shan't
mind if you don't. A drop of booze'll do you good. Your bed's
aired, and I've got a couple of tickets for the theatre tonight. Please
stay!'

Dry-eyed at last, Celia Richards looked sadly at her sister and
smiled bleakly. 'Be kind to me, Betty! You see – you see – I can't
tell you about it, but I've done something terribly wrong.'

Chapter Twenty-seven

The time is out of joint
Hamlet Act I, scene V

Although Morse insisted (that lunch time) that a liquid diet
without blotting-paper was an exceedingly fine nutrient for the
brain cells, Lewis opted for his beloved chips – with sausages
and egg – to accompany the beer. 'Are we making progress?'
he asked, between mouthfuls.

'Progress? Progress, Lewis, is the law of life. You and I would
be making progress even if we were going backwards. And, as
it happens, my old friend, we are actually going *forward* at this
particular stage of our joint investigations.'

'We are?'

'Indeed! I think you'll agree that the main facts hang pretty well together now. Anne Scott goes to a bridge evening the night before she kills herself, and I'm certain she learns something there that's the final straw to a long and cumulative emotional strain. She writes a note to Edward Murdoch, telling him she can't see him for a lesson the next afternoon, and from that point the die is cast. She gets home about 3 a.m. or thereabouts, and we shall never know how she spends the next few hours. But whatever doubt or hesitation she may have felt is finally settled by the Wednesday morning post, when a letter arrives from the birth clinic. She burns the letter and she – hangs herself.

'Now Jackson has been doing some brickwork for her, and he goes over to have a final look at things – and to pick up his trowel. He lets himself in, pushes the kitchen door open, and in the process knocks over the stool on which Anne Scott has stood to hang herself – and finds her swaying there behind the door after he's picked up the stool and put it by the table. Now, just think a minute, Lewis. Anyone, virtually *anyone*, in those circumstances would have rung up the police immediately. So why not Jackson? He's got nothing to worry about. He does lots of odd jobs in the neighbourhood and it must be common knowledge that he's patching up the wall at number 9. So why doesn't he ring the police *at that point*? – because I'm sure it *was* Jackson who rang up later. It's because he *finds* something, Lewis – apart from the body: something which proves too tempting for his cheap and greedy little soul. I thought for a start it may have been money, but I doubt it now. I think she'd written some sort of letter or note and left it on the kitchen table – a letter which Jackson takes. He's anxious to get out of the house quickly, and he forgets to lock the door behind him. Hence all our troubles, Lewis! You see, since Jackson has been coming over regularly – sometimes when she was still in bed – she's got in the habit of locking her front door, then taking the key out, and leaving it on the sideboard, so that he can put his own key in.'

'Surely she wouldn't have done that if she'd already decided to kill herself?'

But Morse ignored the objection and continued. 'Then Jackson goes over to his own home and reads the letter – '

'But you told me he *couldn't* read!'

'It's addressed, Lewis, to one of two people: either to the
police, or to the man who's been her lover – the man she's recently
written to, and the man who's probably been the only real passion
in her life – Charles Richards. And there's something in that letter
that gives Jackson some immediate prospect of personal gain –
a situation he's decided to take full advantage of. But let's get
back to the sequence of events that day. Someone else goes into
number 9 during the afternoon – Celia Richards. Pretty certainly
Jackson sees her going in – as he later sees *me*, Lewis – but he can't
have the faintest idea that she's the wife of the man he's going to
blackmail. He realises one thing, though – that he's forgotten to
lock the door; and so when everything's quiet he goes over and
puts his key through the letter box. That's the way it happened,
Lewis – you can be sure of that.'

'Perhaps,' mumbled Lewis, wiping up the last of the egg yolk
with a final, solitary chip.

'You don't sound very impressed?'

'Well, to be honest, I'd thought very much the same myself,
sir, and I'm pretty sure Bell and his boys – '

'Really?' Morse drained his beer and pushed the glass in
front of Lewis's plate. 'Bags of time for another.'

'I got the last one, sir. Just a half for me, if you don't mind.'

'Now,' resumed Morse (glasses replenished), 'we've got to link
the death of Anne Scott with the murder of Jackson, agreed? Well,
I reckon the connection is fairly obvious, and from what you've just
said I presume that your own nimble mind has already jumped to
a similar conclusion, right?'

Lewis nodded. 'Jackson tried to blackmail Charles Richards
because of what he learned from the letter, and it seems he
succeeded because he took £250 to the Post Office the day before
he was murdered. I reckon he'd written to Richards, or rung him
up, and that Richards decided to cough up to keep him quiet. He
could have arranged to meet Jackson to give him the money and
then just followed him home. And once he knew who he was,
and where he lived – well, that was that. Perhaps he didn't really
mean to kill him at all – just scare him out of his wits and get the
letter, or whatever it was.'

Morse shook his head. It *might* have happened the way Lewis
had just outlined things; but it *hadn't*. 'You may be right most
of the way, Lewis, but you can be absolutely certain about one

thing: *it wasn't Charles Richards who murdered Jackson*. And until somebody proves to us that the earth isn't round or a triangle hasn't got three sides, we'd better bloody face it! He was giving a lecture – with *me* in the audience!'

'Don't you think, perhaps – ?'

'Nonsense! Jackson was in the *pub* at gone eight and the police found his body while Richards was still talking. And he didn't leave that platform for one *second*, Lewis!'

'I'm not saying he did, sir. But he could have got someone else to go and rough Jackson up, couldn't he?'

Morse nodded. 'Carry on!'

'He's got a wife, sir.'

'I can't exactly see her pushing Jackson upstairs, can you? He was no youngster, but he was a tough and wiry little customer, I should think. Though perhaps it might not be a bad idea to find out exactly where she was that night . . . ' His voice drifted off, and characteristically he married a few stray drops of beer on the table with the little finger of his left hand, his eyes seeming to stare into the middle distance.

'He's got a brother, too,' added Lewis, quietly.

Morse's eyes refocused on his colleague immediately and a faint smile formed round his mouth. 'The brother? Yes, indeed! I wondered when you were going to get around to him. I've been giving our Conrad a little bit of thought myself this morning, and I reckon it's time we had a quiet little word with him.'

'We've got some jolly good prints, sir – as good as anything the boys have seen for quite some time. And it wouldn't be much trouble getting Conrad's dabs, would it?'

'No trouble at all.'

'Well' – Lewis looked at Morse rather hesitantly – 'shall we go and see him?'

'Why not? We'll just have another pint and then – '

'No more for me, sir. Do you want – '

'Pint, yes please. You're very kind.'

'I've been thinking, sir,' began Lewis when he came back from the bar.

'So have I. Listen! We'll nip over there together. There are two calls we'd better make. Conrad Richards for one, and then there's that girl-friend Charles Richards told me he was with when – '

'But why see her? You've already – '

'Let's toss up, Lewis. You can drive us out there. Heads you go to see Conrad – tails I do. All right?' Morse took out a 10p piece, flipped it in the air, and then peered cautiously underneath his palm before immediately returning the coin to his pocket. 'Heads it is, Lewis. What was it we agreed? Heads was you to see Conrad, wasn't it? Excellent! I shall have to take it upon myself to visit Mrs Whatsername.'

'Hills, sir.'

'Ah yes.' Morse relaxed and lovingly relished the rest of his beer. Someone had left a copy of the *Daily Mirror* on the next table and he picked it up and turned to the racing page. 'Ever have a flutter these days, Lewis?'

Lewis placed his empty glass in the middle of the plate and lay his knife and fork neatly to the side of it. 'Very seldom, sir. I'm not quite so lucky at gambling as you are.'

As they got up to go, Morse suddenly remembered his bet with the police surgeon. 'Do you think there's *any* way, Lewis, in which Jackson could have been murdered *before* eight o'clock that night?'

'No way at all, sir.'

Morse nodded. 'Perhaps you're right.'

Chapter Twenty-eight

If you have great talents, industry will improve them;
if you have but moderate abilities, industry will supply
their deficiency

Sir Joshua Reynolds

Almost immediately Lewis found himself liking Conrad Richards, the junior partner who worked in an office no smaller than that of his brother's below, though designated by no name-plate on the door. Lewis explained the purpose of his visit, and his reasonable requests met with an amiable co-operation. Conrad had exhibited (as Lewis was later to tell Morse) some surprise, perhaps, when the subject of fingerprints was broached, but he had willingly enough pressed the fingers and thumbs of both hands upon the ink-pad, and thence onto the cards.

'Just a matter of elimination,' Lewis explained.

'Yes, I realise that but . . . '

'I know, sir. It sort of puts you on the record, doesn't it? Everyone feels the same.'

Conrad now held his hands out awkwardly, like a woman just disturbed at the kitchen sink who is looking around for a towel. 'Do you mind if I just go and wash – '

'It's all right, sir. I'll be off now. There's only one more thing – just for the record again, of course. Can you tell me where you were between 8 and 9 p.m. on the evening of the 19th October?'

Conrad looked vague and shook his head. 'I can't, I'm afraid. I can try to find out for you – or try to remember, but I – I don't know. Probably at home reading, I should think, but . . . ' Again he shook his head, his voice level and seemingly unconcerned.

'You live alone, sir?'

'Confirmed bachelor.'

'Well, if you can have a think and let me know.'

'I will. I expect I'll be able to come up with something, but I've got an awful feeling I'm not going to produce any convincing alibi.'

'Few people do, sir. We don't expect it.'

'Well, that's good news.'

Lewis got up to go. 'There *is* just one more thing. I'd like to have a quick word with your brother. Is he – '

'He's in Spain, officer. He's there on business for a week or so.'

'Oh! Well, never mind! We shall have to try to see him when he gets back.'

For five minutes after Lewis had gone, Conrad Richards sat silently at his desk, his features betraying no sign of emotion or anxiety. Then he reached for the phone.

Morse, too, sat waiting, depressed, impatient, and irritated, on a low wooden bench beside the church in Radley. He had told himself (with a modicum of honesty) that he *was* still vaguely worried about Charles Richards' whereabouts on the day of Anne Scott's death; but he could only half convince

himself on the point. Perhaps the simple truth was that he
liked interviewing women whose voices over the phone promised a cloud nine of memorable mouths and leggy elegance. But
whichever way it was, his visit had been fruitless. The house was
locked firmly front and back, the shrill bell echoing through an
ominously vacant property. Pity! A lovely female firmly sunk in
fathoms of leisure – and just at this moment she had to be out!
A bit more than out, too, according to the neighbours. Away.
Abroad.

Morse was still staring glumly at the ground when the white
police car finally drew alongside.

'Any luck?' asked Lewis, as Morse got in beside him.

'Interesting!' Morse feigned a vague indifference and fastened
his seat-belt.

'Nice-looker, sir?' ventured Lewis after a couple of miles.

'I didn't bloody see her, did I?' growled Morse. 'She's in
Spain.'

'Spain?' Lewis whistled loudly. 'Well, well, well! The birds
seem to be flying from their nests, don't they?' He recounted
the details of his own eminently more successful mission and the
impression he'd formed of Conrad Richards; and Morse listened
in silence. Lewis had often noticed it before: over a beer table it
was usually difficult to get the chief to shut up at all, but in a car
he was invariably a taciturn companion.

'What d'you think then, Lewis?'

'Well, we can get those prints checked straightaway – and
I've got the feeling we may just about be there, sir. As I see it,
Charles Richards must have brought his brother along with him
when he came to give his talk; then dropped him somewhere in
Jericho and told him to go and scare the living daylights out of
Jackson.'

'He must have taken him completely into his confidence,
you mean?'

Lewis nodded as he turned onto the A34 and headed north.
'Charles Richards must have traced Jackson – he probably followed him after leaving the money somewhere – and then, as I
say, he must have asked Conrad to help him. Quite neat, really.
Charles is completely in the clear and nobody's going to think
Conrad had anything to do with it. Anyway, things must have
gone wrong, mustn't they? I doubt whether Conrad ever actually

meant to kill Jackson – I reckon he'd have been far more careful
about leaving any prints if he had. In fact, I doubt if he knew
what to do, poor chap. Jackson's bleeding like mad, and Conrad
just panics up there in the bedroom. He gets out quick and
rings the police. Perhaps his one big worry was to save the old
fellow.'

'Mm.' The monosyllable sounded sceptical.

'How else, sir?'

'I dunno,' said Morse. It might have happened the way Lewis
had suggested, but he doubted it. From the look of the dead
Jackson's face it seemed quite clear that someone had definitely
meant business: something more than mere gentle persuasion followed by an accidental bang against a bed-post. The man had
been clouted and punched about the head by someone made of
much sterner stuff than Conrad Richards, surely, for (from the
little Morse had learned of him) Conrad was considered by all to
be one of the mildest and most amenable of men. Everyone, as
Morse supposed, was just about capable of murder, but why
should Conrad be put forward as the likeliest perpetrator of
such uncharacteristic malice? He ought to see Conrad, though;
ought to have seen him that afternoon instead of –

'Turn the car round!'

'Pardon, sir?'

'We're going back there – and put your foot down!'

But Conrad Richards was no longer in his upper-storey office.
According to the young receptionist, he had brought two suitcases
with him that morning, and he had gone off in a taxi about ten
minutes ago. He had mentioned something about a business trip,
but had given no indication of where he was going or when he
would be returning.

Morse was angry with himself and his displeasure was taken
out on the receptionist, she appearing to be the only other person
on the premises. After impressively invoking the awful majesty
of the law, and magisterially demanding whatever keys were available, he stood with Lewis in Charles Richards' office and looked
around: bills in the in-trays, ash in the ash-trays, and the same
serried ranks of box files on the shelves he had seen before. It
seemed a daunting prospect, and leaving Lewis to 'get on with it'
he himself climbed the stairs to Conrad Richards' office.

One way and another, however, it wasn't to be Morse's day. In the (unlocked) drawers of Conrad's desk he found nothing that could raise a twitch from a hyper-suspicious eyebrow: invoices, statements, contracts, costings – it all seemed so futile and tedious. The man had hidden nothing; and might that not be because he had nothing to hide? There were box files galore here, too, but Morse sat back in Conrad's chair and gave up the unequal struggle. On the walls of the office were two pictures only: one a coloured reproduction of a delicate wall-painting from Pompeii; the other a large black-and-white aerial photograph of the mediaeval walled city of Carcassone. And what the hell were *they* supposed to tell him?

It was Lewis who found it – underneath a sheaf of papers in the bottom (locked) drawer of Charles Richards' desk; and as he climbed the stairs he sought to mask the beam of triumph on his face. Putting his nose round the door, he saw Morse seated at the desk, scowling fecklessly around him.

'Any luck, sir?'

'Er, not for the minute, no. What about you?'

Lewis entered the office and sat down opposite his chief. 'Almost all of it business stuff, sir. But I did find *this*.'

Morse took the folded letter and began to read:

Dear Mister Richards
Its about Missis Scott who died, I now all about you and her but does Missis Richards . . .

As they walked out of the office below, Morse spoke to the receptionist once more.

'You weren't here when I called on Tuesday, were you?'

'Pardon, sir?' The young girl seemed very flustered and a red flush spread round her throat.

'You took the day off, didn't you? Why was that?'

'Mr Richards told me I needn't – '

'Which Mr Richards was that?'

'Mr Charles, sir. He said – '

But Morse dismissed her explanation with a curt wave of his hand, and walked down to the street.

'Bit short with her, weren't you, sir?'

'They're all a load of liars, Lewis! Her, too, I shouldn't wonder. Let's get back!'

Morse said nothing on the return drive. The letter that Lewis had found lay on his lap the whole time, and occasionally he looked down to read it yet again. It perplexed him sorely, and by the time the police car pulled into the HQ yard at Kidlington, whatever look of irritation had earlier marked his face had changed to one of utter puzzlement.

'D'you know, Lewis,' he said as they walked into the building together, 'I'm beginning to think we're on the wrong track completely!'

'Pardon, sir?'

'Is everybody going bloody deaf all of a sudden?'

Lewis said no more, and the two men called into the canteen for a cup of tea.

'I'll just be off and see about these prints, sir. Keep your fingers crossed for me. What's the betting?'

'I thought you weren't a gambling man, Lewis? And if you were, I shouldn't put more than a coupla bob on it.'

Lewis shrugged his shoulders, and left his chief staring glumly down at the muddy-brown tea – as yet untouched. He'd frequently seen Morse in this sort of mood, and it worried him no more. Just because one of the chief's fanciful notions took a hefty knock now and then! A bit of bread-and-butter investigation was worth a good deal more than some of that top-of-the-head stuff, and the truth was that they'd found – *he'd* found! – the blackmail letter. Morse might be a brilliant fellow but . . . Well, it hardly called for much brilliance, this case, did it? With the prints confirmed, everything would be all tied up, and Lewis was already thinking of a nationwide alert at the airports, because Conrad Richards couldn't have got very far yet, surely. Luton? Heathrow? Gatwick? Wherever it was, there'd be plenty of time.

Half-an-hour later Lewis was to discover that between the excellent facsimiles of the fingerprints lifted from Jackson's bedroom and those taken only that afternoon from Conrad Richards, *there was not a single line or whorl of correspondence anywhere.*

Chapter Twenty-nine

And Isaac loved Esau, because he did eat of his venison:
but Rebekah loved Jacob

Genesis, XXV. 28

Edward Murdoch felt ill-tempered and sweaty as he cycled home-
wards late that Wednesday afternoon. Much against his will, he
had been roped into making up the number for his house rugby
team, and his own ineffectualness and incompetence had been at
least partly to blame for their narrow defeat. He was almost always
free on Wednesday afternoons, and here was one afternoon he
could have used profitably to get on with those two essays to be
handed in the next morning. The traffic in Summertown was its
usual bloody self, too, with cars seeking to pull into the precious
parking bays, their nearside blinkers flashing as they waited for
other cars to back out. Twice he had to swerve dangerously as
motorists, seemingly oblivious to the rights of any cyclist, cut over
in front of him. It was always the same, of course; but today everything seemed to be going wrong, and he felt increasingly irritated.
He came to the conclusion that his bio-rhythms were heterodyning.
The two words were very new to him, and he rather liked them
both. He was getting hungry, too, and he just hoped that his
mother had got something decent in the oven – for a change!
The last ten days or so, meals had been pretty skimpy: it had
been mince, stew, and baked beans in a dreary cyclical trio, and
he longed for roast potatoes and thinly sliced beef. Not, he knew,
that he ought to blame his mother too much – considering all that
she'd been going through. Yet somehow his own selfish interests
seemed almost invariably to triumph over his daily resolutions to
try to help, even fractionally, during these tragic and traumatic
days in the life of the Murdoch family.

He pushed his bike roughly into the garden shed, ignored
the tin of nails which spilt on to the floor as his handle-bars
knocked it over, unfastened his brief-case from the rack over
the back wheel, and slammed the shed door noisily to.

His mother was in the kitchen ironing one of his white shirts.

'What's for tea?' His tone of voice suggested that whatever
it was it would be viewed with truculent disfavour.

'I've got a nice bit of stew on, with some – '

'Oh Christ! Not stew again!'

Then something happened which took the boy completely by surprise. He saw his mother put down the iron; saw, simultaneously, her shoulders heave and the backs of her two forefingers go up to her tight mouth; and he saw in her eyes a look that was utterly helpless and hopeless, and then the tears soon streaming down her cheeks. A second later she was sitting at the kitchen table, her breath catching itself in short gasps as she fought to stave off the misery that threatened to swamp her. Edward had never for a second seen his mother like this, and the knowledge that she – she, his own solid and ever-dependable mother – was liable, just like anyone else, to be engulfed by waves of desperation, was a deeply felt shock for him. His own troubles vanished immediately, and he was conscious of a long-forgotten love for her.

'Don't be upset, Mum! Please don't! I'm sorry, I really am. I didn't mean . . . '

Mrs Murdoch shook her head vigorously, and wiped her handkerchief across her eyes. 'It's not – ' But she couldn't go on, and Edward put a hand on her shoulder, and stood there, awkward and silent.

'I've not helped much, have I, Mum?' he said quietly.

'It's *not* that. It's – it's just that I can't *cope*. I just can't! Everything seems to be falling to bits and I – I – ' She shook her head once more, and the tears were rolling freely again. 'I just don't know what to *do*! I've tried *so* hard to – ' She put her own hand up on to her son's, and tried to steady her quivering voice. 'Don't worry about me. I'm just being silly, that's all.' She stood up and blew her nose noisily into the paper handkerchief. 'You have a good day?'

'It's Michael – isn't it, Mum?'

Mrs Murdoch nodded. 'I went to see him again this afternoon. He's lost one eye completely and – and they don't really know – they don't really know . . . '

'You don't mean – he'll be *blind*?'

Mrs Murdoch picked up the iron again and seemed to hold it in front of her like some puny shield. 'They're doing the best they can but . . . '

'Don't let's lose hope, Mum! I know I'm not much of a one for church and all that, but hope *is* one of the Christian virtues, isn't it?'

If Mrs Murdoch had followed her instincts at that moment, she would have thrown her arms around her son and blessed him for the words he'd just spoken. But she didn't. Somehow she'd never felt able to express her feelings with any loving freedom, either with Michael or with Edward, and something restrained her even now. She turned off the iron and put two plates under the grill to warm. Where had she gone wrong? Where? If only her husband hadn't died . . . If only they'd never decided to . . . Oh God! Surely, *surely*, things could never get much worse than this? And yet she knew in her heart that they *could*; and as she put on the oven-glove to take out the stew-pot, she guiltily clutched her little secret even closer to herself: the knowledge that she would never be able to love Michael as she had always loved the boy who was now setting the table in the dining-room.

Later that evening the senior ophthalmic surgeon lifted, with infinite care, the bandage round Michael Murdoch's head. Then he took off his wrist-watch and held it about six inches in front of his patient's left eye.

'How are you, Michael?'

'All right. I feel tired, though – ever so tired.'

'Hungry?'

'No, not really. I've had something to eat.'

'That was a little while ago, though, and you've been asleep since then. Have you any idea of the time now?' He still held the watch steadily in front of the boy's remaining eye.

'Must be about teatime, is it? About five?'

The wrist-watch said 8.45, and still the surgeon held it out. But the boy's horridly blood-shot eye stared past the watch, unseeing still, and as the surgeon replaced the bandage he shook his head sadly at the nurse who was standing anxiously beside him.

On his way back from The Friar Bacon at ten minutes to eleven that night, Morse chanced to meet Mrs Murdoch, her labrador straining mightily from her; and for the first time he learned of the tragic fate of her elder boy. He listened dutifully and compassionately, but somehow he couldn't seem to find the appropriate words of comfort, mumbling only the occasional 'Oh dear!', the occasional 'I *am* sorry', as he stood staring blankly at the grass verge. Fortunately the dog came to his rescue, and Morse felt relieved as the sandy coloured beast finally wrenched his mistress off to pastures new.

As he walked the remaining few hundred yards to his home, he pondered briefly upon the Murdoch family and their links with Anne Scott. But he was tired and over-beered, and nothing was to click in Morse's rather muddled mind that night.

Chapter Thirty

An illiterate candidate gives his thoughts. The spelling, punctuation, and sentence structure are chaotic. Examiners should feel no reluctance about giving no marks for such work

Extract from *Specimen Essays at 16+*

Thursday saw Morse late into his office, where he greeted Lewis with a perfunctory nod. He had slept badly, and silently vowed to give the booze a rest that day. Whilst Lewis amateurishly tapped the keys as he typed up a report, Morse forced his attention back to the blackmail note discovered in Charles Richards' desk. At one reading, it seemed a typically semi-literate specimen of the sort of note so often received by blackmail victims – ill-spelt, ill-punctuated, and ill-expressed. And yet, at another reading, it seemed not to fall into the conventional category at all. He handed the note across to Lewis.

'What do you make of it?'

'His spelling's even worse than mine, isn't it? Still, we knew all along he'd never been to Eton.'

'By "he", you mean Jackson, I suppose?'

Lewis turned from the typewriter and frowned. 'Who else, sir?'

'You think Jackson wrote this?'

'Don't *you*?'

'No, I don't. In fact, I'm absolutely sure that Jackson himself couldn't have written one line of this – let alone the whole caboodle. You'll find in Jackson's pathetic little pile of possessions a couple of pamphlets about that telly programme, *On the Move* – and that wasn't a programme for your actual *semi*-literates, Lewis: it was for your *complete* illiterates, who've never managed to read or write and who get embarrassed about ever admitting it to anyone. So I reckon Jackson must have got somebody – '

'But it's pretty *bad*, that letter, sir. Probably get about Grade Five CSE, if you ask me.'

'Really? Well, if you honestly think that, I'm sure the nation is most relieved to know that you're not going to be called up to exercise your ignorant prejudices upon the essays written by most of our sixteen-year-olds! You see, you're quite *wrong*. Here! Look at it again!' Morse thrust the letter across once more, and sat back in his chair like some smug pedagogue. 'What you want a letter to do, Lewis, is to *communicate* – got that? Now the spelling there is a bit weak, and the punctuation's infantile. *But*, Lewis, I'll tell you this: the upshot of that particular letter is so clear, so unequivocal, so *clever*, that no one who read it could have misunderstood one syllable! Mistakes galore, I agree; but when it comes down to telling Richards exactly where and exactly when and the rest of it – why, the letter's a bloody model of clarity! *Look* at it! Is your understanding held up by some dyslexic correspondent who spells "receive" the wrong way round? Never!'

'But – '

'Yes, I know. If you've got some little typist next door who can't spell, you give her the sack. And quite right, too. That's her job, and none of us wants to sign illiterate letters. But I'll say it again: whoever wrote this letter knew *exactly* what he was up to. And it's just the same with the punctuation, if you look a little more closely. Full stops and question marks are all cock-eyed – but they don't affect what's being *said*.' Morse banged the table with a rather frightening intensity. 'No! *Jackson did not write that letter.*'

He wrote two words on the pad in front of him and passed the sheet over. 'What do you make of those?'

Lewis looked down at *egog* and *metantatopi*, but managed to decipher neither of these orthographic monstrosities.

'You've no idea, have you?' continued Morse. 'And I don't blame you, because that's the sort of thing your illiterate johnnies sink to. The first word's supposed to be "hedgehog", and the second's "meat-and-potato-pie" – and they're both genuine!

Chap from the examination board told me. Do you see what I mean?'

Yes, Lewis was beginning to wonder if the chief hadn't got something; but wasn't he assuming that Jackson *was* illiterate? If someone found a book on your shelves entitled *Teach Yourself to Spell*, it didn't automatically mean . . .

But Morse was still going on. 'And then there's this business of the money, isn't there? If Jackson thought he'd got a soft touch for a nice little bit of blackmail, I reckon he'd have asked for one helluva sight more than a measly – '

'Perhaps he did, sir.'

The interjection stopped Morse in his tracks, and he nodded in reluctant agreement. 'Ye-es. You know, I hadn't thought of that.'

'Don't you think, anyway, that it might be better to find out about this? Find out whether Jackson could write?'

'You're right! Get on to that woman at the Post Office down there, Mrs Whatsername – '

'Mrs Beavers.'

'That's her. Get on to her and ask her how Jackson signed for his OAP. And since she's such a nosy old bugger, ask her who Jackson was doing a bit of work for before he died – apart from Anne Scott. Do you know what, Lewis? I reckon you'll find that Jackson was doing one or two other little jobs as well.'

Three-quarters of an hour later Lewis learned that Jackson was able, just, to render in alphabetical characters a tentative resemblance to 'G. Jackson' on his OAP slips. But it wouldn't much have mattered if he'd not even been able to manage that – so Mrs Beavers asserted. There were one or two of the old 'uns who got by with an 'X', provided that it was inscribed on PO premises in view of one of the staff, or vouched for by some close relative or friend. Mrs Beavers herself had often had to read or explain to Jackson some notification of change or renewal, or some information about supplementary benefit or rate rebate. And Jackson had readily understood such things – and acted upon them. He was, it seemed, far from unintelligent. The fact remained, however, that to all intents and purposes Jackson *was* illiterate.

Mrs Beavers was just as well up with the odd-job needs of the local community as with the literary competence of her clientèle. Mrs Jones in Cardigan Street, had found occasion to hire Jackson's services in planing and re-hanging several doors that were sagging and sticking; Mrs Purvis in Canal Reach had asked Jackson if he could rewire the house for her – the estimate from the Electricity Board was quite *ridiculous*. Then there was that couple who'd just moved into Albert Street who wanted pelmets made for the windows . . .

Lewis listened and made his awkward notes. It was, he had to admit, pretty well as Morse had said it would be; and when he reported back to Kidlington the only thing that seemed to interest Morse was, of all things, Mrs Purvis's rewiring.

'Rewiring, eh? I wonder how much Jackson knocked her back for that? My place needs doing and someone told me it'll cost about £250.'

'Well, it's quite a big job, you know.'

'£250 isn't really a lot these days, though, is it?' said Morse slowly.

'Not enough to keep Jackson quiet, you mean?'

'I keep telling you, Lewis – Jackson didn't write the letter!'

'Who do you think did, then?'

Morse tilted his head slightly and opened the palms of his hands. 'I dunno, except that he – or she! – is well enough educated to know how to *pretend* to be uneducated, if you see what I mean. That letter would have been just the sort *I'd* have written, Lewis, if someone had asked me to try to write a semi-literate letter.'

'But you're a *very* well educated man, sir!'

'Certainly so – and don't you forget it! And whilst we're on this education business, I just wonder, Lewis, exactly where Mrs Purvis went to school when she was a girl.'

It seemed to Lewis the oddest question that had so far posed itself to his unpredictable chief, and the reason for it was still puzzling him as he brought the police car to a halt in front of the bollards that guarded Canal Reach.

Chapter Thirty-one

She sat down and wrote on the four pages of a note-
sheet a succinct narrative of those events
Thomas Hardy, *Tess of the D'Urbervilles*

Morse had known – even before he'd noticed the rows of paperback Catherine Cooksons and Georgette Heyers along the two
shelves in the little sitting room.

'His name's Graymalkin,' Mrs Purvis had replied, looking
down lovingly at the grey-haired Persian that wove its feline
figures-of-eight round her legs. 'It's from *Macbeth*, Inspector –
by William Shakespeare, you know.'

'Oh yes?'

Lewis listened patiently whilst Mrs Purvis was duly cosseted
and encouraged, and it was a relief when Morse finally brought
forward the heavier artillery.

'You know, you're making me forget what we called for,
Mrs Purvis. It's about Mr Jackson, of course, and there are
just a few little points to clear up – you know how it is? We're
trying to find out a little bit more about the sort of odd jobs he
was doing – just to check up on the sort of income he had. By
the way, he was doing some work for you, wasn't he?'

'He'd finished. Rewiring the house, it was. He wasn't the
neatest sort of man, but he always did a good job.'

'He'd finished, you say?'

'Yes – when would it be now . . . ?'

'And you'd squared up with him?'

Mrs Purvis leaned down to stroke Graymalkin, and Lewis
thought that her eyes were suddenly evasive. 'I squared up with
him, yes, before . . . '

'Mind telling me how much he charged?'

'Well, he wasn't a *professional*, you know.'

'How much, Mrs Purvis?'

'£75.' (Why, wondered Lewis, did she make it sound like a
guilty admission?)

'Very reasonable,' said Morse.

Mrs Purvis was stroking the Persian again. 'Quite reasonable,
yes.'

'Did he often do jobs for you?'

'Not really. One or two little things. He fixed up the lavatory – '

'Did you ever do any little jobs for *him*?'

Mrs Purvis looked up with startled eyes. 'I don't quite see – '

'Mr Jackson couldn't write very well, could he?'

'Write? I – I don't know really. Of course he hadn't had much education, I knew that, but – '

'You never wrote a letter for him?'

'No, Inspector, I didn't.'

'Not a single letter?'

'Never once in my life! I swear that on the Holy Bible.'

'There's nothing wrong in writing a letter for a neighbour, is there?'

'No, of course there isn't. It's just that I thought – '

'Did you ever *read* a letter for him, though?'

The effect of the question on the poor woman was instantaneous and devastating. The muscles round her mouth were quivering now as two or three times she opened her lips to speak. But no words came out.

'It's all right,' said Morse gently. 'I know all about it, you see, but I'd like to hear it from you, Mrs Purvis.'

The truth came out then, reluctantly confessed but perfectly clear. The bill for rewiring the tiny property had been £100, but Jackson had been willing to reduce it by £25 if she was prepared to help him. All she'd got to do was to read a letter to him – and then to say nothing about it to anyone. That was all. And, of course, it was only after beginning to read it to him that she'd realised it must have been a letter that Ms Scott had left on the kitchen table when she'd hanged herself. There had been four sheets of writing, she recalled that quite clearly, although Jackson had taken the letter from her after she'd read only about half of it. It was a sort of love letter, really (said Mrs Purvis), but she couldn't remember much of the detail. It said that this man she was writing to was the only one she'd ever really loved and that whatever happened she wanted him to know that; and never to blame himself in any way. She said it was all her fault – not his, and . . . But Mrs Purvis could remember no more.

Morse had listened without interruption as the frightened woman exhausted her recollections. 'You didn't do anything else for him – anything else at all?'

'No, honestly I didn't. That was all. I swear on the – '

'You didn't even try to find a telephone number for him?' Morse had spoken evenly and calmly, but Mrs Purvis broke down completely now. Between sobs Morse learned that she *hadn't* looked up a telephone number, but that Jackson had asked her how to get through to directory enquiries, and that she'd told him. It was only later, really, that she'd begun to realise what Mr Jackson might be up to.

'You're not very well off, are you, my love?' said Morse gently, laying a comforting hand on the woman's shoulder. 'I can understand what you did, and we're going to forget all about it – aren't we, Lewis?'

Rather startled at being brought so late into the action, Lewis swallowed hard and made an indeterminate grunt that sounded vaguely corroborative.

'It's just that if you can remember anything – anything at all – about this man Ms Scott was writing to – well, we'd be able to tie the whole thing up, wouldn't we?'

Mrs Purvis nodded helplessly. 'Yes, I see that, but I can't – '

'Do you remember where he lived?'

'I'm sorry, but I didn't see the envelope.'

'Name? There must have been a name somewhere, surely? She must have written "Dear Somebody", or "My dear Somebody", or something? Please try to remember!'

'Oh dear!'

'It wasn't "Charles", was it?'

The light of redemption now beamed in Mrs Purvis's eyes, as though her certain remembrance of things past had atoned at last for her earlier sins. ' "My dearest Charles",' she said, slowly and quietly. 'That's what it was, Inspector: that's how she started the letter!'

Graymalkin's eyes watched the two detectives as they left – eyes that stared after them with indifferent intelligence: neither hostility against the intruders, nor compassion for the mistress. Now left in peace, the cat curled up on the armchair beside the fire, resting its head on its paws and closing its large, all-seeing eyes. It had been another interlude – no more.

That same evening Morse drove up to the JR2 in Headington, and spoke with the sister in the Intensive Care Unit. Silent-footed, they walked to the bed where Michael Murdoch lay asleep.

'I can't let you wake him,' whispered the sister.

Morse nodded and looked down at the boy, his head turbaned in layers of white bandaging. Picking up the chart from the foot of the bed, Morse nodded his ignorant head as his eyes followed the mountain-peaks of pulse-rate and temperature. The top of the chart read *Murdoch, Michael; date of birth: the second of Octo* . . . But Morse's eyes travelled no further, and his mind was many miles away.

The clues were almost all assembled now, although it was not until four hours and a bottle of Teacher's later that Morse finally solved the first of the two problems that the case of the Jericho killings had presented to him. To be more precise, it was at five minutes past midnight that he discovered the name of the man who had killed Ms Anne Scott.

Chapter Thirty-two

A man without an address is a vagabond; a man with
two addresses is a libertine

G. B. Shaw

Detective Constable Walters had experienced little glamour since his appearance on the stage in the first act of the Jericho killings, and his latest assignment, a hefty burglary in North Oxford, had made no great demands on his ratiocinative skills. An upper window had been left open, and the burglars (two of them, perhaps) had helped themselves to the pickings whilst the owners were celebrating their silver wedding at the Randolph. The only fingerprints that might have been left had disappeared with the articles stolen, a list of which Walters had painstakingly made late the previous evening. No clues at all really, except that one of the intruders had urinated over the lounge carpet – an attendant circumstance which had elicited little enthusiasm when reported to the path boys. In fact, even the suggestion that there were two of them had been entertained only because one of the neighbours thought she may have seen a couple of suspicious youngsters walking up and down the road the day before. No, it was going to be one of those unsolved crimes – until perhaps the culprits were caught red-handed, asking for umpteen other offences to be taken into consideration. It was, therefore, a pleasurable relief for Walters when Lewis walked in on Friday morning.

'You want to see the new super, sarge?'

'No. Actually, it's Constable Walters I'm after.'

'Your chief a bit sore about the promotion?'

'Sore? Morse? He looked like he'd won the pools when I last saw him.'

'Can we help you?'

'Morse says you looked into Ms Scott's early marriage, and found where her husband had been living before he was killed.'

'That's right.'

'You spoke to the landlady?'

Walters nodded.

'Tell me all about it,' said Lewis.

'Important, is it?'

'So Morse says.'

By the end of the morning, after a visit to the landlady, after inspecting the medical records in the Radcliffe Infirmary's Accident Department, and after matching his findings with the road accident records in the archives at Police HQ, Lewis knew it all. Yet he felt oddly frustrated about his three hours' research, since Morse – who would never stoop to such fourth-grade clerical stuff himself – had already told him what he'd find: that the other driver involved in the fatal accident with Anne Scott's former husband *had been Michael Murdoch*.

Back in Morse's office, Lewis began to recount his morning's findings, but his reception was surprisingly cool.

'Cut out the weasel words, Lewis! It was just as I said, wasn't it?'

'Just as you said, sir,' replied Lewis mildly.

'And why didn't that incompetent Walters take the trouble to put the landlady's address in his report?'

'I didn't ask him. He probably didn't think it was important.'

'Didn't *think*? What the hell's he got to think *with*?'

'He's only a young fellow – '

'And doubtless *you*, Lewis, with your vast experience, wouldn't have thought it very important either?'

'No, I don't think I would, sir,' replied Lewis, marvelling at his own intrepidity. 'And I know how much you value my own idea of what's important and what isn't.'

'I see.' But there was an icy note in Morse's reply that suddenly alerted Lewis to an imminent gale, force ten. 'I'd always thought, Lewis, that the job of a detective, however feeble-minded he may be, was to produce a faithful and accurate report on whatever facts he'd been able to establish – however insignificant those facts might appear.' The voice was monotonous, didactic, with the slow, refined articulation of a schoolmaster explaining the school rules to a particularly stupid boy. 'You see, it's often the small, seemingly insignificant detail that later assumes a new-born magnitude. You would agree with that, would you not?'

Lewis swallowed hard and nodded feebly. He was in for a carpeting, he knew that. But what had gone wrong?

'So your friend Walters was somewhat remiss, was he not? As you say, I respect your own judgement of what may or may not be important; though, to be honest, I'm disappointed that you don't expect a slightly higher standard of accuracy and thoroughness in your colleagues' reports. But let's forget that. Walters doesn't work for *me*, does he?'

'What have I done wrong, sir?' asked Lewis quietly.

'What have you done wrong? I'll tell you, Lewis. You're bloody careless, that's what! Careless in the way you've been writing your reports – '

'You know my spelling – '

'I'm not talking about your bloody spelling. Listen, man! There are half-a-dozen things here that are purely, simply, plainly, absolutely bloody *wrong*. You're getting *slack*, Lewis. Instead of getting better, you're getting a bloody sight *worse*. Did you *know* that?'

Lewis looked down at the desk and said nothing. He knew, deep down, that he'd rushed a few things; but he'd tried so hard. Whenever Morse picked up his coat for the night and asked, as he often did, for 'a report in the morning', he could have had little idea of how long and difficult a job it was for his sergeant to get the sentences right in his mind, and then tick-tick away on the typewriter until late into the evening while his chief was sitting with his cronies in the local. No, it wasn't fair at all, and Lewis felt a sense of hurt and injustice.

'Let me just see what you mean, if you don't mind, sir. I know I – '

'There's this for a start. Remember it?' Morse's right forefinger flicked the statement taken by Lewis from Mrs Celia Richards. 'And with this one, Lewis, if I remember rightly – as you can be bloody sure I do! – I specifically asked you to take care. *Specifically*.'

Lewis looked down at the statement brusquely thrust across to him and he remembered exactly what Morse had said. He opened his mouth to say something, but Etna was still erupting.

'What the hell's the good of a sergeant who can't even get an address right? A sergeant who can't even copy three figures without getting 'em cock-eyed? And then look at this one here!' Morse had now picked up another sheet and was launching a second front somewhere else – but Lewis was no longer listening. This wasn't just unfair; it was *wrong*. The address on the statement he held was perfectly correct – he was convinced of that. And so he waited, like a deaf man watching a film of Hitler ranting at a Nuremberg rally; and then, when the reverberations had settled, he spoke four simple words, with the massive authority of the Almighty addressing Moses.

'This address is right.'

Morse's mouth opened – and closed. Reaching across the desk, he retrieved Celia Richards' statement, and then fingered through the other documents in front of him until he found what he was looking for.

'You mean to say, Lewis, that she lives at two-*six-one*, and that this address here' – he passed across a Xerox copy of the letter which had accompanied the parking fine – 'is also correct?' The last three words were whispered, and Lewis felt a shiver of excitement as he looked at the copy:

Dear Sirs,
Enclosed herewith please find cheque for £6, being the penalty fixed for the traffic offence detailed on the ticket (also enclosed). I apologise for the trouble caused.
Yours faithfully,
C. Richards.

On the original letterhead, the address had been pre-printed at the top right-hand corner: *216 Oxford Avenue, Abingdon, Oxon.*

It was Lewis who spoke first. 'This means that Celia Richards never paid the fine at all, doesn't it, sir? This is *Conrad* Richards' address.'

Morse nodded agreement. 'That's about it. And I drove past the wretched place myself when . . . ' His voice trailed off, and in his mind at that very moment it was as if a colossal flash of lightning had suddenly illuminated the landscape for a pilot flying lost and blind in the blackest night.

Morse's eyes were still shining as he stood up. 'Calls for a little celebration, don't you think?'

'No, sir. Before we do anything else, I want to know about all those other things in the reports where – '

'Forget 'em! Trivialities, Lewis! Minimal blemishes on some otherwise excellent documentation.' He walked round the table and his right hand gripped Lewis's shoulder. 'We're a team, we are – you realise that, don't you? You and me, when we work together – Christ! We're bloody near invincible! Get your coat!'

Lewis rose reluctantly from his seat. He couldn't really understand why Morse should invariably win, but he supposed it would always be so.

'You reckon you've puzzled it all out, sir?'

'Reckon? *Know*, more like. I'll tell you all about it over a pint.'

'I'd rather you told me now.'

'All right, Lewis. The fact of the matter is that we now not only know who killed Anne Scott, my old friend, but we also know who killed George Jackson. And you want the names? Want 'em now?'

So Morse gave the two different names. The first one left Lewis utterly perplexed, since it was completely unknown to him; the second left him open-mouthed and flabbergasted.

BOOK FOUR

Chapter Thirty-three

What shall be the maiden's fate?
Who shall be the maiden's mate?
Sir Walter Scott, *The Lay of the Last Minstrel*

'There are three basic views about human life,' began Morse.
'One of 'em says that everything happens by pure chance, like
atoms falling through space, colliding with each other occasionally
and cannoning off to start new collisions. According to this view
there's nothing in the scheme of things that has sorted us out –
you and me, Lewis – to sit here in this pub, at this particular time,
to drink a pint of beer together. It's all just a pure fluke – all just
a chancy set of fortuitous circumstances. Then you get those who
reckon that it's ourselves, as people, who determine what happens
– at least to some extent. In other words, it's our own characters
that affect the way things turn out. Sooner or later our sins will
find us out and we have to accept the consequences. It's a bit
like bowls, Lewis. When somebody chucks you down the green,
there's a bias, one way or the other, and you're always going to
drift in a set direction. And then there's another view: the view
that it doesn't matter a bugger what particular circumstances are,
or what individual people do. The future's fixed and firm – just
like the past is. Things are somehow ordained from on high –
pre-ordained, that's the word. There's a predetermined pattern in
life. What's going to be – is going to be; and whatever you do and
whatever your luck is, you just can't avoid it. If your number's up
– your number's up! Fate – that's what they call it.'

'What do *you* believe, sir?'

'Me? Well, I certainly don't go for all this "fate" lark – it's a

153

load of nonsense. I reckon I come somewhere in the middle of the other two. But that's neither here nor there. What *is* important is what Anne Scott believed; and it's perfectly clear to me that she was a firm believer in the fates. She even mentioned the word, I remember, when – when I met her. And then there was that particular row of books just above the desk in her study – all those Penguin Classics, Lewis. It's pretty clear from the look of some of those creased black spines that the works of the Greek tragedians must have made a deep impression on her, and some of those stories – well, let's be more specific. There was one book she'd been re-reading very recently and hadn't put back on the shelf yet. It was lying on her desk, Lewis, and one of the stories in that book – '

'I think I'm getting a bit lost, sir.'

'All right. Listen! Let me tell you a story. Once upon a time – a long, long time ago, in fact – a handsome young prince came to a city and quite naturally he was entertained at the palace, where he met the queen of that city. Soon these two found themselves in each other's company quite a bit, and the prince fell in love with the beautiful and lonely queen; and she, in turn, fell in love with the young prince. And things were easy for 'em. The prince was a bachelor and he found out that the queen was a widow – her husband had recently been killed on a journey by road to one of the neighbouring cities. So they confessed their love – and then they got married. Had quite a few kids, too. And it would've been nice if they'd lived happily ever after, wouldn't it? But I'm afraid they didn't. In fact, the story of what happened to the pair of 'em after that is one of the most chilling and terrifying myths in the whole of Greek literature. You know what happened then, of course?'

Lewis looked down at his beer and reflected sadly upon his lack of any literary education. 'I'm sorry, I don't, sir. We didn't have any of that Greek and Latin stuff when I was at school.'

Morse knew again at that moment exactly why he always wanted Lewis around. The man was so wholesome, somehow: honest, unpretentious, humble, almost, in his experience of philosophy and life. A lovable man; a good man. And Morse continued in a gentler, less arrogant tone.

'It's a tragic story. The prince had plenty of time on his hands and one day he decided to find out, if he could, how the queen's

former husband had died. He spent years digging out eye-witnesses
of what had happened, and he finally discovered that the king
hadn't died in an accident after all: he'd been murdered. And
he kept working away at the case, Lewis, and d'you know what
he found? He found that the murderer had been – ' (the fingers
of Morse's left hand which had been gesticulating haphazardly in
front of him, suddenly tautened and turned dramatically to point
to his own chest) ' – that the murderer had been *himself*. And
he learned something else, too. He learned that the man he'd
murdered had been – *his own father*. And in a blinding, terrifying flash of insight, Lewis, he realised the full enormity of what
he'd done. You see, not only had he murdered his own father –
but he'd married *his own mother*, and had a family by her! And
the truth had to come out – all of it. And when it did, the queen
went and hanged herself. And the prince, when he heard what
she'd done, he – he blinded himself. That's it. That's the myth
of Oedipus.'

Morse had finished, and Lewis felt himself strangely moved
by the story and the way his chief had told it. He thought that if
only his own schoolteachers had been able to tell him about such
top-of-the-head stuff in the way Morse had just done, he would
never have felt so distanced from that intimidating crew who were
listed in the index of his encyclopaedia under 'Tragedians'. He
saw, too, how the legend Morse had just expounded linked up at
so many points with the present case; and he would indeed have
been able to work it all out for himself had not Morse anticipated
his activated musings.

'You can appreciate, Lewis, how Anne Scott's intimate knowledge of this old myth was bound to affect her attitudes and actions.
Just think! As a young and beautiful undergrad here, she had met a
man and married him, just as in the Oedipus myth Queen Jocasta
married King Laius. Then a baby arrived. And just as Jocasta
couldn't keep her baby – because an oracle had told her that
the baby would kill its father – so Anne Scott and her husband
couldn't keep theirs, because they had no permanent home or jobs
and little chance of bringing up the boy with any decent prospects.
Jocasta and Laius exposed the infant Oedipus on some hillside
or other; and Anne and her husband did the modern equivalent
– they found a private adoption society which took the baby off
their hands immediately. I don't know much about the rules and

regulations of these societies, but I'd like to bet that in this case
there was a provision that the mother was not to know who the
future foster-parents were going to be, and that the foster-parents
weren't to know who the actual mother was. Now, Lewis! What
would every mother be absolutely certain to remember about her
only child – even if it was taken from her almost immediately after
it was born. Face and features? Certainly not! Even after a few
weeks any clear-cut visual memory would be getting progressively
more blurred; and after a few months, certainly after a year, the
odds are that she wouldn't even recognise her own offspring. So
what's that one thing that she'll never forget, Lewis? Just think
back a minute. Our friend Bell – *Superintendent* Bell – was quite
right on one point. He believed that something must have happened the night before Anne Scott died that proved to be the
immediate cause of her subsequent actions. He didn't do a bad
job, either, because he came up with two or three very interesting facts.

'He learned, for instance, that the bridge evening happened to
be the club's first anniversary, and whatsername had laid on some
sherry for the occasion; and if you want to get non-boozers a
bit relaxed fairly quickly, a few glasses of sherry isn't a bad
bet. Doubtless tongues began to wag a bit more freely than usual,
and we know a couple of things that cropped up. Vietnam and
Cambodia did, for a start, and I suspect that the only aspect of
those human tragedies that directly impinges on your bourgeois
North Oxford housewife is the question of adopting one or two
of the poor little blighters caught up in refugee camps. All right,
Lewis? I reckon *adoption* was a topic of conversation that night.
Then Bell got to know something else – and bless his heart for
sticking it down! They were talking about *birthdays* – and not
unnaturally so, in view of the fact they were celebrating their
own first birthday; and as I've just said, Lewis, there's one thing
no mother's ever going to forget – and that's when her only baby
was born! So this is how I reckon things were. That night at the
bridge party, somebody who knew Mrs Murdoch pretty well got
a fraction indiscreet, and let it be known to a few people –
including, alas, Anne Scott – that Mrs Murdoch's elder son was
an adopted boy. And then, in the changing circles of conversation, Anne must have heard Mrs Murdoch herself volunteering
the information that her elder son, Michael, was celebrating his

nineteenth birthday on that very day! What a quirk of fate it all was!'

'I thought you didn't believe in fate, sir.'

But Morse was oblivious to the interjection, and continued his fantastic tale. 'When Laius, Jocasta's husband, was killed, it had been on the road between Thebes and Corinth – a road accident, Lewis! When Anne Scott's husband died, it had also been in a road accident, and I'm pretty sure that she knew all about it. After all, she'd known the elder Murdoch boy – and Mrs Murdoch herself, of course – for more than a couple of years. But, in itself, that couldn't have been a matter of any great moment. It had been an *accident*: the inquest had found neither party predominantly to blame. If experience in driving means anything, it means that you have to expect learner drivers – like Michael Murdoch – to do something daft occasionally; and in this case, Anne Scott's husband wasn't careful enough to cope with the other fellow's inexperience. But do you see how things are beginning to build up and develop, Lewis? Everything is beginning to assume a menacing and sinister importance. Young Michael Murdoch was visiting Anne Scott once a week for special coaching; and as they sat next to each other week after week in Canal Reach I reckon that sheer physical proximity got a bit too much for both of 'em. The young lad must have become infatuated by a comparatively mature and attractive woman – a woman with a full and eminently feel-able figure; and the woman herself, who had probably only been in love once in her life – and that with a married man who'd never been willing to run off with her – must surely have felt the attraction of a young, virile lad who worshipped whatever ground she chose to tread. She must have led him on a bit, Lewis; and sure as eggs are eggs, the springs on the old charpoy in the bedroom are soon beginning to creak pretty steadily. Then? Well, then the trouble starts. She misses a period – and then another; and she goes off to the Jericho clinic – where they tell her they'll let her know as soon as they can. It must have been then that she wrote to Charles Richards pleading for a bit of help: a bit of friendly guidance, at the very least – and perhaps for a bit of money so that she could go away and have a quiet, private abortion somewhere. But, as we know, the letter never got through to Charles Richards at all. By some freakish mischance the letter was intercepted by Celia Richards – and that, Lewis, was the source of all the trouble. As

the days pass – and still no reply from her former lover – Anne
Scott must have felt that the fates were conspiring against her.
Michael Murdoch was the very last person in the world she was
going to tell her troubles to: he'd finished his schooling, anyway,
and so there was no longer any legitimate reason for them seeing
each other. Perhaps they met again once or twice after that – I just
don't know. What is perfectly clear is that Anne Scott was growing
increasingly depressed as the days dragged on. Life hadn't been
very kind to her, and looking back on things she saw evidence
only of her failures: her hasty adolescent marriage that had been
short-lived and disastrous; her love for Charles Richards which
had blossomed for a good many years but which had always been
doomed to disappointment; other lovers, no doubt, who'd given
her some physical gratification, but little else; and then Michael
Murdoch . . . '

Morse's voice trailed off, and his eyes drifted along the other
tables in the lounge bar where groups of people sat exchanging
the amusing ephemera of a happier, if somewhat shallower, life
than Anne Scott could ever have known. His glass was empty,
and Lewis, as he picked it up and walked over to the bar, decided
on this occasion not to remind Morse whose turn it was.

'So,' resumed Morse, lapping his lips into the level of his
pint without a word of gratitude, 'Anne Scott's making a bit of a
mess of her life. She's still attractive enough to middle-aged men
like you and me, Lewis; but most of those are already bespoke,
like you, and the ones that are left, like me, are a load of old
remaindered books – out of date and going cheap. But her real
tragedy is that she's still attractive to some of the young pupils
who come along to that piddling little property of hers in Jericho.
She's got no regular income except for the fees from a succession
of half-wits whose parents are rich enough and stupid enough to
cough up and keep hoping. She goes out quite a bit, of course,
and occasionally she meets a nice enough chap but . . . No! Things
don't work out, and she begins to think – she begins to *believe* –
that they never will. She's got a deeply pessimistic and fatalistic
streak in her make-up, and in the end, as you know, she aban-
dons all hope. Charles Richards, as she thinks, doesn't give a sod
about her any longer: just at the time when she desperately needs
a friend, *he* can't even fork out an envelope and stamp. But she
was a pretty tough girl, I should think, and she'd have been able

to cope with her problems – if it hadn't been for that shattering revelation at the bridge evening.

'She'd been reading the Oedipus story again in the Penguin translation – probably with one of her pupils – and the ground's all naked and ready for the seeds that were sown that fateful evening. Adoption and birthdays – they were the seeds, Lewis, and it must have been the most traumatic shock of her whole life when the terrible truth dawned on her: *Michael Murdoch was her own son.* And as the implications whirled round in her mind, she must have seen the whole thing in terms of the fates marking her out as another Jocasta. Everything fitted. Her husband had been killed – killed in a road accident – killed by her own son – a son with whom she'd been having sex – a son who was the father of the child she was expecting. She must have felt utterly powerless against the workings of what she saw as the pre-ordained tragedy of her own benighted life. And so she decided to do the one thing that was left open to her: to stop all the struggling and to surrender to her fate; to co-operate with the forces that were now driving her inexorably to her own death – a death which she determines, as she sits through that long and hopeless night, will be the death that Queen Jocasta chose. And so, my old friend, she hanged herself . . . And had she but known it, the curse had still not finally worked itself out. Michael Murdoch is in the Intensive Care Unit at the JR2, and he's blinded himself, Lewis – just as Oedipus did. The whole wretched thing's nothing less than a ghastly re-enactment of the old myth as you can read it in Sophocles. And as I told you, if there was one man guilty of Anne Scott's death, that man was Sophocles.'

The beer glasses were empty again and the mood of the two men was sombre as Morse took out his wallet and passed a five-pound note over to Lewis.

'My round, I think.'

It was a turn up for the books; an even bigger one when Morse insisted that Lewis kept the change.

'You've been far too generous with your rounds recently, Lewis. I've noticed that. But over-generosity is just as big a fault as stinginess, you know. That's what Aristotle said, anyway.'

Lewis was feeling a little light-headed in the rarefied air of these Greek philosophers and tragedians, but he was anxious to get one thing straight.

'You still don't believe in fate, sir?'

'Course I bloody don't!' snapped Morse.

'But you just think of all those coincidences – '

'What are you talking about? There's only one real coincidence in the business: the fact that Anne Scott should find that one of her pupils is her own son. That's all! And what's so odd about that, anyway? She's had hundreds of pupils, and Oxford's not all that big – '

'What about the accident?'

'Augh! There are millions of accidents every year – thousands of 'em in Oxford – '

'You exaggerate a bit, sir.'

'Nonsense! And that's where the coincidences stop, isn't it? Anne Scott decided to hang herself – *she* decided that. It was a conscious human decision, and had nothing to do with those wretched fates spinning your threads or lopping 'em off or whatever else they're supposed to do. And the fact that Michael Murdoch squirted so much dope into himself and then did what he did – well, that was a sheer fluke, wasn't it? He could have done anything.'

'Fluke, sir? You seem to want to have it all ways. Flukes, coincidences, decisions, fates . . . '

Morse nodded rather sadly. He wasn't quite sure where his own pervasively cynical philosophy of life was leading him, but the facts in this particular case remained what they were; for the life and death of Anne Scott had traced with awesome accuracy those murderous, incestuous, and self-destructive patterns of that early story . . .

'Do you know, Lewis, I could just do justice to some egg and chips.'

Lewis was losing count of his surprises. 'I reckon I'll join you, sir.'

'I'm afraid you'll have to treat me, though. I don't seem to have any money left.'

Chapter Thirty-four

The great advantage of a hotel is that it's a refuge from home life

G. B. Shaw

The hotel room could have been almost anywhere: a neat, well-furnished room, with a white-tiled bathroom annexe, its racks replete with fluffy, white towels. A cosmopolitan room – a little antiseptic and anaemic, perhaps, but moderately expensive and adequately cosy. Two separate lights were fixed to the wall just above the head-board of the double bed, though neither was turned on as Charles Richards lay on his back, his left hand behind his head, smoking silently. He wasn't sure of the exact time, but he thought it must be about 7.30 a.m., and he had been awake for over an hour. Beside him, her back towards him, lay a young woman, the mauve-striped sheet draped closely round her naked body. Occasionally she stirred slightly and once or twice her lips had mumbled some somnolent endearment. But Charles Richards felt no erotic stirrings towards her that morning. For much of the time as he lay there he was thinking of his wife, wondering sadly why it was that now, when she was willing to let him go, his thoughts kept drifting back to her. She had not cried or created any scene when at last the truth of his relations with Anne Scott had been forced into the open. But her eyes had betrayed her hurt and disappointment, and a hardness that made her face seem older and plainer; yet later she had looked so tender and so very vulnerable that he had almost found himself falling in love with her afresh. She had said little, apart from a few practical suggestions about the days immediately ahead: she was proud and wounded. He wondered where exactly she was at that moment? Almost certainly back home from Cambridge by now. And if she was, her bed would already have been made up neatly, the sheets stretched taut across the mattress and lovingly smoothed as she had always smoothed them . . .

And then there was Conrad – his dear and loyal brother Conrad – who had turned up the previous day and managed to book a single room in one of the cheaper hotels across the plaza. Outwardly, Conrad seemed as calm as ever, yet underneath were indications of an unwonted anxiety. Which, of course, was all perfectly understandable, for Conrad had been left with a difficult choice. But, as Charles saw it, his brother had almost certainly made the wrong one. Why come out to Madrid? There was virtually no chance that the police could suspect Conrad of anything; so why hadn't he arranged some quiet little business trip in England? All right, he just *had* to get away, so he'd said – though Charles doubted even that.

There was a light knock on the door, followed by the rattle of a key in the bedroom lock, and a young, heavily moustached Spanish waiter brought in the breakfast tray. But the woman still slept on. And Charles was glad of that, for the previous morning she had suddenly jerked herself up to a sitting position, completely naked to the waist; and for some deeply innate reason, he had felt himself madly jealous as the waiter's dark eyes had feasted on her breasts.

For five minutes the tray by the bedside remained untouched, and then Jennifer turned over towards him, her long, painted fingers feeling inside the top of his pyjama jacket. He knew then beyond doubt that after breakfast he would be making love to her again, and momentarily he despised himself – despised that utterly *selfish* self of his that almost invariably sought some compensating gratification from every situation, just as he had sought out Jennifer Hills after Celia had learned the truth. He shook his head slowly on the pillow, and reached out for the coffee-pot; but the woman's fingertips were detouring tantalisingly towards his pyjama trousers, and he turned himself towards her.

'Can't you even wait till after breakfast?'

'No – o! I want you *now*.'

'You're a sexy bitch, aren't you?'

'Mm. Specially in the mornings. You know that . . . '

When the Spanish chambermaid came in to clean up at 10.30 a.m., she found the toast untouched, as it had been the previous morning; and smiling knowingly to herself she turned her attention to smoothing out the rumpled mauve-striped sheets.

Conrad Richards ate little breakfast, either, for he was a deeply worried man. He'd suspected the previous day that Charles had been most displeased to see him, and now he wished he'd never come. But he needed some advice and reassurance, and for those he had depended on his brother all his life. He walked across to the Tourist Office at nine o'clock and found that if he wanted to he could fly back to Gatwick that same afternoon. Yes, that would probably be the best thing: get back, and see Celia again, and face things . . .

But when, at 11 a.m., the brothers met in the cocktail bar of the Palace Hotel, Charles seemed his bright, ebullient self once more.

'Go back *today*? Nonsense! You've not even had a chance to look round. Look at that!' He pointed out across the plaza to the fountains playing beside the statue of Neptune. 'Beautiful, isn't it? We'll do a bit of sight-seeing together, Conrad. What do you say?'

'What about er – ?'

'Don't worry about her. She's flying back to Gatwick this afternoon – on my instructions.'

Celia, too, had been up early that morning, deciding as she had done to follow Charles's practice of putting some time in at the office on Saturday. The previous day, a measure of greatness had been thrust upon her, for she had found herself making decisions about contracts and payments without the slightest hesitation – and she'd enjoyed it all. Seated in Charles's chair, she'd dictated letters and memoranda, answered the telephone, greeted two prospective clients, and one ineffectual salesman – all with a new-found confidence that had surprised her. Action! That's what she told herself she needed – and plenty of it; and she just said 'No, no, no!' whenever the waves of worry threatened to wash all other thoughts away. Indeed, for some brief periods of time she found herself almost succeeding in her self-imposed discipline. But the currents of anxiety were often too strong, and like her brother-in-law she felt the urgent need of having Charles beside her. Charles, who was so strong and confident; Charles whom, in spite of everything that had happened, she knew the only man she could ever fully love.

She was still in the office when she took the call at ten-past twelve. It was from Madrid. From Charles.

She was at home two hours later when she received another call, this time from Detective Chief Inspector Morse, to whom she was able to report that her husband would be returning home on Monday morning, his flight scheduled to land at Gatwick at 10.40 a.m., and that she herself was driving up to meet him. If it was *really* necessary, yes, they could probably be back by about 2 o'clock – if the plane was on time, of course. Make it 2.30 then? Better still, 3 o'clock, just to be on the safe side. At the Richards' house? All right. Fine!

'Have you any idea where your husband's brother is?'

'Conrad? No, I haven't, I'm afraid. He's off on business somewhere, but no one seems to know where he's gone.'

'Oh, I see.'

Celia could hear the disappointment in the inspector's voice and was clearly anxious to appear co-operative. 'Can I give him a message – when he gets back?'

'No-o.' Morse sounded indecisive. 'Perhaps not, Mrs Richards. It was just – No, it doesn't matter. It's not important.'

Lewis had come into the office during the last part of the telephone conversation, and Morse winked at him broadly as he replaced the receiver.

'Monday, then! That's the big show-down, Lewis. Three o'clock. And you know something? I reckon I'm looking forward to it.'

Lewis, however, was looking unimpressed, and something in his face spelled trouble.

'Aren't *you*, Lewis?'

'I'm afraid I've got some rather odd news for you.'

Morse looked up sharply.

'It was very irregular, they said, and Saturday morning's hardly the best time to make enquiries, is it?'

'But you found out?'

Lewis nodded. 'You're not going to like this much, sir, but the Scott's baby was adopted by a couple in North London: a Mr and Mrs Hawkins. They christened the boy "Joseph", and the poor little fellow died just before his third birthday – meningitis.'

Morse looked utterly blank and his eyes seemed to stare down into some vast abyss. 'You're quite sure about this?'

'Quite sure, sir. You were right about Michael Murdoch being adopted, though. Same society. But his parents were both killed in a road accident just outside – '

But Morse was no longer listening, for if what Lewis had just told him was true . . .

Yet Morse had not been so very far from the truth, and if only he had known it, the final clue in the Anne Scott case lay even now inside his jacket pocket, in the shape of the unopened letter he had so recently picked up from the front-door mat of 9 Canal Reach.

'Does this mean that we're back to the drawing-board, sir?'

'Certainly not!' said Morse.

'Will you want me tomorrow?'

'Sunday? Sunday's a day of rest, Lewis – and I've got to catch up with the omnibus edition of *The Archers*.'

Chapter Thirty-five

Sir: (*n.*) a word of respect (or disapprobation) used in addressing a man
Chambers Twentieth-Century Dictionary

The up-swung door of the wide double garage revealed the incongruous collocation of the Rolls and the Mini as Morse walked across the crunching gravel and rang the bell. Clearly number 261 was in a different class from Conrad's house. It was Celia who answered the door.

'Come in, Inspector.'

'Plane on time, Mrs Richards?'

'A few minutes early, in fact. You know my husband, of course.'

Morse watched them carefully as they stood there, fingers intertwined as though some dramatic reconciliation had recently been enacted – or, at least, as though they wished to give *him* that impression. He nodded rather curtly.

'Afternoon, sir. I'd hoped that we could have a quiet little chat on our own – if, er, your wife – '

'I was just going, Inspector – don't worry. Why don't you go through into the lounge, Charles? You can let me know when you've finished . . . well, finished whatever you've got to discuss.' She sounded remarkably happy, and there was a spring in her step as she walked away.

'She's obviously glad to have you back, sir,' said Morse, as the two men sat opposite each other in the lounge.

'I think she is, yes.'

'Bit surprising, perhaps?'

'We're not here to talk about my personal affairs, I hope?'

'I'm afraid your personal affairs are very much involved, sir.'

'But not my private relations with my wife.'

'No. Perhaps not, sir.'

'And I wish you'd stop calling me "sir"!'

'My sergeant calls me "sir" all the time. It's just a sort of social formality, Mr Richards.' Morse slowly took out a cigarette, as if he were anxious to impose some leisurely tempo on the interview. 'Mind if I smoke?'

'Not a bit.' Richards took an ash-tray from the mantelpiece and placed it on the arm of Morse's chair.

Morse offered the packet across, but Richards shook his head with a show of impatience. 'Not for the minute, thanks. It's about Anne Scott, isn't it?'

'Amongst other things.'

'Well, can we get on with it?'

'Do you know where your brother Conrad is?'

'No. Not the faintest.'

'Did he ring you – while you were in Spain?'

'Yes. He told me one of your men had taken his fingerprints.'

'He didn't object.'

'Why should he, Inspector?'

'Why indeed?'

'Why *did* you take them?'

'I thought he might have murdered Jackson.'

'What *Conrad?* Oh dear! You must be hard up for suspects.'

'Yes. I'm – I'm afraid we are.'

'Do you want *my* fingerprints?'

'No, I don't think so. You see you've got a pretty good alibi for that night. Me!'

'I thought the police were always breaking alibis, though. In detective stories it's usually the person with the cast-iron alibi who commits the murder, isn't it?'

Morse nodded. 'Not in this case, though. You see, I happen to know exactly who killed Jackson – and it wasn't *you*.'

'Well, that's something to be grateful for, I suppose.'

'Did Conrad also tell you that we found the blackmail note in your desk?'

'No. But Celia did. I was a bit daft to keep it, I suppose.'

'But I'm very glad you did. It was the biggest clue in the case.'

'Really?'

'And Jackson didn't write it.'

'*What?*'

'No. Jackson couldn't have written that letter because – '

'But he *rang*, Inspector! It must have been Jackson.'

'Do you remember exactly what he said when he rang?'

'Well – no, not really, but – '

'Please try to think back if you can. It's very important.'

'Well – he seemed to know that er – well, he seemed to know all about me and Anne.'

'Did he actually *mention* the letter?'

'Do you know . . . I don't think he did, no.' Richards frowned and sat forward in his chair. 'So you think, perhaps, that – that the person who rang me . . . But it *was* Jackson, Inspector! I know it was.'

'Do you mind telling me how you can be so sure?' asked Morse quietly.

'You probably know, don't you?' To Morse, Richards' eyes suddenly seemed to show a deeply shrewd intelligence.

'I don't really know anything yet.'

'Well, when Jackson rang, I decided to change things. You know, change the time and the place and all that. I thought it would give me a chance – '

'To follow him?'

'Yes.'

'How much money did you take with you?'

'£250.'

'And where did you arrange to meet him?'

'Woodstock Road. I left the money behind a telephone box there – near Fieldside – Fieldhouse Road, or some such name. I can show you if – '

'Then you waited, and followed him?'

'That's right.'

'In the car?'

Richards nodded. 'It wasn't easy, of course, but – '

'Did you take Conrad with you?'

'Take Conrad? What – what on earth – ?'

'How did Conrad follow Jackson? On his bike?'

'What the hell are you talking about? *I* followed Jackson – in the *car*. I just – '

'There's a folding bicycle in your garage. I just happened to er notice it as I came up the drive. Did he use that?'

'I just *told* you, Inspector. I don't know where you're getting all these cock-eyed notions from but – '

'Did you put the bike in the back seat or in the boot?'

'I *told* you – '

'Look, sir! There can be no suspicion whatever that either you or your brother, Conrad, murdered George Jackson. None! But I'm still faced with a murder, and you've got to tell me the *truth*, if only because then I'll be able to eliminate certain lines of enquiry – and stop meself wasting me bloody time! You've got to understand that! If I can get it quite clear in my own mind exactly what happened that night, I shall be on the right track – I'm certain of that. And I'm certain of something else, and that is that *you* involved Conrad in some way or other. It might not have been on a bike – '

'Yes, it was,' said Richards quietly. 'We put it in the back of the Rolls, and when I parked just off the main road, Conrad got it out. He'd dressed up in a gown and had a few books with him. We thought it would sort of merge into the background somehow.'

'And then Conrad followed him?'

'He followed him to Canal Reach, yes – last house on the right.'

'So?'

'So nothing, Inspector. We knew where he lived and we – well, it was me, actually – I found out his name.'

'Go on!'

'That's the finish, Inspector.'

'You didn't drive Conrad into Oxford the night Jackson was killed? The night you spoke at the Book Association?'

'I swear I didn't!'

'Where *was* Conrad that night?'

'I honestly don't know. I *did* ask him – after we'd heard about this Jackson business. But he said he just couldn't remember. Probably at home all night but – '

'He's got no alibi, you mean?'

'I'm afraid not.'

'Well, I shouldn't worry about that, sir – er Mr Richards, I mean. I'd take it as a good sign rather than a bad one that your brother's a bit hazy about that night.'

'I see, yes. You know, it's not all that easy, is it, remembering where you were a week or so ago?'

'*You'd* surely have no trouble, though? About that night, I mean.'

'No, I haven't. I forget exactly when the meeting finished, but I know I drove straight home, Inspector. I must have been home by – oh, half-past ten, I should think.'

'Would your wife remember?'

'Why don't you ask her?'

'Hardly worth it, is it? You've probably got it all worked out, anyway.'

'I *resent* that, Inspector! All right, my brother and I probably acted like a pair of idiots, I realise that. I should have told the police about the letter and so on straightaway. All right! But please don't drag *Celia* into things! I've treated the poor woman shabbily enough without her having to – '

'I'm sorry! I shouldn't have said that; and it doesn't really matter *when* you got home that night. Why should it?'

'But it's rather nice when someone can confirm what you say, isn't it? And I'm quite sure that Celia – '

'Forget it, please! I think I've got the general picture, and I'm very grateful to you.' Morse stood up to go. 'We shall have to have a statement, of course. But I can send Sergeant Lewis along at some time that's convenient for you.'

'Can't we get it done now, Inspector? I've got a pretty hectic programme these next few days.'

'Not off to Spain again, I hope?'

'No. I'm off to Newcastle first thing in the morning, and I expect to be there a couple of days. Then I'm going – '

'Don't worry about that. There's no rush. As I say, it's not really important. But you know all this bureaucratic business of getting things down on paper: getting people to sign things, and all that. And to be truthful, Mr Richards, we sometimes find that people change their evidence a bit when it actually comes down to having to sign it. Funny, isn't it? And, of course, the memory plays some odd tricks on all of us. Sometimes we find that we suddenly remember a particular detail that we thought we'd quite forgotten it.'

'I'm not sure I like what I think you're trying to say,' said Richards, his voice a degree harsher now.

'No? All I'm saying is that it won't do any harm for you to think things over at your leisure. That's all.'

'Shall I write it all out, and post it to you?'

'No, we can't do that, I'm afraid. We shall need you to sign the statement in front of a police officer.'

'All right.' Richards seemed suddenly relaxed again and rose from his chair. 'Let's arrange something, shall we?'

'I should think the best thing is for you to give Sergeant Lewis a ring at the Kidlington HQ when you've finished your business trips. One day early next week, shall we say?'

'Monday? Will that be all right?'

'Certainly. Well, I'll be off now. I'm sorry to have taken up so much of your time.'

'Would you like a cup of tea?'

'Tea? Er, no thank you – I must be getting back. Please give my regards to Mrs Richards.'

The two men walked to the front door, and Morse asked if he could have a quick look at the Rolls.

'Beautiful!' was his verdict.

'And here's the famous bike,' said Richards ruefully.

Morse nodded. 'I've always had pretty sharp eyes, they tell me.'

They shook hands and Morse walked down to the road where Lewis sat waiting with his usual placid patience.

'Well?' said Morse.

'It was just as you said, sir.'

Morse sat back contentedly as they drove past the last few houses in Oxford Avenue. 'Well, I've thrown in the bait, Lewis. We just sit back now, and wait for the fish to bite.'

'Think he will?'

'Oh, yes! You should have heard me, Lewis. A bloody genius, I was!'

'Really, sir?'

'Why do you call me "sir" all the time?'

'Well, it's just a sort of convention in the Force, isn't it? Just a mark of respect, I suppose.'

'Do you think I deserve some respect?'

'I wouldn't go so far as that, but it's a sort of habit by now and I don't think I could change in a hurry – sir!'

Morse sat back happily, for things were going extraordinarily well. At least on one front.

Chapter Thirty-six

A vauntour and a lyere, al is one
Geoffrey Chaucer, *Troylus and Criseyde*

As instructed, the sister had telephoned Kidlington HQ when the time seemed to her most opportune; and the following evening at 8 p.m. Morse and Lewis sat waiting in a small ante-room just off Dyne Ward in the Eye Hospital at the Radcliffe Infirmary in Walton Street, whither Michael Murdoch had now been transferred. Edward Murdoch, after just leaving his brother's bedside, looked surprised and somewhat flustered as he was ushered into this room and told to sit down. There were no formalities.

'Can you spell "believe"?' asked Morse.

The boy swallowed hard and seemed about to answer when Morse, thrusting the blackmail note across the table, answered the question for him.

'Of course you can. You're a well educated lad, we know that– No! Please don't touch it, Edward! Fingerprints all over it, you see – but whoever wrote that letter couldn't spell "believe", could he? Just have a look at it.'

The boy shifted awkwardly in his chair, his eyes narrowing over the writing in the long, uncomfortable silence that followed.

'Did you write it?' asked Morse slowly. 'Or was it your brother?'

The boy shook his head in apparent bewilderment. 'You must be joking!'

It was Lewis who spoke next, his voice flat and unconcerned. 'You didn't write it yourself – is that what you're saying?'

'Of course I didn't!'

'That's all I wanted to know, Mr Murdoch,' said Lewis with polite finality. He whispered something into Morse's ear; and

Morse, seemingly faced with a decision of some delicacy, finally nodded.

'*Now*, sir?' asked Lewis.

Morse nodded again, and Lewis, taking a pen from his breast pocket and picking up a sheaf of papers from the table, got up and left the ante-room.

Morse himself picked up a copy of *Country Life*, turned to the crossword, and had finished it in eleven minutes – minutes during which Edward Murdoch was showing increasing signs of agitation. Two or three times his mouth had opened as if he were about to speak, and when Morse wrote in the last letter he could stay silent no longer.

'What *is* all this?'

'We're waiting.'

'Waiting for – for *him* to come back?'

Morse nodded. 'Sergeant Lewis – that's his name.'

'How long will he be?'

Morse shrugged his shoulders and turned over a page to survey the features of the Honourable Fiona Forbes-Smithson. 'Difficult to say. Some people are co-operative – some aren't.'

'He's gone to see Michael, hasn't he?'

'He's got his duty to do – just like the rest of us.'

'But it's not *fair*! Michael's *ill*!'

'He's a lot better. Going to see a bit, so they tell me.'

'But it's not – '

'Look, lad!' said Morse very gently and quietly. 'Sergeant Lewis and myself are trying our best to solve a murder. It takes a lot of time and patience and we have to do an awful lot of things we'd rather not do. But if we're lucky and people try to help us – well, sometimes we manage to get to the bottom of things.'

'But I've *told* you, Inspector, I never – '

'You *lie*!' thundered Morse. 'Do you honestly believe it was *my* wish for Sergeant Lewis to go and disturb your brother? You're *right*. He *is* ill. Do you think I don't know all about him? Do you think I'd risk his chances of getting over all this trouble if I didn't *have* to?'

Edward Murdoch did a very strange thing then. Like some frenetic pianist banging away at the same chords, he pressed the fingers of both his hands all over the letter in front of him, and sat back breathing heavily with a look of triumph in his eyes.

'Not *really* very sensible,' said Morse mildly. 'You see, I'm going to have to ask you why you did that, aren't I? And I'll tell you something, lad. You'd better think up something pretty good!'

'You're trying to trick me!' shouted the boy. 'Why don't you just – ?'

'I'm not trying to trick you, lad. I don't need to. You're making enough mistakes without needing me to do much about it.'

'I *told* you. I didn't – '

'Look! Sergeant Lewis'll be back any minute now, because I can't really believe your brother's as stupid as you are. And when he comes in, we'll have a statement, and then we'll take you up to Kidlington and get one from *you*. It's all right. You didn't write the letter, you say. That's fine. All we've got to do is to get it down in writing, then typed up, and signed. It won't take all that long, and I'll give your mum a ring and tell her – '

'What's it got to do with her?'

'Won't she be a bit worried about you, lad? You're all she's got at home now, you know, and she's had one hell of a time these last few weeks, hasn't she?'

It was the final straw, and Edward Murdoch buried his head in his hands and wept.

Morse quietly left the room and beckoned to Lewis, who had been sitting for the last quarter of an hour on a bench at the end of the corridor, making steady progress with the Coffee-Break Crossword in the *Daily Mirror*.

The sordid little story was soon told. It had been Edward who had seen the letter to Charles Richards underneath a pile of books in the study, unsealed but ready to post, with the envelope addressed and stamped. In it Anne Scott had begged for advice, support, and money. She was sure she was pregnant and the father could only be Charles Richards because she had never made love with any other man. She pleaded with Charles to contact her and arrange to see her. She knew he would agree because of what they had meant to each other for so many years; and so very recently, too. She held out no threats, but the very fact that such a thing had crossed her mind served only to show how desperate she was feeling. If he could be her lover no longer, at least he could be a friend – *now*, when she needed him as never before. She treasured all the

letters he had written to her, and re-reading them was about the
only thing that gave her any hope. She would burn them all – as
he'd often asked her to – if only he would help her. If he *wouldn't*
– well, she just couldn't say what she would do.

As best he could remember it, that was the gist of the letter
that Edward had read before hastily replacing it as he heard
Anne climbing the stairs; and that was the gist of what he'd
told his brother Michael the same evening. Not in any fraternal,
conspiratorial sort of way. Just the opposite, in fact; because
Michael had frequently boasted about making love to Anne,
and – yes! – he, Edward, had been angry and jealous about
it. But Michael had laughed it off; after all it wasn't much
good her appealing to *him* for any money, was it? He couldn't
even afford a decent fix every now and again. Then, Anne had
died; and soon after hearing of her death, Michael had asked
Edward whether he could remember the name and address of
the man Anne had written to. And that's how it started. Just
a joke, really – that's what they'd thought, anyway. There was
a chance of some money, perhaps, and money for Michael was
becoming an urgent necessity, because (as Edward knew) he'd
been on drugs for nearly a year. So, almost in a schoolboyish
manner, they had concocted a note together – and, well, that
was all. The next day Michael had been rushed off to hospital,
and Edward himself had felt frightened. Was still frightened –
and agonisedly sorry about the cheap thing he'd done and all
the trouble he'd caused. He'd never rung up Charles Richards,
and he'd never been down to the willow trees to see if anything
had been left there.

Whilst Lewis was laboriously scrawling the last few sentences,
Morse wandered off and walked into the ward where Michael
lay, a large white dressing over his right eye, his left eye, bruised
and swollen, staring up at the ceiling. 'Your brother just told me
that between you you wrote a letter to Charles Richards. Is that
right, Michael?'

'If Ted says so. I forget.' He seemed nonchalant and unconcerned.

'You don't forget other things, perhaps?'

'What's that supposed to mean?'

'You'd always remember getting into bed with Ms Scott, surely?'

To Morse the look that leaped into the single eye of Michael Murdoch seemed distastefully crude and triumphant, but the boy made no direct reply.

'Real honey, wasn't she?'

'Phew! You can say that again.'

'She – er – she took her clothes off, you mean?'

'You kidding? Beautiful body that woman had!'

Morse shrugged his shoulders. 'I wouldn't go so far as that myself. I only saw her after she – after she was dead, but . . . you can't really say she had a beautiful body, can you? With that great birth-mark on her side? Come off it, lad. You can't have seen many.'

'You don't notice that sort of thing too much, though, do you, when – ?'

'You must have noticed it sometimes, though.'

'Well, yes, of course, but – '

'What a cheap and sordid little liar you are, Murdoch!' The anger in Morse's voice was taut and dangerous. 'She had no birth-mark anywhere, that woman! She had one big fault and only one; and that was that she was kind and helpful to such a spineless specimen as you, lad – because you're so full of wind and piss there's room for nothing else!'

The eye was suddenly dull and ashamed, and Morse turned away and walked out. In the corridor he stood at the window for a few minutes breathing heavily until his anger subsided. Perhaps he was a cheap and sordid liar himself, too, for he had seen Anne Scott once – and once only. At a party. Fully dressed. And, as it seemed to him now, such a long, long time ago.

Whilst Morse and Lewis were still at the Eye Hospital, passengers arriving on a British Airways scheduled flight from Madrid were passing through the customs hall at Gatwick, where onlookers might have seen two plain-clothes men walk up on either side of a middle-aged, broad-shouldered man, his dark hair greying at the temples. There was no struggle, no animated conversation: just a wan, helpless sort of half-smile on the face of the man who had just been arrested. Indeed, the exchanges were so quietly spoken, so decorous almost, that even the bearded customs man a few yards away had been able to hear only a little of what was said.

'Mr Conrad Richards?'

The broad-shouldered man had nodded, unemotionally.

'It is my duty as a police officer to arrest you on a charge of murder: the murder of Mr George Jackson of 9 Canal Reach, Jericho . . . '

The customs man frowned, his chalk poised in mid air over the next piece of luggage. Arrests in the hall were commonplace, of course; but Jericho, as it seemed to him, sounded such a long, long way away.

Chapter Thirty-seven

I never saw a man who looked
  With such a wistful eye
Upon that little tent of blue
  Which prisoners call the sky
Oscar Wilde, *The Ballad of Reading Gaol*

Morse had heard of the arrest the previous evening after returning to Kidlington HQ at about 9.45 p.m. He had been pleasurably surprised that things had developed so quickly, and he had promptly despatched a Telex of thanks to Interpol. His decision had been a simple one. The HQ building was non-operational as far as cells were concerned, and he had ordered the police car to drive direct to St Aldates, where a night's solitary confinement might well, in Morse's view, prove beneficial for the prisoner's soul.

The next morning, Morse took his time; and when Lewis drove into the crowded St Aldates' yard it was already 9.45 a.m.

'I'll see him alone first,' said Morse.

'I understand, sir.' Lewis appeared cheerfully indifferent. 'I'll nip along and get a cup of coffee.'

Richards was seated on a narrow bed reading the *Daily Express* when the cell-door was closed behind Morse with a thumping twang.

'Good morning, sir. We haven't met before, have we? I've met your brother several times, of course – but never you. I'm Morse – Detective Chief Inspector Morse.'

'Charles has told me about you, Inspector.'

'Do sit down, please. We've er we've got quite a lot to talk about, haven't we? I told the people here that you were perfectly free, of course, to call your lawyer. They told you that, I hope?'

'I don't need a lawyer, Inspector. And when you let me go – which won't be long, believe me! – I promise I shan't even complain about being cooped up for the night in this wretched cell.'

'I do hope they've treated you reasonably well?'

'Quite well, yes. And it's good to get back to some English food, I must say. Perhaps a prisoner's life isn't too bad – '

'It's pretty grim, I'm afraid.'

'Well, I think you've got a bit of explaining to do, Inspector.'

'Really? I was hoping *you* were going to do all that.'

'I've been accused of murdering a man, I understand?'

'That's it.'

'Don't you think you owe me just a little explanation?'

'All right. Your brother Charles told you about the blackmail note he received, and asked you for your co-operation. You've always been a kindly and good-hearted fellow, and you said you'd do what you could. Then your brother had a phone call about the note – or at least a call he *thought* was about the note – and he arranged to meet the blackmailer, Jackson. He drove his Rolls into Oxford, and he took you with him. When you got near the rendezvous that night, you crouched down in the back seat, and Charles carefully kept the car away from the lighted road whilst you quietly got out, taking Mrs Richards' folding bicycle with you. Then you waited – and you followed the man you'd seen take the money. Luckily he was on a bicycle as well, and you tailed him down to Jericho, where you saw him go in his house. And that was the night's work successfully completed. Charles was waiting for you at some pre-arranged spot and – '

'The Martyrs' Memorial, actually.'

'You – you're not going to deny any of this?'

'No point, is there? It's all true – apart from the fact that I've got a folding bike of my own.'

'Ah well! Even the best of us make little mistakes here and there.'

'Big ones, too, Inspector – like the one I suspect you're about to make. But go on!'

'The plan had worked well, and you decided to repeat it. Charles had agreed to speak to the Oxford Book Association and he took you with him that Friday night. He probably dropped you somewhere near St Barnabas' Church and arranged to pick you up at about a quarter-to-ten or so.'

Richards shook his head in quiet remonstration. 'Look, Inspector. If you really – '

'Just a minute! Hear me out! I don't think you meant to murder Jackson. The idea was that you – '

'I *can't* listen to this! You listen to *me* a minute! You may be right – you probably are – in saying that Charles meant to go and see Jackson. Knowing Charles as I do, I don't think he could have let a thing like that go. He'd like as not have gone to see Jackson and scared the living daylights out of him – because you mustn't underestimate my brother, Inspector. He's as tough and unscrupulous as they come – believe me! But don't you understand? Something put a whacking great full stop to any ideas that Charles may have had. And you know perfectly well what that something was: *Jackson was murdered*. And that, from our point of view, was that! We just felt – well, we needn't worry about him any more.'

'So you didn't go to Jackson's house that night?'

'I certainly did *not*.'

'Where were you that night, sir?' (Had the 'sir' crept in from conditioned reflex? Or was Morse feeling slightly less sure of himself?)

'I don't know,' replied Richards in a hopeless voice. 'I just don't know, Inspector. I don't go out much. I'm not a womaniser like Charles, and if I do go out it's usually only to the local.'

'But you didn't go to the local that night?'

'I may have done, but I can't remember, and it's no good saying I can. If I *had* gone, it would only have been for an hour or so, though.'

'Perhaps you stayed at home and watched the telly?'

'I haven't got a telly. If I was home that night I'd have been reading, I should think.'

'Anything interesting?'

'I've been reading Gibbon recently – and reading him with infinite pleasure, if I may say so – '

'Which volume are you up to?'

'Just past Alaric and the sacking of Rome. Volume Four.'

'Don't you mean Volume Three?'

'Depends which edition you're reading.'

Morse let it go. 'What was the *real* reason for your visit to Jackson's house that night?'

Richards smiled patiently. 'You must have a pretty poor opinion of my intelligence, Inspector.'

'Certainly not! Any man who reads Gibbon has got my vote from the start. But I still think no one actually *intended* murdering Jackson, you see. I think he was after something else.'

'Such as?'

'I think it was a letter – a letter that Jackson had found when he pushed his way through into Anne Scott's kitchen that morning. At first I thought it must have been a letter she'd written for the police – a suicide note – telling the whole story and perhaps telling it a bit too nastily from your brother's point of view. But now I don't think so, somehow. I think the letter Jackson found had probably been received through the post that very morning – a letter from your brother telling Anne Scott that he couldn't and wouldn't help her, and that everything between them was over.'

'Have you got the letter?' asked Richards quietly.

'No,' said Morse slowly. 'No – we haven't.'

'Aren't you going to have to do a bit better than this, Inspector?'

'Well, your brother was looking for *something* – in that shed at the bottom of Jackson's garden. Or was that *you*, sir?'

'In a *shed*?'

Morse ignored the apparent incredulity in Richards' voice and continued: 'That letter would have been a bad thing for your brother, sir. It could have broken up his marriage if – '

'But Celia *knew* about Anne Scott.'

'Only very recently, I think.'

'Yes, that's true.'

'Do you love your sister-in-law?'

Richards looked down sadly at the concrete floor and nodded. 'I shall always love her, I suppose.'

Morse nodded, too, as if he also was not unacquainted with the agonies of unrequited love.

'Where does this leave us, Inspector?'

'Where we started, I'm afraid, sir. You've been charged with the murder of Jackson, and that charge still stands. So we'd better get back to thinking about where you were on the night when – '

Richards got up from the bed, a new note of exasperation in his voice. 'I've told you – I don't *know*! If you like, I'll try – I'll try like hell – to get hold of somebody who may have seen me. But there are millions of people who couldn't prove where they were that night!'

'That's true.'

'Well, why pick on *me*? What possible evidence – ?'

'Ah!' said Morse. 'I wondered when you were going to ask me about the evidence. You can't honestly think we'd have you brought here just because no one saw you reading Gibbon that night? Give us a *little* credit!'

Richards looked puzzled. 'You've *got* some evidence? Against *me*?'

'Well, we're not *absolutely* sure, but – yes, we've got some evidence. You see there were several fingerprints in Jackson's bedroom, and as you know I asked my sergeant to take yours.'

'But he *did*! And I'll tell you one thing, Inspector. My prints could quite definitely *not* have matched up with anything there, because I've never been in the house – never!'

'I think you've missed my point, sir. We didn't really get a chance of matching up your prints at all. I know it's our fault – but you must forgive Sergeant Lewis. You see, he's not very well up in that sort of thing and – well, to be truthful, sir – he mucked things up a bit. But he's a good man, and he's willing to have another go. It's important, don't you think, to give a man a second chance? In fact he's waiting outside now.'

Richards sat down on the bed again, his head between his hands. For several minutes he said nothing, and Morse looked down at a man who now seemed utterly weary and defeated.

'Cigarette?' said Morse.

Richards took one, and inhaled the smoke like a dying man gasping at oxygen.

'When did you find out?' he asked very quietly.

'Find out that you weren't Conrad Richards, you mean? Well, let me see now . . . ' Morse himself inhaled deeply on his own cigarette; and as he briefly told of his discoveries, the same wan and wistful half-smile returned to the face of the man who sat on the edge of the narrow bed.

It was the face of Charles Richards.

Chapter Thirty-eight

Fingerprints are left at the scenes of crime often enough
to put over 10,000 individual prints in the FBI files.
Even the craftiest of perpetrators sometimes forget to
wipe up everywhere

Murder Ink

'When did you find out, Morse?' asked the ACC that afternoon.

'Looking back on it, sir, I think the first inkling *should* have
come when I went to the Book Association and learned that it
had been Anne Scott who had suggested to the committee that
Charles Richards should be invited along to talk about the small
publishing business. Such a meeting would attract a few people,
the committee felt, especially some of the young students from the
Polytechnic who might be thinking of starting up for themselves.
But "small" is the operative word, sir. In a limited and very specialised field the Richards brothers had managed to run a thriving little
concern. But who had heard of them? Who – except for Anne Scott
– *knew* them? Virtually no one in Oxford, that's for certain – just
as virtually no one would recognise the managing directors even
of your big national publishers. And, remember, the Richards
brothers had only just moved into Oxfordshire a few months earlier
– half a dozen miles *outside* Oxford itself – and the chances that anyone would recognise either of them in a small meeting were very
slim indeed. The only person who *would* have known them both
was dead: Anne Scott. So they laid their plan – and decided to
follow the same routine as the one which had proved so successful
earlier in the week, when it was *Conrad* Richards who drove the
Rolls to Oxford and *Charles* Richards who followed Jackson to
Canal Reach.

'Perhaps from the little we've learned about the two brothers'
characters this wasn't surprising: it was Conrad who'd always been
ready to play second fiddle, and Charles who'd always been the
more dynamic. So they decided to swap roles again for the Friday
evening, with Conrad taking his brother's place in a talk which –
very much at the eleventh hour – had been brought forward, thus
almost certainly cutting down what would have been a meagre
audience at the best of times. Charles had already written out his

notes for the speech, and Conrad probably knew more about the workings of the business, anyway. Conrad, I'm sure, was quite happy to do this; what he adamantly refused to do was to go down to Canal Reach. As ever, in his own mild way, he was quite willing to co-operate wherever he felt he could – but it had to be *Charles* who went to face Jackson. Now I'm fairly sure in my own mind, sir, that although Charles Richards wasn't reckoning on murder, he was determined to get that letter back – or else! He tried to scare Jackson and pushed him around from room to room as he tried to find what he wanted – the letter which would implicate him deeply in Anne Scott's death, and pretty certainly put paid to his marriage – and possibly his business, too. And when they got to the bedroom he got so exasperated that he literally shook the life out of Jackson against the bedpost. At that point Charles Richards was in a tight spot. He knew his own name was likely to crop up somewhere in police enquiries into Anne Scott's death, and he realised how vital it was that Conrad, who was at that very moment talking to an audience under the alias of "Charles Richards", should be given an utterly unassailable alibi. So he rang up the police – and then he got the hell out of Jericho and waited at the Martyrs' Memorial for Conrad to pick him up.'

'He didn't find the letter?'

'So he says – and I'm inclined to believe him.'

'What about the change of date for the meeting? Was that deliberate?'

'I don't really see how it could have been, sir. There wasn't the time, I don't think. No. Charles had to go to Spain on business some time this month, and it so happened that one of his girl-friends told him that she could get away, too, and join him. But only during that week. So Charles pleaded urgent business, the meeting was changed, and the brothers took full advantage of – '

'Lucky for them, wasn't it? Keeping the audience down, I mean.'

'Luckier than you realise, sir. Miss Universe or World or some-thing was on the telly that night and – '

'I'm surprised *you* weren't watching it, Morse.'

'Did they pick the right girl, sir?'

'Well, personally I'd have gone for Miss – Go on!'

'I should think things must have looked pretty black as they went home that night and talked over what had happened. But very soon one thing must have become increasingly clear to the pair of them. Perhaps all would be well, *if only they could keep up the pretence*. The real danger would come if the police, in connection with Anne Scott's death, discovered that the "Charles Richards" of the OBA talk was not Charles Richards at all – but his brother Conrad, because *the speaker* that night had an alibi that no one in the world could shake. So the brothers made their decision. Celia Richards had to be brought into the picture straightaway, and Charles had no option but to tell her everything about his affair with Anne Scott and to plead with her to take her part – a pretty big part, too – in the deception that followed.'

The ACC nodded. 'Ye-es. You'd better tell me how they worked that.'

'To an outsider, sir, I think that one thing about this case would seem particularly odd: the fact that Sergeant Lewis and myself had never been *together* when we'd met Conrad Richards; and, at the same time, we'd neither of us met the two brothers when *they* were together. Let me explain, sir. I met Charles Richards – or rather the man I *thought* was Charles Richards – for the first time at the OBA, when his physical appearance was firmly fixed for me *as* Charles Richards. As it happened, I did ring up the *actual* Charles Richards the next day, but the line, as I well remember, was very poor and crackly, and we ended up almost shouting to each other. In any case, I'd only heard him speak the once – and it just didn't occur to me that the man I was speaking to was any other than the man I'd sat listening to on the back row. Then, a day or two later, I rang Charles Richards again; but he was out at the time and so I left a message with his secretary for him to ring back. As we now know, sir, the two brothers were able to solve that little problem without too much trouble. When Charles received the message, he got *Conrad* to ring me back. Easy. But I asked for a meeting with him the next day, and that took a bit more organisation. When I called at Charles Richards' office I was treated to a neat and convincing little charade by Celia – acting as the receptionist, and by Conrad – playing the part of Charles. It was, by the way, sir, at that point that I should have taken more notice of one very significant fact. Celia asked *me* for a cigarette that day – something she surely would never have done if the man who was with her was really her husband, because I was later to learn that Charles Richards was a heavy smoker. Anyway, I suspected nothing at the time, and the

three of them must have felt encouraged about keeping up the pretence if the police were to bother them again.

'Then we were a bit unlucky. Lewis and myself paid a *surprise*
visit to Abingdon one afternoon, to get Conrad's fingerprints.
But I didn't join him for a start, sir. I had another er lead to follow
up, and so I wasn't with Lewis when he called at the office and
met Conrad – the same man who'd twice passed himself off to me
as *Charles*. We had reason to believe that Conrad might have
been involved in things somehow, and we wanted to find whether
his prints matched those found in Jackson's bedroom. So Lewis
got the prints – Conrad's prints – and of course they matched
nothing, because it had been *Charles* who had been in Jackson's
house. That same afternoon we returned to the Richards' firm –
but we were too late. We searched the offices that the brothers
used, and as you know we found the blackmail note in Charles's
desk. But the real clue I missed, I'm afraid. It was pretty clear
from the ash-trays full of stubs that Charles was virtually a chain-
smoker, but in Conrad's room there was no physical sign whatsoever of smoking and not the faintest smell of stale tobacco.
Then we made a final visit to Abingdon, when Celia and Conrad –
this time with ample warning – put on another little performance
for me, playing the parts of a reconciled couple very cleverly.
But they were wasting their time, I'm afraid. You see, there were
two reasons for my visit. First, to get the man I'd been interviewing to the front door so that Lewis could see him and so
corroborate what we'd suspected – that the man I'd been meeting all the time was in fact *Conrad* Richards.'

'But why all the clever-clever stuff, Morse? Why didn't you just
arrest him there and then and get it over with?'

'We'd have run the risk of letting the big fish get away, sir, and
that was the second reason for my going that day. I had to lay the
bait to get Charles Richards back in England, and so I told Conrad
that we had to have a statement from him and that it was going
to be *Sergeant Lewis* who would take it down. You see, Lewis
knew the real Conrad Richards: he'd taken his fingerprints. And
so any statement would have to be made by the *genuine* Charles
Richards; and to do that he'd have to get back from Spain fairly
quickly. As, in fact, he did, sir.'

'And he walked into our men at Gatwick – and then you
walked into *him* at St Aldates.'

'Yes. Once I'd mentioned that we needed to take his prints again and that Sergeant Lewis was going to try to do a better job this time, he realised the game was finally up. Lewis had never taken *his* prints at all, you see – and, well, Charles could see no point in pretending any longer. I offered him a cigarette – and that was that!'

'How kind of you, Morse! I suppose, by the way, the prints *were* Charles Richards'?'

'Er, well, as a matter of fact they weren't, sir. I'm afraid I must have been just a little careless er myself when I examined the head-board and – '

The ACC got to his feet and his face showed pained incredulity. 'Don't – don't tell me they were – '

Morse nodded guiltily. 'I'm afraid so – yes, sir: *they were mine.*'

Chapter Thirty-nine

The troubles of our proud and angry dust
Are from eternity, and shall not fail.
Bear them we can, and if we can we must.
Shoulder the sky, my lad, and drink your ale
                A. E. Housman, *Last Poems*

Apart from a few small details the case of the Jericho killings was solved, but Morse knew as he sat in his office the following morning that it wasn't yet quite the time to pack away the two box files on the shelves of the Record Office. There were two things really that still nagged at his brain. The first was the realisation that his Sophoclean hypothesis about Anne Scott's suicide had been largely undermined by Lewis's patient enquiries . . . (Where was Lewis, by the way? Not like Lewis to be late . . .) The second thing was that the letter Charles Richards had written to Anne Scott had still not been found. Was that important, though? Beyond much doubt it had led directly to Anne's death, but it wasn't difficult to guess at its contents; not difficult to reconstruct the events of that morning when Anne had received one letter from the clinic saying, yes, she *was* pregnant, and another from Charles Richards saying, no, he *wasn't* going to see her again.

Morse nodded to himself: it had been the post that morning that had been the final catalyst – not the previous night's talk at the bridge club of birthdays and adoptions. But why should Anne have been up so early that morning? Usually, as he'd learned, she would stay in bed until about lunch time on a Wednesday, after getting to bed so very late after bridge. And, then again, why had she cancelled her lesson with Edward Murdoch? Had Anne Scott *really* had a morbid sense of the gods' ill-favour as they played their sport with men and women? If not, what had she done when she got home early that morning? What if . . . ? Ye-es. He'd been assuming that she'd stayed awake that terrible night largely because the bed had not been slept in. Or so it had appeared. But surely she *could* have gone to bed? Gone to sleep, got up early, made the bed, and then . . . But *why* had she got up so early that morning?

Morse shook his head. It wasn't quite adding up, he knew that, and he needed to talk to Lewis. (Where the hell *was* Lewis?) Morse reached for another cigarette and his mind wandered back to the night when he had met Anne . . . the night when but for some miserable ill-luck that had taken him away . . . when Lewis had come in and dragged him off . . .

'Morning, sir!' Lewis looked as bright and cheerful as the golden sunlight outside. 'Sorry to be a bit late, but – '

'*Bit* late? You're *bloody* late!' Morse's face was sour.

'But you said – '

'Got your car here?'

'Outside.' Lewis permitted himself a gentle smile and said no more.

'I want to take a last little look at Jericho, Lewis. There's that bloody letter from Richards for a start. Bell's lot looked for it; *you* looked for it; Richards himself looked for it – and nobody can find it, right? So it's about time *I* had a look for it! You all swear it's not there, but the trouble is you've probably all been looking in the wrong *place*. I'm not saying I know where the right place *is*, but I'll be surprised if I don't do a bit better than the rest of you. Can't do worse, can I? You need a bit of *imagination* in these things, Lewis . . . '

'As you wish, sir.'

Morse was unusually talkative as they drove down the

Woodstock Road and turned down the one-way Observatory Street towards Jericho. 'Beautiful morning, Lewis! Almost makes you feel glad to be alive.'

'I'm always glad to be alive.'

'Really?' Morse vaguely looked along the stuccoed fronts of the terraced houses and then, as Lewis waited to turn into Walton Street, he suddenly caught sight of the Jericho Tackle Shop, and a beautiful new idea jumped across the threshold of his mind.

'Jackson was buying his new rod from there, wasn't he?' Morse asked casually.

'That's right.'

Lewis parked the police car by the bollards at Canal Reach. 'Which key do you want first, sir?'

'Perhaps we shan't need either of them.'

The two men walked up the narrow little street, where Morse led the way through to the boat-yard before turning right and climbing over the fence into the back garden which the late George Jackson had fitfully tended. The shed door was still secured only by the rickety latch that Morse had opened once before, and now again he looked inside and surveyed the vast assortment of Jackson's fishing tackle.

'Is that the new rod?' he asked.

'Looks like it, sir.'

Morse carefully disconnected the jointed sections and examined them. 'You see, Lewis? They're hollow inside. Just the place to hide a letter, wouldn't you say? Just roll the letter up into a cylinder and then . . . ' Morse was busily peering and feeling inside the sections, but for the moment, as Lewis stood idly by, he could find nothing.

'It's here, Lewis! It's here somewhere. I know it is.'

But a quarter of an hour later he had still found nothing. And however Morse twisted and pulled and cursed the collection of rods, it soon became clear that no letter was concealed in any of them.

'You've not been much bloody help!' he said finally.

'Never mind, sir – it was a good idea,' said Lewis cheerfully. 'Why don't we nip over the way and have a noggin? What do you say?'

Morse looked at his sergeant in a peculiar way. 'You feeling all right, Lewis?'

'Well, we've solved another case, haven't we? It'll be a little celebration, sort of thing.'

'I don't like these loose ends, though.'

'Forget it, sir!' Lewis led the way through the back yard and out once more into Canal Reach, where Morse stopped and looked up at the bedroom window of number 9. Still no curtains.

'I wonder . . . ' said Morse slowly.

'Pardon, sir?'

'You got the key, you say?'

Lewis fiddled in his pocket and found it.

'I was just wondering,' said Morse, 'if she had an alarm clock in her bedroom. Can you remember?'

'Not off hand, sir. Let's go and have a look.'

Morse opened the door and suddenly stopped. *Déjà vu*. There, on the inside door-mat, was another brown envelope, and he picked it up and looked at it: 'Southern Gas Board' was printed along the bottom of the cover.

'Just nip upstairs then, Lewis, and bring the alarm clock down – if there is one.'

When Lewis had left him, Morse put his hand inside his breast pocket and pulled out the envelope he had previously found – and until this moment forgotten about. Slitting open the top in a ragged tear he took out a single typed sheet of paper:

SUMMERTOWN CURTAINING 8th Oct

Dear Ms Scott,

I am sorry that we were unable to contact you earlier about your esteemed order for curtaining and pelmeting. Unfortunately it proved impossible for our fitters to come as agreed on the 3rd inst., since our suppliers let us down over the yellow material for the study and the front bedroom, and we thought it more sensible to do the whole house in one day rather than doing the jobs in two bits. We regret the inconvenience caused.

I am now able to inform you that all materials are ready and we look forward to hearing from you as soon as possible about a convenient time. We confidently expect, as before, that all the work can be completed in a single day and we shall be happy to begin work at about 9 a.m. if this is again suitable to you.

Yours faithfully,
J. Burkitt (Manager)

As Morse finished reading Lewis was standing beside him, a small, square, black alarm clock in his hand. 'Anything interesting?'

Morse pondered the letter once more, then pointed to the clock. 'I think we've probably got another loose end tied up, yes – if that thing's set for about half-past seven.'

'Quarter-to-eight, actually, sir.'

'Mm.' Morse stood still just inside the door, his mind reconstructing the scene that must have taken place in that very room. He seemed sadly satisfied.

'You know that letter from Charles Richards, sir? Don't you think she probably burnt it with the one from the clinic? Perhaps if we get the path boys to have a look at those ashes in the grate – '

Morse shook his head. 'No. I buggered that up when I started poking around, Lewis. It's no good now.'

'You think he *did* write a letter to her, sir?'

'Well, not in direct answer to hers, no. Celia Richards intercepted that, as we know. But I think she must have got in touch with him somehow, after she'd heard nothing; and I think he wrote to her – yes, I do.'

'He says he *didn't*, though.'

'Pretty understandable, isn't it?'

'You mean he's got one death on his conscience already?'

Morse nodded. 'Not the one you're thinking of, though, Lewis. I don't believe he gives a sod about what he did to Jackson: it's the death of Anne Scott that he'll have on his conscience for ever.'

'I'll get them, sir,' said Lewis as they walked into The Printer's Devil. 'You just sit down and read that.' He handed Morse an envelope which had quite clearly been rolled into a tight cylindrical shape. 'I came here this morning, and I found it inside the new rod, sir. I hope you'll forgive me for not telling you before, but it's not the letter *you* were looking for.'

Lewis walked over to the bar, and Morse sat down and immediately saw the name on the grimy envelope: it was his own.

For Chief Inspector (?) Morse
Thames Valley Police
Absolutely Private, and for the
attention of no one else.

Inside the envelope was a single sheet of writing, together with a further envelope, itself already opened, and addressed 'Charles Richards'. Morse took the single sheet and slowly read it:

Dear Inspector Morse,
Perhaps you will have forgotten me. We met once at a party when you had too much to drink and were very nice to me. I'd hoped you'd get in touch with me – but you didn't. Please, I beg you, be kind to me again now – and deliver the enclosed letter personally and in the strictest confidence. And please, please don't read it. What I am going to do is cowardly and selfish, but somehow I just can't go on any more – and I don't want to go on any more.
     Anne Scott

Lewis had brought the beer over and was sitting quietly opposite.
'Have you read this, Lewis?'
'No, sir. It wasn't addressed to me.'
'But you saw who it was addressed to?'
Lewis nodded, and Morse passed it over.
'You didn't read this one, either?' asked Morse, taking out the envelope addressed to Charles Richards.
'No, sir. But I should think we know roughly what's in it, don't we?'
'Yes,' said Morse slowly. 'And I think – I think I ought to do what she asked me, don't you?' He passed the envelope across. 'Seal it up, Lewis – and see that he gets it straightaway, please.'
Was he doing the right thing? Charles Richards would find the letter terribly hurtful to read – there could be little doubt of that. But, then, life *was* hurtful. Morse had just been deeply hurt himself . . . 'I'd hoped you'd get in touch with me', she'd said, 'but you didn't'. Oh! If only she'd known . . . if only she'd known.
He felt Lewis's hand on his shoulder and heard his kindly words. 'Don't forget your beer, sir!'

Epilogue

Jericho has altered little since the events described in these chapters, although the curious visitor will no longer find Canal Reach marked upon the street map, for the site of the narrow little lane in which Ms Scott and Mr Jackson met their deaths is now straddled by a new block of flats, in which Mrs Purvis (together with Graymalkin) is happily resettled, and where one of her neighbours is the polymath who once regaled Morse on the history of Jericho and who is now a mature student reading Environmental Studies at London University. Some others, too, who played their brief parts in the case have moved – or died; but many remain in the area. Mrs Beavers, for example, continues to run the corner post office, and Mr Grimes to sit amongst his locks and burglar-alarms. And the Italianate campanile of St Barnabas still towers above the terraced streets below.

In the wider confines of Oxford, a few small items of information may be of some interest to the reader. Michael Murdoch, a jauntily-set black patch over his right eye, was able to make a late start to his university studies in the Michaelmas Term, whilst Edward Murdoch's German master confidently predicted a grade 'A' in his Advanced level examination. The bridge club flourished pleasingly, and Gwendola Briggs was heard to boast of twenty-two signatures on the wreath purchased for old Mr Parkes, cremated on the very day that Charles Richards was found guilty at Oxford Crown Court of the murder of George Jackson. Somewhat surprisingly, Detective Constable Walters made up his mind to leave the police and to join the army – a decision which displeased, amongst others, Superintendent Bell, a man who finds his talents now more profitably employed in administration than ever they were in detection. In late November Sergeant Lewis's eldest daughter produced a baby girl, and Mrs Lewis was so overjoyed that she bought a modestly expensive

191

bottle of red wine to accompany her husband's beloved egg and chips.

And what of Morse? He still walks to his local most evenings, and would appear to take most of his calories in liquid form, for no one has seen him buying cans of food in the Summertown supermarkets. In mid-December he was invited to another party in North Oxford; and as he waited in the buffet queue his eyes caressed the slim and curving bottom of the woman just in front of him as she leant across the table. But he said nothing; and after eating his meal alone, he found an easy excuse to slip away, and walked home.

Service of all the Dead

For
John Poole

I had rather be a doorkeeper in the house
of my God: than to dwell in the tents
of ungodliness
(Psalm 84, v.10)

THE FIRST BOOK OF CHRONICLES

Chapter One

Limply the Reverend Lionel Lawson shook the last smoothly gloved hand, the slim hand of Mrs Emily Walsh-Atkins, and he knew that the pews in the old church behind him were now empty. It was always the same: whilst the other well-laundered ladies were turning their heads to chat of fêtes and summer hats, whilst the organist played his exit voluntary, and whilst the now discassocked choirboys tucked their T-shirts into flare-line jeans, Mrs Walsh-Atkins invariably spent a few further minutes on her knees in what had sometimes seemed to Lawson a slightly exaggerated obeisance to the Almighty. Yet, as Lawson knew full well, she had plenty to be thankful for. She was eighty-one years old, but managed still to retain an enviable agility in both mind and body; only her eyesight was at last beginning to fail. She lived in north Oxford, in a home for elderly gentlewomen, screened off from the public gaze by a high fence and a belt of fir-trees. Here, from the front window of her living-room, redolent of faded lavender and silver-polish, she could look out on to the well-tended paths and lawns where each morning the resident caretaker unobtrusively collected up the Coca Cola tins, the odd milk-bottle and the crisp-packets thrown over by those strange, unfathomably depraved young people who, in Mrs Walsh-Atkins' view, had little right to walk the streets at all – let alone the streets of her own beloved north Oxford. The home was wildly expensive; but Mrs W.-A. was a wealthy woman, and each Sunday morning her neatly sealed brown envelope, lightly laid on the collection-plate, contained a folded five-pound note.

'Thank you for the message, Vicar.'

'God bless you!'

This brief dialogue, which had never varied by a single word in the ten years since Lawson had been appointed to the parish of St Frideswide's, was the ultimate stage in non-communication between a priest and his parishioner. In the early days of his ministry, Lawson had felt vaguely uneasy about 'the message' since he was conscious that no passage from his sermons had ever been declaimed with particularly evangelistic fervour; and in any case the rôle of some divinely appointed telegram-boy was quite inappropriate – indeed, quite distasteful – to a man of Lawson's moderately high-church leanings. Yet Mrs Walsh-Atkins appeared to hear the humming of the heavenly wires whatever his text might be; and each Sunday morning she reiterated her gratitude to the un-suspecting harbinger of goodly tidings. It was purely by chance that after his very first service Lawson had hit upon those three simple monosyllables – magical words which, again this Sunday morning, Mrs Walsh-Atkins happily clutched to her bosom, along with her Book of Common Prayer, as she walked off with her usual sprightly gait towards St Giles', where her regular taxi-driver would be waiting in the shallow lay-by beside the Martyrs' Memorial.

The vicar of St Frideswide's looked up and down the hot street. There was nothing to detain him longer, but he appeared curiously reluctant to re-enter the shady church. A dozen or so Japanese tourists made their way along the pavement opposite, their small, bespectacled cicerone reciting in a whining, staccato voice the city's ancient charms, his sing-song syllables still audible as the little group sauntered up the street past the cinema, where the management proudly presented to its patrons the opportunity of witnessing the intimacies of Continental-style wife-swapping. But for Lawson there were no stirrings of sensuality: his mind was on other things. Carefully he lifted from his shoulders the white silk-lined hood (M.A. Cantab.) and turned his gaze towards Carfax, where already the lounge-bar door of The Ox stood open. But public houses had never held much appeal for him. He sipped, it is true, the occasional glass of sweet sherry at some of the diocesan functions; but if Lawson's soul should have anything to answer for when the archangel bugled the final trumpet it would certainly not be the charge of drunkenness. Without disturbing his carefully parted hair, he drew the long white surplice over his head and turned slowly into the church.

Apart from the organist, Mr Paul Morris, who had now reached

the last few bars of what Lawson recognised as some Mozart, Mrs
Brenda Josephs was the only person left in the main body of the
building. Dressed in a sleeveless, green summer frock, she sat
at the back of the church, a soberly attractive woman in her
mid- or late thirties, one bare browned arm resting along the
back of the pew, her finger-tips caressing its smooth surface. She
smiled dutifully as Lawson walked past; and Lawson, in his turn,
inclined his sleek head in a casual benediction. Formal greetings
had been exchanged before the service, and neither party now
seemed anxious to resume that earlier perfunctory conversation.
On his way to the vestry Lawson stopped briefly in order to hook
a loose hassock into place at the foot of a pew, and as he did so
he heard the door at the side of the organ bang shut. A little too
noisily, perhaps? A little too hurriedly?

The curtains parted as he reached the vestry and a gingery-
headed, freckle-faced youth almost launched himself into Lawson's
arms.

'Steady, boy. Steady! What's all the rush?'

'Sorry, sir. I just forgot . . . ' His breathless voice trailed
off, his right hand, clutching a half-consumed tube of fruit gums,
drawn furtively behind his back.

'I hope you weren't eating those during the sermon?'

'No, sir.'

'Not that I ought to blame you if you were. I can get a
bit boring sometimes, don't you think?' The pedagogic tone of
Lawson's earlier words had softened now, and he laid his hand
on the boy's head and ruffled his hair lightly.

Peter Morris, the organist's only son, looked up at Lawson
with a quietly cautious grin. Any subtlety of tone was completely
lost upon him; yet he realised that everything was all right, and
he darted away along the back of the pews.

'Peter!' The boy stopped in his tracks and looked round.
'How many times must I tell you? You're not to run in church!'

'Yes, sir. Er – I mean, no, sir.'

'And don't forget the choir outing next Saturday.'

' 'Course not, sir.'

Lawson had not failed to notice Peter's father and Brenda
Josephs talking together in animated whispers in the north porch;
but Paul Morris had now slipped quietly out of the door after his
son, and Brenda, it seemed, had turned her solemn attention to the

font: dating from 1345, it was, according to the laconic guidebook, number one of the 'Things to Note'. Lawson turned on his heel and entered the vestry.

Harry Josephs, the vicar's warden, had almost finished now. After each service he entered, against the appropriate date, two sets of figures in the church register: first, the number of persons in the congregation, rounded up or down to the nearest five; second, the sum taken in the offertory, meticulously calculated to the last half-penny. By most reckonings, the Church of St Frideswide's was a fairly thriving establishment. Its clientèle was chiefly drawn from the more affluent sectors of the community, and even during the University vacations the church was often half-full. It was to be expected, therefore, that the monies to be totalled by the vicar's warden, then checked by the vicar himself, and thereafter trans-ferred to the church's number-one account with Barclays Bank in the High, were not inconsiderable. This morning's takings, sorted by denominations, lay on Lawson's desk in the vestry: one five-pound note; about fifteen one-pound notes; a score or so of fifty-pence pieces and further sundry piles of smaller coinage, neatly stacked in readily identifiable amounts.

'Another goodly congregation, Harry.' 'Goodly' was a favour-ite word in Lawson's vocabulary. Although it had always been a matter of some contention in theological circles whether the Almighty took any great interest in the counting of mere heads, it was encouraging, on a secular assessment, to minister to a flock that was at least numerically fairly strong; and the word 'goodly' seemed a happily neutral word to blur the distinction between the 'good', by purely arithmetical reckoning, and the 'godly', as assessed on a more spiritual computation.

Harry nodded and made his entries. 'Just check the money quickly if you will, sir. I made it a hundred and thirty-five in the congregation, and I make it fifty-seven pounds twelve pence in the collection.'

'No ha'pennies today, Harry? I think some of the choirboys must have taken my little talk to heart.' With the dexterity of a practised bank-clerk he riffled through the pound notes, and then passed his fingers over the piles of coins, like a bishop blessing heads at a confirmation service. The addition of monies was correct.

'One of these days, Harry, you're going to surprise me and make a mistake.'

Josephs' eyes darted sharply to Lawson's face, but the expression there, as the minister put his signature to the right-hand column of the church register, was one of bland benignity.

Together vicar and warden placed the money in an ancient Huntley & Palmer biscuit-tin. It looked an unlikely repository for any great store of wealth; but when at one of its recent meetings the church council had discussed the problem of security no one had come up with any brighter suggestion, except for the possibility that a slightly later vintage of a similar tin might perhaps more firmly corroborate the notion that the receptacle open to view on the back seat of Josephs' Allegro contained nothing more precious than a few ginger-snaps and arrowroots left over from a recent social.

'I'll be off, then, Vicar. The wife'll be waiting.'

Lawson nodded and watched his warden go. Yes, Brenda Josephs would be waiting; she had to be. Six months previously Harry had been found guilty on a charge of drunken driving, and it was largely through Lawson's plea for mitigation that the magistrate's sentence of a fifty-pound fine and one year's suspension had seemed so comparatively lenient. The Josephs' home was in the village of Wolvercote, some three miles north of the city centre, and buses on Sundays were a rarer sight than five-pound notes on a collection-plate.

The small vestry window looked out on the south side of the church, and Lawson sat down at the desk and stared blankly into the graveyard where the grey, weathered tombstones tilted at their varied angles from the vertical, their crumbling legends long since overgrown with moss or smoothed away by centuries of wind and rain. He both looked and felt a worried man, for the simple truth was that there should have been *two* five-pound notes in the collection that morning. Was there just a possibility, though, that Mrs Walsh-Atkins had at last exhausted her store of five-pound notes and put five separate one-pound notes into the collection? If she had, though, it would have been the first time for – oh, years and years. No. There was a much more probable explanation, an explanation that disturbed Lawson greatly. Yet there was still the slimmest chance that he was mistaken. 'Judge not that ye be not judged.' Judge not – at least until the evidence is unequivocal. He took out his wallet and from it drew a piece of paper on which earlier that same morning he had written down the serial number of the five-pound note which he himself had sealed in a small brown envelope and placed in the morning collection. And only two or three minutes ago he had checked the last three numbers of the five-pound note which Harry Josephs had placed in the biscuit-tin: they were not the numbers he had written down.

Something of this sort Lawson had suspected for several weeks, and now he had proof of it. He should, he knew, have asked Josephs to turn out his pockets on the spot: that was his duty, both as a priest and as a friend (friend?), for somewhere on Josephs' person would have been found the five-pound note he had just stolen from the offertory. At last Lawson looked down at the piece of paper he had been holding and read the serial number printed on it: AN 50 405546. Slowly he lifted his eyes and stared across the churchyard once more. The sky had grown suddenly overcast, and when half an hour later he walked down to the vicarage in St Ebbe's the air was heavy with the threat of rain. It was as if someone had switched off the sun.

Chapter Two

Although he pretended still to be asleep, Harry Josephs had heard his wife get up just before seven, and he was able to guess her movements exactly. She had put on her dressing-gown over her nightdress, walked down to the kitchen, filled the kettle, and then sat at the table smoking her first cigarette. It was only during the past two or three months that Brenda had started smoking again, and he was far from happy about it. Her breath smelt stale, and the sight of an ash-tray full of stubs he found quite nauseating. People smoked a lot when they were worried and tense, didn't they? It was just a drug really, like a slug of aspirin, or a bottle of booze, or a flutter on the horses . . . He turned his head into the pillow, and his own anxieties once more flooded through his mind.

'Tea.' She nudged his shoulder gently and put the mug down on the small table that separated their twin beds.

Josephs nodded, grunted, and turned on to his back, watching his wife as she stood in front of the dressing-table and slipped the nightdress over her head. She was thickening a little round the hips now, but she was still leggily elegant and her breasts were full and firm. Yet Josephs did not look at her directly as she stood momentarily naked before the mirror. Over the past few months he had felt increasingly embarrassed about gazing at her body, as if somehow he were intruding into a privacy he was no longer openly invited to share.

He sat up and sipped his tea as she drew up the zip at the side of her dark-brown skirt. 'Paper come?'

'I'd have brought it up.' She bent forward from the waist and applied a series of cosmetic preparations to her face. Josephs himself had never followed the sequence with any real interest.

'Lot of rain in the night.'

'Still raining,' she said.

'Do the garden good.'

'Mm.'

'Had any breakfast?'

She shook her head. 'There's plenty of bacon, though, if you – ' (she applied a thin film of light pink to her pouting lips) ' – and there's a few mushrooms left.'

Josephs finished his tea and lay back on the bed. It was twenty-five past seven and Brenda would be off in five minutes. She worked mornings only at the Radcliffe Infirmary, at the bottom of the Woodstock Road, where two years ago she had taken up her nursing career once again. Two years ago! That was just after . . .

She came across to his bedside, lightly touched her lips to his forehead, picked up his mug, and walked out of the room. But almost immediately she was back again. 'Oh, Harry. I nearly forgot. I shan't be back for lunch today. Can you get yourself something all right? I really must go and do some shopping in town. Not that I'll be late – three-ish at the latest, I should think. I'll try to get something nice for tea.'

Josephs nodded and said nothing, but she was lingering by the door. 'Anything you want – from town, I mean?'

'No.' For a few minutes he lay quite still listening to her movements below.

'By-ee!'

'Goodbye.' The front door clicked to behind her. 'Goodbye, Brenda.'

He turned the bedclothes diagonally back, got up, and peered round the side of the curtained window. The Allegro was being backed out carefully into the quiet, wet street and then, with a sudden puff of blue exhaust-smoke, was gone. To the Radcliffe was exactly 2.8 miles: Josephs knew that. For three years he had made the identical journey himself, to the block of offices just below the Radcliffe where he had worked as a civil servant after his twenty years' service in the forces. But two years ago the staff had been axed following the latest public-expenditure cuts, and three of the seven of them had been declared redundant, including himself. And how it still rankled! He wasn't the oldest and he wasn't the least experienced. But he was the least experienced of the older men and the oldest of the less experienced. A little silver handshake, a little farewell party, and just a little hope of finding another job. No, that was wrong: almost no hope of finding another job. He had been forty-eight then. Young enough, perhaps, by some standards. But the sad truth had slowly seeped into his soul: no one really wanted him any longer. After more than a year of dispiriting idleness, he had, in fact, worked in a chemist's shop in Summertown, but the branch had recently closed down and he had almost welcomed the inevitable termination of his contract. He – a man who had risen to the rank of captain in the Royal Marine Commandos, a man who had seen active service against the terrorists in the Malayan jungles – standing politely behind the counter handing over prescriptions to some skinny, pale-faced youth or other who wouldn't have lasted five seconds on one of the commando assault-courses! And, as the manager had insisted, saying 'Thank you, sir,' into the bargain!

He shut the thought away, and drew the curtains open.

Just up the road a line of people queued at the bus-stop, their umbrellas raised against the steady rain which filtered down on the straw-coloured fields and lawns. Lines he had learned at school drifted back into his mind, serving his mood and seeming to fit the dismal prospect before him:

> And ghastly thro' the drizzling rain
> On the bald street breaks the blank day.

He caught the 10.30 a.m. bus into Summertown, where he walked into the licensed betting-office and studied the card at

Lingfield Park. He noticed that by some strange coincidence The Organist was running in the two-thirty, and Poor Old Harry in the four o'clock. He wasn't usually over-influenced by names, but when he recalled his lack of success through undue reliance on the form-book he suspected that it might have been more profitable if he had been. In the ante-post betting odds, The Organist was one of the co-favourites, and Poor Old Harry wasn't even quoted. Josephs walked along the series of daily newspapers affixed to the walls of the office: The Organist was napped in a couple of them; Poor Old Harry seemed to have no support whatsoever. Josephs allowed himself a rueful grin: probably neither of them was destined to be first past the post, but . . . why not? Take a chance, Harry boy! He filled in a square white betting-slip and pushed it over the counter with his money:

> Lingfield Park: 4 p.m.
> £2 win: Poor Old Harry.

A year or so previously, after purchasing two tins of baked beans from a supermarket, he had been given change for one pound instead of for the five-pound note he knew he had handed over. His protestations on that occasion had necessitated a full till-check and a nervy half-hour wait before the final justification of his claim; and since that time he had been more careful, always memorising the last three numbers of any five-pound note he tendered. He did so now, and repeated them to himself as he waited for his change: 546 . . . 546 . . . 546 . . .

The drizzle had virtually stopped when at 11.20 a.m. he walked unhurriedly down the Woodstock Road. Twenty-five minutes later he was standing in one of the private car-parks at the Radcliffe where he spotted the car almost immediately. Threading his way through the closely parked vehicles, he soon stood beside it and looked through the off-side window. The milometer read 25,622. That tallied: it had read 619 before she left. And if she now followed the normal routine of any sensible person she would walk down into Oxford from here, and when she got home the milometer would read 625 – 626 at the most. Finding a suitable vantage-point behind a moribund elm-tree he looked at his watch. And waited.

At two minutes past twelve the celluloid doors leading to

E.N.T. Outpatients flapped open and Brenda Josephs appeared and walked briskly to the car. He could see her very clearly. She unlocked the door and sat for a few seconds leaning forward and viewing herself in the driving-mirror, before taking a small scent-bottle from her handbag and applying it to her neck, first to one side, then to the other. Her safety-belt remained unfastened as she backed none too expertly out of the narrow space; then the right blinker on as she drove out of the car-park and up to the Woodstock Road; then the orange blinker flashing left (left!) as she edged into the traffic departing north and away from the city centre.

He knew her next moves. Up to the Northern Ring Road roundabout, there cutting through Five Mile Drive, and then out on to the Kidlington Road. He knew his own move, too.

The telephone-kiosk was free and, although the local directory had long since been stolen, he knew the number and dialled it.

'Hello?' (A woman's voice.) 'Roger Bacon School, Kidlington. Can I help you?'

'I was wondering if I could speak to Mr Morris, Mr Paul Morris, please. I believe he's one of your music teachers.'

'Yes, he is. Just a minute. I'll just have a look at the time-table to see if . . . just a minute . . . No. He's got a free period. I'll just see if he's in the staff-room. Who shall I say?'

'Er, Mr Jones.'

She was back on the line within half a minute. 'No, I'm afraid he doesn't seem to be on the school premises, Mr Jones. Can I take a message?'

'No, it doesn't really matter. Can you tell me whether he's likely to be at school during the lunch-hour?'

'Just a minute.' (Josephs heard the rustling of some papers. She needn't have bothered, though, he knew that.) 'No. He's not on the list for lunches today. He usually stays but— '

'Don't worry. Sorry to have been a nuisance.'

He felt his heart pounding as he rang another number – another Kidlington number. He'd give the bloody pair a fright! If only he could drive a car! The phone rang and rang and he was just beginning to wonder . . . when it was answered.

'Hello?' (Just that. No more. Was the voice a little strained?)

'Mr Morris?' (It was no difficulty for him to lapse into the broad Yorkshire dialect of his youth.)

'Ye-es?'

'Electricity Board 'ere, sir. Is it cónvénient for us to come along, sir? We've— '

'Today, you mean?'

'Aye. This lunch-taime, sir.'

'Er – er – no, I'm afraid not. I've just called in home for a second to get a – er – book. It's lucky you caught me, really. But I'm due back at school – er – straightaway. What's the trouble, anyway?'

Josephs slowly cradled the phone. That would give the sod something to think about!

When Brenda arrived home at ten minutes to three, he was clipping the privet-hedge with dedicated precision. 'Hello, love. Have a good day?'

'Oh. Usual, you know. I've brought something nice for tea, though.'

'That's good news.'

'Have any lunch?'

'Mouthful of bread and cheese.'

She knew he was telling a lie, for there was no cheese in the house. Unless, of course, he'd been out again . . . ? She felt a sudden surge of panic as she hurried inside with her shopping-bags.

Josephs continued his meticulous clippings along the tall hedge that separated them from next door. He was in no hurry, and only when he was immediately alongside the off-side front door of the car did he casually glance at the fascia dials. The milometer read 25,633.

As he always did, he washed up after their evening meal by himself, but he postponed one small piece of investigation until later, for he knew that as surely as night follows day his wife would make some excuse for retiring early to bed. Yet, strange as it seemed, he felt almost glad: it was he who was now in control of things. (Or, at least, that is what he thought.)

She was on cue, all right – just after the news headlines on BBC1: 'I think I'll have a bath and an early night, Harry. I – I feel a bit tired.'

He nodded understandingly. 'Like me to bring you a cup of Ovaltine?'

'No, thanks. I shall be asleep as soon as I hit the pillow. But thanks anyway.' She put her hand on his shoulder and gave it the slightest squeeze, and for a few seconds her face was haunted by the twin spectres of self-recrimination and regret.

When the water had finished running in the bathroom, Josephs went back into the kitchen and looked in the waste-bin. There, screwed up into small balls and pushed right to the bottom of the débris, he found four white paper-bags. Careless, Brenda! Careless! He had checked the bin himself that same morning, and now there were four newcomers, four white paper-bags, all of them carrying the name of the Quality supermarket at Kidlington.

After Brenda had left the next morning, he made himself some coffee and toast, and sat down with the *Daily Express*. Heavy overnight rain at Lingfield Park had upset a good many of the favourites, and there were no congratulatory columns to the wildly inaccurate prognostications of the racing tipsters. With malicious glee he noticed that The Organist had come seventh out of eight runners; and Poor Old Harry – had won! At sixteen to one! Whew! It hadn't been such a blank day after all.

Chapter Three

The last lesson of the week could hardly have provided a more satisfactory envoi. There were only five of them in the O-Level music group, all reasonably anxious to work hard and to succeed, all girls; and as they sat forward awkwardly and earnestly, their musical scores of Piano Sonata Opus 90 on their knees, Paul Morris vaguely reminded himself how exquisitely Gilels could play Beethoven. But his aesthetic sense was only minimally engaged, and not for the first time during the past few weeks he found himself wondering whether he was really cut out for teaching. Doubtless, these particular pupils would all get decent O-Level grades, for he had sedulously drilled the set works into them – their themes, their developments and recapitulations. But there was, he knew, little real radiance either in his own exposition of the works or in his pupils' appreciation of them; and the sad truth was that what until so recently had been an all-consuming passion was now becoming little more than pleasurable background listening. From Music to Muzac – in three short months.

Morris had moved from his previous post (it was almost three years ago now) primarily to try to forget that terrible day when the young police constable had come to tell him that his wife had been killed in a car accident; when he had gone along to the primary school to collect Peter and watched the silent, tragic tears that sprang from the boy's eyes; and when he had wrestled with that helpless, baffled anger against the perversity and cruelty of the Fates which had taken his young wife from him – an anger which over those next few dazed and despairing weeks had finally settled into a firm resolve at all costs to protect his only child whenever and wherever he could. The boy was something – the only thing – that he could cling to. Gradually, too, Morris had become convinced that he had to get away, and his determination to move – to move anywhere – had grown into an obsession as weekly the Posts Vacant columns in *The Times Educational Supplement* reminded him of new streets, new colleagues, a new school – perhaps even a new life. And so finally he had moved to the Roger Bacon Comprehensive School on the outskirts of Oxford, where his breezy interview had lasted but fifteen minutes, where he'd immediately found a quiet little semi-detached to rent, where everyone was very kind to him – but where his life proved very much the same as before. At least, until he met Brenda Josephs.

It was through Peter that he had established contact with St Frideswide's. One of Peter's friends was a keen member of the choir, and before long Peter had joined, too. And when the aged choirmaster had finally retired it was common knowledge that Peter's father was an organist, and the invitation asking him to take over was accepted without hesitation.

Gilels was lingering *pianissimo* over the last few bars when the bell sounded the end of the week's schooling. One of the class, a leggy, large-boned, dark-haired girl, remained behind to ask if she could borrow the record for the week-end. She was slightly taller than Morris, and as he looked into her black-pencilled, languidly amorous eyes he once more sensed a power within himself which until a few months previously he could never have suspected. Carefully he lifted the record from the turntable and slipped it smoothly into its sleeve.

'Thank you,' she said softly.

'Have a nice week-end, Carole.'

'You, too, sir.'

He watched her as she walked down the steps from the stage and clattered her way across the main hall in her high wedge-heeled shoes. How would the melancholy Carole be spending her week-end? he wondered. He wondered, too, about his own.

Brenda had happened just three months ago. He had seen her on many occasions before, of course, for she always stayed behind after the Sunday morning service to take her husband home. But that particular morning had not been just another occasion. She had seated herself, not as usual in one of the pews at the back of the church, but directly behind him in the choir-stalls; and as he played he'd watched her with interest in the organ-mirror, her head slightly to one side, her face set in a wistful, half-contented smile. As the deep notes died away around the empty church, he had turned towards her.

'Did you like it?'

She had nodded quietly and lifted her eyes towards him.

'Would you like me to play it again?'

'Have you got time?'

'For you I have.' Their eyes had held then, and for that moment they were the only two beings alive in the world.

'Thank you,' she whispered.

Remembrance of that first brief time together was even now a source of radiant light that shone in Morris's heart. Standing by his side she had turned over the sheet-music for him, and more than once her arm had lightly brushed his own . . .

That was how it had begun, and how, he told himself, it had to end. But that couldn't be. Her face haunted his dreams that Sunday night, and again through the following nights she would give his sleeping thoughts no rest. On the Friday of the same week he had rung her at the hospital. A bold, irrevocable move. Quite simply he had asked her if he could see her some time – that was all; and just as simply she had answered 'Yes, of course you can' – words that re-echoed round his brain like the joyous refrain of the Seraphim.

In the weeks that followed, the frightening truth had gradually dawned on him: he would do almost anything to have this woman for his own. It was not that he bore any malice against Harry Josephs. How could he? Just a burning, irrational jealousy, which no words from Brenda, none of her pathetic pleas of reassurance could assuage. He wished Josephs out of the way – of course he did! But only recently had his conscious mind accepted the stark reality of his position. Not only did he wish Josephs out of the way: he would be positively happy to see him dead.

'You stayin' much longer, sir?'

It was the caretaker, and Morris knew better than to argue. It was a quarter past four, and Peter would be home.

The regular Friday evening fish and chips, liberally vinegared and blotched with tomato sauce, were finished, and they stood together at the kitchen sink, father washing, son drying. Although Morris had thought long and hard about what he would say, it was not going to be easy. He had never before had occasion to speak to his son about matters connected with sex; but one thing was quite certain: he had to do so now. He remembered with devastating clarity (he had only been eight at the time) when the two boys next door had been visited by the police, and when one of the local ministers had been taken to court, and there convicted and sentenced to prison. And he remembered the new words he had then learned, words that his school-fellows had learned, too, and laughed about in lavatory corners: slimy words that surfaced ever after in his young mind as if from some loathsome, reptilian pool.

'I think we may be able to get you that racing bike in a couple of months.'

'*Really*, Dad?'

'You'd have to promise me to be jolly careful . . . '

But Peter was hardly listening. His mind was racing as fast as the bike was going to race, his face shining with joy . . .

'Pardon, Dad?'

'I said, are you looking forward to the outing tomorrow?'

Peter nodded, honestly, if comparatively unenthusiastically. ' 'Spect I'll get a bit fed up on the way back. Like last year.'

'I want you to promise me something.'

Another promise? The boy frowned uncertainly at the serious

tone in his father's voice, and rubbed the tea-towel quite unnecessarily round and round the next plate, anticipating some adult information, confidential, and perhaps unwelcome.

'You're still a young lad, you know. You may think you're
getting a bit grown-up, but you've still got a lot to learn. You
see, some people you'll meet in life are very nice, and some
aren't. They may seem nice, but – but they're not nice at all.'
It sounded pathetically inadequate.

'Crooks, you mean?'

'In a way they're crooks, yes, but I'm talking about people
who are bad inside. They want – strange sort of things to satisfy
them. They're not normal – not like most people.' He took a deep
breath. 'When I was about your age, younger in fact . . . '

Peter listened to the little story with apparent unconcern.
'You mean he was a queer, Dad?'

'He was a homosexual. Do you know what that means?'

' 'Course I do.'

'Listen, Peter, if any man ever tries anything like that –
anything! – you have nothing at all to do with it. Is that clear?
And, what's more, you'll tell me. All right?'

Peter tried so very hard to understand, but the warning seemed
remote, dissociated as yet from his own small experience of life.

'You see, Peter, it's not just a question of a man – touching'
(the very word was shudderingly repulsive) 'or that sort of thing.
It's what people start talking about or – or photographs that kind
of— '

Peter's mouth dropped open and the blood froze in his freckled
cheeks. So *that* was what his father was talking about! The last
time had been two weeks ago when three of them from the youth
club had gone along to the vicarage and sat together on that long,
black, shiny settee. It was all a bit strange and exciting, and there
had been those photographs – big, black and white, glossy prints
that seemed almost clearer than real life. But they weren't just
pictures of *men*, and Mr Lawson had talked about them so – so
naturally, somehow. Anyway, he'd often seen pictures like that
on the racks in the newsagent's. He felt a growing sense of bewilderment as he stood there by the sink, his hands still clutching the
drying-cloth. Then he heard his father's voice, raucous and ugly,
in his ears, and felt his father's hand upon his shoulder, shaking
him angrily.

'Do you hear me? Tell me about it!'

But the boy didn't tell his father. He just couldn't. What was there to tell anyway?

Chapter Four

The coach, a wide luxury hulk of a thing, was due to leave Cornmarket at 7.30 a.m., and Morris joined the group of fussy parents counterchecking on lunch-bags, swimming-gear and pocket-money. Peter was already ensconced between a pair of healthily excited pals on the back seat, and Lawson once more counted heads to satisfy himself that the expedition was fully manned and could at last proceed. As the driver heaved round and round at the huge horizontal steering-wheel, slowly manoeuvring the giant vehicle into Beaumont Street, Morris had his last view of Harry and Brenda Josephs sitting silently together on one of the front seats, of Lawson folding his plastic raincoat and packing it into the overhead rack, and of Peter chatting happily away and like most of the other boys disdaining, or forgetting, to wave farewell. All *en route* for Bournemouth.

It was 7.45 a.m. by the clock on the south face of St Frideswide's as Morris walked up to Carfax and then through Queen Street and down to the bottom of St Ebbe's, where he stopped in front of a rangy three-storeyed stuccoed building set back from the street behind bright yellow railings. Nailed on to the high wooden gate which guarded the narrow path to the front door was a flaking notice-board announcing in faded capitals ST FRIDESWIDE'S CHURCH AND OXFORD PASTORATE. The gate itself was half-open; and as Morris stood self-consciously and indecisively in the deserted street a whistling paper-boy rode up on his bicycle and inserted a copy of *The Times* through the front door. No inside hand withdrew the newspaper, and Morris walked slowly away from the house and just as slowly back. On the top floor a pale yellow strip of neon lighting suggested the presence of someone on the premises, and he walked cautiously up to the front door where he rapped gently on the ugly black knocker. With no sound of movement from within, he tried again, a little louder. There must be someone, surely, in the rambling old vicarage. Students up on the top floor, probably? A housekeeper, perhaps? But again as he held his ear close to the door he could hear no movement; and conscious that his heart was beating fast against his ribs he tried the door. It was locked.

The back of the house was enclosed by a wall some eight or nine feet high; but a pair of gates, with NO PARKING amateurishly painted in white across them, promised access to somewhere, and turning the metal ring Morris found the gate unlocked. He stepped inside. A path led alongside the high stone wall beside an ill-tended stretch of patchy lawn, and quietly closing the gates behind him Morris walked up to the back door, and knocked with a quiet cowardice. No answer. No sound. He turned the door-knob. The door was unlocked. He opened it and went inside. For several seconds he stood stock-still in the wide hallway, his eyes unmoving as an alligator's. Across the hall *The Times* protruded downwards through the front-door letter-box like the tongue of some leering gargoyle, the whole house as still as death. He forced himself to breathe more naturally and looked around him. A door on his left was standing ajar, and he tiptoed across to look inside. 'Anyone there?' The words were spoken very softly, but they gave him an odd surge of confidence as though, should anyone be there, he was obviously trying to be noticed. And someone was there; or had been, until very recently. On a formica-topped table lay a knife, stickily smeared with butter and marmalade, a solitary plate strewn with toast-crumbs, and a large mug containing the dregs of cold tea. The remains, no doubt, of Lawson's breakfast. But a sudden shudder of fear climbed up Morris's spine as he noticed that the grill on the electric cooker was turned on full, its bars burning a fierce orange-red. Yet there was the same eerie stillness as before, with only the mechanical tick-tock of the kitchen clock to underline the pervasive silence.

Back in the hallway, he walked quietly across to the broad staircase, and as lightly as he could climbed up to the landing. Only one of the doors was open; but one was enough. A black-leather settee was ranged along one side of the room, and the floor was fully carpeted. He walked noiselessly across to the roll-top desk beside the window. It was locked, but the key lay on the top. Inside, two neatly written sheets of paper – on which he read

the text and notes for some forthcoming sermon – lay beneath
a paper-knife, curiously fashioned in the shape of a crucifix,
the slitting-edge, as it seemed to Morris, wickedly (and quite
needlessly?) sharp. He tried first the drawers on the left – all of
them gliding smoothly open and all of them apparently fulfilling
some innocent function; and the same with the top three drawers
on the right. But the bottom one was locked, and the key to it
was nowhere to be seen.

As a prospective burglar Morris had anticipated the stubborn-
ness of locks and bolts only to the extent of a small chisel which
he now took from his pocket. It took him more than ten minutes,
and when finally the bottom drawer lay open the surrounding
oblong frame was irreparably chipped and bruised. Inside lay an
old chocolate-box, and Morris was slipping off the criss-cross of
elastic bands when a slight sound caused him to whip round, his
eyes wide with terror.

Standing in the doorway was a man with a lathered face,
his right hand holding a shaving-brush, his left clutching a dirty
pink towel about his neck. For a second Morris felt a shock that
partly paralysed his terror, for his immediate impression was that
the man was Lawson himself. Yet he knew he must be mistaken,
and the logic that for a moment had threatened to disintegrate was
swiftly reasserting itself. The man was about the same height and
build as Lawson, yes. But the face was thinner and the hair was
greyer; nor was the man's voice, when finally he spoke, in any
way like Lawson's own, but a voice and a mode of expression
that seemed to mask a curious combination of the cultured and
the coarse:

'May I ask what the 'ell you're doing 'ere, mate?'

Morris recognised him then. He was one of the drop-outs
who sometimes congregated in Bonn Square or Brasenose Lane.
Indeed, Lawson had brought him to church a few times, and there
was a whisper of rumour that the two men were related. Some had
even suspected that the man was Lawson's brother.

At Bournemouth the sun shone brightly out of a clear sky, but
the wind was chill and blustery, and Brenda Josephs, seated in
an open deck-chair, envied the other holiday-makers who sat so
snugly, it seemed, behind their striped wind-breaks. She felt cold
and bored – and more than a little disturbed by that little remark

of Harry's on the coach: 'Pity Morris couldn't make it.' That was all. That was all . . .

The boys had thrown themselves around with phenomenal energy: playing beach football (Harry had organised that), running into the sea, clambering up and down the rocks, guzzling Coke, guttling sandwiches, crunching crisps, then back into the sea. But for her – what an empty, fruitless day! She was officially the 'nurse' of the party, for invariably someone would feel sick or cut his knee. But she could have been with Paul all day. All day! No risk, either. Oh God! She couldn't bear to think of it . . .

The farther stretches of the sea twinkled invitingly in the sun, but along the shore-line the crashing breakers somersaulted into heavy spray. It was no day for tentative paddlers, but huge fun for the boys who were still leaping tirelessly against the waves, Lawson with them, white-skinned as a fish's underbelly, laughing, splashing, happy. It all seemed innocent enough to Brenda, and she couldn't really believe all that petty church gossip. Not that she liked Lawson much; but she didn't dislike him, either. In fact she'd thought more than once that Lawson must suspect something about herself and Paul; but he'd said nothing . . . so far.

Harry had gone for a walk along the esplanade, and she was glad to be left to herself. She tried to read the newspaper, but the sheets flapped and billowed in the breeze, and she put it back into the carrier-bag, alongside the flask of coffee, the salmon sandwiches, and her white bikini. Yes. Pity about the bikini . . . She had become increasingly conscious of her body these past few months, and she would have enjoyed seeing the young lads gawping up at her bulging breasts. What was happening to her . . . ?

When Harry returned an hour or so later it was quite clear that he had been drinking, but she made no comment. As a concession to the English summer he had changed into a pair of old shorts – long, baggy service-issue in which (according to Harry) he and his men had flushed the Malaysian jungles of all the terrorists. His legs had grown thinner, especially round the thighs, but they were still muscular and strong. Stronger than Paul's, but . . . She stemmed the gathering flood of thoughts, and unfolded the tin-foil round the sandwiches.

She averted her eyes from her husband as he slowly masticated the tinned salmon. What *was* happening to her? The poor fellow couldn't even eat now without her experiencing a mild disgust. She would have to do something, she knew that. And soon. But what *could* she do?

It was not on that joyless day at Bournemouth (although it was very soon after) that Brenda Josephs recognised the ugly fact that had been standing at the threshold of her mind: she now hated the man she had married.

'Have you heard that somebody might be helping himself from the collection? It's only a rumour but . . . ' It was the following morning when Morris heard the first whisperings; but in his mind – as in many others' – the alleged hebdomadal thefts were already firmly substantiated in the higher courts of heaven and now stood only in need of a little terrestrial corroboration. There were – surely – only two obvious opportunities, and two possible suspects: Lawson at the altar and Josephs in the vestry. And during the penultimate verse of the offertory hymn Morris turned the organ-mirror slightly to the right and adjusted the elevation so that he had a good view of the large, gilt crucifix standing on the heavily brocaded altar-cloth; and of Lawson holding high the collection-plate, then lowering it and leaning forward in a tilted benediction before handing it back to the vicar's warden. It had been impossible to see Lawson's hands clearly, but nothing had been taken – Morris could have sworn to it. So it must be that contemptible worm Josephs! Much more likely – counting the cash all alone in the vestry. Yes. And yet . . . And yet, if the church funds *were* being pilfered, wasn't there a much likelier culprit than either? The scruffy-looking man from the Church Army hostel, the man who had been there again this morning, sitting next to Josephs at the back of the church, the man Lawson had befriended – and the man whom Morris himself had encountered the previous morning in the vicarage.

A few minutes later he closed the organ-door quietly behind him and managed a cheerful 'Good morning' to Mrs Walsh-Atkins as she finally rose from her knees. But in truth he was far from cheerful; and as he walked slowly up the central aisle his mind for once was not wholly preoccupied with thoughts of Brenda Josephs, whom he could now see waiting for him by the font. Like Lawson at this time a week ago, he felt a very worried man.

Chapter Five

On Wednesday of the same week, no one seemed to mind the woman as she stood by the shop-window examining with slow deliberation one bulky sample-book after another. 'Just looking,' she told the assistant. She'd known what would happen, of course: from the bus-stop in Woodstock Road he would walk down South Parade (where Cromwell had once arranged his Roundheads), turn right into Banbury Road, and then go into the licensed betting-office just opposite the carpet-shop. And he had already done so. She knew, too, that he would have to come out sooner rather than later, since he was due home for lunch – lunch with *her* – at about one o'clock; and he had another call to pay before then, had he not?

It was 11.20 a.m. when Harry Josephs at last emerged, and his wife drifted quietly behind a line of vertically stacked linoleum rolls, watching him. Back up to South Parade, where he pushed the button at the pelican crossing and waited to cross the Banbury Road. Just as she'd thought. She left the shop with a guilty 'Thank you', and kept well behind him as he walked with his slightly splay-footed gait up towards north Oxford, his brown suit clearly visible beyond the other pedestrians. He would turn right very soon now (how much she knew!) into Manning Terrace; and she skipped and waltzed her way in and out of the prams as soon as he disappeared. He was on the right-hand side of the terrace, about seven or eight houses along, and he would be stopping just about there (yes!) and walking up the short path to one of the front doors. She knew not only the number of the house but also the woman who lived there; knew the style and colour of her hair even – long and prematurely grey, like the strand she'd found on Harry's suit one day the previous week. Ruth Rawlinson! That was the name of the woman who lived at number 14, the woman whom her husband had been seeing; and it was all just as Lionel Lawson had told her it was. She hurried back to the Summertown car-park. She would just have time to put in a brief appearance at the Radcliffe Infirmary, and to tell the nursing officer that her dental appointment had taken much longer than expected and that she'd make up the time tomorrow.

As she drove down into Oxford her lips were curled in a cruelly contented smile.

At 8 p.m. on the Wednesday of the following week, Ruth Rawlinson took little notice when she heard the click and the creak of the north door opening. People often came in to look around, to admire the font, to light a candle, to pray even; and she silently wiped her wet cloth over the wooden floor of the pew behind one of the pillars in the south aisle. The stranger, whoever he might be, was now standing still, for the echo of his footsteps had died away in the empty, darkening church. This was just about the time when the place could get almost eerie – and time for Ruth to go home. Of indeterminate age, anywhere between mid-thirties and late forties, she wiped her pale forehead with the back of her wrist and brushed back a wisp of straggling hair. She'd done enough. Twice a week, on Mondays and Wednesdays, she spent about two hours in St Frideswide's (usually in the mornings), cleaning the floors, dusting the pews, polishing the candlesticks, turning out the dying flowers; and once every three months washing and ironing all the surplices. For these good works her motives were obscure, not least to Ruth herself: sometimes she suspected they sprang from an almost pathological need to escape for a brief while her demanding, discontented, self-centred invalid of a mother, with whom she shared house; at other times, especially on Sundays, she felt her motives sprang from a deeper source, for she found herself profoundly moved in spirit by the choral mass, especially by Palestrina, and then she would approach the altar of the Lord to partake the host with an almost mystical sense of wonder and adoration.

The footsteps had started again, and as they moved slowly up the central aisle she peered over the top of the pew. He looked somehow familiar, but he was half turned away from her and for a while she failed to recognise him: his subfusc suit seemed of good quality cloth, though loose-fitting and shabby; and his face (so far as she could see it) was matted with greyish stubble. He peered vaguely across the pews, first to the left, then to the right, before stopping at the chancel steps. Was he looking for something – or someone? Instinctively Ruth felt it better if he remained unaware of her presence, and very very quietly she wiped the cloth over the winking suds.

The north door clicked and groaned again, and she dipped the soapy cloth more boldly into the dirty water; but almost immediately her body froze over the bucket.

'You came, then?'

'Keep your voice down!'

'There's nobody here.'

The newcomer walked down the central aisle and the two men met half-way. They spoke in hushed voices, but the few snatches of their conversation that carried to Ruth's ears were readily and frighteningly comprehensible.

' . . . given you more than enough already and you're not getting a penny more . . . '

' . . . *told* you, Mister Morris. It's just to tide me over, that's all. And I'm sure you wouldn't want me to tell my brother. . . . ' The voice seemed a curious combination of the cultured and the coarse.

The ugly word 'blackmail' rose to the surface of Ruth's mind; but before she could learn more the door had opened again to admit a small group of tourists, one of whom in a nasal twang was soon admiring 'that cute lil farnt'.

Half of the long school holiday had now passed and the August sun shone gloriously. Brenda and Harry Josephs were in Tenby for a week; Lawson had just come back from a brief holiday in Scotland; Peter Morris was away at scout camp; and his father was decorating the staircase – amongst other things.

It was at 1.30 p.m. that he was sitting in the Old Bull at Deddington and deciding that he oughtn't to drink any more. After all, he had to drive home. And he had the additional responsibility of a passenger.

'I think we ought to go now,' he said.

Carole nodded, and drained her third Babycham. From the start she had felt embarrassment at being with him, and things hadn't been helped much by the way he'd been speaking to her – so naturally! So unendearingly! It wasn't at all what she'd expected. Or hoped. She'd been in a pub before, of course – quite a few times; but only for a giggle round the juke-box with some of the others from school. But this? The whole thing had been a ghastly mistake, somehow; and yet it could have been so very different. . . .

The car was parked at the far end of the tarmac behind the pub, and Morris politely unlocked and opened the door for his passenger before getting into the driver's seat and fitting the key into the ignition.

'You won't say anything at all about this, will you?'

' 'Course I won't.'

'You mustn't tell anyone.'

'I shan't tell a soul,' she said. Her eyes, the lids shaded in a lurid blue, were dull with disappointment.

Morris took a deep breath. 'Put your safety belt on, my girl. Better safe— '

He leaned over to help fix the awkward thing, and was aware of the softness of her breast against his arm. With what seemed almost paternal affection he took her hand in his; and as she turned her head towards him he put his mouth lightly to hers and felt her full lips softly cushioning his own. He had meant no more than that; but he lingered there as the girl's lips gently – yet so perceptibly! – pushed forward against his own. And still he lingered, savouring long the sensual delight. He put his arm along the seat, easing her more closely towards him; and then the tip of her tongue tentatively tried the entrance to his mouth, and the smouldering smoke burst forth in a blazing flame. . . . Eagerly she pulled down his hand to her naked thigh, and her legs opened slowly and invitingly, like the arms of a saint in a holy benediction.

They broke away from each other guiltily as a car backed into the space beside them, and Morris drove off to Kidlington, dropping her (where he had picked her up) on the north side of the village.

'Would you like to come to see me sometime?' They were the first words that either of them had spoken on the way back.

'When do you mean?'

'I dunno.' His throat was very dry. 'Now?'

'All right.'

'How long will it take you from here?'

'Ten minutes.'

'You'd better come in the back way.'

'All right.'

'I want you, Carole!'

'I want you, sir.' ('Sir'! My God! What was he doing?)

'Be as quick as you can.'

'I will, don't worry.'

In the kitchen he opened a bottle of Beaujolais, fetched two glasses from the living-room, and looked yet again at his watch. Just another five minutes. Come on, Carole! . . . Already in his mind he was unfastening the buttons down the front of her white blouse, and his hands were slipping inside to fondle her breasts. . . . He breathed deeply and waited with an almost desperate impatience.

When finally he heard the timid knock, he walked to the back door like a man newly ushered through the gates of Paradise.

'Good afternoon,' said Lawson. 'I hope I've not called at an inconvenient time? I wonder if I can come in and talk to you. It's – er – it's rather important.'

THE SECOND BOOK OF CHRONICLES

Chapter Six

But for his dilatoriness and indecisiveness Detective Chief Inspector Morse would have been cruising among the Greek islands. Three months earlier, in January, he had discussed Easter bookings with the Town and Gown travel agency, taken home a Technicolor brochure, rung up his bank manager to discover the going rate for the drachma, bought a slim Modern Greek phrase-book, and even managed to find his passport again. He had never been to Greece; and now, a bachelor still, forty-seven years old, he retained enough romance in his soul to imagine a lazy liaison with some fading film-star beside the wine-dark waves of the Aegean. But it was not to be. Instead, on this chilly Monday mid-morning in early April, he stood at a bus-stop in north Oxford, with a fortnight's furlough before him, wondering exactly how other people could organise their lives, make decisions, write a letter even.

Still no bus in sight.

A heavily pregnant mother pushed a rickety, collapsible pram into the shelter, unstrapped the infant within it, and then stuck her head out to admonish her slightly older offspring, already exhibiting, as it seemed to Morse, the lively potential of a fully fledged criminal. 'Stop frowin' dem bricks, Jason!'

Jason! Jason and the Argonauts sailing up to the Hellespont. . . . Morse felt he could have done without the reminder – the second reminder, in fact, that morning; for Radio Oxford had just broadcast an interview with the new vicar of St Frideswide's, recently returned from a fortnight in a monastery on the island of Patmos.

Morse stood aside to allow Jason's formidable mother to enter

225

the bus first. She asked for 'St Frideswide's', and as she fiddled one-handedly in her purse the other passengers watched in helpless silence as the hero of the *Argosy* wiped his filthy shoes over the nearest seat-cover.

Morse knew where St Frideswide's was, of course: one of the string of ecclesiastical edifices along Cornmarket . . . where there had been some rather curious occurrences the previous autumn . . . when he himself had been away on an eight-week secondment in west Africa. . . .

'Where to, mate?'

'Er' (it was more than a year since Morse had been on a bus) 'St Frideswide's, please.' It was as good a stop as any for the Ashmolean, and Morse had promised himself an hour or so in the galleries: it would be good to see the Tiepolo again; and the Giorgione.

But he saw neither that morning.

Whilst Mrs Jason was extricating her push-chair from the luggage-rack, the triumphant young vandal himself was already at large in the street, and very soon the bottom half of a notice affixed to the church railings was torn from its moorings.

' 'Ow many times 'ave I *told* you, Jason?' This rhetorical question was accompanied by a clumping clout across the youngster's ears, and the bawling brat was finally dragged away.

The notice now read: ST FRIDESWIDE'S EASTER JUMBLE SALE. That was all. Any details of date, time and place had vanished with the passing of Jason.

Morse was a believer neither in the existence of God nor in the fixity of the Fates. About such things he never quite knew what he should think; and, like Hardy's, his philosophy of life amounted to little more than a heap of confused impressions, akin to those of a bewildered young boy at a conjuring show. Yet, as he looked back, it seemed somehow pre-ordained that his steps should take him on only one course that morning; and he took that course now as, in obedience to some strangely compelling impulse, he walked the few steps across the pavement and unlatched the door at the north porch of St Frideswide's.

Chapter Seven

As a schoolboy, Morse had once paid a few shillings for a book on architecture and had traipsed around a good many churches, earnestly tracing the development of Early English into Gothic. But the enthusiasm, like so many, had been short-lived. And as he stood in the vaulted silence, looking down the central aisle towards the altar, with the heavily curtained vestry to the right behind him, few of the architectural features were familiar any longer; and his mind, whilst not uninformed, remained maddeningly blank – like that of an amnesic ornithologist at a duck-pond. A ring of candles burned around the effigy of some saint or other, and an occasional elongated asterisk of light was reflected in a gleaming flash from an adjacent crucifix. The air was heavy with incense.

As he walked slowly towards the chancel, Morse realised that he'd been wrong about the silence, though. Somewhere he could hear a quiet, rhythmic scratching noise, like that of a church mouse scampering about in the wainscoting. But the noise was too regular for that; and suddenly Morse knew that he was not alone. A grey head rose above the level of the front pew and nodded neutrally as the visitor stopped alongside. She wiped her pale forehead with the back of her wrist and blew a stray hair from her vision before bending over her work once more, the concentric rings of soap on the wooden floor dissolving beneath her wiping-cloth, the bucket rattling as she moved to the next rectangle.

'Good morning.' Morse smiled amiably as he looked down at her. 'You don't seem to have got any of those brochure things – you know, telling people what to look at.'

'No. We ran out last week, but the Vicar's having some more printed.'

'The Vicar? That's Mr Lawson, isn't it?'

'No, it isn't.' Her large brown eyes looked up at him cautiously, and she suddenly seemed a good deal younger than he'd thought. 'It's Mr Meiklejohn. He's been here since last November.'

'I must have been thinking of one of the other churches.'

'No. Mr Lawson *was* here.' She hesitated. 'He – he died last October.'

'Oh dear. I'm sorry about that.'

For a few seconds there was silence between them.

'I think you knew he was dead,' said the woman quietly.

Morse blinked at her happily. 'Did I?'

'You're another one of those reporters, aren't you?'

Morse shook his head and told her. He was a police officer attached to the Thames Valley Police H.Q. in Kidlington – not to the City Police in St Aldates; he'd heard vaguely about the case but had never been on it himself; in fact, he'd been out of the country at the time.

'Were you involved in any way?' he asked.

'As a matter of fact I was, yes.'

'Pardon?' She spoke so very quietly now that Morse took a step nearer to her.

'I was here in the church on the night of the murder.'

'I see. Do you mind telling me something about it?'

She dried her hands along her faded blue jeans, worn almost threadbare at the knees, and stood up. 'Wait a minute.'

There was a natural elegance about her walk, and Morse's eyes followed her with a slightly quickened interest as she disappeared somewhere at the back of the church, and re-emerged a minute later carrying a brown handbag. She had taken the opportunity to arrange her straggling hair, and Morse began to realise that she must once have been an attractive woman.

'Here you are.' She handed him a cheap brown envelope containing several cuttings from the *Oxford Mail*, and Morse sat down in the pew opposite her and carefully unfolded the thin sheets. The first cutting was dated Tuesday, 27 September of the previous year:

CHURCHWARDEN MURDERED DURING SERVICE

Whilst the congregation was singing the last hymn, Mr H.A. Josephs was last night stabbed to death in the vestry of St Frideswide's Church, Cornmarket. Chief Inspector Bell of the Oxford City Police, who is in charge of the murder enquiries, told our reporter that Mr Josephs, one of the two churchwardens at St Frideswide's, had just taken the collection and was almost certainly counting it as he was attacked.

When the police arrived there was no sign of the collection-plate itself or of the money. Inspector Bell said that if robbery had been the sole motive the murder was doubly tragic, since only a dozen or so people had attended the evening service, and the offertory could have amounted at most only to about two or three pounds.

Several members of the congregation had heard sounds of some disturbance at the back of the church, but no one suspected that anything was seriously wrong until Mr Josephs had shouted for help. The vicar, the Reverend L. Lawson, immediately suspended the service and summoned the police and the ambulance, but Mr Josephs died before either could arrive.

The knife used by the murderer was of a dull, golden colour, cast in the shape of a crucifix, with the blade honed to a razor sharpness. Police are anxious to hear from anyone who has knowledge of such a knife.

Mr Josephs, aged 50, was married and lived in Port Meadow Drive, Wolvercote. He came to Oxford after serving as a regular officer in the Royal Marine Commandos and saw active service in Malaya. left-foot shot was brilliantly pushed over the bar by Until two years ago he worked for the Inland Revenue Department. There are no children. The inquest is to be held next Monday.

Morse quickly read through the article again, for there were a couple of things, quite apart from the extraordinary typography of the last paragraph, that puzzled him slightly.

'Did you know him very well?'

'Pardon?' The woman stopped her scrubbing and looked across at him.

'I said did you know Josephs well.'

A flicker of unease in those brown eyes? Had she heard him the first time?

'Yes, I knew him quite well. He was a churchwarden here. It says so, doesn't it?'

Morse let it go and turned his attention to the second cutting, dated Tuesday, 4 October:

INQUEST RIDDLE

The inquest on Mr H.A. Josephs, who was stabbed to death last week at St Frideswide's Church, was adjourned yesterday after a twenty-minute hearing, but not before the court had heard some startling new evidence. The post-mortem report on Mr Josephs showed that a lethal quantity of morphine was present in the stomach, but it seemed clear that it was the stab-wound which had been the immediate cause of death.

Earlier, Mr Paul Morris, of 3 Home Close, Kidlington, had given evidence of formal identification. He had been the organist during the service and was in fact playing the last hymn when Mr Josephs was murdered.

Another witness, Miss Ruth Rawlinson, of 14 Manning Terrace, Summertown, said that she heard noises coming from the vestry during the singing of the last hymn, and had turned to see Mr Josephs call out and slump beside the vestry curtains.

Chief Inspector Bell, of the Oxford City Police, informed the Coroner that he was as yet unable to report on any firm developments in the case but that enquiries were proceeding. The Coroner extended his deepest sympathy to Mrs Brenda Josephs, the deceased's wife.

The funeral service will be held at St Frideswide's on Thursday at 2.30 p.m.

The narrative was bald, but interesting enough, wasn't it? What was morphine doing in the poor beggar's innards? Somebody must have wanted him out of the way pretty badly, and that somebody had so far got away with it and was still walking around – probably walking around the streets of Oxford – a free man. Or a free woman perhaps, he reminded himself, as he glanced across the aisle.

Morse looked about him with renewed interest. He was actually sitting a few yards from the scene of the crime, and he tried to imagine it all: the organ playing, the few members of the congregation standing, heads bowed over their hymn-books – one minute, though! Where was the organ? He got to his feet and walked up the broad, shallow steps of the chancel. Yes. There it was, on the left-hand side behind two rows of choir-stalls, with a blue curtain stretched across in front of it to hide the body of the organist; and a mirror, too, fixed just above the high top manual, so that, however much he was concealed from the view of all others, the organist himself could keep an observant eye on the minister and the choir – and on the congregation as well, if he wanted to. If you swung the mirror round a bit. . . . Morse sat himself behind the curtain on the organ-seat and looked into it. He could see the choir-stalls behind him and the main body of the chancel. Mm. Then, like a nervous learner before starting off on a driving test, he began adjusting the mirror, finding that it moved easily and noiselessly: up and down, right and left – wherever he wanted it. First, to the right and slightly down, and he found himself looking straight at the intricately woven gold design on the front of the green altar-cloth; then to the left and down, and he could see the head and shoulders of the cleaning woman, her elbows circling sedulously over the soap-suds; then further still to the left and up slightly, almost as far as the mirror would go – and Morse suddenly stopped, a needle-sharp sensation momentarily flashing across

his temples. So very clearly he could now see the front curtains of
the vestry, could even see the fold where they would swing back
to let the choir on its way; the fold where they had once opened
– perhaps only slightly? – to reveal the figure of a man shouting
desperately above the swell of the organ notes, a man with a knife
stuck firm and deep through his back, a man with only a moment
or two to live. . . . What if the organist – Morris, wasn't it? – had
actually been looking at the vestry curtains during those fateful,
fatal seconds? What if he'd seen something? Something like. . . .

The rattle of the pail brought his airborne fancies down to earth.
What possible reason could Morris have had for turning the mirror
to such an improbable angle as he played the last hymn? Forget
it! He turned on the smooth bench and looked over the curtain.
The cleaner was packing up by the look of things, and he hadn't
read the other cuttings yet. But before he got off the bench his
mind again took wing and was floating as effortlessly as a kittiwake
keeling over the cliffs. It was the organ-curtain. . . . He was himself a man of just over medium height, but even someone three or
four inches taller would be fairly well concealed behind that curtain. The back of the head would be showing, but little else; and if
Morris was a small man he would have been almost completely
concealed. Indeed, as far as the choir and congregation were concerned, the organist might . . . might not have been Morris at all!

He walked down the chancel steps. 'Mind if I keep these
cuttings? I'll post them back to you, of course.'

The woman shrugged. 'All right.' It seemed a matter of little
concern to her.

'I don't know your name, I'm afraid,' began Morse, but a
small middle-aged man had entered the church and was walking
briskly towards them.

'Morning, Miss Rawlinson.'

Miss Rawlinson! One of the witnesses at the inquest. Well,
well! And the man who had just come in was doubtless Morris,
the other witness, for he had already seated himself at the organ,
where a few switches were clicked on and where a whirr of some
hidden power was followed by a series of gruff bass blasts, as if
the instrument were breaking wind.

'As I say, I can post 'em,' said Morse, 'or pop 'em through
your letter-box. 14 Manning Road, isn't it?'

'Manning *Terrace*.'

'Oh yes.' Morse smiled at her good-naturedly. 'Memory's not what it was, I'm afraid. They tell me we lose about 30,000 brain cells a day once we're past thirty.'

'Just as well we all have plenty to start with, Inspector.' There was perhaps just a hint of mockery in her steady eyes, but Morse's light-heartedness had evoked no reciprocal response.

'I'll just have a quick word with Mr Morris before— '

'That's not Mr Morris.'

'Pardon?'

'That's Mr Sharpe. He was deputy organist when Mr Morris was here.'

'And Mr Morris isn't here any longer?' said Morse slowly.

She shook her head.

'Do you know where he's gone?'

Did she? Again there seemed some hesitation in the eyes. 'N-no, I don't. He's left the district. He left last October.'

'Surely he must have— '

'He left his post at the school and, well, he just went.'

'But he must have— '

She picked up the bucket and prepared to leave. 'Nobody knows where he went.'

But Morse sensed she was lying. 'It's your duty to tell me, you know, if you've any idea at all where he went.' He spoke now with a quiet authority, and a flush arose in the woman's cheeks.

'It's nothing really. Just that he – he left at the same time as someone else. That's all.'

'And it was fairly easy to put two and two together?'

She nodded. 'Yes. You see, he left Oxford the same week as Mrs Josephs.'

Chapter Eight

Morse left the church and strolled over to the snack bar.

'One coffee, please,' he said to the girl lounging by the pay-desk.

'If you go an' si' down, one of the girls'll come.'

'Oh.' It all seemed a roundabout business.

He sat and stared abstractedly through the large window, flecked now with drizzle, and watched the people walking to and fro along Cornmarket. Immediately opposite him, fencing in the church and the churchyard, were the sharply pointed, black-painted railings of St Frideswide's, against which a bearded, damp-looking tramp was leaning uncertainly, a bottle of something hanging loosely in his left hand.

'Order, please?' It was the same waitress.

'You just had it,' snapped Morse.

'I'm sorry, sir, bu'— '

'Forget it, luv.'

He left and walked back across the street.

'How goes it, brother?'

The tramp looked at Morse warily through an incongruous pair of dark sun-glasses: unsolicited interest in his well-being was quite clearly no everyday occurrence. 'Could do wiv a cup o' tea, guv.'

Morse pushed a couple of ten-pence pieces into a surprisingly clean hand. 'Do you usually stand here?'

'Nah. Usually be'ind Brasenose College. Makes a change, though, don't it?'

'Some nice kind people come out of the church, do they?'

'Sometimes.'

'You know the minister here?'

'Nah. Tell yer to push off, like as not, this one. Knew the other one, though. Real gent he was, guv. Sometimes 'e'd take yer down to the vicarage an' give yer a real square meal, 'e would.'

'Is he the one who died?'

The tramp looked at Morse with what could have been a glint of suspicion behind the dark lenses, and took a swig on the bottle. 'Christ, you can say that again, mister.' He shuffled along the railings towards Carfax, and was gone.

Morse crossed the road yet again, and walked past the snack bar, past a well-stocked bicycle-shop, past the cinema, and then turned left into the curving sweep of Beaumont Street. Momentarily he debated between the Ashmolean, just opposite on his right, and the Randolph, immediately on his left. It wasn't a fair contest.

The cocktail-bar was already quite full as Morse waited rather impatiently for a group of Americans to sort out their gins and tarnics. The barmaid wore a low-cut dress and Morse watched with what he told himself was a fascinated indifference as she finally leaned forward over the beer-pump to pull his order. She was too young, though – no more than twenty-odd – and Morse was beginning to formulate the philosophy that men were attracted to women of roughly their own age – well, give or take ten years or so either way.

He sat down, savoured his beer, and took out cutting number three from his pocket. It was dated Wednesday, 19 October.

TRAGIC FALL FROM CHURCH TOWER

Yesterday morning the Reverend Lionel Lawson fell to his death from the tower of St Frideswide's Church in Cornmarket. Only ten minutes earlier he had conducted the regular 7.30 a.m. Communion Service, and two members of the congregation were among the first to discover the tragedy.

The church tower, formerly a favourite viewing-point for tourists, has been closed to the public for the last two years as signs of crumbling have become evident in the stone fabric on the north side. But the tower was not considered unsafe, and only a week ago workmen had been up to check the leads.

Mr Lawson, a bachelor, aged 41, had been vicar of St Frideswide's for almost eleven years. He will be remembered above all, perhaps, for his social work, since in addition to his deep involvement with the church's flourishing youth activities he invariably took a compassionate interest in the plight of the homeless, and there can be few regular down-and-outs in Oxford who have not at some time or another enjoyed his hospitality.

As a churchman he made no apologies for his High Anglican views, and although his strongly voiced hostility towards the ordination of women was not universally popular his large and loyal congregation will mourn the death of a dear friend and pastor. He studied theology at Christ's College, Cambridge, and later at St Stephen's House, Oxford.

Only last month Mr H. A. Josephs, churchwarden of St Frideswide's, was found stabbed to death in the church vestry.

Mm. Morse looked at the last sentence again and wondered why the reporter had deemed it his duty to stick it in. Wasn't there a bit too much of that *post hoc, propter hoc* suspicion about it? Yet a murder followed very shortly afterwards by a suicide was by no means uncommon, and the reporter would hardly have been the only one to suspect some causal connection. For if Lawson had somehow managed to murder Josephs, then it was surely only honourable and proper for a servant of the Lord to be stricken so sorely in conscience as to chuck himself off the nearest or most convenient pinnacle, was it not?

Morse drained his beer, fiddled in his pockets for some more change, and looked vaguely around him. A woman had just walked up to the bar and he studied her back view with growing interest. A good deal nearer his own age than the barmaid, certainly: black-leather, knee-length boots; slim figure; tight-belted, light-fawn raincoat; spotted red headscarf. Nice. On her own, too.

Morse sauntered up beside her and heard her order a dry Martini; and the thought crossed his mind that all he had to do was to pay for her drink, ask her over to his lonely corner, and talk of this and that in a quiet, unassuming, intelligent, fascinating, masterly way. And then – who knows? But a middle-aged customer had risen from his seat and clapped a hand on her shoulder.

'I'll get that Ruth, love. You sit down.'

Miss Rawlinson unfastened her headscarf and smiled. Then, as she appeared to notice Morse for the first time, the smile was gone. She nodded – almost curtly, it seemed – and turned away.

After his third pint, Morse left the cocktail-bar and from the foyer rang through to the City Police Station. But Chief Inspector Bell was on holiday, he was told – in Spain.

It was a long time since Morse had undertaken any extended exercise, and he decided on impulse to walk up to north Oxford. Only half an hour, if he stepped it out. As if to deride his decision, bus after bus passed him: Cutteslowe buses, Kidlington buses, and the eternally empty Park and Ride buses, subsidised at huge cost by the City Fathers in the vain hope of persuading shoppers to leave their cars on the outskirts. But Morse kept walking.

As he came up to the Marston Ferry cross-roads he watched, almost mesmerised, as a north-bound car pulled out of the inside lane into the path of an overtaking motor-cycle. The rider was thrown slithering to the other side of the road where his white helmet hit the kerb with a sickening thwack, and where the near-side wheel of a south-bound lorry, for all its squealing brake-power, ran over the man's pelvis with an audible crunch.

Others on that scene showed, perhaps for the first time in their lives, a desperate courage born of the hour: figures knelt by the dying man, and coats were laid over his crushed body; a young man with greasy shoulder-length hair took upon himself the duties of a traffic policeman; a doctor was on his way from the Summertown Health Centre on the corner; the ambulance and police were already being summoned.

But Morse felt his stomach tighten and twist in a spasm of pain. A light sweat had broken out on his forehead, and he thought he was going to vomit as he averted his eyes and hurried away. The sense of his inadequacy and cowardice disgusted him, but the physical sickness prowling in his bowels drove him on, farther and farther up the road, past the Summertown shops, and at last to his home. Even the Levite had taken a quick look before passing by on the other side.

What it was about road accidents that threw him so completely off balance, Morse had never quite been able to understand. Many a time he had been on the scene of a murder, and examined a brutally mutilated corpse. With an ugly distaste, certainly; but with nothing worse. Why was it, then? Perhaps it was something to do with the difference between death and the *process* of dying, certainly of dying in a writhing agony after a road accident. Yes, it was the *accidental* angle of things; the flukey, fortuitous nature of it all; the 'if only' of being just a few yards, just a few inches even, from safety; of being just a second, just a fraction of a second, earlier – or later. It was all that Lucretian business about the random concourse of the atoms, hurtling headlong through the boundless void, colliding occasionally like billiard balls, colliding like a car against a motor-bike. All so pointless, somehow; all so cruelly haphazard. Occasionally Morse considered the ever-decreasing possibility of having a family himself, and he knew that he might be able to face some terrible illness in those he loved; but never an accident.

In the distance sounded the urgent two-toned siren of an ambulance, like some demented mother wailing for her children.

Morse picked up his one pint of milk and shut the door of his bachelor flat behind him. Not the best of starts to a holiday! He selected Richard Strauss's *Vier Letzte Lieder*; but a sudden thought flashed through his mind, and he put the record down again. In the Randolph he had quickly read through cutting number four, the newspaper account of the inquest on Lawson; little of interest there, he'd thought. But had he been right? He read it through again now. The poor fellow had obviously been a terrible sight, his body violently crushed by his fall, his skull – Yes! That is what had clicked in Morse's mind as he had lifted the lid of the record-player. If he himself had been unwilling to look at the face of a dying motor-cyclist, had those two witnesses looked as closely as they should have done at that sadly shattered skull? All he needed now was a little information from the official report of the coroner's hearing; and, knowing the coroner very well, he could get that little information straightaway – that very afternoon.

Ten minutes later he was asleep.

Chapter Nine

Avoiding the man's look, Ruth Rawlinson finished her second Martini and stared at the slice of lemon at the bottom of her glass.

'Another?'

'No, I mustn't. Really. I've had two already.'

'Go on! Enjoy yourself! We only live once, you know.'

Ruth smiled sadly. It was just the sort of thing her mother kept saying: 'You're missing out on life, Ruthie dear. Why don't you try to meet more people? Have a good time?' Her mother! Her grumbling, demanding, crippled mother. But still her mother; and she, Ruth, her only child: forty-one years old (almost forty-two), a virgin until so recently, and then not memorably deflowered.

'Same again, then?' He was on his feet, her glass held high in his hand.

Why *not*? She felt pleasantly warm somewhere deep down inside her, and she could always go to bed for a few hours when she got home. Monday afternoon was her mother's weekly bridge session, and nothing short of a nuclear attack on north Oxford could ever disturb those four mean old women as they grubbed for penalty points and overtricks at the small green-baize table in the back room.

'You'll have me drunk if you're not careful,' she said.

'What do you think I'm trying to do?'

She knew him fairly well now, and she watched him as he stood at the bar in his expensively cut suit: a few years older than herself, with three teenage children and a charming, intelligent, trusting wife. And he wanted *her*.

Yet for some reason she didn't want him. She couldn't quite bear the thought of being intimate with him – not (she reminded herself) that she really knew what intimacy was all about. . . .

Her eyes wandered round the room once more, in particular to a point in the farthest corner of the room. But Morse had gone now, and for some unfathomable reason she knew she had wanted him to stay – just to *be* there. She'd recognised him, of course, as soon as she'd walked in, and she had been conscious of his presence all the time. Could she get into bed with *him*? It was his eyes that fascinated her; bluey-grey, cold – and yet somehow vulnerable and lost. She told herself not to be so silly; told herself she was getting drunk.

As she slowly sipped the third Martini, her companion was busily writing something on the back of a beer-mat.

'Here we are, Ruth. Be honest with me – please!'

She looked down at what he had written:

> Tick the box which
> in your opinion is nearest
> to your inclinations. Will
> you let me take you to bed
> this week?   ☐
> next week?   ☐
> this year?   ☐
> next year?   ☐
> sometime?   ☐
> never?   ☐

It made her smile, but she shook her head slowly and helplessly. 'I can't answer that. You know I can't.'

'You mean it's "never"?'

'I didn't say that. But – but you *know* what I mean. You're married, and I know your wife. I respect her. Surely— '

'Just tick one of the boxes. That's all.'

'But— '

'But you'll disappoint me if you tick the last one, is that it? Go on, then. Disappoint me. But be honest about it, Ruth. At least I shall know where I stand.'

'I like you – you know that. But— '

'You've got plenty of choice.'

'What if none of the answers is the right one?'

'One of 'em must be right.'

'No.' She took out her own pen and wrote in a single word before 'sometime': the word 'perhaps'.

Unlike Morse, she didn't sleep that afternoon. She felt fresh and alive, and would have done a few odd jobs in the garden but for the persistent drizzle. Instead she revised the lines for her part in the play. Friday was looming frighteningly near, and the cast was rehearsing at 7.30 p.m. that evening. Not that a tuppenny-ha'penny play at a church social was all that grand; but she was never happy about doing even the smallest things half-heartedly – and they always had a good audience.

Morse himself woke up with a shudder and a grunt at 3 p.m., and slowly focused upon life once more. The newspaper cuttings still lay on the arm of his chair, and he collected them together and put them back in their envelope. Earlier in the day he had allowed things to get out of perspective. But no longer. He was on holiday, and he was going to *have* a holiday. From his bookshelf he hooked out a thick volume; and just as the Romans used to do it with the Sibylline Books, just as the fundamentalists still do it with the Holy Scriptures – so did Morse do it with the *AA Hotels of Britain*. He closed his eyes, opened the book at random, and stuck his index finger half-way down the left-hand page. There she was. Derwentwater: *Swiss Lodore Hotel*. Keswick, three miles S. along the. . . . He rang the number immediately. Yes, they had a single room with private bath. How long for? Four or five nights, perhaps. All right. He'd be leaving straightaway, and be there about – oh, about nine or ten. Good.

Evesham – about an hour, if he was lucky. Along the old Worcester Road. M5 and M6 – 80 m.p.h. in the fast lane. Easy! He'd be there in time for a slap-up meal and a bottle of red wine. Lovely. *That's* what holidays were all about.

Chapter Ten

The Reverend Keith Meiklejohn exuded a sort of holy enthusiasm as he stood at the door of the church hall. Obviously there was going to be a big audience, and in between the unctuous Good evenings, how nice of you to comes, he debated the wisdom of fetching some of the old chairs from the store-room. It was only 7.20 p.m., but already the hall was two-thirds full. He knew why, of course: it was the Sunday School infant classes' tap-dance troupe, with its gilt-edged guarantee of attracting all the mums and aunts and grandmas. 'Hello, Mrs Walsh-Atkins. How very nice of you to come. Just a few seats left near the front. . . . ' He despatched two reluctant choirboys for the extra chairs, and was ready with his beam of ecclesiastical bonhomie for the next arrival. 'Good evening, sir. How nice of you to come. Are you a visitor to Oxford or—?'

'No, I live here.'

The newcomer walked into the hall and sat down at the back, a slightly sour expression on his face. He gave five pence to the pretty pig-tailed girl who came up to him and stuck the programme in his pocket. What a day! Almost six hours from Keswick to the Evesham exit: single-lane traffic north of Stoke; a multiple pile-up just after Birmingham, with all lanes closed for almost an hour on the south-bound carriageway; flood warnings flashing for the last thirty miles and the juggernaut lorries churning up spray like speedboats. . . . And what a so-called holiday! On fine days (he had little doubt) the view from his bedroom at the Swiss Lodore would have been most beautiful; but the mist had driven down from the encircling hills, and it was as much as he could do to spot the grass on the lawn below his window, with its white chairs and tables – all deserted. Some of his fellow-guests had taken to their cars and driven (presumably) in search of some less-bedraggled scenery; but the majority had just sat around and read paperback thrillers, played cards, gone swimming in the heated indoor pool, eaten, drunk, talked intermittently, and generally managed to look rather less miserable than Morse did. He could find no passably attractive women over-anxious to escape their hovering husbands, and the few who sat unattended in the cocktail-lounge were either too plain or too old. In his bedroom Morse found a leaflet on which was printed Robert Southey's 'How the Waters Come Down at Lodore'; but he felt that even a poet laureate had seldom sunk to such banality. And anyway, after three days, Morse knew only too well how the waters came down at Lodore: they came down in bucketfuls, slanting incessantly in sharp lines from a leaden sky.

On Friday (it was 7 April) *The Times* was brought into his room with his early-morning tea; and after looking at the week-end weather forecast he decided to leave immediately after breakfast. It was as he was taking out his cheque-book at the reception-desk that the folded white leaflet fluttered to the floor: he had pocketed it absentmindedly from the literature set out on the table at the entrance to St Frideswide's, but it was only now that he read it.

CONCERT

At the Church Hall, St Aldates
Friday, April 7th, at 7.30 p.m.
TAP-DANCE TROUPE (Sunday School)
GILBERT & SULLIVAN MEDLEY (Church Choir)
A VICTORIAN MELODRAMA (Drama Group)
Entrance Fee 20p. Programme 5p.
ALL WELCOME
(Proceeds in aid of the Tower Restoration Fund)

It was that last line, pregnant with possibilities, that had monopolised Morse's thoughts as he drove the Jaguar south. Were the crenellations really crumbling after all? *Had* they crumbled, when Lawson looked his last over the familiar landmarks of the city? Whenever possible, juries were keen to steer away from 'suicide' verdicts, and if the tower had been at all unsafe the point would have been a crucial one. What Morse really needed was the coroner's report: it would all be there. And it was to the coroner's office that Morse had immediately driven when he finally reached Oxford at 4.30 p.m.

The report, apart from the detailed descriptions of Lawson's multiple mutilations, was vaguer than Morse had hoped, with no mention whatsoever of the parapet from which Lawson had plummeted to earth. Yet there was one section of the report that firmly gripped his interest, and he read it through again. 'Mrs Emily Walsh-Atkins, after giving formal evidence of identification, said that she had remained alone for some minutes in the church after the service. She then waited for about five minutes outside the church, where she had arranged to be picked up by taxi: the service had finished slightly earlier than usual. At about 8.10 a.m. she heard a terrible thud in the churchyard and had looked round to find Lawson's body spread-eagled on the railings. Fortunately two police officers had soon appeared on the scene and Mr Morris' (Morris!) 'had taken her back inside the church to sit down and recover. . . . ' Morse knew that he would have little mental rest until he had seen Mrs W.-A., and it was that lady who was the immediate cause of his attendance at the Church Concert. (Was she the *only* reason, Morse?) He had just missed her at the Home for Ageing Gentlefolk, but they knew where she had gone.

Meiklejohn had finished his long-winded, oily introduction, the lights had been switched off, and now the stage-curtains were jerkily wound back to reveal the Tap-Dance Troupe in all its bizarre glory. For Morse the whole thing was embarrassingly amusing; and he was quite unprepared for the wild applause which greeted the final unsynchronised kneelings of the eleven little girls, plumed plastic headgear and all, who for three minutes or so had braved inadequate rehearsal, innate awkwardness, and the appallingly incompetent accompaniment of the pianist. To make matters worse, the troupe had started with a complement of twelve, but one small child had turned left instead of right at a crucial point in the choreography, and had promptly fled to the wings, her face collapsing in tearful misery. Yet still the audience clapped and clapped, and was not appeased until the appearance of the troupe's instructress, alias the piano-player, leading by the hand the unfortunate, but now shyly smiling, little deserter – the latter greeted by all as if she were a prima ballerina from the Sadler's Wells.

The Gilbert and Sullivan selections were excellently sung, and Morse realised that the St Frideswide's choir contained some first-rate talent. This time, fortunately, the piano was in the hands of an infinitely more able executant – Mr Sharpe, no less, former deputy to Mr Morris (that name again!). Morris . . . the man who had been on the scene when Josephs was murdered; had been on the scene, too, when Lawson was – when Lawson was found. Surely, surely, it shouldn't be at all difficult to trace him? Or to trace Mrs Brenda Josephs? They must be somewhere; must be earning some money; must have insurance numbers; must have a house. . . . With clinical precision the choir cut off the last chord from the finale of *The Mikado*, and their turn was complete – greeted by appreciative if comparatively short-lived applause.

It took a good five minutes for the Victorian melodrama to materialise; minutes during which could be heard the squeaking and bumping of furniture, during which the curtains were twice prematurely half opened, and during which Morse once more looked through the coroner's digest on Lawson's death. There was this fellow Thomas's evidence, for example: 'He had just parked his car in St Giles' and was walking down towards Broad Street when he noticed someone on the tower of St Frideswide's. He could not recall seeing anyone standing there before, but it was not unusual to see people looking out over Oxford from St Mary's in the High, or from Carfax tower. He thought that the figure was dressed in black, looking down, his head leaning over the parapet. . . . ' That was all, really. Only later had he heard of the morning's tragedy and had reluctantly rung up the police – at his wife's suggestion. Not much there, but the man must have been the very last person (Morse supposed) to see Lawson alive. Or was he? He might just have been the first – no, the second – person to see Lawson *dead*. Morse found the key words again: 'looking down, his head leaning over the parapet. . . .' How high *were* those parapets? No more than three feet or so, surely. And why bring Lawson's head into it? Why not just 'leaning over the parapet'? And why 'looking down'? Was a man about to leap to his death likely to be all that worried about the place he was going to land? A minister, surely – more than most of his fellow-mortals – might be expected to seek a little consolation from more ethereal realms, whatever the depths of his despair. But if . . . if Lawson had been dead already; if someone had—

The melodrama was under way at last, and in Morse's view a more crudely amateurish production could seldom have merited a public presentation. The play appeared to have been chosen to embrace the largest possible cast, and to allow to all of its participants the briefest possible exposure on the boards, in order to minimise their breathtaking incompetences. The bearded one-armed hero, who at least had learned his lines and spoke them audibly, clumped around in a pair of squeaky army boots, and at one point conducted a crucial telephone conversation by speaking into the ear-piece – of an incongruously modern-looking instrument at that; whilst one of the numerous housemaids was every other line reduced to referring to a copy of her part pasted on the underside of her dustpan. The only feature which prevented the whole thing from degenerating into a farcical shambles was the performance of the heroine herself, a young blonde who acted with a charm and sophistication hopelessly at variance with the pathetically inadequate crew around her. She appeared to know everyone else's part, and covered their lapses and stumbles with impressive aplomb. She even managed, at one stage, to prevent one of the butlers (blind fool! thought Morse) from tripping over an intervening chair as he carried in her ladyship's tea. Mercifully many of the lines (as originally written) must have been extremely amusing, and even voiced by these clowns could elicit a little polite laughter; and when the final curtain drew its veil over the proceedings there seemed to Morse not the slightest sign of embarrassed relief amongst the audience. Perhaps all church concerts were the same.

The Vicar had earlier announced that tea would be served at the end of the entertainment, and Morse felt certain that Mrs W.-A. would not be leaving without a cup. All he had to do was find out which one she was. He looked around in vain for Miss Rawlinson, but it seemed clear that she'd given the evening a miss – enough of a penance, no doubt, her scrubbing the pews. But he felt a certain disappointment. . . . People were leaving the hall fairly quickly now, but Morse decided to wait a minute or two. He took out his programme and looked at it vaguely, but with no real purpose other than that of seeming not to be lonely.

'I hope you'll have a cup of tea with us?' Even at this late stage Meiklejohn was not neglecting his pastoral duties.

Tea? It had never occurred to Morse that he might be drinking tea at 9 p.m. 'Yes; thank you. I wonder if you happen to know a Mrs Walsh-Atkins. I want— '

'Yes, yes. This way. Wonderful concert, wasn't it?'

Morse mumbled inaudibly and followed his guide into the crowded vestibule where a stout lady was coaxing a dark-brown liquid from a formidable urn. Morse took his place in the queue and listened to the conversation of the two women in front of him.

'You know, it's the fourth time now he's been in one of them. His dad would have been ever so proud of him.'

'No one would ever suspect he was blind, would they? Coming on the way he does and all that.'

'It's lots of rehearsal that does it, you know. You have to sort of picture where everything is— '

'Yes. You really must be proud of him, Mrs Kinder.'

'They've asked him to be in the next one, anyway, so he must be all right, mustn't he?'

So the poor devil *had* been blind after all. And learning a part and stepping out on to the stage had probably been about as much of an ordeal as for a sighted person walking through a swamp of crocodiles. Morse suddenly felt very moved, and very humbled. When it came to his turn, he slipped a fifty-pence piece on to the tea-money plate, and hoped that nobody had noticed. He felt oddly out of place there. These were good people, who rejoiced in the simple ties of family and Christian fellowship; who thought of God as a father, and who never in a month of Sabbaths could begin to understand the aberrations of the new theology which thought of Him (if it thought of Him at all) as the present participle of the verb 'to be'. Morse sipped his tea self-consciously, and once more took out his programme and looked for the name of Her Ladyship's butler, whose mother (with what sweet justification!) was feeling so happy and proud. But once again he was interrupted. Meiklejohn was at his shoulder, and with him a diminutive old lady munching a digestive biscuit.

'Mr – er?'

'Morse.'

'You said you wanted to meet Mrs Walsh-Atkins?'

Morse stood above her, acutely conscious of her smallness, and suggested they should sit down back in the hall. He explained who he was, why he was there, and what he wanted to know; and she readily told him of her own part in that dreadful day's events when she'd found Lawson dashed to pieces from the tower, repeating virtually verbatim the words she had used at the inquest.

Nothing! Morse had learned nothing. Yet he thanked her politely and asked if he could fetch her another cup of tea.

'One's enough for me these days, Inspector. But I must have left my umbrella somewhere. If you would be kind enough to. . . . '

Morse felt his scalp tingling in the old familiar way. They were seated at a small table at the back of the hall, and there was the umbrella, large as life, lying diagonally across it. There could be little doubt about it: *the old lady must be going blind.*

'Do you mind me asking how old you are, Mrs Walsh-Atkins?'

'Can you keep a secret, Inspector?'

'Yes.'

'So can I,' she whispered.

Whether Morse's decision to patronise the cocktail-lounge of the Randolph was determined by his thirst, or by some wayward wish to find out if Miss Rawlinson might be there, he didn't stop to think. But he recognised no one, left after only one pint, and caught a bus outside the Taylorian. Back home, he poured himself a large neat whisky and put on *Vier Letzte Lieder*. Marvellous. 'Melismatic', as it said on the sleeve. . . .

It was time for an early night, and he hung up his jacket in the hallway. The programme stuck out of one of the pockets and, third time lucky, he opened it and read it.

'Her Ladyship's Butler – Mr John Kinder.' And then his pulse raced as he looked at the top of the cast: 'Her Ladyship, the Hon. Amelia Barker-Barker – Miss Ruth Rawlinson.'

Chapter Eleven

Mediums and clairvoyants claim enhanced scope for their talents if they can be physically present in a room where the absent ones – the missing or the plain dead – may have left a few stray emanations behind. Murderers, likewise, have the reputation of nursing an uncontrollable urge to revisit the scene of death, and on Sunday morning Morse found himself wondering whether the murderer of Josephs had ever set foot in St Frideswide's again since the day of his crime. He thought that the answer was probably 'yes', and it was one of the very few positive thoughts he had managed to generate since Friday evening. Somehow his mind had gone completely stale, and on the Saturday he had firmly resolved to abandon all idea of further investigation into a mysterious affair which was none of his business anyway. In the morning he had consulted the Sibyl once more, but had drawn the line at Inverness. In the afternoon he had wasted two idle hours in front of the television set watching the racing from Doncaster. He was restless and bored: there were so many books he could read, so many records he could play – and yet he could summon up no enthusiasm for anything. What *did* he want? His listless mood persisted through to Sunday morning, when not even the few erotic titbits in the *News of the World* could cheer him. He sprawled gloomily in his armchair, his eyes vaguely scanning the multi-coloured spines along the bookshelves. Baudelaire might match his mood, perhaps? What was that line about the prince in 'Les Fleurs du Mal'? 'Riche, mais impuissant, jeune et pourtant très vieux. . . . ' And quite suddenly Morse felt better. Bloody nonsense! He was neither impotent nor senile – far from it! It was time for action.

He rang the number and she answered.

'Hello?'

'Miss Rawlinson?'

'Speaking.'

'You may not remember me. I – I met you in St Frideswide's last Monday.'

'I remember.'

'I was – er – thinking of going to church this morning— '

'Our church, you mean?'

'Yes.'

'You'd better get a move on – it starts at half-past ten.'

'Oh. I see. Well – er – thank you very much.'

'You're very interested in us all of a sudden, Inspector.' There was a suggestion of friendly amusement in her voice, and Morse wanted to keep her on the phone.

'Did you know I came to the social on Friday evening?'

'Of course.' Morse felt a silly juvenile joy about that 'of course'. Keep going, lad!

'I – er – I didn't see you afterwards. In fact I didn't realise that it was you in the play.'

'Amazing what a blonde wig does, isn't it?'

'Who is it?' Someone called behind her voice.

'Pardon?' said Morse.

'It's all right. That was my mother – asking who you are.'

'Oh, I see.'

'Well, as I say, you'd better hurry up if you're going— '

'Are *you* going? Perhaps I could give you— '

'No, not this morning. Mother's had one of her asthma attacks, and I can't leave her.'

'Oh.' Morse hid his disappointment beneath a cheerful fare-well, and said 'Bugger it!' as he cradled the phone. *He* was going, though. It wasn't Ruth Rawlinson he wanted to see. He just wanted to get the feel of the place – to pick up a few of those stray emanations. He told himself that it didn't matter two hoots whether the Rawlinson woman was there or not.

Looking back on his first church attendance for a decade, Morse decided that it was quite an experience. St Frideswide's must, he thought, be about as 'spikey' as they come in the Anglican var-ieties. True, there was no Peter's Pence at the back of the church, no bulletin from the pulpit proclaiming the infallibility of his Holiness; but in other respects there seemed little that separated the church from the Roman fold. There'd been a sermon, all right, devoted to St Paul's humourless denunciation of the lusts of the flesh, but the whole service had really centred round the Mass. It had not started all that well for Morse who, two minutes late, had inadvertently seated himself in the pew reserved for the churchwarden, and this had necessitated an awkward, whispered exchange as the people knelt to confess their wrongdoings. Fortu-nately, from his vantage-point at the rear, Morse was able to sit and stand and kneel in concert with the rest, although many of the crossings and genuflections proved equally beyond his reflexes as his inclinations. What amazed him more than anything was the number of the cast assembled around the altar, each purposefully pursuing his part: the celebrant, the deacon, the sub-deacon, the incense-swinger and the boat-boy, the two acolytes and the four torch-bearers, and conducting them all a youngish, mournful-faced master of ceremonies, his hands sticking out horizontally before him in a posture of perpetual prayer. It was almost like a floor-show, with everyone so well trained: bowing, crossing, kneeling, rising, with a synchronised discipline which (as Morse saw it) could profitably have been emulated by the Tap-Dance Troupe. To these manoeuvres the equally well-disciplined congregation would match its own reactions, suddenly sitting, as suddenly on its feet again, and occasionally giving mouth to mournful responses. The woman seated next to Morse had soon spotted him for the green-horn that he was, and was continually thrusting the appropriate page of the proceedings under his nose. She herself sang in a shrill soprano, and was so refined in her diction that the long 'o' vowels issued forth as bleating 'ew's: thus, all the 'O Lords' became 'You Lords', and three times at the start of the service, whilst Meiklejohn walked briskly up and down the aisles sprinkling everything in sight with holy water, she had implored the Almighty to wash her from her sins and make her waiter yea waiter than snew. But there was one thing in Morse's favour – he knew most of the hymns; and at one point he thought he almost managed to drown the 'Hewly Hewly Hewly' on his right. And he learned something, too. From Meiklejohn's notices for the week's forthcoming attractions, it was clear that this Mass business was rather more complicated than he'd imagined. There must be three types, it seemed – 'low', 'high' and 'solemn'; and if, as Morse suspected, the low variety wasn't all that posh, if no choir was involved – no organist even? – then what in heaven's name was Morris doing in church when the unhappy Lawson dashed himself to pieces from the tower? People perhaps did sometimes go to church because they wanted to but. . . . Anyway, it might be worthwhile finding out a bit more about those different masses. And there was something else; something very suggestive indeed. With the exception of Morse himself, all the congregation partook of the blessed bread and the blessed wine, ushered quietly and firmly to the chancel-rails by that same churchwarden who had so nearly lost his seat, and who – doubtless by venerable tradition – *was himself the very last to receive the sacrament*. Josephs had been churchwarden. Josephs must have been the last to kneel at the chancel-rails on the evening of his death. Josephs had drunk some of the communion wine that same night. And Josephs – so the pathologist said – had finished up with some very queer things in his stomach. Was it possible? Was it possible that Josephs had been poisoned at the altar? From his observation of the final part of the ritual, it was clear to Morse that any celebrant with a chalice in his hands could wreak enormous havoc if he had the inclination to do so, for when he'd finished *he could get rid of every scrap of evidence*. Nor did he need any excuse for this, for it was part of the drill: rinse the cup and wipe it clean and stick it in the cupboard till the next time. Yes. It would be tricky, of course, with all those other stage-hands standing around, like they were now; but on the evening of Josephs' murder, the cast must surely have been very much smaller. Again, it was something worth looking into. There was another snag, though, wasn't there? It seemed that the celebrant himself was called upon to drain the dregs that were left in the chalice, and to do it in front of the whole congregation. But couldn't he just pretend to do that? Pour it down the piscina later? Or, again, there might have been nothing left in the chalice at all. . . .

There were so very many possibilities . . . and Morse's fancies floated steeple-high as he walked out of the cool church into the sunlit reach of Cornmarket.

Chapter Twelve

It was some relief for Morse to recognise the fair countenance of Reason once more, and she greeted him serenely when he woke, clear-headed, on Monday morning, and told him that it would be no bad idea to have a quiet look at the problem itself before galloping off towards a solution. Basically there were only two possibilities: either Lawson had killed Josephs, and thereafter committed suicide in a not surprising mood of remorse; or else some unknown hand had killed Josephs and then compounded his crime by adding Lawson to his list. Of these alternatives, the first was considerably the more probable; especially so if Josephs had in some way been a threat to Lawson, if the dagger found in Josephs' back had belonged to Lawson, and if Lawson himself had betrayed signs of anxiety or distress in the weeks preceding

Josephs' death, as well as in the days that followed it. The trouble was that Morse had no one to talk to. Yet someone, he felt sure, knew a very great deal about his three 'ifs', and at 9.45 a.m. he found himself knocking rather hesitantly on the door of number 14 Manning Terrace. Such hesitancy was attributable to two causes: the first, his natural diffidence in seeming on the face of it to be so anxious to seek out the company of the fair Ruth Rawlinson; the second, the factual uncertainty that he was actually knocking on the right door, for there were two of them, side by side; the one to the left marked 14B, the other 14A. Clearly the house had been divided – fairly recently by the look of it – with one of the doors (Morse presumed) leading directly to the upper storey, the other to the ground floor.

'It's open,' shouted a voice behind 14A. 'I can't get any farther.'

For once, Sod's Law had been inoperative, and he had chosen right. Two steps led up to the narrow carpeted passage which served as a hallway (the staircase was immediately behind the boarded-up wall to the left, and the conversion had left little room for manoeuvre here), and at the top of these steps sat Mrs Alice Rawlinson in her wheelchair, a rubber-tipped walking-stick held firmly across her lap.

'What d'you want?' Her keen eyes looked up at him sharply.

'I'm sorry to bother you – Mrs Rawlinson, isn't it?'

'I said what d'you want, Inspector.'

Morse's face must have betrayed his astonishment, and the old lady read his thoughts for him. 'Ruthie told me all about you.'

'Oh. I just wondered if— '

'No, she's not. Come in!' She worked her chair round in an expertly economical two-point turn. 'Close the door behind you.'

Morse obeyed quietly, and found himself pushed brusquely aside as he tried to help her through the door at the end of the passage. She waved him to an upright armchair in the neatly furnished sitting-room, and finally came to rest herself only about four feet in front of him. The preliminaries were now completed, and she launched into the attack immediately.

'If you want to cart my daughter off for a dirty week-end, you can't! We'd better get that straight from the start.'

'But Mrs Raw— ' He was silenced by a dangerously close wave of the stick. (Belligerent old bitch! thought Morse.)

'I disapprove of many aspects of the youth of today – young men like yourself, I mean – especially their intolerable lack of manners. But I think they're quite right about one thing. Do you know what that is?'

'Look, Mrs Raw— ' The rubber ferule was no more than three inches from his nose, and his voice broke off in mid-sentence.

'They've got enough sense to have a bit of sex together before they get married. You agree?'

Morse nodded a feeble acquiescence.

'If you're going to live with someone for fifty years— ' She shook her head at the prospect. 'Not that I was married for fifty years. . . . ' The sharp voice had drifted a few degrees towards a more wistful tone, but recovered immediately. 'As I say, though. You can't have her. I need her and she's my daughter. I have the prior call.'

'I do assure you, Mrs Rawlinson, I hadn't the slightest intention of— '

'She's had men before, you know.'

'I'm not sur— '

'She was a very lovely girl, was my Ruthie.' The words were more quietly spoken, but the eyes remained shrewd and calculating. 'She's not a spring chicken any more, though.'

Morse decided it was wise to hold his peace. The old girl was going ga-ga.

'You know what her trouble is?' For a distasteful moment Morse thought her mind must be delving into realms of haemorrhoids and body-odour; but she sat there glaring at him, expecting an answer.

Yes, he knew full well what Ruth Rawlinson's trouble was. Too true, he did. Her trouble was that she had to look after this embittered old battle-axe, day in and day out.

'No,' he said. 'You tell me.'

Her lips curled harshly. 'You're lying to me, Inspector. You know her trouble as well as I do.'

Morse nodded. 'You're right. I don't think I could stick you for very long.'

Now her smile was perfectly genuine. 'You know, you're beginning to sound like the man Ruthie said you were.' (Perhaps, thought Morse, she's not so ga-ga after all?)

'You're a bit formidable sometimes, aren't you?'

'All the time.'

'Would Ruth have married – but for you?'

'She's had her chances – though I didn't think much of her choices.'

'Real chances?'

Her face grew more serious. 'Certainly one.'

'Well.' Morse made as if to rise, but got no farther.

'What was *your* mother like?'

'Loving and kind. I often think of her.'

'Ruthie would have made a good mother.'

'Not too old now, is she?'

'Forty-two tomorrow.'

'Hope you'll bake her a cake,' muttered Morse.

'What?' The eyes blazed now. 'You don't understand, either, do you? Bake? Cook? How can I do anything like that? I can't even get to the front door.'

'Do you try?'

'You're getting impertinent, Inspector. It's time you went.' But as Morse rose she relented. 'No, I'm sorry. Please sit down again. I don't get many visitors. Don't deserve 'em, do I?'

'Does your daughter get many visitors?'

'Why do you ask that?' The voice was sharp again.

'Just trying to be pally, that's all.' Morse had had his fill of the old girl, but her answer riveted him to the chair.

'You're thinking of Josephs, aren't you?'

No, he wasn't thinking of Josephs. 'Yes, I was,' he said, as flatly as his excitement would allow.

'He wasn't her sort.'

'And he had a wife.'

She snorted. 'What's that got to do with it? Just because you're a bachelor yourself— '

'You know that?'

'I know a lot of things.'

'Do you know who killed Josephs?'

She shook her head. 'I don't know who killed Lawson, either.'

'I do, Mrs Rawlinson. He killed himself. You'll find the information in the coroner's report. It's just the same as cricket, you know: if the umpire says you're out, you're out, and you can check it up in the papers next morning.'

'I don't like cricket.'

'Did you like Josephs?'

'No. And I didn't like Lawson, either. He was a homosexual, you know.'

'Really? I hadn't heard of any legal conviction.'

'You're surely not as naïve as you sound, Inspector?'

'No,' said Morse, 'I'm not.'

'I hate homosexuals.' The stick lifted menacingly, gripped tight in hands grown strong from long years in a wheelchair. 'I'd willingly strangle the lot of 'em.'

'And I'd willingly add you to the list of suspects, Mrs Rawlinson, but I'm afraid I can't. You see, if someone killed Lawson, as you're suggesting, that someone must have gone up the church tower.'

'Unless Lawson was killed in the church and *someone else* carried him up there.'

It was an idea; and Morse nodded slowly, wondering why he hadn't thought of it himself.

'I'm afraid I shall have to kick you out, Inspector. It's my bridge day, and I always spend the morning brushing up on a few practice hands.' She was winning every trick here, too, and Morse acknowledged the fact.

Ruth was fixing the lock on her bicycle when she looked up to see Morse standing by the door and her mother sitting at the top of the steps behind him.

'Hello,' said Morse. 'I'm sorry I missed you, but I've had a nice little chat with your mother. I really came to ask if you'd come out with me tomorrow night.' With her pale face and her untidy hair, she suddenly seemed very plain, and Morse found himself wondering why she'd been so much on his mind. 'It's your birthday, isn't it?'

She nodded vaguely, her face puzzled and hesitant.

'It's all right,' said Morse. 'Your mother says it'll do you good. In fact she's very pleased with the idea, aren't you, Mrs Rawlinson?' (One trick to Morse.)

'Well, I – I'd love to but— '

'No buts about it, Ruthie! As the Inspector says, I think it would do you the world of good.'

'I'll pick you up about seven, then,' said Morse.

Ruth gathered up her string shopping-bag, and stood beside Morse on the threshold. 'Thank you, Mother. That was kind of you. But' (turning to Morse) 'I'm sorry. I can't accept your invitation. I've already been asked out by – by someone else.'

Life was a strange business. A few seconds ago she'd looked so ordinary; yet now she seemed a prize just snatched from his grasp, and for Morse the day ahead loomed blank and lonely. As it did, if only he had known, for Ruth.

Chapter Thirteen

'What the 'ell do *you* want?' growled Chief Inspector Bell of the City Police. A fortnight in Malaga which had coincided with a strike of Spanish hotel staff had not brought him home in the sweetest of humours; and the jobs he had gladly left behind him had (as ever) not gone away. But he knew Morse well: they were old sparring partners.

'The Spanish brothels still doing a roaring trade?'

'Had the wife with me, didn't I?'

'Tell me something about this Lawson business.'

'Damned if I will. The case is closed – and it's got nothing to do with you.'

'How're the kids?'

'Ungrateful little buggers. Shan't take 'em again.'

'And the Lawson case is closed?'

'Locked and bolted.'

'No harm in just— '

'I've lost the key.'

'All kids are ungrateful.'

'Especially mine.'

'Where's the file?'

'What d'you want to know?'

'Who killed Josephs, for a start.'

'Lawson did.'

Morse blinked in some surprise. 'You mean that?'

Bell nodded. 'The knife that killed Josephs belonged to Lawson. The woman who charred for him had seen it several times on his desk in the vicarage.'

'But Lawson was nowhere near Josephs when —' Morse stopped in his tracks, and Bell continued.

'Josephs was just about dead when he was knifed: acute mor-phine poisoning, administered, as they say, at the altar of the Lord. What about that, Morse? Josephs was a churchwarden and he was always last at the altar-rail, and he finished up with some pretty queer things in his belly, right? It seems pretty obvious, then, that. . . . ' It was a strange experience for Morse. *Déjà vu*. He found himself only half-listening to Bell's explanation – no, not Bell's, his own explanation. ' . . . rinse the utensils, wipe 'em clean, stick 'em in the cupboard till next time. Easy! Proof, though? No.'

'But how did Lawson— '

'He's standing in front of the altar, waiting for the last hymn to finish. He knows Josephs is counting up the collection in the vestry as he always does, and Lawson's expecting him to be lying there unconscious; dead, probably, by now. But suddenly Josephs shouts for help, and Lawson comes swooping down the aisle in his batman outfit – '

'Chasuble,' mumbled Morse.

' – and covers him up under his what's-it; he keeps the others – there aren't many of 'em, anyway – away from the vestry, sends for help, and then when he's alone he sticks his knife in Josephs' back – just to make sure.'

'I thought the collection was pinched.'

Bell nodded. 'There was one of those down-and-out fellows at the service: Lawson had helped him occasionally – put him up at the vicarage, given him his old suits – that sort of thing. In fact, this fellow had been kneeling next to Josephs at the communion-rail— '

'So *he* could have put the stuff in the wine.'

Bell shook his head. 'You should go to church occasionally, Morse. If he had done, Lawson would have been poisoned just like Josephs, because the minister has to finish off what's left of the wine. You know, I reckon your brain's getting addled in your old age.'

'Someone still pinched the collection,' said Morse feebly.

'Oh yes. And I'm sure it was this fellow – Swan, or something like that, his name was. He just saw the money in the vestry and – well, he just nicked it.'

'I thought you said Lawson kept all the others outside.'

'For a start, yes. He had to.'

Morse looked far from convinced, but Bell sailed happily on. 'A reasonably well-educated fellow, by all accounts. We put out a description of him, of course, but. . . . They all look much of a muchness, those sort of fellows: none of 'em shave or get their hair cut. Anyway, he'd only be up for petty larceny if we found him. Two or three quid, at the outside – that's all he got. Funny, really. If he'd had a chance to go through Josephs' pockets, he'd have found nearly a hundred.'

Morse whistled softly. 'That means that Lawson couldn't have gone through his pockets, either, doesn't it? They tell me the clergy aren't exactly overpaid these days, and Lawson couldn't have been rolling in— '

Bell smiled. 'Lawson was hellish lucky to get the chance to knife him – let alone go through his pockets. But that's neither here nor there. Lawson *was* rolling in it. Until a few weeks before he died, his deposit account at the bank stood at over £30,000.'

This time Morse's whistle was loud and long. 'Until a few weeks . . . ?'

'Yes. Then he took his money out. Almost all of it.'

'Any idea— '

'Not really.'

'What did the bank manager have to tell you?'

'He wasn't allowed to tell me anything.'

'What *did* he tell you?'

'That Lawson had told him he was going to make an anonymous donation to some charity, and that's why he wanted cash.'

'Some bloody donation!'

'Some people are more generous than others, Morse.'

'Did he take out all this cash before, or after, Josephs was murdered?'

For the first time Bell seemed slightly uneasy. 'Before, actually.'

Morse was silent for a short while. The new pieces of evidence were not fitting at all neatly. 'What was Lawson's motive for killing Josephs?'

'Blackmail, perhaps?'

'Josephs had some hold over him?'

'Something like that.'

'Any ideas?'

'There were a few rumours.'

'Well?'

'I prefer facts.'

'Was Lawson buggering the choirboys?'

'You always did put things so nicely.'

'What facts, then?'

'Lawson had made out a cheque for £250 to Josephs a couple of weeks earlier.'

'I see,' said Morse slowly. 'What else?'

'Nothing.'

'Can I look through the files?'

'Certainly not.'

Morse spent the next hour in Bell's office looking through the files.

Considering the limited number of personnel available, the investigations into the deaths of Josephs and Lawson had been reasonably thorough, although there were a few surprising omissions. It would have been interesting, for example, to read the evidence of every single member of the congregation present when Josephs died, but it seemed that several of them had been only casual visitors – two American tourists amongst them – and Lawson had quite innocently informed them that perhaps they needn't stay. Understandable, no doubt – but very careless and quite improper. Unless . . . unless, thought Morse, Lawson wasn't over-anxious for all of them to tell the police what they'd seen? It was sometimes just those little details, just those little inconsistencies. . . . Of the statements that were available, all cleanly set out, all neatly typed, only one arrested Morse's attention: the one, duly signed in the dithery hand of Mrs Emily Walsh-Atkins, attesting to the identification of Lawson.

'Did you interview this old girl?' asked Morse, pushing the statement across the table.

'Not personally, no.'

So far Bell had shown himself a jump or two ahead all round the course, but Morse thought he now saw himself coming through pretty fast on the rails. 'She's as blind as a bloody bat, did you know that? What sort of identification do you think this is? I met her the other night and— '

Bell looked up slowly from the report he'd been reading. 'Are you suggesting that fellow we found draped over the railings *wasn't* Lawson?'

'All I'm suggesting, Bell, is that you must have been pretty hard up for witnesses if you had to rely on her. As I say, she's— '

'She's as blind as a bat – almost your own words, Morse; and, if I remember rightly, exactly the words of my own Sergeant Davies. But don't be too hard on the old dear for wanting to get into the act – it was the most exciting thing that ever happened to her.'

'But that doesn't mean— '

'Hold your horses, Morse! We only needed one identification for the coroner's court, so we only *had* one. Right? But we had another witness all ready, and I don't think *he's* as blind as a bat. If he is, he must have one helluva job when he plays the organ in six sharps.'

'Oh, I see.' But Morse didn't see. What was Morris doing at St Frideswide's that morning? Ruth Rawlinson would know, of course. Ruth. . . . Huh! Her birthday today, and she would be all dolled up for a date with some lecherous lout. . . .

'Why was Morris at church that morning?'

'It's a free country, Morse. Perhaps he just wanted to go to church.'

'Did you find out if he was playing the organ?'

'As a matter of fact, I did, yes.' Bell was thoroughly enjoying himself again – something he'd seldom experienced in Morse's company before. 'He *was* playing the organ.'

After Morse had gone, Bell stared out of his office window for several minutes. Morse was a clever beggar. One or two questions he'd asked had probed a bit deeper than was comfortable; but most cases had a few ragged ends here and there. He tried to switch his mind over to another channel, but he felt hot and sticky; felt he might be sickening for something.

Ruth Rawlinson had lied to Morse – well, not exactly lied. She did have an assignation on the evening of her birthday; but it wouldn't last for long, thank goodness! And then? And then she could meet Morse – if he still wanted to take her out.

At 3 p.m. she nervously flicked through the *m*s in the blue Oxford Area Telephone Directory, and found only one 'Morse' in north Oxford: Morse, E. She didn't know his christian name, and she vaguely wondered what the 'E' stood for. Irrationally, as she heard the first few rings, she hoped that he wasn't in; and then, as they continued, she prayed that he was.

But there was no answer.

Chapter Fourteen

From the City Police H.Q. Morse walked up past Christ Church to Cornmarket. To his left he noticed that the door of Carfax tower stood open, and beside it a notice inviting tourists to ascend and enjoy a panoramic view of Oxford. At the top of the tower he could see four or five people standing against the sky-line and pointing to some of the local landmarks, and a teenage youth actually sitting on the edge, with one of his boots wedged against the next parapet. Morse, feeling a twinge of panic somewhere in his bowels, lowered his eyes and walked on. He joined the small bus-queue just outside Woolworth, thinking again of what he'd just been reading: the life-histories of Josephs and Lawson, the accounts of their deaths, the subsequent investigations. But for the moment the filters of his brain could separate out no new nugget of precious information, and he turned towards St Giles' and looked up at the tower of St Frideswide's. No one up there, of course. . . . Just a minute! Had anyone been up there – recently? Suddenly a curious thought came into his mind – but no, it must be wrong. There'd been something in Bell's file about it: 'Each November a group of volunteers go up to sweep the leaves.' It had just been a thought, that's all.

A Banbury Road bus nudged into the queue, and Morse sat upstairs. As they passed St Frideswide's he looked up again at the tower and made a guess at its height: eighty, ninety feet? The trees ahead of him in St Giles' had that long-distance look of green about them as the leaves began to open; and the bus, as it pulled into the lay-by outside the Taylorian Institute, was scraping against some of their budded branches, when something clicked in Morse's mind. How tall were the trees here? Forty, fifty feet? Not much more, certainly. So how in the name of gravity did the autumnal leaves ever manage to dance their way to the top of St Frideswide's tower? Wasn't there perhaps a simple answer, though. They *didn't*. The November leaf-sweeping brigade had no need to go up to the main tower at all: they just cleared the lower roofs over the aisle and the Lady Chapel. That must be it. And so the curious thought grew curiouser still: since the time of Lawson's death, when doubtless Bell's minions had sieved every leaf and every fragment of stone, had *anyone* been up to the roof of the tower?

The bell pinged for the bus to stop at the Summertown shops; and simultaneously another bell rang in Morse's mind, and he joined the exodus. In Bell's notes (it was all 'bells' now) there'd been a few tactful mentions of Josephs' weakness for gambling on the horses, and the intelligent early suggestion (before Bell's visit to Josephs' bank manager) that the £100 or so found in the dead man's wallet might have had a fairly simple provenance – the licensed betting-office in Summertown.

Morse pushed open the door and immediately registered some surprise. It was more like a branch of Lloyds Bank than the traditional picture of a bookmaker's premises. A counter faced him along the far wall, with a low grille running the length of it, behind which two young women were taking money and stamping betting-slips. Round the three other walls the racing pages of the daily newspapers were pinned, and in front of them were placed black plastic chairs where clients could sit and study the form-guides and consider their own fancies or the tipsters' selections. There were about fifteen people there, all men – sitting or standing about, their minds keenly concentrated on the state of the going, the weights and the jockeys, their ears intent on the loudspeaker which every few minutes brought them the latest news of the betting direct from the courses. Morse sat down and stared vacantly at a page of the *Sporting Chronicle*. To his right, a smartly dressed Chinaman twisted the knob on a small machine affixed to the wall and tore off a betting-slip. And from the corner of his eye Morse could see exactly what he wrote: '3.35 Newmarket – £20 win – The Fiddler'. Phew! Surely most of the punters here had to be satisfied with a modest fifty pence or so each way? He turned his head and watched the Chinaman at the pay-in counter, four crisp fivers fanned out neatly in his right hand; watched the girl behind the grille, as she accepted the latest sacrifice with the bland indifference of a Buddhist deity. Two minutes later the loudspeaker woke up again, and without enthusiasm an impersonal voice announced, the 'off'; announced, after a period of silence, the order of the runners at the four-furlong marker; then the winner, the second, the third – The Fiddler not amongst them. To Morse, who as a boy had listened to the frenetically exciting race-commentaries of Raymond Glendenning, the whole thing seemed extraordinarily flat, more like an auctioneer selling a Cézanne at Sotheby's.

The Chinaman resumed his seat beside Morse, and began to tear up his small yellow slip with the exaggerated delicacy of one who practises the art of origami.

'No luck?' ventured Morse.

'No,' said the Chinaman, with a polite oriental inclination of the head.

'You lucky sometimes?'

'Sometime.' Again the half-smile, the gentle inclination of the head.

'Come here often?'

'Often.' And, as if to answer the query on Morse's face, 'Me pretty rich man, you think so?'

Morse took the plunge. 'I used to know a fellow who came in here most days – fellow called Josephs. Used to wear a brown suit. About fifty.'

'Here now?'

'No. He died about six months ago – murdered, poor chap.'

'Ah. You mean Harree. Yes. Poor Harree. I know heem. We often talk. He murdered, yes. Me verree sorree.'

'He won quite a bit on the horses, I've heard. Still, some of us are luckier than others.'

'You wrong. Harree verree unluckee man. Always just not there quite.'

'He lost a lot of money, you mean?'

The Chinaman shrugged. 'Perhaps he rich man.' His narrow eyes focused on the 4.00 card at Newmarket, his right hand reaching up automatically for the knob on the wall machine.

Probably Josephs had been losing money pretty consistently, and not the sort of money he could hope to recoup from the unemployment exchange. Yet he'd got money from somewhere, by some means.

Morse considered a little wager of his own on the Chinaman's next selection, but squint as he would he couldn't quite see the name, and he left and walked thoughtfully up the hill. It was a pity. A few minutes after Morse had let himself into his flat, the little Chinaman stood smiling a not particularly inscrutable smile at the pay-out counter. He hadn't really got his English syntax sorted out yet, but perhaps he'd coined as fitting an epitaph for Harry Josephs as any with those five disjointed adverbs: 'Always just not there quite.'

Chapter Fifteen

'No, I'm sorry, Inspector – he isn't.' It was ten-past seven and Mrs Lewis regretted the interruption to *The Archers*: she hoped that Morse would either come in or go away. 'Oxford are playing tonight, and he's gone to watch them.'

The rain had been falling steadily since tea-time, and still pattered the puddles in the Lewises' front drive. 'He must be mad,' said Morse.

'It's working with you, Inspector. Are you coming in?'

Morse shook his head and a raindrop dripped from his bare head on to his chin. 'I'll go and see if I can find him.'

'You must be mad,' muttered Mrs Lewis.

Morse drove carefully through the rain up to Headington, the windscreen-wipers sweeping back and forth in clean arcs across the spattered window. It was these damned holidays that upset him! Earlier this Tuesday evening he had sat in his armchair, once again in the grip of a numbing lethargy that minute by minute grew ever more paralysing. The Playhouse offered him a Joe Orton farce, hailed by the critics as a comedy classic. No. The Moulin Rouge announced that the torrid Sandra Bergson was leading a sexy, savage, insatiable all-girl gang in *On the Game*: an X trailer, no doubt, advertising a U film. No. Every prospect seemed displeasing, and even women, temporarily, seemed vile. Then he'd suddenly thought of Sergeant Lewis.

It had been no problem parking the Jaguar in Sandfield Road, and Morse now pushed through the stiff turnstile into the Manor

Road ground. Only a faithful sprinkling of bedraggled spectators was standing along the west-side terrace, their umbrellas streaked with rain; but the covered terrace at the London Road end was tightly packed with orange-and-black-scarved youngsters, their staccato 'Ox-ford – clap-clap-clap' intermittently echoing across the ground. One row of brilliant floodlights was suddenly switched on, and the wet grass twinkled in a thousand silvery gleams.

A roar greeted the home team, yellow-shirted, blue-shorted, leaning forward against the slanting rain, and kicking and flicking a series of white footballs across the sodden pitch until they shone like polished billiard balls. Behind him, as Morse turned, was the main stand, under cover and under-populated; and he walked back to the entrance and bought himself a transfer ticket.

By half-time Oxford were two goals down, and in spite of repeated scrutinies of those around him, Morse had still not spotted Lewis. Throughout the first half, when the centre of the pitch and the two goal-mouths had churned up into areas of squelchy morass reminiscent of pictures of Passchendaele, Morse's thoughts had given him little rest. An improbable, illogical, intuitive notion was growing ever firmer in his mind – a mind now focused almost mesmerically on the tower of St Frideswide's; and the fact that he himself was quite unable to check his forebodings served only to reinforce their probability. He needed Lewis badly – there could be no doubt of that.

Greeted by a cacophony of whistles and catcalls, his black top and shorts shining like a skin-diver's suit, the referee came out to inspect the pitch again, and Morse looked at the clock by the giant scoreboard: 8.20 p.m. Was it really worth staying?

A firm hand gripped his shoulder from behind. 'You must be mad, sir.'

Lewis clambered over the back of the seat and sat himself down beside his chief.

Morse felt indescribably happy. 'Listen, Lewis. I want your help. What about it?'

'Any time, sir. You know me. But aren't you on— ?'

'*Any* time?'

A veil of slow disappointment clouded Lewis' eyes. 'You don't mean— ?' He knew exactly what Morse meant.

'You've lost this one, anyway.'

'Bit unlucky, weren't we, in the first half?'

'What are you like on heights?' asked Morse.

Like the streets around the football ground, St Giles' was comparatively empty, and the two cars easily found parking-spaces outside St John's College.

'Fancy a beefburger, Lewis?'

'Not for me, sir. The wife'll have the chips on.' Morse smiled contentedly. It was good to be back in harness again; good to be reminded of Mrs Lewis' chips. Even the rain had slackened, and Morse lifted his face and breathed deeply, ignoring Lewis' repeated questions about their nocturnal mission.

The large west window of St Frideswide's glowed with a sombre, yellow light, and from inside could be heard the notes of the organ, muted and melancholy.

'We going to church?' asked Lewis; and in reply Morse unlatched the north door and walked inside. Immediately on their left as they entered was a brightly-painted statue of the Virgin, illumined by circles of candles, some slim and waning rapidly, some stout and squat, clearly prepared to soldier on throughout the night; and all casting a flickering kaleidoscopic light across the serene features of the Blessed Mother of God.

'Coleridge was very interested in candles,' said Morse. But before he could further enlighten Lewis on such enigmatic subject-matter a tall, shadowy figure emerged from the gloom, swathed in a black cassock.

'I'm afraid the service is over, gentlemen.'

'That's handy,' said Morse. 'We want to go up the tower.'

'I beg your pardon.'

'Who are you?' asked Morse brusquely.

'I am the verger,' said the tall man, 'and I'm afraid there's no possibility whatsoever of your going up to the tower.'

Ten minutes later with the verger's key, and the verger's torch, and the verger's warning that the whole thing was highly irregular, Morse found himself on the first few steps of the ascent – a narrow, steep, scalloped stairway that circled closely upwards to the tower above. With Lewis immediately behind he shone the torch ahead of him, and, increasingly breathless from exertion and apprehension, gritted his teeth and climbed. Fifty-five, fifty-six, fifty-seven. . . . On the sixty-third step a small narrow window loomed on the left, and Morse shut his eyes, hugging the right-hand wall ever more closely; and ten steps higher, steps still religiously counted, he reached the inexorable conclusion that he would climb one step higher, make an immediate U-turn, descend to the bottom, and take Lewis for a pint in the Randolph. A cold sweat had broken out on his forehead, and the planes registering the vertical and horizontal realities were merging and sliding and slanting into a terrifying tilt. He craved only one thing now: to stand four-square on the solid ground outside this abominable tower and to watch the blessedly terrestrial traffic moving along St Giles'. To stand? No, to sit there; to lie there even, the members of his body seeking to embrace at every point the solid, fixed contours of the flat and comforting earth.

'Here you are, Lewis. You take the torch. I'm – I'm right behind you.'

Lewis set off ahead of him, easily, confidently, two steps at a time, upwards into the spiralling blackness; and Morse followed. Above the bell chamber, up and up, another window and another dizzying glimpse of the ground so far below – and Morse with a supreme effort of will thought only of one step upwards at a time, his whole being concentrating itself into the purely physical activity of lifting each leg alternately, like a victim of locomotor ataxia.

'Here we are, then,' said Lewis brightly, shining the torch on a low door just above them. 'This must be the roof, I think.'

The door was not locked and Lewis stepped through it, leaving Morse to sit down on the threshold, breathing heavily, his back tight against the door-jamb and his hands tight against his clammy forehead. When finally he dared to look about him, he saw the tessellated coping of the tower framed against the evening sky and then, almost fatally, he saw the dark clouds hurrying across the pale moon, saw the pale moon hurrying behind the dark clouds, saw the tower itself leaning and drifting against the sky, and his head reeled vertiginously, his gut contracted, and twice he retched emptily – and prayed that Lewis had not heard him.

From the north side of the tower Lewis looked down and across the broad, tree-lined expanse of St Giles'. Immediately below him, some eighty or ninety feet, he guessed, he could just make out the spiked railing that surrounded the north porch, and beyond it the moonlit graves in the little churchyard. Nothing much of interest. He shone the torch across the tower itself. Each of the four sides was about ten or twelve yards in length, with a gully running alongside the outer walls, and a flat, narrow walk, about a yard in width, between these walls and the leaded roof which rose from each side in a shallow pyramid, its apex some eight or nine feet high, on which a wooden post supported a slightly crooked weather-vane.

He walked back to the door. 'You all right, sir?'

'Yes, fine. Just not so fit as you, that's all.'

'You'll get a touch of the old Farmer Giles sitting there, sir.'

'Find anything?'

Lewis shook his head.

'You looked all round?'

'Not exactly, no. But why don't you tell me what we're supposed to be looking for?' Then, as Morse made no reply: 'You *sure* you're all right, sir?'

'Go and – go and have a look all the way round, will you? I'll – er – I'll be all right in a minute.'

'What's wrong, sir?'

'I'm scared of bloody heights, you stupid sod!' snarled Morse.

Lewis said nothing more. He'd worked with Morse many times before, and treated his outbursts rather as he had once treated the saddeningly bitchy bouts of temper from his own teenage daughters. Nevertheless, it still hurt a bit.

He shone the torch along the southern side of the tower and slowly made his way along. Pigeon-droppings littered the narrow walk, and the gully on this side was blocked somewhere, for two or three inches of water had built up at the south-east corner. Lewis took hold of the outer fabric of the tower as he tried to peer round the east side, but the stonework was friable and insecure. Gingerly he leaned his weight against the slope of the central roofing, and shone the torch round. 'Oh Christ!' he said softly to himself.

There, stretched parallel to the east wall, was the body of a man – although even then Lewis realised that the only evidence for supposing the body to be that of a man was the tattered, sodden suit in which the corpse was dressed, and the hair on the head which was not that of a woman. But the face itself had been picked almost clean to the hideous skull; and it was upon this non-face that Lewis forced himself to shine his torch again. Twice in all – but no more.

Chapter Sixteen

At lunch-time on the following day, Morse sat alone in The
Bulldog, just opposite Christ Church, and scanned an early
copy of the *Oxford Mail*. Although the main headline and three
full columns of the front page were given over to COMPONENTS
STRIKE HITS COWLEY MEN, 'Body Found on Church Tower' had
been dramatic enough news to find itself half-way down the left-
hand column. But Morse didn't bother to read it. After all, he'd
been sitting there in Bell's office a couple of hours previously
when one of the *Mail*'s correspondents had rung through and when
Bell's replies had been guarded and strictly factual: 'No, we don't
know who he is.' 'Yes, I did say a "he".' 'What? Quite a long
time, yes. Quite a long time.' 'I can't say at the minute, no.
They're holding the post-mortem this afternoon. Good headline
for you, eh? P.M. THIS P.M.' 'No, I can't tell you who found
him.' 'Could be a link-up, I suppose, yes.' 'No, that's the lot.
Ring up tomorrow if you like. I might have a bit more for you
then.' At the time Morse had felt that this last suggestion was
a bit on the optimistic side, and he still felt so now. He turned
to the back page and read the sports headline: UNITED COME
UNSTUCK ON PITCH LIKE GLUE. But he didn't read that account,
either. The truth was that he felt extremely puzzled, and needed
time to think.

Nothing had been found in the dead man's pockets, and
the only information imparted by the dark-grey suit, the under-
clothing, and the light-blue tie was 'Burton', 'St Michael' and
'Munro Spun' respectively. Morse himself had declined to view
what Bell had called 'a sticky, putrescent mess', and had envied
the perky *sang-froid* of the police surgeon who reported that
whoever he was he wasn't quite such a gruesome sight as some
of the bodies they used to fish out of the water at Gravesend.
One thing was clear. It was going to be a tricky job to identify
the corpse: tricky for Bell, that was. And Bell had not been in
the best of humours as he'd glared across the table at Morse and
reminded him that he *must* have some idea who the fellow was.
It was Morse who had taken Lewis to the exact spot, wasn't it?
And if he was pretty sure he was going to find a corpse he must
have got a jolly good idea whose corpse it was!

But Morse hadn't – it was as simple as that. A peculiar combination of circumstances had concentrated his thoughts on to the tower of St Frideswide's, and all he'd done (whatever Bell suspected) was to obey a compelling instinct which had proved too strong even for his chronic acrophobia. But he'd not expected to find a corpse up there, had he? Or had he? When Lewis had shouted the grim discovery over the roof to him, Morse's mind had immediately jumped to the shadowy figure of the tramp and his miserably thin pickings from the collection-plate. All along he'd felt that it should have been comparatively easy for the police to pick up such a character. People like that had to depend almost entirely on charitable and welfare services of some kind, and were usually well known to the authorities wherever they went. Yet extensive enquiries had led nowhere, and might there not have been a very very simple reason for that?

Morse bought himself another pint and watched the glass as the cloudy sedimentation slowly cleared; and when he sat down again his brain seemed to have cleared a little, too. No; it wasn't the tramp they'd found, Morse felt sure of that. It was the clothes, really – especially that light-blue tie. Light-blue . . . Cambridge . . . graduates . . . teachers . . . Morris. . . .

Bell was still in his office.

'What happened to Paul Morris?' asked Morse.

'Beggered off with Josephs' wife, like as not.'

'You don't *know*?'

Bell shook his head. He looked tired and drawn. 'We tried, but— '

'Did you find *her*?'

Again Bell shook his head. 'We didn't push things too far. You know how it is. What with Morris teaching at the same school as his son and— '

'His *what*? You didn't tell me Morris had a son!'

Bell sighed deeply. 'Look, Morse. Whadya want from me? You find me another body last night, and I'm deeply grateful, aren't I? That'll be another half-dozen of my lads out of circulation. And I've just had a call to say somebody's been fished out of the river at Folly Bridge, and we've got more trouble with some squatters down in Jericho.' He took out a handkerchief and sneezed heavily. 'And I'm sickening for the flu, and you want me to go chasing after some fellow who was known to be seein' Josephs' missus pretty regularly long before— '

'Really?' said Morse. 'Why didn't I read that in the report?'

'Come off it!'

'He could have killed Josephs. Jealousy! Best motive of the lot.'

'He was sittin' – playin' the bleedin' organ – when— ' Bell sneezed noisily again.

Morse settled back in his chair, for some unfathomable reason looking very pleased with himself. 'You still think it really *was* Lawson you found on the railings?'

'I told you, Morse, we had two identifications.'

'Oh yes, I remember. One from a blind woman and one from the man who ran away with Brenda Josephs, wasn't it?'

'Why don't you go home?'

'You know,' said Morse quietly, 'when you've finished with your squatters, you'd better get a squad of lads to dig up old Lawson's coffin, because I reckon – just reckon, mind – that *you might not find old Lawson in it.*' Morse's face beamed with a mischievous pleasure, and he got up to go.

'That's a bloody fool's thing to say.'

'Is it?'

'Not all that easy, either.' It was Bell who was enjoying himself now.

'No?'

'No. You see, they cremated him.'

The news appeared to occasion little surprise or disappointment on Morse's face. 'I knew a minister once— '

'Well, well!' mumbled Bell.

' – who had one of his feet amputated in the First World War. He got it stuck in a tank, and they had to get him out quick because the thing was on fire. So they left his foot there.'

'Very interesting.'

'He was very old when I knew him,' continued Morse. 'One foot already in the grave.'

Bell pushed his own chair back and got up. 'Tell me about it some other time.'

'He was in a discussion one day about the respective merits of burial and cremation, and the old boy said he didn't mind two hoots what they did with him. He said he'd sort of got a foot in *both* camps.'

Bell shook his head in slow bewilderment. What the hell was *that* supposed to mean?

'By the way,' said Morse. 'What was the name of Paul Morris' son?'

'Peter, I think. Why— ?'

But Morse left without enlightening Bell on the point.

P.M. THIS P.M., Bell had said; and as he drove the Jaguar up to Carfax the initials kept repeating themselves to his mind: post-mortem, post meridiem, prime minister, Paul McCartney, Post Master, putrefying mess, Perry Mason, Provost Marshal, Peter Morris. . . . The lights were red at the end of Cornmarket, and as Morse sat waiting there for them to change he looked up yet again at the tower of St Frideswide's looming overhead, and at the great west window which only last night had glowed in the dark when he and Lewis. . . . On a sudden impulse he pulled round the corner into Beaumont Street and parked his car outside the Randolph. A uniformed young flunkey pounced upon him immediately.

'You can't leave your car here.'

'I can leave the bloody car where I like,' snapped Morse. 'And next time you speak to me, lad, just call me "sir", all right?'

The north porch was locked, with a notice pinned to it: 'Due to several acts of wanton vandalism during the past few months, we regret that the church will now be closed to the public from 11 a.m. to 5 p.m. on weekdays.' Morse felt he would have liked to recast the whole sentence, but he satisfied himself by crossing through 'due' and writing 'owing'.

Chapter Seventeen

Morse rapped briskly on the door marked 'Enquiries', put his head round the door, and nodded 'Hello' to a nice-looking school secretary.

'Can I help you, sir?'

'Headmaster in?'

'Is he expecting you?'

'Doubt it,' said Morse. He walked across the narrow office, tapped once on the study door and entered.

Phillipson, headmaster of the Roger Bacon School, was only too pleased to be of help.

Paul Morris, it seemed, had been a music master of the first water. During his short stay at the school, he'd been popular both with his teaching colleagues and with his pupils, and his G.C.E. O-Level and A-Level results had been encouragingly good. Everyone had been mystified – for a start anyway – when he'd left so suddenly, without telling a soul; right in the middle of term, too, on (Phillipson consulted his previous year's diary) 26 October, a Wednesday. He had turned up for school perfectly normally in the morning and presumably gone off, as he often did on Wednesdays, to have lunch at home. And that was the last they'd seen of him. His son, Peter, had left the school just after lessons finished at a quarter to four, and that was the last they'd seen of *him*. The next day several members of staff had pointed out that both of them were absent from school, and no doubt someone would have gone round to the Morris residence if it hadn't been for a call from the Oxford City Police. It seemed that some anonymous neighbour had tipped them off that Morris and his son had left Kidlington and gone off to join a woman ('I suppose you know all about this, Inspector?') – a Mrs Josephs. Inspector Bell had called personally to see Phillipson and told him that a few enquiries had already been made, and that several of Morris' neighbours had seen a car answering the description of Mrs Josephs' Allegro parked somewhere nearby several times during the previous months. In fact, the police had learned from other sources that in all probability Morris and Mrs Josephs had been lovers for some time. Anyway, Bell had asked Phillipson to soft-pedal the whole thing; make up some story about Morris having to be away for the rest of the term – death of one of his parents – anything he liked. Which Phillipson had done. A temporary stand-in had taken over Morris' classes for the remainder of the autumn term, and a new woman appointed from January. The police had visited the house that Morris had rented furnished, and found that most of the personal effects had been taken away, although for some reason a fair number of books and an expensive record-player had been left behind. And that was all, really. Phillipson had heard nothing more from that day to this. To the best of his knowledge no one had received any communication from Morris at all. He had not applied for a reference, and perhaps, in the circumstances, was unlikely to do so.

Not once had Morse interrupted Phillipson, and when finally he did say something it was totally irrelevant. 'Any sherry in that cupboard, Headmaster?'

Ten minutes later Morse left the headmaster's study and leaned over the young secretary's shoulder.

'Making out a cheque for me, miss?'

' "Mrs"; Mrs Clarke.' She wound the yellow cheque from the typewriter carriage, placed it face downwards on her desk, and glared at Morse defiantly. His lack of manners when he'd come in had been bad enough, but—

'You look pretty when you're cross,' said Morse.

Phillipson called her through to his study. 'I've got to go out, Mrs Clarke. Take Chief Inspector Morse along to the first-year-sixth music group, will you? And wash up these glasses when you get back, please.'

Tight-lipped and red-cheeked, Mrs Clarke led the way along the corridors and up to the music-room door. 'In there,' she said.

Morse turned to face her and laid his right hand very gently on her shoulder, his blue eyes looking straight into hers. 'Thank you, Mrs Clarke,' he said quietly. 'I'm awfully sorry if I made you angry. Please forgive me.'

As she walked back down the steps, she felt suddenly and marvellously pleased with life. Why had she been so silly? She found herself wishing that he would call her back about something. And he did.

'When do the staff get their cheques, Mrs Clarke?'

'On the last Friday in the month. I always type them the day before.'

'You weren't typing them just now, then?'

'No. We're breaking up tomorrow, and I was just typing an expenses cheque for Mr Phillipson. He had a meeting in London yesterday.'

'I hope he's not on the fiddle.'

She smiled sweetly. 'No, Inspector. He's a very nice man.'

'You're very nice, too, you know,' said Morse.

She was blushing as she turned away, and Morse felt inordinately envious of Mr Clarke as he watched the secretary's legs disappearing down the stairs. Last Friday in the month, she'd said. That would have been 28 October, and Morris had left two days before his cheque was due. Very strange!

Morse knocked on the music-room door and entered.

Mrs Stewart stood up immediately and made as if to turn off the record-player; but Morse held up his right hand, waved it slightly, and sat down on a chair by the wall. The small class was listening to Fauré's *Requiem*; and with an almost instant ecstasy Morse closed his eyes and listened again to the ethereal sweep of the 'In Paradisum': *aeternam habeas requiem* . . . 'that thou mayest have eternal rest'. . . . Too quickly the last notes died away into the silence of the room, and it occurred to Morse that rather too many people had all too recently had a premature dose of that eternal rest thrust forcibly upon them. The score stood at three at the minute; but he had a grim foreboding that soon it might be four.

He introduced himself and his purpose, and was soon surveying the seven girls and the three boys who were in the first year of their A-Level music course. He was making enquiries about Mr Morris; they'd all known Mr Morris; there were various business matters which had to be cleared up, and the police weren't sure where Mr Morris had gone to. Did any of them know anything at all about Mr Morris that might just possibly be of any help? The class shook their heads, and sat silent and unhelpful. So Morse asked them a lot more questions, and still they sat silent and unhelpful. But at least two or three of the girls were decidedly decorative – especially one real honey at the back whose eyes seemed to flash the inner secrets of her soul across the room at him. Morris must have looked at her lustfully just once in a while? Surely so. . . .

But he was getting nowhere slowly, that was obvious; and he changed his tactics abruptly. His target was a pallid-looking, long-haired youth in the front row. 'Did you know Mr Morris?'

'Me?' The boy swallowed hard. 'He taught me for two years, sir.'

'What did you call him?'

'Well, I – I called him "Mr Morris".' The rest of the class smirked silently to each other, as if Morse must be a potential idiot.

'Didn't you call him anything else?'

'No.'

'You never called him "sir"?'

'Well, of course. But— '

'You don't seem to realise the seriousness of this business, lad. So I'll have to ask you again, won't I? What else did you call him?'

'I don't quite see what you mean.'

'Didn't he have a nickname?'

'Well, most of the teachers— '

'What was his?'

It was one of the other boys who came to the rescue. 'Some of us used to call him "Dapper".'

Morse directed his gaze towards the new voice and nodded wisely. 'Yes. So I've heard. Why was it, do you think?'

It was one of the girls now, a serious-looking soul with a large gap between her front teeth. 'He alwayth drethed very nithely, thir.' The other girls tittered and twittered amongst themselves, and nudged each other knowingly.

'Any more contributions?'

It was the third boy who took up the easy theme. 'He always wore a suit, you see, sir, and most of the staff – well' (more sniggering) 'well, you know, most of 'em have beards, the men, I mean' (a great guffaw from the class now) 'and wear jeans and sweaters and all that. But Mr Morris, he always wore a suit and looked – well, smart, like.'

'What sort of suits did he wear?'

'Well' (it was the same boy) 'sort of dark, you know. Party suits, sort of thing. So, well, we called him "Dapper" – like we said.'

The bell rang for the end of the lesson, and several members of the class began to gather their books and file-cases together.

'What about his ties?' persisted Morse. But the psychological moment had passed, and the colour of Morris' ties seemed to have faded from the collective memory.

As he walked up the drive to his car, Morse wondered if he ought to talk to some of the staff; but he hadn't quite enough to go on yet, and decided it would be better to wait for the pathologist's report.

He had just started the engine when a young girl appeared at the driving-window. 'Hello, beautiful,' he said. It was the girl from the back row, the girl with the radar eyes, who leaned forward and spoke. 'You know you were asking about ties? Well, I remember one tie, sir. He often wore it. It was a light-blue tie. It sort of went with the suits he used to wear.'

Morse nodded understandingly. 'That's most helpful. Thank you very much for telling me.' He looked up at her and suddenly realised how tall she was. Strange how all of them looked about the same size when they were sitting down, as if height were determined not so much from the bottom to the shoulder as by the length of the legs – in this case by the length of some very beautiful legs.

'Did you know Mr Morris well?'

'Not really, no.'

'What's your name?'

'Carole – Carole Jones.'

'Well, thank you, Carole. And good luck.'

Carole walked thoughtfully back to the front entrance and made her way to the next lesson. She wondered why she so often felt so attracted to the older men. Men like this inspector fellow; men like Mr Morris. . . . Her mind went back to the time they'd sat in the car together; when his hand had lightly touched her breasts, and when her own left hand had gently pushed its way between the buttons of his white shirt – beneath the light-blue tie he'd worn that day; the time when he'd asked her to his house, when he'd answered the door and told her that an unexpected visitor had just arrived and that he'd get in touch with her again – very soon.

But he never had.

Chapter Eighteen

Morse was still asleep the next morning when his bedside phone rang. It was Superintendent Strange of the Thames Valley Police H.Q.

'I've just had a call from the City Police, Morse. You still in bed?'

'No, no,' said Morse. 'Decorating the lavatory, sir.'

'I thought you were on holiday.'

'A man's got to use his leisure hours profitably— '

'Like clambering over church roofs at the dead of night, you mean.'

'You heard?'

'Heard something else, too, Morse. Bell's got flu. And since you seem to have taken over the case already I just wondered whether you'd like to sort of – take over the case. Officially, I mean.'

Morse shot upright in bed. 'That's good news, sir. When— ?'

'From now. It'll be better if you work from St Aldates. All the stuff's there, and you can work from Bell's office.'

'Can I have Lewis?'

'I thought you'd already got him.'

Morse's face beamed with pleasure. 'Thank you, sir. I'll just slip a few clothes on and— '

'Decorating in your pyjamas, Morse?'

'No. You know me, sir. Up with the lark— '

'And to bed with the Wren. Yes, I know. And it wouldn't be a bad thing for morale here if you got to the bottom of things, would it? So what about getting out of bed?'

Five minutes later Morse got through to Lewis and reported the good news. 'What are you doing today, old friend?'

'My day off, sir. I'm going to take the wife over to— '

'Were you?' The change of tense was not lost on Lewis, and he listened cheerfully to his instructions. He'd been dreading another visit to his ancient mother-in-law.

The Jaguar took only one and a half hours to cover the eighty-odd miles to Stamford in Lincolnshire, where the Lawson clan had lived for several generations. The speedometer had several times exceeded 85 m.p.h. as they drove along, up through Brackley, Silverstone and Towcester, then by-passing Northampton and twisting through Kettering before looking down from the top of Easton Hill on to the town of Stamford, its grey stone buildings matching the spires and towers of its many old churches. *En route* Morse had cheerfully sketched in the background of the St Frideswide's murders; but the sky had grown overcast and leaden, and the sight of thousands of dead elm-trees along the

Northamptonshire roads seemed a sombre reminder of reality.

'They say those trees commit suicide,' Lewis had ventured at one point. 'They secrete a sort of fluid to try to— '

'It's not always easy to tell suicide from murder,' muttered Morse.

By late afternoon the two men had uncovered a fairly solid body of information about the late and (it seemed) little-lamented Lionel Lawson. There had been two Lawson brothers. Lionel Peter and Philip Edward, the latter some eighteen months the younger. Both had won scholarships to a public school some ten miles distant, and both had been weekly boarders, spending their Saturday evenings and Sundays during term-time with their parents, who ran a small local business specialising in the restoration of ancient buildings. Academically (it appeared) the two boys were more than competent, with Philip potentially the abler – if also the lazier and less ambitious. After leaving school each of them had spent eighteen months on National Service; and it was during his time in the Army that Lionel, always the more serious-minded of the two, had met a particularly persuasive psalm-singing padre, and been led to the conviction that he was called to the ministry. After demobilisation, he had studied hard on his own for a year before gaining acceptance at Cambridge to read theology. During this period Philip had worked for his father for a few years, but seemingly with little enthusiasm; and finally he had drifted away from home, occasionally revisiting his parents, but with no firm purpose in life, no job, and with little prospect of discovering either. Five years ago Mr Lawson senior and his wife had been killed in the Zagreb air-crash whilst returning from a holiday in southern Yugoslavia, and the family business had been sold, with each of the two sons inheriting about £50,000 net from the estate.

For most of the day Morse and Lewis had worked separately, each pursuing a different line of enquiry; and it was only on the last visit, to the ex-headmaster of the Lawson boys' public school, that they came together again.

Doctor Meyer's speech was that of an old schoolmaster, deliberate, over-latinised, with an apparent dread of imprecision. 'He was a clever boy, young Philip. With a modicum of dedication and perseverance – who knows?'

'You've no idea where he is now?'

The old man shook his head. 'But Lionel, now. He worked like a Trojan – although exactly why the Trojans are proverbially accredited with a reputation for industriousness has always been a mystery to me. His ambition was always to win a scholarship to Oxford, but— ' He broke off suddenly as if his memory could take him no farther along that avenue of recollection. But Morse was clearly anxious to push him past a few more trees.

'How long was Lionel in the sixth form?'

'Three years, as I recall it. Yes, that's right. He took his Higher School Certificate at the end of his second year, and got it all right. He took the Oxford entrance examination just after that, in the Michaelmas term, but I had little real hope for him. His mind was not quite – not quite alpha potential. They wrote to me about him, of course. They said they were unable to offer him a place, but the boy's work had not been without merit. They advised him to stay on for a further year in the sixth and then to try again.'

'Was he very disappointed?'

The old man eyed Morse shrewdly and relit his pipe before replying. 'What do you think, Inspector?'

Morse shrugged his shoulders as if the matter were barely of consequence. 'You said he was ambitious, that's all.'

'Yes,' replied the old man slowly.

'So he stayed on another year?'

'Yes.'

Lewis shuffled a little uncomfortably in his chair. At this rate of progress they wouldn't be home before midnight. It was as if Morse and Meyer were at the snooker table, each of them playing his safety shots. Your turn, Morse.

'He took his Higher again?'

Meyer nodded. 'He didn't do quite so well as in the previous year, if I remember rightly. But that is not unusual.'

'You mean he was more worried about preparing for his Oxford entrance?'

'That was probably the reason.'

'But he didn't make it to Oxford?'

'Er – no.'

Something seemed to be puzzling Morse, Lewis could see that. Was he on to something? But it appeared not. Morse had got to his feet and was pulling on his coat. 'Nothing else you can tell me about him?'

Meyer shook his head and prepared to see his visitors out. He was a short man, and now well over eighty; yet there was still an air of authority in his bearing, and Lewis could well understand (what he'd heard earlier in the day) that Meyer had ruled his school with a rod of iron, and that pupils and staff alike had trembled at his coming.

'Nothing at all?' repeated Morse as they stood at the door.

'There's nothing more I can tell you, no.'

Was there slightly more emphasis on the 'can' than there need have been? Lewis wasn't sure. He was lost as usual anyway.

For the first part of their return journey, Morse seemed rapt in thought; and when he finally did say something Lewis could only wonder what those thoughts had been.

'What was the exact day when Lionel Lawson left school?'

Lewis looked through his notebook. 'November the eighth.'

'Mm.' Morse nodded slowly. 'Tell me when you spot a phone-box.'

When, ten minutes later, Morse got back into the car, Lewis could see that he was very pleased with himself.

'Are you letting me in on this one, sir?'

'Of course!' Morse looked sideways at his sergeant in mild surprise. 'We're partners, aren't we? We do things together, you and me. Or "you and I", as I've no doubt old man Meyer would say. You see, young Lionel Lawson was an ambitious little swot, right? He's not been over-endowed by the Almighty with all that much up top, but he makes up for it by sheer hard work. More than anything else he wants to go up to Oxford. And why not? It's a fine ambition. Let's just recap on Master Lionel, then. He tries once – and he fails. But he's a sticker. He stays on for another year – another year of grind on his set books and the rest of it, and all the time he's being groomed by his masters for his entrance exam. I shouldn't think he's too bothered about not doing so well in his other exams that summer – he's set his sights on higher things. Remember he's already done three years in the sixth form, and he goes back in the autumn term because that's when the entrance exams are always taken. He's all ready for the final furlong – agreed?'

'But he didn't make it.'

'No, you're right. But he didn't *fail* to get in, Lewis – and that's the interesting point. Lawson, L., left school on November the eighth, you tell me. And I'll tell *you* something. That year the entrance papers were sat in the first week of December – I just rang up the Registry at Oxford – *and Lawson, L., didn't sit the examination.*'

'Perhaps he changed his mind.'

'And perhaps somebody changed it for him!'

A light flickered dimly in the darkness of Lewis' mind. 'He was expelled, you mean?'

'That's about it, I reckon. And that's why old man Meyer was so cagey. He knew a good deal more than he was prepared to tell us.'

'But we have no real evidence— '

'Evidence? No, we haven't. But you've got to use a bit of imagination in this job, Lewis, haven't you? So let's use a bit. Tell me. Why do boys usually get expelled from public schools?'

'Drugs?'

'They had no drugs in those days.'

'I don't know, sir. I never went to a public school, did I? There was none of that Greek and Latin stuff for me. We had enough trouble with the three Rs.'

'It's not the three Rs we're worried about now, Lewis. It's the three Bs: bullying, beating and buggery! And Lawson, L., from what we've learned of him, was a quietly behaved little chap, and I doubt he got expelled for bullying or beating. What do you think?'

Lewis shook his head sadly: he'd heard this sort of thing before. 'You can't just – you can't just make up these things as you go along, sir. It's not fair!'

'As you wish.' Morse shrugged his shoulders, and the needle on the speedometer touched 90 m.p.h. as the Jaguar skirted Northampton on the eastern by-pass.

Chapter Nineteen

Back in Oxford at about 4.30 p.m. that same afternoon, two men were walking slowly down Queen Street from Carfax. The elder, and slightly the taller of the two, a growth of greyish stubble matting his long vacant face, was dressed in an old blue pin-striped suit which hung loosely on his narrow frame. In his right hand he carried a bull-necked flagon of Woodpecker cider. The younger man, bearded and unkempt, anywhere in age (it seemed) between his mid-forties and mid-fifties, wore a long army-issue greatcoat, buttoned up to the neck, its insignia long since stripped off or lost. He carried nothing.

At Bonn Square they turned into the circle of grass that surrounds the stone cenotaph, and sat down on a green-painted bench beneath one of the great trees girdling the tiny park. Beside the bench was a wire waste-paper basket, from which the younger man pulled out a copy of the previous day's edition of the *Oxford Mail*. The elder man unscrewed the liquor with great deliberation and, having taken a short swig of its contents, wiped the neck of the bottle on his jacket sleeve before passing it over. 'Anything in the paper?'

'Nah.'

Shoppers continuously criss-crossed one another in the pedestrian precinct in front of the park, many of them making their way down the covered arcade between the light-beige brickwork of the Selfridges building and the duller municipal stone of the public library. A few casual glances swept the only two people seated on the park-benches – glances without pity, interest or concern. Lights suddenly blazed on in the multi-storeyed blocks around and the evening was ushered in.

'Let's look at it when you've finished,' said the elder man, and immediately, without comment, the paper changed hands. The bottle, too, was passed over, almost rhythmically, between them, neither man drinking more than a mouthful at a time.

'This is what they were talking about at the hostel.' The elder man pointed a thin grubby finger at an article on the front page, but his companion made no comment, staring down at the paving-stones.

'They've found some fellow up the top of that tower, you

know, just opposite— ' But he couldn't quite remember what it was opposite to, and his voice trailed off as he slowly finished the article. 'Poor sod!' he said finally.

'We're all poor sods,' rejoined the other. He was seldom known to communicate his thoughts so fully, and he left it at that, hunching himself down into his greatcoat, taking a tin of shredded tobacco from one of its large pockets and beginning to roll himself a cigarette.

'P'haps you weren't here then, but a fellow got hisself murdered there last – when was it now? – last. . . . Augh! Me memory's going. Anyway, a few days later the minister there, he chucks hisself off the bloody tower! Makes you think.'

But it was not apparent that the younger man was given cause to think in any way. He licked the white cigarette-paper from left to right, repeated the process, and stuck the ill-fashioned cylinder between his lips.

'What was his name? Christ! When you get older your memory. . . . What was his name?' He wiped the neck of the bottle again and passed it over. 'He knew the minister there. . . . I wish I could think of. . . . He was some sort of relation or something. Used to stay at the vicarage sometimes. What *was* his name? You don't remember him?'

'Nah. Wasn't 'ere then, was I?'

'He used to go to the services. Huh!' He shook his head as if refusing credence to such strange behaviour. 'You ever go to church?'

'Me? Nah.'

'Not even when you was a lad?'

'Nah.'

A smartly dressed man carrying a brief-case and umbrella walked past them on his way from the railway station.

'Got a coupla bob for a cup o' tea, mister?' It was a long sentence for the younger man, but he could have saved his breath.

'I've not seen him around at all recently,' continued the other. 'Come to think of it, I've not seen him since the minister chucked hisself. . . . Were you there when the police came round to the hostel?'

'Nah.'

The elder man coughed violently and from his loose, rattling

chest spat out a gob of yellowish phlegm on to the paving. He
felt tired and ill, and his mind wandered back to his home, and
the hopes of his early years. . . .

'Gizz the paper 'ere!' said his companion.

Through thin purplish lips the elder man was now whistling
softly the tune to 'The Old Folks at Home', lingering long over
the melody like a man whose only precious pleasure now is the
maudlin stage of drunkenness. 'Wa-a-ay down upon the— ' Suddenly he stopped. 'Swan-something. *Swanpole* – that was it! Funny
sort of name. I remember we used to call him Swanny. Did you
know him?'

'Nah.' The younger man folded the *Oxford Mail* carefully
and stuck it through the front of his coat. 'You oughta look
after that cough o' yours,' he added, with a rare rush of words,
as the elder man coughed up again – revoltingly – and got to his
feet.

'I think I'll be getting along. You coming?'

'Nah.' The bottle was now empty, but the man who remained
seated on the bench had money in his pockets, and there may
have been a glint of mean gratification in his eyes. But those eyes
were shielded from public view behind an incongruous pair of dark
glasses, and seemed to be looking in the opposite direction as the
elder man shuffled unsteadily away.

It was colder now, but the man on the bench was gradually
getting used to that. It was the first thing he'd discovered. After
a time you learn to forget how cold you are: you accept it and
the very acceptance forms an unexpected insulation. Except
for the feet. Yes, except for the feet. He got up and walked
across the grass to look at the inscriptions on the stone obelisk.
Among the buglers and privates whose deeds were commemorated
thereon, he noticed the odd surname of a young soldier killed
by the mutineers in Uganda in 1897: the name was Death.

Chapter Twenty

At 4.30 p.m. on the Friday of the same week, Ruth Rawlinson wheeled her bicycle through the narrow passageway and propped it against the side of the lawn-mower in the cluttered garden-shed. Really, she must tidy up that shed again soon. She took a white Sainsbury carrier-bag from the cycle-basket, and walked back round to the front door. The *Oxford Mail* was in the letter-box, and she quietly withdrew it.

Just a little bit today, but still on page one:

CORPSE STILL UNIDENTIFIED

Police still have no positive clue about the identity of the body found on the tower-roof of St Frideswide's Church. Chief Inspector Morse today repeated that the dead man was probably in his late thirties, and revealed that he was wearing a dark-grey suit, white shirt and light-blue tie. Anyone who may have any information is asked to contact the St Aldates Police Station, Oxford 49881. Enquiries have not as yet established any link with the still unsolved murder of Mr Harry Josephs in the same church last year.

Ruth's body gave an involuntary little jerk as she read the article. 'Anyone who may have. . . . ' Oh God! She had information enough, hadn't she? Too much information; and the knowledge was weighing ever more heavily upon her conscience. And was Morse in charge now?

As she inserted the Yale key, Ruth realised (yet again) how sickeningly predictable would be the dialogue of the next few minutes.

'Is that you, Ruthie dear?'

Who else, you silly old crow? 'Yes, Mother.'

'Is the paper come?'

You know it's come. Your sharp old ears don't miss a scratch, do they? 'Yes, Mother.'

'Bring it with you, dear.'

Ruth put the heavy carrier-bag down on the kitchen-table, draped her mackintosh over a chair and walked into the lounge. She bent down to kiss her mother lightly on an icy cheek, placed the newspaper on her lap, and turned up the gas-fire. 'You never have this high enough, you know, Mother. It's been a lot colder this week and you've got to keep yourself warm.'

'We've got to be careful with the bills, dear.'

Don't start on that again! Ruth mustered up all her reserves of patience and filial forbearance. 'You finished the book?'

'Yes, dear. *Very* ingenious.' But her attention was fixed on the evening paper. 'Anything more about the murder?'

'I don't know. I didn't know it *was* a murder anyway.'

'Don't be childish, dear.' Her eyes had pounced upon the article and she appeared to read it with ghoulish satisfaction. 'That man who came here, Ruthie – they've put him in charge.'

'Have they?'

'He knows far more than he's letting on – you mark my words.'

'You think so?'

The old girl nodded wisely in her chair. 'You can still learn a few things from your old mother, you know.'

'Such as what?'

'You remember that tramp fellow who murdered Harry Josephs?'

'Who said he murdered— ?'

'No need to get cross, dear. You know you're interested. You still keep all the newspaper clippings, I know that.'

You nosey old bitch! 'Mother, you must *not* go looking through my handbag again. I've told you before. One of these days— '

'I'll find something I shouldn't? Is that it?'

Ruth looked savagely into the curly blue line of flame at the bottom of the gas-fire, and counted ten. There were some days now when she could hardly trust herself to speak.

'Well, that's who it is,' said her mother.

'Pardon?'

'The man up the tower, dear. It's the tramp.'

'Bit elegantly dressed for a tramp, wouldn't you say, Mother? White shirt and a— '

'I thought you said you hadn't seen the paper, dear.' The charge was levelled with a silky tongue.

Ruth took a deep breath. 'I just thought you'd like to find it for yourself, that's all.'

'You're beginning to tell me quite a few little lies, Ruthie, and you've got to stop it.'

Ruth looked up sharply. What was that supposed to mean?

Surely her mother couldn't know about . . . ? 'You're talking nonsense, Mother.'

'So you don't think it *is* the tramp?'

'A tramp wouldn't be wearing clothes like that.'

'People can change clothes, can't they?'

'You've been reading too many detective stories.'

'You could kill someone and then change his clothes.'

'Of course you couldn't.' Again Ruth was watching her mother carefully. 'Not just like that anyway. You make it sound like dressing up a doll or something.'

'It would be difficult, dear, I know that. But, then, life is full of difficulties, isn't it? It's not impossible, that's all I'm saying.'

'I've got two nice little steaks from Sainsbury's. I thought we'd have a few chips with them.'

'You could always change a man's clothes *before* you killed him.'

'What? Don't be so silly! You don't identify a body by the clothes. It's the face and things like that. You can't change— '

'What if there's nothing left of his face, dear?' asked Mrs Rawlinson sweetly, as if reporting that she'd eaten the last piece of Cheddar from the pantry.

Ruth walked over to the window, anxious to bring the conversation to a close. It was distasteful and, yes, worrying. And perhaps her mother wasn't getting quite so senile after all. . . . In her mind's eye Ruth still had a clear picture of the 'tramp' her mother had been talking of, the man she'd known (though she'd never actually been told) to be Lionel Lawson's brother, the man who had usually looked exactly what he was – a worthless, feckless parasite, reeking of alcohol, dirty and degraded. Not quite always, though. There had been two occasions when she'd seen him looking more than presentable: hair neatly groomed, face shaven freshly, finger-nails clean, and a decently respectable suit on his back. On those occasions the family resemblance between the two brothers had been quite remarkable. . . .

' . . . if they ask me, which doubtless they won't— ' Mrs Rawlinson had been chattering non-stop throughout, and her words at last drifted through to Ruth's consciousness.

'What would you tell them?'

'I've *told* you. Haven't you been listening to me, dear? Is there something wrong?'

Yes, there's a lot wrong. You, for a start. And if you're

not careful, Mother dear, I'll strangle you one of these days, dress you up in someone else's clothes, carry your skinny little body up to the top of the tower, and let the birds have a second helping! 'Wrong? Of course there isn't. I'll go and get tea.'

Rotten, black blotches appeared under the skin of the first potato she was peeling, and she took another from the bag she had just bought – a bag marked with the words 'Buy British' under a large Union Jack. Red, white and blue. . . . And she thought of Paul Morris seated on the organ-bench, with his red hood, white shirt and blue tie; Paul Morris, who (as everyone believed) had run off with Brenda Josephs. But he hadn't, had he? Someone had made very, very sure that he hadn't; someone who was sitting somewhere – even now! – planning, gloating, profiting, in some way, from the whole dreadful business. The trouble was that there weren't many people left. In fact, if you counted the heads of those that *were* left, there was really only one who could conceivably. . . . Surely not, though. Surely Brenda Josephs could have nothing to do with it, could she?

Ruth shook her head with conviction, and peeled the next potato.

Chapter Twenty-one

Although her husband (unbeknown to her) had borrowed on the mortgage of their house in Wolvercote, Mrs Brenda Josephs was now comfortably placed financially, and the nurses' hostel in the General Hospital on the outskirts of Shrewsbury provided more than adequate accommodation. On Paul's specific instructions, she had not written to him once, and she had received only that one letter from him, religiously guarded under the lining of her handbag, much of which she knew by heart: ' . . . and above all don't be impatient, my darling. It will take time, perhaps quite a lot of time, and whatever happens we must be careful. As far as I can see there is nothing to worry us, and we must keep it that way. Just be patient and all will be well. I long to see you again and to feel your beautiful body next to mine. I love you, Brenda

– you know that, and soon we shall be able to start a completely new life together. Be discreet always, and do nothing until you hear from me again. Burn this letter – now!'

Brenda had been working since 7.30 a.m. on the women's surgical ward, and it was now 4.15 p.m. Her Friday evening and the whole of Saturday were free, and she leaned back in one of the armchairs in the nurses' common room and lit a cigarette. Since leaving Oxford her life (albeit without Paul) had been fuller and freer than she could ever have hoped or imagined. She had made new friends and taken up new interests. She had been made aware, too, happily aware, of how attractive she remained to the opposite sex. Only a week after her appointment (she had given, as her referee, the name of the matron for whom she had worked prior to her nursing at the Radcliffe) one of the young married doctors had said to her, 'Would you like to come to bed with me, Brenda?' Just like that! She smiled now as she recollected the incident, and an unworthy thought, not for the first time, strayed across the threshold of her mind. Did she *really* want Paul all that badly now? With that son of his, Peter? He was a nice enough young boy, but. . . . She stubbed out her cigarette and reached for the *Guardian*. There was an hour and a half to wait before the evening meal, and she settled down to a leisurely perusal of the day's news. Inflation figures seemed mildly encouraging for a change; but the unemployment figures were not, and she knew only too well what unemployment could do to a man's soul. Middle East peace talks were still taking place, but civil wars in various parts of Africa seemed to be threatening the delicate balance between the superpowers. In the Home News, at the bottom of page three, there was a brief item on the discovery of a body on the tower of an Oxford church; but Brenda didn't reach it. The young doctor sat down beside her, unnecessarily but not distressingly close.

'Hello, beautiful! What about us doing the crossword together?'

He took the paper from her, folded it over to the crossword, and unclipped a biro from the top pocket of his white coat.

'I'm not much good at crosswords,' said Brenda.

'I bet you're good in bed, though.'

'If you're going to— '

'One across. Six letters. "Girl takes gun to district attorney." What's that, do you think?'

'No idea.'

'Just a minute! What about BRENDA? Fits, doesn't it? Gun
– "bren"; district attorney – "D.A." Voilà!'

Brenda snatched the paper and looked at the clue: Girl in bed
– censored. 'You're making it up,' she laughed.

'Lovely word "bed", isn't it?' He printed the letters of 'Brenda'
on the margin of the paper, and then neatly ringed the three letters
'b', 'e', 'd' in sequence. 'Any hope for me yet?'

'You're a married man.'

'And you ran away.' He underlined the three remaining letters
'r', 'a', 'n', and turned impishly towards her. 'No one'll know.
We'll just nip up to your room and— '

'Don't be silly!'

'I'm not silly. I can't help it, can I, if I lust after you every time
I see you in your uniform?' His tone was light and playful, but he
suddenly became more serious as the door opened and two young
nurses came in. He spoke softly now. 'Don't get cross with me if
I keep trying, will you? Promise?'

'Promise,' whispered Brenda.

He wrote BANNED into the squares for 1 Across, and read
out the clue for 1 Down. But Brenda wasn't listening. She didn't
wish to be seen sitting so closely to the young doctor as this, and
soon made up an excuse to go to her room, where she lay back on
her single bed and stared long and hard at the ceiling. The door was
locked behind her, and no one would have known, would they?
Just as he'd said. If only. . . . She could hardly bring herself to
read her own thoughts. If only he'd just walk up the stairs, knock
on the door and ask her again in his simple, hopeful, uncomplicated way, she knew that she would invite him in, and lie down –
just as she lay there now – gladly unresistant as he unfastened
the white buttons down the front of her uniform.

She felt tired, and the room was excessively stuffy – the
radiator too hot to touch. Gradually she dozed off, and when
she awoke her mouth was very dry. Something had woken her;
and now she heard the gently reiterated knock-knock at the door.
How long had she slept for? Her watch told her it was 5.45 p.m.
She fluffed her hair, straightened her uniform, lightly smeared on
a little lipstick and, with a little flutter of excitement in her tummy,
walked across to the door of her room, newly painted in dazzling
white gloss.

* * *

It was lying by the same door that a member of the cleaning staff found her the next morning. Somehow she had managed to crawl across from the centre of the small room; and it was clear that her fingers had groped in vain for the handle of the door, for the lower panels were smeared with the blood coughed up from her throat. No one seemed to know exactly where she came from, but the letter the police found beneath the lining of her handbag suggested strongly that she was, or had been, on the most intimate terms with a man called 'Paul', who had given his address only as 'Kidlington', and who had urged the recipient to burn the evidence immediately.

Chapter Twenty-two

It was on Saturday morning, and in the middle of page two of the long-delayed post-mortem report on the corpse found on the tower, that Morse came to the conclusion he might just as well be reading the *Chinese People's Daily*. He appreciated, of course, the need for some technical jargon, but there was no chance whatsoever for a non-medical man to unjumble such a farrago of physiological labellings. The first paragraph had been fairly plain sailing, though, and Morse handed the report over to Lewis:

The body is that of an adult Caucasian male, brachycephalic. Height: 5 ft 8½ in. Age: not easy to assess with accuracy, but most likely between 35 and 40. Hair: light brown, probably cut a week or so before death. Eyes: colouring impossible to determine. Teeth: remarkably good, strongly enamelled, with only one filling (posterior left six). Physical peculiarities: none observable, although it cannot be assumed that there were no such peculiarities, since the largest patch of skin, taken from the lower instep (left), measures only. . . .

Lewis passed the report back, for he had little wish to be reminded too vividly of the sight picked out so recently by the narrow beam of the verger's torch. Moreover, his next job promised to be quite gruesome enough for one morning, and for the next half-hour he sifted through the half-dozen transparent plastic bags containing the remnants of the dead man's clothes. Morse himself declined to assist in the unsavoury operation and expressed only mild interest when he heard a subdued whistle of triumph from his subordinate.

'Let me guess, Lewis. You've found a label with his name and telephone number.'

'As good as, sir.' In a pair of tweezers, he held up a small rectangular bus-ticket. 'It was in the breast-pocket of the jacket – 30p fare on 26 October. I reckon the fare from Kidlington to Oxford's about 30p – '

'Probably gone up by now,' muttered Morse.

' – and surely' (Lewis' eyes suddenly sparkled with excitement) 'that was the day when Paul Morris disappeared, wasn't it?'

'Never my strong point – dates,' said Morse.

For the moment, however, nothing was going to dampen Lewis' enthusiasm. 'Pity his teeth were so good, sir. He's probably not been near a dentist for years. Still, we ought to be able to— '

'You're taking an awful lot for granted, you know. We neither of us have the slightest proof about who the fellow is, agreed? And until— '

'No, we haven't. But there's not much sense in closing our eyes to the obvious.'

'Which is?'

'That the man we found is Paul Morris,' replied Lewis with firm confidence.

'Just because a young girl in one of his classes says he used to wear a dark suit – '

'And a blue tie.'

' – and a blue tie, all right, that makes him Paul Morris, you say? Lewis! You're getting as bad as I am.'

'Do you think I'm wrong?'

'No, no. I wouldn't say that. I'm just a little more cautious than you, shall we say?'

This was ridiculous. Morse, as Lewis knew only too well, was a man prepared to take the most prodigious leaps into the dark; and yet here he was now – utterly blind to the few simple facts that lay staring him in the face in broad daylight. Forget it, though!

It took Lewis no more than ten minutes to discover that Paul Morris had been a patient at the Kidlington Health Centre, and after a little quiet but urgent pressure the senior partner of that consortium was reading through the details on his medical card.

'Well?' asked Morse, as Lewis cradled the receiver.

'Fits pretty well. Thirty-eight years old, five feet nine inches, light-brown hair— '

'Fits a lot of people. Medium height, medium colouring, medium— '

'Don't you *want* to find out who he is?' Lewis stood up and looked down at Morse with unwonted exasperation in his voice. 'I'm sorry if all this doesn't fit in with any clever little theory you've thought up, but we've got to make some sort of start, haven't we?'

Morse said nothing for a few moments, and when he did speak his quiet words made Lewis feel ashamed of the tetchiness which had marked his own.

'Surely you can understand, can't you, Lewis, why I'm hoping that rotting corpse isn't Paul Morris? You see, if it is, I'm afraid we'd better start looking round pretty quickly, hadn't we? We'd better start looking round for yet another corpse, my old friend – a corpse aged about twelve.'

Like Bell, the landlord of 3 Home Close, Kidlington, had flu, but he gave Morse a sneezy blessing to look over the property, rented out (since Morris left) to a young married couple with one baby daughter. But no one answered Lewis' repeated knockings. 'Probably shopping,' he said as he sat down again next to Morse in the front of the police car.

Morse nodded and looked vaguely around him. The small crescent had been built some time in the early 1930s – a dozen or so red-brick, semi-detached properties, now beginning to look their age, with the supports of their slatted wooden fences virtually sopped and sapped away. 'Tell me, Lewis,' he said suddenly. 'Who do *you* think murdered Josephs?'

'I know it's not a very original idea, sir, but I should think it must have been this down-and-out fellow. Like as not he decided to pinch the collection-money, and Josephs got in his way, and he knifed him. Another possibility— '

'But why didn't Josephs yell the place down?'

'He did try to shout for help, sir, if you remember. Couldn't make himself heard above the organ, perhaps.'

'You could be right, you know,' said Morse, almost earnestly, as if he'd suddenly woken up to the fact that the obvious way of looking at things wasn't necessarily the wrong one. 'What about Lawson? Who killed him?'

'You know better than I do, sir, that the majority of murderers either give themselves up or commit suicide. There's surely not much doubt that Lawson committed suicide.'

'But Lawson didn't kill Josephs, did he? You just said— '

'I was going on to say, sir, that there was another possibility. I don't think Lawson himself actually killed Josephs, but I think he may have been *responsible* for killing him.'

'You do?' Morse looked across at his subordinate with genuine interest. 'I think you'd better take it a bit more slowly, Lewis. You're leaving me a long way behind, I'm afraid.'

Lewis allowed himself a mild grin of modest gratification. It wasn't often that Morse was the back-marker – just the opposite in fact: he was usually about three or four jumps ahead of his stable-companion. 'I think there's more than a possibility, sir, that Lawson got this down-and-out fellow to kill Josephs – probably by giving him money.'

'But why should Lawson want to kill Josephs?'

'Josephs must have had some hold over him.'

'And Lawson must have had some hold on this down-and-out fellow.'

'How right you are, sir!'

'Am I?' Morse looked across in a semi-bewildered way at his sergeant. He remembered how when he was taking his eleven-plus examination he was seated next to a boy renowned for his vacuous imbecility, and how this same boy had solved the tenth anagram whilst Morse himself was still puzzling over the third.

'As I see it,' continued Lewis, 'Lawson must have been looking after him all ways: meals, clothes, bed, everything.'

'He must have been like a sort of brother to him, you mean?'

Lewis looked at Morse curiously. 'Bit more than that, wasn't he, sir?'

'Pardon?'

'I said it was a bit more than being like a brother to him. He *was* a brother, surely.'

'You mustn't believe every piece of gossip you hear.'

'And you mustn't automatically disbelieve it, either.'

'If only we had a bit more to go on, Lewis!' And then the truth hit him, as it usually did, with a flash of blinding simplicity. Any corroboration he'd wanted had been lying under his nose since his visit with Lewis to Stamford, and a shiver of excitement ran along his scalp as at last he spotted it. 'Swanpole' had appeared several times in Bell's files as the probable name of the man who had been befriended by the Reverend Lionel Lawson, the man who had so strangely disappeared after the murder of Josephs. But, if all the rumours were right, that man's real name was Philip Edward Lawson, and whether you were a rather timid little fellow trying your eleven-plus question-paper, or whether you were a souring middle-aged detective sitting in a panda-car, *Swanpole was an anagram of P. E. Lawson.*

'I reckon this'll be mother and infant,' said Lewis under his breath. And indeed the heavily pregnant, dowdily dressed young woman dragging a two-year-old child along the pavement duly announced that she herself was the present occupier of 3 Home Close and that this was her daughter, Eve. Yes, she said, since the landlord had no objections, they could come in and have a look round the house. With pleasure.

Morse declined the offer of a cup of tea, and went out into the back garden. Clearly someone had been very busy, for the whole plot showed every evidence of a systematic and recent digging-over; and in the small garden-shed the tines of the fork and the bottom half of the spade were polished to a silvery smoothness.

'I see your husband's keen on growing his own veg.,' said Morse lightly, as he wiped his shoes on the mat by the back door.

She nodded. 'It was all grass before we came, but, you know, with the price of things these days— '

'Looks as if he's been doing a bit of double-digging.'

'That's it. Took him ages, but he says it's the only way.'

Morse, who hardly knew a sweet pea from a broad bean, nodded wisely, and gratefully decided he could forget about the garden.

'Mind if we have a quick look upstairs?'

'No. Go ahead. We only use two of the bedrooms – like the people who was here before us did. But – well, you never know. . . . ' Morse glanced down at her swollen belly and wondered how many bedrooms she might need before her carrying days were over.

Young Eve's bower, the smallest of the bedrooms, was redolent of urine, and Morse screwed up his nose in distaste as he
cursorily bent down over the uncarpeted floorboards. A dozen
Donald Ducks on the newly decorated walls seemed to mock his
aimless investigations, and he quickly left the room and closed the
door behind him.

'Nothing in either of the other rooms, sir,' said Lewis, joining
Morse on the narrow landing, where the walls had been painted
in a light Portland beige, with the woodwork cleanly finished off
in white gloss. Morse, thinking the colours a good match, looked
up at the ceiling – and whistled softly. Immediately above his head
was a small rectangular trap-door, some 3 feet by $2^1/_2$ feet, painted
as lovingly as the rest of the woodwork.

'You got a step-ladder?' Morse shouted downstairs.

Two minutes later Lewis was poking his head over the dusty
beams and shining a torch around the rafters. Here and there a
little of the early afternoon light filtered through ill-fitting joints
in the tiles, yet the surprisingly large roof-space seemed dismal
and darkly silent as Lewis took his weight on his wrists, gently
levered himself up into the loft, and warily trod from beam to
beam. A large trunk occupied the space between the trap-door
and the chimney-stack, and as Lewis opened the lid and shone
his torch on the slightly mildewed covers of the books inside a
black, fat-bellied spider scurried its way out of reach. But Lewis
was no arachnophobe, and quickly satisfying himself that the
trunk was packed only with books he prodded around amid the
rest of the débris: a furled Union Jack on a long blue pole, its
colours faded now and forlorn; an old camp-bed probably dating
from the Baden-Powell era; a brand-new lavatory-pan, patched
(for some unfathomable purpose) with strips of gummed brown
paper; an antiquated carpet-sweeper; two rolls of yellow insulation
material; and a large roll of something else – surely? – pushed up
tight between the beams and the roof-angle. Bending forward as
low as he could, and groping in front of him, Lewis managed to
reach the bundle, where his finger-tips prodded something soft
and where his torch-light shone on to a black shoe sticking out
of one end, the toe-cap filmed with a layer of grey dust.

'Anything there?' Lewis heard the quiet urgent voice from
below, but said nothing. The string tying the bundle together
broke as he tugged at it, and there unrolled before him a collection

of good-quality clothes: trousers, shirts, underclothes, socks, shoes and half a dozen ties – one of them a light Cambridge blue.

Lewis' grim face appeared suddenly framed in the darkened rectangle. 'You'd better come up and have a look, sir.'

They found another roll of clothes then, containing very much the same sort of items as the first. But the trousers were smaller, as indeed were all the other garments, and the two pairs of shoes looked as if they might have fitted a boy of about eleven or twelve. There was a tie, too. Just the one. A brand-new tie, with alternate stripes of red and grey: the tie worn by the pupils of the Roger Bacon Comprehensive School.

Chapter Twenty-three

A good many of the gradually swelling congregation were acid-faced spinsters of some fifty or sixty summers, several of whom glanced round curiously at the two strangers who sat on the back row of the central pews, next to the empty seat now clearly marked CHURCHWARDEN. Lewis both looked and felt extraordinarily uncomfortable, whilst Morse appeared to gaze round him with bland assurance.

'We do what everybody else does, understand?' whispered Morse, as the five-minute bell ceased its monotonous melancholy toll, and the choir set out in procession from the vestry and down the main aisle, followed by the incense-swinger and the boat-boy, the acolytes and torch-bearers, the master of ceremonies, and three eminent personages, similarly but not identically dressed, the last wearing, amongst other things, alb, biretta and chasuble – the ABC of ecclesiastical rig as far as Morse as yet had mastered it. In the chancel, the dramatis personae dispersed to their appropriate stations with practised alacrity, and suddenly all was order once more. Ruth Rawlinson, in a black, square choir-hat, took her place just beneath a stone-carved angel, and the assembled choir now launched into the Mass. During this time the churchwarden had slipped noiselessly into his seat, and handed Morse a little scrap of paper: 'Setting, *Iste Confessor*

– Palestrina'; at which Morse nodded wisely before passing it on to Lewis.

At half-time, one of the eminent personages temporarily doffed his chasuble and ascended the circular steps of the pulpit to admonish his flock against the dangers and follies of fornication. But Morse sat throughout as one to whom the admonition was not immediately applicable. Once or twice earlier his eyes had caught Ruth's, but all the female members of the choir were now sheltered from view behind a stout octagonal pillar, and he leaned back and contemplated the lozenge-shaped panes of stained glass – deepest ruby, smoky blue and brightest emerald – his mind drifting back to his own childhood, when he had sung in the choir himself. . . .

Lewis, too, though for different reasons, very soon lost all interest in fornication. Being, in any case, the sort of man who had seldom cast any lascivious glances over his neighbour's wife, he let his mind wander quietly over the case instead, and asked himself once more whether Morse had been right in his insistence that another visit to a church service would be certain to spark off a few flashes of association, 'to give the hooked atoms a shake', as Morse had put it – whatever that might mean. . . .

It took some twenty minutes for the preacher to exhaust his anti-carnal exhortations; after which he descended from the pulpit, disappeared from view through a screen in the side of the Lady Chapel, before re-emerging, chasuble redonned, at the top of the main chancel. This was the cue for the other two members of the triumvirate to rise and to march in step towards the altar where they joined their brother. The choir had already picked up their Palestrina scores once more, and amid much genuflexion, crossing and embracing the Mass was approaching its climactic moment. 'Take, eat, this is my body,' said the celebrant, and his two assistants suddenly bowed towards the altar with a perfect syn-chronisation of movement and gesture – just as if the two were one. Yes, just as if the two were one. . . . And there drifted into Morse's memory that occasion when as a young boy he'd been taken to a music-hall show with his parents. One of the acts had featured a woman dancing in front of a huge mirror, and for the first few minutes he had been unable to fathom it out at all. She wasn't a particularly nimble-bodied thing, and yet the audience had seemed enthralled by her performance. Then his mind had clicked: the dancer wasn't in front of a mirror at all! The apparent reflection was in reality another woman, dancing precisely the same steps, making precisely the same gestures, dressed in precisely the same costume. There were two women – not one. So? So, if there had been two dancers, could there not have been two priests on the night when Josephs was murdered?

The kittiwake was soaring once again. . . .

Five minutes after the final benediction, the church was empty. A cassocked youth had finally snuffed out the last candle in the galaxy, and even the zealous Mrs Walsh-Atkins had departed. *Missa est ecclesia*.

Morse stood up, slid the slim red *Order of Service* into his raincoat pocket, and strolled with Lewis into the Lady Chapel, where he stood reading a brass plaque affixed to the south wall:

In the vaults beneath are interred the terrestrial remains of Jn. Baldwin Esq., honourable benefactor and faithful servant of this parish. Died 1732. Aged 68 yrs. Requiescat in pace.

Meiklejohn smiled without joy as he approached them, surplice over his left arm. 'Anything else we can do for you, gentlemen?'

'We want a spare set of keys,' said Morse.

'Well, there *is* a spare set,' said Meiklejohn, frowning slightly. 'Can you tell me why— ?'

'It's just that we'd like to get in when the church is locked, that's all.'

'Yes, I see.' He shook his head sadly. 'We've had a lot of senseless vandalism recently – mostly schoolchildren, I'm afraid. I sometimes wonder. . . . '

'We shall only need 'em for a few days.'

Meiklejohn led them into the vestry, climbed on to a chair, and lifted a bunch of keys from a hook underneath the top of the curtain. 'Let me have them back as soon as you can, please. There are only four sets now, and someone's always wanting them – for bell-ringing, that sort of thing.'

Morse looked at the keys before pocketing them: old-fashioned keys, one large, three much smaller, all of them curiously and finely wrought.

'Shall we lock the door behind us?' asked Morse. It was meant to be lightly jocular, but succeeded only in sounding facetious and irreverent.

'No, thank you,' replied the minister quietly. 'We get quite a lot of visitors on Sundays, and they like to come here and be quiet, and to think about life – even to pray, perhaps.'

Neither Morse nor Lewis had been on his knees throughout the service; and Lewis, at least, left the church feeling just a little guilty, just a little humbled; it was as if he had turned his back on a holy offering.

'C'm on,' said Morse, 'we're wasting good drinking-time.'

At 12.25 p.m. the same day, a call from the Shrewsbury Constabulary came through to the Thames Valley Police H.Q. in Kidlington, where the acting desk-sergeant took down the message carefully. He didn't *think* the name rang any bells, but he'd put the message through the appropriate channels. It was only after he'd put the phone down that he realised he hadn't the faintest idea what 'the appropriate channels' were.

Chapter Twenty-four

Morse was lingering longer than usual, and it was Lewis who drained his glass first.

'You feeling well, sir?'

Morse put the *Order of Service* back in his pocket, and finished his beer in three or four gargantuan gulps. 'Never better, Lewis. Fill 'em up.'

'Your round, I think, sir.'

'Oh.'

Morse leaned his elbows beside the replenished pints and continued. 'Who murdered Harry Josephs? That's the key question really, isn't it?'

Lewis nodded. 'I had a bit of an idea during the service— '

'No more ideas, please! I've got far too many already. Listen! The prime suspect's got to be the fellow Bell tried to trace.

Agreed? The fellow who'd stayed several times at Lawson's vicarage, who was at the church when Josephs was murdered, and who disappeared afterwards. Agreed? We're not *quite* certain about it, but there's every chance that this fellow was Lionel Lawson's brother, Philip Lawson. He's hard up and he's a wino. He sees some ready cash on the collection-plate and he decides to pinch it. Josephs tries to stop him, and gets a knife in the back for his trouble. Any problems?'

'How did Philip Lawson come to have the knife?'

'He'd seen it lying around the vicarage, and he decided to pocket it.'

'Just on the off chance?'

'That's it,' said Morse, as he turned unblinking towards Lewis.

'But there were only a dozen or so people at the service, and the collection wouldn't have come to more than a couple of quid.'

'That's it.'

'Why not wait till one of the Sunday-morning services? Then he'd have the chance of fifty-odd quid.'

'Yes. That's true.'

'Why didn't he, then?'

'I dunno.'

'But no one actually *saw* him in the vestry.'

'He skipped it as soon as he'd knifed Josephs.'

'Surely someone would have seen him – or heard him?'

'Perhaps he just hid in the vestry – behind the curtain.'

'Impossible!'

'Behind the door to the tower, then,' suggested Morse. 'Perhaps he went up to the tower – hid in the bell-chamber – hid on the roof – I dunno.'

'But that door was locked when the police arrived – so it says in the report.'

'Easy. He locked it from the inside.'

'You mean he had – he had the key?'

'You say you read the report, Lewis. Well? You must have seen the inventory of what they found in Josephs' pockets.'

The light slowly dawned in Lewis' mind, and he could see Morse watching him, a hint of mild amusement in the inspector's pale-blue eyes.

'You mean – they didn't find any keys,' he said at last.

'No keys.'

'You think he took them out of Josephs' pocket?'

'Nothing to stop him.'

'But – but if he looked through Josephs' pockets, why didn't he find the money? The hundred quid?'

'Aren't you assuming,' asked Morse quietly, 'that that was all there was to find. What if, say, there'd been a *thousand*?'

'You mean— ?' But Lewis wasn't sure what he meant.

'I mean that everyone, *almost* everyone, Lewis, is going to think what you did: that the murderer didn't search through Josephs' pockets. It puts everyone on the wrong scent, doesn't it? Makes it look as if it's petty crime – as you say, a few pennies off the collection-plate. You see, perhaps our murderer wasn't really much worried about *how* he was going to commit the crime – he thought he could get away with that. What he didn't want was anyone looking too closely at the *motive*.'

Lewis was growing increasingly perplexed. 'Just a minute, sir. You say he wasn't much worried about how he murdered Josephs. But how *did* he? Josephs was poisoned as well as stabbed.'

'Perhaps he just gave him a swig of booze – doctored booze.'

Again Lewis felt the disconcerting conviction that Morse was playing a game with him. One or two of the points the chief had just made were more like those flashes of insight he'd learned to expect. But surely Morse could do better than this? He could do better himself.

'Josephs could have been poisoned when he took communion, sir.'

'You think so?' Morse's eyes were smiling again. 'How do you figure that out?'

'I reckon the churchwarden is usually the last person to take communion – '

'Like this morning, yes.'

' – and so this tramp fellow is kneeling there next to him and he slips something into the wine.'

'How did he carry the poison?'

'He could have had it in one of those rings. You just unscrew the top – '

'You watch too much television,' said Morse.

' – and sprinkle it in the wine.'

'It would be a whitish powder, Lewis, and it wouldn't dissolve immediately. So the Rev. Lionel would see it floating on top. Is that what you're saying?'

'Perhaps he had his eyes closed. There's a lot of praying and all that sort of thing when— '

'And Josephs himself? Was he doing a lot of praying and all that sort of thing?'

'Could have been.'

'Why wasn't Lawson poisoned, then? It's the minister's job to finish off any wine that's left and, as you say, Josephs was pretty certainly the last customer.'

'Perhaps Josephs swigged the lot,' suggested Lewis hopefully; and then his eyes irradiated a sudden excitement. 'Or perhaps, sir – or perhaps the two of them, the two Lawson brothers, were in it together. That would answer quite a lot of questions, wouldn't it?'

Morse smiled contentedly at his colleague. 'You know, Lewis, you get brighter all the time. I think it must be my company that does it.'

He pushed his glass across the table. 'Your turn, isn't it?'

He looked around him as Lewis waited patiently to be served: it was half-past one and Sunday lunch-time trade was at its peak. A man with a rough beard, dressed in a long ex-army coat, had just shuffled through the entrance and was standing apprehensively by the bar; a man in latish middle-age, it seemed, wearing that incongruous pair of sun-glasses, and grasping an empty flagon of cider in his hand. Morse left his seat and walked over to him.

'We met before, remember?'

The man looked slowly at Morse and shook his head. 'Sorry, mate.'

'Life not treating you so good?'

'Nah.'

'Been roughing it long?'

'Last back-end.'

'You ever know a fellow called Swanpole?'

'Nah. Sorry, mate.'

'Doesn't matter. I used to know him, that's all.'

'I knew somebody who did,' said the tramp quietly. 'Somebody who knew the fellah you was just talking about.'

'Yes?' Morse fumbled in his pockets and pushed a fifty-pence piece into the man's hand.

'The old boy I used to go round with – 'e mentioned that name recently. "Swanny" – that's what they called 'im, but 'e's not round these parts any more.'

'What about the old boy? Is he still around?'

'Nah. 'E's dead. Died o' pneumonia – yesterday.'

'Oh.'

Morse walked back thoughtfully to the table, and a few minutes later watched a little sadly as the landlord showed the tramp the way to the exit. Clearly there was no welcome for the poor fellow's custom here, and no cider slowly to be sipped on one of the city's benches that Sunday afternoon; not from this pub anyway.

'One of your pals?' grinned Lewis, as he placed two more pints on the table.

'I don't think he's got any pals.'

'Perhaps if Lawson were still alive— '

'He's just the man we've got to talk about, Lewis – suspect number two. Agreed?'

'You mean he suddenly disappeared from in front of the altar, murdered Josephs, and then came and carried on with the service?'

'Something like that.'

The beer was good, and Lewis leaned back, quite happy to listen.

'Come on, sir. I know you're dying to tell me.'

'First, let's just follow up your idea about the poisoned chalice. There are too many improbabilities in the way you looked at it. But what if the Rev. Lionel himself put the morphine in the wine? What then? After his brother's had a swig, he can pretend that the chalice is empty, turn round to the altar, slip in the powder, pour in a drop more wine, give it a quick stir – no problem! Or else he could have had two chalices – one of 'em already doctored – and just put the one down and pick up the other. Easier still! Mark my words, Lewis. If it was either of the two brothers who poisoned Josephs, I reckon the odds are pretty heavily on the Rev. Lionel.'

'Let me get it straight, sir. According to you, Lionel Lawson tried to kill Josephs, only to find that someone had done a far neater job a few minutes later – with a knife. Right?' Lewis shook his head. 'Not on, sir, is it?'

'Why not? The Rev. Lionel knows that Josephs'll go straight to the vestry, and that in a few minutes he's going to be very

dead. There's one helluva dose of morphine in the communion
wine and the strong probability is that Josephs is going to die
all nice and peaceful like, because morphine poisoning isn't a
painful death – just the opposite. In which case, Josephs' death
may well pose a few problems; but no one's going to be able to
pin the murder on the Rev. Lionel. The chalice has been carefully
washed out and dried, in strict accord with ecclesiastical etiquette
– a wonderful example of a criminal actually being encouraged to
destroy the evidence of his crime. Beautiful idea! But then things
began to go askew. Josephs must have guessed that something
was desperately wrong with him, and before he collapsed in the
vestry he just managed to drag himself to the curtains and shout
for help – a shout that all the congregation heard. But someone,
someone, Lewis, was watching that vestry like a hawk – the Rev.
Lionel himself. And as soon as he saw Josephs there he was off
down the aisle like an avenging Fury; and he was down there in
the vestry before anyone else had the nous or the guts to move;
and once inside he stabbed Josephs viciously in the back, turned
to face the congregation, and told 'em all that Josephs was lying
there – murdered.' (Morse mentally congratulated himself on an
account that was rather more colourful and dramatic than Bell's
prosaic reconstruction of exactly the same events.)

'He'd have got blood all over him,' protested Lewis.

'Wouldn't have mattered much if he'd been wearing the sort
of outfit they were wearing this morning.'

Lewis thought back to the morning service and those deep-
crimson vestments – the colour of dark-red blood. . . . 'But why
finish Josephs off with a knife? He'd be almost dead by then?'

'Lionel was frightened that Josephs would accuse him of doing
the poisoning. Almost certainly Josephs would have guessed what
had happened.'

'Probably everyone else would, too.'

'Ah! But if you stabbed Josephs in the back as well, people
are going to ask who did *that*, aren't they?'

'Yes. And they're going to think that was Lawson, too. After
all, it was Lawson's knife.'

'No one knew that at the time,' said Morse defensively.

'Did Bell think that's how it happened?'

Morse nodded. 'Yes, he did.'

'And do *you*, sir?'

Morse seemed to be weighing the odds in the mental balance. 'No,' he said finally.

Lewis leaned back in his chair. 'You know, when you come to think of it, it's a bit improbable that a minister's going to murder one of his own congregation, isn't it? That sort of thing doesn't happen in real life.'

'I rather hope it does,' said Morse quietly.

'Pardon, sir?'

'I said I rather hope it *does* happen. You asked me if Lionel Lawson killed Josephs in a particular way, and I said I didn't think so. But I reckon it *was* Lionel Lawson who killed Josephs, though in a rather more simple way. He just walked down to the vestry, knifed poor old Harry Josephs— '

'And then he walked back!'

'You've got it!'

Lewis' eyes rolled towards the tobacco-stained ceiling and he began to wonder if the beer had not robbed the inspector of his wits.

'With all the congregation watching him, I suppose.'

'Oh, no. They didn't see him.'

'They didn't?'

'No. The service at which Josephs was killed was held in the Lady Chapel. Now, if you remember, there's an archway in the screen separating this chapel from the central chancel, and I reckon that after the bread and wine had been dished out Lawson took a few of the utensils across from the altar in the Lady Chapel to the main altar – they're always doing that sort of thing, these priests.' (Lewis was hardly listening any more, and the landlord was wiping the tables, collecting glasses and emptying the ash-trays.) 'You want to know how he performed this remarkable feat, Lewis? Well, as I see it, the Rev. Lionel and his brother had got everything worked out, and that night the pair of 'em were all dressed up in identical ecclesiastical clobber. Now, when the Rev. Lionel walked out of the Lady Chapel for a few seconds, it wasn't the Rev. Lionel who walked back! There are only a few prayerful old souls in the congregation, and for that vital period the man standing in front of the altar, kneeling there, praying there, *but never actually facing the congregation*, is brother Philip! What do you think, Lewis? You think anyone looking up could have suspected the truth?'

'Perhaps Philip Lawson was bald.'

'Doubt it. Whether you go bald depends on your grandfather.'

'If you say so, sir.' Lewis was growing increasingly sceptical about all this jiggery-pokery with duplicate chalices and chasubles; and, anyway, he was anxious to be off home. He stood up and took his leave.

Morse remained where he was, the forefinger of his left hand marrying little droplets of spilt beer on the table-top. Like Lewis, he was far from happy about his possible reconstructions of Josephs' murder. But one idea was growing even firmer in his mind: there must have been some collaboration somewhere. And, like as not, that collaboration had involved the two brothers. But how? For several minutes Morse's thoughts were chasing round after their own tails. For the thousandth time he asked himself where he ought to start, and for the thousandth time he told himself that he had to decide who had killed Harry Josephs. All right! Assume it was the Rev. Lionel – on the grounds that *something* must have driven him to suicide. But what if it wasn't Lionel who had thrown himself from the tower? What if it was Philip who had *been* thrown? Yes, that would have been very neat. . . . But there was a virtually insuperable objection to such a theory. The Rev. Lionel would have to dress up his brother's body in his own clothes, his own black clerical front, his dog-collar – everything. And that, in such a short space of time after the morning service, was plain physically impossible! But what if . . . ? Yes! What if Lionel had somehow managed to persuade his brother to change clothes? Was it possible? Phew! Of course it was! It wasn't just possible – it was eminently probable. And why? *Because Philip Lawson had already done it before*. He'd agreed to dress up in his brother's vestments so that he could stand at the altar whilst Josephs was being murdered! Doubtless he'd been wonderfully well rewarded for his troubles on that occasion. So why not agree to a second little charade? Of course he would have agreed – little thinking he'd be dressing up for his own funeral. But with one seemingly insuperable problem out of the way, another one had taken its place: two people had positively identified the body that had fallen from the tower. Was that a real problem, though? Had Mrs Walsh-Atkins really had the stomach to look all that carefully at a face that was as smashed and bleeding as the rest of that mutilated body? Had her presence outside the church just been an accidental fluke? Because someone else had been there, had he not? Someone all ready to testify to the identity – the false identity – of the corpse: Paul Morris. And Paul Morris had subsequently been murdered because he knew too much: knew, specifically, that the Reverend Lionel Lawson was not only still in the land of the living, but was also a murderer, to boot! A double-murderer. A triple-murderer. . . .

'Do you mind drinking up, sir?' said the landlord. 'We often get the police round here on Sunday mornings.'

Chapter Twenty-five

On the same day, just after eight o'clock in the evening, a middle-aged man, his white shirt open at the neck, sat waiting in a brightly lit, well-furnished room. He was lounging back on a deep sofa, its chintz covers printed in a russet-and-white floral design, from which, smoking a king-sized Benson & Hedges cigarette, he vaguely watched the television. She was a little late tonight; but he had no doubts that she would come, for she needed him just as much as he needed her. Sometimes, he suspected, even more so. A bottle of claret, already opened, and two wine-glasses stood on the coffee-table beside him, and through the half-opened bedroom door he could see the hypotenuse of white sheet drawn back from the pillows.

Come on, girl!

It was eight-ten when the key (she had a key – of course she did!) scraped gently in the Yale lock and she entered. Although a steady drizzle persisted outside, her pale-blue mackintosh seemed completely dry as she slipped it from her shoulders, folded it neatly across its waist, and put it over the back of an armchair. The white cotton blouse she wore was drawn tight across her breasts, and the close-fitting black skirt clung to the curve of her thighs. She said nothing for a while; merely looked at him, her eyes reflecting no affection and no joy – just a simmering animal sensuality. She walked across the room and stood in front of him – provocatively.

'You told me you were going to stop smoking.'

'Sit down and stop moaning, woman. Christ! You make me feel sexy in that outfit.'

The woman did exactly as she was told, almost as if she would do anything he asked without demur; almost as if she thrived on the brusque crudity of his commands. There were no tender words of preliminary love-play on either side, yet she sat close to him as he poured two full glasses of wine, and he felt the pressure of her black-stockinged leg (good girl – she'd remembered!) against his own. In token of some vestigial respect they clinked their glasses together, and she leaned back against the sofa.

'Been watching the telly all night?' Her question was commonplace, uninterested.

'I didn't get back till half-past six.'

She turned to look at him for the first time. 'You're a fool going out like that. Especially on Sundays. Don't you realise— ?'

'Calm down, woman! I'm not a fool, and you know it. Nobody's seen me slipping out of here yet. And what if they did? Nobody's going to recognise me now.' He leaned across her and his fingers deftly unfastened the top button of her blouse. And then the next button.

As always with this man, the woman experienced that curious admixture of revulsion and attraction – compulsive combination! Until so very recently a virgin, she was newly aware of herself as a physical object, newly conscious of the power of her body. She lay back passively as he fondled her far beyond the point which a few months previously would have been either pleasing or permissible; and she seemed almost mesmerised as he pulled her up from the sofa and led the way through to the bedroom.

Their coitus was not exceptionally memorable – certainly not ecstatic; but it was satisfactory and satisfying. It usually was. As usual, too, the woman now lay between the sheets silently, feeling cheap and humiliated. It was not only her body that was naked, but her soul, too; and instinctively she drew the top of the sheet up to her neck and prayed that for a little while at least he would keep his hands and eyes away from her. How she despised him! Yet not one half, not one quarter as much as she had learned to despise herself.

It had got to stop. She hated the man and the power he had come to wield over her – yet she needed him, needed the firm virility of

his body. He had kept himself wonderfully fit . . . but, then, that
wasn't . . . wasn't surprising . . . not really . . . not really. . . .

Briefly she fell asleep.

He spoke to her as she stood by the door, the mackintosh
loosely over her shoulders. 'Same time on Wednesday?'

Once more the humiliation of it all settled heavily upon her,
and her lip was shaking as she replied.

'It's got to stop! You know it has!'

'Stop?' His mouth was set in a conceited sneer. 'You couldn't
stop. You know that as well as I do.'

'I can stop seeing you whenever I like, and there's nothing
you or anybody else— '

'Isn't there? You're in this as deeply as I am – don't you
ever forget that!'

She shook her head, almost wildly. 'You said you'd be going
away. You promised!'

'And I shall be. I'll be going very soon now, my girl, and that's
the truth. But until I do go, I keep seeing you – understand? I see
you when I want, as often as I want. And don't tell me you don't
enjoy it, because you do! And you know you do.'

Yes, she knew it, and she felt her eyes prickling with hurt at
his cruel words. How could she do this? How could she hate a
man so much – and yet allow him to make love to her? No! It
just couldn't go on like this! And the solution to all her troubles
was so childishly simple: she just had to go and see Morse, that
was all; tell him everything and face the consequences, whatever
they were. She still had a bit of courage left, didn't she?

The man was watching her carefully, half-guessing what was
going through her mind. He was used to taking swift decisions –
he always had been; and he saw his next moves as clearly as if he
were a grandmaster playing chess with a novice. He had known
all along that he would have to deal with her sooner or later; and,
although he had hoped it would be later, he realised now that the
game must be finished quickly. For him, sex had always come –
would always come – a poor second to power.

He walked over to her, and his face for once seemed kind
and understanding as he placed his hands so very lightly on her
shoulder, his eyes looking searchingly into hers.

'All right, Ruth,' he said quietly. 'I'll not be a nuisance to you

any more. Come and sit down a minute. I want to talk to you.'
Gently he took her arm and led her unresisting to the sofa. 'I won't
make any more demands on you, Ruth – I promise I won't. We'll
stop seeing each other, if that's what you really want. I can't bear
to see you unhappy like this.'

It had been many weeks since he had spoken to her in such
a way, and for a while, in the context of her wider grief, she felt
infinitely grateful for his words.

'As I say, I'll be going away soon and then you can forget me,
and we can both try to forget what we've done. The wrong we've
done – because it *was* wrong, wasn't it? Not about us going to bed
together – I don't mean that. That was something lovely for me
– something I shall never regret – and I'd hoped . . . I'd hoped
it was lovely for you, too. But never mind that. Just promise me
one thing, Ruth, will you? If you ever want to come to me – while
I'm here, I mean – please come! Please! You know I'll be wanting
you – and waiting.'

She nodded, and the tears trickled down her cheeks at the
bitter-sweet joy of his words as he cradled her head against his
shoulder and held her firmly to him.

She stayed there for what seemed to her a long, long time;
yet for him it was little more than a functional interspace, his
cold eyes staring over her shoulder at the hateful wallpaper behind
the television. He would have to kill her, of course: that decision
had been taken long ago anyway. What he was quite unable to
understand was the delay. Surely the police were not so stupid
as they seemed? Nothing so far – *why?* – about the Shrewsbury
murder. Nothing definite about the body on the tower. Nothing
at all about the boy. . . .

'Your mother all right?' He asked it almost tenderly.

She nodded and sniffed. It was time she was back home
with that mother of hers.

'Still cleaning the church?'

She nodded again, continued her sniffing, and finally broke
away from him.

'Mondays, Wednesdays and Fridays?'

'Just Mondays and Wednesdays now, I'm getting a bit slack
in my old age.'

'Still in the mornings?'

'Mm. I usually go about ten. And I've been going for a drink in

the Randolph when I've finished, I'm afraid.' She laughed nervously, and blew her nose loudly into her sopping handkerchief. 'I
could do with a quick drink now if— '

'Of course.' He fetched a bottle of Teacher's whisky from
the sideboard and poured a good measure into her wine-glass.
'Here you are. You'll feel better soon. You feel better *now*,
don't you?'

'Yes, I do.' She took a sip of the whisky. 'You – you remember
when I asked you whether you knew anything about – about what
they found up on the church tower?'

'I remember.'

'You said you hadn't any idea at all— '

'And I hadn't – haven't. Not the faintest idea. But I expect
the police will find out.'

'They just say they're – they're making enquiries.'

'They've not been bothering you again, have they?'

She breathed deeply and stood up. 'No. Not that I could
tell them anything about *that*.'

For a moment she thought of Morse with his piercing eyes.
Sad eyes, though, as if they were always looking for something
and never quite finding it. A clever man, as she realised, and a
nice man, too. Why, oh why, hadn't someone like Morse found
her many years ago?

'What are you thinking about?' His voice was almost brusque
again.

'Me? Oh, just thinking how nice you can be when you want.
That's all.'

She wanted to get away from him now. It was as if freedom
beckoned her from behind the locked door, but he was close
behind her and his hands were once again fondling her body; and
soon he had forced her to the floor where, within a few inches of
the door, he penetrated her once again, snorting as he did so like
some animal, whilst she for her part stared joylessly at a hair-line
crack upon the ceiling.

Chapter Twenty-six

'They tell me you can start a fibroblast from the commercial banger,' said Morse, rubbing his hands delightedly over the crowded plate of sausages, eggs and chips which Mrs Lewis had placed before him. It was half-past eight on the same Sunday evening.

'What's a fibroblast?' asked Lewis.

'Something to do with taking a bit of tissue and keeping it alive. Frightening really. Perhaps you could keep a bit of somebody alive – well, indefinitely, I suppose. Sort of immortality of the body.' He broke the surface of one of his eggs and dipped a golden-brown chip into the pale-yellow yolk.

'You won't mind if I have the telly on?' Mrs Lewis sat down with a cup of tea, and the set was clicked on. 'I don't really care what they do to me when I'm gone, Inspector, just as long as they make absolutely certain that I'm dead, that's all.'

It was an old fear – a fear that had prompted some of the wealthier Victorians to arrange all sorts of elaborate contraptions inside their coffins so that any corpse, revivified contrary to the expectations of the physicians, could signal from its subterranean interment immediate intelligence of any return to consciousness. It was a fear, too, that had driven Poe to write about such things with so grisly a fascination; and Morse refrained from mentioning the fact that those whose most pressing anxiety was they might be lowered living into their graves could have their minds set at rest: the disturbing medical truth was they quite certainly *would* be so lowered.

'What's on?' mumbled Morse, his mouth full of food.

But Mrs Lewis didn't hear him. Already, Svengali-like, the television held her in its holy trance.

Ten minutes later Lewis sat checking his football pools from the *Sunday Express*, and Morse leaned back on the sofa and closed his eyes, his mind preoccupied with death and people being lowered . . . lowered into their graves. . . .

Where – where was he?

Morse's head and shoulders jerked backwards, and he blinked himself awake. Lewis was still engrossed in the back page of the

Sunday Express, and on the television screen a head butler was walking sedately down some stairs to a wine-cellar.

That was it! Silently Morse cursed himself for his own stupidity. The answer had stared him in the face that very same morning: 'In the vaults beneath are interred the terrestrial remains. . . . ' A wave of excitement set his senses tingling as he stood up and drew back the edge of the curtain from the window. It was dark now, and the pane was spattered with fine drizzle. Things could wait, surely? What on earth was going to be gained by another nocturnal visit to a dark, deserted church, that couldn't wait until the light of the morning? But inevitably Morse knew that he couldn't wait and wouldn't wait.

'Sorry about this, Mrs Lewis, but I shall have to take the old man away again, I'm afraid. We shouldn't be long, though; and thanks again for the meal.'

Mrs Lewis said nothing, and fetched her husband's shoes from the kitchen. Lewis himself said nothing, either, but folded the newspaper away and resigned himself to the fact that his Lit-plan permutations had once more failed to land him a fortune. It was the 'bankers' that always let him down, those virtual certainties round which the plan had to be constructed. Like this case, he thought, as he pulled on his shoes: no real certainties at all. Not in his own mind anyway; and from what Morse had said at lunch-time no real certainties in *his* mind, either. And where the Dickens, he wondered, were they off to now?

As it happened, the church was neither dark nor deserted, and the main door at the north porch creaked open to reveal a suffused light over the quiet interior.

'Do you think the murderer's here, sir – confessing his sins?'

'I reckon somebody's confessing something,' muttered Morse.

His ears had caught the faintest murmurings and he pointed to the closed curtains of the confessional, set into the north wall.

Almost immediately an attractive young woman emerged, her sins presumably forgiven, and with eyes averted from the two detectives click-clacked her way out of the church.

'Nice-looking girl, sir.'

'Mm. She may have what you want, Lewis; but do you want what she's got?'

'Pardon, sir?'

The Reverend Canon Meiklejohn was walking silently towards them on his rubber-soled shoes, removing a long, green-embroidered stole from round his neck.

'Which of you wants to be first, gentlemen?'

'I'm afraid I've not been sinning much today,' said Morse. 'In fact there's many a day when I hardly get through any sinning at all.'

'We're all sinners, you know that,' said Meiklejohn seriously. 'Sin, alas, is the natural state of our unregenerate humanity— '

'Is there a crypt under the church?' asked Morse.

Meiklejohn's eyes narrowed slightly. 'Well, yes, there is, but – er – no one goes down there. Not as far as I know anyway. In fact I'm told that no one's been down there for ten years or so. The steps look as if they've rotted away and— '

Again Morse interrupted him. 'How can we get down there?'

Meiklejohn was not in the habit of being spoken to so sharply, and a look of slight annoyance crossed his face. 'I'm afraid you can't, gentlemen. Not now anyway. I'm due at Pusey House in about— ' He looked down at his wristwatch.

'You don't really need me to remind you what we're here for, do you, sir? And it's not to inspect your Norman font, is it? We're investigating a murder – a series of murders – and as police officers we've every right to expect a bit of co-operation from the public. And for the minute *you're* the public. All right? Now. How do we get down there?'

Meiklejohn breathed deeply. It had been a long day and he was beginning to feel very tired. 'Do you really have to talk to me as if I were a naughty child, Inspector? I'll just get my coat, if you don't mind.'

He walked off to the vestry, and when he returned Morse noticed the shabbiness of the thick, dark overcoat; the shabbiness, too, of the wrinkled black shoes.

'We shall need this,' said Meiklejohn, pointing to a twenty-foot ladder against the south porch.

With a marked lack of professionalism, Morse and Lewis manoeuvred the long ladder awkwardly out of the south door, through the narrow gate immediately opposite, and into the churchyard, where they followed Meiklejohn over the wet grass along the south side of the outer church wall. A street lamp threw a thin light on to the irregular rows of gravestones to their right, but the wall itself was in the deepest gloom.

'Here we are,' said Meiklejohn. He stood darkly over a horizontal iron grille, about six feet by three feet, which rested on the stone sides of a rectangular shaft cut into the ground. Through the grille-bars, originally painted black but now brown-flaked with rust, the torch-light picked out the bottom of the cavity, about twelve feet below, littered with the débris of paper bags and cigarette-packets. To the side of the shaft furthest from the church wall was affixed a rickety-looking wooden ladder, and parallel to it an iron hand-rail ran steeply down. Set just beneath the church wall was a small door: the entrance to the vaults.

For a minute or so the three men looked down at the black hole, similar thoughts passing through the mind of each of them. Why not wait until the sane and wholesome light of morning – a light that would dissipate all notions of grinning skulls and gruesome skeletons? But no. Morse put his hands beneath the bars of the grille and lifted it aside easily and lightly.

'Are you sure no one's been down here for ten years?' he asked.

Lewis bent down in the darkness and felt the rungs of the ladder.

'Feels pretty firm, sir.'

'Let's play it safe, Lewis. We don't really want any more corpses if we can help it.'

Meiklejohn watched as they eased down the ladder, and when it was resting firmly on its fellow Lewis took the torch and slowly and carefully made his way down.

'I reckon someone's been down here fairly recently, sir. One of the steps near the bottom here's broken, and it doesn't look as if it happened all that long ago.'

'Some of these hooligans, I expect,' said Meiklejohn to Morse. 'Some of them would do anything for what they call a "kick". But look, Inspector, I really must be going. I'm sorry if I – er. . . . '

'Forget it,' said Morse. 'We'll let you know if we find anything.'

'Are you – are you expecting to find something?'

Was he? In all honesty the answer was 'yes' – he was expecting to find the body of a young boy called Peter Morris. 'Not really, sir. We just have to check out every possibility, though.'

Lewis' voice sounded once more from the black hollow. 'The door's locked, sir. Can you— ?'

Morse dropped his set of keys down. 'See if one of these fits.'

'If it doesn't,' said Meiklejohn, 'I'm afraid you really will have to wait until the morning. My set of keys is just the same as yours and— '

'We're in, Meredith,' shouted Lewis from the depths.

'You get off, then, sir,' said Morse to Meiklejohn. 'As I say, we'll let you know if – er – if. . . . '

'Thank you. Let's just pray you don't, Inspector. This is all such a terrible business already that— '

'Goodnight, sir.'

With infinite pains and circumspection Morse eased himself on to the ladder, and with nervously iterated entreaties that Lewis make sure he was holding 'the bloody thing' firmly he gradually descended into the shaft with the slow-motion movements of a trainee tight-rope walker. He noted, as Lewis had just done, that the third rung from the bottom of the original wooden ladder had been snapped roughly in the middle, the left-hand half of it drooping at an angle of some forty-five degrees. And, judging from the yellowish-looking splintering at the jagged fracture, someone's foot had gone through the rung comparatively recently. Someone fairly heavy; or someone not so heavy, perhaps – with an extra weight upon his shoulder.

'Do you think there are any rats down here?' asked Morse.

'Shouldn't think so. Nothing to feed on, is there?'

'Bodies, perhaps?' Morse thought yet again of leaving the grim mission until the morning, and experienced a little shudder of fear as he looked up at the rectangle of faint light above his head, half-expecting some ghoulish figure to appear in the aperture, grinning horridly down on him. He breathed deeply.

'In we go, Lewis.'

The door creaked whiningly on its rusted hinges as inch by inch Lewis pushed it open, and Morse splayed his torch nervously to one side and then to the other. It was immediately clear that the main supporting pillars of the upper structure of the church extended down to the vaults, forming a series of stone recesses and dividing the subterranean area into cellar-like rooms that seemed (at least to Lewis) far from weird or spooky. In fact the second alcove on the left could hardly have been less conducive to thoughts of some skeletal spectre haunting these nether regions. For within its walls, dry-surfaced and secure, was no more than a large heap of coke (doubtless for the church's earlier heating system) with a long-handled spatulate instrument laid across it.

'Want a bit of free coke, sir?' Lewis was leading the way, and now took the torch from Morse and shone it gaily around the surprisingly dry interior. But as they progressed deeper into the darkness it became increasingly difficult to form any coherent pattern of the layout of the vaults, and Morse was already hanging back a little as Lewis shone the torch upon a stack of coffins, one piled on top of another, their lids warped and loose over the shrunken, concave sides.

'Plenty of corpses here,' said Lewis.

But Morse had turned his back and was staring sombrely into the darkness. 'I think it'll be sensible to come back in the morning, Lewis. Pretty daft trying to find anything at this time of night.' He experienced a deeper shudder of fear as he grew aware of something almost tangibly oppressive in the dry air. As a young boy he'd always been afraid of the dark, and now, again, the quaking hand of terror touched him lightly on the shoulder.

They retraced their way towards the entrance, and soon Morse stood again at the entrance to the vaults, his forehead damp with cold sweat. He breathed several times very deeply, and the prospect of climbing the solid ladder to the ground above loomed like a glorious release from the panic that threatened to engulf him. Yet it was a mark of Morse's genius that he could take hold of his weaknesses and almost miraculously transform them into his strengths. If anyone were going to hide a body in these vaults, he would feel something (surely!), at least *something*, of this same irrational fear of the dark, of the dead, of the deep-seated terror that forever haunted the subconscious mind? No one, surely, would venture too far, alone and under the cover of night, into these cavernous, echoing vaults? His foot kicked a cigarette-packet as he walked past the heap of coke, and he picked it up and asked Lewis to shine the torch on it. It was a golden-coloured empty packet of Benson & Hedges, along the side of which he read: 'Government health warning. Cigarettes can seriously damage your health. Middle tar.' When had the Government decided to stipulate such a solemn warning to cigarette addicts? Three, four, five years ago? Certainly not – what had Meiklejohn said? – ten years!

'Have a look under the coke, will you?' said Morse quietly.

Five minutes later Lewis found him. He was a young boy, aged about eleven or twelve, well preserved, just over five feet in height, and dressed in school uniform. Round his neck was a school tie, a tie tightened so viciously that it had dug deep into the flesh around the throat; a tie striped alternately in the regulation red and grey of the Roger Bacon School, Kidlington.

In the Pending file of the duty-sergeant's tray at Thames Valley H.Q., there still lay the handwritten message taken down from Shrewsbury.

Chapter Twenty-seven

Lewis reached Bell's office at 9.15 a.m. the following morning, but Morse had beaten him to it and was sitting behind the desk shouting into the phone with a livid fury.

'Well, get the stupid bugger, then. Yes! *Now*.' He motioned Lewis to take a seat, the fingers of his left hand drumming the desk-top in fretful impatience.

'You?' he bellowed into the mouthpiece at last. 'What the hell do you think you're playing at? It's been sitting under your bloody nose since yesterday lunch-time! And all you can do is to sit on that great fat arse of yours and say you're sorry. You'll be sorry, my lad – you can be sure of that. Now, just listen to me carefully. You'll go along to the Super's office as soon as I give you permission to put that phone down, and you tell him exactly what you've done and exactly what you've *not* done. Is that understood?'

The unfortunate voice at the other end of the line could only have mumbled something less than propitiatory, and Lewis sat almost fearfully through the next barrage of abuse.

'What are you going to tell him? I'll tell you what you're

going to tell him, my lad. First, you tell him you deserve the
bloody V.C. All right? Second, you tell him it's about time
they made you chief constable of Oxfordshire. He'll understand.
Third, you tell him you're guilty of the blindest bloody stupidity
ever witnessed in the history of the force. That's what you tell
him!' He banged down the phone and sat for a minute or so still
seething with rage.

Sensibly Lewis sat silent, and it was Morse who finally spoke.

'Mrs Josephs was murdered. Last Friday, in a nurses' hostel
in Shrewsbury.'

Lewis looked down at the threadbare carpet at his feet and
shook his head sadly. 'How many more, sir?'

Morse breathed deeply and seemed suddenly quite calm again.
'I dunno.'

'Next stop Shrewsbury, sir?'

Morse gestured almost hopelessly. 'I dunno.'

'You think it's the same fellow?'

'I dunno.' Morse brooded in silence and stared blankly at
the desk in front of him. 'Get the file out again.'

Lewis walked across to one of the steel cabinets. 'Who was
on the other end of the rocket, sir?'

Morse's face broke into a reluctant grin. 'That bloody fool,
Dickson. He was sitting in as duty-sergeant yesterday. I shouldn't
have got so cross with him really.'

'Why did you, then?' asked Lewis, as he put the file down
on the desk.

'I suppose because I ought to have guessed, really – guessed
that she'd be next on the list, I mean. Perhaps I was just cross
with myself, I dunno. But I know one thing, Lewis: I know that
this case is getting out of hand. Christ knows where we are; I
don't.'

The time seemed to Lewis about right now. Morse's anger
had evaporated and only an irritable frustration remained to
cloud his worried features. Perhaps he would welcome a little
bit of help.

'Sir, I was thinking when I got home last night about what
you'd been saying in the Bulldog. Remember? You said that
Lawson, the Reverend Lawson, that is, might just have walked
straight down— '

'For God's sake, Lewis, come off it! We're finding corpses

right, left and centre, are we not? We're in the biggest bloody muddle since God knows when, and all you can do is to— '

'It was you who said it – not me.'

'I *know* – yes. But leave me alone, man! Can't you see I'm trying to think? *Somebody's* got to think around here.'

'I was only— '

'Look Lewis. Just forget what I said and start thinking about some of the *facts* in the bloody case. All right?' He thumped the file in front of him viciously. 'The facts are all in here. Josephs gets murdered, agreed? All right. Josephs gets murdered. The Reverend Lionel Lawson jumps off the bloody tower. Right? He jumps off the bloody tower. Morris senior gets murdered and gets carted off to the same bloody tower. Right? Exit Morris senior. Morris junior gets strangled and gets carted off down the crypt. Right? Why not just accept these facts, Lewis? Why fart around with all that piddling nonsense about— Augh! Forget it!'

Lewis walked out, making sure to slam the door hard behind him. He'd had just about enough, and for two pins he'd resign from the force on the spot if it meant getting away from this sort of mindless ingratitude. He walked into the canteen and ordered a coffee. If Morse wanted to sit in peace – well, let the miserable blighter! He wouldn't be interrupted this side of lunch-time. Not by Lewis anyway. He read the *Daily Mirror* and had a second cup of coffee. He read the *Sun* and had a third. And then he decided to drive up to Kidlington.

There were patches of blue in the sky now, and the overnight rain had almost dried upon the pavements. He drove along the Banbury Road, past Linton Road, past Belbroughton Road, and the cherry- and the almond-trees blossomed in pink and white, and the daffodils and the hyacinths bloomed in the borders of the well-tended lawns. North Oxford was a lovely place in the early spring; and by the time he reached Kidlington Lewis was feeling slightly happier with life.

Dickson, likely as not would be in the canteen. Dickson was almost always in the canteen.

'I hear you got a bit of a bollocking this morning,' ventured Lewis.

'Christ, ah! You should have heard him.'

'I did,' admitted Lewis.

'And I was only standing in, too. We're so short here that they asked me to take over on the phone. And then this happens! How the hell was I supposed to know who she was? She'd changed her name anyway, and she only *might* have lived in Kidlington, they said. Huh! Life's very unfair sometimes, Sarge.'

'He can be a real sod, can't he?'

'Pardon?'

'Morse. I said he can be a real— '

'No, not really.' Dickson looked far from down-hearted as he lovingly took a great bite from a jam doughnut.

'You've not been in to the Super yet?'

'He didn't mean that.'

'Look, Dickson. You're in the force, you know that – not in a play-school. If Morse says— '

'He didn't. He rang me back half an hour later. Just said he was sorry. Just said forget it.'

'He didn't!'

'He bloody did, Sarge. We had quite a pally little chat in the end, really. I asked him if I could do anything to help, and d'you know what he said? Said he just wanted me to find out from Shrewsbury C.I.D. whether the woman was killed on Friday. That's all. Said he didn't give a monkey's whether she'd been knifed or throttled or anything, just so long as she was killed on Friday. Funny chap, ain't he? Always asking odd sort of questions – never the questions you'd think he'd ask. Clever, though. Christ, ah!'

Lewis stood up to go.

'It wasn't a sex murder, Sarge.'

'Oh?'

'Nice-looker, they said. Getting on a little bit, but it seems quite a few of the doctors had tried to get off with her. Still, I've always thought those black stockings are sexy – haven't you, Sarge?'

'Was she wearing black stockings?'

Dickson swallowed the last of his doughnut and wiped his fingers on his black trousers. 'Don't they all wear— ?'

But Lewis left him to it. Once more he felt belittled and angry. Who was supposed to be helping Morse anyway? Himself or Dickson? Aurrgh!

It was 11.45 a.m. when Lewis re-entered St Aldates Police Station and walked into Bell's office. Morse still sat in his chair, but his head was now resting on the desk, pillowed in the crook of his left arm. He was sound asleep.

Chapter Twenty-eight

Mrs Rawlinson was getting more than a little anxious when Ruth had still not arrived home at five minutes to one. She suspected – knew, really – that Ruth's visits to the Randolph were establishing themselves into a regular lunch-time pattern, and it was high time she reminded her daughter of her filial responsibilities. For the moment, however, it was the primitive maternal instinct that was paramount; and increasingly so, as the radio news finished at ten-past one with still no sign of her daughter. At a quarter-past one the phone rang, shattering the silence of the room with a shrill, abrupt urgency, and Mrs Rawlinson reached across for the receiver with a shaking hand, incipient panic welling up within her as the caller identified himself.

'Mrs Rawlinson? Chief Inspector Morse here.'

Oh my God! 'What is it?' she blurted out. 'What's happened?'

'Are you all right, Mrs Rawlinson?'

'Yes. Oh, yes. I – I just thought for a moment. . . . '

'I assure you there's nothing to worry about.' (But didn't *his* voice sound a little worried?) 'I just wanted a quick word with your daughter, please.'

'She's – she's not in at the moment, I'm afraid. She— ' And then Mrs Rawlinson heard the key scratching in the front door. 'Just a minute, Inspector.'

Ruth appeared, smiling and fresh-faced, round the door.

'Here! It's for you,' said her mother as she pushed the receiver into Ruth's hand, and then leaned back in her wheelchair, luxuriating in a beautifully relieved anger.

'Hello?'

'Miss Rawlinson? Morse here. Just routine, really. One of

those little loose ends we're trying to tie up. I want you to try to remember, if you can, whether the Reverend Lawson wore spectacles.'

'Yes, he did. Why— ?'

'Did he wear them just for reading or did he wear them all the time?'

'He always wore them. Always when I saw him anyway. Gold-rimmed, they were.'

'That's very interesting. Do you – er – do you happen to remember that tramp fellow? You know, the one who sometimes used to go to your church?'

'Yes, I remember him,' replied Ruth slowly.

'Did he wear spectacles?'

'No-o, I don't think he did.'

'Just as I thought. Good. Well, that's about all, I think. Er – how are you, by the way?'

'Oh, fine; fine, thanks.'

'You still engaged on your – er – your good works? In the church, I mean?'

'Yes.'

'Mondays and Wednesdays, isn't it?'

'Ye-es.' It was the second occasion she'd been asked the same question within a very short time. And now (she knew) he was going to ask her what time she usually went there. It was just like hearing a repeat on the radio.

'Usually about ten o'clock, isn't it?'

'Yes, that's right. Why do you ask?' And why did she suddenly feel so frightened?

'No reason, really. I just – er – I just thought, you know, I might see you again there one day.'

'Yes. Perhaps so.'

'Look after yourself, then.'

Why couldn't *he* look after her? 'Yes, I will,' she heard herself say.

'Goodbye,' said Morse. He cradled the phone and for many seconds stared abstractedly through the window on to the tar-macadamed surface of the inner yard. Why was she always so tight with him? Why couldn't she metaphorically open her legs for him once in a while?

'You ask some very odd questions,' said Lewis.

'Some very important ones, too,' replied Morse rather pompously. 'You see, Lawson's specs were in his coat pocket when they found him – a pair of gold-rimmed specs. It's all here.' He tapped the file on the death of the Reverend Lionel Lawson which lay on the desk in front of him. 'And Miss Rawlinson said that he always wore them. Interesting, eh?'

'You mean – you mean it wasn't Lionel Lawson who— '

'I mean exactly the opposite, Lewis. I mean it *was* Lionel Lawson who chucked himself off the tower. I'm absolutely sure of it.'

'I just don't understand.'

'Don't you? Well, it's like this. Short-sighted jumpers invariably remove their specs and put 'em in one of their pockets before jumping. So any traces of glass in a suicide's face are a sure tip-off that it wasn't suicide but murder.'

'But how do you know Lawson was short-sighted. He may have been— '

'Short-sighted, long-sighted – doesn't matter! It's all the same difference.'

'You serious about all this?'

'Never more so. It's like people taking their hearing-aids off before they have a bath or taking their false teeth out when they go to bed.'

'But the wife never takes hers out when she goes to bed, sir.'

'What's your wife got to do with it?'

Lewis was about to remonstrate against the injustice of such juvenile logic, but he saw that Morse was smiling at him. 'How do you come to know all this stuff about suicides anyway?'

Morse looked thoughtful for a few seconds. 'I can't remember. I think I read it on the back of a match-box.'

'And that's enough to go on?'

'It's something, isn't it? We're up against a very clever fellow, Lewis. But I just can't see him murdering Lawson, and then very carefully taking off his specs and putting 'em back in their case. Can you?'

No, Lewis couldn't see that; couldn't see much at all. 'Are we making any progress in this case, sir?'

'Good question,' said Morse. 'And, as one of my old school-masters used to say, "Having looked that problem squarely in the face, let us now pass on." Time we had a bit o' lunch, isn't it?'

The two men walked out of the long three-storey stone building that forms the headquarters of the Oxford Constabulary, up past Christ Church, across Carfax, and turned into the Golden Cross, where Morse decided that, for himself at least, a modicum of liquid refreshment was all that would be required. He had always believed that his mind functioned better after a few beers, and today he once again acted on his customary assumption. He should, he realised, be off to Shrewsbury immediately, but the prospect of interviewing hospital porters and nurses and doctors about times and places and movements and motives filled him with distaste. Anyway, there was a great deal of routine work to be done in Oxford.

Lewis left after only one pint, and Morse himself sat back to think. The flashing shuttles wove their patterns on the loom of his brain, patterns that materialised in different shapes and forms, but patterns always finally discarded. After his third pint, there was nothing to show for his cerebrations except the unpalatable truth that his fanciful theories, all of them, were futile, his thinking sterile, his progress nil. Somewhere, though, if only he could think where, he felt convinced that he had missed something – something that would present him with the key to the labyrinth. Yes, that's what he needed: the key to the— He had the key to the *church*, though. Was it there, in the church itself, that he had overlooked some simple, obvious fact that even at this very second lay waiting to be discovered?

Chapter Twenty-nine

Morse relocked the door in the north porch after him, conscious that he must try to look upon the interior of the church somehow differently. Previously he had gazed vaguely across the pews, his mind wafted away to loftier things by the pervasive sickly-sweet smell of the incense and the gloomy grandeur of the stained-glass windows. Not so now. He fingered through half a dozen devotional tracts, neatly stacked side by side on a wall-ledge just inside the door to the left; he examined a sheaf of leaflets to be filled in by those who wished to be added to the electoral roll; he drew back a curtain just behind the font and noticed a bucket, a scrubbing-brush and two sweeping-brushes. This was much better – he felt it in his bones! He examined postcards (6p each), which carried exterior views of the church taken from several angles, large close-ups of the famous font (much admired, it seemed, by all save Morse), and full frontal photographs of one of the grinning gar-goyles on the tower (how on earth had anyone taken those?); then he turned his attention to a stack of Guides to St Frideswide's (10p each), and another stack of Parish Notes (2p each) in which details of the current month's activities were fully listed; then, beside the west wall, he noted again the heaps of prayer-books with their dull-red covers and the heaps of hymn-books with their— He suddenly stopped, experiencing the strange conviction that he had already overlooked the vital clue that he'd been looking for. Was it something he'd just seen? Something he'd just heard? Something he'd just smelt? He went back to the door, retraced his few steps around the porchway, and then duplicated as far as he could his exact actions since entering the church. But it was no use. Whatever it was – if it was anything – was still eluding his grasp. Maddeningly. Slowly he paced his way up the central aisle and there stood still. The hymns from the previous evening's service were there, white cards with their red numbers, slotted into a pair of hymn-boards, one on either side of him. Odd! Why hadn't they been taken down? Was that one of Ruth Rawlinson's jobs? The bucket and the scrubbing-brush looked as if they had been used very recently, almost certainly by Ruth herself that very morning. Had she forgotten the hymn-boards? Or was that the job of the Vicar? Or one of the choir? Or one of the supernumerary assistants? For someone had to look after such matters. Come to think of it, someone had to decide the hymns, the psalms, the collects, epistles and gospels and the rest. Morse knew nothing about it, but he presumed that it was all laid down in some great holy book available for the guidance of the clergy. Must be. Like all those saints' days and other religious festivals. No one could carry all that stuff around in his head. What was more, someone would have to keep some sort of record of all the services every week – surely so! – especially when you had as many services as— *That* was it! He walked quickly back to the north porch and picked up a copy of the Parish Notes, and stared with curious excitement at the front page:

CHURCH OF ST FRIDESWIDE, OXFORD

Services: Sundays   Mass and Holy Communion 8 a.m.
10.30 a.m. (High) and 5.30 p.m.
Evening Service 6 p.m.
Weekdays Mass on Tuesdays and Fridays 7.30 a.m.
On Feast Days 7.30 a.m. and 7.30 p.m.
(Solemn)
Confessions: Tuesdays, Fridays and Saturdays, all at midday.
Or by arrangement with the clergy.
Clergy: The Revd. Canon K. D. Meiklejohn (Vicar), St
Frideswide's Vicarage.
The Revd Neil Armitage (Curate), 19 Port Meadow
Lane.

April

1st   In Octave of Easter
2nd   LOW SUNDAY. Preacher at 10.30 a.m.
The Bishop of Brighton. Annual Parish
Meeting 6.15 p.m.
3rd   ST RICHARD OF CHICHESTER
Mass at 8 a.m. and 7.30 p.m.
4th   Holy Hour 11 a.m.
5th   Mothers' Union 2.45 p.m.
6th   Deanery Synod 7.45 p.m.
8th   Holy Hour 5 to 6 p.m.
9th   EASTER II . . .

So it went on, through the whole month, with one major Feast Day (Morse noted) in two of the other three weeks. But so what? Was there anything here that was of the slightest interest or value? The name 'Armitage' was new to Morse, and he suspected that the Curate was probably a fairly recent acquisition, and had almost certainly been one of the three wise men in the purple vestments. Still, with all those services on the programme, there'd be need of a helping hand, wouldn't there? It would be a pretty hefty assignment for one poor fellow, who presumably was entrusted, in addition, with the pastoral responsibilities of visiting the lame and the sick and the halt and the blind. My goodness, yes! Meiklejohn would certainly need a co-labourer in such an extensive vineyard. And then a little question posed itself to Morse's mind, and for a second or two the blood seemed to freeze in his cheeks. *Did Lawson have a curate?* It should be easy enough to find out, and Morse had a peculiar notion that the answer might be important, though exactly *how* important he had, at this point, no real idea at all.

He pocketed the Parish Notes, and turned back into the church. A long tasselled rope barred access to the altar in the Lady Chapel, but Morse stepped irreverently over it and stood before the heavily embossed and embroidered altar-cloth. To his immediate left was the arched opening to the main altar, and slowly he walked through it. In a niche to the left of the archway was an Early English piscina, and Morse stopped to look at it carefully, nodding slowly as he did so. He then turned left, made his way along the high carved screen which separated the Lady Chapel from the main nave, skipped lightly across the entrance to the Lady Chapel, and came to a halt outside the vestry. For some reason he looked quite pleased with himself and nodded his head again several times with a semi-satisfied smile.

He stood where he was for several minutes looking around him once more; and, indeed, had he but realised it, he was now within a few yards of the clue that would smash some of his previous hypotheses into a thousand pieces; but for the moment the Fates were not smiling upon him. The north door was opened and Meiklejohn entered, carrying a carton of electric-light bulbs, in the company of a young man balancing an extending ladder on his shoulder.

'Hello, Inspector,' said Meiklejohn. 'Discovered anything more yet?'

Morse grunted non-committally, and decided that the investigation of the vestry could, without any cosmic ill-consequence, be temporarily postponed.

'We're just going to change the bulbs,' continued Meiklejohn. 'Have to do it, you know, every three or four months. Quite a few have gone already, I'm afraid.'

Morse's eyes travelled slowly up to the tops of the walls where, about forty feet above the floor he could see a series of twin electric-light bulbs, each pair set about twenty feet apart.

Meanwhile the ladder had been propped up beneath the nearest lights, and in a progressively more precarious stutter of elongations the two men were pushing the ladder even higher until the slimly converging top of the third extension now rested about two or three feet below the first pair of bulbs.

'I'm afraid,' said Morse, 'that I just haven't got the stomach to stop and witness this little operation any further.'

'Oh, it's not so bad, Inspector, as long as you're careful. But I must admit I'm always glad when it's over.'

'He's a better man than I am,' said Morse, pointing to the young man standing (rather nervously?) on the second rung and gently manoeuvring the ladder on to a more firmly based vertical.

Meiklejohn grinned and turned to Morse quietly. 'He's about as bad as you are – if not worse. I'm afraid I have to do the job myself.'

And may the good Lord be with you, thought Morse, as he made his rapid exit, completely forgetting that he was debtor to church funds to the sum of 2p; forgetting, too, that there was a most important question he had yet to put to the dare-devil incumbent of St Frideswide's.

In all there were twenty bulbs to change, and as always the job was taking an unconscionably long time to complete. To any observer of the scene, it would have appeared that the young man who stood dutifully with his foot placed firmly on the bottom rung of the ladder seemed quite incapable of raising his eyes above the strict horizontal as Meiklejohn repeatedly ascended to the dizzy heights above him where, standing on the antepenultimate rung, he would place his left hand for support against the bare wall, stretch up to twist out one of the old bulbs, place it carefully in his coat pocket, and then insert one of the new bulbs with an upward thrust of his right arm which virtually lifted his body into unsupported space. With the merest moment of carelessness, with the slightest onset of giddiness, the good vicar would have lost his precarious balance and plunged to his death on the floor so far below; but mercifully the task was now almost complete, and the ladder was in place below the last pair of bulbs when the door (which had remained unlocked) creaked open to admit a strange-looking man whose beard was unkempt, who was dressed in a long, shabby greatcoat, and who wore an incongruous pair of sun-glasses. For a moment or two he looked about him, unaware of the presence of the other two men. The afternoon had grown dull and the electricity had been turned off whilst the bulbs were being changed.

'Can I help you?' asked Meiklejohn.

'What?' The man started nervously. 'Cor, you frightened me, guv.'

'Please do have a look around. You're most welcome.'

'Sorright. I just – I just wanted to – er. . . . '

'I can show you around myself in a minute if you can— '

'Nah. Sorright, guv.' He shuffled out, and Meiklejohn raised his eyebrows to the young man. The ladder was ready again now and he put his right hand up to the rung just above his head – and then stopped.

'You remember my predecessor here – poor Mr Lawson? He had a way with these down-and-outs, they tell me. Often used to have one or two of them staying with him for a few days. You probably know that anyway. Perhaps I should make more of an effort than I do. Still, we're all different, Thomas. Just as the good Lord made us.' He smiled, rather sadly, and began to climb. 'Perhaps poor Mr Lawson wasn't very good at changing light-bulbs, eh?'

Thomas managed a ghostly-weak smile in response and took up his guardian rôle on the bottom rung, his eyes once more averted from the fast-disappearing soles of the vicar's black shoes. Funny, really! He'd joined St Frideswide's church just over a year ago (he was an undergraduate at Hertford College) and he remembered the previous vicar very well indeed. He thought he remembered other things, too. For example, he thought he remembered the tramp who'd just walked in. Hadn't he seen him in church once or twice?

Chapter Thirty

The decision to travel to Shrewsbury was taken, momentarily and arbitrarily, when Morse had walked out of the church on his way back to St Aldates; and as Lewis drove the police car round the Woodstock Road roundabout and headed out on to the A34 both men were mentally calculating the possible time-schedule. It was already 4.20 p.m. Two hours, say, to get there – if the traffic was reasonable; two hours actually there; another two hours back. So, with a bit of luck, they could be back in Oxford by about 10.30 p.m.

Morse, as was his wont, spoke little in the car, and Lewis was quite happy to give his whole attention to the motoring. They had started in time to miss the diurnal mass exodus from Oxford which begins at about a quarter to five and continues its semi-paralytic progress for almost another hour. It was good fun, too, driving in a conspicuously marked POLICE car. As always other road-users immediately became punctilious about speed-restrictions as they spied the pale-blue and white car in their mirrors, and ostentatiously shunned the slightest suspicion of sub-standard driving, behaving with a courtesy and care that were wildly at variance with their customary frenetic aggression.

So it was now.

Lewis turned left off the A34 through Chipping Norton, up through Bourton-on-the-Hill, through Moreton-in-Marsh, and then, with the Vale of Evesham opening out in a vast panorama before them, down the long, steep hill into Broadway, its houses of mellowed Cotswold stone gleaming a warm yellow in the late afternoon sun. At Evesham, Morse insisted that they took the road to Pershore, in which town he enthused lovingly over the red-brick houses with their white-painted window-frames; and at Worcester he directed Lewis along the Bromyard Road.

'I've always thought,' said Morse, as they turned north from Leominster on to the A49, 'that this is one of the prettiest roads in England.'

Lewis sat silent. It was also a pretty long way round, and at this rate it would be about seven before they reached Shrewsbury. Yet as they drove past Church Stretton it seemed to Lewis that Morse was perhaps right; and even more so as they left the Long Mynd behind them, when the sun, still hovering over the Welsh hills far off on the western horizon, suffused the early evening sky with a fiery glow and turned the white clouds to the softest shade of purple.

It was half-past seven when finally the two Oxford detectives were seated in the Superintendent's office at the Salop Police H.Q.; and it was half-past eight when they emerged.

Morse had said little, and Lewis less, and neither man felt that the meeting was of more than routine value. There were no grounds for suspecting anyone, and not the slightest whisper of a likely motive. The dead woman had been quietly popular with her fellow-nurses, slightly less quietly popular with the surgeons and housemen, and it was difficult to believe that even Florence Nightingale herself could have found too many faults with her efficient and experienced nursing. One of the doctors had spoken to her the previous evening, had sat in the nurses' common room with her doing a crossword puzzle; but, although he was probably the last person (apart from the murderer) to see her alive, there was no reason whatsoever to suspect that he'd had anything to do with her death. But somebody had. Somebody had strangled her brutally with her own belt and left her for dead on the floor by the side of her bed, from where she had later managed to crawl to the door of her room to try desperately to call for help. But no one had heard her, and no one had come.

'I suppose we'd better see her?' said Morse dubiously, as they all trooped out of the Superintendent's office.

In the cream-tiled police morgue, a constable pulled out a sliding container from a stainless-steel structure, and turned back the sheet from the face – white, waxy-textured and washed, the lolling bloodshot eyes bearing their chilling witness to the agony of her death. At the base of her neck and running up to her right ear was the hideous groove left by the belt.

'Probably left-handed,' muttered Lewis, 'if he strangled her from the front, that is.' He turned towards Morse as he spoke, and noticed that the great man had his eyes shut.

Five minutes later Morse was looking immeasurably happier as he sat in the anteroom surveying the contents of the murdered woman's pockets and handbag.

'We should be able to check the handwriting easily enough,' said Lewis, as he saw Morse studying the letter from Kidlington.

'We hardly need to, do we?' said Morse, putting it to one side and turning to the other contents of the handbag. There were two pocket diaries, a lady's handkerchief, a leather purse, three luncheon vouchers, and the usual bric-à-brac of feminine toiletry: perfume, nail-file, comb, hand-mirror, eye-shadow, lipstick and tissues.

'Was she wearing much make-up when you found her?' asked Morse.

The Superintendent frowned slightly and looked less than comfortable. 'I think she was wearing some, but – er. . . . '

'I thought you said she'd just come off duty. They don't let 'em slink round the wards all tarted up, surely?'

'You think she might have been expecting somebody?'

Morse shrugged his shoulders. 'Possibility, isn't it?'

'Mm.' The Superintendent nodded thoughtfully, and wondered why he hadn't thought of that himself; but Morse had brushed aside the cosmetics as if whatever interest they might momentarily have exercised over him was now a thing of the past.

The purse contained six one-pound notes, about fifty pence in small change, and a local bus timetable. 'No driving licence' was Morse's only comment, and the Superintendent confirmed that as far as they knew she'd had no car since coming to work at the hospital.

'She was pretty anxious to cover up her tracks, Super. Perhaps,' he added quietly, 'perhaps she was frightened that somebody would find her.' But again he seemed to lose interest in the line of thought upon which he had embarked, and proceeded to turn his attention to the two slim diaries, one for the current, one for the previous year.

'She wasn't exactly a Samuel Pepys, I'm afraid,' said the Superintendent. 'The odd jotting here and there, but not much to go on as far as I can see.'

Mrs Brenda Josephs had certainly started off the two years with admirable intentions, and the first few days of each of the two Januarys were fairly fully documented. But, even then, such *aide-mémoire* entries as her 'Six fish fingers' or '8.30 Nurses' Social' seemed hardly likely to lead the Salop or the Oxon constabulary very much nearer to the apprehension of her murderer. The expression on Morse's face was mildly sour as he flicked rather aimlessly through the pages, and in truth he found little to hold his attention. On the day of Brenda's death he noticed the single entry 'Periods due'; rather pathetic, but of little consequence.

Lewis, who hitherto had felt his contribution to the visit to have been less than positively constructive, picked up the diary for the previous year and examined it with his usual exaggerated care. The writing was neatly and clearly charactered, but for the

most part so small that he found himself holding the diary at
arm's length and squinting at it lop-sidedly. Against virtually
every Sunday throughout the year up to mid-September were
the letters 'SF', and these same letters were repeated at irregular
intervals and on irregular week-days throughout the same period.
'SF'? The only thing he could think of was Science Fiction, but
that was obviously wrong. There was something else, though.
From July up until late September there was a series of 'P's,
written (almost imperceptibly) in pencil in the ruled blue lines
which separated the days of the month from each other. And
the day was always a Wednesday.

'What does "SF" stand for, sir?'

'Saint Frideswide's,' said Morse without a moment's thought.

Yes. That must be it. Harry Josephs (as Lewis now recalled)
had been disqualified from driving, and it was his wife's duty to
take him down to the church in her own car. That fitted all right.
Sunday mornings for the big service of the week, and then, at
intermittent intervals, the mid-week days whenever some prestigious saint or other held an anniversary. That was it. No doubt
about it.

'What does "P" stand for, sir?'

Morse reeled them off with the fluency of a man who had
devoted too many hours of his life to the solving of crosswords:
'soft', 'president', 'prince', 'page', 'participle'.

'Nothing else?'

'Phosphorus?'

Lewis shook his head. 'Probably the initial of someone's name.
It's a capital "P".'

'Let's have a look, Lewis.'

'Could be "Paul", sir? Paul Morris?'

'Or Peter Morris – if she's a paedophile.'

'Pardon?'

'Nothing.'

'Always on Wednesdays, though, sir. Perhaps she suddenly
decided she wanted to see him more often— '

'And her old man was in the way and so she bumped him off?'

'I've heard of odder things. She said she'd nipped off to
the pictures that night, didn't she?'

'Mm.' Morse's interest appeared to be engaged at last. 'How
much does it cost to go to the pictures these days?'

'Dunno, sir. A quid? One-fifty?'

'Expensive for her, wasn't it? She couldn't have been there much more than an hour, at the most.'

'*If* she went, sir. I mean, she mightn't have gone to the pictures at all. She might have just crept quietly back into the church and— '

Morse nodded. 'You're quite right. She probably had the best motive of the lot of 'em. But you're forgetting something. The door creaks like hell.'

'Only the north door.'

'Really?' But Morse had clearly lost all interest in creaking doors, and Lewis found himself once more wondering why they'd bothered to come all this way. Nothing had been learned. No progress had been made.

'There's another "P", isn't there?' said Morse suddenly. 'We've forgotten Philip Lawson.'

Yes, Lewis had forgotten Philip Lawson; but where on earth was *he* supposed to fit into this particular picture?

The constable packed up Brenda Morris' possessions, replaced them in their plastic bags, and redeposited the bags in a labelled cabinet. Morse thanked the Superintendent for his co-operation, shook hands with him, and got into the car beside Lewis.

It was on the Kidderminster road about six or seven miles south of Shrewsbury that a wave of chilling excitement, starting from the bottom of the back, gradually crept up to the nape of Morse's neck. He tried to conceal the agitation of his mind as he questioned Lewis. 'Did you say that Brenda Josephs marked off the days when she took her husband to church?'

'Looked like it, sir. And quite a few times apart from Sundays.'

' "SF", you said. She put "SF"?'

'That's about it, sir. As you said, it's "St Frideswide's". Not much doubt about that.' He turned suddenly and glanced at Morse, who was staring with extraordinary intensity into the outer darkness of the night. 'Unless, of course, you think it stands for something else?'

'No, no. It doesn't stand for anything else.' And then, very quietly, he said. 'Turn round, please. We're going back.'

The luminous dial on the fascia board showed half-past ten, just gone, and things were running way behind even the most pessimistic schedule. But Lewis turned round at the earliest possible opportunity. He also was a man under authority.

The constable in the police mortuary re-opened the cabinet and shook out the contents of the plastic bags once more. They were always a funny lot – these fellows from other forces.

Morse managed to keep his hand from shaking as he picked up the earlier of the two diaries and turned to the one specific page. And as he looked at the page the blood seemed to congeal in his jowls, and a slow smile of joyous satisfaction formed about his mouth.

'Thank you very much, constable. Thank you very much. You don't think I could take this diary?'

'I don't know about that, sir. The Super's gone off now and— '

Morse held up his right hand like a priest delivering the benediction. 'Forget it! Doesn't matter!' He turned quickly to Lewis. 'See that?' He pointed to the space for Monday, 26 September, the day on which Harry Josephs had been murdered; and Lewis' forehead creased into a frown as he looked at it, and then looked at it again. The space was completely blank.

'You remember your Sherlock Holmes, Lewis?' But whether or not Lewis was familiar with the works of that great man was not immediately apparent, for clearly Morse himself had a good many passages of Holmesian dialogue by heart, and before Lewis could reply he proceeded to recite one:

' "Is there any point to which you would wish to draw my attention."

' "To the curious incident of the dog in the night-time."

' "The dog did nothing in the night-time."

' "That was the curious incident." '

'I see,' said Lewis, seeing not.

'How fast will she go?' asked Morse as he clambered into the police car once more.

'About ninety – bit more – on the straight.'

'Well, put the flasher on and start the siren up. We must get back to Oxford quickly, all right?'

The car sped through the darkened countryside, down through Bridgnorth and Kidderminster, along the old Worcester Road to Evesham, and then in an almost incredibly short time back to Oxford. An hour and a half – almost to the minute.

'Back to the station, is it?' asked Lewis as he turned into the Northern Ring Road.

'No. Take me straight home, Lewis. I'm tired out.'

'But I thought you said— '

'Not tonight, Lewis. I'm dead beat.' He winked at Lewis and slammed the door of the Ford behind him. 'Good fun, wasn't it? Sleep tight! We've got work to do in the morning.'

Lewis himself drove off home happily. His honest soul had very few vices – but fast driving was certainly one of them.

Chapter Thirty-one

Perhaps the events of the past few days had disturbed the Reverend Keith Meiklejohn rather less than they should have done; and being an honest man the realisation of this was worrying to him. It was true that, inducted as he had been only in the previous November, he had not known the Morris family personally, and could not therefore be expected to react too keenly to the tragic discoveries of what (if rumour were to be believed) were the bodies of father and son. Yet as he sat in his study at 9.30 a.m. on Tuesday morning he knew that his compassion should have been engaged more deeply, and he wondered about himself; wondered about his church, too.

Meiklejohn was a robust, well-built man, forty-one years of age and happily unmarried. His childhood had been spent in a family household brimming with evangelical piety, and one forever frequented by inveterate god-botherers and born-again Baptists. From his earliest years the promises of eternal life and the terrors of the lake that burneth with fire and brimstone had been as real to him as liquorice allsorts and the landscape of his Dorset home. In his early youth, whilst his classmates discussed the prospects of their favourite football teams or the merits of their new racing bikes, young Keith had grown zealous over matters ecclesiastical and theological, and by the age of sixteen the way ahead was quite clear: he was destined to take holy orders. As a young curate he had at first been moderately low-church in his views on the liturgy and the sacraments; but gradually he had been more and more attracted towards the doctrines of the Oxford

Movement, and at one point he had come within a communion wafer of conversion to the Roman Church. But all that was in the past. With a new-found balance, he discovered he could tread the tight-rope of High Anglicanism with security and confidence, and it was pleasing to him that his congregation appeared to think well of him for doing so. His predecessor, Lionel Lawson, had not (it seemed) found universal favour with an ecclesiastical stance that was decidedly more middle-and-leg than middle-and-off. In fact, when Lawson's curate, some five years earlier, had been promoted to a parish of his own there had been no request to the Bishop for a replacement, and Lawson himself had coped single-handed with the manifold duties of St Frideswide's parish. Inevitably, of course, there had been cuts in services, and it was Meiklejohn's resolve to restore as soon as possible the daily masses at 11.15 a.m. and 6.15 p.m. which were a wholly necessary feature (as he saw things) of a church that was dedicated to the glory of God.

Yet, as he sat at the ancient roll-top desk, the page over which his pen had been poised for several minutes remained blank. It was high time he preached again on transubstantiation: a tricky issue, of course, but one that was vital for the spiritual health of the brethren. But could that sermon wait, perhaps? His limp-leather copy of the Holy Writ lay open before him at the book of Hosea. A marvellous and memorable piece of writing! It was almost as if the Almighty himself had not really known what to do with his people when their goodness and mercy were as evanescent as the mists or the early dews that melted away in the morning sun. Was the Church in danger of losing its love? For without love the worship of God and the care of the brethren was little more than sounding brass and tinkling cymbals. . . . Yes, a possible sermon was just beginning to shape itself nicely. Not too forcefully expressed: nothing to smack too strongly of the stumping pulpit-thumper. But then another verse caught his eye from an earlier chapter of the same prophecy: 'Ephraim is joined to idols; let him alone.' Another striking verse! Idolaters were, after all, those within the Church – not those outside it. Those who worshipped, but who worshipped a false representation of God. And not just the golden calf, either. There was always a danger that other representations could get in the way of true worship: yes – he had to admit it! – things like incense and candles and holy water and crossings and genuflections, and all the sheer apparatus of ceremonial which could perhaps clog up the cleansing power of the Holy Spirit. It was possible, too – only too easy, in fact – to be blinded to the spiritual health of the Church by the arithmetical aggregation of its membership, especially when he considered (as he did with pride) the undoubted increase in the numbers attending divine worship since his own arrival. The records showed that there had been times under Lawson's régime when attendance had been just a little disappointing; and indeed some occasions in mid-week when it had been difficult to muster much of a congregation at all! But God didn't just count heads – or so Meiklejohn told himself; and he pondered again the central problem that had dominated his earlier thinking: should he not be more concerned than he was about the spiritual health of his church?

He was still undecided about the text of his next sermon, the page still blank beneath his pen, the disturbing words of the prophet Hosea still lying before him, when the door-bell rang.

Had it been the will of Providence that he had been pondering the state of St Frideswide's soul? At the very least, it was an uncanny coincidence that his visitor was soon asking him the very same questions he had been asking himself; asking them pretty bluntly, too.

'You had a big congregation last Sunday, sir.'

'About usual, Inspector.'

'I've heard that you get even more people than Lawson did.'

'Perhaps so. Certainly in the week, I think.'

'The crowds are flocking back, so to speak?'

'You make it sound like a football match.'

'Bit more interesting than the last football match I saw, I hope.'

'And one doesn't have to queue up at the turnstiles, Inspector.'

'You keep a fairly accurate record of the congregations, though?'

Meiklejohn nodded. 'I've continued my predecessor's practice in that respect.'

'Not in all respects?'

Meiklejohn was aware of the Inspector's blue eyes upon him. 'What are you trying to say?'

'Was Lawson lower-church in his views than you are?'

'I didn't know him.'

'But he was?'

'He had views, I believe, which were – er. . . . '

'Lower-church?'

'Er – that might be a way of putting it, yes.'

'I noticed you had three priests in church on Sunday morning, sir.'

'You've still got quite a lot to learn about us, Inspector. There were myself and my curate. The sub-deacon need not be in holy orders.'

'Three's a bit more than the usual ration, though, isn't it?'

'There are no ration-books when it comes to divine worship.'

'Did Lawson have a curate?'

'For the first part of his time here, he did. The parish is a large one, and in my view should always have a curate.'

'Lawson was on his own, then – for the last few years?'

'He was.'

'Did you ever hear, sir, that Lawson might have been a fraction too fond of the choirboys?'

'I – I think it quite improper for you or for me to— '

'I met his former headmaster recently,' interrupted Morse, a new note of authority in his voice. 'I felt he was concealing something, and I guessed what it was: the fact that Lionel Lawson had been expelled from school.'

'You're sure of that?'

Morse nodded. 'I rang the old boy up today and put it to him. He told me I was right.'

'Expelled for homosexuality, you say?'

'He refused to confirm that,' said Morse slowly. 'He also refused to deny it, I'm afraid, and I'll leave you to draw your own conclusions. Look, sir. I want to assure you that whatever you may have to tell me will be treated in the strictest confidence. But it's my duty as a police officer to ask you once again. Have you heard any rumours that Lawson was at all inclined to that sort of thing?'

Meiklejohn looked down at his feet and picked his words with uneasy care. 'I've heard one or two rumours, yes. But I don't myself think that Lawson was an active homosexual.'

'Just a passive one, you mean.'

Meiklejohn looked up, and spoke with quiet conviction: 'It is my view that the Reverend Mr Lawson was not a homosexual.

I am, of course, sometimes wrong, Inspector. But in this case I think I am right.'

'Thank you,' said Morse, in the tone of a man who says 'Thank you for nothing'. He looked round the room at the bookshelves, lined with rows of theological works, the spines of most of them either dark-blue or brown. It was in this dark and sombre room that Lawson himself would have sat, probably for several hours each day, during his ten-year ministry at St Frideswide's. What had *really* gone wrong here? What strange tales of the human heart and the deep abyss of human consciousness could these walls and these books tell, if only they had tongues to speak to him? Could Meiklejohn tell him any more? Oh, yes, he could. There was just that one final question, the most vital question he would ask in the whole case. It was the question which had suddenly sprung to life in his mind the previous evening on the road just a few miles south of Shrewsbury.

He took from his pocket the now-crumpled Parish Notes for April.

'You print one of these every month?'

'Yes.'

'Do you' – this was it, and his mouth seemed suddenly to grow dry as he asked it – 'do you keep copies of them from previous years?'

'Of course. It's a great help in compiling the Parish Notes to have the previous year's copy. Not so much with the Easter period, of course, but— '

'Can I look at last year's Notes, please, sir?'

Meiklejohn walked over to one of the bookshelves and took out a loose-leafed folder. 'Which month's copy do you want?' His eyes reflected a shrewd intelligence. 'September, perhaps?'

'September,' said Morse.

'Here we are, yes. July, August. . . . ' He stopped and looked a little puzzled. 'October, November. . . . ' He turned back to January and went very carefully through the issues once more. 'It's not here, Inspector,' he said slowly. 'It's not here. I wonder. . . . '

Morse was wondering, too. But – please! – it wouldn't be too difficult to find a copy somewhere, would it? They must have printed a few hundred – whoever 'they' were.

'Who prints these for you, sir?'

'Some little man in George Street.'

'He'd surely keep the originals, wouldn't he?'

'I'd have thought so.'

'Can you find out for me – straightaway?'

'Is it that urgent?' asked Meiklejohn quietly.

'I think it is.'

'You could always check up from the church register, Inspector.'

'The *what*?'

'We keep a register in the vestry. Every service – I think it *is* a service you're looking for? – every service is recorded there. The time, the type of service, the minister officiating, the offertory – even the number of the congregation, although I must admit that's a bit of a rough guess sometimes.'

Morse allowed himself an exultant grin. His hunch had been right, then! The clue for which he'd been searching was where he'd always thought it would be – under his very nose inside the church itself. The next time he had a hunch, he decided, he would pursue it with a damned sight more resolution than he had done this one. For the moment, however, he said nothing. He was there – almost there anyway – and he felt the thrill of a man who knows that he has seven draws up on the football pools and is just going out to buy a sports paper to discover the result of the eighth match.

The two men walked down the wide staircase and into the hallway, where Meiklejohn took his coat from the clothes-stand, stained dark brown like almost every other item of furniture in the large, echoing vicarage.

'A lot of room here,' said Morse as they stepped out into the street.

Again the Vicar's eyes flashed with intelligence. 'What you mean to say is that I ought to turn it into a hostel, is that it?'

'Yes, I do,' replied Morse bluntly. 'I understand your predecessor used to take in a few waifs and strays now and then.'

'I believe he did, Inspector. I believe he did.'

They parted at George Street, and Morse, in a state of suppressed excitement, and already fingering the heavy church-keys in his raincoat pocket, walked on down Cornmarket to St Frideswide's.

Chapter Thirty-two

Just as Meiklejohn had said, the bulky, leather-bound register stood on its shelf in the vestry, and Morse felt the same
amalgam of anxiety and expectation with which as a schoolboy
he had opened the envelopes containing his examination results:
any second – and he would know. The pages of the register were
marked in faded blue lines, about a third of an inch apart, with
each line, stretched across the double page, quite sufficient to
accommodate the necessary information. On the left-hand page
were written the day, the date, and the time of the service,
followed by some brief specification of the particular saint's
day, feast day, et cetera; on the right-hand page the record
was continued with details of the type of service celebrated,
the number present in the congregation, the amount taken at
the offertory, and lastly the name (almost always the signature)
of the minister, or ministers, officiating. Doubtless in a church
permeated by a more fervent evangelicalism, there would have
been the biblical reference of the text which the preacher had
sought to propound; but Morse was more than delighted with the
information he found in front of him. The register had fallen open
at the current month and he noted the last entry: 'Monday, 3rd
April. 7.30 p.m. St Richard of Chichester. Low Mass. 19. £5.35.
Keith Meiklejohn M.A. (Vicar).' Then he turned back a thickish
wadge of the book's heavy pages. A little too far, though: July,
the previous year. On through August, and his heart suddenly
seemed to sink within him as the thought flashed into his mind
that someone might well have torn out the page he was seeking.
But no! There it was now, staring him in the face: 'Monday, 26th
Sept. 7.30 p.m. The Conversion of St Augustine. Solemn Mass.
13. – . Lionel Lawson M.A. (Vicar).' For several minutes Morse
stared at the entry with a blank fixity. Had he been wrong after
all? For there it was, all printed out in Lawson's own hand – the
precise details of the service at which Josephs had been murdered:
the date and time, the occasion, the type of service (which, of
course, accounted for Paul Morris' presence), the number in the
congregation, the offertory (the sum quite naturally unknown and
unrecorded, except perhaps for a few brief seconds in Josephs'
brain before he met his death), and then Lawson's signature. All

there. All in order. What had Morse hoped to find there? Surely he had not expected the amount of the offertory to be recorded? That would have been an elementary mistake of such monumental stupidity on Lawson's part that if repeated in other aspects of his crime would have led to an arrest within a few hours by any even moderately competent detective. No. Morse had not been looking for any such mistake. The simple truth of the matter was that *he'd expected there to be no entry at all.*

The door at the north porch creaked open, and Morse felt a sudden brief surge of primitive fear as he stood alone in the silent church. Somewhere, perhaps somewhere very near, there was a murderer still at large, watching every latest development with a vicious, calculating mind; watching even now, perhaps, and sensing that the police might be hovering perilously close to the truth. Morse walked on tiptoe to the heavy red curtain which cloaked the entrance to the vestry and cautiously peered through.

It was Meiklejohn.

'This is what you want, Inspector,' he said breezily. 'You must excuse me, if you will. We've got a service here at eleven.'

He handed to Morse a single sheet of paper, printed on both sides in faded black ink, with rows of asterisks dividing up the Parish Notes for the previous September into a series of closely typed paragraphs, of which the first, in double columns, gave full details of that month's forthcoming (and, in one case, fatal) functions. Morse sat down in the back pew and looked down intently at the sheet.

He was still looking down at the sheet several minutes later when Mrs Walsh-Atkins made her careful way down the central aisle, passing her left hand from pew-head to pew-head as she progressed, until finally settling herself in her accustomed seat where she knelt down, her forehead resting on the crook of her left arm, for a further protracted audience with the Almighty. A few other faithful souls had come in, all of them women, but Morse had not heard their entrances, and it was clear to him that the hinges on the door at the south porch had received a more recent oiling than those of its fellow at the north porch. He registered the point, as if it might be of some importance.

Morse sat through the devotional service – literally 'sat'. He made no pretence to emulate the gestures and movements of the sprinkling of ageing ladies; but a neutral observer would have marked a look of faintly smiling contentment on his features long before Meiklejohn's solemn voice at last, at very long last, intoned the benediction.

'It *was* what you wanted, I hope, Inspector?' Meiklejohn was leaning forward over the low table in the vestry, writing down the details of the service in the register with his right hand, his left unfastening the long row of buttons down his cassock.

'Yes, it was, and I'm most grateful to you. There's just one more thing, sir. Can you tell me anything about St Augustine?'

Meiklejohn blinked and looked round. 'St Augustine? Which St Augustine?'

'You tell me.'

'There were two St Augustines. St Augustine of Hippo, who lived about A.D. 400 or thereabouts. He's chiefly famous for his *Confessions* – as you'll know, Inspector. The other one is St Augustine of Canterbury, who lived a couple of hundred years or so later. He's the one who brought Christianity to Britain. I've got several books you could borrow if— '

'Do you know when either of 'em was converted?'

'Converted? Er – no, I'm afraid I don't. In fact I wasn't aware that there was any such biographical data – certainly not about our own St Augustine anyway. But as I say— '

'Which one of 'em do you celebrate here, sir?' Upon Meiklejohn's answer, as Morse now knew, hung all the law and the prophets, and the light-blue eyes that fixed the Vicar were almost hostile in their unblinking anticipation.

'We've never celebrated either of them,' said Meiklejohn simply. 'Perhaps we should. But we can't have an unlimited succession of special days. If we did, none of them would be "special", if you follow me. "When everyone is somebody, then no one's anybody." '

Phew!

After Meiklejohn had left, Morse hurriedly checked the three previous years' entries for September in the register, and almost purred with pleasure. The institution of any celebration to mark the conversion of one or other of the great Augustines had only begun – if it had begun at all – in the September of the previous year. Under the Reverend Lionel Lawson!

As Morse was about to leave the church, he saw that Mrs

Walsh-Atkins had finally risen from her knees, and he walked back to help her.

'You're a faithful old soul, aren't you?' he said gently.

'I come to all the services I can, Inspector.'

Morse nodded. 'You know, it's surprising really that you weren't here the night when Mr Josephs was murdered.'

The old lady smiled rather sadly. 'I suppose I must have forgotten to look at the Parish Notes that week. That's one of the troubles of growing old, I'm afraid – your memory just seems to go.'

Morse escorted her to the door and watched her as she walked away up to the Martyrs' Memorial. Had he wished, he could have told her not to worry too much about forgetting things. At the very least there had been no error of memory on her part over the Parish Notes for the previous September. For in those same notes, the notes which Meiklejohn had just found for him, *there was not a single word about the service at which Josephs would be murdered.*

Chapter Thirty-three

Lewis had spent a busy morning. He had co-ordinated arrangements with the Coroner's Sergeant for the forthcoming inquests on the Morrises, *père et fils*; he had written a full report on the Shrewsbury trip; and he had just come back from acquainting a rapidly recovering Bell with the latest developments in the case when Morse himself returned from St Frideswide's, looking tense yet elated.

'What time does the *Oxford Mail* go to press, Lewis?'

'First edition about now, I should think.'

'Get me the editor on the blower, will you? Quick! I've got some news for him.'

Morse very hastily scribbled a few notes, and when Lewis handed him the phone he was ready.

'I want this in tonight's *Mail*, is that clear? Absolutely vital. And what's more it's got to go on the front page somewhere.

Got your pencil ready? Here goes. Headline: ARREST IMMINENT IN ST FRIDESWIDE'S MURDER HUNT. Got that? Good. Now, here's your copy. Exactly as I tell you. I don't want any sub-editor buggering about with so much as a comma. "The Oxford police today reported that their long investigation into the murder last September of Mr Harry Josephs is now virtually complete stop The further deaths at St Frideswide's reported in these columns last week are now known to be connected with the earlier murder comma and the bodies discovered comma one on the tower and one in the crypt of the church comma have been positively identified as those of Mr Paul Morris comma formerly music-master of the Roger Bacon School Kidlington comma and of his son Peter Morris comma former pupil of the same school and a member of the church choir stop The police confirmed also that a woman found murdered last week in a nurses' genitive plural hostel in Shrewsbury was Mrs Brenda Josephs comma wife of Mr Harry Josephs stop Chief Inspector Morse capital M-o-r-s-e of the Thames Valley Constabulary told reporters today that public response to earlier appeals for information had been extremely encouraging comma and that evidence is now almost complete." No. Change that last bit: "and that only one more key witness remains to come forward before the evidence is complete stop In any case an arrest is confidently expected within the next forty hyphen eight hours stop" End of copy. You got all that? Front page, mind, and give it a good big headline – about the same size type you use when Oxford United win.'

'When did that last happen?' asked the editor.

Morse put down the phone and turned to Lewis. 'And here's a little printing job for you. Get it typed and stick it on the outside of the south door at St Frideswide's.'

Lewis looked down at what Morse had written: 'Because of imminent danger from falling masonry immediately above the inside of the porch, this door must on no account be opened until further notice.'

'Come back as soon as you've done that, Lewis. There are a few things I've got to tell you.'

Lewis stood up and tapped the note with his fingers. 'Why don't we just lock the door, sir?'

'Because there's only one lock on it, that's why.'

For once Lewis refused to rise to the bait, put a clean white sheet of paper into the typewriter carriage, and turned the ribbon to 'red'.

The hump-backed surgeon put his head round the door of Bell's office just after 3 p.m., and found Morse and Lewis in earnest conversation.

'Won't interrupt you, Morse. Just thought you ought to know we're not much forrader with that fellow you found up the tower. I dunno as we're ever going to be certain, you know.'

Morse seemed neither surprised nor overmuch interested. 'Perhaps you're getting too old for the job.'

'Not surprising, Morse, old son. We're all ageing at the standard rate of twenty-four hours *per diem*, as you know.'

Before Morse could reply, he was gone, and Lewis felt glad that the interruption was so brief. For once in the case he knew exactly (well, almost exactly) where they were and why they were there.

It was just after half-past four when one of the paper-boys from the Summertown Newsagents turned into Manning Terrace on his racing-bicycle, the drop handlebars (in one of the stranger perversions of fashion) turned upward. Without dismounting he took a copy of the *Oxford Mail* from the canvas bag thrown over his shoulder, folded it expertly in one hand, rode up to the door of number 7, and stuck it through the letter-box. Four doors in a row next, all on the right-hand side, starting with number 14A, where Ruth Rawlinson was just inserting her Yale key after an afternoon's shopping in Oxford.

She took the paper from the boy, put it under her right arm, and carried the two fully laden shopping-bags into the house.

'Is that you, Ruthie dear?'

'Yes, Mother.'

'Is the paper come?'

'Yes, Mother.'

'Bring it with you, dear.'

Ruth put her carrier-bags down on the kitchen table, draped her mackintosh over a chair, walked into the lounge, bent down to kiss her mother lightly on the cheek, placed the newspaper on her lap, turned up the gas-fire, almost commented on the weather, wondered why she hadn't already gone mad, realised that tomorrow was Wednesday – oh God! How much longer would she be able to stand all this – her mother, and him? Especially *him*. There was little enough she could do about her mother, but she could do something about him. She just wouldn't go – it was as simple as that.

'Ruth! Come and read this!' said her mother.

Ruth read through the front-page article. Oh my God!

The man seated on the deep sofa, its chintz covers designed in the russet-and-white floral pattern, was not surprised by the factual material reported in the front-page article, but he was deeply worried by its implications. He read the article through many, many times and always would his eyes linger on the same lines: 'only one more key witness remains to come forward before evidence is complete. In any case an arrest is confidently expected within the next forty-eight hours.' It was the piece about the 'key witness' which he found the more disturbing. Himself he could look after without help from anyone, but. . . . In a flash, as always, the decision was taken. Yes, it had to be tomorrow – tomorrow morning. It *would* be tomorrow morning.

It was not only Ruth Rawlinson, therefore, who had decided to miss the regular Wednesday-evening rendezvous. Someone else had now made exactly the same decision for her.

Chapter Thirty-four

At five minutes past ten the next morning, Ruth Rawlinson was not so wholly preoccupied with other things that she failed to notice and to admire the baskets of daffodils that bedecked the lamp-standards all the way along St Giles'. But if the morning was bright and sunny, her own mood was full of dark foreboding, for affairs were getting terrifyingly out of hand. Having been informed of the identities of the two bodies found at St Frideswide's, having learned of the death of Brenda Josephs, and knowing in any case far more than the police could know, her thoughts were in constant and grievous agitation. What was to stop her, at this very second, from cycling straight on through Cornmarket and down St Aldates to the Oxford City Police H.Q.? In any case, it was her duty to do so. It had always been her moral duty, but it was something more than that now: it was a personal cry for help as the walls began to close in around her. Five minutes earlier, when she had left Manning Terrace, her firm resolve had been to go to see Morse immediately and tell him the whole tragic tale. But that resolution was now crumbling, and she told herself that she needed a chance to think things out a little more clearly; a chance to brace herself emotionally, before plunging her own life, and thereby her mother's life, too, into utter ruin and desolation. Yes. She needed time – just a little more time. She propped her bicycle against the wall of the south porch, fastened the lock through the rear wheel, and then saw the notice on the door, pinned rather too high and typed in red capitals. Registering no particular surprise, Ruth Rawlinson walked round to the door at the north porch. It was open.

From the sub-manager's office on the top floor of the large store almost opposite, Lewis followed Ruth's progress with his binoculars – just as he had followed the progress of the others who had entered the church since 8.45 a.m., when the door at the north porch had first been unlocked. But they had been few, and his task had been far easier than he could have imagined. A flamboyantly dressed group of what looked from above like American tourists had gone in at 9.10 a.m.: ten of them. And at 9.22 a.m. ten of them had emerged into the sunlight and drifted off towards Radcliffe Square. At 9.35 a.m. a solitary white-haired lady had gone in, and had come out, her morning devotions completed, about ten minutes later. During the same time, a tall, bearded youth, carrying an extraordinarily large transistor radio, had gone in, only to make his exit some twenty seconds later, doubtless (as it appeared to Lewis) having mistaken the place for somewhere else. That was all – until Lewis recognised Ruth Rawlinson. He'd accepted the offer of a cup of coffee five minutes after she'd gone in, but had kept his binoculars trained on the north entrance, even refusing to turn round to express his thanks. This, if Morse were right (and Lewis thought he was), could be the vital time. Yet half an hour later it hardly seemed as if it were going to be so. There had been no further visitors, if one discounted, that is, an innocent-looking white-haired terrier which had urinated against the west wall.

Some of the daffodils on the sides of the altar steps were now well past their prime, and Ruth picked them out, neatly rearranging the remainder, and mentally deciding to buy some more. She then walked boustrophedon along the pews on either side of the main aisle, replacing on their hooks whatever loose hassocks had been left on the floor, flicking the pew-ledges with a yellow duster, and at the same time collecting a few stray hymn-books and prayer-books. At one point she peered curiously up at the stonework above the south porch, but was unable to identify any visible signs of impending collapse.

Morse watched her with mixed emotions. He watched her large eyes and her full sensitive lips, and he realised once again how attractive she could have been to him. Even her little mannerisms were potentially endearing: the way she would blow a stray wisp of hair away from her face; the way she would stand, her hands on her waist, with something approaching pride on her face after completing one of her humble tasks. And yet, at the same time, he was conscious that she was in far more imminent danger than the masonry above the south porch was ever likely to be. If he was right (which after 10.20 a.m. he was beginning to doubt somewhat), Ruth Rawlinson was not likely to die in her nightdress, but in the very church in which he was now sitting, carefully concealed behind the dull-red curtain of the confessional. His intermittent fears that she would decide to spring-clean his own observation-post had hitherto proved groundless; but now, arms akimbo, she was looking searchingly around her. Did it matter all that much, though, if she did find him? He could explain as best he could – even take her over to the Randolph for a drink, perhaps. Yet he was glad when he heard the tell-tale clatterings and the drumming of cold water into the bottom of the scrubbing-bucket.

Several members of the public had entered the church during this time, and at each clinking of the latch and creaking of the door Morse felt the tension rise within him – only to fall again as the visitors stared rather vacantly around them, fumbled through the church literature, and without exception departed again within ten minutes of their arrival. Lewis had seen them go in; seen them leave, too – the coffee long since cold at his elbow. But Morse's own vigilance was becoming progressively less keen, and he began to feel just a little bored. The only book within arm's reach was a stiff-backed Bible, whose pages he now turned desultorily, thinking back as he did so to his youth. Something had gone sadly wrong somewhere with his own spiritual development, for he had almost completely lost his early ebullient faith and he now had to confess that when faced with the overwhelming difficulties of forming any coherent philosophy of life and death he had come to regard the teachings of the Church as so much gobbledegook. He could be wrong, of course. Probably *was* wrong – just as he was probably wrong about this morning. Yet it had seemed such a logical time – certainly the time *he* would have chosen had he found himself in the murderer's shoes.

At some point in his musings, he thought he had heard a twanging metallic noise, but only now did it register fully. Could it have been the north door being locked? If so, it must surely have been locked from the outside. Yes. Blast it! He'd forgotten that notice about the recent vandalism, and someone must have come and locked the place up. But surely that someone would have looked into the church first? There was Ruth in there, for a start, although she probably had a key herself. *Did* she have a set of keys? What about any others who were in the church? If Ruth hadn't got a key, they'd all be shut up in there, wouldn't they?

Morse was only too conscious how woolly and confused his thinking was becoming – when he suddenly froze in his seat. He heard a man's voice, very close to him. It said, 'Hello, Ruth!' That was all. Quite a pleasant voice by the sound of it, but it seemed to turn Morse's blood to ice. Someone must have locked the door all right. *From the inside.*

Chapter Thirty-five

'What are you doing in here?' she asked sharply. 'I didn't hear you come in.'

'No, you wouldn't would you? I've been here a long time. Up on the tower. It's cold up there; but you get a wonderful view, and I like looking down on things – and people.'

(Oh, Lewis! If only your eyes had not been focused quite
so closely on the door!)

'But you must go! You can't stay here! You shouldn't be
out at all!'

'You *worry* too much.' He laid a hand on her shoulder as they
stood together in the central aisle, and pulled her towards him.

'Don't be silly!' she whispered harshly. 'I've told you – we
agreed— '

'The door's locked, my beauty, have no fear. I locked it
myself, you see. There's only the two of us here, so why don't
we sit down for a little while?'

She pushed his hand from her. 'I've told you. It's got to
finish.' Her lips were quivering with emotion, and she was very
close to tears. 'I can't take any more of this, I just can't! You've
got to go away from here. You've got to!'

'Of course I have. That's exactly what I've come to see you
for – can't you understand that? Just sit down, that's all. Not too
much to ask, is it, Ruth?' His voice was silkily persuasive.

She sat down and the man sat next to her, no more than ten
feet or so from the confessional. (The man's heavy brown shoes,
as Morse could now see, were of good quality, but appeared not
to have been cleaned for many weeks.) For some time neither of
them spoke as the man's left arm rested across the back of the
pew, the hand lightly gripping her shoulder. (The finger-nails, as
Morse could now see, were clean and well manicured, reminding
him of a clergyman's nails.)

'You read the article,' she said flatly. It was not a question.

'We both read the article.'

'You must tell me the truth – I don't care what you say, but
you must tell me the truth. Did you – ' (her voice was faltering
now) ' – did you have anything to do with all that?'

'Me? You must be joking! You can't honestly believe that –
surely you can't, Ruth!' (The man, as Morse could now see, wore
a pair of dingy grey flannels, and above them a large khaki-green
jumper, with leather shoulder-patches, reaching up to the neck in
such a way that it was not clear whether or not he wore a tie.)

Ruth was leaning forward, her elbows on the top edge of
the pew in front of her, her head in her hands. From the look
of her she might well be praying, and Morse guessed that she
probably was. 'You're not telling me the truth. You're *not*. It

was *you* who killed them! All of them! I *know* you did.' She was a lost soul now, uncaring in the bitter depths of her misery as she buried her head in her hands. Morse, as he watched her, felt a profound and anguished compassion welling up within him; yet he knew that he must wait. The previous day he had guessed at the truth behind the grim succession of tragedies, and here and now that very same truth was working itself out, not more than a few yards away from him.

The man made no denial of the charges spoken against him, but his right hand seemed to be working round his throat, his face momentarily turned away. (The face, as Morse had already noticed, was that of a man in his late forties – or early fifties perhaps, for both the long, unkempt, blackish hair and the beard which covered his face were heavily streaked with white and grey.)

Here it all was, then – in front of him. It was all so very simple, too – so childishly simple that Morse's mind, as always, had refused to believe it and had insisted instead on trying to find (and, indeed, almost finding) the weirdest, most complex solutions. Why, oh, why, just for once in a while was he not willing to accept and come to terms with the plain, incontrovertible facts of any case – the facts that stared him point-blank in the face and simply shrieked out for a bit of bread-and-butter common sense and application? The man sitting here now, next to Ruth Rawlinson? Well, Morse? Of course it was! It was Lionel Lawson's brother – *Philip Lawson*; the man so despised in the stories of clever detection, the man so despised by Morse himself; the man who committed a not-very-clever crime for the very meanest of rewards; the layabout, the sponger and the parasite, who had bedevilled his longsuffering brother's life from their earliest schooldays together; the cleverer boy, the more popular boy, the favourite – the boy who had grown up without a thread of moral fibre in his being, the boy who had wasted his considerable substance on riotous living, and who had come back to prey once more upon his wretched brother Lionel; come back, with a complete knowledge of his brother's life and his brother's weaknesses; come back with threats of betrayal and public exposure – threats which Lionel had paid off with help and kindness and compassion and, doubtless, with money, too. And then – yes, and then came the time when Lionel himself, for once in his life, had desperately needed the help of his worthless brother, and was more than prepared to pay for it; the time when the two brothers had planned the execution and arranged the subsequent cover-up of Harry Josephs' murder, a murder planned meticulously at the very moment when Paul Morris had just opened the diapason stop on the organ, and was doubtless drowning the church with the last verse of 'Praise to the Holiest in the Height' or something. *fff.*

These were the thoughts that flashed across Morse's mind in that instant, with the multiple murderer sitting there just in front of him, his left arm still resting along the back of the pew, his right hand still fumbling with something round his neck; and Ruth still bending forward in her posture of semi-supplication, still so pathetically vulnerable.

Then, even as he watched, Morse felt his every muscle tense in readiness as the adrenalin coursed through his body. The fingers of the man's left hand were holding the narrower end of a tie, a dark navy-blue tie with broad diagonal scarlet stripes bordered by very much thinner ones of green and yellow; and as Morse watched the scene being enacted immediately before his eyes his mind came to a dead stop in its tracks, seemed to turn a reverse somersault and to land in a state of complete stupefaction.

But the time for thought was past; already the man's left hand had looped the tie round the woman's neck; already the right hand was moving to meet it – and Morse acted. It was ill luck that the low door of the confessional opened inwards, for he had to clamber awkwardly in the narrow space and by the time he was out the element of surprise was gone; and as the tourniquet was already tightening about Ruth's throat she cried a terrible cry.

'Keep your distance!' snarled the man, springing to his feet and dragging Ruth up with him, the tie cutting cruelly into her neck. 'You heard me! Keep it there! Not a step farther or else— '

Morse hardly heard him. He lunged desperately at the pair of them, and Ruth fell heavily in the central aisle as Morse seized the man's right arm and tried with all his considerable strength to twist it behind his back. But with almost ridiculous ease his adversary shook himself clear and stood there, a vicious hatred blazing in his eyes.

'I know you,' said Morse, panting heavily. 'And you know who I am, don't you?'

'Yes, I know you, you bastard!'

'There's no sense in trying anything – I've got my men all round the church – ' (the words were coming out in a series of breathless snatches) 'there's no way for you to get out of here – no way at all – now – now please be sensible – I'm going to take you from here – there's nothing to worry about.'

For a while the man stood quite motionless, only his eyes roving about in their sockets as if weighing the situation with a frenetic logicality, as if searching for some desperate remedy. Then something seemed to snap in the man, as if the glaze that suddenly dilated the eyes had effaced the very last vestiges of any rational thought. He turned swiftly, almost athletically, on his heel, and with his descending peal of maniacal laughter echoing under the vaulted roof he ran to the back of the church and disappeared behind the curtains of the vestry.

At that point (as Lewis later protested) Morse could have chosen several more logical courses of action than the one which he in fact pursued. He could have gone to the door at the north porch and signalled Lewis immediately; he could have led Ruth from the church and locked the door behind him, with his quarry cornered and powerless; he could have sent Ruth, if sufficiently recovered, to get help, and himself stayed where he was, performing no more than a watchdog brief until that help arrived. But Morse did none of these things. He felt that strangely compelling and primitive instinct of the hunter for the hunted, and he walked almost boldly to the vestry where in a sudden flurry he flung the curtains aside on their rollers. No one was there. The only other doorway from the vestry led to the tower, and Morse walked across the parquet floor and tried the door. Locked. He took out his keys, selected the right one first time, unlocked the door and, standing cautiously to one side, pulled it open. On the lowest of the circular stone steps, he saw a man's greatcoat, long, shabby and dirty; and, placed neatly on top of it, a pair of dark sunglasses.

Chapter Thirty-six

Traceries of blackened cobwebs lined the under-lintels of the stone steps above his head as step by step Morse ascended the circular stairway. He was conscious of no fear: it was as if his paranoiac acrophobia was temporarily suspended, subsumed by the saner, more immediate danger from the man somewhere above him. Up and up he climbed, the door to the bell-chamber just appearing on his right when he heard the voice from high above him.

'Keep going, Mr Morse. Lovely view from the top.'

'I want to talk to you,' shouted Morse. He put his hands out to the walls on either side of him and looked upwards towards the tower. For a second his balance threatened to desert him as he caught sight, through the small low window to his left, of the shoppers walking along Cornmarket, far, far below him. But a raucous laugh from above served only to restore his equilibrium.

'I only want to talk to you,' repeated Morse, and climbed another six steps. 'I only want to *talk* to you. As I told you, my men are outside. Be sensible, man. For Christ's sake, be sensible!'

But there was no reply.

Another window, again to his left, and the angle down on to the stream of shoppers was now virtually vertical. Strangely, however, Morse realised that he could now look down without that wave of incipient panic. What for the life of him he was unable to do was to look across at the store almost opposite, where he knew that the faithful Lewis would still be watching the door at the north porch with his wonted, unwavering vigilance.

Another six steps. And another six steps.

'The door's open, Mr Morse. Not much farther.' Then again the almost insane laugh, but softer this time – and more menacing.

On the second step from the top of the tower and with the door (as the man had asserted) wide open, Morse stopped.

'Can you hear me?' he asked. He was breathing heavily, and he realised sadly how ill-conditioned he had allowed his body to become.

Again, there was no reply.

'It must have been heavy work carting a body up here.'

'I've always kept fit, Mr Morse.'

'Pity the ladder collapsed, though. You could have hidden 'em both in the crypt then, couldn't you?'

'Well, well! How observant we are!'

'Why did you have to kill the boy?' asked Morse. But if there was a reply a sudden tugging gust of wind cut across the words and whipped them away.

It was clear to Morse that the man was not concealed behind the tower door and after taking one further step he could now see him, standing facing him at the northern wall of the tower, about thirty feet away, on the narrow gully that divided the sides of the tower from the shallow central eminence. With a peculiarly detached inconsequentiality, Morse noticed how very large the weather-vane was, and for a second or two he wondered whether he would soon be waking from a terrifying dream.

'Come down. We can't talk here. Come on.' Morse's tone was gentle and persuasive. He knew the whole truth at last, and his one remaining duty was to get this man down safely. 'Come on. Come down. We can talk then.' Morse climbed the final step, and felt the wind pulling at his thinning hair.

'We'll talk now, Mr Morse, or we won't talk at all. Do you understand what I mean?' The man hitched himself up and sat on the coping between two of the crenellations, his feet dangling loosely above the tower floor.

'Don't do anything stupid!' shouted Morse, his voice betraying a sudden panic. 'That solves nothing. That's no way out for you. Whatever else you are, you're not a coward.'

The last word seemed to strike a chord which could still vibrate with something of its former attunement, for the man jumped lightly down and his voice was steady now. 'You're right, Mr Morse. Dangerous sitting there like that, especially in the wind.'

'Come on!' Morse's mind was racing now. This was the time when it mattered so desperately that he said and did exactly the right things. He felt sure that there must be some suitable phrases in the psychiatrist's hand-book that would soothe the raging of a maddened lion; but his own brain was quite incapable of formulating any such irenic incantations. 'Come on,' he said again; then, as a minor variant, 'Come along.' And, in spite of the bankruptcy of these banal exhortations, Morse felt that he was adopting the right sort of approach, for there now seemed some hesitation in the other's manner, some indication of a slightly saner attitude.

'Come along,' repeated Morse, and took one slow step towards the man. Then another step. Then another. And still the man stood motionless, his back to the north wall of the tower. Only five or six yards now separated them, and Morse took yet a further step towards him. 'Come along.' He held out his hand as if to lend support to one who has passed the dangers of a long walk along a tight-rope, and now is only a few feet from final safety.

With a snarl on his bearded lips, the man launched himself at Morse and pinned him round the shoulders with a vicious vice-like power. 'No one's ever called me a coward,' he hissed. 'No one!'

Morse managed to grab hold of the man's beard with both hands and to force his head back inch by inch until they both lost their balance and fell heavily against the leaded slope of the central roofing. Morse felt himself pinned beneath the other man's body, his legs and shoulders utterly powerless. He felt strong hands at his throat, the thumbs digging deep into the flesh; and his own hands were now frantically gripping the man's wrists, temporarily staying the irresistible thrust, his lips stretched to their widest extremity over his gritted teeth, his eyes closed with a desperate tightness, as though somehow this might lend him a few extra seconds of time, an extra ounce of strength. The blood thudded in his ears like someone pounding against a heavy door that would admit no entrance, and from somewhere he heard what sounded like the tinkling crash of a broken milk-bottle; and the noise registered coolly and clinically in his brain, as if his mind was now outside himself, contemplating events with an objective detachment that was wholly devoid of panic or fear. He saw the scene with such clearly focused clarity. He was driving through the night along the fast, straight, narrow stretch of road from Oxford to Bicester, a long stream of cars coming towards him, ever coming towards him, their twin headlights staggered slightly in a continuous double line of yellow circles, ever approaching – and then flashing past him. And now there was another vehicle coming straight towards him, coming on the wrong side of the road, its off-side blinker flashing as it closed upon him. Yet (amazingly!) his hands remained firm and steady on the driving-wheel. . . . Perhaps that was one of death's most guarded secrets? Perhaps the fear of dying, per- haps even death itself, was nothing but a great deception after all. . . . The headlights turned to spinning yellow circles in his brain, and then as he opened his eyes he could see only the dull sky above him. His knees were drawn up under the man's stomach; but so oppressive was the weight upon him that he could gain no leverage at all. If only he could find the strength to co-ordinate his arms and his knees, there might just be the chance of unbalancing the man and turning him sideways, and thus for a few seconds relieving the overpowering pressure of the hands at his throat. But his strength was almost gone, and he knew that his body, any second now, would almost gladly capitulate as the aching muscles in his arms screamed out for rest. He was relaxing already, his head resting almost comfortably now against the cold surface of the central roofing. That weather-vane really was enormous! How on earth could anyone have carried such a weight up here, up the circling staircase, up and up and up, with such a great weight upon his shoulder?

The full realisation of his situation registered for the last time, and for a few seconds longer his grip on the man's wrists held firm as he dredged up the very last drop of his energy. But he had nothing more to offer. His grip on the steering-wheel slowly relaxed and as he closed his eyes the lights from the oncoming cars were dazzlingly bright. He thought of the final words of Richard Strauss's last song: 'Ist dies etwa der Tod?'

Chapter Thirty-seven

Morse realised that something miraculous had occurred. The body so inexorably pressing down upon him had become, in the self-same moment of time, both heavier and lighter; the grip at his throat both tighter and looser. The man groaned as if in some intolerable agony, and as he did so Morse's knees thrust him away, almost lightly and easily. The man reeled away towards the side of the tower where he frantically reached out to the nearest crenellation to stay himself. But his impetus was too great. The stonework crumbled away as his right hand jarred into it for support; and head first the man plunged over the parapet.

Then was to be heard the diminuendo of a terrifying 'Yaooh' as the man's body fell somersaulting to the ground far below, and finally a deadly thump followed by the terrified shrieks of those passing by at the foot of the tower.

Lewis stood there still clutching the top end of a long brass candlestick. 'You all right, sir?'

Morse remained where he was, blissfully breathing in the heady air in mighty gulps. The pain in his arms was like raging toothache, and he spread them out beside him, lying there on the gently sloping roof like a man who is crucified.

'Are you all right?' It was another voice now, a gentler, softer voice, and slim cool fingers pressed themselves against his wet forehead.

Morse nodded, and looked up at her face. He saw that there was a slight down of very fair hair upon her cheeks and light-brown freckles on either side of her nose. She was kneeling beside him, her large eyes brimming with happy tears. She held his head in her arms and pressed him closely to her for what to Morse seemed many days and many hours.

They said nothing to each other. When they slowly descended from the tower, she leading but only so little a way in front that their hands could remain firmly clasped, they still said nothing. When a few minutes later Lewis saw them they were sitting in the back pew of the Lady Chapel, her tear-stained face resting happily on his shoulder. And still they said nothing.

Lewis had seen the two men on the tower, had almost broken his own neck clambering down the five flights of stairs, had knocked several young ladies out of the way as he had run through the ground-floor cosmetic department, and finally, like some frustrated Fury, had hammered and hammered with his fists against the north door. The woman was still in there, he knew that, but it occurred to him that something might have happened to her; and in desperation he had hurled a large stone through the lowest and most convenient window with the dual purpose of making himself heard and of creating a possible means of entry. And the woman had heard him. The door was unlocked and, grabbing a candlestick from the shrine of the Blessed Virgin, he had taken the tower staircase three steps at a time and once on the roof he had smashed the candlestick with

all his force across the middle of the back of Morse's bearded
assailant.

Two duty-policemen were already on the scene when Lewis
emerged. A ring of people, standing some four or five yards off,
surrounded the dead body, and an ambulance, already summoned,
was whining its way down St Giles' from the Radcliffe Infirmary.
Lewis had plucked a cassock from one of the hooks in the vestry,
and now draped it over the dead man.

'Do you know who he is?' asked one of the policemen.

'I think so,' said Lewis.

'You all right?' The hump-backed police surgeon was the third
person to have asked the same question.

'Fine. Few weeks on the Riviera and I'll be fine. Nothing
serious.'

'Huh! That's what they all say. Whenever I ask my patients
what their parents died of, they all say the same – "Oh, nothing
serious".'

'I'd tell you if I wasn't all right.'

'You know, Morse, don't you, that every single person ever
born has at least one serious illness in life – the last one?'

Mm. It was a thought.

Lewis came back into the church: things were almost ready
outside. 'You all right, sir?'

'Oh, for Christ's sake!' said Morse.

Ruth Rawlinson still sat on the rear pew of the Lady Chapel,
her eyes staring blankly ahead of her – composed, silent and
passive.

'I'll see her home,' said Lewis quietly. 'You just— '

But Morse interrupted him. 'She can't go home, I'm afraid.
You'll have to take her down to the station.' He breathed heavily
and looked away from her. 'She's under arrest, and I want you
personally to take her statement.' He turned to Lewis with inexplicable anger in his voice. 'Is that clear? You! Personally!'

Unspeaking and unresisting Ruth was led away to a police
car by one of the constables; and after she was gone Morse,
Lewis and the police surgeon followed.

The crowd outside, now standing three or four deep around
the covered body, watched their emergence with deep interest,

as if the principal protagonists in a drama had just walked on to the stage: the hump-backed, rather elderly man, who looked (had he been around in 1555) as if he might have viewed unmoved the sight of Ridley and Latimer as they had burned to death in front of Balliol, only a few hundred yards away; next, the placid-looking, rather thick-set man, who earlier had seemed to be in charge of all the operations but who now appeared to fade a little into the background as if he were in the presence of his superiors; and finally a slimmer, balding, pale-faced man with piercing eyes, in whose sombre mien – if in any of the trio's – lay the look of a natural authority.

They stood there, these three, over the covered body.

'You want to look at him, Morse?' asked the police surgeon.

'I've seen enough of him,' muttered Morse.

'His face is all right – if you're feeling squeamish.'

The surgeon pulled back the top of the cassock from the dead man's face, and Lewis looked down at it with great interest and intensity.

'So that's what he looked like, sir.'

'Pardon?' said Morse.

'Lawson's brother, sir. I was just saying that— '

'That's not Lawson's brother,' said Morse quietly; so quietly in fact that neither of the other men seemed to hear him.

THE BOOK OF RUTH

Chapter Thirty-eight

Statement given by Miss Ruth Rawlinson, 14A Manning Terrace, Oxford, dictated by Miss Rawlinson, signed by the same, and witnessed by Sergeant Lewis, Thames Valley Police (C.I.D.)

Perhaps it is easier to start twenty years ago. I was then in the first-year sixth at Oxford High School studying for my A Levels in English and History and Economics. The headmistress came into the class one morning and called me outside. She told me that I must be a brave girl because she had some very sad news for me. My father who worked as a printer with Oxford University Press had suffered a massive coronary thrombosis and had died within an hour of being admitted to the Radcliffe Infirmary. I remember a feeling of numbness more than anything and little real grief. In fact for the next few days I felt almost a sense of pride as the mistresses and the other girls treated me with a kindness I had never really known before. It was just as if I were a heroine who had suffered much misfortune with great fortitude. But that wasn't the case at all really. I didn't dislike my father but we had never been close to each other. A perfunctory kiss when I went up to bed or a pound note sometimes when I'd done well in examinations but he had shown little real interest and no real love. Perhaps it wasn't his fault. My mother had been struck down with multiple sclerosis and although at that time she was still reasonably mobile my father's first and every thought was for her welfare and happiness. He must have loved her very dearly and his death was a terrible blow to her. Almost from that day onwards she seemed to change. It was as if the woman she had been could never come to terms with such bereavement and therefore had to become a different person.

Something happened to me too. I suddenly began to lose all pride in my school work and I began to lose all love for my mother. I suspected that she exaggerated her physical handicaps and all the cooking and washing and cleaning and shopping I did for her were accepted with less and less gratitude. I stayed on at school and took my A Levels the next year but I didn't apply for a university place although oddly enough my mother wanted me to. Instead I took a year's course at the Marlborough Secretarial College in the High and soon found that I had a real aptitude for the work. Even before I left the college I had been offered three posts and I finally accepted a very good offer from Oxford University Press as a personal and confidential secretary to a man who had known my father slightly. He was a very kind boss and a very clever man and the five years I spent with him were the happiest of my life. He was a bachelor and a year or so after starting with him he began to ask me out for an occasional meal or a visit to the Playhouse and I accepted. He never tried to take the slightest advantage of me and only when he used to take my arm through his as we walked to the car was there the slightest physical contact between us. Yet I fell in love with him – quite hopelessly as I thought. Then two things happened almost within a few days of each other. My boss asked me if I would marry him and there was a sudden sharp deterioration in my mother's condition. Whether these two things were connected it is impossible for me to say. I had told her about the proposal of marriage and she had told me what she thought about it in typically forthright terms. He was just a dirty old man looking for a bit of regular sex and look at the huge difference in our ages. Ridiculous! I should find myself some nice young man about my own age – that is if I had finally decided to leave her to rot away in some lonely home for chronic invalids. She worked herself up into a most distraught state and I realise that I am perhaps being less than fair in doubting her genuine shock at the news I had brought her. Anyway her G.P. told me that she was very poorly indeed and would have to go into hospital immediately. Then two more things happened almost at once. My mother returned home now needing a great deal of daily attention and I told my boss that I couldn't accept his proposal and that in the circumstances it would be better for me to leave. I remember the look of childlike sadness and disappointment in his eyes. When I left three weeks later he took me out for a marvellous meal at the Elizabeth and he talked quite happily all the evening. When he took me home and we sat in the car trying to say our very awkward farewells I turned to him and kissed him freely and lovingly on the mouth. From that day I grew my own shell round me just as my mother had grown hers. Doubtless I am much more like my mother than I would want to believe. Anyway Mother had probably been quite right. When I left work I was twenty-four and my boss was forty-nine. I met him once or twice after that just casually in the street. We asked the usual polite questions and went our ways. He never married. Two years afterwards he died of a brain haemorrhage and I went to his funeral. Looking back on it I feel no deep regrets that we didn't marry but I shall always regret that I never offered to become his mistress. These facts may seem irrelevant but I mention them only in the hope that someone may be able to understand why things began to go wrong and not in order to exonerate myself in any degree for my own part in the terrible business that was to come.

I must now talk about money. With my own quite handsome little salary now cut off, our financial situation had to be considered carefully and my mother thought that my own C-grade pass in A Level Economics was a sure guarantee of prudence and wizardry in monetary matters. Soon therefore I came to have a very full knowledge of all our financial affairs and it wasn't long before my mother gladly handed over all the responsibility to me. There was no problem with the house since my father had taken out a combined mortgage and life-insurance policy on it. It was far too big for the two of us but its market value was now about ten times greater than when my father had bought it twenty-five years earlier and with his death it was ours. At that time too my mother had realisable assets of about £2,000 in various stock-market equities and my own deposit account with Lloyds stood at over £800. In addition my mother had a small widow's pension accruing from a policy my father had taken out with the Press and from this time I also began to claim a dependency allowance from the Department of Social Security. For the next ten years or so I took on quite a lot of typing duties at home – mostly theses for doctorates and manuscripts for hopeful authors and that sort of thing. So we lived with a reasonable degree of comfort and security. And then two years ago came the stock-market slump and I was persuaded to realise my mother's stock capital for less than £500. If only I had held on for another six months all would have been well or at least not half so disastrous but there were great fears at the time of a complete collapse in the market. As the shares plummeted even lower in the weeks that followed it seemed that I had been wise to act as I had done but the truth was that I had been badly advised and that I had acted disastrously. I kept all this from my mother as best I could and this was not difficult. She had no real knowledge about financial affairs. Whilst my father was alive he had managed his small resources with a shrewd competence and would never let my mother worry about such things or enquire too closely into them. Since his death the burden of responsibility had fallen on my own slimmer shoulders and my mother fully expected that all was still well. I was too ashamed of my own incompetence to let her think otherwise. I decided then (and remember this was only two years ago) to put all our remaining assets into my one idea of a sound investment. I've already mentioned that our house was far too big for the two of us and I had my plans for it. We would divide the house into two with Mother and myself living on the ground floor and another family on the first floor. My idea was to partition the front hall so that the stairs to the upper floor led directly to a completely self-contained residence. The bathroom and toilet were already on that floor anyway and the only major reconstruction necessary was a kitchen sink upstairs and a small bathroom downstairs with a second front door so that there need be no sharing of keys or door-bells and no postal complications. A friend from St Frideswide's (yes I shall be coming to that soon) drew up some neat little plans for me and after finding out that no planning permission was required I asked for estimates. They all seemed to me surprisingly high but I decided we could just manage the lowest estimate of £1,500. So I went ahead and the work began a few months later with heaps of sand and piles of bricks and builders' planks appearing in the front driveway. Everything was going well until a year last February when my mother received a letter from an old friend of hers who had heard of a marvellous clinic in Switzerland which specialised in the treatment and care of multiple sclerosis. No magical cures were promised but there were glowing reports from satisfied clients and the brochure included with the letter gave full details of the three-week course together with technicolour pictures of the clinic itself overlooking Lake Thun with the snowy summits of the Alps behind and the foothills alive with saxifrage and eidelweiss. The cost was £630 which included the return air fare from Heathrow to Basel and transport to and from the clinic. Never before this time had I fully understood the terrible tyranny of money. If I had it my mother could go. If I didn't she couldn't go. There were no gradations of merit or need. I was rather sceptical about any treatment for my mother's illness but the clinic was obviously a reputable one and I knew that a period abroad would do my mother some good. She had not stirred out of the house for more than eighteen months and often couldn't even be bothered to get out of bed and into her wheel-chair. But now for the first time in years she had taken a firm decision herself. She wanted to go and was excited at the prospect. She went. Although I spent the three weeks of her absence working as hard and as long as I could as a temporary typist by day and as a waitress in the evenings I found the time exhilarating and I once more discovered some of the joy of living. But things were not working out at all well. The builders were finding unexpected snags and I received a letter from the head of the firm saying that if the work was to be properly carried out the estimate would have to be increased by £350. My mother's return did nothing to help of course and when it was discovered that the waste pipes on the ground floor would quite definitely have to be replaced I was compelled to ask the builders to lay off work for a few weeks since I was unable to meet the next monthly instalment. By the middle of the summer I was at my wits' end. It was then I went to see the Reverend Lionel Lawson.

Chapter Thirty-nine

Statement given by Miss Ruth Rawlinson (continued)

The first time I had been in St Frideswide's was as a girl in the High School choir when we had sung the Stainer Crucifixion with the Oxford augmented choirs. Several of us sang there again

especially when the choir was short of sopranos and contraltos
for the Palestrina masses. So I got to know some of the people
there and began to feel quite at home. Soon I became a regular
member of the choir not because I had any deep conviction about
High Anglicanism but because I enjoyed having a different ambit
of action and acquaintances. There was an old woman there who
cleaned the church every morning of the week – a woman so
crippled with arthritis that the carrying of mops and buckets was
in itself a positive affirmation of her faith and will. I got to know
her well and one day I asked her about herself and she said ever so
simply and happily that she hoped God would one day reward her
for what she was doing but that if He decided she was not worthy
then she still wished to praise and glorify Him for the blessings he
had given her. Instead of feeling surprised or cynical about this
I felt myself most profoundly moved and when she died I vowed
that I would try to take upon myself at least some part of her
good works. And so I found myself scrubbing and polishing and
the rest and discovering just a little bit of the fulfilment in life
that the old woman had experienced. In the course of this self-
imposed pennance I naturally got to know Lionel Lawson quite
well and as I say it was to him that I went for help and advice
when I could no longer cope with our financial crisis. I had
one of the great surprises of my life when he told me that if all
I was worrying about was money I could and should forget my
worries immediately. He asked me what I needed and when I
told him he sat down at his desk (where I noticed a paper-
knife in the form of a crucifix) and wrote out a cheque for
£500. It was just like a miracle and when I told him that I had
no idea of when I could repay him or how I could thank him
enough he just said that he might be in trouble himself one day
and if he was he'd like to know that I would try to help him in
any way I could. Of course I promised that I would do absolutely
anything for him, and I remember clearly how at the time I
hoped and prayed that I would one day be able to do some
really big favour for him in return. As I was leaving the vicarage that day I saw a man coming out of the kitchen downstairs.
For a moment I didn't recognise him although his face looked
familiar. He was rather shabbily dressed but he was freshly
shaven and his hair had been recently trimmed. I knew that
Lionel had a few of the men from the Church Army Hostel

to stay with him for a day or two and sometimes he would persuade them to come along to church services. Then I recognised him. He was much the same age and build as Lionel but the last time I'd seen him he'd had a week or so's growth of stubble on his face and his hair had been long and dirty. It was only later that I learned that this man was Lionel's brother Philip.

It was shortly after this time that Harry Josephs came into my life. One way and another tensions were growing between various members of the church at the end of last summer. It was then that I first heard a nasty rumour about Lionel possibly liking the company of choirboys rather more than he should but I couldn't bring myself to believe it. Even now I am quite convinced that if Lionel was in some way homosexually inclined his weakness was a very gentle and a completely passive one. But there was another rumour almost everyone seemed to have heard about to the effect that Paul Morris the church organist was very much too fond of Harry Josephs' wife Brenda who almost always brought Harry to the services. Harry himself had been disqualified from driving for some reason. Brenda was often seen talking to Paul although she herself would rarely stay in the church for a service and one of the women in the congregation told me she had once seen them holding hands. I must admit that although I had no direct evidence to go on I began to suspect more and more that this second rumour might be true. And then I knew it was true because Harry Josephs told me so. The first time he had called at my home there were the three of us because Mother happened to be up that day and he was very pleasant and polite and he stayed for about two hours. After that he called quite regularly always in the morning and we took to sitting together in the lounge when Mother was in bed. In some ways he reminded me a bit of my old boss because he made no attempt at all to take the slightest advantage of me. Not then anyway. But he couldn't hide the fact that he was a lonely and disappointed man and before long he told me that he knew all about his wife's affair with Paul Morris. At first I think he must have come to see me just to find a little sympathy because he never once asked my opinion of what he should do. But then one day as we walked to the front door he just turned to me and told me that he found me attractive and that he would love to go to bed with me. Of course I felt a little bit flattered and certainly I had no moral scruples about the situation. We had been drinking sherry together and I was feeling rather more vivacious and daring than I normally do. What was I to say? I was still a virgin. I was forty-one. I had turned down the only man I had so far fallen in love with. I knew that life was passing me by and that if I didn't get to know something about sex fairly soon I never would. Not that I said any of this to Harry. In other circumstances I think I would have reminded him that he was married and that I liked and respected his wife too much to think of anything between us. As it was I think I just smiled and told him not to be so silly. He didn't say anything else but he looked so dejected and humiliated as he stood at the front door that I suddenly felt terribly sorry for him. Immediately to our right was the newly installed door to 14B which had just been painted Cambridge blue. I had the key in my pocket and I asked him if he'd like to have a look at the flat. He made love to me on the mattress of the unmade bed in the back room. It wasn't a particularly happy initiation for me but I experienced little regret. In fact I almost felt a sense of satisfaction and for the next few months we made love together once a week. As I became a little more practised in the physical side of it all I found myself enjoying the act of sex itself more and more. But I knew that something was sadly wrong because I felt so shoddy and cheap after it was over and I began to hate myself for wanting sex at all. I tried to stop it but looking back I think my try was half-hearted. The man seemed to have some power over me and I began living more and more on my nerves. I started worrying about my mother finding out although she seemed to suspect nothing. I started worrying about the neighbours too but goodness knows why because the houses on either side of us were multi-occupied with an ever-changing stream of temporary tenants or undergraduates. Above all I was worried about myself. The truth was that I now needed Harry more than he needed me and he knew this. Whatever agonies of self-reproach I suffered after he was gone I knew that I would be thinking all the time about our next meeting. I began to hate him as well as myself. He was like a drug to which I was fast becoming an addict.

It is perhaps important for you to know all this if you are to understand what happened to me later.

Chapter Forty

Statement given by Miss Ruth Rawlinson (continued)

One Wednesday morning in early September my mother had a bad attack and I decided I had to put off my cleaning visit from the Wednesday morning to the Wednesday evening. But I had keys to the church and could get in whenever I wanted to so a break in my regular routine didn't matter. I locked the door behind me (I almost always used the south door because I could leave my bicycle in the porch there) and I was cleaning the confessional when I heard the north door being unlocked. Paul Morris and Lionel Lawson's brother (as I now knew) Philip came in. For some reason I felt frightened and I sat quietly where I was. I couldn't hear anything they said but it was clear to me that Paul was being blackmailed and that he couldn't and wouldn't pay up very much longer. I didn't understand too much of what was going on and I felt confused and worried. I just kept sitting where I was and I'm not sure exactly what happened next. But a few minutes later it was clear to me that Paul must have gone and that Lionel himself had come into the church because I could now hear the two brothers talking to one another. Again I didn't catch too much of what they were saying but the little I managed to pick up hit me like a thunderbolt. They were talking about murdering Harry Josephs. I was so astounded that the scrubbing-brush I was holding fell clattering to the floor – and they found me. Philip Lawson left almost immediately and then Lionel talked to me for a long long time. I am not prepared even now to disclose everything he told me then but the simple fact is that he begged me for my co-operation. He reminded me of course of my earlier promise to him and he offered to write me a cheque for £5,000 immediately (£5,000!) if I would do as he asked. He said that this payment was for me to keep the upstairs flat free so that his brother Philip could live there for what was likely to be no more than a month at the outside. I felt completely dumbfounded and could hardly begin to realise the implications of all this. At home things were going from bad to worse. The £500 loan from Lionel had all gone and although the flat was now virtually ready our own part of the house was living on borrowed time. According to the builders the whole of the ground floor badly needed rewiring and the water tank was corroded and likely to burst any day. To cap it all the gas central-heating had broken down completely only that very week after a few days of fitful functioning. I had not taken into account either the decoration of the converted kitchen upstairs and the only estimate I'd had on that was a horrifying £200. Just imagine my feelings then! But there was something else. I should have mentioned it much earlier but since it is the one thing in the whole case which inescapably incriminates me you will perhaps understand my reluctance – my refusal almost – to mention it. Lionel explained to me that I could now discharge my obligation to him and that this would involve me in the telling of one lie. No. Even now I am not being quite truthful. He made me swear on my most solemn honour I would tell this one lie. He emphasised repeatedly that it would only be one lie – it would involve me in nothing more than that and he insisted that it would be perfectly simple for me to carry out. I didn't care! I was desperately glad to be able to help him and I agreed without a second's hesitation. My mind was in a complete whirl as I left the church that evening. Of Harry Josephs I tried not to think at all. I suppose I almost managed to persuade myself that I had misheard the whole thing. But of course I hadn't. I knew that for some reason or other Harry Josephs was going to die and that my own commitment to tell one simple lie was quite certainly going to be associated with that (for me) not unwelcome event. Where did Philip Lawson fit in? I couldn't then be sure but if money was involved with me – surely it would be involved with him too. The conviction gradually grew in my mind that Lionel had hired his brother to murder Harry Josephs and if this was the case my own part in the business – my own lie – would have something to do with being with a certain person at a certain time. An alibi. Yes. I began to feel convinced that such was the case – and again I didn't care! During this time I felt no burden of conscience. It was money now that played the tyrant. Sex was no longer the dominating force and even if it had been I had plenty of opportunity. Several times I had met a man in the Randolph cocktail-bar who showed he was obviously attracted towards me. He was a sales consultant for some prestigious firm and I had little doubt that the room he had in the Randolph would leave little to ask for in terms of physical comfort. I suspect he had taken up with another woman but it was

me that he really wanted. At this time too I was becoming
increasingly mean with money. Now I had far more than ever
before in my whole life I found myself not even offering to pay
for any drinks and accepting expensive meals and generally being
an utterly selfish parasite. I bought no new clothes no perfume
no special tit-bits for meals. As I grew mean with money I grew
mean in other ways too. The same week I rang Harry Josephs and
told him that our weekly date was off because my mother was
very ill again. Lying like that was ridiculously easy for me now.
Good practice! At home the boiler they said could just about be
repaired and so I refused to buy a new one. I regarded the first
rewiring estimate as ridiculously high so I got a local odd-job
man in to do it for half the price. Not that he made a wonderful
success of it. I decided to redecorate the upstairs kitchen myself
and I found I thoroughly enjoyed doing it. For years I had put
50p in the collection-plate each Sunday morning. Now I put in
20p. But I still cleaned the church. It was my one pennance and
I seemed to take more pride than ever in my self-imposed duties.
You will think all of this very strange yet it is exactly how I
felt and acted. From the way I have just been talking I am conscious that I have made it sound as if it all took place over
a long time. But of course it didn't. It was only just over three
weeks until the 26th September.

On that day the five of us met at 7 p.m. at St Frideswide's:
Brenda Josephs and Paul Morris and Lionel Lawson and Philip
Lawson and myself. The doors were locked and I received my
instructions. The candles were to be lit in the Lady Chapel and
prayer books set out as if for thirteen members of a congregation
– including the churchwarden's pew! I think that last thing was the
worst of all really. Paul was playing something on the organ and
he seemed to me to look more strained than any of us. Brenda
was standing by the font dressed in a smart two-piece green suit
and looking quite expressionless. Lionel was busying himself with
what appeared to be the usual preparations for a mass – his face
quite normal as far as I could tell. Lionel's brother was just as
spruce as when I had last seen him and was sitting in the vestry
drinking from a bottle which Lionel had no doubt provided for
him. At about 7.15 Lionel asked Brenda and myself to go and
stand up at the altar in the Lady Chapel and to stay there until
he told us. Almost immediately we heard the key being fitted into

the north door and Harry Josephs walked in carrying a fairly large brown-paper parcel under his arm. He looked flushed and excited and it was obvious that he had been drinking quite heavily. He saw the pair of us and nodded – but whether to me or to Brenda I couldn't tell. We sat down on the steps of the altar and I think that both of us were trembling. Then the organ suddenly stopped and Paul came through and pressed his hand lightly on Brenda's shoulder before walking up towards the vestry. For several minutes we could hear the men's mumbled voices and then there was a scuffling of feet followed by a dull low sort of moan. When Lionel fetched us he was dressed in surplice and cope. He was breathing heavily and looked very shaken. He said that when the police came I was to tell them that there had been about a dozen or more in the congregation mostly American visitors and that I had heard Harry cry out for help from the vestry during the playing of the last hymn. Whether Brenda was still with me I can't remember. I just walked slowly down to the vestry in a daze. I could see him clearly. He lay there quite still in his brown suit and the cassock he always wore in church with Lionel Lawson's paper knife stuck deep in his back.

Of the other deaths in this nightmarish business I know nothing at all. But I am convinced that Lionel himself committed suicide unable to face what he had done. I am only too glad that at least he cannot be accused of the murders of Brenda Josephs and the Morrises. As I now finish this long statement my thoughts are with my mother and I beg of you to look after her for me and to tell her – but I can't think what you can tell her. I suppose it will have to be the truth.

Signed: RUTH RAWLINSON

Morse put down the statement and looked at Lewis with some distaste. He had been away from the station for more than six hours and had left word of his whereabouts to no one. It was now 8 p.m., and he looked tired. 'Whoever typed that isn't very fond of commas, is she?'

'She's a jolly good girl, sir. Wish we had her up at Kidlington.'

'She can't spell "penance".'

'She can take about 130 words a minute, though.'

'Did Miss Rawlinson speak as fast as that?'

'Pretty fast, yes.'

'Strange,' said Morse.

Lewis looked at his chief with an air of weary puzzlement. 'Clears the air a bit, doesn't it, sir?'

'That?' Morse picked up the statement again, separated the last few sheets, tore them across the middle, and deposited them in the wastepaper basket.

'But you can't just tear— '

'What the hell? The factual content of those pages isn't worth a sheet of lavatory paper! If she's decided to persist in her perjury, she'll get twice as long! Surely you can see that, man?'

Lewis saw very little. He'd been pleased with his day's work – still was; but he, too, felt very tired now and shook his head without bitterness. 'I reckon I could do with a bit of rest, sir.'

'Rest? What the hell are you talking about? You save my life for me and all you want to do is indulge in a bit of Egyptian P.T.! Rubbish! We're going to celebrate, you and me.'

'I think I'd rather— '

'But don't you want to hear what I've been up to, old friend?' He looked slyly for a minute at Lewis, and then smiled – a smile which but for a slight hint of sadness could have been called wholly triumphant.

THE BOOK OF REVELATION

Chapter Forty-one

The Friar Bacon stands a little way back from the A40 Northern Ring Road, its name commemorating the great thirteenth-century scientist and philosopher, and its beer pleasing to the critical palate of Chief Inspector Morse. The sign outside this public house depicts a stout, jolly-looking man in Franciscan habit, pouring out what appears at first glance to be a glass of Guinness, but what on closer scrutiny proves to be a quantity of some chemical liquid being poured from one glass phial to another. Well, that's what Morse said. Inside they ordered beer and sat down. And then Morse spoke as follows.

'There are some extremely odd points in this case, Lewis – or rather there were – each of them in itself suggestive but also puzzling. They puzzled all of us, and perhaps still do to some extent, because by the time we'd finished we'd got no less than five bodies on our hands and we were never in a position to learn what any of the five could have told us. So, if first of all we look for motive, it's likely to be little more than intelligent guesswork, although we've got some little bits of evidence here and there to help us on our way. Let's start with Harry Josephs. He's getting desperately short of money, and what little he manages to get hold of he promptly donates to his bookmaker. Unbeknown to his wife he borrows money from his insurance company against his house – and he's soon through that, too. Then – as I strongly suspect, Lewis – he starts embezzling church funds, of which there are temptingly large sums and to which he has easy access. Then – I'm guessing again – Lionel Lawson must have found out about this; and if he reports the matter we've got the humiliating prospect of a highly respected ex-officer caught pilfering from the till. It would surely

378

be the last straw for a man who's already lost his job and his money, and who's in real danger of losing his wife as well. Then take Lionel Lawson. Rumours are beginning to spread about him – nasty rumours about his relations with the choirboys, and someone soon made him very much aware of them – pretty certainly Paul Morris, whose son Peter was actually in the choir. Again we've got the prospect of public humiliation: a highly respected minister of the C. of E. caught interfering with the choirboys. Then there's Paul Morris himself. He's having what he hopes is a discreet affair with Harry Josephs' wife, but rumours are beginning to spread about that, too, and it's not very long before Harry gets to know what's going on. Next we come to Ruth Rawlinson. She's got her eyes and ears open more than most, and very soon she gets to know a great deal – in fact a great deal more than is good for her. But she's got a good many problems herself, and it's directly because of them that she becomes caught up in the case. Last, there's Lawson's brother, Philip, who as far as I can see only comes permanently on to the Oxford scene last summer. He's been an idle beggar all his life, and he still was then – absolutely on his uppers and looking yet again to his brother for help. Lionel has him to stay at the vicarage, and it isn't long before the old tensions begin to mount again. By the way, Lewis, I'm not making that last bit up, but I'll come back to it later. What have we got then? We've got enough miscellaneous motive here for a multitude of murders. Each of those involved has some cause to fear at least one of the others, and at the same time some hope he might profit from it all. There's enough potential blackmail and hatred to boil up into a very, very ugly situation. The only thing needed to set the whole reaction off is a catalyst, and we know who that catalyst was – the Reverend Lionel Lawson. It's he who's got the one priceless asset in the case – money: about forty thousand pounds of it. What's more, this money means very little to him personally. He's perfectly happy to struggle along on the miserable little stipend he's allowed by the mean-minded Church Commissioners, because whatever weaknesses he may have the love of money is not among 'em. So, he carefully tests the ice, and after a few tentative steps he finds that the ice on the pond is thick enough to hold all of 'em. What does he offer? To his brother Philip – money, and the chance to perpetuate his dissolute life-style for a few more years to come. To Josephs –

money, and the chance to clear up his financial affairs and get away to start a new life somewhere else, minus his wife. To Morris – again, doubtless, money, if that's what Morris wanted; but he can also probably ensure that Morris gets Brenda Josephs as well, and the chance for both of 'em to get away and start a new life together, with a healthy bank balance into the bargain. To Ruth Rawlinson – money, and the chance to settle once and for all her chronic anxiety over her domestic problems. So Lionel Lawson sets up his scheme, with the others as his willing accomplices. He fixes up a bogus service to celebrate some non-existent feast – and then the deed is done. The witnesses happily perjure themselves and at the same time vouch for one another's alibis. Lionel is standing at the altar. Paul Morris is playing the organ, Ruth Rawlinson is sitting in the congregation, and Brenda Josephs is across the road at the cinema. If they all stick to their stories, they're all in the clear. All the suspicion, of course, is going to fall on brother Philip; but Lionel has told him – and probably told everyone else – that everything has been most carefully arranged for him: within a few minutes of the murder, he will have caught a train from Oxford station and will be on his way to some pre-arranged hotel booking, with several thousand pounds in his pocket for his troubles. And for all that a little suspicion is a cheap price to pay, wouldn't you say?'

Morse finished his beer and Lewis, who for once had beaten him to it, walked up to the bar. It was quite clear to him, as Morse had said, that there was a whole host of motives in the case interlocking and (if Morse were right) mutually complementary and beneficial. But where did all this *hatred* against Harry Josephs spring from? All right, the lot of them were getting into a terrible mess, but (again, if Morse were right) money seemed to be coping quite adequately with all their problems. And why, oh, why, all this peculiar palaver in the church? It all seemed a ridiculously complicated and quite unnecessary charade. Why not just kill Josephs and dump his body somewhere? Between them that would have been infinitely simpler, surely? And what about the actual murder itself? Morphine poisoning *and* a knife in the back. No. It didn't really add up.

He paid for the beer and walked circumspectly back to their table. He wouldn't be thanked if he slopped as much as a cubic millimetre on to the carpet.

Morse took a mighty swallow from his beer and continued. 'We've now got to ask ourselves the key question: how can we account for enough hatred – on somebody's part – against Harry Josephs? Because unless we can answer that question we're still groping about in the dark. And closely connected with it we've got to ask ourselves why there was all this clumsy kerfuffle at the phoney service, and also why Josephs was killed twice over. Well, let's deal with the last question first. I'm sure you've heard of those firing squads when you get, say, four men with rifles, all quite happy to shoot the poor fellow tied to the post, but three of 'em have blanks up the barrel and only one has a live bullet. The idea is that none of 'em will ever know which one actually fired the fatal shot. Well, I thought that something of the sort may have happened here. There were three of 'em, remember, and let's say none of 'em is too keen on being solely responsible for the killing. Now, if Josephs, as well as being poisoned and stabbed, had also been bashed on the head, I reckon the evidence would have pointed strongly to my being right. But we learned from the post-mortem that there were two causes of death, and not three. Somebody gives Josephs morphine in some red wine; and then somebody, either the same somebody or somebody else, stabs him in the back. Why bother to kill him twice over? Well, it may well be that two of 'em *were* involved in the actual murder; a division of labour could have been agreed for the reason I've just mentioned. But there was a far more important reason than that. Are you ready for a bit of a shock, Lewis?'

'Ready for anything, sir.'

Morse drained his glass. 'By Jove, the beer's good here!'

'It's your turn, sir.'

'Is it?'

The landlord had come through into the lounge-bar, and for a few minutes Lewis could hear him discussing with Morse the crass stupidity of the selectors of the England football team.

'These are on the house,' said Morse, planting the two pints carefully on the Morrell's beer-mats. (For a man proposing to treat his junior officer for services rendered, he seemed to Lewis to be getting away with things extremely lightly.) 'Where was I now? Ah, yes. You didn't ask me where I'd been today, did you? Well, I've been up to Rutland again.'

'Leicestershire, sir.'

Morse appeared not to hear. 'I made one bad blunder in this case, Lewis. Only one. I listened too much to rumour, and rumour's a terrible thing. If I tell everybody that you're having an affair with that comma-less typist of yours, you'd suddenly find yourself trying like hell to prove you weren't – even though there was absolutely no truth in it. Like they say, you throw enough mud and some of it'll stick. Well, I reckon that's what happened with Lionel Lawson. If he was a homosexual, he must have been one of the very mildest variety, I think. But once the charge had been suggested he found himself in the middle of a good deal of suspicion, and I was one of those prepared to think the worst of him. I even managed to convince myself, without the slightest shred of evidence, that when he was expelled from school it must have been because he was buggering about with some of the younger lads there. But suddenly I began to wonder. What if I'd been quite wrong? What if Lionel Lawson's old headmaster wasn't too unhappy about letting me believe what I did – *because the truth of the matter was far worse?* I thought I knew what this truth was, and I was right. Today I met Meyer again, as well as Lionel's old housemaster. You see, the Lawson brothers were an extremely odd mixture. There was Lionel, the elder brother, a hard-working, studious swot, not too gifted academically, struggling along and doing his best, bespectacled even then, lacking in any confidence – in short, Lewis, a bit of a bore all round. And then there was Philip, a clever little beggar, with all the natural gifts any boy could ask for – a fine brain, good at games, popular, good-looking, and yet always idle and selfish. And the parents dote on – guess who? – young, glamour-pants Philip. It doesn't require much imagination to see the situation from Lionel's point of view, does it? He's jealous of his brother – increasingly and, finally, furiously jealous. From what I've been able to learn there was a young girl mixed up in it all, when Lionel was eighteen and Philip a year or so younger. She wasn't a brilliant looker by all accounts – but she was Lionel's girl. Until, that is, Philip decided to step in; and probably for no other reason than to spite his brother he took her away from him. It was from that point that the whole of the tragedy dates. At home, one week-end, *Lionel Lawson tried to kill his brother*. He tried to use the kitchen-knife, and in fact he wounded him quite seriously – *in the back*. Things were hushed up as far as possible and the police were quite happy to leave the situation in the hands of the school and the parents. Some arrangement was worked out, with both the boys being taken away from the school. No charge was brought, and things, so it seemed, settled down. But the records couldn't be altered, could they, Lewis? The fact was that at the age of eighteen Lionel Lawson had tried unsuccessfully to murder his brother. So if, as I said, we're looking for any festering, insatiable hatred in this case, then we've found it: the hatred that existed between Lionel Lawson and his younger brother.'

It was all very interesting and suggestive, Lewis could see that; but he couldn't really see how it affected many of the problems in the present case. Morse was going on, though, and the shock he'd spoken of was imminent.

'At first I thought that Lionel Lawson had killed Harry Josephs and had then faked his own suicide by dressing up his brother in clerical get-up and chucking him from the top of the tower. What could be neater? All you'd want was someone who would agree to a wrong identification of the body, and such a person was readily available in Paul Morris, a man who would have profited twofold from the murder of Josephs: first, by pocketing a considerable sum of money; and, second, by having Josephs' wife for himself. But you made the point to me yourself, Lewis, and you were absolutely right: it's one helluva job to dress up a dead man in someone else's clothes. But it's not an *impossible* job, is it? Not if you're all prepared for the difficulties and if you've got plenty of time. But in this particular instance you were right, I'm convinced of that. It was Lionel Lawson, not his brother Philip, who fell from the tower last October. In his own conscience Lionel must have realised that he'd done something so terrible and so unforgivable that he just couldn't live with it any longer. So he took his spectacles off, put them in their case – and jumped. And while we're on this identification business, Lewis, I must confess I had my fair share of doubts about whether the body we found on the tower really was Paul Morris. If it wasn't, the possibilities were staggeringly interesting. But, although we've no satisfactory identification as yet, you can take my word for it that it *was* Paul Morris. Yes, indeed. And so at long last I began to shelve all these fanciful theories, and I just looked at the simple possibility that all of us had completely ignored from the very beginning. Ruth Rawlinson herself came very near to telling the truth and giving the game away in that ridiculous statement of hers when she said that she was prepared to tell one lie – *one lie*. She told us, as you'll remember, that this lie was about the service in St Frideswide's that never took place, and about her silence in the plotting of Harry Josephs' murder. But listen, Lewis! That wasn't the real lie at all. The real lie was about something else: she lied about the identification of the body lying dead in St Frideswide's vestry that night in September! *That* was her one big lie. Because, you see, the body found murdered that night was not the body of Harry Josephs at all! *It was the body of Lionel Lawson's brother – Philip Lawson*.'

Chapter Forty-two

Extract from the transcript of proceedings held on 4 July at Oxford Crown Court against Miss Ruth Isabel Rawlinson on the charges of perjury and conspiracy, Mr Gilbert Marshall, Q.C., prosecuting for the Crown, Mr Anthony Johns, Q.C., acting for the defence.

Marshall: Let us turn, if we can, away from these rather nebulous areas of motive, and come to the events of last September, specifically to the evening of Monday the twenty-sixth of that month. The Court will be glad, I know, to hear your own explanation of the events which took place that unholy night.

Morse: It is my view, sir, that a conspiracy had been formed to murder Mr Philip Lawson, and that this conspiracy involved the Reverend Lionel Lawson, Mr Paul Morris and Mr Harry Josephs. I am quite sure in my own mind that the statement made by the defendant about the events of that evening is substantially correct. Correct, that is, as far as it goes, since I am convinced that Miss Rawlinson was not in a position to know the detailed sequence of events, being neither an active party in, nor an actual witness to, the murder itself.

Marshall: Try to confine yourself to the question, Inspector, will you? It is for the Court to determine the degree of the defendant's involvement in this crime – not for you. Please continue.

Morse: If I were to guess the sequence of events that night, sir, it would have to be something like this. Lionel Lawson was able somehow to persuade his brother Philip that it would be greatly to his advantage to be in the church at a certain time that evening. It would have been no great problem to persuade him to drink a glass of red wine whilst they waited there – wine that had already been doctored with morphine. The fact that the man found dead at the church that night could have died, or certainly would have died, of morphine poisoning was clearly established by the post-mortem findings; but the provenance of the morphine itself was never discovered, in spite of extensive police enquiries. However, there was one of the three men who had earlier had direct and daily access to a complete pharmacopoeia, a man who had worked for eighteen months as a chemist's assistant in Oxford. That man, sir, was Harry Josephs. And it was Josephs, who, in my view, not only suggested but actually administered the lethal dose of morphine in the wine.

Marshall: Can you tell us why, if the man was already dead, it was necessary to stab him into the bargain?

Morse: I don't think he was already dead, sir, although I agree he would have been unconscious fairly soon after drinking the wine. Whatever happened, though, he had to be dead when the police arrived, because there might always be the outside chance of his recovering and telling the police what he knew. Hence the knife. And so if I may say so, sir, the key question is not why he was stabbed in the back – but why he was given morphine. And in my considered view the reason was this: it was absolutely vital from Lionel Lawson's point of view that his brother's clothes should be changed, and you can't stab a man in the back and then change his clothes without removing the knife and stabbing him again. By arrangement, Josephs had changed from the brown suit which by all accounts he always wore and brought it with him to the church that night. Without any doubt, I should think, the suit was wrapped up in the brown-paper parcel which Miss Rawlinson mentions in her statement. The police would obviously examine the dead man's clothes in the minutest detail, and an actual change of clothes would be the one certain way of making the deception appear absolutely authentic. And so, when Philip Lawson had slumped unconscious in the vestry, his own clothes were removed and Josephs' clothes put on him –

a difficult and lengthy job, I should imagine, but there were three of them to do it and time was very much on their side. Then they dressed him in Josephs' cassock and the moment of truth had now arrived for Lionel Lawson. I suspect that he asked the other two to leave him, and then he completed a task which he had attempted once before and in which he had failed so disastrously. He looked down on the brother he had hated for so long, and he stabbed him in the back with his paper-knife. As I say, I don't myself think that Philip Lawson was dead at that point, and the defendant's statement tends to confirm this view, since what she heard must almost certainly have been the dying man's final groans. The police were summoned immediately, the body wrongly identified, both by the defendant and by Paul Morris, and I think you know the rest, sir.

Marshall: Doesn't all this seem to you an extraordinarily complicated business, Inspector? To me, at least, it seems quite ludicrously so. Why didn't the Reverend Lionel Lawson just murder his brother himself?

Judge: It is my duty to remind prosecuting counsel that it is not the Reverend Mr Lawson who is on trial in this court, and it is improper for the witness to answer the question in the form in which it has been phrased.

Marshall: Thank you, m'lord. Will the witness please explain to the Court why, in his view, the Reverend Mr Lawson, supposing him to have been responsible for his brother's death, did not proceed in this matter in a significantly more simple manner?

Morse: In my opinion, sir, two things were absolutely imperative for the Reverend Lawson. First that his brother should die – a matter which, as you suggest, he could perhaps have coped with singlehandedly all right if he'd tried. But the second imperative need was far trickier, and one which he could never have coped with by himself, however hard he tried. He had to have someone who was willing to be identified as the dead man and who was also prepared to disappear immediately from the Oxford scene. Let me explain, sir, why I think this was so. Philip Lawson had let it be known to several people, including the defendant, for example, that he was Lionel Lawson's brother. So if he had been murdered and identified as the man who had often been seen at the vicarage, in the church, and so on, it would only have been a matter of time before the police discovered his true identity. And once that was known other facts would have been swift to follow. An attempt had already been made upon the man's life once before – with a knife – by his elder brother. Police enquiries would very quickly have been channelled in the right direction and virtually certain suspicion would have centred on the Reverend Lawson. As I say, sir, it was absolutely vital not only that Philip Lawson should die but also that he should be wrongly identified. As the Court now knows, he was indeed wrongly identified – as Harry Josephs; and Harry Josephs himself disappeared from the scene, although as it happens he didn't disappear very far. That same night he moved into the upstairs flat at 14B Manning Terrace, and he lived there until he died. He'd taken Philip Lawson's clothes from the church and no doubt the idea was that he should destroy them. But for various reasons Josephs grew restless—

Marshall: Before you go on with your evidence, Inspector, I must ask you if it is your view that the defendant's relations with Mr Josephs had ever been in any way more – shall we say? – more intimate than merely providing him with the daily necessities of living?

Morse: No.

Marshall: You are aware, no doubt, of the evidence before the Court from an earlier witness of several visits by Mr Josephs to Manning Terrace during the course of last summer?

Morse: I am, sir.

Marshall: And it is your view that these visits were of a purely – er – purely social nature?

Morse: It is, sir.

Marshall: Please continue, Inspector.

Morse: I think the idea must have been for Josephs to stay where he was until the dust had settled and then to get right away from Oxford somewhere. But that again has to be guesswork. What is certain is that he very soon learned that the Reverend Lionel Lawson had committed suicide and—

Marshall: I'm sorry to interrupt you again, but is it your view that in that death, at least, the late Mr Josephs could have had no hand whatsoever?

Morse: It is, sir. News of Lawson's death, as I say, would have been a big shock to Josephs. He must have wondered what on earth had gone wrong. Specifically he must have wondered many times whether Lawson had left a note and, if so, whether the note in any way incriminated himself and the others. Quite apart from that, though, Josephs had been dependent on Lawson. It was Lawson who had arranged his present hide-out and it was Lawson who was arranging his impending departure from Oxford. But now he was on his own, and he must have felt increasingly isolated. But again that's guesswork. What is clear is that he started going out into Oxford during the early winter months. He wore Philip Lawson's old clothes, with the long dirty greatcoat buttoned up to the neck; he wore a pair of dark glasses; he grew a beard; and he found that he could merge quite anonymously into the Oxford background. It was about this time, too, I think, that he must have realised that there was now only one other person who knew exactly what had taken place in the vestry that September evening; and that person was Paul Morris, a man who had robbed him of his wife, a man who was probably going to live with her after the end of the school term, and a man who had done very nicely out of the whole thing, without actually doing very much at all himself. It is my own view, by the way, sir, that Paul Morris may not have been quite so eager to get away with Mrs Josephs as he had been. But Josephs himself could have no inkling of that, and his hatred of Morris grew, as did his sense of power and his rediscovered capacity for the sort of action he had once known as a captain in the Royal Marine Commandos. On some pretext or other Josephs was able to arrange a meeting with Paul Morris at St Frideswide's, where he killed him and hid his body – though probably not, at that point, on the roof of the tower. Remember that no keys had been found in the clothing of the man murdered in the vestry; and it is clear that Josephs kept them for himself, and was therefore able to use the church for the murders of Paul Morris and his son Peter. Not only that, though. He was compelled to use the church. He was disqualified from driving, and without a licence, of course, he couldn't even hire a car. If he'd had a car, he would probably have tried to dispose of the bodies elsewhere; but in this respect, at least, he was a victim of circumstance. Later the same day – at tea-time in fact – he also arranged to meet Peter Morris, and there can be little doubt that the young boy was also murdered in St Frideswide's. I'm pretty sure his first idea was to hide both bodies in the crypt, and as soon as it was dark he put the boy in a sack and opened the door at the south porch. Everything must have seemed safe enough and he got to the grilled entrance to the crypt in the south churchyard all right – it's only about fifteen yards or so from the door. But then something happened. As he was carrying the body down, the ladder snapped and Josephs must have had an awkward fall. He decided that he couldn't or daren't repeat the process with a much bigger and heavier body; so he changed his plans and carried Paul Morris' body up to the tower roof.

Marshall: And then he decided to murder his wife?

Morse: Yes, sir. Whether at this point he knew exactly where she was; whether he had actually been in touch with her; whether he was able to find out anything from Paul Morris – I just don't know. But once the bodies – or just one of them – were found, he was going to make absolutely sure that *she* didn't talk, either; and, in any case, with Paul Morris now out of the way, his jealous hatred was directing itself ever more insanely against his wife. For the moment, however, he had a dangerous job on his hands. He had to get to the Morrises' house in Kidlington and try to make everything there look as if they'd both left in a reasonably normal manner. It was no problem getting into the house. No keys were found on either of the Morrises, although each of them must have had a latchkey. Once inside—

Marshall: Yes, yes. Thank you, Inspector. Could you now tell the Court exactly where the defendant fits into your scheme of things?

Morse: I felt reasonably certain, sir, that Miss Rawlinson would be safe only so long as she herself had no knowledge of the identities of the bodies found in St Frideswide's.

Marshall: But as soon as she did – tell me if I am wrong, Inspector – Josephs decided that he would also murder the defendant?

Morse: That is so, sir. As you know, I was an eye-witness to the attempted murder of Miss Rawlinson, and it was only at that point that I was convinced of the true identity of the murderer – when I recognised the tie he tried to strangle her with: the tie of the Royal Marine Commandos.

Marshall: Yes, very interesting, Inspector. But surely the defendant was always just as much of a threat to the murderer as Brenda Josephs was? Don't you think so? And, if she was, why do you think he treated the two women so differently?

Morse: I believe that Josephs had grown to hate his wife, sir. I made the point earlier in my evidence.

Marshall: But he didn't feel the same hatred towards the defendant – is that it?

Morse: I don't know, sir.

Marshall: You still wish to maintain that there was no special relationship between the defendant and Mr Josephs?

Morse: I have nothing to add to my earlier answer, sir.

Marshall: Very well. Go on, Inspector.

Morse: As I say, sir, I felt convinced that Josephs would attempt to kill Miss Rawlinson almost immediately, since it must have been clear to him that things were beginning to move very fast indeed, and since Miss Rawlinson was the only person left, apart from himself, who knew something of the truth – far too much of it, he must have felt. So my colleague, Sergeant Lewis, and myself decided we would try to bring the murderer out into the open. We allowed a slightly inaccurate report on the case to appear prominently in the *Oxford Mail* with the sole purpose of making him suspect that the net was already beginning to close on him. I thought that wherever he was – and remember that I had no idea whatsoever that he was living in the same house as Miss Rawlinson – he was almost certain to use the church once more. He would know exactly the times when Miss Rawlinson would be cleaning there, and he had his plans all ready. In fact, he got to church very early that morning, and managed to ruin the precautions which we had so carefully taken.

Marshall: But fortunately things worked out all right, Inspector.

Morse: I suppose you could say that. Thanks to Sergeant Lewis.

Marshall: I have no more questions.

Johns: I understand, Inspector, that you heard the conversation between my client and Mr Josephs before the attempt to strangle her was made.

Morse: I did.

Johns: In that conversation, did you hear anything which might be considered by the Court to be mitigating evidence in the case against my client?

Morse: Yes. I heard Miss Rawlinson say that she—

Judge: Will the witness please speak up for the Court?

Morse: I heard Miss Rawlinson say that she had decided to go to the police and make a full statement of all she knew.

Johns: Thank you. No further questions.

Judge: You may stand down, Inspector.

Chapter Forty-three

'What beats me,' said Bell, 'is how many crooks there are around – in a church, too! I always thought those sort of people walked straight down the middle of the paths of righteousness.'

'Perhaps most of them do,' said Lewis quietly.

They were sitting in Bell's office just after the verdict and sentence had been passed on Miss Ruth Rawlinson. Guilty; eighteen months' imprisonment.

'It still beats me,' said Bell.

Morse was sitting there, too, silently smoking a cigarette. He either smoked addictively or not at all, and had given up the habit for ever on innumerable occasions. He had listened vaguely to the mumbled conversation, and he knew exactly what Bell had meant, but. . . . His favourite Gibbon quotation flashed across his mind, the one concerning the fifteenth-century Pope John XXIII, which had so impressed him as a boy and which he had committed to memory those many years ago: 'The most scandalous charges were suppressed; the vicar of Christ was only accused of piracy, murder, rape, sodomy, and incest.' It was no new thing to realise that the Christian church had a great deal to answer for, with so much blood on the hands of its temporal administrators, and so much hatred and bitterness in the hearts of its spiritual lords. But behind it all, as Morse knew – and transcending it all – stood the simple, historical, unpalatable figure of its founder – an enigma with which Morse's mind had wrestled so earnestly as a youth, and which even now troubled his pervasive scepticism. He remembered his first visit to a service at St Frideswide's, and the woman singing next to him: 'Wash me, and I shall be whiter than snow.' Wonderful possibility! The Almighty, as it were, wiping the slate clean and not just forgiving, but forgetting, too. And it was forgetting that was the really hard thing. Morse could find it even in his own cynical soul to forgive – but not to forget. How could he forget? For a few blissful moments on that day in St Frideswide's he had felt such a precious affinity with a woman as he had felt only once before; but their orbits, his and hers, had crossed too late in the day, and she, like all other lost souls, like the Lawsons and Josephs and Morris, had erred and strayed from the ways of acceptable human behaviour. But how could his mind not be haunted by the revelations she had made? Should he go to see her now, as she had asked? If he *was* to see her, it would have to be very soon.

Dimly and uninterestedly his mind caught up with the conversation once more: 'Doesn't reflect very well on me, does it, Sergeant? I'm in charge of the case for months, and then Morse here comes along and solves it in a fortnight. Made me look a proper Charley, if you ask me.' He shook his head slowly. 'Clever bugger!'

Lewis tried to say something but he couldn't find the right words. Morse, he knew, had the maddeningly brilliant facility for seeing his way through the dark labyrinths of human motive and human behaviour, and he was proud to be associated with him; proud when Morse had mentioned his name in court that day. But such matters weren't Lewis' forte; he knew that, too. And it was almost a relief – after Morse – to get back to his usual pedestrian and perfunctory duties.

Morse heard his own name mentioned again and realised that Bell was talking to him.

'You know, I still don't understand— '

'Nor do I,' interrupted Morse. Throughout the case he had made so many guesses that he could find no mental reserve to fabricate more. The words of St Paul to the Corinthians were writ large in his brain: 'There is a manifestation and there is a mystery'; and he felt sure that whatever might be puzzling Bell was not likely to be one of the greater mysteries of life. Wasn't one of the real mysteries the source of that poison which had slowly but inexorably dripped and dripped into Lionel Lawson's soul? And that was almost as old as the seed of Adam himself, when Cain and Abel had presented their offerings before the Lord. . . .

'Pardon?'

'I said the pubs'll soon be open, sir.'

'Not tonight for me, Lewis. I – er – I don't feel much like it.'

He got up and walked out of the office without a further word, Lewis staring after him in some bewilderment.

'Odd bugger!' said Bell; and for the second time within a few minutes Lewis felt he had to agree with him.

Obviously Ruth had been crying, but she was now recovered, her voice dull and resigned. 'I just wanted to thank you, Inspector, that's all. You've been – you've been so kind to me, and – and I think if anyone could ever understand me it might have been you.'

'Perhaps so,' said Morse. It was not one of his more memorable utterances.

'And then— ' She sighed deeply and a film of tears enveloped her lovely eyes. 'I just wanted to say that when you asked me out that time – do you remember? – and when I said – when I— ' Her face betrayed her feelings completely now, and Morse nodded and looked away.

'Don't worry about it. I know what you're going to say. It's all right. I understand.'

She forced herself to speak through her tears. 'But I *want* to say it to you, Inspector. I want you to know that— ' Again, she was unable to go on; and Morse touched her shoulder lightly, just as Paul Morris had touched Brenda Josephs lightly on the shoulder on the night of Philip Lawson's murder. Then he got up and made his way quickly out along the corridor. Yes, he understood – and he forgave her, too. But, unlike the Almighty, he was unable to forget.

Mrs Emily Walsh-Atkins had been called upon to identify the battered corpse of Harry Josephs. (It was Morse's idea.) She had done so willingly, of course. What an exciting time this last year had been! And the goldfish flashed its tail almost merrily in her mind as she recalled her own part in the tragic events which had centred upon her chosen church. Her name had appeared once more in the *Oxford Mail* – in the *Oxford Times*, too – and she had cut out the paragraphs carefully, just as Ruth Rawlinson before her, and kept them in her handbag with the others. One Sunday morning during the hot summer which followed these events, she prayed earnestly for forgiveness for her sins of pride, and the Reverend Keith Meiklejohn, standing benignly beside the north porch, was kept waiting even longer than usual until she finally emerged into the bright sunshine.

Mrs Alice Rawlinson had been taken to the Old People's Home in Cowley immediately after her daughter's arrest. When Ruth was freed, after serving only eleven of her eighteen months' sentence, the old lady returned to 14A Manning Terrace, still going strong and looking good for several years to come. As she was helped into the ambulance on her way home, one of the young housemen was heard to murmur that anyone who predicted how long a patient had got to live was nothing but a bloody fool.

A few books had been found in Harry Josephs' upstairs flat at 14B Manning Terrace; and after the case was over these had been given to Oxfam, and were slowly sold, at ridiculously low prices, at the second-hand charity bookshop in north Oxford. A seventeen-year-old boy (by some curious coincidence, a boy named Peter Morris) bought one of them for five pence in the early summer. He had always been interested in crime, and the large, fat, glossy volume entitled *Murder Ink* had immediately attracted his attention. That same night whilst browsing through the assorted articles, he came to a piece about suicides on page 349, heavily underlined in red biro: *Myopic jumpers invariably remove their eyeglasses and put them in a pocket before jumping*.

Chapter Forty-four

Morse took his holidays later the following year and decided, again, to go to the Greek islands. Yet somehow his passport remained unrenewed in its drawer, and one sunny morning in mid-June the chief inspector caught a bus down from north Oxford into the city. For an hour he wandered contentedly around the Ashmolean where amongst other delights he stood for many minutes in front of the Giorgione and the Tiepolo. Just before midday he walked across to the cocktail-bar at the Randolph and bought a pint of beer, for he would never lend his lips to anything less than that measure. Then another pint. He left at half-past twelve, crossed Cornmarket, and walked into St Frideswide's. The north door creaked no longer, but inside the only sign of life was the flickering candles that burned around the statue of the Virgin. The woman he was seeking was not there. As once before, he decided to walk up to north Oxford, although this time he witnessed no accident at the Marston Ferry

cross-roads. Reaching the Summertown shops, he called into the
Dew Drop, drank two further pints of beer, and continued on
his way. The carpet-shop, from which Brenda Josephs had once
observed her husband, had now been taken over by an insurance
firm, but otherwise little seemed to have changed. When he came
to Manning Terrace, Morse turned into it, paused at one point for
a second or two, and then continued along it. At number 14A he
stopped, knocked briskly on the door, and stood there waiting.

'You!'

'I heard you'd come home.'

'Well! Come in! Come in! You're the first visitor I've had.'

'No, I won't do that. I just called by to tell you that I've
been thinking a lot about you since you've been – er – away,
and you'd blush if I told you what happened in my dreams.'

'Of course I wouldn't!'

'Don't take any notice of me – I've had too much beer.'

'*Please* come in.'

'Your mother's there.'

'Why don't you take me to bed?'

Her large eyes held his, and in that moment a sparkling
mutual joy was born.

'Can I use your "gents"?'

'There's one upstairs – it's a "ladies", too.'

'Upstairs?'

'Just a minute!'

She was back almost immediately with a Yale key labelled
14B in her hand.

'Hadn't you better tell your mother— ?'

'I don't think so,' she said, and a slow smile spread across
her lips as she closed the door of 14A quietly behind her and
inserted the key into 14B.

Morse's eyes followed her slim ankles as she climbed the
carpeted stairs ahead of him.

'Bedroom or lounge?'

'Let's go into the lounge a few minutes first,' said Morse.

'There's some whisky here. Do you want a drink?'

'I want you.'

'And you can have me. You know that, don't you?'

Morse took her in his arms as they stood there, and kissed her
tenderly on her sweet, full lips. Then, as if the moment were too

unbearably blissful to be prolonged, he pressed her body tightly to him and laid his cheek against hers.

'I dreamed about you, too,' she whispered in his ear.

'Did I behave myself?'

'I'm afraid so. But you're not going to behave yourself now, are you?'

'Certainly not.'

'What's your Christian name?' she asked.

'I'll tell you afterwards,' said Morse quietly, as his fingers lingered lightly on the zip at the back of her brightly patterned summer dress.

The Silent World
of Nicholas Quinn

for Jack Ashley

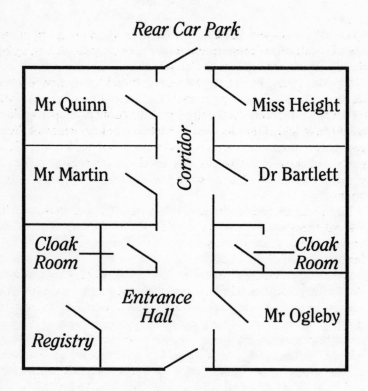

Rear Car Park

Mr Quinn

Miss Height

Mr Martin

Dr Bartlett

Corridor

Cloak Room

Cloak Room

Entrance Hall

Mr Ogleby

Registry

Front Car Park

Prologue

'Well? What do you think?' The Dean of the Foreign Examinations Syndicate addressed his question directly to Cedric Voss, the Chairman of the History Committee.

'No, no, Dean. I think the Secretary should be the first to have his say. After all, it's the permanent staff who'll have to work with whoever we appoint.' In slightly less distinguished company, Voss would have added that he didn't give two monkeys which of them got the job. As it was, he reassumed a characteristically somnolent posture in his comfortable blue-leather chair, and prayed they'd all get their fingers out. The meeting had already lasted almost three hours.

The Dean turned to the person sitting on his immediate left, a small twinkling man in his middle or late fifties, who blinked boyishly behind his rimless spectacles. 'Well, Dr Bartlett, let's hear what you've got to say.'

Bartlett, permanent Secretary of the Foreign Examinations Syndicate, glanced good-naturedly round the tables before looking down briefly at his neatly-written notes. He was used to this sort of thing. 'It seems to me, Dean, that generally speaking, by and large' (the Dean and several senior members of the Syndicate visibly winced) 'and on the whole, we would all agree that the short-list has been a very good one. All the applicants seemed pretty competent, and most of them sufficiently experienced to take on the work. But— ' He looked down again at his notes. 'Well, to be truthful, I would not myself wish to appoint either of the two women. The one from Cambridge was, I thought, a little er a little *strident*, shall we say?' He beamed expectantly round the Appointments Committee and a few heads nodded fairly vigorous assent. 'The other woman I thought just a *little* inexperienced, and I er didn't feel much inner surge of conviction about some of her answers.' Again there was no visible sign of dissent from the silent tables, and Bartlett stroked his ample belly with mild satisfaction. 'So. Let's come to the three

men. Duckham? Just a little vague, I thought. Nice chap and all
that, but I wonder if he's got quite the snap and zip that I'd welcome
in the Humanities Department here. He's third, in my book. Then
there's Quinn. I liked him: honest, intelligent fellow; firm views;
clear brain. Not quite the ideal experience, perhaps, and then—
Well, let me be quite honest about it. I think that er I think his er
– *handicap* may be a bit too much of a liability here. You know what
I mean: phone calls, meetings, that sort of thing. It's a pity, but
there it is. Anyway, I'd put him second. That leaves Fielding, and
he's the man I'd go for every time: damn good schoolmaster; excellent results from his pupils; just the right age; modest; likeable;
and a first in History from Balliol. References quite outstanding. I
don't honestly think we could have hoped for a better applicant,
and he's my first choice, Dean, without the slightest doubt.'

Not unostentatiously the Dean closed his appointments folder
and gently nodded his agreement, noting with gratification that
several other heads were nodding too. Including the Dean himself,
the full complement of Syndics was present. Twelve of them, each
a prominent fellow of his or her college within the University of
Oxford, and each called upon to attend the meetings held twice a
term at the Syndicate building for the purpose of formulating official examination policy. None of them was on the permanent staff
of the Syndicate, and none was paid a penny (apart from travelling
expenses) for attendance at these meetings. Yet most of them took
an active part on the various Subject Committees, were happy to
adopt a policy of enlightened self-interest towards the profitable
procedures of public examinations, and during the months of June
and July, after their own undergraduates had departed for the
long vac, acted as chief examiners and moderators in the GCE
Ordinary- and Advanced-level examinations. Of the permanent
officers of the Syndicate only Bartlett was automatically invited to
participate in the counsels of this governing body (though even he
was not entitled to cast a vote), and it was Bartlett who brought the
number in the room up to thirteen. Thirteen . . . Yet the Dean was
not a superstitious man, and he looked round the committee with
a degree of mild affection. Tried and trusted colleagues almost all
of them, although one or two of the younger dons he'd not yet got
to know particularly well: hair rather too long, and one of them had
a beard. Quinn had a beard, too . . . Come on! The appointment
would be settled very quickly now, and with a bit of luck he could

be back in Lonsdale College before six. Tonight was a 'gaudy' and
. . . Get it over with! 'Well, if I'm right in assuming that the committee agrees to the appointment of Fielding, there's only the
matter of his starting salary to settle. Let's see, he's thirty-four. I
should think the bottom of the B Lecturers' Scale might— '

'Could I just make one point before you go on, Dean?' It was
one of the younger dons. One of the long-haired ones. The one
with the beard. A chemist from Christ Church.

'Yes, of course, Mr Roope. I didn't mean to give the impression— '

'If I may say so, I think you're presuming that we all agree
with the Secretary's views; and, of course, it may be that everyone
else does. But *I* don't, and I thought the whole purpose of this
meeting— '

'Quite so, quite so, Mr Roope. As I say, I'm sorry if I
gave you the impression that er – you know . . . I certainly
didn't mean to do that. It was just that I thought I sensed a
feeling of general agreement. But we're in your hands. If you
feel— '

'Thank you, Dean. I do feel strongly about this, and I just can't
agree with the order of merit the Secretary has given. If I'm going
to be frank about it, I thought that Fielding was too much of a
yes-man, too much of a smoothie for me. In fact if he got the job, it
wouldn't be so much a matter of taking the rough with the smooth
as taking the smooth with the smooth.' A gentle murmur of amusement rippled round the tables, and the slight tension, perceptible
only a minute before, was visibly relaxed. And as Roope continued, some of his senior colleagues listened to him with slightly
more interest and attention. 'I agree with the Secretary about the
rest, though I can't say I completely agree with his reasons.'

'You mean you'd put Quinn first, is that it?'

'I would, indeed. He's got sound views on examinations, and
he's got a good mind. But what's more important, I reckon he's
got a genuine streak of integrity, and these days— '

'You didn't feel the same about Fielding?'

'No.'

The Dean ignored the Secretary's audible mumble of 'Nonsense!' and thanked Roope for his views. His eyes swept vaguely
over the committee, inviting comments. But none was immediately
forthcoming. 'Anyone else wish to er—?'

'I think it quite unfair for us to make too many cosmic character-judgements on the strength of a few brief interviews, Dean.' The speaker was the Chairman of the English Committee. 'We must all make our own assessments of these people; of course we must. That's the only reason we're here. But I agree with the Secretary. My order of merit was the same as his: exactly so.'

Roope leaned back and stared at the white ceiling, a yellow pencil balanced between his teeth.

'Anyone else?'

The Vice-Dean sat shuffling uneasily in his chair, profoundly bored, and anxious to be on his way. His notes consisted of an extraordinarily intricate doodle of whorls and scrolls; and he added a further florid curve to the flowing tracery as he made his first and final contribution to the day's deliberations: 'They're both good men, that's obvious. Doesn't seem to me to matter which we go for. If the Secretary wants Fielding, I want Fielding. A quick vote, perhaps, Dean?'

'If that's er, that's er . . . '

A few members of the committee interjected their muted bleats of approval, and in a vaguely disconsolate voice the Dean called the division lobbies. 'All right. A show of hands, then. All those in favour of appointing Fielding, please?'

Seven or eight hands were being raised when Roope suddenly spoke again, and the hands were slowly lowered.

'Just before we vote, Dean, I would like to ask the Secretary for some information. I'm quite sure he'll have it at his fingertips.'

From behind his spectacles the Secretary eyed Roope with chill distaste, and several committee members could scarcely conceal their impatience and irritation. Why had they co-opted Roope? He was certainly a brilliant chemist and his two years with the Anglo-Arabian Oil Co had seemed a decided asset in view of the Syndicate's commitments. But he was too young, too cocky; too loud and splashy, like a vulgar speedboat churning through the placid waters of the Syndicate regatta. This wasn't the first time he'd clashed with the Secretary, either. And he didn't even serve on the Chemistry Committee; didn't do a scrap of examining. Always said he was too busy.

'I'm sure the Secretary will be glad to er— What were you thinking of, Mr Roope?'

'Well, as you know, Dean, I've not been with you very long

yet, but I've been looking at the Syndicate's Constitution, and as it happens I've got a copy with me here.'

'Oh God!' mumbled the Vice-Dean.

'In paragraph 23, Dean – would you like me to read it?' Since half the committee had never even seen a copy of the Constitution, let alone read it, it seemed wholly inappropriate to dissemble any phoney familiarity, and the Dean nodded reluctant assent.

'Not er too long, I hope, Mr Roope?'

'No, it's very brief. Here's what it says, and I quote: "The Syndicate will endeavour at all times to remember that, wholly dependent as it is for its income on public monies, it owes and must seek to discharge a corresponding responsibility both to society at large and to its own permanent employees. Specifically, it will undertake to employ in its services a small percentage of persons who are variously handicapped, should the disabilities of such persons prove not substantially to interfere with the proper discharge of the duties entrusted to them." ' Roope closed the slim document and put it aside. 'Now, my question is this: can the Secretary please tell us how many handicapped people are at present employed by the Syndicate?'

The Dean turned once more to the Secretary, whose customary bonhomie had now apparently returned.

'We used to have a one-eyed fellow in the packing depart-ment— ' In the ensuing laughter the Vice-Dean, whose own particular handicap was a weak bladder, shuffled out of the room, where Roope was pursuing his point with humourless pedantry.

'But presumably he's no longer employed here?'

The Secretary shook his head. 'No. Unfortunately he turned out to have an uncontrollable weakness for stealing toilet rolls, and we— ' The rest of the sentence was drowned in a ribald cackle of lavatory laughter, and it was some little while before the Dean could bring the meeting to order again. He reminded the com-mittee that paragraph 23 was not, of course, a statutory injunction – merely a marginal recommendation in the interests of normal civi-lized er living. But somehow it was the wrong thing to say. Far wiser to have allowed the Secretary a few more anecdotes about his less-than-fortunate experiences with the unfortunately afflicted few. As it was, the subtle shift had been made. The man with the handi-cap was coming into the betting once more, his odds shortening further as Roope pressed his point neatly and tellingly home.

'You see, Dean, all I really want to know is this: do we feel that Mr Quinn's deafness is going to be a significant liability in the job? That's all.'

'Well, as I said,' replied Bartlett, 'there's the telephone for a start, isn't there? Mr Roope perhaps isn't fully aware of the vast number of incoming and outgoing telephone calls here, and he must excuse me if I suggest that I know slightly more about this than he does. It's a very tricky problem when you're deaf— '

'Surely not. There are all sorts of gadgets these days. You can wear one of those behind-the-ear things, where the microphone is— '

'Does Mr Roope actually know someone who's deaf and who—?'

'As a matter of fact, I don't but— '

'Then I suggest he is in real danger of underestimating the sort of problems— '

'Gentlemen, gentlemen!' The exchanges were becoming increasingly tetchy, and the Dean intervened. 'I think we all agree that it would be *something* of a problem. The real question is – how much of one?'

'But it's not just the telephone, is it, Dean? There are meetings – dozens and dozens of 'em a year. A meeting like this one, for instance. You get stuck in a meeting with somebody on the same side of the table, sitting three or four places away . . . ' Bartlett warmed to the point, and made his case without interruption. He was on safer ground, he knew that. He was getting just a little deaf himself.

'But it's not beyond the wit of man to arrange the seating of a meeting— '

'No, it isn't,' snapped Bartlett. 'And it's not beyond the wit of man either to rig up a convenient little system of headphones and microphones and God knows what else; and we could all learn the deaf-and-dumb alphabet, if it came to that!'

It was becoming increasingly obvious that there was a festering, strangely personal antipathy between the two men, and few of the older Syndics could understand it. Bartlett was usually a man of wonderfully equable temperament. And he hadn't finished yet: 'You all saw the report from the hospital. You all saw the audiographs. The fact of the matter is that Quinn is very deaf. *Very* deaf.'

'He seemed to be able to hear us all perfectly well, didn't he?' Roope spoke the words quietly, and if Quinn himself had been there he would almost certainly have missed them. But the committee didn't, and it became perfectly clear that Roope had a point. A strong point.

The Dean turned again to the Secretary. 'Mm. You know it's amazing that he *did* seem to hear us so well, isn't it?'

A desultory discussion broke out, gradually drifting further and further away from the immediate decision that still remained to be taken. Mrs Seth, the Chairman of the Science Committee, thought about her father . . . He had gone deaf very quickly when he was in his late forties and when she was only a schoolgirl; and he had been dismissed from his job. Redundancy money, and a meagre disability pension from his firm – oh yes, they'd tried to be sympathetic and fair. But he'd had such a clear brain, and he'd never worked again. Confidence irreparably shattered. He could still have done a whole host of jobs infinitely more efficiently than half the layabouts sitting idling on their backsides on office stools. It made her so very sad and so very cross to think of him . . .

Suddenly she was aware that they were voting. Five hands went up almost immediately for Fielding, and she thought, as the Secretary did, that he was probably the best of the bunch. She would vote for him too. But for some curious reason her hand remained on the blotting paper in front of her.

'And those for Quinn, please?'

Three hands, including Roope's, were raised; and then a fourth. The Dean began counting from the left: 'One, two, three . . . four . . . ' Another hand, and the Dean started again: 'One, two, three, four, five. It looks— ' And then, slowly and dramatically, Mrs Seth raised her own hand.

'Six.'

'Well, you've made your decision, ladies and gentlemen. Quinn has been appointed. Close vote: six–five. But there it is.' He turned rather awkwardly to his left. 'Are you happy, Mr Secretary?'

'Let's just say we all have our own views, Dean, and the view of the Appointments Committee is not mine. But, as you say, the committee has made its decision and it's my job to accept that decision.'

Roope sat back once more staring vaguely at the ceiling, the yellow pencil once more between his teeth. He may have been inwardly gloating over his minor triumph, but his face remained impassive – detached almost.

Ten minutes later the Dean and the Secretary walked side by side down the flight of stairs that led to the ground floor and to Bartlett's office. 'You really think we've made a bad mistake, Tom?'

Bartlett stopped and looked up at the tall, grey-haired theologian. 'Oh, yes, Felix. Make no mistake about that. We have!'

Roope pushed his way past them on the stairs and volunteered a vague 'Cheerio'.

'Er – goodnight,' said the Dean; but Bartlett remained darkly silent, and watched Roope go before slowly walking down the few remaining stairs and entering his office.

Above his door was a twin-coloured light, similar to the sort found in hospitals, which was operated from two switches on the desk inside. The first switch turned on a red light, signifying that Bartlett was in session with someone, and did not wish to be (and would not be) disturbed; a second switch turned on a green light, indicating that one was free to knock and enter. When neither switch was depressed, no light showed, and the conclusion thence to be drawn was that the room was empty. Since his appointment to the Secretaryship, Bartlett had firmly maintained that if any-one wished to discuss a matter of importance with him, he himself should have the courtesy to ensure an uninterrupted, confidential chat; and his staff fully appreciated and almost invariably observed the arrangement. On the very few occasions that the rule had been infringed, Bartlett had displayed quite uncharacteristic anger.

Once inside the Secretary snapped down the red switch before opening a small cabinet and pouring himself a glass of gin and dry vermouth. Then he sat down behind his desk, opened a drawer and took out a packet of cigarettes. He never smoked at meet-ings, but he lit one now, inhaled deeply, and sipped his drink. He would send a telegram to Quinn in the morning: it was too late to send one now. He opened his appointments' folder once more and reread the information on Quinn. Huh! They'd picked the wrong fellow – of course they had! All because of Roope, the bloody idiot!

He put the papers away neatly, cleared his desk and sat back in his chair – a curious half-smile forming on his lips.

WHY?

Chapter One

Whilst the other four took their seats in the upstairs lounge of the Cherwell Motel, he walked over to the bar and ordered the drinks: two gins and tonics, two medium sherries, one dry sherry – the latter for himself. He was very fond of dry sherry.

'Put them all down to the Foreign Examinations Syndicate, will you? And we shall be having lunch. If you can tell the waiter we're here? Sitting over there.' His north-country accent was still noticeable, though less so than it had been.

'Have you booked a table, sir?'

He enjoyed the 'sir'. 'Yes. The name's Quinn.' He grabbed a handful of peanuts, took the drinks over on a tray, and sat down with the other members of the History Committee.

It was his third Revision meeting since joining the Syndicate, and there were several others fixed for later in the term. He sat back in the low leather chair, drained half his sherry at a gulp, and looked out at the busy lunchtime traffic along the A40. This was the life! A jolly good meal to come, wine, coffee – and then back for the afternoon session. Finish with a bit of luck about five or even earlier. The morning session had been a concentrated, unremitting slog; but they'd done well. Question papers covering the periods from the Continental Crusades to the English Civil War had now assumed the final and definitive form in which they would appear before the following summer's Advanced-level History candidates. Just the five papers left, from the Hanoverians to the Treaty of Versailles; and he felt much more at home with the recent periods. At school History had been his favourite subject, and it was in History that he had won his exhibition to Cambridge. But after prelims he'd changed over to English, and it had been

411

as an English teacher that he had been subsequently appointed to the staff of Priestley Grammar School, Bradford, only twenty-odd miles from the Yorkshire village in which he was born. Looking back on it, he realized how lucky the switch to English had been: the advertisement for the post with the Syndicate had stressed the need for some qualification in both History and English, and he'd realized that he might stand a pretty good chance, although even now he couldn't quite believe that he had landed the job. Not that his deafness . . .

'Your menu, sir.'

Quinn had not heard the man approach, and only when the inordinately large menu obtruded itself into his field of vision was he aware of the head-waiter. Yes, perhaps his deafness would be slightly more of a handicap than he'd sometimes assumed; but he was managing wonderfully well so far.

For the moment he sat back, like the others, and studied the bewildering complexity of permutations on the menu: expensive – almost all the dishes; but as he knew from his two previous visits, carefully cooked and appetizingly garnished. He just hoped that the others wouldn't plump for anything *too* exotic, since Bartlett had quietly mentioned to him after the last jollification that perhaps the bill was a *little* on the steep side. For himself, he decided that soup of the day, followed by gammon and pineapple would not be beyond the Syndicate's means – even in these hard days. A drop of red wine, too. He knew it would be red wine whatever happened. Many of them drank red wine all the time in Oxford – even with Dover sole.

'We've got time for another drink, haven't we?' Cedric Voss, Chairman of the History Committee, passed his empty glass across the table. 'Drink up, men. We shall need something to keep us going this afternoon.'

Quinn dutifully collected the glasses and walked over to the bar once more, where a group of affluent-looking executives had just arrived and where a five-minute wait did nothing to quell the vague feeling of irritation which had begun to fester quietly in a corner of his mind.

When he returned to the table, the waiter was taking their orders. Voss, after discovering that the cherries were canned, the peas frozen, and the steak delivered the previous weekend, decided that he would revise his original ideas and go for the escargots and the lobster, and Quinn winced inwardly as he noted the prices. Three times his own modest order! He had pointedly *not* bought a second drink for himself (although he could have tossed another three or four back with the greatest relish) and sat back rather miserably, staring at the vast aerial photograph of central Oxford on the wall beside him. Very impressive, really: the quads of Brasenose and Queen's and—

'Aren't you drinking, Nicholas, my boy?' Nicholas! It was the first time that Voss had called him by his Christian name, and the irritation disappeared like a lizard's eyelid.

'No. I er— '

'Look, if old Tom Bartlett's been griping about the expense, forget it! What do you think it cost the Syndicate to send him to the Oil States last year, eh? A month! Huh! Just think of all those belly-dancers— '

'You wanted wine with your meal, sir?'

Quinn passed the wine list over to Voss, who studied it with professional avidity. 'All red?' But it was more a statement than a question. 'That's a nice little wine, my boy.' He pointed a stubby finger at one of the Burgundies. 'Good year, too.'

Quinn noted (he'd known it anyway) that it was the most expensive wine on the list, and he ordered a bottle.

'I don't think one's going to be much good, is it? With five of us— '

'We ought to have a bottle and a half, you think?'

'I think we ought to have two. Don't you, gentlemen?' Voss turned to the others and his proposal was happily approved.

'Two bottles of number five,' said Quinn resignedly. The irritation was nagging away again.

'And open them straightaway, please,' said Voss.

In the restaurant Quinn seated himself at the left-hand corner of the table, with Voss immediately to his right, two of the others immediately opposite, and the fifth member of the party at the top of the table. It was invariably the best sort of arrangement. Although he could see little of Voss's lips as he was speaking, he was just about near enough to catch his words; and the others he could see clearly. Lip-reading had its limitations, of course: it was of little use if the speaker mumbled through unmoving lips, or held a hand over his mouth; and absolutely useless when the speaker turned his back, or when the lights went out. But in normal circumstances, it was quite wonderful what one *could* do. Quinn had first attended lip-reading classes six years previously, and had been amazed to discover how easy it was. He knew from the outset that he must have been blessed with a rare gift: he was so much in advance of the first-year class that his teacher had suggested, after only a fortnight, that he should move up to the second-year class; and even there he had been the star pupil. He couldn't really explain his gift, even to himself. He supposed that some people were talented in trapping a football or in playing the piano: and he had a talent for reading the lips of others, that was all. Indeed, he had become so proficient that he could sometimes almost believe that he was in fact 'hearing' again. In any case, he hadn't completely lost his hearing. The expensive aid at his right ear (the left was completely nerve-less) amplified sufficient sound at reasonably close quarters, and even now he could hear Voss as he pronounced the benediction over the escargots just placed before him.

'Remember what old Sam Johnson used to say? "The fellow who doesn't mind his belly can't be trusted to mind anything." Well, something like that.' He tucked a napkin into his waist-band and stared at his plate with the eyes of a Dracula about to ravish a virgin.

The wine was good and Quinn had noticed how Voss had dealt with it. Quite beautifully. After studying the label with the intensity of a backward child trying to get to grips with the Initial Teaching Alphabet, he had taken the temperature of the wine, lightly and lovingly laying his hands around the bottle-neck; and then, when the waiter had poured half an inch of the ruby liquid into his glass, he had tasted not a drop, but four or five times sniffed the bouquet suspiciously, like a trained alsatian sniffing for dynamite. 'Not bad,' he'd said finally. 'Pour it out.' Quinn would remember the episode. He would try it himself next time. 'And turn the bloody music down a bit, will you,' shouted Voss, as the waiter was about to depart. 'We can't hear each other speak.' The music was duly diminished a few decibels, and a solitary diner at the next table came over to express his thanks. Quinn himself had been completely unaware that any background music was being played.

When the coffee finally arrived Quinn himself was feeling

more contented, and a little befuzzled. In fact, he couldn't quite remember whether it was Richard III on the First Crusade or Richard I on the Third Crusade. Or, for that matter, whether either Richard had been on either Crusade. Life was suddenly very good again. He thought of Monica. Perhaps he would call in – just for a second – before they started the business of the afternoon. Monica . . . It must have been the wine.

They finally arrived back at the Syndicate building at twenty minutes to three; and whilst the others were making their leisurely way back to the Revision Room upstairs, Quinn himself walked quickly along the corridor and gently knocked on the furthest door on the right, whereon the name plate read MISS M. M. HEIGHT. He tentatively opened the door and looked in. No one. But he saw a note prominently displayed beneath a paperweight on the neatly cleared desk, and he stepped inside to read it. 'Gone to Paolo's. Back at three.' It was typical of their office life together. Bartlett never minded his staff coming and going just when and how they liked, so long as their work was adequately done. What he did insist upon, however (almost pathologically), was that everyone should keep him informed about exactly where they could be found. So, Monica had gone to have her comely hair coiffured. Never mind. He didn't know what he would have said, anyway. Yes, it was just as well: he would see her in the morning.

He walked up to the Revision Room, where Cedric Voss was leaning back in his chair, his eyes half-closed, an inane grin upon his flabby, somnolent features. 'Well, gentlemen. Can we please try to turn our attention to the Hanoverians?'

Chapter Two

By the middle of the nineteenth century radical reforms were afoot in Oxford; and by its end a series of Commissions, Statutes, and Parliamentary Bills had inaugurated changes which were to transform the life of both Town and Gown. The University syllabuses were extended to include the study of the emergent sciences, and of modern history; the high academic standards set by Benjamin Jowett's Balliol gradually spread to other colleges; the establishment of professorial chairs increasingly attracted to Oxford scholars of international renown; the secularization of the college fellowships began to undermine the traditionally religious framework of university discipline and administration; and young men of Romanist, Judaic, and other strange persuasions were now admitted as undergraduates, no longer willy-nilly to be weaned on Cicero and Chrysostom. But, above all, university teaching was no longer concentrated in the hands of the celibate and cloistered clergymen, some of whom, as in Gibbon's day, well remembered that they had a salary to receive, and only forgot that they had a duty to perform; and many of the newly-appointed fellows, and some of the old, forswore the attractions of bachelor rooms in college, got themselves married, and bought houses for themselves, their wives, their offspring, and their servants, immediately outside the old spiritual centre of Holywell and the High, the Broad and St Giles'; especially did they venture north of the great width of tree-lined St Giles', where the Woodstock and the Banbury Roads branched off into the fields of North Oxford, towards the village of Summertown.

A traveller who visits Oxford today, and who walks northward from St Giles', is struck immediately by the large, imposing houses, mostly dating from the latter half of the nineteenth century, that line the Woodstock and the Banbury Roads and the streets that cross their ways between them. Apart from the blocks of weathered yellow stone round the white-painted window frames, these three-storeyed houses are built of attractive reddish brick, and are roofed with small rectangular tiles, more of an orange-red, which slope down from the clustered chimney stacks aslant the gabled windows. Today few of the houses are occupied by single families. They are too large, too cold, and too expensive to maintain; the rates are too high and salaries (it is said) are too low, and the fast-disappearing race of domestic servants demands a colour telly in the sitting-room. So it is that most of the houses have been let into flats, converted into hotels, taken over by doctors, by dentists, by English Language schools for foreign students, by University faculties, by hospital departments – and, in the case of one large and

well-appointed property in Chaucer Road, by the Foreign Examinations Syndicate.

The Syndicate building stands some twenty yards back from
the comparatively quiet road which links the busy Banbury and
Woodstock thoroughfares, and is modestly sheltered from inquisitive eyes behind a row of tall horse-chestnut trees. It is approached
from the front (there is no back entrance) by a curving gravelled
drive, allowing space sufficient for the parking of a dozen or so
cars. But the Syndicate staff has grown so much of late that this
space is now inadequate, and the drive has been extended along
the left-hand side of the building, leading to a small concreted
yard at the rear, where it has become the custom of the graduates
themselves to park their cars.

There are five graduates on the permanent staff of the Syndicate, four men and one woman, severally superintending the
fields of study corresponding, in the main, to the disciplines
which they had pursued for their university degrees, and to
the subjects taught in their subsequent careers. For it is an
invariable rule that no graduate may apply for a post with
the Syndicate unless he (or she) has spent a minimum of five
years teaching in the schools. The names of the five graduates
are printed in bold blue letters at the top of the Syndicate's
official notepaper; and on such notepaper, in a large converted
bedroom on the first floor, on Friday, 31st October (the day
after Quinn's deliberations with the History Committee), four
of the five young shorthand typists are tapping out letters to
the headmasters and headmistresses of those overseas schools
(a select, but growing band) who are happy to entrust the
public examination of their O- and A-level candidates to the
Syndicate's benevolence and expertise. The four girls pick at
their typewriters with varying degrees of competence; frequently
one of them leans forward to delete a mis-spelling or a careless
transposition of letters; occasionally a sheet is torn from a typewriter carriage, the carbon salvaged, but the top sheet and the
under-copies savagely consigned to the waste-paper basket. The
fifth girl has been reading *Woman's Weekly*, but now puts it
aside and opens her dictation book. She'd better get started.
Automatically she reaches for her ruler and neatly crosses through
the third name on the headed notepaper. Dr Bartlett has insisted
that until the new stocks are ready the girls shall manually correct

each single sheet – and Margaret Freeman usually does as she is told:

T. G. Bartlett, PhD, MA Secretary
P. Ogleby, MA Deputy Secretary
~~G. Bland, MA~~
Miss M. M. Height, MA
D. J. Martin, BA

Beneath the last name she types 'N. Quinn, MA' – her new boss.

After Margaret Freeman had left him, Quinn opened one of his filing cabinets, took out the drafts of the History question-papers, deciding that a further couple of hours should see them ready for press. All in all, he felt quite pleased with life. His dictation (for him, a completely new skill) had gone well, and at last he was beginning to get the knack of expressing his thoughts directly into words, instead of first having to write them down on paper. He was his own boss, too; for Bartlett knew how to delegate, and unless something went sadly askew he allowed his staff to work entirely on their own. Yes, Quinn was enjoying his new job. It was only the phones that caused him trouble and (he admitted it) considerable embarrassment. There were two of them in each office: a white one for internal extensions, and a grey one for outside calls. And there they sat, squat and menacing, on the right-hand side of Quinn's desk as he sat writing; and he prayed they wouldn't ring, for he was still unable to quell the panic which welled up within him whenever their muted, distant clacking compelled him to lift up one or other (he never knew which). But neither rang that morning, and with quiet concentration Quinn carried through the agreed string of amendments to the History questions. By a quarter to one he had finished four of the question papers, and was pleasantly surprised to find how quickly the morning had flown by. He locked the papers away (Bartlett was a martinet on all aspects of security) and allowed himself to wonder whether Monica would be going for a drink and a sandwich at the Horse and Trumpet – a pub he had originally misheard as the 'Whoreson Strumpet'. Monica's office was immediately opposite his own, and he knocked lightly and opened the door. She was gone.

* * *

In the lounge bar of the Horse and Trumpet a tall, lank-haired man pushed his way gingerly past the crowded tables and made for the furthest corner. He held a plate of sandwiches in his left hand, and a glass of gin and a jug of bitter in his right. He took his seat beside a woman in her mid-thirties who sat smoking a cigarette. She was very attractive and the appraising glances of the men who sat around had already swept her more than once.

'Cheers!' He lifted his glass and buried his nose in the froth.

'Cheers!' She sipped the gin and stubbed out her cigarette.

'Have you been thinking about me?' he asked.

'I've been too busy to think about anybody.' It wasn't very encouraging.

'I've been thinking about *you*.'

'Have you?'

They lapsed into silence.

'It's got to finish – you know that, don't you?' For the first time she looked him directly in the face, and saw the hurt in his eyes.

'You said you enjoyed it yesterday.' His voice was very low.

'Of course I bloody well enjoyed it. That's not the point, is it?' Her voice betrayed exasperation, and she had spoken rather too loudly.

'Shh! We don't want everybody to hear us, do we?'

'Well – you're so silly! We just can't go on like this! If people don't suspect something by now, they must be blind. It's got to stop! You've got a *wife*. It doesn't matter so much about me, but— '

'Couldn't we just—?'

'Look, Donald, the answer's "no". I've thought about it a lot – and, well, we've just got to stop, that's all. I'm sorry, but— '

It *was* risky, and above all she worried about Bartlett finding out. With his Victorian attitudes . . .

They walked back to the office without speaking, but Donald Martin was not quite so heart-broken as he appeared to be. The same sort of conversation had taken place several times before, and always, when he picked his moment right, she was only too eager again. So long as she had no other outlet for her sexual frustrations, he was always going to be in with a chance. And once they were in her bungalow together, with the door locked and the curtains drawn – God! What a hot-pants she could be.

He knew that Quinn had taken her out for a drink once; but he didn't worry about that. Or did he? As they walked into the Syndicate building at ten minutes to two, he suddenly wondered, for the first time, whether he *ought* perhaps to be a fraction worried about the innocent-looking Quinn, with his hearing aid, and his wide and guileless eyes.

Philip Ogleby heard Monica go into her office and gave her no second thought today. He occupied the first room on the right-hand side of the corridor, with the Secretary's immediately next door, and Monica's next to that – at the far end. He drained his second cup of coffee, screwed up his thermos flask, and closed an old copy of *Pravda*. Ogleby had been with the Syndicate for fourteen years, and remained as much a mystery to his present colleagues as he had done to his former ones. He was fifty-three now, a bachelor, with a lean ascetic face, and a perpetually mournful, weary look upon his features. What was left of his hair was grey, and what was left of his life seemed greyer still. In his younger days his enthusiasms had been as numerous as they were curious: Morris dancing, Victorian lamp-posts, irises, steam-locomotives and Roman coins; and when he had come down from Cambridge with a brilliant first, and when he had walked directly into a senior mathematics post in a prestigious public school, life had seemed to promise a career of distinguished and enviable achievement. But he had lacked ambition, even then; and at the age of thirty-nine he had drifted into his present position for no other reason than the vague conviction that he had been in one rut for so long that he might as well try to climb out and fall as gently as possible into another. There remained but few joys in his life, and the chief of these was travel. Though his six weeks annual holiday allowed him less time than he would have wished, at least his fairly handsome salary allowed him to venture far afield, and only the previous summer he had managed a fortnight in Moscow. As well as deputizing for Bartlett, he looked after Mathematics, Physics and Chemistry; and since no one else in the office (not even Monica Height, the linguist) was his equal in the unlikelier languages, he did his best to cope with Welsh and Russian as well. Towards his colleagues he appeared supremely indifferent; even towards Monica his attitude seemed that of a mildly tolerant husband towards his mother-in-law. For their part, the rest of the staff accepted him for what he was: intellectually superior to them all; administratively more than competent; socially a nonentity. Only one person in Oxford was aware of a different side to his nature . . .

At twenty past three Bartlett rang extension five.

'Is that you, Quinn?'

'Hullo?'

'Come along to my office a minute, will you?'

'I'm sorry. I can't hear you very well.'

'It's Bartlett here.' He almost shouted it into the phone.

'Oh, sorry. Look, I can't quite hear you, Dr Bartlett. I'll come along to your office right away.'

'That's what I asked you to do!'

'Pardon?'

Bartlett put the phone down and sighed heavily. He'd have to stop ringing the man; and so would everybody else.

Quinn knocked and entered.

'Sit down, Quinn, and let me put you in the picture. When you were at your meeting yesterday, I gave the others some details of our little er jamboree next week.'

Quinn could follow the words fairly easily. 'With the oil sheiks, you mean, sir?'

'Yes. It's going to be an important meeting. I want you to realize that. The Syndicate has only just broken even these last few years, and – well, but for these links of ours with some of the new oil states, we'd soon be bankrupt, like as not, and that's the truth of the matter. Now, we've been in touch with our schools out there, and one of the things they'd like us to think about is a new History syllabus. O-level only for a start. You know the sort of thing: Suez Canal, Lawrence of Arabia, colonialism, er, cultural heritage, development of resources. That sort of thing. Hell of a sight more relevant than Elizabeth the First, eh?'

Quinn nodded vaguely.

'The point is this. I want you to have a think about it before next week. Draft out a few ideas. Nothing too detailed. Just the outlines. And let me have 'em.'

'I'll try, sir. Could you just say one thing again, though? Better than "a list of metaphors", did you say?'

'Elizabeth the First, man! Elizabeth the First!'

'Oh yes. Sorry.' Quinn smiled weakly and left the room deeply embarrassed. He wished Bartlett would occasionally try to move his lips a little more.

When Quinn had gone, the Secretary half-closed his eyes, drew back his mouth as though he had swallowed a cupful of vinegar, and bared his teeth. He thought of Roope once more. Roope! What a bloody fool that man had been!

Chapter Three

Throughout the month of October the health of the pound sterling was a topic of universal, if melancholy, interest. Its effective devaluation against the dollar and against other European currencies was solemnly reported (to two points of decimals) in every radio and TV news bulletin: the pound had a poor morning, but recovered slightly in later dealings; the pound had a better morning, but was later shaky against its Continental competitors. The pound, it seemed, occasionally sat up in its sick bed to prove to the world that reports of its death had been somewhat exaggerated; but almost invariably the effort appeared to have been overtaxing and very soon it was once more lying prostrate, relapsing, slipping, falling, collapsing almost – until finally it struggled up on to its elbow once more, blinked modestly around at the anxious foreign financiers, and moved up a point or two in the international money market.

Yet although, during that autumn, the gap in the balance of payments grew ever wider; although the huge oil deficit could be made up only by massive loans from the IMF; although the number of the unemployed rose sickeningly to unpredicted heights; although the bankruptcy courts were enjoying unprecedented business; although foreign investors decided that London was no longer a worthy recipient for their ever-accumulating cash surpluses – still, in spite of it all, there remained among our foreign friends a firm and charming faith in the efficiency and efficacy of the British educational system; and, as a corollary to this, in the integrity and fair-mindedness of the British system of public examinations. Heigh-ho!

On the night of Monday, 3rd November, many were making their ways to hotel rooms in Oxford: commercial travellers and small business men; visitors from abroad and visitors from home – each selecting his hotel with an eye to business expenses, subsistence allowances, travellers' cheques or holiday savings. Cheap hotels and posh hotels; but mostly of the cheaper kind, though they (Lord knew) were dear enough. Rooms where the cisterns groaned and gurgled through the night; rooms where the window sashes sagged and the floorboards creaked beneath the flimsy matting. But the five emissaries from the Sheikdom of Al-jamara were safely settled in the finest rooms that even the Sheridan had to offer. Earlier in the evening they had eaten gloriously, imbibed modestly, tipped liberally; and each in turn had made his way upstairs and slipped between the crisp white sheets. Domestic problems, personal problems, health problems – certainly any or all of these might ruffle the waters of their silent dreams; but money was a problem which worried none of them. In the years immediately after the Second World War, oil, of high quality and in large accessible deposits, had been discovered beneath their seemingly barren sands; and a benevolent and comparatively scrupulous despot, in the person of the uncle of Sheik Ahmed Dubal, had not only secured American capital for the exploitation of the wells, but had immeasurably enriched the lives of most of the inhabitants of Al-jamara. Roads, hospitals, shopping centres, swimming pools and schools had not only been planned – but built; and in such an increasingly westernized society the great demand of the wealthier citizens was for the better education of their children; and it was now five years since the first links with the Foreign Examinations Syndicate had been forged.

The two-day conference started at 10.30 a.m. on Tuesday, 4th, and at the coffee session beforehand there was much shaking of hands, many introductions, and all was mutual smiles and general bonhomie. The deeply-tanned Arabs were dressed almost identically in dark-blue suits, with sparklingly laundered white shirts and sober ties. Quinn had earlier viewed the day with considerable misgivings, but soon he found to his very great relief that the Arabs

spoke a beautifully precise and fluent brand of English, marred, it
was true, by the occasional lapse from purest idiom, but distinct
and (to Quinn) almost childishly comprehensible. In all, the two
days passed rapidly and delightfully: plenary sessions, individual
sessions, general discussions, private discussions, lively conversations, good food, coffee, sherry, wine. The whole thing had
been an enormous success.

On Wednesday evening the Arabs had booked the Disraeli suite
at the Sheridan for a farewell party, and all the Syndicate's permanent staff, together with wives and sweethearts, and all the
Syndicate's governing council, were invited to the junketing. Sheik
Ahmed himself, resplendent in his middle-eastern robes, took his
seat beside a radiant Monica Height, exquisitely dressed in a pale-
lilac trouser-suit; and Donald Martin, as he sat next to his plain-
looking little wife, her white skirt creased and her black jumper
covered with dandruff, was feeling progressively more miserable.
The Sheik had clearly commandeered the fair Monica for the evening and was regularly flashing his white and golden smile as he
leaned towards her – intimate, confiding. And she was smiling back
at him – attentive, flattered, inviting . . . Quinn noticed them, of
course, and as he finished his shrimp cocktail he watched them
more closely. The Sheik was in full flow, but whether his words
were meant for Monica alone, Quinn was quite unable to tell.

'As one of your own Englishmen told me one day, Miss Height,

> "Oysters is amorous,
> Lobsters is lecherous,
> But Shrimps – Christ!" '

Monica laughed and said something close beside the Sheik's
ear which Quinn could not follow. How foolish he had been to
harbour any hope! And then he was able to follow another brief
passage of their conversation, and he knew that the words must
certainly have been whispered *pianissimo*. He felt his heart beat
thicker and faster. He must surely have been mistaken . . .

Towards midnight the party had dwindled to about a third
of its original number. Philip Ogleby, who had drunk more
than anyone, seemed the only obviously sober one amongst
them; the Martins had left for home some time ago; Monica and
Sheik Ahmed suddenly reappeared after an unexplained absence

of over half an hour; Bartlett was talking rather too loudly, and his large solicitous wife had already several times reminded him that gin always made him slur his words; one of the Arabs was in earnest negotiation with one of the barmaids; and of the Syndics, only the Dean, Voss, and Roope appeared capable of sustaining the lively pace for very much longer.

At half-past midnight Quinn decided that he must go. He felt hot and vaguely sick, and he walked into the Gentlemen's, where he leaned his head against the coolness of the wall mirror. He knew he would feel rough in the morning, and he still had to drive back to his bachelor home in Kidlington. Why hadn't he been sensible and ordered a taxi? He slapped water over his face, turned on the cold tap over his wrists, combed his hair, and felt slightly better. He would say his thank-yous and good-byes, and be off.

Only a few were left now, and he felt almost an interloper as he re-entered the suite. He tried to catch Bartlett's eye, but the Secretary was deep in conversation with Sheik Ahmed, and Quinn stared rather fecklessly around for a few minutes before finally sitting down and looking again towards his hosts. But still they talked. And then Ogleby joined them; and then Roope walked over, and Bartlett and Ogleby moved away; and then the Dean and Voss went across; and finally Monica. Quinn felt almost mesmerized as he watched the changing groupings and tried to catch the drift of what they were talking about. He felt a simultaneous sense of guilt and fascination as he looked at their lips and followed their conversations, as though he were standing almost immediately beside them. He knew instinctively that some of the words must have been whispered very quietly; but to him most of them were as clear as if they were being shouted through a megaphone. He remembered one occasion (his hearing had been fairly good then) when he had picked up a phone and heard, on a crossed line, a man and his mistress arranging a clandestine rendezvous and anticipating their forthcoming fornication with lascivious delight . . .

He felt suddenly frightened as Bartlett caught his eye and walked over, with Sheik Ahmed just behind him.

'Well? You enjoyed yourself, my boy?'

'Yes, indeed. I – I was just waiting to thank you both— '

'That is a great pleasure for us, too, Meester Queen.' Ahmed smiled his white and golden smile and held out his hand. 'We shall be meeting you again, we hope so soon.'

Quinn walked out into St Giles'. He had not noticed how keenly one of the remaining guests had been watching him for the past few minutes; and it was with considerable surprise that he felt a hand on his shoulder and turned to face the man who had followed him to his car.

'I'd like a word with you, Quinn,' said Philip Ogleby.

At 12.30 the following day, Quinn looked up from the work upon which, with almost no success, he had been trying to concentrate all morning. He had heard no knock, but someone was opening the door. It was Monica.

'Would you like to take me out for a drink, Nicholas?'

Chapter Four

On Friday, 21st November, a man in his early thirties caught the train from Paddington back to Oxford. He found an empty first-class compartment with little difficulty, leaned back in his seat, and lit a cigarette. From his briefcase he took out a fairly bulky envelope addressed to himself ('If undelivered please return to the Foreign Examinations Syndicate'), and extracted several lengthy reports. He unclipped his ballpoint pen from an inside pocket, and began to make sporadic notes. But he was left-handed, and with an ungenerous margin, and that only on the right of the closely-typed documents, the task was awkward; and progressively so, as the Inter-City train gathered full speed through the northern suburbs. The rain splashed in slanting parallel streaks across the dirty carriage window, and the telegraph poles snatched up the wires ever faster as he found himself staring out abstractedly at the thinning autumn landscape; and even when he managed to drag his attention back to the tedious documents he found it difficult to concentrate. Just before Reading he walked along to the buffet car and bought a Scotch; then another. He felt better.

At four o'clock he put the papers back into their envelope, crossed out his own name, C. A. Roope, and wrote T. G. Bartlett on the cover. Bartlett, as a man, he disliked (he could not disguise that), but he was honest enough to respect the man's experience, and his flair for administration; and he had promised to leave the papers at the Syndicate that afternoon. Bartlett would never allow a single phrase in the minutes of a Syndicate Council meeting to go forward before the relevant draft had been circulated to every member who had attended. And (Roope had to admit) this meticulous minuting had frequently proved extremely wise. Anyway, the wretched papers were done now, and Roope snapped his briefcase to, and looked out at the rain again. The journey had passed more quickly than he could have hoped, and within a few minutes the drenched grey spires of Oxford came into view on his right, and the train drew into the station.

Roope walked through the subway, waited patiently behind the queue at the ticket barrier, and debated for a second or two whether he should bother. But he knew he would. He took the second-class day-return from his wallet and passed it to the ticket collector. 'I'm afraid I owe you some excess fare. I travelled back first.'

'Didn't the ticket inspector come round?'

'No.'

'We-ll. Doesn't really matter then, does it?'

'You sure?'

'Wish everybody was as honest as you, sir.'

'OK then, if you say so.'

Roope took a taxi and after alighting at the Syndicate tipped the driver liberally. Rectangles of pale-yellow light shone in the upper storeys of nearby office blocks, and the giant shapes of the trees outside the Syndicate building loomed black against the darkening sky. The rain poured down.

Charles Noakes, present incumbent in the key post of care-taker to the Syndicate, was (for the breed) a comparatively young and helpful man, whose soul was yet to be soured by years of cumulative concern about the shutting of windows, the polishing of floors, the management of the boiler, and the setting of the burglar alarm. He was replacing a fluorescent tube in the downstairs corridor when Roope entered the building.

'Hello, Noakes. The Secretary in?'

'No, sir. He's been out all the afternoon.'

'Oh.' Roope knocked on Bartlett's door and looked in. The light was on; but then Roope knew that the lights would be on in every room. Bartlett always claimed that the mere switching-on of a fluorescent tube used as much electricity as leaving it on for about four hours, and consequently the lights were left on all day throughout the office – 'for reasons of economy'. For a brief second Roope thought he heard a noise inside the room, but there was nothing. Only a note on the desk which read: 'Friday p.m. Off to Banbury. May be back about five.'

'Not there, is he, sir?' Noakes had descended the small ladder and was standing outside.

'No. But never mind. I'll have a word with one of the others.'

'Not many of 'em here, I don't think, sir. Shall I see for you?'

'No. Don't worry. I'll do it myself.'

He knocked and put his head round Ogleby's door. No Ogleby.

He tried Martin's room. No Martin.

He was knocking quietly on Monica Height's door, and leaning forward to catch any response from within, when the caretaker reappeared in the well-lit, well-polished corridor. 'Looks as if Mr Quinn's the only graduate here, sir. His car's still out the back, anyway. I think the others must have gone.'

When the cat's away, thought Roope . . . He opened Monica's door and looked inside. The room was tidiness itself, the desk clear, the leather chair neatly pushed beneath it.

It was the caretaker who tried Quinn's room, and Roope came up behind him as he looked in. A green anorak was draped over one of the chairs, and the top drawer of the nearest cabinet gaped open to reveal a row of buff-coloured file-cases. On the desk, placed under a cheap paperweight, was a note from Quinn for his typist's attention. But Quinn himself was nowhere to be seen.

Roope had often heard tell of Bartlett's meticulous instructions to his staff not only about their paramount duty for ensuring the strictest security on all matters concerning question-papers, but also about the importance of leaving some notification of their whereabouts. 'At least he's left a note for us, Noakes. More than some of the others have.'

'I don't think the Secretary would be very happy about this, though.' Noakes gravely closed the top drawer of the cabinet and pushed in the lock.

'Bit of a stickler about that sort of thing, isn't he, old Bartlett?'

'Bit of a stickler about everything, sir.' Yet somehow Noakes managed to convey the impression that if he were on anyone's side, it would be Bartlett's.

'You don't think he's too much of a fusspot?'

'No, sir. I mean, all sorts of people come into the office, don't they? You can't be too careful in a place like this.'

'No. You're absolutely right.'

Noakes felt pleasantly appeased, and having made his point he conceded a little to Roope's suspicions. 'Mind you, sir, I reckon he might have picked a warmer week for practising the fire drill.'

'Gives you those, does he?' Roope grinned. He hadn't been on a fire drill since he was at school.

'We had one today, sir. Twelve o'clock. He had us all there, standing in the cold for something like a quarter of an hour. Freezing, it was. I know it's a bit too hot in here but . . . ' Noakes was about to embark on an account of his unequal struggle with the Syndicate's antiquated heating system, but Roope was far more interested in Bartlett, it seemed.

'Quarter of an hour? In *this* weather?'

Noakes nodded. 'Mind you, he'd warned us all about it earlier in the week, so we had our coats and everything, and it wasn't raining then, thank goodness, but— '

'Why as long as that, though?'

'Well, there's quite a lot of permanent staff now and we had to tick our names off a list. Huh! Just like we was at school. And the Secretary gave us a little talk . . . '

But Roope was no longer listening; he couldn't stand there talking to the caretaker all night, and he began walking slowly up the corridor. 'Bit odd, isn't it. Everybody here this morning and nobody here this afternoon!'

'You're right, sir. Are you sure I can't help you?'

'No, no. It doesn't matter. I only came to give this envelope to Bartlett. I'll leave it on his desk.'

'I'm going upstairs for a cup o' tea in a minute, sir, when I've fixed this light. Would you like one?'

'No, I've got to be off. Thanks all the same, though.'

Roope took advantage of the Gentlemen's lavatory by the entrance and realized just how hot it was in the building: like walking into a Turkish bath.

Bartlett himself had been addressing a group of Banbury headmasters and headmistresses on the changing pattern of public examinations; and the last question had been authoritatively (and humorously) dispatched at almost exactly the same time that Roope had caught his taxi to the Syndicate. He was soon driving his pride and joy, a dark-brown Vanden Plas, at a steady sixty down the twenty-odd-mile stretch to Oxford. He lived out at Botley, on the western side of the city, and as he drove he debated whether to call in at the office or to go straight home. But at Kidlington he found himself beginning to get caught up in the regular evening paralysis, and as he negotiated the roundabouts on Oxford's northern perimeter he decided to turn off right along the ring-road instead of carrying straight over towards the city centre. He would call in the office a bit later, perhaps, when the evening rush-hour had abated.

When he arrived home, at just gone five his wife informed him that there had been several phone calls; and even as she was giving him the details the wretched thing rang again. How she wished they had a number ex-directory!

On Saturday, 22nd November (as on most Saturdays), the burglar alarm system was switched off at 8.30 a.m., one hour later than on weekdays. During the winter months there were only occasional Saturday workings, and on this particular morning the building was, from all appearances, utterly deserted. Ogleby was on foot, and let himself in quietly. The smell of floor polish, like the smell of cinema seats and old library books, took him back tantalizingly to his early schooldays, but his mind was on other things. Successively he looked into each room on the ground floor in order to satisfy himself that no one was around. But he was aware of this instinctively: there was an eerie, echoing emptiness about the building which the quiet clickings-to of the doors served merely to re-emphasize. He went into his own room and rang a number.

'Morning, Secretary. Hope I didn't get you out of bed? No? Ah, good. Look. I know it sounds a bit silly, but can you remind me when the alarm's turned off on Saturday mornings? I've got to . . . 8.30? Yes, I thought so, but I just wanted to make sure. I didn't want . . . No. Funny, really. I'd somehow got it into my head that there'd been some change . . . No, I see. Well, sorry to trouble you. By the way, did the Banbury meeting go off all right? . . . Good. Well, I'll be off.'

Ogleby walked into Bartlett's room. He looked around quickly and then took out his keys. Botley was at least twenty minutes' drive away: he could probably allow himself at least half an hour. But Ogleby was a cautious soul, and he allowed himself only twenty minutes.

Twenty-five minutes later, as he was sitting at his own desk, he heard someone enter the building, and almost immediately, it seemed, his door was opened.

'You got in all right then, Philip?'

'Yes thanks. No bells ringing in the police station this morning.'

'Good.' Bartlett blinked behind his spectacles. 'I've er got a few things I want to clear up myself.' He closed the door and walked into his own office. He knew what had been happening, of course. For a clever man, Ogleby's excuse about the burglar alarm had been desperately thin. But what had he been looking for? Bartlett opened his cabinets and opened his drawers; but everything was in order. Nothing seemed to have been taken. What *was* there to take? He sat back and frowned deeply: the whole thing was strangely disturbing. He walked up the corridor to Ogleby's room, but Ogleby had gone.

Chapter Five

Morse looked directly into the large mirror in front of him, and there surveyed the reflection of the smaller hand mirror held behind him, in which, in turn, he considered the occipital regions of what he liked to think of as a distinguished skull. He nodded impassively as the hand mirror was held behind the left side of his neck, nodded again as it was switched to the right, declined the suggested application of a white, greasy-looking hair oil which stood on the surface before him, arose, like a statue unveiled, from the chair, took the proffered tissue, rubbed his face and ears vigorously, and reached for his wallet. That felt much better! He was never happy when his hair began to grow in untidy, curly profusion just above his collar, and he wondered sadly why it now failed to sustain a similar luxuriance upon the top of his head. He tipped the barber generously and walked out into Summertown. Although not so cold as in recent days, it was drizzling slightly, and he decided to wait for a bus up to his bachelor flat at the top of North Oxford. It was 10.15 a.m. on Tuesday, 25th November.

It would be unlikely that anything of importance should require his immediate attention at HQ, and he had to call in home anyway. It was a ritual with Morse. As a young recruit in the army he had been driven almost mad by the service issue of prickly vests, prickly shirts, and prickly trousers. His mother had told him that he had an extremely sensitive skin; and he believed her. It was always the same after a haircut. He would take off his shirt and vest, and dip his head into a basin full of hot water. Bliss! He would shampoo his hair twice, and then flannel his face and ears thoroughly. He would then rub his back with a towel, dry his hair, wash down the short, black hairs from the sides of the basin, select a clean vest and shirt, and finally comb his hair with loving care in front of the bathroom mirror.

But this morning it *wasn't* quite the same. He was just about to rinse off the second application of medicated shampoo when the phone rang. He swore savagely. Who the hell?

'Hoped I might find you at home, sir. I couldn't find anyone who'd seen you at the office.'

'So what? I've had a haircut. Not a crime, is it?'

'Can you get here straightaway, sir?' Lewis's tone was suddenly grave.

'Give me five minutes. What's up?'

'We've got a body, sir.'

'Whereabouts are you?'

'I'm phoning from the station. Do you know Pinewood Close?'

'No.'

'Well, I think you'd be best to call here first anyway, sir.'

'OK. Wait for me there.'

* * *

Chief Superintendent Strange was waiting for him, too. He stood impatiently on the steps outside the Thames Valley Police HQ in Kidlington, as Morse hurriedly parked the Jaguar and jumped out.

'Where have you been, Morse?'

'Sorry, sir. I've had a haircut.'

'You *what*?'

Morse said nothing, not the slightest flicker of guilt or annoyance betraying itself in the light-blue eyes.

'A fine advertisement, eh? Citizens under police care and protection getting themselves bumped off, and the only Chief Inspector I've got on duty is having his bloody hair cut!'

Morse said nothing.

'Look, Morse. You're in charge of this case – is that clear? You can have Lewis here if you want him.' Strange turned away, but suddenly remembered something else. 'And you won't get another haircut until you've sorted this little lot out – that's an order!'

'Perhaps I shan't need one, sir.' Morse winked happily at Lewis and led the way into his office. 'What's it look like from behind?'

'Very nice, sir. They've cut it very nicely.'

Morse sat back in his black-leather armchair and beamed at Lewis. 'Well? What have you got to tell me?'

'Chap called Quinn, sir. Lives on the ground floor of a semi-detached in Pinewood Close. He's been dead for a good while by the look of him. Poisoned, I shouldn't wonder. He works' ('worked', muttered Morse) 'at the Foreign Examinations Syndicate down the Woodstock Road somewhere; and one of his colleagues got worried about him and came out and found him. I got the call about a quarter to ten, and I went along straightaway with Dickson and had a quick look round. I left him there, and came back to call you.'

'Well, here I am, Lewis. What do you want me to do?'

'Knowing you, sir, I thought you might want me to arrest the chap who found him.'

Morse grinned. 'Is he here?'

'In the Interview Room. I've got a rough statement from him, but it'll need a bit of brushing up before he signs it. You'll want to see him, I suppose?'

'Yes, but that can wait. Got a car ready?'

'Waiting outside, sir.'

'You've not called the path. boys in yet, I hope?'

'No. I thought I ought to wait for you.'

'Good. Go and get your statement tarted up and I'll see you outside in ten minutes or so.'

Morse made two phone calls, combed his hair again, and felt inordinately happy.

Several faces peeped from behind ground-floor lace-curtained windows as the police car drove into Pinewood Close, a small, undistinguished crescent wherein eight semi-detached houses, erected some fifty years previously, stood gently fading into a semi-dignified senescence. Most of the wooden fences that bordered the properties managed to sustain only a precarious pretence to any upright posture, the slats uncreosoted and insecure, the crossrails mildewed, sodden with rain, and rotten. Only at each end of the crescent had the original builder left sufficient sideroom for the erection of any garage, and it was at the house at the extreme left that the bulky figure of Constable Dickson stood, stamping his feet on the damp concrete in front of a prefabricated unpainted garage, and talking to a woman in her early fifties, the owner of the property and rentier of some half a dozen other houses in the neighbourhood. But whatever other benefits her various incomes conferred upon her, her affluence appeared not to be reflected in her wardrobe: she wore no stockings and was pulling a shabby old coat more closely over a grubby white blouse as Morse and Lewis stepped out of the car.

' 'Ere come the brains, missus,' muttered Dickson, and stepped forward to greet the Chief Inspector. 'This is Mrs Jardine, sir. She owns the property and she's the one who let us in.'

Morse nodded a friendly greeting, took the Yale key from Dickson, and instructed him to take Mrs Jardine to the police car and get a statement from her. He himself stood for a while in silence with his back to the house, and looked around him. In a kerbed oval plot, a thick cluster of small trees and variegated bushes sheltered the houses from the main road and gave to the crescent the semblance of partial privacy. But the small curved stretch of road itself was poorly maintained and unevenly surfaced, with a long, irregular black scar, running parallel to the pavement, where the water mains had recently been dug up again. The gutter was full of sopping brown leaves, and the lamp-post immediately outside No 1 had been vandalized. The front door of the next house opened a few inches and a middle-aged woman directed inquisitive eyes towards the centre of activity.

'Good morning,' said Morse brightly.

The door was closed in a flash, and Morse turned round to survey the garage. Although the claw of the lock which secured the doors was not pushed home, he touched nothing, contenting himself with a quick glance through the glass panels at the top. Inside he saw a dark-blue Morris 1300 which allowed little more than a foot of space between the wall and the driver's door. He walked over to the front porch and inserted the key. 'Good job he doesn't drive a Cadillac, Lewis.'

'Didn't,' corrected Lewis quietly.

The front door of No 1 Pinewood Close opened on to a narrow hallway, with a row of clothes pegs at the foot of the staircase which climbed the wall to the left. Morse stood inside and pointed to the door immediately to his right. 'This the one?'

'Next one, sir.'

The door was closed and Morse took out his pen and depressed the handle carefully. 'I hope you haven't left your prints all over the place, Lewis?'

'I opened it the same way as you, sir.'

Inside the room the electric light was still turned on; the dull-orange curtains were drawn; the gas fire was burning low; and lying in a foetal posture on the carpet was the body of a young man. The fire was flanked by two old, but comfortable-looking armchairs; and beside the one to the right, on a low french-polished coffee-table, stood a bottle of dry sherry, almost full, and a cheap-looking sherry glass, almost empty. Morse bent forward and sniffed the pale, clear liquid. 'Did you know, Lewis, that about eighteen per cent of men and about four per cent of women can't smell cyanide?'

'It *is* poison, then?'

'Smells like it. Peach blossom, bitter almonds – take your pick.'

The dead man's face was turned towards them, away from the fire, and Morse knelt down and looked at it. A small quantity of dry froth crusted the twisted mouth, and the bearded jaw was tightly clenched in death; the pupils of the open eyes appeared widely dilated, and the skin of the face was a morbid, blotchy blue. 'All the classic symptoms, Lewis. We hardly need a post-mortem on this one. Hydrocyanic acid. Anyway the path boys should be here any minute.' He stood up and walked over to the curtains, which had obviously shrunk in a not particularly recent wash, and which gaped open slightly towards the top. Outside Morse could see the narrow garden, with its patchy, poor-quality grass, a small vegetable plot at the far end, and a section of fencing missing on the left. But the view appeared to convey little of significance to his mind, and he turned his attention back to the room itself. Along the wall opposite the fire were a dozen or so bundles of books, neatly tied with stout cord, and a dark mahogany sideboard, the left-hand door of which stood open to reveal a small collection of assorted tumblers and glasses, and an unopened bottle of whisky. Everywhere seemed remarkably clean and tidy. A small waste-paper basket stood in the shallow alcove to the left of the fire; and inside the basket was a ball of paper, which Morse picked out and smoothed gently on the top of the sideboard:

Mr Quinn. I can't do all the cleaning this afternoon because Mr Evans is off sick and I've got to get him a prescription from the doctor. So I'll call back and finish just after six if that's convenient for you.
   A. Evans (Mrs)

Morse handed the note over to Lewis. 'Interesting.'
'How long do you think he's been dead, sir?'
Morse looked down at Quinn once more and shrugged his shoulders. 'I dunno. Two or three days, I should think.'
'It's a wonder someone didn't find him earlier.'
'Ye-es. You say he just has these downstair rooms?'
'So Mrs Jardine says. There's a young couple living upstairs usually, but she's in the John Radcliffe having a baby, and he works nights at Cowley and he's been staying with his parents in Oxford somewhere.'
'Mm.' Morse made as if to leave, but suddenly stopped. The bottom of the door had been amateurishly planed to enable it to ride over the carpet and a noticeable draught was coming beneath it, occasionally setting the low, blue gas-jets flickering fitfully into brighter yellow flames.

'Funny, isn't it, Lewis? If I lived in this room I wouldn't choose the armchair immediately in line with the draught.'

'Looks as if he did, sir.'

'I wonder, Lewis. I wonder if he did.'

The front-door bell rang and Morse sent Lewis to answer it. 'Tell 'em they can start as soon as they like.' He walked out of the room and through into the kitchen at the back of the house. Again, everywhere was tidy. On a red Formica-topped table stood a stack of recently purchased provisions: half a dozen eggs in their plastic container; ½ lb butter; ½ lb English Cheddar; two generous slices of prime steak under a cellophane wrapper; and a brown-paper bag full of mushrooms. Beside the groceries was a curling pay-out slip from the *Quality* supermarket, and a flicker of excitement showed in Morse's eyes as he looked it through.

'Lewis!'

Nothing else here looked particularly interesting: a sink unit, a gas cooker, a fridge, two kitchen stools, and by the side of the back door, filling the space under the stairs, a small larder. Lewis, who had been chatting to the police surgeon, appeared at the door. 'Sir?'

'What's going on in there?'

'Doc says he's been poisoned.'

'Amazing thing – medical science, Lewis! But we've got other things to worry about for the minute. I want you to make a complete inventory of the food in the fridge and in this larder here.'

'Oh.' Lewis was almost thinking that a man of his own rank and experience should be above such fourth-grade clerical chores; but he had worked with Morse before, and knew that whatever other faults he had the Chief Inspector seldom wasted his own or other people's time on trivial or unnecessary tasks. He heard himself say he would get on with it – immediately.

'I'm going back to the station, Lewis. You stay here until I get back.'

Outside, Morse found Dickson and Mrs Jardine standing beside the police car. 'I want you to drive me back to HQ, Dickson.' He turned to Mrs Jardine. 'You've been very kind and helpful. Thank you very much. You've got a car?'

The landlady nodded and walked away. In truth, she felt disappointed that her small part in the investigation seemed

now to be over, and that she had warranted no more than
a cursory question from the rather abrupt man who appeared
to be in charge. But as she drove away from the crescent her
thoughts soon veered to other, more practical considerations.
Would anyone be over-anxious to move into the rooms so lately
rented by that nice young Mr Quinn? People didn't like that sort
of thing. But as she reached the outskirts of Oxford she comforted
herself with the salutary thought that the dead are soon forgotten.
Yes, she would soon be able to let the rooms again. Just give it
a month or so.

Morse read the statement aloud to the youngish man seated
rather nervously at the small table in Interview Room No 1.

I have known Nicholas Quinn for three months. He came to work
at the Foreign Examinations Syndicate as an assistant secretary on
1st September this year.
   On Monday, 24th November, he did not appear at the office and did
not ring in to say that anything was wrong. It is not unusual for the
graduates to take a day or two off when they can, but the Secretary,
Dr Bartlett, always insists that he should be kept fully informed
of any such arrangement. None of my colleagues saw Mr Quinn on
Monday, and no one knew where he was. This morning, Tuesday, 25th
November, Dr Bartlett came to my office and said that Mr Quinn had
still not arrived. He said that he had tried to phone him, but that there
was no reply. He then asked me to drive round to Mr Quinn's house
and I did so, arriving at about 9.30 a.m. The front door was locked
and no one answered the doorbell. I could see that Mr Quinn's car
was still in the garage, so I proceeded to the back of the house. The
light was on in the ground-floor room and the curtains were drawn;
but there was a gap in the curtains and I looked inside. I could see
someone lying quite still on the floor in front of the fireplace, and I
knew that something was seriously wrong. I therefore rang the police
immediately from the public call box in the main street, and was told
to wait at the house until the police came. When Sergeant Lewis
arrived with a constable, they discovered who owned the house. The
landlady turned up with the key about ten minutes later. The police
then proceeded into the house for a short while, and when Sergeant
Lewis came out he told me that I must prepare myself for a shock.
He said that Mr Quinn was dead.

'You happy to sign this?' Morse pushed the statement across
the table.

'I didn't use the word "proceeded".'

'Ah, you must forgive us, sir. We never "go" anywhere in the Force, you know. We always "proceed".'

Donald Martin accepted the explanation with a weak smile and signed the statement with a nervy flourish.

'How well did you know Mr Quinn, sir?'

'Not very well really. He's only been with us— '

'So you say in your statement. But why did the Secretary send you – not one of the others?'

'I don't know. I suppose I knew him as well as any of them.'

'What did you expect to find?'

'Well, I thought he was probably ill or something, and couldn't let us know.'

'There's a phone in the house.'

'Yes, but it could have – well, it could have been a heart attack, or something like that.'

Morse nodded. 'I see. Do you happen to know where his parents live?'

'Somewhere in Yorkshire, I think. But the office could— '

'Of course. Did he have a girl-friend?'

Martin was aware of the Inspector's hard eyes upon him and his mouth was suddenly very dry. 'Not that I know of.'

'No pretty fillies he fancied at the office?'

'I don't think so.' The hesitation was minimal but, for Morse, sufficient to set a few fanciful notions aflutter.

'I'm told such things are not unknown, sir. He was a bachelor, I take it?'

'Yes.'

'You a married man, sir?'

'Yes.'

'Mm. Perhaps you've forgotten what it's like to be single.' Morse would have been happier if Martin had told him not to talk such drivel. But Martin didn't.

'I don't quite see what you're getting at, Inspector.'

'Oh, don't worry about that, sir. I often don't know what I'm getting at myself.' He stood up, and Martin did the same, fastening his overcoat. 'You'd better get back to the office, or they'll be getting worried about you. Tell the Secretary I'll be in touch with him as soon as I can – and tell him to lock up Mr Quinn's room.'

'You've no idea—?' said Martin quietly.

'Yes, I'm afraid I have, sir. He was almost certainly murdered.'
The sinister word seemed to hang on the air, and the room was
suddenly and eerily still.

Chapter Six

During the previous decade the Foreign Examinations Syndicate
had thrown its net round half the globe; and for its hundred or
so oversea centres the morning of Tuesday, 25th November, had
been fixed for the 'retake' of the Ordinary-level English Language
papers. For the vast majority of the foreign candidates involved,
the morning afforded the chance of a second bite at the cherry;
and such was the importance of a decent grade in English
Language, either for future employment or for admission to higher
education, that there were very few of the candidates who were
treating the two question papers (Essay and Comprehension) with
anything but appropriate respect. Only those few who had been ill
during the main summer examination were taking the examination
for the first time; the remainder were the 'returned empties' who,
either through some congenital incapacity or a prior history of
monumental idleness, had yet to succeed in persuading the examiners that they had reached a standard of acceptable competence
in the skills of English usage.

At 11.55 a.m. this same morning, in strict accord with the
explicit instructions issued by the examining body, invigilators
in Geneva, in East and West Africa, in Bombay, and in the
Persian Gulf, were reminding their candidates that only five
minutes remained before scripts would be collected; that all candidates should ensure that their full names and index numbers
appeared on each sheet of their work; and that all sheets must
be handed in in the correct order. Some few candidates were
now scribbling furiously and for the most part fruitlessly; but
the majority were having a final look through their answers,
shuffling their sheets into order, and then leaning back in more
relaxed postures, shooting the occasional grin at fellow examinees

who sat at desks (the regulation five-feet apart) in commandeered classrooms or converted gymnasia.

At twelve noon, in an air-conditioned, European-style classroom in the Sheikdom of Al-jamara, a young Englishman, who was invigilating his first examination, gave the order to 'stop writing'. There were only five pupils in the room, all Arabs, all of whom had finished writing several minutes previously. One of the boys (not a pupil of the school, but the son of one of the sheiks) had in fact finished his work some considerable time earlier, and had been sitting back in his chair, arms folded, an arrogant, self-satisfied smirk upon his dark, semitic features. He was the last of the five candidates, and handed in his script without saying a word.

Left alone, the young Englishman filled in the invigilation form with great care. Fortunately, no candidate had failed to turn up for the examination, and the complexities of the sections dealing with 'absentees' could be ignored. In the appropriate columns he filled in the names and index numbers of the five candidates, and prepared to place the attendance sheet, together with the scripts, in the official buff-coloured envelope. As he did so his eyes fell momentarily upon the work of Muhammad Dubal, Index Number 5; and he saw immediately that it was very good – infinitely better than that of the other four. But then the sheik's son had doubtless had the privilege of high-class private tuition. Ah well. There would be plenty of opportunity for him to try to jack up the standards of his own pupils a bit before next summer . . .

He left the room, licking the flap of the envelope as he did so, and walked through to the school secretary's office.

It was just after noon, too, that Morse returned to Pinewood Close. He made no effort to move on the curious crowd who thronged the narrow crescent, for he had never understood why the general public should so frequently be castigated for wishing to eye-witness those rare moments of misfortune or tragedy that occurred in their vicinity. (He would have been one of them himself.) He threaded his way past the three police cars, past the ambulance, its blue light flashing, and entered the house once more. There were almost as many people inside as outside.

'Sad thing, death,' said Morse.

'*Mors, mortis*, feminine,' mumbled the ageing police surgeon.

Morse nodded morosely. 'Don't remind me.'

'Never mind, Morse. We're all dying slowly.'

'How long's he been dead?'

'Dunno. Could be four, five days – not less than three, I shouldn't think.'

'Not too much help, are you?'

'I shall have to take a closer look at him.'

'Have a guess.'

'Unofficially?'

'Unofficially.'

'Friday night or Saturday morning.'

'Cyanide?'

'Cyanide.'

'You think it took long?'

'No. Pretty quick stuff if you get the right dose down you.'

'Minutes?'

'Much quicker. I'll have to take the bottle and the glass, of course.'

Morse turned to the two other men in the room who had been brushing the likeliest-looking surfaces with powder.

'Anything much?'

'Seems like his prints all over the place, sir.'

'Hardly surprising.'

'Somebody else's, though.'

'The cleaner's, most likely.'

'Just the one set of prints on the bottle, sir – and on the glass.'

'Mm.'

'Can we move the body?'

'Sooner the quicker. I suppose we'd better go through his pockets, though.' He turned again to the surgeon. 'You do it, will you?'

'You getting squeamish, Morse? By the way, did you know he wore a hearing aid?'

At one minute to two, Morse got to his feet and looked down at Lewis.

'Time for another if you drink that up smartish.'

'Not for me, sir. I've had enough.'

'The secret of a happy life, Lewis, is to know when to stop and then to go that little bit further.'

'Just a half, then.'

Morse walked to the bar and beamed at the barmaid. But in truth he felt far from happy. He had long since recognized the undoubted fact that his imagination was almost invariably fired by beer, especially by beer in considerable quantities. But today, for some reason, his mind seemed curiously disengaged; sluggish even. After the body had been removed he had spent some time in the downstairs front room, used by Quinn as a bedroom-cum-study; he had opened drawers, looked through papers and folders, and half-stripped the bed. But it had all been an aimless, perfunctory exercise, and he had found nothing more incriminating than the previous month's copy of *Playboy*; and it was whilst sitting on the uncovered mattress scanning a succession of naked breasts and crotches that Lewis, after completing his tedious inventories, had found him.

'Anything interesting, sir?'

'No.' Morse had guiltily returned the magazine to the desk and fastened up his overcoat.

Just as they were about to leave, Morse had noticed the green anorak on one of the clothes pegs in the narrow hallway.

Chapter Seven

Bartlett knew that the man had been drinking and found himself feeling surprised and disappointed. He had been expecting the call all the afternoon, but it had not come through until half past three. The four of them had been seated in his office since lunchtime (the red light on outside) talking in hushed voices amongst themselves about the shattering news. Graphically Martin had recounted again and again the details of his morning discovery, and had taken some muted pleasure, even in these grim moments, at finding himself, quite unprecedentedly, at the centre of his colleagues' attention. But invariably the conversation had reverted to the perplexing question of who had been the last to see Quinn alive – and where. They all agreed, it seemed, that it had been on Friday, but exactly when and exactly where no one seemed able to remember. Or cared to tell . . .

Monica Height watched the Inspector carefully as he came in, and told herself, as they were briefly introduced, that his eyes held hers a fraction longer than was strictly necessary. She liked his voice, too; and when he informed them that each would be interviewed separately, either by himself or by Sergeant Lewis (standing silently by the door), she found herself hoping that in her case it would be him. Not that she need have worried on that score: Morse had already mentally allocated her to himself. But first he had to see what Bartlett could tell him.

'You've locked Quinn's door, I hope, sir.'

'Yes. Immediately I got your message.'

'Well, I think you'd better tell me something about this place: what you do, how you do it, anything at all you think may help. Quinn was murdered, sir – little doubt about that; and my job's to find out who murdered him. There's just a possibility, of course, that his murder's got nothing at all to do with this place, or with the people here; but it seems much more probable that I may be able to find something in the office here that will give me some sort of lead. So, I'm afraid I shall be having to badger you all for a few days – you realize that, don't you?'

Bartlett nodded. 'We shall all do our best to help you, Inspector. Please feel completely free to carry out whatever inquiries you think fit.'

'Thank you, sir. Now, what can you tell me?'

During the next half-hour Morse learned a great deal. Bartlett told him about the purpose, commitments, and organization of the Syndicate, about the personnel involved at all stages in the running of public examinations. And Morse found himself surprised and impressed: surprised by the unexpected complexities of the operations involved; and, above all, impressed by the extraordinary efficiency and grasp of the Pickwickian little Secretary sitting behind his desk.

'What about Quinn himself?'

Bartlett opened a drawer and took out a folder. 'I looked this out for you, Inspector. It's Quinn's application for the job here. It'll tell you more than I can.'

Morse opened the folder and his eyes hurriedly scanned the

contents: curriculum vitae, testimonials, letters from three referees, and the application form itself, across the top of which Bartlett had written: 'Appointed w.e.f. 1st Sept'. But again Morse's mind remained infuriatingly blank. The cogs in the machine were beginning to turn all right, but somehow they refused to engage. He closed the folder, defensively mumbling something about studying it later, and looked again at Bartlett. He wondered how that clear and supremely efficient mind would be tackling the problem of Quinn's murder, and it appeared that Bartlett could almost read his thoughts.

'You know that he was deaf, don't you, Inspector?'

'Deaf? Oh yes.' The police surgeon had mentioned it, but Morse had taken little notice.

'We were all very impressed by the way he coped with his disability.'

'How deaf was he?'

'He would probably have gone completely deaf in a few years' time. That was the prognosis, anyway.'

For the first time since Bartlett had been talking the merest flicker of interest showed itself in Morse's eyes. 'Little surprising you appointed him, perhaps, sir?'

'I think it's you who would have been surprised, Inspector. You could hardly tell he was deaf, you see. Apart from dealing with the phone, which *was* a problem, he was quite remarkable. He really was.'

'Did you er did you appoint him, you know, because he *was* deaf?'

'Did we feel sorry for him, you mean? Oh no. It seemed to the er the er committee that he was the best man in the field.'

'Which committee was that?'

Did Morse catch a hint of guardedness in Bartlett's eyes? He wasn't sure. What he did know was that the teeth of the smallest cog had now begun to bite. He sat back more happily in his chair.

'We er had all twelve Syndics on that committee – plus myself, of course.'

'Syndics? They're er— ?'

'They're like governors of a school, really.'

'They don't work here?'

'Good gracious, no. They're all university dons. They just

meet here twice a term to see if we're doing our job properly.'

'Have you got their names here?'

Morse looked with interest down the typed list that Bartlett handed to him. Printed beside the name of each of the Syndics were full details of university, college, degrees, doctorates and other academic honours, and one name in the list jumped out at him. 'Most of them Oxford men, I see, sir.'

'Natural enough, isn't it?'

'Just one or two from Cambridge.'

'Ye-es.'

'Wasn't Quinn at Magdalene College, Cambridge?' Morse began to reach for the folder, but Bartlett immediately confirmed the fact.

'I see that Mr Roope was at the same college, sir.'

'Was he? I'd never noticed that before.'

'You notice most things, if I may say so.'

'I always associate Roope with Christ Church, I suppose. He's been appointed a fellow there: "student", rather, if we want to be pedantic, Inspector.' His eyes were utterly guileless now, and Morse wondered if he might earlier have been mistaken.

'What's Roope's subject?'

'He's a chemist.'

'Well, well.' Morse tried to suppress the note of excitement in his voice, but realized that he wasn't succeeding. 'How old is he? Do you know?'

'Youngish. Thirty or so.'

'About Quinn's age, then?'

'About that.'

'Now, sir. Just one more thing.' He looked at his watch and found that it was already a quarter to five. 'When did you last see Quinn? Can you remember?'

'Last Friday, sometime. I know that. But it's a funny thing. Before you came in, we were all trying to think when we'd last seen him. Very difficult, you know, to pinpoint it exactly. I certainly saw him late on Friday morning; but I can't be sure about Friday afternoon. I had to go to a meeting in Banbury at three o'clock, and I'm just not sure if I saw him before I went.'

'What time did you leave the office, sir?'

'About a quarter-past two.'

'You must drive pretty fast.'

'I've got a fast car.'

'Twenty-two, twenty-three miles?'

Bartlett's eyes twinkled. 'We've all got our little weaknesses, Inspector, but I try to keep within the speed limits.'

Morse heard himself say he hoped so, and decided it was high time he saw Miss Monica Height. But before he did so he had a very much more urgent call to pay. 'Where's the nearest Gents? I'm dying for— '

'There's one right here, Inspector.' He got up and opened the door to the right of his desk. Inside was a tiny lavatory with a small wash basin tucked away behind the door; and as Morse blissfully emptied his aching bladder, Bartlett was reminded of the mighty out-pourings of Niagara.

After only a few minutes with Monica Height, Morse found himself wondering how the rest of the staff could ever manage to keep their hands off her, and cynically suspected that perhaps they didn't. The bright-green, flower-patterned dress she wore was stretched too tightly across her wide thighs, yet somehow managed to mould itself softly and suggestively around her full breasts. Biddable, by the look of it – and eminently beddable. She wore little make-up, but her habit of passing her tongue round her mouth imparted a moist sheen to her slightly pouting lips; and she exuded a perfume that seemed to invite instant and glorious gratification. Morse felt quite sure that at certain times and in certain moods she must have proved well-nigh irresistible to the young and the susceptible. To Martin, perhaps? To Quinn? Yes, surely the temptation must always have been there. Morse knew that he himself, the middle-aged and the susceptible . . . But he pushed the thought to the back of his mind. What about Ogleby? Or even Bartlett, perhaps? Whew! It was a thought! Morse recalled the passage from Gibbon about one of the tests designed for the young novitiate: stick him in a sack all night with a naked nun and see if . . . Morse shook his head abruptly and passed his hand over his eyes. It was always the same when he'd had a lot of beer.

'Do you mind if I just ring my daughter, Inspector?' (Daughter?) 'I'm usually on my way home by this time, and she'll probably wonder where I've got to.' Morse listened as she rang a number and explained her whereabouts.

'How old is your daughter, Miss er er Miss Height?'

She smiled understandingly. 'It's all right, Inspector. I'm divorced, and Sally's sixteen.'

'You must have married young.' (Sixteen!)

'I was foolish enough to marry at eighteen, Inspector. I'm sure you had much more sense than that.'

'Me? Oh yes, er no, I mean. I'm not married myself, you see.' Their eyes held again for a brief second and Morse sensed he could be living dangerously. It was time he asked the fair Monica a few important questions.

'When did you last see Mr Quinn?'

'It's funny you should ask that. We were only . . . ' It was like listening to a familiar record. She'd seen him on Friday morning – quite sure of that. But Friday afternoon? She couldn't quite remember. It was difficult. After all, Friday was – what? – five days ago now. ('Could have been four, five days' – hadn't the police surgeon said?)

'Did you like Mr Quinn?' Morse watched her reaction carefully, and suspected that this was one question for which she hadn't quite prepared herself.

'I haven't known him all that long, of course. What is it? Two or three months? But I liked him, yes. Very nice sort of person.'

'Did he like you?'

'What do you mean by that, Inspector?'

What *did* he mean? 'I just thought – well, I just thought— '

'You mean did he find me attractive?'

'I don't suppose he could help that.'

'You're very nice, Inspector.'

'Did he ever ask you out with him?'

'He asked me out to the pub once or twice at lunchtimes.'

'And you went?'

'Why not?'

'What did he drink?'

'Sherry, I think.'

'What about you?'

Her tongue moistened her lips once more. 'I've got slightly more expensive tastes myself.'

'Where did you go?'

'The Horse and Trumpet – just at the end of the road. Nice, cosy little place. You'd love it.'

'Perhaps I'll see you in there one day.'

'Why not?'

'Your tastes are expensive, you say?'

'We could work something out.'

Again their eyes met and the danger bells were ringing in Morse's brain. He stood up: 'I'm sorry to have kept you so long, Miss Height. I hope you'll apologize for me to your daughter.'

'Oh, she'll be all right. She's been home a lot of the time recently. She's retaking a few O-levels, and the school lets her go home when she hasn't got an examination.'

'I see.' Morse stood at the door, and seemed reluctant to leave. 'We shall be seeing each other again, no doubt.'

'I hope so, Inspector.' She spoke pleasantly and quietly and – damn it, yes! – sexily.

Her last words re-echoed in Morse's mind as he walked abstract-edly down the corridor.

'At last!' muttered Lewis to himself. He had been sitting in the entrance foyer for the past twenty minutes with Bartlett, Ogleby and Martin. All three had their overcoats and briefcases with them but were obviously reluctant to depart until Morse came and said the word. The death of Quinn had obviously thrown a pall of gloom over everything, and they had little to say to each other. Lewis had liked Ogleby, but had learned little from him: he'd remembered seeing Quinn the previous Friday morning, but not in the early afternoon; and to each of Lewis's other questions he had appeared to answer frankly, if uninformatively. Martin, though, had seemed a completely different proposition: intense and nervous now, as the shock of the whole business seemed to catch up with him, he'd said he couldn't really remember seeing Quinn at all on Friday.

Rather awkwardly, Morse thanked them for their cooperation, and gathered from Bartlett that it would be perfectly in order for himself and Lewis to stay in the building: the caretaker would be on the premises until at least 7.30 p.m., and naturally the build-ing would be kept open for them as long as they wished. But before handing over the keys to Quinn's office and to his filing cabinets, Bartlett gave the policemen a stern-faced little lecture on the strictly confidential nature of most of the material they would find; it was of the greatest importance therefore that they should remember . . . Yes, yes, yes, yes. Morse realized how he would have hated working under Bartlett, a man for whom the sin against the Holy Ghost was clearly that of leaving filing cabinets unlocked whilst nipping out to pee.

After they had gone, Morse suggested a quick stroll round the block, and Lewis responded willingly. The building was far too hot, and the cool night air was clean and refreshing. On the corner of the Woodstock Road they passed the Horse and Trumpet and Morse automatically consulted his watch.

'Nice little pub, I should think, Lewis. Ever been in?'

'No, sir, and I've had enough beer, anyway. I'd much rather have a cup o' tea.' Relieved that it still wanted ten minutes to opening time, he told Morse of his interviews, and Morse in turn told Lewis of his. Neither of them, it seemed, felt unequivocally convinced that he had stared into the eyes of a murderer.

'Nice-looker, isn't she, sir?'

'Uh? Who do you mean, Lewis?'

'Come off it, sir!'

'I suppose she is – if you go for that sort.'

'I notice you kept her all to yourself.'

'One o' the perks, isn't it?'

'I'm a bit surprised you didn't get a bit more out of her, though. Of the lot of 'em she seemed to me the one most likely to drop her inhibitions pretty quickly.'

'Drop her knickers pretty smartish, too, I shouldn't wonder.'

Lewis sometimes felt that Morse was quite unnecessarily crude.

Chapter Eight

Quinn's office was large and well-furnished. Two blue-leather chairs, one on each side, were neatly pushed beneath the writing desk, the surface of which was clear, except for the in- and out-trays (the former containing several letters, the latter empty) and a large blotter, with an assortment of odd names and numbers, and meaningless squiggles scribbled round its perimeter in black Biro. Lining two complete walls, right up to the ceiling, were row upon row of History texts and editions of the English classics, with the occasional yellow, red, green and white spine adding a further splash of colour to the brightly-lit and cheerful room. Three dark-green filing cabinets stood along the third wall, whilst the fourth carried a large plywood notice board and, one above the other, reproductions of Atkinson Grimshaw's paintings of the docks at Hull and Liverpool. Only the white carpet which covered most of the floor showed obvious signs of wear, and as Morse seated himself magisterially in Quinn's chair he noticed that immediately beneath the desk the empty waste-paper basket covered a patch that was almost threadbare. To his right, on a small black-topped table stood two telephones, one white, one grey, and beside them a pile of telephone directories.

'You go through the cabinets, Lewis. I'll try the drawers here.'

'Are we looking for anything in particular, sir?'

'Not that I know of.'

Lewis decided to plod along in his own methodical manner: at least it promised to be a bit more interesting than listing tins of rice pudding.

Almost immediately he began to realize what an enormous amount of love and labour went into the final formulation of question papers for public examinations. The top drawer of the first cabinet was stuffed with bulky buff-coloured folders, each containing copies of drafts, first proofs, first revises, second revises – even third revises – of papers to be set for the Ordinary-level English syllabuses. 'I reckon I could get a few quick O-levels this way, sir.'

Morse mumbled something about not being worth the paper they were printed on, and carried on with his own desultory investigation of the top right-hand drawer of Quinn's desk, wherein it soon became abundantly clear that he was unlikely to make any cosmic discoveries: paper-clips, bulldog-clips, elastic bands, four fine-pointed black Biros, a ruler, a pair of scissors, two birthday cards ('Love, Monica' written in one of them – well, well!), a packet of yellow pencils, a pencil sharpener, several letters from the University Chest about the transfer of pension rights to the University Superannuation Scheme, and a letter from the *Centre for the Deaf* informing Quinn that the lip-reading classes had been transferred from Oxpens to Headington Tech. After poking haphazardly around, Morse turned to the books behind him and found himself in the middle of the M's. He selected *Marvell's Collected Poems*, and as if someone else had recently been studying the same page, the book fell open of its own accord at the poem written 'To His Coy Mistress', and Morse read again the lines which had formed part of his own mental baggage for rather more years than he wished to remember:

> 'The grave's a fine and private place,
> But none, I think, do there embrace . . . '

Yes, Quinn was lying in the police mortuary, and Quinn had hoped his hopes and dreamed his dreams as every other mortal soul . . . He slotted the book back into its shelf, and turned with a slightly chastened spirit to the second drawer.

The two men worked for three-quarters of an hour, and Lewis felt himself becoming progressively more dispirited. 'Do you think we're wasting our time, sir?'

'Are you thirsty, or something?'

'I just don't know what I'm looking for, that's all.'

Morse said nothing. He didn't either.

By seven o'clock Lewis had looked through the contents of two of the three cabinets, and now inserted the key into the third, whence he took a further armful of thick folders and once again sat down to his task. The first file contained many carbons of letters, stretching back over two years, all marked GB/MF, and the replies from various members of the Syndicate's English Committee, all beginning 'Dear George'.

'This must be the fellow Quinn took over from, sir.'

Morse nodded cursorily and resumed his study of a black Letts desk diary which was the only object of even minimal interest he had so far unearthed. But Quinn had obviously shown no inclination to emulate an Evelyn or a Pepys, and little more than the dates and times of various meetings had been entered. 'Birthday' (under 23rd October), and 'I owe Donald £1' seemed to form the only concession to an otherwise autobiographical blank. And since he could think of nothing more purposeful to pursue, Morse idly counted the meetings: ten of them, almost all for the revisions of various question papers, within twelve weeks or so. Not bad going. And one or two other meetings: one with the English Committee on 30th September and one, a two-day meeting, with AED – whatever that was – on the 4th and 5th November.

'What's AED stand for, Lewis?'

'Dunno, sir.'

'Have a guess.'

'Association of Eccentric Dentists.'

Morse grinned and shut the diary. 'You nearly finished?'

'Two more drawers.'

'Think it's worth it?'

'Might as well go through with it now, sir.'

'OK.' Morse leaned back in the chair, his hands behind his head, and looked across the room once more. Not a particularly memorable start to a case, perhaps; but it was early days yet. He decided to put a call through to HQ. The grey telephone seemed the one used for outside calls, and Morse pulled it towards him. But as soon as he had picked up the receiver he put it down again. Underneath the orange code book he saw a letter which had escaped his notice hitherto. It was written on the official notepaper of the Frederic Delius School, Bradford, and was dated Monday, 17th November:

Dear Nick,

Don't forget me when you sort out your examining teams for next year. I trust you've had the form back by now. Gryce wasn't all that cooperative about the testimonial at first, but you'll have noticed that I'm 'a man of sound scholarship, with considerable experience of O- and A-level work.' What more can you ask for? Martha sends her love, and we all hope you'll be up here on your old stamping ground this Christmas. We've decided we can't please both lots of parents, and so we are going to please neither – and stay at home. By the way, old sour-guts has applied for the headship of the new Comprehensive! O tempora! O mores!

As ever,

Brian.

The letter was ticked through in black Biro, and Morse considered it carefully for a moment. Had Quinn rung up his friend? A former colleague, possibly? If so, when? It might be worth while finding out.

But it was Lewis who, quite accidentally, was to stumble through the trip-wire and set off the explosive that blew the case wide open, although he himself was quite unaware at the time of his momentous achievement. As he was about to jam the latest batch of files back into its cabinet he caught sight of an envelope, squashed and crumpled, which had become wedged beneath the moveable slide designed to keep the file cases upright. He worked it out and took the single sheet of paper from the envelope. 'I can tell you what AED stands for, sir.' Morse looked up without enthusiasm and took the letter from him. It was an amateurishly-typed note, written on the official, headed notepaper of the Al-jamara Education Department, and dated 3rd March:

Dear George,
Greetings to all at Oxford. Many thanks for your
letter and for the Summer examination package.
All Entry Forms and Fees Forms should be ready
for final dispatch to the Syndicate by Friday
20th or at the very latest, I'm told, by the 21st.
Admin has improved here, though there's room
for improvement still; just give us all two or three
more years and we'll really show you! Please
don't let these wretched 16+ proposals destroy
your basic O- and A-pattern. Certainly this
sort of change, if implemented immediately,
would bring chaos.
Sincerely yours,

Apart from the illegibly scrawled signature, that was all.

Morse frowned slightly as he looked at the envelope, which was addressed to G. Bland, Esq, MA, and marked 'STRICTLY PRIVATE AND CONFIDENTIAL' in bold red capitals. But his face quickly cleared, and he handed the letter back to Lewis without a word. It really was time they went.

Idly he opened the Letts diary again and his eyes fell upon the calendar inside the front page. And suddenly the blood began to freeze in his arms, and from the quiet, urgent tone of his voice Lewis immediately realized that the Inspector was strangely excited.

'What's the date of the postmark on that envelope, Lewis?'

'Third of March.'

'This year?'

Lewis looked again. 'Yes, sir.'

'Well, well, well!'

'What is it?'

'Funny, wouldn't you say, Lewis. Friday the 20th, it says in the letter. But *which* Friday the 20th?' He looked down at the calendar again. 'Not March. Not April. Not May. Not June. Not July. And it must refer to entry forms for last summer's examinations.'

'Somebody could have made a mistake over the date, sir. Could have been using last year's— '

But Morse wasn't listening. He picked up the letter again and studied it for several minutes with a fierce intensity. Then he nodded slowly to himself and a quiet smile spread over his face. 'Lewis, my boy, you've done it again!'

'I have, sir?'

'I'm not saying we're much nearer to finding out the identity of the person who murdered Nicholas Quinn, mind you. But I'll tell you one thing: I'm beginning to think we've got a pretty good idea *why* he was murdered! Unless it's a cruel coincidence— '

'Hadn't you better explain, sir?'

'Look at the letter again, Lewis, and ask yourself why such a seemingly trivial piece of correspondence was marked "Strictly Private and Confidential". Well?'

Lewis shook his head. 'I agree, sir, that it doesn't seem very important but— '

'But it *is* important, Lewis. That's just the point! *We* start reading from the left and then go across, agreed? But they tell me that some of these cockeyed foreigners start from the right and read down!'

Lewis studied the letter once more and his eyes gradually widened. 'You're a clever old bugger, sir.'

'Sometimes, perhaps,' conceded Morse.

At 7.35 p.m. the caretaker knocked deferentially and put his head round the door. 'I don't want to interrupt, sir, if—'

'Don't, then,' snapped Morse, and the door was quietly reclosed. The two policemen looked across the table at each other – and grinned happily.

WHEN?

Chapter Nine

Morse had never been in the slightest degree interested in the technicalities of the science of pathology, and on Wednesday morning he read the reports before him with the selectivity of a dedicated pornophilist seeking out the juiciest crudities. 'The smallest dose which has proved fatal is a ½ drachm of the pharmacopoeial acid, or 0.6 gram of anhydrous hydrocyanic acid . . . rapidly altered in the body after death, uniting with sulphur . . . ' Ah, here we are: ' . . . and such in this instance were the post-mortem appearances that there is reason to believe that death must have occurred almost immediately . . . fruitless, in the absence of scratches or abrasions, to speculate on the possibility of the body having been moved after death . . . ' Interesting. Morse skipped his way along. ' . . . would suggest a period of between 72–120 hours before the body was discovered. Any greater precision about these time limits is precluded in this case . . . ' As in *all* cases you ever have, muttered Morse. He had never ceased to wonder why, with the staggering advances in medical science, all pronouncements concerning times of death remained so disconcertingly vague. For that was the real question: *when* had Quinn died? If Aristotle could be believed (why not?) the truth would probably lie somewhere in the middle: 94 hours, say. That meant Friday lunchtime or thereabouts. Was that possible? Morse put the report aside, and reconsidered the little he as yet knew of Quinn's whereabouts on the previous Friday. Yes. Perhaps he should have asked Quinn's colleagues where *they* were on Friday, not when they had last seen Quinn. But there was plenty of time; he would have to see them all again soon, anyway. At least one thing was clear. Whoever had tinkered with Quinn's sherry bottle had known something about poison – known a great deal about poison, in fact. Now who . . . ? Morse went to his shelves, took down Glaister and Rentoul's bulky and definitive tome on *Medical Jurisprudence and Toxicology*, and looked up 'Hydrocyanic Acid' (page 566); and as he skimmed over the headings he smiled to himself. The compiler of the medical report he had just read had beaten him to it: some of the sentences were lifted almost verbatim. Why not, though? Cyanide wasn't going to change much over the years. . . . He recalled Hitler and his clique in the Berlin bunker. That was cyanide, wasn't it? Cyanide. Suicide! Huh! The obvious was usually the very last thing that occurred to Morse's mind; but he suddenly realized that the most obvious answer to his problem was this: that Quinn had committed suicide. Yet, come to think of it, that was no real answer either. For if he had, why on earth . . . ?

Lewis was surprised when half an hour later Morse took him to his home in North Oxford. It was two years since he had been there, and he was pleasurably surprised to find how comparatively neat and clean it was. Morse disappeared for a while, but put his head round the door and told Lewis to help himself to a drink.

'I'm all right, sir. Shall I pour one for you?'

'Yes. Pour me a sherry. And pour one for yourself.'

'I'd rather— '

'Do as you're told for a change, man!'

It wasn't unusual for Morse suddenly to turn sour, and Lewis resigned himself to the whims of his superior officer. The cabinet was well-stocked with booze, and Lewis took two small glasses and filled them from a bottle of medium sherry, sat back in an armchair, and wondered what was in store for him now.

He was sipping his sherry effeminately when Morse reappeared, picked up his own, lifted it to his lips and then put it down. 'Do you realize, Lewis, that if that sherry had been poisoned, you'd be a goner by now?'

'So would you, sir.'

'Ah, no. I've not touched mine.'

Lewis slowly put down his own glass, half-empty now, and began to understand the purpose of the little charade. 'And there'd be my prints on the bottle and on the glass . . . '

'And if I'd carefully wiped them both before we started, I've just got to pour my own sherry down the sink, wash the glass – and Bob's your uncle.'

'Somebody still had to get into Quinn's place to poison the sherry.'

'Not necessarily. Someone could have given Quinn the bottle as a present.'

'But you don't give someone a bottle that's been opened! You'd have a hell of a job trying to reseal a sherry bottle. In fact, you couldn't do it.'

'Perhaps there wasn't any need for that,' said Morse slowly; but he enlightened Lewis no further. For a moment he stood quite still, his eyes staring into the hazy past where a distant memory lingered on the threshold of his consciousness but refused the invitation to come in. It was something to do with a lovely young girl; but she merged into other lovely young girls. There had been so many of them, once . . . Think of something else! It would come. He drained his sherry at a gulp and poured himself another. 'Bit like drinking lemonade, isn't it, Lewis?'

'What's the programme, sir?'

'Well – I think we've got to play things a bit delicately. We might be on to something big, you must realize that; but it's no good rushing things. I want to know what all of 'em in the office were doing on Friday, but I want 'em to *know* what I'm going to ask them.'

'Wouldn't it be better—?'

'No. It wouldn't be fair, anyway.'

Lewis was getting lost. 'You think one of the four of them murdered Quinn?'

'What do you think?'

'I don't know, sir. But if you let them know beforehand— '

'Yes?'

'Well, they'd have something ready. Make something up— '

'That's what I want them to do.'

'But surely if one of them murdered Quinn—?'

'He'd have an alibi all ready, you mean?'

'Yes.'

Morse said nothing for a few seconds and then suddenly changed tack completely. 'Did you see me last Friday, Lewis?' Lewis opened his mouth and shut it again. 'Come on! We work in the same building, don't we?' Lewis tried hard, but he couldn't get hold of the problem at all. Friday. It seemed a long way away. What had he done on Friday? Had he seen Morse?

'You see what I mean, Lewis? Not easy, is it? We ought to give 'em a chance.'

'But as I say, sir, whoever killed Quinn will have something pretty good cooked up for last Friday.'

'Exactly.'

Lewis let it go. Many things puzzled him about the chief, and he felt even more puzzled as Morse pulled the front door to behind him: 'And what makes you so sure that Quinn was murdered on Friday?'

Margaret Freeman was unmarried – a slim, rather plain girl, with droopy eyelashes, who had worked for the Syndicate for just over three years. She had earlier been confidential secretary to Mr Bland, and had automatically been asked to transfer her allegiance to Mr Quinn. She had slept little the previous night, and not until the late grey dawn had she managed to rein in the horses of her terror. But Morse (who thought he understood such things) was still surprised when she broke down and wept after only a few minutes of gentle interrogation. She had certainly seen Quinn on Friday morning. He had dictated a whole sheaf of letters to her at about 10.45, and these had kept her busy until fairly late that same afternoon, when she had taken them into Quinn's office and put them in the in-tray. She hadn't seen him that Friday afternoon; yet she'd had the feeling that he was about somewhere, for she could almost positively recall (after some careful prodding) that Quinn's green anorak had been draped over the back of one of the chairs; and yes! there had been that little note for her, with her initials on it, MF, and then the brief message ('Dr Bartlett liked them to leave messages, sir'); but she couldn't quite remember . . . something like . . . no. Just something about 'going out', she thought. About being 'back soon', perhaps? But she couldn't really remember – that was obvious.

Morse had interviewed her in Quinn's office, and after she had gone he lit a cigarette and considered things anew. It was certainly interesting. Why wasn't the note still there? Quinn must have come back, crumpled up the note . . . But the waste-paper basket was empty. Cleaners! But Quinn had been alive at about 11 or 11.15 that Friday morning. That was something to build on, anyway.

To Lewis was entrusted the task of finding the caretaker and of discovering what happened to the Syndicate's rubbish.

And for once the luck was with him. Two large, black plastic sacks of wastepaper were standing in a small loading bay at the side of the building, awaiting collection, and the job of sifting through the papers was at least a good deal more congenial than delving into rubbish bins. Comparatively quick, too. Most of the wastepaper was merely torn across the middle, and not screwed into crumpled balls: outdated forms mostly and a few first drafts of trickier letters. No note from Quinn to his confidential secretary, though, and Lewis felt disappointed, since that was the prime object of the search. But there were several (identical) notes from Bartlett, which Lewis immediately sensed might well be of some interest; and he took them along to Quinn's office, where the receiver that Morse held to his ear was emitting the staccato bleeps of the 'engaged' signal. He further smoothed out one of the notes, and Morse put down the receiver and read it:

Mon, 17th Nov
Notice to all Staff
PRACTICE FIRE DRILL

The fire alarm will ring at 12 noon, on Friday, 21st Nov, when all staff must immediately stop working, turn off all fires, lights and other electrical appliances, close all windows and doors, and walk through the front door of the building and out into the front parking area. No one is to remain in the building *for any reason*, and normal work will not be resumed until everyone is accounted for. Since the weather seems likely to be cold and wet, staff are advised to take their coats, etc., although it is hoped that the practice will take no longer than ten minutes or so. I ask and expect your full co-operation in this matter.
Signed T. G. Bartlett (Secretary)

'He's a careful soul, isn't he, Lewis?'
'Seems pretty efficient, sir.'
'Not the sort to leave anything to chance.'
'What's that supposed to mean?'
'I was just wondering why he didn't tell me about this fire drill, that's all.' He smiled to himself, and Lewis knew that that *wasn't* all.

'Perhaps he didn't tell you because you didn't ask him.'

'Perhaps so. Anyway, go along and ask him if there was a roll-call. You never know – we may be able to postpone Quinn's execution from 11.15 to 12.15.'

The red light showed outside Bartlett's office, and as Lewis stood undecided before the door, Donald Martin walked past.

'That light means he's got somebody with him, doesn't it?'

Martin nodded. 'He'd be very annoyed if any of the staff interrupted him, but – I mean . . . ' He seemed extremely nervous about something, and Lewis took the opportunity (as Morse had instructed him) of disseminating the news that Quinn's colleagues would all soon be asked to account for their whereabouts the previous Friday.

'But what— ? He can't really think— '

'He thinks a lot of things, sir.'

Lewis knocked on Bartlett's door and went in. Monica Height turned round with some annoyance on her face, but the Secretary himself, smiling benignly, made no reference whatsoever to the infraction of the golden rule. In answer to his query, Lewis was informed that he'd better see the chief clerk upstairs, who had been in charge of the whole operation and who almost certainly would have kept the register of all those who had been present for the fire drill.

After Lewis had left the room, Monica turned around and looked hard at Bartlett. 'What's all that about, pray?'

'You know you mustn't blame the police for trying to find out when Mr Quinn was last seen alive. I must admit I'd not mentioned the fire drill— '

'But he was alive last Friday *afternoon* – there's not much doubt about that, is there? His car was here until about twenty to five. So Noakes says.'

'Yes, I know all about that.'

'Don't you think we ought to tell the police straightaway?'

'I've got a strong suspicion, my dear, that Chief Inspector Morse is going to find out far more than some of us may wish.'

But whatever might have been the cryptic implication of this remark, Monica appeared not to notice it. 'Don't you agree it may be very important, though?'

'Certainly. Especially if they think that Mr Quinn was murdered last Friday.'

'Do *you* think he was murdered on Friday?'

'Me?' Bartlett looked at her with a gentle smile. 'I don't think it matters very much what I think.'

'You haven't answered my question.'

Bartlett hesitated and stood up. 'Well, for what it's worth the answer's "no".'

'When—?'

But Bartlett held up his finger to his lips and shook his head. 'You're asking as many questions as they are.'

Monica rose to her feet and walked to the door. 'I still think you ought to let them know that Noakes— '

'Look,' he said in a kindly way. 'If it'll make you happier, I'll let them know straightaway. All right?'

As Monica Height left the room, Martin came up to her and said something urgently into her ear. Together they disappeared into Monica's office.

The chief clerk remembered the fire drill well, of course. Everything had gone according to plan and the Secretary had scrutinized the final list himself before allowing his staff to resume their duties. Of the twenty-six permanent staff, only three had not ticked themselves off. But all had been accounted for: Mr Ogleby was down at the Oxford University Press; one of the typists had 'flu; and one of the junior clerks was on holiday. Against Quinn's name was a bold tick in black Biro. And that was that. Lewis walked downstairs and rejoined Morse.

'Have you noticed how everyone in this office uses black Biro, Lewis?'

'Bartlett's got 'em all organized, sir – even down to the pens they use.'

Morse seemed to dismiss the matter as of no importance, and picked up the phone once more. 'You'd have thought this bloody school would have more than one line, wouldn't you?' But this time he heard the ringing tone, and the call was answered almost immediately. Morse heard a cheerful north-country voice telling him that she was the school secretary and asking if she could help. Morse explained who he was and what information he required.

'Friday, you say? Yes, I remember. From Oxford, that's right

. . . Oh, must have been about twenty past twelve. I remember I looked on t'time-tairble and Mr Richardson was teaching until a quarter to one . . . No, no. He said not to bother. Just asked me to give him t'message, laik. He said he would be inviting Mr Richardson to do some marking this summer . . . No, I'm sorry. I can't remember t'name for the minute, but Mr Richardson would know, of course . . . Yes. Yes, I'm sure that was it. Quinn – that's right. I hope there's nothing . . . Oh dear . . . Oh dear . . . Shall I tell Mr Richardson? . . . All right . . . All right, sir. Goodbye.'

Morse cradled the phone and looked across at Lewis. 'What do you think?'

'I think we're making progress, sir. Just after eleven he finishes dictating his letters; he's here for the fire drill at twelve; and he rings up the school at twenty past.' Morse nodded and Lewis felt encouraged to go on. 'What I'd really like to know is whether he left the note for Miss Freeman *before* or *after* lunch. So perhaps we'd better try to find out where he had a bite to eat, sir.'

Morse nodded again, and seemed to be staring at nothing. 'I'm beginning to wonder if we're on the right track, though, Lewis. You know what? I wouldn't be at all surprised if— '

The internal phone rang and Morse listened with interest. 'Well, thank you for telling me, Dr Bartlett. Can you ask him to come along straightaway?'

When the sycophantic Noakes began his brief tale, Morse wondered why on earth he had not immediately sought the caretaker's confidence; for he knew full well that in institutions of all kinds throughout the land it was the name of the caretaker which should appear at the top of all official notepaper. Wherever his services were called upon (including Police HQ) it seemed to be the caretaker, with his strangely obnoxious combination of officiousness and servility, whose goodwill was prized above all; whose co-operation over rooms, teas, keys and other momentous considerations, was absolutely indispensable. On the face of it, however, Noakes seemed one of the pleasanter specimens of the species.

'Yes, sir, his coat *was* there – I remember it distinct like, because his cabinet was open and I closed it. The Secketary wouldn't 'ave wanted that, sir. Very particular he is, about that.'

'Was there a note on his desk?'

'Yes, we saw that as well, sir.'

' "We", you say?'

'Mr Roope, sir. He was with me. He'd just— '

'What was he doing here?' said Morse quietly.

'He wanted to see the Secketary. But he was out, I knew that, sir. So Mr Roope asked me if any of the assistant secketaries was in – he had some papers, you see, as he wanted to give to somebody.'

'Who did he give them to?'

'That's just it. As I was going to say, sir, we tried all the other secketaries' offices, but there was nobody in.'

Morse looked at him sharply. 'You're quite sure about that, Mr Noakes?'

'Oh yes, sir. We couldn't find anybody, you see, and Mr Roope left the papers on the Secketary's desk.'

Morse glanced at Lewis and his eyebrows rose perceptibly. 'Well, well. That's very interesting. Very interesting.' But if it was as interesting as Morse would have the caretaker imagine, it prompted no further questions. At least not immediately so. The plain truth was that the information was, for Morse, completely unexpected, and he now regretted his earlier (stupidly theatrical) decision of allowing word to be spread on the office grape-vine (it had surely got round by now?) that he would be asking all of them to account for their movements on Friday afternoon. The last thing he had expected was that they'd *all* need an alibi. Bartlett, he knew, had been out at Banbury. But where had the others been that fateful afternoon? Monica, Ogleby, Martin, and Quinn. *All of them out of the office.* Whew!

'What time was all this, Mr Noakes?'

' 'Bout half-past four, sir.'

'Had any of the others left a note?'

'I don't think so.'

'Could any of them have been upstairs, do you think?'

'Could 'ave been, sir, but – well, I was here quite a long while. I was in the corridor, you see, fixin' this broken light when Mr Roope came in.'

Morse still seemed temporarily blown off course, and Lewis decided to see if he could help. 'Could any of them have been in the lavatory?'

'Must have been in there a long time!' It was quite clear from the slightly contemptuous smirk that crossed Noakes's face that he was not prepared to pay any particular respect to the suggestions of a mere sergeant, and the almost inevitable 'sir' was noticeably absent.

'It was raining on Friday afternoon, wasn't it?' said Morse at last.

'Yes, sir. Rainin', blowin' – miserable afternoon it was.'

'I hope Mr Roope wiped his feet,' said Morse innocently.

For the first time Noakes seemed uneasy. He passed his hands one over the other, and wondered what on earth *that* was supposed to mean.

'Did you see any of them at all – later on, I mean?'

'Not really, sir. I mean, I saw Mr Quinn leave in his car about— '

'You *what*?' Morse sat up and blinked at Noakes in utter bewilderment.

'You saw him *leave*, you say?'

'Yes, sir. About ten to five. His car was— '

'Were there any other cars here?' interrupted Morse.

'No, sir. Just Mr Quinn's.'

'Well, thank you, Mr Noakes. You've been very helpful.' Morse got up and walked to the door. 'And you didn't see anyone else – anyone at all – after that?'

'No, sir. Except the Secketary himself. He came back to the office about half-past five, sir.'

'I see. Well, thank you very much.' Morse had scarcely been able to hide his mounting excitement and he fought back the strong impulse to push Noakes out into the corridor.

'If I can be of any help any time, sir, I hope you . . . ' He stood fawning at the door like a liegeman taking leave of his lord. But Morse wasn't listening. A little voice within his brain was saying 'Bugger off, you obsequious little creep,' but he merely nodded good-naturedly and the caretaker finally sidled through the door.

'Well, Lewis? What do you make of that little lot?'

'I expect we shall soon find somebody who saw Quinn in a pub on Friday night. About chucking-out time.'

'You think so?' But Morse wasn't really interested in what Lewis was making of it. The previous day the cogs had started turning all right, but turning, it now appeared, in the wrong direction; and whilst Noakes had been speaking they'd temporarily stopped turning altogether. But they were off again now, in forward gear, with two or three of them whirring furiously. He looked at his watch, and saw that the morning was over. 'What swill do they slop out at the Horse and Trumpet, Lewis?'

Chapter Ten

Few of the buildings erected in Oxford since the end of the Second World War have met with much approval from either Town or Gown. Perhaps it is to be expected that a public privileged with the daily sight of so many old and noble buildings should feel a natural prejudice against the reinforced concrete of the curious post-war structures; or perhaps all modern architects are mad. But it is generally agreed that the John Radcliffe Hospital on Headington Hill is one of the least offensive examples of the modern design – except, of course, to those living in the immediate vicinity who have found their expensive detached houses dwarfed by the gigantic edifice, and who now view from the bottom of their gardens a broad and busy access road instead of the green and open fields of Manor Park. The seven-storeyed hospital, built in gleaming, off-white brick, its windows painted chocolate brown, is set in spacious, tree-lined grounds, where royal-blue notice-boards in bold white lettering direct the strangers towards their destinations. But few are strangers here, for the John Radcliffe Hospital is dedicated to the safe delivery of all the babies to be born beneath the aegis of the Oxfordshire Health Authority, and in it almost all the pregnant mums have suffered their precious embryos to be coddled and cosseted, turned and tested many many times before. Joyce Greenaway has. But with her ('one in a thousand', they'd said) things have not gone quite according to the gynaecological guarantee.

Frank Greenaway had Wednesday afternoon free and he drove into the hospital car park at 1 p.m. He was feeling much happier than he had done, for it now looked as if everything was going to be all right after all. But it still annoyed him that the incompetent nitwit of a foreman at Cowley had not been able to get the message to him the previous Friday evening, and he felt that he had let his wife down. Their first, too! Not that Joyce had been over-worried: when things seemed to her to be getting to the critical stage, she had shown her usual good sense and contacted the hospital direct. But it still niggled a bit; he couldn't pretend it didn't. For when he had finally arrived at the hospital at 9.30 p.m., their underweight offspring – some three weeks premature – was already putting up its brave and successful little fight in the Intensive Care Unit. It wasn't *his* fault, was it? But for Frank (who had little imagination, but a ready sympathy) it was something like arriving ten minutes late for an Oxford United fixture and finding he'd missed the only goal of the match.

He, too, was no stranger now. The doors opened for him automatically, and he walked his way confidently down the wide, blue-carpeted entrance hall, past the two inquiry desks, and made straight for the lift, where he pressed the button and, with a freshly-laundered nightie, a box of Black Magic, and a copy of *Woman's Weekly*, he ascended to the sixth floor.

Both Joyce and the baby were still isolated – something to do with jaundice ('Nothing to worry about, Mr Greenaway'), and Frank walked once more into Private Room 12. Why he felt a little shy, he could hardly begin to imagine; but he knew full well that he had every cause for continued apprehension. The doctors had been firmly insistent that he should as yet say nothing whatsoever about it. ('Your wife has had a pretty rough time, Mr Greenaway.') She would have to know *soon*, though; couldn't *help* getting to know. But he had willingly agreed to play the game, and the sister had promised to have a word with each of Joyce's visitors. ('The post-natal period can be very difficult, Mr Greenaway.') No *Oxford Mail* either, of course.

'How are we then, love?'

'Fine.'

'And the little one?'

'Fine.'

They kissed, and soon began to feel at ease again.

'Has the telly-man been yet? I meant to ask you yesterday.'

'Not yet, love. But he'll fix it – have no fear.'

'I should hope so. I shan't be in here much longer – you realize that, don't you?'

'Don't you worry about that.'

'Have you put the cot up yet?'

'I keep telling you. Stop *worrying*. You just get on your feet again and look after the little fellah – that's all that matters.'

She smiled happily, and when he stood up and put his arm around her she nestled against his shoulder lovingly.

'Funny, isn't it, Frank? We'd got a name all ready, if it was a girl. And we were so sure it would be.'

'Yeah. I been thinking, though. What about "Simon"? Nice name, don't you think. "Simon Greenaway" – what about that? Sounds sort of – distinguished, if you know what I mean.'

'Yeah. Perhaps so. Lots of nice names for boys, though.'

'Such as?'

'Well. You know that chap downstairs – Mr Quinn? His name's "Nicholas". Nice name, don't you think? "Nicholas Greenaway." Yeah. I quite like that, Frank.' Watching his face closely, she could have sworn there was *something* there, and for a second she felt a surge of panic. But he *couldn't* know. It was just her guilty conscience: she was imagining things.

The Horse and Trumpet was quite deserted when they sat down in the furthest corner from the bar, and Lewis had never known Morse so apparently uninterested in his beer, over which he lingered like a maiden aunt sipping homemade wine at a church social. They sat for several minutes without speaking, and it was Lewis who broke the silence. 'Think we're getting anywhere, sir?'

Morse seemed to ponder the question deeply. 'I suppose so. Yes.'

'Any ideas yet?'

'No,' lied Morse. 'We've got to get a few more facts before we start getting any fancy ideas. Yes . . . Look, Lewis. I want you to go along and see Mrs What's-her-name, the cleaner woman. You know where she lives?' Lewis nodded. 'And you might as well call on Mrs Jardine – isn't it? – the landlady. You can take my car: I expect I'll be at the Syndicate all afternoon. Pick me up there.'

'Anything particular you want me to—?'

'Christ man! You don't need a wet nurse, do you? Find out all you bloody well can! You know as much about the case as I do!' Lewis sat back and said nothing. He felt more angry with himself than with the Inspector, and he finished his pint in silence.

'I think I'll be off then, sir. I'd just like to nip in home, if you don't mind.'

Morse nodded vaguely and Lewis stood up to go. 'You'd better let me have the car-keys.'

Morse's beer was hardly touched and he appeared to be staring with extraordinary intensity at the carpet.

Mrs Evans had been cleaning the ground floor of No 1 Pinewood Close for several years, and had almost been part of the tenancy for the line of single men who had rented the rooms from Mrs Jardine. Most of them had been on the look-out for something a little better and had seldom stayed long; but they'd all been pleasant enough. It was chiefly the kitchen that would get so dirty, and although she dusted and hoovered the other rooms, her chief task always lay in the kitchen, where she usually spent half an hour cleaning the stove and another half-hour ironing the shirts, underwear and handkerchiefs which found their weekly way into the local launderette. It was just about two hours' work – seldom more, and often a little less. But she always charged for two hours, and none of the tenants had ever demurred. She liked to get things done whilst no one was about; and, with Quinn, 3–5 p.m. on Fridays was the regularly appointed time.

It was about poor Mr Quinn, she knew that, and she invited Lewis in and told him the brief story. She had usually finished and gone before he got back home. But the previous Friday she had to call at the Kidlington Health Centre for Mr Evans, who had bronchitis and was due to see the doctor again at 4.30 that day. But the weather was so dreadful that she thought he ought to stay in. So she went herself to get Mr E another prescription, called in at the dispensing chemist, and then went home and got the tea. She got back to Quinn's house at about a quarter-past six and stayed about half an hour to do the ironing.

'You left a note for him, didn't you, Mrs Evans?'

'I thought he'd wonder why I hadn't finished.'

'That was at about four o'clock, you say?'

She nodded, and felt suddenly nervous. Had poor Mr Quinn died on *Friday night*, just after she'd left, perhaps?

'We found the note in the waste-paper basket, Mrs Evans.'

'I suppose you would, sir. If he screwed it up, like.'

'Yes, of course.' Lewis found himself wishing that Morse was there, but he put the thought aside. A few interesting ideas were beginning to develop. 'You left the note in the lounge?'

'Yes. On the sideboard. I always left a note there at the end of the month – when me four weeks' cleaning was up, like.'

'I see. Can you remember if Mr Quinn's car was in the garage when you got back?'

'No, Sergeant. I'm sorry. It was raining, and I was on me bike and I just got in as fast as I could. Anyway, why should I look in the garage? I mean— '

'You didn't see Mr Quinn?'

'No, I didn't.'

'Ah well. Never mind. We're obviously anxious— '

'You think he died on Friday night, then?'

'No, I wouldn't say that. But if we could find what time he got back from the office – well, it would be a great help. For all we know, he didn't get back home at all on Friday night.'

Mrs Evans looked at him with a puzzled frown. 'But *I* can tell you what time he got home.'

The room was suddenly very quiet and Lewis looked up tensely from his notes. 'Will you say that again, Mrs Evans?'

'Oh yes, Sergeant. You see, I left this note for him and he must have seen it.'

'He *must* have done, you say?'

'Must have done. You just said it was in the waste-paper basket.'

Lewis sank back in the sofa, his excitement ebbing away. 'He could have found the note any time, I'm afraid, Mrs Evans.'

'Oh no. You don't understand. He'd seen the note before I got back at quarter-past six.' Lewis was sitting very still again and listening intently. 'You see, he left a note for me, so— '

'*He left a note for you?*'

'Yes. Said he'd gone shopping, or something. I forget exactly – but something like that.'

'So you— ' Lewis started again. 'You left the note at four o'clock and went back there at quarter-past six, you say?'

'That's right.'

'So you think he must have got home – when? About five?'

'Well, yes. He usually got home about then, I think.'

'You're sure the note was for you?'

'Oh yes. It got me name on it.'

'Can you – can you remember *exactly* what it said?'

'Not really. But I tell you what, Sergeant: I might still have got it. I probably put it in me pinny, or something. I always wear— '

'Can you try to find it for me?'

As Mrs Evans went out into the kitchen, Lewis found himself praying to the gods that for once they would smile upon him, and he felt almost sick with relief when she came with a small folded sheet of paper, and handed it to him. He read it with the awesome reverence of a druid brooding on the holy runes:

Mrs E,
Just off shopping – shan't be long. NQ

It couldn't have been much briefer and it puzzled him a little; but he was fully aware of its huge importance.

' "Shopping", he says. Funny time for shopping, isn't it?'

'Not really, sir. The supermarket's open till nine of a Friday night.'

'The *Quality* supermarket, is that?'

'Yes, sir. It's only just behind the house, really. There's a pathway by the side of the crescent, and now that the fence is down you can get on to it from the side of the garden.'

Five minutes later Lewis thanked her fulsomely and left. By Jove, old Morse was going to be pleased!

It was just after one when Monica walked into the lounge bar. She spotted Morse immediately (though he appeared not to notice her) and after buying a gin and Campari she walked across and stood beside him.

'Can I get you a drink, Inspector?'

Morse looked up and shook his head. 'I seem to be off the beer today.'

'You weren't yesterday.'

'I wasn't?'

She sat down beside him and brought her lips close to his ear. 'I could smell your breath.'

'You smelled pretty good, too,' said Morse, but he knew that this was not to be a time for high romance. He could read the signs a mile away.

'I thought I might find you here.'

Morse shrugged non-committally. 'What have you got to tell me?'

'You don't beat about the bush, do you?'

'Sometimes I do.'

'Well, it's – it's about Friday afternoon.'

'News gets around.'

'You wanted to know what we were all doing on Friday afternoon, is that right?'

'That's it. Seems none of you were in the office, wherever else you were.'

'Well, I don't know about the others – no, that's not quite true. You see – Oh dear! You don't make it very easy for me. I was out all the afternoon and, well – I was with somebody else; and I suppose sooner or later you'll have to know who I was with, won't you?'

'I think I know,' said Morse quietly.

Monica's face dropped. 'You can't know. Have you already spoken—?'

'Have I spoken to Mr Martin? No, not yet. But I shall be doing so very soon, and I suppose he'll tell me the whole story, with the usual dose of reluctance and embarrassment – perhaps with a bit of anxiety, too. He *is* married, isn't he?'

Monica put her hand to her forehead and shook her head rather sadly. 'Are you a clairvoyant?'

'I'd solve all my cases a bit quicker if I were.'

'Do you want to hear about it?' She looked at him unhappily.

'Not now. I'd rather hear it from your boy-friend. He's not a very good liar.' He stood up and looked down at her empty glass. 'Gin and Campari, was it?'

She nodded, and thanked him; and as Morse walked over to the bar, she lit another cigarette and inhaled deeply, her immaculately plucked eyebrows narrowing into a worried frown. What on earth was she going to do if . . . ?

Morse was soon back again, and placed her drink neatly on to a beer mat. 'I see what you mean about expensive tastes, Miss Height.'

She looked up at him and smiled feebly. 'But – aren't you going to join me?'

'No. Not now, thank you. I'm a bit busier than usual this

week, you know. I've got a murder to investigate, and I don't usually mix much with tarts, anyway.'

After he had gone Monica felt utterly miserable, her thoughts a pallid multitude that drifted along the sunless waters. How cruel he had been just now! Only yesterday she had experienced an unwonted warmth of pleasure in his company. But how she hated him now!

Morse, too, was far from happy with himself. He shouldn't really have treated her as callously as that. How stupid it was, anyway – feeling so childishly jealous! Why, he'd only met her once before. He could go back, of course, and buy her another drink . . . and say he was sorry. Yes, he could do that. But he didn't; for interwoven with the jealousy motif was something else: he sensed intuitively that Monica had lied to him.

Chapter Eleven

Apart from the fact that Mrs Greenaway, the upstairs tenant, had been delivered of a baby boy the previous Friday evening, Lewis had learned nothing much of interest from Mrs Jardine. She was unable to add anything of substance to the statement made to Constable Dickson the previous day, and Lewis had stayed with her no more than ten minutes. But he'd had his earlier triumph. Oh yes! And as that same afternoon he recounted to Morse his interview with Mrs Evans – and presented his prize – he felt very pleased with himself indeed. Yet Morse's reactions seemed decidedly luke-warm; certainly he'd looked long and hard at Quinn's brief note, but in general he appeared preoccupied with other things.

'You don't seem very happy with life, sir.'

'The majority of men lead lives of quiet desperation.'

'But if this doesn't cheer you up— '

'What? Don't be daft!' Almost physically Morse tried to shake off his mood of temporary gloom, and he looked down at the note once more. 'I couldn't have done much better myself.' He said it flippantly, but Lewis knew him better.

'Let's have it, sir.'

'What do you mean?'

'What would you have asked her?'

'Just what you did – I told you.'

'What else?'

Morse appeared to consider the question carefully. 'Perhaps one or two other things.'

'Such as?'

'Perhaps I'd have asked her if she'd looked in the waste-paper basket.'

'Really?' Lewis sounded unimpressed.

'Perhaps I'd have asked her if Quinn's anorak was there.'

'But— ' Lewis let it ride.

'I'd certainly have asked her if the gas fire was on.'

Lewis began to catch the drift of Morse's mind, and he nodded slowly to himself. 'I suppose we'd better see her again, sir.'

'Oh yes,' said Morse quietly. 'We shall have to see her again. But that's no problem, is it? The main thing is that we seem to have got Quinn alive till about six o'clock. I wonder . . . ?' His thoughts floated away again, but suddenly he sat upright and took out his Parker pen. 'There's still a good deal to do here, though, Lewis. Nip and see if he's back from lunch.'

'Who do you mean, sir?'

'I just told you – Martin. You going deaf?'

As Martin painfully corroborated Monica's story, Morse's facial expression was that of a man with a rotten egg stuck just beneath his nose. The pair of them had left the office at about 1.10 p.m. No, not together – in separate cars. Yes, to Monica's bungalow. Yes, to bed. (Putrescent, fetid egg!) That was all really. (All! Christ! That was *all*, he'd said.)

'What time did you leave?'

'About a quarter to four.'

'And you didn't come back to the office at all?'

'No. I went straight home.'

'Nice little surprise for your wife.'

Martin was silent.

'Lewis! Go and see Miss Height. You've heard what this man says. Get her story, and see if it fits.'

After Lewis had gone Morse turned to Martin and looked him hard in the eyes. 'You're a cock-happy young sod, aren't you?'

The young man shook his head sadly. 'I'm not really, you know, Inspector. I've only been unfaithful with Monica, never anyone else.'

'You in love with her?'

'I don't know. This business has – I don't know, Inspector. She's— Ah, what's it matter now!'

'Why did you leave so early?'

'There's Sally – that's Monica's daughter. She usually gets home from school about quarter-past four.'

'And you didn't want her to find you shagging her mother, is that it?'

Martin looked up miserably. 'Haven't you ever been unfaithful, Inspector?'

Morse shook his head. 'No, lad. I've never had to be faithful, you see.'

'There's – there's no need for all this to come out, is there?'

'Not really, no. Unless— '

'Unless what?' A look of alarm sprang into Martin's eyes, and Morse did nothing to dispel it.

'Tell me. This girl Sally: is she at school in Oxford?'

'Oxford High School.'

'Bit awkward with examinations, isn't it? I mean, with her mother— '

'No. You don't quite understand, Inspector. This Board doesn't examine in England at all.'

'Who examines Oxford High?'

'Oxford Locals, I think.'

'I see.'

After Martin had gone, Morse rang HQ and gave Constable Dickson his instructions; and he was smiling contentedly to himself when Lewis returned.

'She confirms what Martin says, sir.'

'Does she now?'

'You sound a bit dubious.'

'Do I?'

'You don't believe 'em?'

'For what it's worth, Lewis, I think they're a pair of bloody

liars. But I may be wrong, of course. As you know, I often am.'
He had that deprecatingly-conceited look on his face which many
found the Chief Inspector's least attractive trait, and Lewis was
determined not to demean himself by trying to delve further into
that cocky logic. For his part, he believed them, and high-and-
mighty Morse could mumble away as he pleased.

'Didn't you hear me, Lewis?'

'Pardon sir?'

'What the hell's up with you today, man? I said go and
get Ogleby. Can you do that small thing for me?'

Lewis slammed the door behind him and walked out into
the corridor.

Morse had spoken no more than half a dozen words to Ogleby
when they had been formally introduced the previous day, yet he
had felt an instinctive liking for the man; and this impression was
confirmed as Ogleby began to chat informatively and authoritatively about the work of the Syndicate.

'What about security?' asked Morse cautiously, like a timid
skater testing the ice.

'It's a constant problem, of course. But everyone's conscious
of it, and so in an odd sort of way the problem solves itself – if
you see what I mean.'

Morse thought he did. 'I gather the Secretary's pretty keen
on that side of things.'

'Yes, I suppose you could say that.'

Morse eyed him sharply. Had there been a tinge of irony –
or even jealousy, perhaps – in Ogleby's reply? 'Is there *never*
any malpractice?'

'Oh, I wouldn't say that. But that's a completely different
question.'

'Is it?'

'You see if a candidate decided to cheat in the examination
room, either by taking notes in with him or copying from someone
else, then we've just got to rely on the invigilators keeping a very
careful eye on things, and reporting anything suspicious directly
to us.'

'That happens, does it?'

'Two or three times a year.'

'What do you do about it?'

'We disqualify the candidates concerned from every subject in the examinations.'

'I see.' Morse tried another angle. 'You send out the question papers before the examination, don't you?'

'Wouldn't be much good holding the examinations if we didn't, would it?'

Morse realized what a stupid question he'd asked, and continued rather hastily. 'No. I mean – if one of the teachers was dishonest, or something?'

'The question-papers are sent out directly to examination departments, and then distributed to heads of centres – not to individual teachers.'

'But let's take a headmaster, then. If he was a crook – let's say he opened a particular package of question-papers and showed them to his pupils— '

'It's as good a way as any for the headmaster to slit his throat.'

'You'd know, you mean?'

Ogleby smiled. 'Gracious, yes. We've got examiners and awarders who'd smell anything like that a mile away. You see we've got records going back over the years of percentage passes for all the subjects examined, and so we know the sort of pupils we're examining, the types of schools – all that sort of thing. But that's not really the point. Like all the examining Boards we inspect our centres regularly after they've been accepted, and they have to meet pretty high standards of integrity and administrative competence before they're recognized in the first place.'

'The schools are regularly inspected then?'

'Oh yes.'

'Is that the sort of job Mr Bland does in Al-jamara?'

Morse watched Ogleby carefully, but the deputy sailed serenely on. 'Among other things, yes. He's in charge of the whole administrative set-up there.'

Morse decided that he might as well tackle the problem from the other end, and he delicately tip-toed his way over the ice again.

'Would it be possible for an outsider, one of the cleaners, say, to get into the cabinets in this office? And get the papers he wanted?'

'Technically, I suppose, yes. If he had the keys, knew where to look, knew the complicated system of syllabus numbering, had the intelligence to understand the various amendments and printing symbols. Then he'd have to copy what he'd got, of course. Every page of proofs and revises is carefully numbered, and no one could get away with just *pinching* a page.'

'Mm. What about examiners? Let's say they put a high mark down for a particular candidate who's as thick as a plank.'

'Wouldn't work, I'm afraid. The arithmetic of every single script is checked against the marksheet.'

'Well, let's say an examiner gives high marks for all of the answers on the script – even if they're rubbish.'

'If an examiner did that, he would have been kicked out years ago. You see the examiners are themselves examined by a team of what we call "awarders", who report on all the members of the various panels after each examination.'

'But the awarders could . . . ' No, Morse, let it go. He began to see that it was all far more complex than he had imagined.

But Ogleby finished the thought for him. 'Oh, yes, Inspector. If one of the people *at the top* was crooked, it would be very easy. Very easy indeed. But why are you asking me all this?'

Morse pondered a while, and then told him. 'We've got to find a motive for Quinn's murder, sir. There are a hundred and one possibilities, of course, but I was just wondering if – if perhaps he'd found some er some suggestion of jiggery-pokery, that's all. Anyway, you've been very helpful.'

Ogleby stood up to go, and Morse too rose from his chair. 'I've been asking the others what they were doing last Friday afternoon. I suppose I ought to ask you too. If you can remember, that is.'

'Oh, yes. That's easy enough. I went down to the Oxford University Press in the morning, had a pretty late lunch at the Berni place there with the chief printer, and got back here about, oh, about half-past three, I should think.'

'And you spent the rest of the afternoon in the office here?'

'Yes.'

'Are you sure about that, sir?'

Ogleby looked at him with steady eyes. 'Quite sure.'

Morse hesitated, and debated whether to face it now or later.

'What is it, Inspector?'

'It's a bit awkward, sir. I understand from er from other sources that there was no one here in the latter part of Friday afternoon.'

'Well, your sources of information must be wrong.'

'You couldn't have slipped out for a while? Gone up to see the chief clerk or something?'

'I certainly didn't go out of the office. I might have gone upstairs, but I don't think so. And if I had, it would only have been for a minute or two, at the very outside.'

'What would you say, then, sir, if someone said there was no one here on Friday afternoon between a quarter-past four and a quarter-to five?'

'I'd say that someone was mistaken, Inspector.'

'But what if he insisted—?'

'He'd be a liar, then, wouldn't he?' Ogleby smiled serenely, and gently closed the door behind him.

Or *you* would, thought Morse, as he sat alone. And although you don't know it, my good friend Ogleby, there are two some-ones who say you weren't here. And if you weren't here, where the hell *were* you?

Chapter Twelve

The police car, white with a broad, pale-blue stripe along its middle, stood parked by the pavement, and Constable Dickson knocked at the spruce detached bungalow in Old Marston. The door was immediately opened by a smartly-dressed, attractive woman.

'Miss Height?'

'Yes?'

'Is your daughter in?'

Miss Height's features crumpled into a girlish giggle. 'Don't be silly! I'm only sixteen!'

Dickson himself grinned oafishly, and accepted the young lady's invitation to step inside.

'It's about Mr Quinn, isn't it? Ever so exciting. Coo. Just think. He worked in the same office as Mummy!'

'Did you ever meet him, miss?'

'No, worse luck.'

'He never came here?'

She giggled again. 'Not unless Mummy brought him here while I was slaving away at school!'

'She wouldn't do that, would she?'

She smiled happily. 'You don't know Mummy!'

'Why aren't you at school today, miss?'

'Oh, I'm taking some O-levels again. I took them in the summer but I'm afraid I didn't do too well in some of them.'

'What subjects are they?'

'Human Biology, French and Maths. Not that I've got much chance in Maths. We had Paper Two this morning – a real stinker. Would you like to see it?'

'Not now, miss. I er – I was just wondering why you weren't at school, that's all.' It wasn't very subtle.

'Oh, they let us off when we haven't got an exam. Great really. I've been off since lunchtime.'

'Do you always come home? When you're free, I mean?'

'Nothing else to do, is there?'

'You revise, I suppose?'

'A bit. But I usually watch telly. You know, the kiddies' programmes. Quite good, really. Sometimes I don't think I've grown up at all.'

Dickson felt he shouldn't argue. 'You've been here most days recently, then?'

'Most afternoons.' She looked at him innocently. 'I shall be here again tomorrow afternoon.'

Dickson coughed awkwardly. He'd done the bit of homework that Morse had told him to. 'I watched one of those kiddies' films, miss. About a dog. Last Friday afternoon, I think it was.'

'Oh yes. I watched that. I cried nearly all the way through. Did it make *you* cry?'

'Bit of a tearjerker, I agree, miss. But I mustn't keep you from your revising. As I say, it was your mother I really wanted to see.'

'But you said – you said you wanted to see *me*!'

'I got it a bit muddled, miss, I'm afraid. I sort of thought— '
He gave it up and got to his feet. He hadn't done too badly at
all really, and he thought the Chief Inspector would be pleased
with him.

At 7 p.m. the same evening Morse sat alone in his office.
A single tube of white strip-lighting threw a harsh unfriendly
glare across the silent room, and a single yellow lamp in the yard
outside the uncurtained window did little more than emphasize
the blackness of the night. Occasionally, especially at times like
this, Morse wished he had a home to welcome him, with a wife
to have his slippers warmed and ready. It was at times like this,
too, that murder seemed a crude and terrifying thing . . . Dickson
had reported on his visit to Sally Height, and the silhouettes on the
furthest walls of the darkened cave were now assuming a firmer
delineation. Monica had lied to him. Martin had lied to him. It
was odds-on that Ogleby had lied to him. Had Bartlett lied as
well? Stocky, cautious little Bartlett, meticulous as a metronome.
If *he* had murdered Nicholas Quinn . . .

For half an hour he let his thoughts run wild and free, like
randy rabbits in orgiastic intercourse. And then he put a stop to
it. He needed a few more facts; and facts were facing him, here and
now, in the dark-blue plastic bag containing the items found in
Quinn's pockets, in Quinn's green anorak, and in Lewis's inventories. Morse cleared the top of his desk and set to work. Quinn's
pockets had thrown up little of surprise or interest: a wallet, a
grubby handkerchief, half a packet of Polo, a diary (with not a
single entry), 43½p, a pink comb, one half of a cinema ticket,
two black Biros, a strip of tired-looking Green Shield stamps, and
a statement from Lloyds Bank (Summertown branch), showing a
current account balance of £114.40. That was the lot, and Morse
arranged each item neatly before him and sat surveying them for
minutes, before finally taking a sheet of notepaper and listing
each item carefully. Ye-es. The thought had flashed across his
mind a few minutes earlier. Decidedly odd . . . Next he picked
up the anorak and took a further selection of objects from each
side pocket: another grubby handkerchief, car keys, a black key-
case, two ancient raffle tickets, a further 23p, and an empty white
envelope addressed to Quinn, with the word 'Bollox' written on
the flap in pencil. 'Well, well,' mumbled Morse to himself. His

randy rabbits could have a field day with *that*, but he decided to give them no chance. Again he listed each item with great precision and again sat back. It was just as he had thought, but it was too late to go back to the lonely rooms in Pinewood Close that night. A bit too creepy, anyway.

Having completed a synoptic review of the evidence before him, Morse systematically tackled each item severally. The wallet first: a driving licence, RAC membership card, Lloyds Bank cheque card, an out-of-date NHS prescription for Otosporon, the previous month's pay-slip, a blue outpatients' appointment card for the ENT department at the Radcliffe Infirmary, one five-pound note, three one-pound notes, and a Syndicate acknowledgement card on which were written two telephone numbers. Morse picked up the phone and dialled the first, but his ears were greeted only by a continuous high-pitched monotone. He dialled the second.

'Hello? Monica Height here.'

Morse hastily put down the receiver. It was naughty of him, he knew, but he had the feeling that Monica would not be very happy with him for the moment. Or with Constable Dickson. Yet it made him wonder exactly what the pattern of cross-relationships in the Syndicate had been.

It was the buff-coloured right-hand half of the cinema ticket which next attracted Morse's attention. Across the top were the numbers 102, beneath them the words 'Rear Lounge', and along the right edge, running down, the numbers 93550. On the back of the ticket was the design of a pentagram. Somebody must know which cinema it was, he supposed. Job for Lewis, perhaps . . . And then it struck him. Fool of a fool! It wasn't 102 across the top at all. There was just the slightest gap between the 0 and the 2 and Morse saw the name of the cinema staring up at him: STUDIO 2. He knew the place – in Walton Street. Morse had bought a copy of the previous day's *Oxford Mail* (wherein the Quinn murder had been briefly reported) and he turned the pages and found that Tuesday was the critics' day for reporting to the citizens of Oxford on the quality of the entertainments currently available. Yes, there it was:

It is all too easy to see why *The Nymphomaniac* has been retained for a further week at Studio 2. The afficionados have been flocking to see the Swedish sexpot, Inga Nielsson, dutifully exposing her 40″ bosom at the slightest provocation. Flock on.

Morse read the review with mixed feelings. Clearly, the critics hadn't yet gone metric, and this particular aficionado couldn't even spell the word. Yet big Inga seemed to Morse a most inviting prospect; and doubtless to many another like him. Especially perhaps when the boss was away one Friday afternoon . . . ? He flicked through the telephone directory, found the number, and asked to speak to the manager who surprisingly turned out to be the manageress.

'Oh yes, sir. All our tickets are traceable. Buff, you say? Rear circle? Oh yes. We should be able to help you. You see all the blocks of tickets are numbered and a record is kept at the start of each matinée, and then at six o'clock, and then at ten o'clock. Have you got the number?'

Morse read out the number and felt curiously excited.

'Just one minute, sir.' It turned into three or four, and Morse fiddled nervously with the directory. 'Are you there, sir? Yes, that's right. Last Friday. It's one of the first tickets issued. The doors opened at 1.15 and the programme started at 1.30. The first rear lounge number is 93543, so it must have been issued in the first five or ten minutes, I should think. There's usually half a dozen or so waiting for the doors to open.'

'You quite sure about this?'

'Quite sure, sir. You could come down and check if you wanted to.' She sounded young and pretty.

'Perhaps I will. What film have you got on?' He thought it sounded innocent enough.

'Not quite your cup of tea, I don't think, Inspector.'

'I wouldn't be too sure about that, miss.'

'*Mrs*. But if you do come, ask for me and I'll see you get a free seat.'

Morse wondered sadly how many more gift horses he'd be looking in the mouth. But it wasn't that at all really. He was just frightened of being seen. Now if she'd said . . .

But she said something else, and Morse jolted upright in his chair. 'I think I ought to mention, Inspector, that someone else asked me the very same sort of thing last week and . . .'

'*What?*' He almost screamed down the phone, but then his voice became very quiet. 'Say that again, will you, please?'

'I said someone else had— '

'When was this, do you remember?'

'I'm not quite sure; sometime – let's see, now. I ought to remember. It's not very often— '

'Was it Friday?' Morse was excited and impatient.

'I don't know. I'm trying to remember. It was in the afternoon, I remember that, because I was doing a stint in the ticket office when the phone rang, and I answered it myself.'

'Beginning of the afternoon?'

'No, it was much later than that. Just a minute. I think it was . . . Just a minute.' Morse heard some chattering in the background, and then the manageress's voice spoke in his ear once more. 'Inspector, I think it was in the late afternoon, sometime. About five, perhaps. I'm sorry I can't— '

'Could have been Friday, you think?'

'Ye-es. Or Saturday, perhaps. I just— '

'A man, was it?'

'Yes. He had a nice sort of voice. Educated – you know what I mean.'

'What did he ask you?'

'Well, it was funny really. He said he was a detective-story writer and he wanted to check up on some details.'

'What details.'

'Well, I remember he said he'd got to put some numbers on a ticket his detective had found, and he wanted to know how many figures there were – that sort of thing.'

'And you told him?'

'No, I didn't. I told him he could come round to see me, if he liked: but I felt a bit – well, you know, you can't be too careful these days.'

Morse breathed heavily down the phone. 'I see. Well, thank you very much. You've been extremely kind. I think, as I say, I shall probably have to bother you again— '

'No bother, Inspector.'

Morse put down the phone, and whistled softly to himself. Whew! Had someone else found Quinn's body and the cinema ticket before Tuesday morning? Long before? Saturday; the manageress had said it might have been Saturday. And it couldn't have been Friday, could it? About five, she'd said. Morse looked quickly again at the *Oxford Mail* and saw the times: *The Nympho-maniac*. 1.30 to 3.20 p.m. Until twenty-past three on Friday Quinn had been feasting his eyes on Inga Nielsson's mighty bosom and few things, surely, would have dragged him out of Studio 2 before the film had finished. Unless, of course . . . At long last it struck him: *the pretty strong probability that Quinn had not been sitting alone in Studio 2 that Friday afternoon.*

Chapter Thirteen

As Morse stood with Lewis in Pinewood Close at 2 p.m. on the following afternoon, awaiting the arrival of Mrs Jardine, he tried with little success to draw a veil over the harrowing events of the morning. Mr and Mrs Quinn had trained down from Huddersfield, and somewhere amid the wreckage of their lives, somewhere amid the tears and the heartbreak, they had managed to find reserves of quiet dignity and courage. Morse had accompanied Mr Quinn senior to the mortuary for the formal identification of his son, and then spent over an hour with them both in his office, unable to tell them much, unable to offer anything except the usual futile words of sympathy. And as Morse had watched the tragic couple climb into the police car for Oxford, he felt great admiration – and even greater relief. The whole interview had upset him, and apart from a few brief minutes with a reporter from the *Oxford Mail*, he had not been in the mood to grapple with the perpetually multiplying clues to the last hours lived by Nicholas Quinn.

Two men were repairing the street lamp in front of No 1, and Morse strolled over to them. 'How long before they come and smash it up again?'

'You never know, sir. But, to be truthful, we don't get too much vandalism round 'ere, do we, Jack?'

But Morse had no chance of hearing Jack's views on the local yahoos, for Mrs Jardine drew up in her car and the three of them disappeared into the house, where for half an hour they sat together in the front room. Mrs Jardine told them as much as she knew about her former tenant: about his coming to see her in mid-August; about her chat with Bartlett (Quinn's choice as referee); about his tidy habits and his punctuality in paying his rent; about his usual weekend routine; and about any and every thing Morse could think of asking her that might add to his picture of Mr Quinn alive. But he learned nothing. Quinn had been a model tenant, it seemed. Quiet, orderly, and no gramophone. Girl-friends? Not that she knew of. She couldn't stop that sort of thing, of course, but it was much better if her tenants – well, you know, *behaved* themselves. The others – upstairs? Oh, they got along well with Mr Quinn, she thought, though she couldn't really *know*, could she? What a good job Mrs Greenaway hadn't been there on Tuesday, though! You could never tell – with the *shock*. Yes, that had been a real blessing.

It was another chilly afternoon, and Morse got up to light the fire, turning the automatic switch on the side as far as he could. But nothing happened.

'You'll have to use a match, Inspector. Those things never seem to work. How the manufacturers get away with it— '

Morse struck a match and the fire exploded into an orange glow.

'Do you make any extra charge for gas and electricity?'

'No. It's included in the rent,' replied Mrs Jardine. But as if to dispel any possible suspicion of excessive generosity, she hastily added that the tenants had to share the telephone bill, of course.

Morse was puzzled. 'I don't quite follow you.'

'Well, there's a shared line between them, you see. There's a phone upstairs in the Greenaways' bedroom and one here in this room.'

'I see,' said Morse quietly.

After the landlady had left them, Morse and Lewis went into the room where Quinn had been found. Although the curtains were now drawn back, it seemed no less sombre than when they were in it last; and certainly colder. Morse bent down and tried turning the switch on the gas fire. He tried again; and again. But nothing.

'Probably no batteries in it, sir.' Lewis unfastened the side panel, and produced two stumpy Ever Ready batteries, now covered with a slimy, mildewed discharge.

* * *

The same Thursday morning Joyce Greenaway had been moved from the Intensive Care Unit at the John Radcliffe Hospital; and when one of her old schoolfriends came to see her at 2.30 p.m. she was in a pleasant ward, two storeys below, in the company of three other recently-delivered mothers. Conversation was babies, babies, babies, and Joyce felt buoyant. She should be out in a few days, and she felt a strangely-satisfying surge of maternal emotions developing deep within herself. How she loved her darling little boy! He was going to be fine – there was no doubt of that now. But the problem of what to call him remained unresolved. Frank had decided that he didn't really like 'Nicholas' all that much, and Joyce wanted *him* to make the choice. She herself wasn't all that smitten with the name, anyway. It had been awfully naughty of her to mention the name in the first place. But she'd just *had* to see if Frank had suspected anything; and despite her earlier fears she now felt convinced that he hadn't. Not that there was *much* to suspect.

It had started just after Nicholas had come, at the beginning of September, when he'd always seemed to be running out of matches, or sugar, or milk tokens; and he'd been so grateful, and so attentive towards her – and she over six months gone! Then that Saturday morning when *she* had been out of milk, with Frank on one of his everlasting shifts, and she had gone down in her nightie and housecoat, and they had sat for a long time drinking coffee together in the kitchen, and she had longed for him to kiss her. And he had, standing beside her with his hands on her shoulders, and then, after delicately unfastening her housecoat, putting his right hand deep inside her nightie and gently fondling her small firm breasts. It had happened three times after that, and she'd felt a deep tenderness towards him, for he made no other demands upon her body than to pass the tips of his fingers silkily over her legs and over her swollen belly. And just that once she had done more than passively lean back and surrender herself to the exquisite thrill that his hands could bring to her. Just the once – when so diffidently and so lightly, her outstretched fingers had caressed him. Oh yes, so very, very lightly! She had felt an enormous inner joy as he had finally buried his head on her shoulder, and the things she'd whispered to him then were now the focus of her conscience-stricken thoughts. But

Frank would never know, and she promised herself that never, never again would she . . . would she . . .

She was awoken by the clatter of cups at four o'clock, and a quarter of an hour later the trolley came round with books and newspapers. She bought the *Oxford Mail*.

Morse was a few minutes early for his appointment, but the Dean of the Syndicate was ready for him in his oak-panelled rooms on the Old Staircase in the inner quad, and the two men were chatting vaguely of this and that when at five past four a scout knocked and came in with a tray.

'I thought we'd have a drop of Darjeeling. All right with you?' The voice, like the man, was syrupy and civilized.

'Lovely,' said Morse, wondering what Darjeeling was.

The white-coated scout poured the dark-brown liquid into bone-china cups, embossed with the crest of Lonsdale College. 'Milk, sir?'

Morse watched it all with an amused detachment. The Dean, it seemed, always had a slice of lemon, and one half-teaspoonful of sugar, which the scout himself measured out, almost to the grain, and stirred in with high seriousness. The old boy probably got his scout to tie his shoe-laces up for him! Cloudcuckooland! Morse took a sip of the tea, sat back, and saw the Dean smiling at him shrewdly.

'You don't really approve, I see. Not that I blame you. He's been with me almost thirty years now, and he's almost— But, I'm sorry, I'm forgetting. You've come to see me about Mr Quinn. What can I tell you?'

The Dean was clearly a sensitive and cultured soul: he was due to retire in one year's time, at sixty-five, and was clearly saddened that the tragedy of Quinn's murder should have clouded a long and distinguished connection with the Syndicate. To Morse, it seemed a curiously self-centred commiseration.

'Would you say the Syndicate is a happy sort of place, sir?'

'Oh yes. I think everybody would tell you that.'

'No hostility? No er personal animosities?'

The Dean looked a little uneasy, and it was clear that he might have one or two reservations – minor ones, of course. 'There are always a few er difficulties. You find them in every er— '

'What difficulties?'

'Well – basically, I think, there'll always be just a little er friction, shall we say, between the older generation – my generation – and some of the younger Syndics. You always get it. It was just the same when I was their age.'

'The younger ones have their own ideas?'

'I'm glad they have.'

'Are you thinking of any particular incident?'

Again the Dean hesitated. 'You know the sort of thing as well as I do, surely? One or two people get a bit hot under the collar now and again.'

'Has this got anything to do with Mr Quinn?'

'Quite honestly, Chief Inspector, I think not. You see, one of the incidents I'm thinking of happened before Quinn was appointed – in fact it happened when we were appointing him.' He gave a brief account of the interviewing committee's disagreement over the choice of candidates, and Morse listened with deep interest.

'You mean Bartlett didn't want to appoint Quinn?'

The Dean shook his head. 'You misunderstand me. The Secretary was quite happy about him. But, as I say, personally he would have given the job to one of the others.'

'What about you, sir? What did you feel?'

'I er I thought the Secretary was right.'

'So Mr Roope was the fly in the ointment?'

'No, no. You still misunderstand me. Quinn was appointed by the *committee* – not by Roope.'

'Look, sir. Please be quite frank with me. Would I be right in saying that there's not much love lost between Bartlett and Roope?'

'Aren't you enjoying your tea, Chief Inspector? You've hardly touched a drop yet.'

'You're not going to answer my question, sir?'

'I really do think it would be fairer if you asked *them*, don't you?'

Morse nodded, and drained the luke-warm liquid. 'What about the permanent staff? Any er friction there?'

'Amongst the graduates, you mean? N-o, I don't think so.'

'You sound a bit dubious.'

The Dean sat back and slowly finished his own tea, and Morse realized he would have to push his luck a bit.

'Miss Height, for instance?'

'A lovely girl.'

'You mean we can't blame the others too much if . . . '

'If there's any of er of that sort of thing going on, I can only say that I know nothing about it.'

'Rumours, though?'

'We've all got more sense than to listen to rumours.'

'Have we?' But it was clear that the Dean was not to be drawn, and Morse switched the line of his questioning once more. 'What about Bartlett? Is he well liked?'

The Dean looked at Morse keenly, and carefully poured out more tea. 'What do you mean?'

'I just wondered if any of the other graduates had any cause to – to, you know— ' Morse didn't know what he wondered; but the Dean, it seemed, did.

'I suppose you're thinking of Ogleby?'

Morse nodded sagely, and tried to ooze omniscience. 'Yes, it was Mr Ogleby I was wondering about.'

'That's ancient history, though, isn't it? It's a long time ago, now. Huh! I remember at the time thinking that Ogleby was potentially the better man. In fact, I voted for him. But with hindsight I'm sure that Bartlett was the wiser choice, and we were all very glad that Ogleby was willing to accept the post of Deputy Secretary. Very able man. I'm quite sure that if he'd wanted to, he . . . ' The Dean talked freely now, and Morse felt his own attention drifting further and further away. So. Bartlett and Ogleby had applied for the Secretaryship together, and Ogleby had been turned down; and perhaps the slight had rankled on and on over the years – might still be rankling on. But what on earth could that have to do with the murder of Quinn? If Bartlett had been murdered – or even Ogleby – yes! But . . .

The Dean stood at the window and watched Morse walk briskly around the quad. He knew that for the last ten minutes his words had fallen on deaf ears, and for the life of him he was completely unable to fathom the look of quiet contentment which had so suddenly appeared on the Chief Inspector's face.

Lewis finished his own cup of tea and was leaving the police canteen as Dickson walked in.

'I see you're appealing for help, Sarge. Old Morse stuck, is he?'

He handed Lewis the *Oxford Mail* and pointed to a paragraph at the bottom of the front page:

MURDER INQUIRY

Police investigating the murder of Mr N. Quinn, 1 Pinewood Close, Kidlington, whose body was found on Tuesday morning by a colleague from the Foreign Examinations Syndicate, are appealing to anyone who may have seen the murdered man on either the evening of Friday, 21st November, or on Saturday, 22nd November, to come forward. Chief Inspector Morse, who is heading the inquiry, said today that any such information could be vital in establishing the time of Mr Quinn's death. An inquest will be held next Monday.

Lewis looked at the photograph beside the article, and handed the paper back to Dickson. In his inside pocket was the original which Morse had asked the Quinns to bring with them from Huddersfield. Sometimes, he had to agree, Morse *did* take on the dirty work; compared to which his present little assignment was a doddle.

He soon found the young manager and learned that the flimsy short roll of paper he had brought with him was a richly-seamed mine of information: the date at the top; the 'customer-reading' number on the right; the items purchased, each classified according to the various departments, and designated by one of the Roman numerals I-IV; the number of the till at the bottom. 'Customer flow' (Lewis learned) was fairly constant on Fridays, with high takings for most of the day, and (though the manager refused to be precise) the items listed had doubtless been purchased in the late afternoon or early evening. If he had to guess? Well, between 5 and 6.30 p.m. Unfortunately, however, the plump waddling little woman who was summoned in her capacity as i/c Till 3 could remember nothing, and failed to register even the vaguest recollection of ever having seen the face on the photograph she was shown. It was the goods she always watched, you see; seldom the faces.

Ah well!

Lewis thanked the manager and left the Kidlington premises of the *Quality* supermarket. Morse wouldn't be too pleased, perhaps, but all the clues seemed to be fitting into a firm, clear pattern.

* * *

'But why why *why* didn't you tell me? You must have realized— '

'Come off it, Joyce! You *know* why. It would have upset you, and we've— '

'It wouldn't have been half such a shock as reading about it in the paper!'

He shook his head sadly. 'I just thought I was doing right, luv. That's all. Sometimes you just can't win, can you?'

'No, I suppose not.' She understood all right, but she knew that *he* didn't. How could he?

'As I say, there's no need to worry about *anything*. When you're better again, we can talk about things. But not now. It'll soon all blow over – you see; and we're all fixed up for the time being.'

No, he couldn't begin to understand. He was trying hard not to put it into so many words, but he'd got it all wrong. The fact was that she hadn't as yet given a single thought as to whether they should go back to live in Pinewood Close or not. No. There was something much more urgent on her mind for the minute, and of that she would tell him nothing. Not yet anyway.

Chapter Fourteen

Christopher Roope had willingly agreed to meet Morse, on Friday just after 12 noon, at the Black Dog in St Aldates, just opposite the great portal of Christ Church. Roope had mentioned that he might be a few minutes late – he had a tutorial until twelve – but Morse waited happily with a pint of beer in front of him. He looked forward to meeting the young chemist, for if any outsider was involved in the murder of Quinn, he'd decided that Roope was the likeliest candidate, and already he had gleaned a few significant facts about him. First, he had learned that Roope had spent some time with one of the Gulf Petroleum companies, and might therefore have been in some sort of liaison with the men of power. For a deal there must have been at some stage, doubtless (though later) involving Bland at the Oxford end, in a perverse, though infinitely profitable, betrayal of public trust. It was certainly a possibility. Second, Roope was a chemist: and whoever had murdered Quinn had a great deal of technical knowledge about the fatal dosages of cyanide. Who better than Roope? Third, it was Roope who had suddenly materialized in the Syndicate building at a very, very crucial time – 4.30 p.m. or thereabouts (according to Noakes) on the previous Friday; and it was Roope who had looked into the rooms of each of the graduate staff in turn. What exactly had he been doing there? And what had he done after Noakes had gone upstairs for tea . . . ? Fourth, there was the strange animosity that existed between Roope and Bartlett, and it appeared to Morse that the explanation for such animosity probably lay deeper, far deeper, than any temporary clash of views over the appointment of Quinn. Yes . . . It was interesting that the clash had been over *Quinn*. And that fitted well with the fifth fact, which Morse had patiently unearthed earlier that morning in the University Registry: the fact that Roope had been educated at a public school in Bradford, the city where Quinn had lived almost all his short life, first as a pupil and then as a teacher. Had the two men known each other before Quinn was appointed to the Syndicate? And why had Roope been so obviously anxious to get Quinn appointed? (Morse found himself dismissing the Dean's charitable view of his colleague's social conscience.) Why, then? Now, Quinn had been thirty-one and Roope was thirty, and if they had been friends . . . Yet where was the logic in that? One didn't go around murdering one's friends. Unless, that is—

A trio of laughing, long-haired, bearded undergraduates came into the bar, T-shirted and bejeaned, and Morse pondered on the changing times. He had worn a scarf and a tie himself – and sometimes a blazer. But that seemed a long time ago. He drained his glass and looked at his watch.

'Chief Inspector Morse?' It was one of the bearded trio and Morse realized that he was a good deal further out of touch than he had imagined.

'Mr Roope?'

The young man nodded. 'Can I get you a refill?'

'I'll get them— '

'No, no. My pleasure. What are you drinking?'

Over their beer a somewhat bemused Morse explained as

much of the situation as he deemed prudent, and stressed the importance of trying to fix the exact time of Quinn's death. And when he came to ask about the visit to the Syndicate on the previous Friday, Morse was pleasantly impressed to find how carefully and indeed (if Noakes could be believed) how accurately Roope retraced his steps from the moment he had entered the building. All in all, Roope and Noakes appeared to corroborate each other's evidence neatly at almost every juncture. Yet there were several points on which Roope's memory seemed somewhat less than clear, and on which Morse immediately pressed him further.

'You say there was a note on Quinn's desk?'

'Yes. I'm sure the caretaker must have seen it too. We both— '

'But you don't remember exactly what it said?'

Roope was silent for a few seconds. 'Not really. Something about – oh, I don't know – "being back soon", I think.'

'And Quinn's anorak was on one of the chairs?'

'That's right. Over the back of the chair behind his desk.'

'You didn't notice if it was wet?'

Roope shook his head.

'And the cabinets were open, you say?'

'One of them was, I'm sure of that. The caretaker pushed it to and locked it.'

'Bit unusual for a cabinet to be left open – with Bartlett around, I mean?' Morse watched the chemist closely, but discerned no reaction.

'Yes.' And then Roope grinned disarmingly. 'Bit of a sod, you know, old Bartlett. Keeps 'em all on their toes.' He lit himself a cigarette and put the spent match carefully back into the box with his left hand.

'How do *you* get on with him, sir?'

'Me?' Roope laughed aloud. 'We don't see eye to eye, I'm afraid. I suppose you've heard—?'

'I gathered you weren't exactly bosom pals.'

'Oh, I wouldn't put it like that. You mustn't believe everything you hear.'

Morse let it ride. 'Mr Ogleby wasn't in his room, you say?'

'Not while I was there.'

Morse nodded, and believed him. 'How long *were* you there, sir?'

'Quarter of an hour, I suppose. Must have been. If Ogleby

or any of the others were there – well, I just didn't see them, that's all. And I'm pretty sure I would have done if they *had* been there.'

Morse nodded again. 'I think you're right, sir. I don't think anyone *was* there.' His mind drifted off, and for a brief second one of the silhouettes on the cavern wall focused in full profile – a profile that Morse thought he could recognize without much difficulty . . .

Roope interrupted his thoughts. 'Anything else I can tell you?'

Morse drained his beer and said there was. He asked Roope to account for his activities during the whole of the previous Friday, and Roope gladly obliged: he had caught the 8.05 to London; arrived at Paddington at 9.10; caught the Inner Circle tube to Mansion House; conferred with his publishers about the final proofs of a forthcoming opus on Industrial Chemistry; left about 10.45; had a chicken salad in the Strand somewhere; spent an hour or so in the National Portrait Gallery in Trafalgar Square; and then returned to Paddington, where he'd caught the 15.05 for Oxford.

Morse himself couldn't have specified the reason, but suddenly he became convinced that somehow, somewhere, Roope was lying. It was all too pat, too slick. A good deal of it must be true (the bit about the publishers, for instance). Mm. He'd obviously gone to London all right; but exactly when had he returned? Roope said he'd left his publishers at about 10.45 a.m. A taxi to Paddington, perhaps? Easy! *Roope could have been back in Oxford before lunchtime.* 'Just as a matter of interest, sir' (he asked it very mildly), 'do you think you could prove all that?'

Roope looked at him sharply. 'I don't suppose I could, no.' The eyes were steady and steely.

'You didn't meet anyone you knew in London?'

'I told you. I went to see— '

'Of course. But I meant later.'

'No, I didn't.' The words were slow and evenly spaced, and Morse sensed that in spite of his slim build and his rather mannered trendiness, Roope was probably considerably tougher, both physically and mentally, than he appeared to be. One thing was sure: he wasn't very happy when his word was questioned. Was that perhaps why he and Bartlett . . . ?

'Well, never mind that now, sir. Tell me something else,

if you will. Did you know Quinn before he came to Oxford?'
'No.'
'You come from that part of the country though, don't you?'
'You mean I haven't got an Oxford accent?'
'I'd put you down as a Yorkshireman.'
'You've done your homework, I see.'
'That's what they pay me for, sir.'
'I'm from Bradford, and so was Quinn. But let me spell it out.
I'd never set eyes on him until he came before the interviewing
committee. Do you believe that?'
'I believe everything you tell me, sir. Why shouldn't I?'
'You'd be a fool to believe everything some people told you.'
There was little pretence now at masking the hostility in his voice,
and Morse was beginning to enjoy himself.
'I think you ought to know,' said Morse quietly, 'that whatever
else I am, I'm not a fool, sir.'
Roope made no reply and Morse resumed his questioning.
'Have you got a car?'
'No. I used to have, but I only live just up the Woodstock
Road— '
'That's the bachelor flats, isn't it?'
Roope suddenly relaxed and smiled ingenuously. 'Look, Inspec-
tor, why don't you ask me something you *don't* know?'
Morse shrugged his shoulders. 'All right. Tell me this. Was
it raining when you came back from London?'
'Raining like hell, yes. I— ' Suddenly the light dawned in
his eyes. 'Yes. I got a *taxi* from the station – straight to the
Syndicate. There'll be a record of that somewhere, surely?'
'Do you remember the driver?'
'No. But I think I remember the cab firm.'
Roope was right, of course. It shouldn't be all that difficult.
'We could try to— '
'Why not?' Roope got to his feet and picked up a pile of
books. 'No time like the present, they say.'
As they walked up to Carfax and then left into Queen Street,
Morse felt that he had gone wrong somewhere, and he said nothing
until they reached the railway station, where a line of taxis was
parked alongside the pavement. 'You'd better leave it to me, sir.
I've got a bit of experience— '
'I'd rather do it myself, if you don't mind, Inspector.'

So Morse left him to get on with it; and stood there waiting under the 'Buffet' sign, feeling (he told himself) like the proverbial spare part at a prostitute's wedding.

Five minutes later a crestfallen Roope rejoined him: it wasn't going to be so easy as he'd thought, though he'd still like to do it himself, if Morse didn't mind, that was. But why should Morse mind? If the young fellow was as anxious as all that to justify himself . . . 'Like another beer?'

They walked through the ticket area and came to the barrier.

'We only want a beer,' explained Morse.

' 'Fraid you'll need platform tickets, sir.'

'Ach, bugger that,' said Morse. He turned to Roope: 'Let's walk down to the Royal Oxford.'

'Just a minute!' said Roope quietly. His eyes were shining again, and he retraced his steps and tapped the ticket collector on the shoulder. 'Do you remember me?'

'Don't think so, mate.'

'Were you here on duty last Friday afternoon?'

'No.' (Dismissive.)

'Do you know who was?'

'You'd have to ask in the office.'

'Where's that?'

The man pointed vaguely. 'Not much good now, though. Lunchtime, isn't it?'

Clearly it wasn't Roope's day, and Morse put a sympathetic hand on his shoulder, and turned to the ticket collector. 'Give us two of your platform tickets.'

Half an hour later, after Roope had left him, Morse sat deep in thought and, to the teenaged couple who came to sit opposite him at the narrow buffet table, his face seemed quite impassive. Yet had they looked more carefully at him, and rather less eagerly towards each other, they might just have spotted the mildest hint of a satisfied smile trying to hide itself around the corners of his mouth. He sat quite still, his eyes staring unblinkingly into some great blue beyond, as the unresting birds of thought winged round and round his brain . . . until the London train came lumbering massively alongside the platform and finally broke the spell.

The young couple got up, kissed briefly but passionately, and said their fond farewells.

'I won't come on the platform,' he said. 'Always makes me miserable.'

'Yeah. You ge' off now. See you Sat'day.'

'You bet!'

The girl walked off in her high-heeled boots towards the door leading to Platform 1, and the boy watched her as she went, and fished for his platform ticket.

'Don't forge'. *I'll* bring the drinks this time.' She almost mouthed the words, but the boy understood and nodded. Then she was gone; and Morse felt the icy fingers running down from the top of his spine. *That* was the memory that had been eluding him. Yes! It all came back in a rushing stream of recollection. He'd been an undergraduate then and he'd invited the flighty little nurse back to his digs in Iffley Road and she'd insisted on bringing a bottle because her father kept a pub and she'd asked him what his favourite drink was and he'd said Scotch and she'd said it was hers too not so much because she enjoyed the taste but because it made her feel all sexy and . . . Christ, yes!

Morse shut off the distant, magic memories. The main silhouette was growing blurred again; but others now appeared upon the wall of the darkened cave, and together they fell into a more logical grouping. Much more logical. And as Morse handed in his platform ticket and walked out into the bright afternoon, he was more firmly convinced than ever that *someone else* had been in Studio 2 that Friday afternoon. He looked at his watch: 1.45 p.m. Tempting. By Jove, yes! The cinema was only three or four minutes' walk away, and Inga would be showing 'em all a few tricks. Ah well.

He signalled for a taxi: 'Foreign Examinations Syndicate, please.'

Chapter Fifteen

'I don't care what you ask her,' snapped Morse. 'When I've fetched her in here, just keep her talking for ten minutes, that's all I ask.' Lewis, who half an hour previously had been summoned to the Syndicate building once more, looked inordinately uncomfortable. 'What do you want me to find out, though?'

'Anything you like. Ask her what her measurements are.'

'I wish you'd try to be serious, sir.'

'Well, ask her whether gin goes straight to her tits, or something.'

Lewis decided he would get nowhere with Morse in such a mood. What had happened to him? Something, surely; for suddenly he seemed as chirpy as a disc jockey.

Morse himself crossed the corridor, knocked on Monica's door, and went in. 'Can you spare a minute, Miss Height? Won't take long.' He escorted her politely to Quinn's office, showed her to the chair that faced Lewis, her reluctant interlocutor, and himself stood idly aside.

The phone went a few moments later and Lewis answered it. 'For you, sir.'

'Morse here.'

'Ah, Inspector. Can I see you for a minute? It's er rather important. Can you come along straightaway?'

'I'm on my way.'

Both Lewis and Monica had heard the voice plainly, and Morse excused himself without further explanation.

Once inside Monica's office, he worked swiftly. First, the bulky sheepskin jacket hanging up in the wall cupboard. Nothing much in either pocket – nothing much of interest, anyway. Next, the handbag. It would surely be here, if anywhere. Make-up, cheque book, diary, Paper-mate pen, comb, small bottle of perfume, pair of ear-rings, programme for a forthcoming performance of *The Messiah*, packet of Dunhill cigarettes, matches – and a purse. His hands trembled slightly as he opened the catch and poked his fingers amidst the small change and the keys and the stamps and – *there it was*. Ye gods. He'd been right! He was breathing nervously and noisily as he closed the handbag, placed it carefully back in its former position, left the room, closed the door quietly behind

him, and stood alone in the corridor. He saw the implications –
the extraordinarily grave implications – of the discovery he had
just made. Certainly he'd been fairly sure that with a bit of luck
he might find something. Yet now he'd found it, he knew there
was something wrong, something that rang untrue, something that
had not occurred to him before. Still, there was a quick way of
finding out.

He hadn't been away for more than two or three minutes,
and Lewis was relieved to see him back so soon. He sat on
the corner of the table and looked at her. There were times (not
very frequent, he admitted) when he seemed to lose all interest in
the female sex, and this was one of them. She might as well have
been a statue cast in frigid marble for all the effect she was having
on him now. It happened to all men – or, at least, so Morse had
heard. The womenopause, they called it. He took a deep breath.
'Why did you lie to me about last Friday afternoon?'

Monica's cheeks flushed a deep crimson, but she was not,
it appeared, excessively surprised. 'It was Sally, wasn't it? I
realized, of course, what your man was up to.'

'Well?'

'I don't know. I suppose it sounded less – less sordid, somehow,
saying we went to my place.'

'Less sordid than what?'

'You know – motoring around, stopping in lay-bys and hoping
no one else would pull in.'

'And that's what you did?'

'Yes.'

'Would Mr Martin back you up?'

'Yes. If you explained to him why— '

'You mean *you* haven't done that already?' The tone of Morse's
voice was becoming increasingly harsh, and Monica coloured
deeply again.

'Don't you think we ought to ask him?'

'No I don't! You've got him round your little finger, woman!
Anyone can see that. I'm not interested in your web of lies. I
want the truth! We're investigating a murder – not a bloody
parking offence!'

'Look, Inspector. I can't do much more than tell you— '

'Of course you can! You can tell me the *truth*.'

'You seem terribly sure of— '

'And so I am, woman! What the hell do you think *that* is?'
He banged his right hand furiously on the top of the desk, and
revealed the torn-off half of a cinema ticket. Across the top were
the letters IO, and almost immediately after them the number 2;
beneath were the words 'Rear Lounge', and along the right-hand
edge, running downwards, were the numbers 93556.

Monica looked down at the ticket as if mesmerized.

'Well?'

'I suppose it was *you* who arranged the little charade on
the phone with Dr Bartlett?'

'I've done worse in my time,' said Morse. And suddenly,
and quite inexplicably, he felt a surge of sympathy and warmth
towards her, and his tone softened as he looked into her eyes:
'It'll come out in the end – you know that. Please let me have
the truth.'

Monica sighed deeply. 'Do you mind getting me a cigarette,
Inspector. As I think you know, mine are in my handbag.'

Yes (she said) Morse had been right. With Sally back from
school that afternoon, there was no chance of going home, and
she wasn't that keen, in any case. The whole thing was her fault
quite as much as Donald's, of course; but recently she had been
increasingly anxious to end the futile and dangerous affair. It was
Donald who suggested they should go to the cinema and she had
finally agreed. It would be an unnecessary risk to be seen going
in together, and so it was arranged that he should go in at twenty
past one, and she a few minutes later. They would each buy a ticket
separately, and he would sit on the back row of the rear lounge
in Studio 2 and watch out for her. And that's what they'd done.
Everything had gone as planned, and they had left the cinema at
about half-past three. They'd each taken their car, and hers had
been parked in Cranham Terrace, at the side of the cinema. She
herself had gone straight home afterwards, and so, for all she
knew, had Donald. Naturally they'd both been worried when they
heard that the police wanted to know their whereabouts on Friday
afternoon, and so they'd foolishly – well, Morse knew what they'd
done. It wasn't all that far from the truth, though, was it? But, yes,
they'd lied about that Friday afternoon. Of course, they had.

'Do you mind if we get your boy-friend in?' asked Morse.

'I think it would be better if you did.' She looked a little
happier now, in spite of the jibe – certainly happier than Morse.

* * *

Pathetically Martin himself began to repeat the unauthorized version, but Monica stopped him. 'Tell them the truth, Donald. *I* just have. They know exactly where we both were on Friday afternoon.'

'Oh. Oh, I see.'

Morse felt his morale sagging ever lower as Martin stumbled his way through the same cheap little story. No discrepancy anywhere. He, like Monica it seemed, had gone straight home afterwards. And that was that.

'One more question.' Morse got up from the edge of the table and leaned against the nearest cabinet. It was a vital question – *the* vital question, and he wanted to witness their immediate reactions. 'Let me ask you both once again – did either of you see Mr Quinn on Friday afternoon? Please think very, very carefully before you answer.'

But it seemed that neither of them had any wish to think unduly carefully. Their faces registered blank. They shook their heads, and with apparent simplicity and earnestness they said that they hadn't.

Morse took another deep breath. He might as well tell them, he thought – that is, if they didn't know it already. 'Would it surprise you both if I told you that . . . ' (Morse hesitated – dramatically, he hoped) 'that there was another of your colleagues in Studio 2 last Friday afternoon?'

Martin turned deathly pale, and Monica opened her mouth like a chronic asthmatic fighting for breath. Morse (as he later realized) would have been wiser if he had allowed his little speech to take its full effect. But he didn't. 'You may well look surprised. You see, we know exactly where Mr Quinn was on Friday afternoon. He was sitting along with the pair of you – in the rear lounge of Studio 2!'

Donald Martin and Monica Height stared at him in stupefied astonishment.

After they had gone, Morse turned to Lewis: 'That'll give 'em something to think about.'

But Lewis was feeling far from happy, and he said so. 'I hope you'll forgive me, sir, but— '

'C'mon, Lewis. Out with it!'

'Well. I don't think you handled it very well.' He sat back and waited for the explosion.

'Nor do I,' said Morse quietly. 'Go on.'

'You see, sir, I had the impression that when you said one of the others was in the cinema – well, they didn't seem *surprised* at all. It was almost as if— '

'I know what you mean. It was almost as if they expected me to say someone else, wasn't it?'

Lewis nodded vigorously. 'But they really *were* surprised when you said it was Quinn.'

'Ye-es. You're right. And there's only one other person it could have been, isn't there? Bartlett was in Banbury that afternoon.'

'We haven't checked on that.'

'I don't think we shall have much trouble in finding a few headmasters to back up his alibi. No, I don't think there's much doubt where Bartlett was that afternoon.'

'That leaves Ogleby, then, sir.'

Morse nodded.

'Shall I go and fetch him, sir?'

'What do you think?' Morse's customary confidence had deserted him, and Lewis got up and walked to the door. 'No, Lewis. Leave it a while, please. I want to think things through a bit more carefully.'

Lewis shrugged his shoulders with some impatience and sat down again. Morse didn't seem quite the man he had been, one way or another; but Lewis knew from previous experience that it wouldn't be long before something happened. Something was always happening when Morse was around.

And even as Lewis righteously reviewed the perfectly valid points he had just been making, Morse himself was conscious of an even greater failure in his own powers of logical analysis. Clown of a clown! Martin and Monica Height! Why had they ever told that abject lie in the first place? There was every risk (with Sally home so often) that even a moderately competent detective would pretty soon ferret out the truth about that. Why, then? And suddenly the answer presented itself, pellucidly clear: *there was an even greater risk about telling the truth*. If they had gone to the cinema together, why not say so? It seemed an infinitely less reprehensible piece of behaviour than the sordid liaison to which they had both been prepared to admit. People *did* go to the pictures together. It would cause a bit of talk – of course it would – if someone saw them. But . . . The silhouetted figures once again reformed, and they were all now grouping around one man. Around Philip Ogleby.

'You're right, you know, Lewis. Go and fetch him straightaway.'

After they had left Quinn's office, Donald and Monica had stood silent for a few seconds in the polished corridor. 'Come in a second,' whispered Monica. She closed her own office door behind her, and looked at him fiercely. She spoke clearly and quietly, and with a force that was impressive. 'We don't say a word about it. Is that clear? *Not a single word!*'

Chapter Sixteen

Ogleby looked tired, and Morse decided he might as well be short and sharp. He knew he was taking a risk, but he'd played longer shots before – *and* won.

'You say, sir, that you came back to the office after lunch last Friday afternoon?'

'We've been over that before.'

Morse ignored him and continued. 'But you lied to me. You were seen outside this office last Friday afternoon. To be precise, you were seen going into Studio 2 in Walton Street.'

Ogleby sat placidly in his chair. He seemed in no way surprised; indeed, if anyone were surprised it was Morse, who expected almost anything except the answer he received, 'Who saw me?'

'You don't deny it?'

'I asked you who it was that saw me.'

'I'm afraid I can't tell you that, sir. I'm sure you understand why.'

Ogleby nodded disinterestedly. 'As you wish.'

'We also have evidence, sir, that Mr Quinn was in Studio 2 that afternoon.'

'Really? Did somebody see him, too?'

Morse felt progressively less at ease with the man. It was one of the troubles with lies – his own lies; but he solved the problem by ignoring it. 'What time did you go to the cinema, sir?'

'Don't you know?' (There it was again!)

'I'd like your own statement.'

For a few seconds Ogleby appeared to be weighing the pros and cons of coming clean. 'Look, Inspector. In a way I suppose I lied to you a little.' (Lewis was scribbling as fast as he could.) 'We finish here, officially that is, at five. I try to put in my time as honestly as I can, and I think anyone you speak to here will confirm that. I'm never late, and I often work well after the rest have gone. On Friday, I agree, I left a bit early. I should think about a quarter-to five or so.'

'And you went to Studio 2.'

'I live in Walton Street, you know. It's not far away.'

'You went there?'

Ogleby shook his head. 'No.'

'Will you tell me why you went?'

'I didn't.'

'Have you ever been?'

'Yes.'

'Why?'

'I'm a lecherous old man.'

Morse switched his line of attack. 'Were you still here when Mr Roope came into the building?'

'Yes. I heard him talking to the caretaker.'

Again it was the answer that Morse had least expected, and he felt increasingly bewildered. 'But you weren't in your room. Your car— '

'I didn't come in a car on Friday.'

'You didn't see Quinn – in the cinema, I mean?'

'I wasn't in the cinema.'

'Did you see Miss Height and Mr Martin there?'

Surprise certainly registered now. 'Were *they* there?' Morse could have sworn that Ogleby had not known of *that*, at any rate, and in a blindingly perverse sort of way, he felt very tempted to believe the man. 'Did you enjoy the film, sir?'

'I didn't see it.'

'You enjoy pornographic films, though?'

'I've sometimes thought that if I were a film producer I'd make something *really* erotic, Inspector. I think I've got the right sort of imagination.'

'You didn't keep your ticket?'
'I didn't have a ticket.'
'Will you look for it, sir?'
'Not much point, is there?'
Whew!

Morse decided that he might as well go the whole hog now.
Few secrets could be kept for long in a place like the Syndicate,
and he realized that he would be losing nothing – might in fact
be gaining – by coming out into the open.

With Ogleby gone, he invited Bartlett along to Quinn's office,
and told him what he had learned that afternoon: told him of the
deserted office he had left behind him when he'd gone to Banbury;
told him of the mammary magnetism of Miss Inga Nielsson; told
him of his difficulties in establishing the whereabouts of everyone
on that Friday afternoon; told him, indeed, most of what he
knew, or suspected, to be true. It wasn't really giving much away,
for most of it would have to come out in the wash fairly soon
anyway. Finally, he told Bartlett that he would be grateful of a
more accurate timetable of *his* movements; and all in all Bartlett
hadn't taken things too badly. He could (he said) so very easily
establish his own whereabouts; and there and then he rang the
Head of Banbury Polytechnic and put him straight on to Morse.
Yes, Bartlett had addressed a meeting of Heads; had arrived about
five to three; together they had taken a glass of sherry; and the
meeting was over about twenty, twenty-five past four. That was
that, it seemed.

Bartlett asked if he was allowed to make his own observations
on what he'd been told, and it was quite obvious that he was a
far shrewder judge of his fellows than Morse had given him credit
for. 'I'm not *all* that surprised, Inspector, about Miss Height and
Martin. She's a very attractive girl: she's attractive to me, and
I'm getting an old man; and Martin hasn't had the happiest of
marriages, so I'm led to believe. There have been the occasional
rumours, of course; but I've said nothing. I hoped it was just one
of those brief infatuations – we've all had them in our time, and
I thought it best to let it blow itself out. But – but, I must be
honest, I'm very surprised by what you told me about Ogleby.
It just doesn't seem to fit in. I've known him many years now,
and he's – well, he's not like that.'

'We've all got our little weaknesses, sir.'

'No, you misunderstand me. I didn't mean whether he'd want to go to a sexy film or not. I've often . . . Well, never mind about that. No. It was about him saying he was *here*. You see, he's just not the sort of man who lies about things, and yet you say he insists that he was here when Roope came.'

'That's what he says.'

'And Roope says he wasn't in his own office, or anywhere around?'

'The caretaker backs him up.'

'He might have been upstairs.'

'I don't think so. Mr Ogleby himself says he heard Roope come in.'

Bartlett shook his head slowly and frowned. 'What do the girls say?'

'What girls?'

'The girls who collect the out-trays.'

Morse mentally kicked himself. 'What time are the trays collected?'

'Four o'clock every afternoon. The Post Office van is usually here about four-fifteen, and we like to have everything ready before then.'

I bet you do, thought Morse.

Bartlett rang through to the Registry and almost immediately a young, fair-haired girl came in and tried to keep her head as Morse questioned her. She had collected the trays on Friday afternoon. Yes, at four o'clock. And no one was there. Neither Ogleby, nor Miss Height, nor Martin, nor Quinn. No, she was *quite* sure. She'd mentioned to the other girls how odd it seemed.

Bartlett watched her distastefully as she left. He was wondering exactly how much work the 'other girls' had been doing when his back was turned.

Morse, as he walked slowly up the corridor with Bartlett, realized how very little he knew about the tangled complexity of relationships within the office. 'I'd like to have a long chat with you sometime, sir – about the office, I mean. There are so many things— '

'Why not come out and have a meal with us? My wife's a jolly good cook, you'll find. What about it?'

'That's very kind of you, sir. When do you suggest?'

'Well. Any time, really. Tonight, if you like.'

'Your wife— '

'Oh, don't worry about that. Leave it to me.' He disappeared into his office, and returned a couple of minutes later. 'Do you like steak, Inspector?'

As they walked to the car, both Lewis and Morse were deep in thought. The case was throwing up enough clues to solve a jumbo crossword, but somehow they wouldn't quite fit into the diagram.

'Nice fellow, Bartlett,' ventured Lewis, as they drove along the Woodstock Road towards the ring-road perimeter.

Morse did not reply. Bit too nice, perhaps, he was thinking. Far too nice, really. Like one of those suspects in a detective story who like as not turns out to be the crook. Was it possible! Was there any way in which the sturdy, shrewd, efficient little Secretary could have contrived the murder of Nicholas Quinn? As Lewis picked up speed down the long hill towards Kidlington, Morse began to see that there *was* a way. It would have been fiendishly clever; but then for all Morse knew . . . Oxford was full of clever people, wasn't it? And all at once it occurred to Morse that he was in very real danger of underestimating *all* of those he'd interviewed so far. Why, even now, perhaps, they were all sitting there quietly laughing at him.

Chapter Seventeen

Morse sat alone in his office. It was over two and a half hours before he was due at the Bartletts' and he welcomed the solitude and the chance to think.

The groceries which Quinn had purchased and the list of the provisions found in his kitchen proved more interesting than Morse had expected. Two pieces of steak and a bag of mushrooms, for instance. Bit extravagant, for one person? Might it have been for *two*? Two lovers? Morse pictured again the girl at the buffet door that led to Platform 1, and she merged into the figure of Monica Height. Could it have worked? Monica now admitted going to the cinema – with Martin, though. Could he forget Martin? Spineless creature. And so besotted with Monica that he'd say anything – if she told him to, or bribed him to. Think on, Morse! Monica and *Quinn*, then. Back row of the rear lounge; awkward unfastenings and frenetic fondlings, with the promise of still more glorious things in store – later. Later, yes. But where? Not at her place: impossible with Sally around. Why not at *his*? He could get some food in (steak? mushrooms?), and she would cook it for him. She'd love to. 'And don't forget, Nick, *I'll* bring the drinks this time. Sherry, isn't it? Dry sherry? I like that, too. And I'll bring a bottle of Scotch, as well. It always does things to me . . . ' Possible. A starting point anyway.

Morse looked at the two lists again, and noticed a fact he'd missed before. Quinn already had two ½-pound packs of butter in his fridge, yet for some reason he'd bought another. Different brand, too. Very odd. Like a few other facts. He took a piece of paper and wrote them down:

(a) Position of Quinn's coffee table indicated that he'd probably been sitting in the draught. (Steady, Sherlock!)
(b) No spent matches found in either kitchen or living room; no matches found in Quinn's pockets (Remember: Mrs E had already cleaned; she'd only returned for the ironing and had *not* cleared the waste-paper basket again.)
(c) More butter bought, when plenty in stock. (Forget it?)
(d) Note left by Quinn for Mrs E: vague enough to fit virtually any occasion? (Not *all* that vague though.)

Morse sat back and looked at his handiwork. Individually each point seemed pretty thin; but collectively – did they add up to something? Something like assuming that *Quinn did not return from work at all that Friday evening*? Had it been somebody else who lit the fire, and bought the groceries, and wrote a note for Mrs Evans? Think on, Morse! Think on, my boy! It was possible. Another starting point. Could the mysterious somebody have been Monica? (His mind kept coming back to her.) But she must have gone home to Sally sometime. (Job for Lewis – check.) Martin? He must have gone home to his wife sometime. When? (Job for Lewis – check.) And anyway, neither of them knew enough about cyanide, did they? Poisoning was a highly specialized job. (A woman's weapon, though.) Now, Roope was a chemist. And Ogleby knew enough . . . Roope or Ogleby – a much likelier pair to choose from. But Roope was out of Oxford until about 4.15 p.m. (Or so he said.) And Ogleby went home a bit early. (Or so he said.) Mm. And what about Bartlett? Kidlington was on the main road from Banbury, and the main road passed no more than thirty yards from Pinewood Close. If he'd left Banbury at 4.25 p.m. and really pushed it, 70 mph say, he could have been in Kidlington by, well, ten to five? Opportunity enough for any of them really. For if Quinn had discovered that one of the four . . .

Morse knew he wasn't getting very far. It was the *method* he couldn't fathom. But one thing was becoming an ever firmer conviction in his mind: whoever had come to Pinewood Close that Friday evening, *it hadn't been Nicholas Quinn*. Leave it there for the minute, Morse. Think of something else. Always the best way, and there was one thing he could check on straightaway.

He called in Peters, the handwriting pundit, showed him the note written to Mrs Evans, and gave him one of the sheets of Quinn's writing taken from Pinewood Close.

'What do you think?'

Peters hesitated. 'I'd need to study— '

'What's stopping you?'

Nothing had ever been known to hurry or ruffle Peters, an ex-Home Office pathologist, who in his younger days had made a considerable name and a considerable income for himself by disobeying the two cardinal rules for success – of thinking quickly and of acting decisively. For Peters thought at the speed of an arthritic tortoise and acted with the decisiveness of a soporific sloth. And Morse knew him better than to do anything but sit quietly and wait. If Peters said it was, it was. If Peters said that Quinn had definitely written the note, Quinn had definitely written the note. If he said he wasn't sure, hhe wasn't sure: and no one else in the world would be sure.

'How long will you be, Peters?'

'Ten, twelve minutes.'

Morse therefore knew that in about eleven minutes he would have his answer, and he sat quietly and waited. The phone went a few minutes later.

'Morse. Can I help you?'

It was the switchboard. 'It's a Mrs Greenaway, sir. From the John Radcliffe. Says she wants to talk to the man in charge of the Quinn murder.'

'That's me,' said Morse, without much enthusiasm. Mrs Greenaway, eh? The woman above Quinn. Well, well.

She had read the report in the *Oxford Mail* (she said) and felt that she ought to ring the police. Her husband wouldn't be very happy but – (Come on, girl, come on!). Well, she wasn't to have the baby until December, but she'd known – about four o'clock on Friday. The contractions – (Come on, girl!). Well, she'd rung up the works where Frank ('my husband, Inspector'), where Frank worked, and tried to get a message to him. But something must have gone wrong. She'd sat there by the window, watching and waiting, but no one came; and then she'd rung the works again about a quarter to five. She wasn't really worried, but she'd feel happier if Frank . . . Anyway she could always ring the hospital herself. They would send an ambulance straightaway; and she wasn't *absolutely* sure. It could have been just – (Come *on*!). Anyway, she saw Quinn come in, in his car, just after five.

'You *saw* him?'

'Yes. About five past five, it must have been. He drove in and put his car in the garage.'

'Was anybody with him?'

'No.'

'Go on, Mrs Greenaway.'

'Well, there's nothing else, really.'

'Did he go out again.'

'I didn't see him.'

'*Would* you have seen him?'

'Oh yes. As I say, I was looking out of the window all the time.'

'We think he went out to the shops, Mrs Greenaway. But you say— '

'Well, he could have gone out the back way, I suppose. You can get through the fence and on to the path, but— '

'But you don't think he did?'

'Well, I didn't hear him, and he wouldn't have gone over the back. It's ever so muddy.'

'I see.'

'Well, I hope— '

'Mrs Greenaway, are you absolutely sure you *saw* Mr Quinn?'

'Well, perhaps I didn't actually . . . I *heard* him on the phone, though.'

'You *what*?'

'Yes. We've got a shared line, and it was just after he came in. I was really getting worried, and I thought I'd try the works again; but I couldn't get through, because Mr Quinn was using the phone.'

'Did you listen to what he was saying?'

'No, I'm sorry, I didn't. I'm not nosy like that.' (Of course not!) 'You see I just wanted him to get off the line, that's all.'

'Was he talking for long?'

'Quite a while. I picked up the phone two or three times and they were still— '

'You don't remember a name, *any* name, that Mr Quinn used? Christian name? Surname? Anything at all that could help us?'

Joyce Greenaway was silent for a minute. There *was* a very vague recollection, but it slipped away from her. 'I—No, I can't remember.'

'Not a woman, was it?'

'Oh no. It was a man all right. Sounded an educated sort of man – well, you know what I mean, it wasn't a common sort of voice.'

'Were they having a row?'

'No. I don't think so. But I didn't listen in. I didn't *really*. I was just getting impatient, that's all.'

'Why didn't you go down and tell Mr Quinn what the situation was?'

Joyce Greenaway hesitated a little, and Morse wondered exactly why. 'Well, we weren't, you know, as friendly as all *that*.'

'Look, Mrs Greenaway. Please think very hard. It's vitally important – do you understand? If you could remember – even the slightest thing.'

But nothing would come, although the outline of that name still lurked subliminally. If only—

Morse did it for her. 'Ogleby? Mr Ogleby? Does that ring any bells?'

'No-o.'

'Roope? Mr Roope? Bartlett? Dr Bartlett? Mar— '

Joyce's scalp tingled. She'd been fishing for a verbal shape like 'Bartlett'. Could it have been? She wasn't really listening to Morse now. 'I can't be sure, Inspector, but it might have been Bartlett.'

Whew! What a turn-up for the books! Morse said somebody would be in to see her, but it would have to be the next day; and Joyce Greenaway, feeling a strange mixture of relief and trepidation, walked slowly back to the maternity ward.

Peters had been sitting quite motionless for the past two or three minutes, openly listening to the conversation, but he made no comment. 'Well?' said Morse.

'Quinn wrote it.'

Morse opened his mouth, but closed it again. Any protestation was futile. Peters said it was; so it *was*.

Why not go with the evidence, Morse, and fling your flimsy fancies aside? Quinn got back home about five; he wrote a note for Mrs Evans; and he rang somebody up – a well-spoken somebody, whose name may have been Bartlett.

Chapter Eighteen

Mrs Bartlett was something of a surprise. She was three or four inches taller than her husband, and she ordered him around as if he were a naughty but lovable little schoolboy. There was another surprise, too. No one had mentioned to Morse that the Bartletts had a son, and the rather slovenly-dressed, sullen-looking, bearded young man who was introduced as Richard seemed not particularly anxious to make an immediately favourable impression. But whilst the four of them sat rather awkwardly drinking their sherry, it became apparent that under his skin young Richard had a pleasant and attractive personality. As the ice thawed, he spoke with an easy humour and a total lack of self consciousness; and as he and Morse discussed the respective merits of the Solti and Furtwängler recordings of *The Ring*, Mrs Bartlett slipped away to push a cautious fork into the Brussels sprouts, and summoned her husband to open the wine. The table was immaculately set for the four of them, the silver cutlery winking and sparkling on the white tablecloth in the dimly lit room. The vegetables were almost ready.

Bartlett himself refilled Morse's glass. 'Nice little sherry, isn't it?'

'Indeed,' said Morse. He noticed that the label was different from that on the sherry bottle found in Quinn's rooms.

'Any more for you, Richard?'

'No.' It sounded oddly abrupt, as though there lurked some dark and hidden enmity within the Bartlett clan.

The soup was ready now, and Morse tossed back the last of his sherry, got to his feet, and walked across the wide room rubbing his hands together.

'Come on then, Richard.' His mother said it pleasantly, but Morse could hear the underlying note of tension.

'Don't worry about me. I'm not hungry.'

'But you *must*, Richard. I've— '

The young man stood up, and a strange light momentarily blazed in his eyes. 'I've just told you, Mother, I'm not hungry.'

'But I've got it all ready for you. Just have a— '

'I don't want any bloody food. How many times do you want telling, you stupid woman?' The words were cruel and harsh, the tone one of scarcely repressed fury. He stalked out of the room, and almost immediately the front door slammed with a thudded finality.

'I'm awfully sorry, Inspector.'

'Don't worry about me, Mrs Bartlett. Some of the youngsters these days, you know— '

'It's not that, Inspector. You see . . . you see, Richard suffers from schizophrenia. He can be absolutely charming, and then – well, he gets like you saw him just now.' She was very near to tears and Morse tried hard to say the right things; but inevitably the incident had cast its shadow deep across the evening, and for a while they ate in awkward silence.

'Can it be treated?'

Mrs Bartlett smiled sadly. 'Good question, Inspector. We've spent literally thousands, haven't we, Tom? He's a voluntary patient at Littlemore at the moment. Sometimes he comes home at the weekends, and just occasionally, like tonight, he'll drop in and sit around or have something to eat.' Her voice was wavering and her husband patted her affectionately on the shoulder.

'Don't worry about it, my dear. We didn't ask the Inspector along to talk about *our* problems. He's got enough of his own, I should think.'

Only when Mrs Bartlett was washing the pots were the two men able to talk, and Morse's earlier impression that the Secretary knew exactly what was going on in his own office was cumulatively confirmed: if anyone had any ideas about who had been prepared to prostitute the integrity of the Syndicate, Morse felt it would be Bartlett. But he didn't, it seemed. With every subtlety he knew, Morse tried to draw out any suspicion of secret doubts; but the Secretary was deeply loyal to his staff, and Morse knew that he was tip-toeing too delicately. He decided the time had come.

'What did Mr Quinn want when he rang you up?'

Bartlett blinked behind the window frames; and then looked down at his coffee, and was silent for a while. Morse knew perfectly well that if Bartlett denied that Quinn had spoken to him, that would be the end of it, for there was no hard evidence on the point. Yet the longer Bartlett hesitated (surely Bartlett must realize it?), the more obvious it became.

'You know that he did ring me, then?'

'Yes, sir.' He might as well push his luck a little.

'Do you mind telling me how you know?'

It was Morse's turn to hesitate, but he decided to come reasonably clean. 'Quinn's telephone is on a shared line. Someone overheard you.'

Did Morse catch a sudden flash of alarm behind the friendly lenses? If he did, it was gone as quickly as it had appeared.

'You want me to tell you what the conversation was about?'

'I think you should have told me before, sir. It would have saved a great deal of trouble.'

'Would it?' Bartlett looked the Inspector in the eye, and Morse suspected that he was still a long, long way from reaching to the bedrock of the mystery.

'The truth's going to come out sometime, sir. I honestly think you'd be sensible to tell me all about it.'

'Haven't you got that information, though? You say someone was listening in? Despicable attitude of mind, isn't it? Eavesdropping on other people— '

'Perhaps it is, sir; but, you see, the er person wasn't really listening in at all – just trying to get a very important call through, that's all. There was no question of deliberately— '

'So you *don't* know what we were talking about?'

Morse breathed deeply. 'No, sir.'

'Well, I'm er I'm not going to tell you. It was a very personal matter, between Quinn and myself— '

'Perhaps it was a personal matter that led to him being murdered, sir.'

'Yes, I realize that.'

'But you're not going to tell me?'

'No.'

Morse slowly drained his coffee. 'I don't think you realize exactly how important this is, sir. You see, unless we can find out where Quinn was and what he was doing that Friday evening— '

Bartlett looked at him sharply. 'You said nothing about Friday before.'

'You mean—?'

'I mean that Quinn rang me up one evening last week, yes. But it wasn't Friday.'

Clever little bugger! Morse had let the cat out of the bag – about not really knowing what the conversation had been about – and now the cat had jumped away over the fence. Bartlett was right, of course. He *hadn't* actually mentioned Friday, but—

Mrs Bartlett came through with the coffee pot and refilled the cups. She appeared quite unaware of breaking the conversation at a vital point, sat down, and innocently asked Morse how he was getting on with his inquiries into the terrible terrible business of poor poor Mr Quinn.

And Morse was game for anything now. 'We were just talking about telephone calls, Mrs Bartlett. The curse of the times, isn't it? I should think you must get almost as many as I do.'

'How right you are, Inspector. I was only saying last week – when was it, Tom? Do you remember? Oh yes. It was the day you went to Banbury. The phone kept ringing all the afternoon, and I said to Tom when he came in that we ought to get an ex-directory number and – do you know what? – just as I said it, the wretched thing rang again! And you had to go out again, do you remember, Tom?'

The little Secretary nodded and smiled ruefully. Sometimes life could be very unfair. Very unfair indeed.

Just after 8.15 p.m. that same evening a man was taking the lid off the highly-polished bronze coal-scuttle when he heard the knock, and he got slowly to his feet and opened the door.

'Well, well! Come on in. I shan't be a minute. Take a seat.' He knelt down again by the fire and extracted a lump of shiny black coal with the tongs.

In his own head it sounded as if he had taken an enormous bite from a large, crisp apple. His jaws seemed to clamp together, and for a weird and terrifying second he sought frantically to rediscover some remembrance of himself along the empty, echoing corridors of his brain. His right hand still held the tongs, and his whole body willed itself to pull the coal towards the bright fire. For some inexplicable reason he found himself thinking of the lava from Mount Vesuvius pouring in an all-engulfing flood towards the streets of old Pompeii; and even as his left hand began slowly and instinctively to raise itself towards the shattered skull, he knew that life was ended. The light snapped suddenly out, as if someone had switched on the darkness. He was dead.

Chapter Nineteen

Mrs Bartlett got up to answer the phone at a quarter to eleven and Morse realized that it would be as good an opportunity as he would get of taking a reasonably early leave of his hosts.

'It's probably Richard,' said Bartlett. 'He often feels a bit sorry later on, and tries to apologize. I shouldn't be surprised if— '

Mrs Bartlett came back into the room. 'It's for you, Inspector.'

Lewis told him as quickly and as clearly as he could what had happened. The Oxford City Police had been called in about nine o'clock – Chief Inspector Bell was in charge. It was only later that they realized how it might all tie in, and they'd tried to get Morse, and had finally got Lewis. The man had been killed instantly by a savage blow with a poker across the back of the skull. No prints or anything like that. The drawers had been ransacked, but not in any methodical way, it seemed. Probably the murderer had been interrupted.

'I'll see you there as soon as I can manage it, Lewis.'

As Morse came back into the room his face was pale with shock and he tried to keep his voice steady as he told the Bartletts the tragic news. 'It's Ogleby. He's been murdered.'

Mrs Bartlett buried her head in her hands and wept, whilst the Secretary himself, as he showed Morse to the front door, had difficulty in putting his words together coherently. He suddenly seemed an old man, shattered and uncomprehending. 'You asked about Quinn – when he rang – when he rang me – you asked about it – I said— '

Morse put his hand gently on the little man's shoulders. 'Yes. You tell me.'

'He said that – he said that he'd found out something I ought to know – he said that – that someone from the office was deliberately leaking question papers.'

'Did he say who it was?' asked Morse quietly.

'Oh yes, Inspector. *He said it was me.*'

When Morse arrived at the neat little terraced house in Walton Street, Lewis was engaged in low conversation with Bell. It was an ugly sight, and Morse turned his head away, closed his eyes, and felt the nausea rising in his gorge. 'Look, Lewis. I want you to get on to one or two things straightaway. Phone, if you like, or go around to see 'em – but I want to know exactly where Roope was tonight, where Martin was, where Miss Height was, where— '

Bell interrupted him. 'I've just been telling the Sergeant. We know where Miss Height was. She was here. She was the one who found him.'

It was not what Morse had expected, and the news appeared to confound whatever provisional procedure he had planned. 'Where is she now?'

'She's in a pretty bad way, I'm afraid. She rang through on a 999 call and then fainted, it seems. Somebody found her slumped by the public telephone box just up the road. She's been seen by the doc and they've taken her to the Radcliffe for the night.'

'She's got a young daughter.'

Bell put his hand on Morse's shoulder. 'Relax, old boy. We've seen to all that. Give us a *bit* of credit.'

Morse sat down in an armchair and wondered about himself. He seemed to be losing his grip. He closed his eyes again, and breathed deeply several times. 'Do as I tell you, anyway, Lewis. Get on to Roope and Martin straightaway. And there's something else. You'd better go up to the Littlemore hospital sometime, and find out what you can about Richard Bartlett – got that? Richard Bartlett. He's a voluntary patient there. Find out what time he got in tonight – *if* he got in, that is.'

Morse forced himself to look once more at the liquid squelch of brains and blood commingled on the carpet, beyond which the fire was now no more than an ashen glow. 'And try to find out if any of them changed their clothes, tonight. What do you think, Bell? Blood must have spurted all over the place, mustn't it?'

Bell shrugged his shoulders. 'The girl had blood on her hands and sleeves.'

'I'd better see her,' said Morse.

'Not tonight, old boy, I'm afraid. Doc says she's to see nobody. She's in a state of deep shock.'

'Why did she come here? Did she say?'

'Said she wanted to talk to him about something important.'

'Was the door unlocked?'

'No. She says it was locked.'

'How the hell did she get in then?'

'She's got a key.'

Morse let it sink in. 'Has she now! She certainly spreads the joys around, doesn't she?'

'Pardon?' said Bell.

It was in the early hours of Saturday morning that Morse found what he was looking for and he whistled incredulously. Only he and Lewis remained, apart from the two Oxford City constables standing guard outside.

'Come here, Lewis. Look at this.' It was the diary found in Ogleby's hip pocket. Bell had earlier flipped cursorily through it, but had found no entries whatsoever, and had put it down again. It was a blue University diary with a small flap at the back which could be used for railway tickets and the like. And as Morse had prised open the flap, he could hardly believe his eyes. It was a ticket, torn roughly in half, with IO 2 printed across the top, 'Rear Lounge' beneath it, and along the right edge, running down, the numbers 93587.

'What do you make of it?'

'He *was* there after all, then, sir.'

'*Four* of them. Just think of it. Four out of the five!'

Lewis himself picked up the diary and looked with his usual thorough care at every page in turn. It was clear that Ogleby had never used the diary during the year. But on a page headed 'Notes' at the back of the diary, Lewis saw something that made his eyeballs bulge. 'Sir!' He said it very quietly, as though the slightest noise might frighten it away. 'Look at this.'

Morse looked at the diary, and felt the familiar constriction of the temples as an electric charge seemed to flash across his head. There, drawn with accuracy and neatness, was a small diagram:

'My God!' said Morse. '*It's the same number as the ticket we found on Quinn.*'

Half an hour later, as the two policemen left the house in Walton Street, Morse found himself recalling the words of Dr Hans Gross, one-time Professor of Criminology at the University of Prague. He had them by heart: 'No human action happens by pure chance unconnected with other happenings. None is incapable of explanation.' It was a belief that Morse had always cherished. Yet as he stepped out into the silent street, he began to wonder if it were really true.

No more than fifty or sixty yards down the street he saw the building which housed both Studio 1 and Studio 2. The neon lighting still illuminated the white boards above the foyer, the red and royal-blue lettering garish and bright in the almost eerie stillness: *The Nymphomaniac* X (Strictly Adults Only). Was she trying to tell him something? He walked down to the cinema with Lewis and stood looking at the stills outside. She was certainly a big and bouncy girl, although a series of five-pointed stars had been superimposed by some incomparable idiot over the incomparable Inga's nipples.

Chapter Twenty

Morse was in his office at 7.30 a.m. the next morning, tired and unshaven. He had tried to catch a few hours' sleep, but his mind would give him no rest, and he had finally given up the unequal struggle. He knew that he would be infinitely better able to cope with his problems if he had a complete change. But while there was no chance of that, at least he could sharpen his brain on the crossword; and he folded over the back page of *The Times*, looked at his watch, wrote the time in the left-hand margin, and began. It took him twelve and a half minutes. Not his best, this week; but not bad. And barring that one clue, he would have been within ten minutes: *In which are the Islets of Langerhans* (8). –A–C–E–S had been staring him in the face for well over two minutes before he'd seen the answer. He'd finally remembered it from a quiz programme on the radio: one contestant had suggested the South China Sea, another the Baltic, and a third the Mediterranean; and what a laugh from the studio audience when the question master had told them the answer!

During the morning the seemingly endless flood of news poured in. Lewis had managed to see Martin who (so he said) had felt restless and worried the previous evening, gone out about 7.30 p.m., and got back home at about a quarter to eleven. He had taken his car, called at several pubs near Radcliffe Square, and on his return had been banished by his wife to the dog-house. Roope (so he said) had been at home working all evening. No callers – seldom did have any callers. He was preparing a series of lectures on some aspect of Inorganic Chemistry which Lewis had been unable to understand at the time, and was unable to remember now. 'So far as I can see, sir, they're both very strongly in the running. The trouble is we seem to be running out of suspects. Unless you think Miss Height— '

'It's a possibility, I suppose.'

Lewis grudgingly conceded the point. 'That's still only three, though.'

'Aren't you forgetting Ogleby?'

Lewis stared at him. 'I don't follow you, sir.'

'He's still on my list, Lewis, and I see no earthly or heavenly reason why I should cross him off. Do you?'

Lewis opened his mouth but shut it again. And the phone went.

It was the Dean of the Examinations Syndicate, phoning from Lonsdale. Bartlett had rung him up the previous evening. What a terrible business it all was! Frightening. He just wanted to mention a little thing that had occurred to him. Did Morse remember asking about relationships within the Syndicate? Well, somehow the murders of Quinn and Ogleby had brought it all back. It had been just a *little* odd, he'd thought. It was the night when they'd had the big do at the Sheridan, with the Al-jamara lot. Some of them had stayed very late, long after the others had gone off to bed. Quinn was one of them, and Ogleby another; and the Dean had felt at the time (he could be *totally* wrong, of course) that Ogleby had been waiting for Quinn to go; had been watching him in a rather curious way. And when Quinn had left, Ogleby had followed him out almost immediately. It was only a *very* small thing, and actually putting it into words made it seem even smaller. But there it was. The Dean had now unburdened himself, and he hoped he hadn't wasted the Inspector's time.

Morse thanked him and put the phone down. As the Dean said, it didn't seem to add up to much.

In mid-morning Bell rang from Oxford. The medical evidence suggested that Ogleby had died only minutes before he was found. There were no prints other than Ogleby's on the poker or on the desk where the papers had been strewn around; Morse could re-examine whatever he wanted at any time, of course, but there seemed (in Bell's view) little that was going to help him very much. The blow that had crushed Ogleby's thin skull must have been struck with considerable ferocity, but may have required only minimal strength. It had probably been delivered by a right-handed person, and the central point of impact was roughly five centimetres above the occipital bone, and roughly two centimetres to the right of the parietal foramen. The result of the blow— '

'Skip it,' said Morse.

'I know what you mean.'

'Is Miss Height still—?'

'You can't see her till lunchtime. Doc's orders.'

'Still in the Radcliffe?'

'Yep. And you'll be the second person to see her, I promise.'

A young nurse put her head round the screens curtaining the bed on the women's accident ward. 'You've got another visitor.'

Monica appeared drawn and nervous as Morse looked down at her, sitting up against the pillow, her ample hospital nightie softening the contours of her lovely body. 'Tell me about it,' said Morse simply.

Her voice was quiet but firm: 'There's not much to tell, really. I called to see him about half-past eight. He was just lying— '

'You had a key?'

She nodded. 'Yes.' Her eyes seemed suddenly very sad, and Morse pressed the point no further. Whether Philip Ogleby had been to see *The Nymphomaniac* was a question still in doubt; but it was perfectly clear that the nymphomaniac had been to see *him* – at fairly regular intervals.

'He was lying there—?'

She nodded. 'I thought he must have had a heart attack or something. I wasn't frightened, or anything like that. I knelt down and touched his shoulder – and his – his head was – was almost in the fireplace, and I saw the blood— ' She shook her head, as though to rid herself of that horrific sight. 'And I got blood and – and stuff, over my hands – and I didn't know what to do. I just couldn't stay in that terrible room. I knew there was a phone there but – but I went out into the street and rang the police from the phone box. I don't remember any more. I must have stepped out of the box and just – fainted. The next thing I remember was being in the ambulance.'

'Why did you go to see him?' (He had to ask it.)

'I – I hadn't really had any chance to talk to him about – about Nick and— ' (Lying again!)

'You think he knew something about Quinn's murder?'

She smiled sadly and wearily. 'He was a very clever man, Inspector.'

'You didn't see anyone else?'

She shook her head.

'Could there have been anyone else – in the house?'

'I don't know. I just don't know.'

Should he believe her? She'd told so many lies already. But there must have been *some* cause for the lies; and Morse was convinced that if only he could discover that cause he would make the biggest leap forward in the case so far . . . It was the Studio 2 business that worried him most. Why, he repeated to himself, *why* had Monica and Donald Martin lied so clumsily about it? And as he wrestled with the problem once again, he began to convince himself that all four of them – Monica, Martin, Ogleby, and Quinn – must have had some collective reason for being in Studio 2 that Friday afternoon, for he just could not bring himself to believe that their several paths had converged for purely fortuitous reasons. Even Morse, who accepted the majority of improbable coincidences with a curiously credulous gullibility, was not prepared to swallow that! Something – *something* must have happened at Studio 2 that afternoon. What? Think of anything, Morse, anything – it wouldn't matter. Quinn had got there early, just after the doors opened. Then Martin had come in, sneaking into the back row and waiting and looking nervously around. Had he seen Quinn? Had Quinn seen *him*? The lights must have been dim; but not so dim as all that, especially as the eyes slowly accustomed themselves to the gloom. *Then*, what? Monica had come in, and Martin saw her, and they sat there together, and Martin told her that he had seen *Quinn*. What would they do? They'd leave. Pronto! Go *on*, Morse. If Martin had seen Quinn – and Quinn had not seen him – he would have left the cinema immediately, waited outside for Monica, told her that they couldn't stay there, and suggested somewhere else . . . Yes. But where had Ogleby fitted in? The number on his ticket, some forty-odd numbers after Quinn's, suggested (if the manageress had done her sums right) that Ogleby had not appeared in Studio 2 until about four or five o'clock. How did *that* fit into the pattern, though? Augh! It didn't fit. Try again, Morse. Something must have frightened *Monica* off, perhaps. Yes. That was a slightly more promising hypothesis. Had she seen something? Someone? The cause of all the lies? After learning that Quinn had been in Studio 2, she had told another lie, and . . . Oh Christ! What a muddle his mind was in!

The pictures flickered fitfully upon the wall, the faces fading and changing, and fading again . . .

'You've been a long way away, Inspector.'

'Mm? Oh, sorry. Just daydreaming.'

'About me?'

'Among others.'

On the table beside the bed was a copy of *The Times*, folded at the crossword page; but only three or four words were written into the diagram, and Morse found himself wondering and wandering off again. Wondering if Monica knew where the Islets of Langerhans were situated . . . Well, if she didn't, the nurse could soon— *Just a minute!* His thinning hair seemed to be standing on end, and his scalp suddenly tingled with a thousand tiny prickles. Oh yes! It was a beautiful idea, and the old questions flooded his brain. In what sea are the Islets of Langerhans? When was George Washington assassinated? Who was Kansas-Nebraska Bill? In what year did R.A. Butler become prime minister? Who composed the Trout Quartet? By what name was the Black Prince known when he became King? *The questions were all non-questions*. Georgie W. wasn't assassinated, and K.–N. Bill wasn't *anybody*; he was a Bill before the Senate. The same with all of them. They were questions which couldn't be answered, because they were questions which couldn't be asked. Morse had become besotted with trying to find out who had been at Studio 2, when they had been there, why they had been there. But what if they were all non-questions? What if *no one* had been in Studio 2? Everything in the case had been designed to mislead him into thinking that they had been there. Some of them – all of them, perhaps – *wanted* him to think so. And he had blindly stumbled along the gangway down the darkened cinema, groping his way like a blind man, and trying to see (O fool of a fool!) who was sitting there. But perhaps there was no one, Morse. No one!

'Who did you see going into Studio 2, Miss Height?'

'Why don't you call me "Monica"?'

The nurse put her head through the curtains, and told Morse that he really ought to leave now; he'd already gone way over his time. He stood up and looked down at her once more, and kissed the top of her head gently.

'You didn't see anyone going into Studio 2, did you, Monica?'

For a second there was hesitation in her eyes, and then she

looked at him earnestly. 'No. I didn't. You must believe that.'

She took Morse's hand and squeezed it gently against her soft breast. 'Come again, won't you? And try to look after me.' Her eyes sought his and he realized once more how desperately desirable she would always be to lonely men – to men like him. But there was something else in her eyes: the look of the hunted fleeing from the hunter; the haunted look of fear. 'I'm frightened, Inspector. I'm so very frightened.'

Morse was thoughtful as he walked the long corridors before finally emerging through the flappy celluloid doors into the entrance road by the side of the Radcliffe, where the Jaguar stood parked on an 'Ambulance Only' plot. He started up the engine and was slowly steering through the twisting alleys that led down into Walton Street when he saw a familiar figure striding up towards the hospital. He stopped the car and wound down the window.

'I'm glad to see you, Mr Martin. In fact I was just coming along to see you. Jump in.'

'Sorry. Not now. I'm going to see— '

'You're not.'

'Who says?'

'No one's going in to see her until I say so.'

'But when—?'

'Jump in.'

'Do I have to?'

Morse shrugged his shoulders. 'Not really, no. You please yourself. At least, you please yourself until I decide to take you in.'

'What's that supposed to mean?'

'What it says, sir. Until I decide to take you in and charge you— '

'*Charge* me? What with?'

'Oh, I could think up something pretty quickly, sir.'

The dull eyes stared at Morse in anxious bewilderment. 'You must be joking.'

'Of course I am, sir.' He leaned across and opened the Jaguar's nearside door, and Donald Martin sullenly eased his long body into the passenger seat.

The traffic was heavy as they drove up the narrow street, and Morse decided to turn right and cut straight across to Woodstock

Road. As he stopped at yet another Pelican crossing, he realized just how close the Syndicate building was to Studio 2. And as the lights turned to flashing amber, he held the car on half-clutch as a late pedestrian galloped his way across: a bearded young man. He was in too much of a rush to recognize Morse; but Morse recognized *him*, and the last words that Monica had spoken re-echoed in his mind. In his rear mirror he could see that the man was walking briskly down the right-hand side of Woodstock Road towards the Radcliffe Infirmary, and he swung the Jaguar sharp left at the next turning, furiously cursing the crawling stream of cars. He parked on the double yellow lines at the back of the Radcliffe, told Martin to stay where he was, and ran like a crippled stag to the accident ward. She was still there: still sitting up prettily amid the pillows as he peeped behind the screens. Phew! He rang up HQ from the Sister's office, told Dickson he was to get there immediately, and stood breathing heavily.

'You all right, Inspector?'

'Just about, thank you, Sister. But listen. I don't want anyone to talk to Miss Height or to get anywhere near her. All right? And if anyone *does* try to visit her, I want to know who it is. One of my men will be here in ten minutes.'

He paced impatiently up and down the corridor waiting for Dickson's arrival. Like Pilgrim he seemed to be making but sluggish progress – up the hill of difficulty and down into the slough of despond. But there was no sign whatsoever of Richard Bartlett. Perhaps Morse was imagining things.

Chapter Twenty-one

Three-quarters of an hour later, with the office clock showing half-past two, Morse's irritation with the young philanderer was mounting towards open animosity. What a flabby character Donald Martin was! He admitted most things, albeit with some reluctance. His relationship with Monica had sputtered into sporadic passion, followed by the usual remorse and the futile promises that the affair had got to finish. Certainly it was he who had always tried to force the pace; yet when they were actually making love together (Morse drew the blinds across his imagination) he knew that she was *glad*. She could surrender herself so completely to physical love; it was wonderful, and he had known nothing like it before. But when the passion was spent, she would always retreat into indifference – callousness, almost. Never had she made any pretence about her reasons for letting him take her: it was purely physical. Never had she spoken of love, or even of deep affection . . . His wife (he was sure of it) had no suspicions of his unfaithfulness, although she must have sensed (of course she must!) that the careless rapture of their early married days had gone – perhaps for ever.

How despicable the man was! His dark, lank hair, his horn-rimmed glasses, his long, almost effeminate fingers. Ugh! Nor was Morse's dark displeasure dissipated as Martin repeated what he had already told Lewis about his whereabouts the previous evening. He'd been lucky to find a parking space in the Broad, and he'd gone to the King's Arms first, where he thought the barmaid would probably remember him. Then to the White Horse, where he didn't know anyone. Another pint. Then down to the Turl Bar. Another pint. No he didn't often go out for a binge: very rarely in fact. But the last few days had been a nightmarish time. He'd found he couldn't sleep at all well, and beer had helped a bit; it usually did. But why did Morse keep on and on at him about it? He'd gone nowhere near Ogleby's! Why should he! What, for heaven's sake, could he have had to do with Ogleby's murder! He'd not even known him very well. He doubted if anybody in the office knew him very well.

Morse said nothing to enlighten him. 'Let's come back to last Friday afternoon.'

'Not again, surely! I've told you what happened. All right, I lied for a start, but— '

'You're lying now! And if you're not careful you'll be down in the cells until you *do* tell me the truth.'

'But I'm *not* lying.' He shook his head miserably. 'Why can't you believe me?'

'Why did you say you spent the afternoon at Miss Height's house?'

'I don't know, really. Monica thought . . . ' His voice trailed off.

'Yes. She's told me.'

'Has she?' His eyes seemed suddenly relieved.

'Yes,' lied Morse. 'But if you don't want to tell me yourself, we can always wait, sir. I'm in no great rush myself.'

Martin looked down at the carpet. 'I don't know why she didn't want to say we'd been to the pictures. I don't – honestly! But I didn't think it mattered all that much, so I agreed to what she said.'

'It's a bit odd to say you'd been to bed when all you'd done was sit together in the cinema!'

Martin seemed to recognize the obvious truth of the assertion, and he nodded. 'But it's the truth, Inspector. It's the honest truth! We stayed in the cinema till about a quarter to four. You've got to believe that! I had nothing at all – nothing! – to do with Nick's death. Nor did Monica. *We were together* – all the afternoon.'

'Tell me something about the film.'

So Martin told him, and Morse knew that he could hardly be fabricating such entirely gratuitous obscenities. Martin *had* seen the film; seen it sometime, anyway. Not necessarily that Friday, not necessarily with Monica, but . . .

Martin was convincing him, he knew that. Assume he *was* there that Friday afternoon. With Monica? Yes, assume that too. Sit them down there on the back row of the rear lounge, Morse. Martin had been waiting for her, and she'd come in. Yes, keep going! She'd come in and . . . and they had stayed after all! Who, if anyone, had they seen? No. Go back a bit. Who had Martin seen going in? No. Who had Monica seen? Going in? Or . . . ? Yes. Yes!

Think of it the other way for a minute. Ogleby had gone into the cinema at about quarter to five, say. But he must have known all about Quinn's ticket, mustn't he? In fact he must have *seen* it. When? Where? Why had he made a careful freehand drawing of that ticket? Ogleby must have known, or at least suspected, that the ticket was vitally important. All right. Agree that Monica and Martin had seen the film together. But had *Quinn* gone? Or had someone just wished to make everyone else *think* that he'd gone? Who? Who knew of the ticket? Who had drawn it? Where had he found it, Morse? My god, yes! What a stupid blind fool he'd been!

Martin had stopped talking minutes before, and was looking curiously at the man in the black-leather chair, sitting there smiling serenely to himself. It had all happened, as it always seemed to do with Morse, in the twinkling of an eye. Yes, as he sat there, oblivious to everything about him, *Morse felt he knew when Nicholas Quinn had met his death.*

HOW?

Chapter Twenty-two

Early on Saturday evening Mr Nigel Denniston decided to begin.
He found that the majority of his O-level English Language scripts
had been delivered, and he began his usual preliminary task of putting the large buff-coloured envelopes into alphabetical order, and
of checking them against his allocated schedule. The examiners'
meeting was to be held in two days' time, and before then he had
to look at about twenty or so scripts, mark them provisionally in
pencil, and present them for scrutiny to the senior examiner, who
would be interviewing each of his panel after the main meeting. Al-
jamara was the first school on his list, and he slit open the carefully-
sealed envelope and took out the contents. The attendance sheet
was placed on top of the scripts, and Denniston's eyes travelled
automatically and hopefully down to the 'Absentee' column. It was
always a cause of enormous joy to him if one or two of his candidates had been smitten with some oriental malady; but Al-Jamara
was a disappointment. According to the attendance sheet there
were five candidates entered, and all five were duly registered as
'present' by the distant invigilator. Never mind. There was always
the chance of finding one or two of those delightful children who
knew nothing and who wrote nothing; children for whom the wells
of inspiration ran dry after only a couple of laboured sentences.
But no. No luck there, either. None of the five candidates had prematurely given up the ghost. Instead, it was the usual business:
page after page of ill-written, unidiomatic, irrelevant twaddle,
which it was his assignment to plough through (and almost certainly to plough), marking in red ink the myriad errors of grammar,
syntax, construction, spelling and punctuation. It was a tedious
chore, and he didn't really know why year after year he took it on.

Yet he did know. It was a bit of extra cash; and if he didn't mark, he would only be sitting in front of the TV, forever arguing with the family about which of the channels they should watch . . . He flicked through the first few sheets. Oh dear! These foreigners might be all right at Mathematics or Economics or that sort of thing. But they couldn't write *English* – that was a fact. Still, it wasn't really surprising. English was their second language, poor kids; and he felt a little less jaundiced as he took out his pencil and started.

An hour later he had finished the first four scripts. The candidates had tried – of course they had. But he felt quite unjustified in awarding the sort of marks that could bring them anywhere near the pass range. Tentatively he had written his own provisional percentages at the top right-hand corner of each script: 27%, 34%, 35%, 19%. He decided to finish off the last one before supper.

This was a better script. My goodness, it was! And as he read on he realized that it was very good indeed. He put aside his pencil and read through the essay with genuine interest, bordering on delight. Whoever the boy was, he'd written beautifully. There were a few awkward sentences, and a sprinkling of minor errors; but Denniston doubted whether he himself could have written a better essay under examination conditions. He had known the same sort of thing before, though. Sometimes a candidate would memorize a whole essay and trot it out: beautiful stuff, lifted lock, stock and paragraph from one of the great English prose stylists; but almost invariably in such cases, the subject matter was so wildly divorced from the strict terms of the question set as to be completely irrelevant. But not here. Either the lad was quite exceptionally able, or else he had been extraordinarily fortunate. That wasn't for Denniston to decide, though; his job was to reward what was on the script. He pencilled in 90%; and then wondered why he hadn't given it 95%, or even 99%. But like almost all examiners, he was always frightened of using the full range of marks. The lad would fly through, anyway. Wonderful lad! Perfunctorily Denniston looked at the name: Dubal. It meant nothing to him at all.

In Al-jamara itself, the last of the Autumn examinations, crowded into just the one week, had finished the previous afternoon, and George Bland relaxed with an iced gin-and-tonic in his air-conditioned flat. It had taken him only a few weeks to regret his move. Better paid, certainly; but only away from Oxford had he begun fully to appreciate the advantages of his strike-ridden, bankrupt, beautiful homeland. He missed, above all, the feeling of belonging somewhere which, however loosely, he could think of as his home: the pub at night; the Cotswold villages with their greens and ancient churches; the concerts, the plays, the lectures, and the general air of learning; the oddities forever padding their faddish, feckless paths around the groves of the Muses. He'd never imagined how much it all meant to him . . . The climate of Al-jamara was overwhelming, intolerable, endlessly enervating; the people alien – ostensibly hospitable, but secretly watchful and suspicious . . . How he regretted the move now!

The news had worried him; would have worried anyone. It was for information only, really – no more; and it had been thoughtful of the Syndicate to keep him informed. The International Telegram had arrived on Wednesday morning: TRAGIC NEWS STOP QUINN DEAD STOP MURDER SUSPECTED STOP WILL WRITE STOP BARTLETT. But there had been another telegram, received only that morning; and this time it was unsigned. He had burned it immediately, although he realized that no one could have suspected the true import of the brief, bleak lines. Yet it had always been a possibility, and he was prepared. He walked over to his desk and took out his passport once more. All was in order; and tucked safely inside was his ticket on the scheduled flight to Cairo, due to leave at noon the following day.

Chapter Twenty-three

There was a car outside No 1 Pinewood Close as Frank Greenaway pulled into the crescent; but he didn't recognize it and gave it no second thought. He could fully understand Joyce's point of view, of course. He wasn't too keen to go back there himself, and it wasn't right to expect her to be there on her own while he was out at work. She'd have the baby to keep her company, but— No. He agreed with her. They would find somewhere else, and in the meantime his parents were being very kind. Not that he wanted to stay with them *too* long. Like somebody said, fish and visitors began to smell after three days . . . They could leave most of their possessions at Pinewood Close for a week or two, but he had to pick up a few things for Joyce (who would be leaving the John Radcliffe the next morning), and the police had said it would be all right.

As he got out of his car, he noticed that the street lamp had been repaired, and the house where he and Joyce had lived, and wherein Quinn had been found murdered, seemed almost ordinary again. The front gate stood open, and he walked up to the front door, selecting the correct key from his ring. The garage doors stood open, propped back by a couple of house bricks. Frank opened the front door very quietly. He was not a nervous man, but he felt a slight involuntary shudder as he stepped into the darkened hallway, the two doors on his right, the stairs almost directly in front of him. He would hurry it up a bit; he didn't much fancy staying there too long on his own. As he put his hand on the banister he noticed the slim line of light under the kitchen door: the police must have forgotten . . . But then he heard it, quite distinctly. Someone was in the kitchen. Someone was quietly moving around in there . . . The demon fear laid its electrifying hand upon his shoulder, and without conscious volition he found himself a few seconds later scurrying hurriedly along the concrete drive towards his car.

Morse heard the click of the front door, and looked out into the passageway. But no one. He was imagining things again. He returned to the kitchen, and bent down once more beside the back door. Yes, he *had* been right. There was no mud on the carpets in the other downstairs rooms, and they had been hoovered only an hour or so before Quinn was due to return. But beside the back door there *were* signs of mud, and Morse knew that someone had taken off his shoes, or her shoes, and left them beside the doormat. And even as he had stood there his own shoes crunched upon the gritty, dried mud with the noise of someone trampling on corn flakes.

He left the house and got into the Jaguar. But then he got out again, walked back, closed the garage doors, and finally the garden gate behind him.

* * *

Ten minutes later he drew up outside the darkened house in Walton Street, where a City constable stood guard before the door.

'No one's tried to get in, Constable?'

'No, sir. Few sightseers always hanging around, but no one's been in.'

'Good. I'll only be ten minutes.'

Ogleby's bedroom seemed lonely and bleak. No pictures on the walls, no books on the bedside table, no ornaments on the dressing table, no visible signs of heating. The large double-bed monopolized the confined space, and Morse turned back the coverlet. Two head pillows lay there, side by side, and a pair of pale-yellow pyjamas were tucked just beneath the top sheet. Morse picked up the nearer pillow, and there he found a neatly-folded négligée – black, flimsy, almost transparent, with a label proclaiming 'St Michael'.

No one had yet bothered to clean up the other room, and the fire which had blazed merrily the night before was nothing now but cold, fine ash into which some of the detectives had thrown the tipped butts of their cigarettes. It looked almost obscene. Morse turned his attention to the books which lined the high shelves on each side of the fireplace. The vast majority of them were technical treatises on Ogleby's specialisms, and Morse was interested in only one: *Medical Jurisprudence and Toxicology*, by Glaister and Rentoul. It was an old friend. A folded sheet of paper protruded from the top, and Morse opened the book at that point: page 566. In heavy type, a quarter of the way down the page, stood the heading 'Hydrocyanic Acid'.

At the Summertown Health Clinic, Morse was shown immediately into Dr Parker's consulting room.

'Yes, Inspector, I'd looked after Mr Ogleby for – oh, seven or eight years now. Very sad really. Something may have turned up, but I very much doubt it. Extremely rare blood disease – nobody knows much about it.'

'You gave him about a year, you say?'

'Eighteen months, perhaps. No longer.'

'He knew this?'

'Oh yes. He insisted on knowing everything. Anyway, it would have been useless trying to keep it from him. Medically speaking, he was a very well-informed man. Knew more about his illness than I did. Or the specialists at the Radcliffe, come to that.'

'Do you think he told anybody?'

'I doubt it. Might have told one or two close friends, I suppose. But I knew nothing about his private life. For all I know, he didn't have any close friends.'

'Why do you say that?'

'I don't know. He was a – a bit of a loner, I think. Bit uncommunicative.'

'Did he have much pain?'

'I don't think so. He never said so, anyway.'

'He wasn't the suicidal sort, was he?'

'I don't think so. Seemed a pretty balanced sort of chap. If he *were* going to kill himself, he would have done it simply and quickly, I should have thought. He would certainly have been in his right mind.'

'What would you say is the simplest and quickest way?'

Parker shrugged his shoulders. 'I think I'd have a quick swig of cyanide, myself.'

Morse walked thoughtfully to the car: he felt a sadder, if not a much wiser man. Anyway, one more call to make. He just hoped Margaret Freeman hadn't gone off to a Saturday night hop.

Although earlier in the evening Lewis had been quite unable to fathom the Inspector's purposes, he had quite looked forward to the duties assigned to him.

Joyce Greenaway was pleasantly cooperative, and she tried her best to answer the Sergeant's strange questions. As she had told Inspector Morse, she couldn't be certain that the name *was* Bartlett, and she could see no point whatsoever in trying (although she did try) to remember whether he'd been addressed as Bartlett or Dr Bartlett. She was quite sure, too, that she could never hope to recognize the voice again: her hearing wasn't all that good at the best of times and – well, you couldn't recognize a voice again just like that, could you. What were they talking about? Well, as a matter of fact, she did just have the feeling that they were arranging to meet somewhere. But further than that – when, where, why – no. No ideas at all.

Lewis got it all down in his notebook; and when he'd finished he made the appropriate noises to the little bundle of life that lay beside the bed.

'Have you got any family, Sergeant?'

'Two daughters.'

'We had a name all ready if it had been a girl.'

'There's a lot of nice boys' names.'

'Yeah, I suppose so. But somehow— What's your Christian name, Sergeant?'

Lewis told her. He'd never liked it much.

'What about the Inspector? What's his Christian name?'

Lewis frowned for a few seconds. Funny, really. He'd never thought of Morse as having one. 'I don't know. I've never heard anyone call him by his Christian name.'

From the John Radcliffe Lewis drove down to the railway station. There were four taxi firms, and Lewis received conflicting pieces of advice about the best way to tackle his assignment. It really should have been a comparatively easy job to find out who (if anyone) had taken Roope from the station to the Syndicate building at about 4.20 p.m. on the 21st November. But it wasn't. And when Lewis had finally completed his rounds he doubted whether the answer he'd come up with was the one that Morse had expected or hoped for.

It was after half-past eight before Lewis reached Littlemore Hospital.

Dr Addison, who was on night duty, had not himself had a great deal to do with Richard Bartlett's case, although he knew *of* it, of course. He fetched the file, but refused to let Lewis look through it himself. 'There are some very *personal* entries, you know, Officer, and I think that I can give you the information you want without— '

'I don't really want any details about Mr Bartlett's mental troubles. Just a list of the institutions that he's stayed in over the past five years, the clinics he's been to, the specialists he's seen – and the dates, of course.'

Addison looked annoyed. 'You want all that? Well, I suppose, if it's really necessary . . . ' The file contained a wadge of papers two inches thick, and Lewis patiently made his notes. It took them almost an hour.

'Well, many thanks, sir. I'm sorry to have taken up so much of your time.'

Addison said nothing.

As Lewis finally got up to leave he asked one last question, although it wasn't on Morse's list.

'What's the trouble with Mr Bartlett, sir?'

'Schizophrenia.'

'Oh.' Lewis thanked him once again, and left.

Morse was not in his office when Lewis arrived back. They'd arranged to meet again at about ten if each could manage it. Had Morse finished his own inquiries yet? Like as not he had, and gone out for a pint. Lewis looked at his watch: it was just after ten-past ten, and he might as well wait. Morse must have been looking up something for his crossword, for the *Chambers* lay on the cluttered desk. Lewis opened it. 'Ski-'? No. 'Sci-'? No. He'd never been much of a hand at spelling. 'Sck-'? Ah! There it was: '*ski-zo-freni-a*, or *skid-zo*, n., dementia praecox or kindred form of insanity, marked by introversion and loss of connexion between thoughts, feelings and actions.'

Lewis had moved on to 'dementia' when Morse came in, and it was quite clear that for once in a lifetime he had *not* been drinking. He listened with great care to what Lewis had to tell him, but seemed neither surprised nor excited in any way.

It was at a quarter to eleven that he dropped his bombshell. 'Well, Lewis, my old friend. I've got a surprise for you. We're going to make an arrest on Monday morning.'

'That's when the inquest is.'

'And that's when we're going to arrest him.'

'Can you do that sort of thing at an inquest, sir? Is it legal?'

'Legal? I know nothing about the law. But perhaps you're right. We'll make it just *after* the inquest, just as he's— '

'What if he's not there?'

'I think he'll be there all right,' said Morse quietly.

'You're not going to tell me who he is?'

'What? And spoil my little surprise? Now, what do you say we have a pint or two? To celebrate, sort of thing.'

'The pubs'll be shut, sir.'

'Really?' Morse feigned surprise, walked over to a wall cupboard, and fetched out half a dozen pint bottles of beer, two glasses, and an opener.

'You've got to plan for all contingencies in our sort of job, Lewis.'

Margaret Freeman had been tossing and turning since she went to bed at eleven, and she finally got up at 1.30 a.m. She tiptoed past her parents' room, made her way silently to the kitchen, and put the kettle on. It was no longer a matter of being frightened, as it had been earlier in the week, when she had blessed the fact that she didn't live on her own like some of the girls did; it was more a matter of being puzzled now: puzzled about what Morse had asked her. The other girls thought that the Inspector was a bit dishy; but she didn't. Too old – and too vain. Combing his hair when he'd come in, and trying to cover up that balding patch at the back! Men! But she'd liked Mr Quinn – liked him rather more than she should have done . . . She poured herself a cup of tea and sat down at the kitchen table. Why had Morse asked her that question? It made it seem as if she held the secret to something important; it *was* important, he'd said. But why did he want to know? She had lain awake thinking and thinking, and asking herself just why he should have asked her *that*. Why was it so important for him to know if Mr Quinn had put her own initials on the little notes he left? Of course he had! She was the one who most needed to know, wasn't she? After all, she *was* his confidential secretary. Had been, rather . . . She poured herself a second cup of tea, took it back to her room, and turned on the bedside reading lamp. Menacing shadows seemed to loom against the far wall as she settled herself into bed. She tried to sit very still, and suddenly felt very frightened again.

Chapter Twenty-four

On Monday morning Lewis was waiting outside as the door of Superintendent Strange's office opened, and he caught the tail-end of the conversation.

' . . . cock-eyed, but— '

'Have I ever let you down, sir?'

'Frequently.'

Morse winked at Lewis and closed the door behind him. It was 10.30 a.m. and the inquest was due to start at eleven. Dickson was waiting outside with the car, and together the three policemen drove down into Oxford.

The inquest was to be held in the courtroom behind the main Oxford City Police HQ in St Aldates, and a small knot of people was standing outside, waiting for the preceding hearing to finish. Lewis looked at them. He had written (as Morse had carefully briefed him) to all those concerned in any way with Quinn's murder: some would have to take the stand anyway; others ('but your presence will be appreciated') would not. The Dean of the Syndicate stood there, his hands in his expensive dark overcoat, academically impatient; the Secretary, looking duly grave; Monica Height looking palely attractive; Martin prowling around the paved yard like a nervous hyaena; Roope, smoking a cigarette and staring thoughtfully at the ground; Mr Quinn senior, lonely, apart, staring into the pit of despair; and Mrs Evans and Mrs Jardine, leagues apart in the social hierarchy, yet managing to chat away quite merrily about the tragic events which had brought them together.

It was ten minutes past eleven before they all filed into the court, where the coroner's sergeant, acting as chief usher, quietly but firmly organized the seating to his liking, before disappearing through a door at the back of the court, and almost immediately reappearing with the coroner himself. All rose to their feet as the sergeant intoned the judicial ritual. The proceedings had begun.

First the identification of the deceased was established by Mr Quinn senior; then Mrs Jardine took the box; then Martin; then Bartlett; then Sergeant Lewis; then Constable Dickson. Nothing was added to, nothing subtracted from, the statements the coroner had before him. Next the thin humpbacked surgeon gave evidence of the autopsy, reading from a prepared script at such a breakneck speed and with such a wealth of physiological detail that he might just as well have been reciting the Russian creed to a class of the educationally subnormal. When he had reached the last fullstop, he handed the document perfunctorily to the coroner, stepped carefully down, and walked briskly out of the courtroom and out of the case. Lewis wondered idly what his fee would be . . .

'Chief Inspector Morse, please.'

Morse walked to the witness-box and took the oath in a mumbled gabble.

'You are in charge of the investigation into the death of Mr Nicholas Quinn.'

Morse nodded. 'Yes, sir.'

Before the coroner could proceed, however, there was a slight commotion at the entrance door; and a series of whispered exchanges, which resulted in a bearded young man being admitted and taking his place next to Constable Dickson on one of the low benches. Lewis was glad to see him: he had begun to wonder if his letter to Mr Richard Bartlett had gone astray.

The coroner resumed: 'Are you prepared to indicate to the court the present state of your investigations into this matter?'

'Not yet, sir. And with your honour's permission, I wish to make formal application for the inquest to be adjourned for a fortnight.'

'Am I to understand, Chief Inspector, that your inquiries are likely to be completed within that time?'

'Yes, sir. Quite shortly, I hope.'

'I see. Am I right in saying that you have as yet made no arrest in this case?'

'An arrest is imminent.'

'Indeed?'

Morse took a warrant from his inside pocket and held it up before the court. 'It may be somewhat unusual to introduce such a note of melodrama into your court, your honour; but immediately after the adjournment of this inquest – should, of course, your honour allow the adjournment – it will be my duty to make an arrest.' Morse turned his head slightly and ran his eyes along the front bench: Dickson, Richard Bartlett, Mrs Evans, Mrs Jardine, Martin, Dr Bartlett, Monica Height, Roope, and Lewis. Yes, they were all there, with the murderer seated right amongst them! Things were going according to plan.

The coroner formally adjourned the inquest for two weeks and the court stood as the august personage reluctantly departed. Now there was a hush over the assembly; no one seemed to breathe or to blink as Morse slowly stepped down from the witness-box, and stood momentarily before Richard Bartlett, and then walked on; past Mrs Evans; past Mrs Jardine; past Martin; past Bartlett; past

Monica Height; and then stood in front of Roope. And stayed there.

'Christopher Algernon Roope, I have here a warrant for your arrest in connection with the murder of Nicholas Quinn.' The words echoed vaguely around the hushed court, and still nobody seemed to breathe. 'It is my duty to tell you— '

Roope stared at Morse in disbelief. 'What the *hell* are you talking about?' His eyes darted first to the left and then to the right, as if calculating his chances of making a quick dash for it. But to his right stood the bulky figure of Constable Dickson; and immediately to his left Lewis laid a heavy hand upon his shoulder.

'I hope you'll be sensible and come quietly, sir.'

Roope spoke in a harsh whisper. 'I hope you realize what a dreadful mistake you're making. I just don't know— '

'Leave it for later,' snapped Morse.

All eyes were on Roope as he walked out, Dickson on his right and Lewis on his left; but still no one said a word. It was as if they had all been struck dumb, or just witnessed a miracle, or stared into the face of the Gorgon.

Bartlett was the first to move. He looked utterly dumbfounded and walked like an automaton towards his son. Monica's eyes crossed the gap that Bartlett had left, and found Donald Martin's looking directly into her own. It was the merest imperceptibility, perhaps; but it was there. The slightest shaking of her head; the profound, dead stillness of her eyes: 'Shut up, you fool!' they seemed to say. 'Shut up, you stupid fool!'

Chapter Twenty-five

'You had mixed luck in this wicked business, Roope. You had a bit of good luck, I know; and you made the most of it. But you also had some bad luck: things happened that no one, not even you, could have foreseen. And although you tried to cope as best you could – in fact, you almost succeeded in turning it to your own advantage – you had to be just that little bit *too* clever. I realized that I was up against an exceptionally cunning and resourceful murderer, but in the end it was your very cleverness that gave you away.'

The three of them, Morse, Lewis, Roope, sat together in Interview Room No 1. Lewis (who had been firmly cautioned by Morse to keep his mouth shut, whatever the provocation) was seated by the door, whilst Morse and Roope sat opposite each other at the small table. Morse, the hunter, seemed supremely confident as he sat back on the wooden chair, his voice calm, almost pleasant. 'Shall I go on?'

'If you must. I've already told you what a fool you're making of yourself, but you seem determined to listen to no one.'

Morse nodded. 'All right. We'll start in the middle, I think. We'll start at the point where you walked into the Syndicate building at about 4.25 p.m. a week last Friday. The first person you saw was the caretaker, Noakes, mending a broken light-tube in the corridor. But it was soon clear to you that there was no one else in the downstairs offices at all. No one! You concocted some appropriate tale about having to leave some papers with Dr Bartlett, and since he was out you had the best reason in the world for trying to find one of the others and for looking into their offices. You looked into Quinn's, of course, and everything was just as you'd known it would be – as you'd *planned* it would be. Everything was cleverly arranged to give the clear impression to anyone going into his room that Quinn was *there* – in the office; or, at least, would be there again very soon. It was raining heavily all day Friday – a piece of good luck! – and there, on the back of Quinn's chair, was his green anorak. Who would leave the office on a day like that without taking his coat? And the cabinets were left *open*. Now cabinets contain question papers, and the Secretary would have been down like a hawk on any of his colleagues who showed the slightest carelessness over security. But what are we asked to believe in Quinn's case? Quinn? Recently appointed; briefed, doubtless *ad nauseam*, about the need for the strictest security at every second of every day. And what does he do, Roope? He goes out and leaves his cabinets open! Yet, at the very same time, we find evidence of Quinn's punctilious adherence to the Secretary's instructions. Since he took up his job a few months previously, he has been told, very pointedly told, that it doesn't matter in the slightest if he takes time off during the day. *But* – if he does go out, he's to leave a note informing anyone who might want him exactly where he is or what he's doing. In other words, what Bartlett says is all the law and the commandments. Now, I find the combination of these two sets of circumstances extremely suggestive, Roope. Some of us are idle and careless, and some of us are fussy and conscientious. But very few of us manage to be both at the same time. Wouldn't you agree?'

Roope was staring through the window on to the concrete yard. He was watchful and tensed, but he said nothing.

'The caretaker told you that he was going off for tea, and before long you were alone – *or so you thought* – on the ground floor of the Syndicate building. It was still only about half-past four, and although I suspect you'd originally planned to wait until the whole office was empty, this was too good a chance to miss. Noakes, quite unwittingly, had given you some very interesting information, though you could very easily have found it out for yourself. The only car left in the rear car park was *Quinn's*. Well, what happened then was this, or something very like it. You went into Quinn's room once more. You took his anorak, and you put it on. You kept your gloves on, of course, and you folded up the plastic mac you'd been wearing. Then you saw that note once more, and you decided that you might as well pocket it. Certainly Quinn wouldn't have left it on the desk if he'd returned, and from this point on you had to think and act exactly as Quinn would have done. You walked out of the back door and found – as you knew you would – that Quinn's car keys were in his anorak pocket. No one was around, of course: the weather was still foul – though ideal for you. You got into the car and you drove away from the building. Noakes in fact saw you leave as he sat upstairs having a cup of tea. But he thought – why shouldn't he? – that it was Quinn. After all, he could only see the top of the car. So? That was that. The luck was on your side at this stage, and you made the most of it. The first part of the great deception was over, and you'd come through it with flying colours!'

Roope shuffled uneasily on his hard wooden chair, and his eyes looked dangerous; but again he said nothing.

'You drove the car to Kidlington and you parked it safely in Quinn's own garage in Pinewood Close, and here again you had a curious combination of good and bad luck. First the good luck. The rain was still pouring down and no one was likely to look too carefully at the man who got out of Quinn's car to unlock his own garage doors. It was dark, too, and the corner of Pinewood Close was even darker than usual because someone – *someone*, Roope, had seen to it that the street lamp outside the house had been recently and conveniently smashed. I make no specific charges on that point, but you must allow me to harbour my little suspicions. So, even if anyone *did* see you, hunched up in Quinn's green anorak, head down in the rain, I doubt whether any suspicions would have been aroused. You were very much the same build as Quinn, and like him you had a beard. But in another way the luck was very much against you. It so happened, and you couldn't help noticing the fact, that a woman was standing at the upstairs front window. She'd been waiting a long time, frightened that her baby was going to be born prematurely; she had rung her husband at Cowley several times, and she was impatiently expecting him at any minute. Now, as I say, this was not in itself a fatal occurrence. She'd seen you, of course, but it never occurred to her for a second that the person she saw was anyone but Quinn; and you yourself must have totted up the odds and worked on exactly that assumption. Nevertheless, she'd seen you go *into the house*, where you immediately discovered that Mrs Evans – you must have had a complete dossier on all the domestic arrangements – as I say, Mrs Evans, by a sheer fluke, had not finished the cleaning. What's more, she'd left a note to say she would be coming back! That was bad luck, all right, and yet you suddenly saw the chance of turning the tables completely. You read the note from Mrs Evans, and you screwed it up and threw it into the waste-paper basket. You lit the gas fire, putting the match you used carefully back into your matchbox. You shouldn't have done that, Roope! But we all make mistakes, don't we? And then – the masterstroke! You had a note in your pocket – a note written by Quinn himself, a note which not only looked genuine; it *was* genuine. Any handwriting expert was going to confirm, almost at a glance, that the writing was Quinn's. Of course he'd confirm it. The writing *was* Quinn's. You were hellishly lucky, though, weren't you? The note was addressed to Margaret Freeman, Quinn's confidential secretary. But not by name. By initials. MF. You found a black thin-point Biro in Quinn's anorak, and very carefully you changed the initials. Not too difficult, was it? A bit of a squiggle for "rs" after the M, and an additional bar at the bottom of the F, converting it into an E. The message was good enough – vague enough, anyway – to cover the deception. How you must have smiled as you placed the note carefully on the top of the cupboard. Yes, indeed! And then you went out again. You didn't want to take any risks, though; so you went via the back door, out into the back garden, through the gap in the fence and over the path across the field to the *Quality* supermarket. You had to get out of the house anyway, so why not carry through with the bluff? You bought some provisions, and even as you walked round the shelves your brain was working non-stop. Buy something that made it look as though Quinn was having someone in for a meal that evening! Why not? Another clever touch. Two steaks and all the rest of it. But you shouldn't have bought the butter, Roope! You got the wrong brand, and he had plenty in the fridge, anyway. As I say, it was clever. But you were getting a bit *too* clever.'

'Like you are, Inspector.' Roope bestirred himself at last. He took out a cigarette and lit it, putting the match carefully into the ashtray. 'I can't honestly think that you expect me to believe such convoluted nonsense.' He spoke carefully and rationally, and appeared much more at ease with himself. 'If you've nothing better to talk about than such boy-scout fancy-dress twaddle, I suggest you release me immediately. But if you want to persist with it, I shall have to call in my lawyer. I refused to do this when you told me of my rights earlier – I knew my rights, anyway, Inspector – but I thought I'd rather have my own innocence at my side than any pettifogging lawyer. But you're driving me a bit too far, you know. You've not the slightest shred of evidence for any of these fantastic allegations you've made against me. Not the slightest! And if you can't do any better than this I suggest that it may be in your own interests, not just mine, to pack in this ridiculous charade immediately.'

'You deny the charges then?'

'Charges? *What* charges? I'm not aware that you've made any charges.'

'You deny that the sequence of events— '

'Of *course*, I deny it! Why the hell should anyone go to all that trouble—?'

'Whoever murdered Quinn had to try to establish an alibi. And he did. A very clever alibi. You see all the indications in this case seemed to point to Quinn being alive on Friday evening, certainly until the early evening, and it was vital— '

'You mean Quinn *wasn't* alive on Friday evening?'

'Oh no,' said Morse slowly. '*Quinn had been dead for several hours.*'

There was a long silence in the small room, broken finally by Roope. 'Several hours, you say?'

Morse nodded. 'But I'm not *quite* sure exactly when Quinn was murdered. I rather hoped you might be able to tell me.'

Roope laughed aloud, and shook his head in bewilderment. 'And you think *I* killed Quinn?'

'That's why you're here, and that's why you're going to stay here – until you decide to tell me the truth.'

Roope's voice suddenly became high-pitched and exasperated. 'But – but I was in London that Friday. I *told* you that. I got back to Oxford at four-fifteen. Four-fifteen! Can't you believe that?'

'No, I can't,' said Morse flatly.

'Well, look, Inspector. Let's just get one thing straight. I don't suppose I could account for my movements – at least not to your satisfaction – from, let's say, five o'clock to about eight o'clock that night. And you wouldn't believe me, anyway. But if you're determined to keep me in this miserable place much longer, at least charge me with something I *could* have done. All right! I drove Quinn's car and did his shopping and God knows what else. Let's accept all that bloody nonsense, if it'll please you. *But charge me with murdering Quinn as well.* At twenty-past four – whenever you like, I don't care! Five o'clock. Six o'clock. Seven o'clock. Take your pick. But for Christ's sake show *some* sense. *I was in London until three o'clock or so, and I was on the train until it reached Oxford.* Don't you understand that? Make something up, if you like. But please, *please* tell me when and how I'm supposed to have murdered the man. That's all I ask.'

As Lewis looked at him, Morse seemed to be growing a little less confident. He picked up the papers in front of him and shuffled them around meaninglessly. Something seemed to have misfired somewhere – that was for sure.

'I've only got your word, Mr Roope' (it was *Mr* Roope now) 'that you caught that particular train from London. You were at your publishers', I know that. We've checked. But you could— '

'May I use your phone, Inspector?'

Morse shrugged and looked vaguely disconsolate. 'It's a bit unusual, I suppose, but— '

Roope looked through the directory, rang a number, and spoke rapidly for a few minutes before handing the receiver to Morse. It was the Cabriolet Taxi Services, and Morse listened and nodded and asked no questions. 'I see. Thank you.' He put down the phone and looked across at Roope. 'You had more success than we did, Mr Roope. Did you find the ticket collector, too?'

'No. He's had flu, but he'll be back at work this week sometime.'

'You've been very busy.'

'I was worried – who wouldn't be? You kept asking me where I was, and I thought you'd got it in for me, and I knew it would be sensible to try to check. We've all got an instinct for self-preservation, you know.'

'Ye-es.' Morse ran the index finger of his left hand along his nose – many, many times; and finally came to a decision. He dialled a number and asked for the editor of the *Oxford Mail*. 'I see. We're too late then. Page one, you say? Oh dear. Well, it can't be helped. What about Stop Press? Could we get anything in there? . . . Good. Let's say er "Murder Suspect Released. Mr C. A. Roope (see page 1), arrested earlier today in connection with the murder of Nicholas Quinn, was released this afternoon. Chief Inspector— " What? No more room? I see. Well, it'll be better than nothing. Sorry to muck you about . . . Yes, I'm afraid these things do happen sometimes. Cheers.'

Morse cradled the phone and turned towards Roope. 'Look, sir. As I say, things like this do— '

Roope got to his feet. 'Forget it! You've said enough for one day. Can I assume I'm free to go now?' There was a sharp edge on his voice.

'Yes, sir. And, as I say . . . ' Roope looked at him with deep contempt as the feeble sentence whimpered away. 'Have you a car here, sir?'

'No. I don't have a car.'

'Oh no, I remember. If you like, Sergeant Lewis here will— '

'No, he won't! I've had quite enough of your sickening hospitality for one day. I'll bus it, thank you very much!'

Before Morse could say more, he had left the room and was walking briskly across the courtyard in the bright and chilly afternoon.

* * *

During the last ten minutes of the interview Lewis had felt himself becoming progressively more perplexed, and at one stage he had stared at Morse like a street-idler gaping at the village idiot. What *did* Morse think he was doing? He looked again at him now, his head down over the sheets of paper on the table. But even as Lewis looked, Morse lifted his head, and a strangely self-satisfied smile was spreading over his face. He saw that Lewis was watching him, and he winked happily.

Chapter Twenty-six

The man inside the house is anxious, but reasonably calm. The phone rings stridently, imperiously, several times during the late afternoon and early evening. But he does not answer it, for he has seen the post-office van repairing (repairing!) the telephone wires just along the road. Clumsy and obvious. They must think him stupid. Yet all the time he knows that *they* are not stupid, either, and the knowledge nags away in his mind. Over and over again he tells himself that they cannot *know*; can only guess; can never prove. The maze would defeat an indefatigable Ariadne, and the ball of thread leads only to blind and bricked-up alleyways. Infernal phone! He waits until the importunate caller has exhausted a seemingly limitless patience, and takes the receiver off its stand. But it purrs – intolerably. He turns on the transistor radio at ten minutes to six and listens, yet with only a fraction of his conscious faculties, to the BBC's City correspondent discussing the fluctuations in the *Financial Times* index, and the fortunes of the floating pound. He himself has no worries about money. No worries at all.

The man outside the house continues to watch. Already he has been watching for over three and a half hours, and his feet are damp and cold. He looks at his luminous watch: 5.40 p.m. Only another twenty minutes before his relief arrives. Still no movement, save for the shadow that repeatedly passes back and forth across the curtained window.

* * *

If sleep be defined as the relaxation of consciousness, the man inside the house does not sleep that night. He is dressed again at 6 a.m. and he waits. At 6.45 a.m. he hears the clatter of milk-bottles in the darkened road outside. But still he waits. It is not until 7.45 a.m. that the paper boy arrives with *The Times*. It is still dark, and the little business is speedily transacted. Uncomplicated; unobserved.

The man outside the house has almost given up hope when at 1.15 p.m. the door opens and the man emerges and walks unhur-riedly down towards Oxford. The man outside switches to 'trans-mission' and speaks into his mobile radio. Then he switches to 'reception', and the message is brief and curt: 'Follow him, Dickson! And don't let him see you!'

The man who had been inside the house walks to the railway station, where he looks around him and then walks into the buffet, orders a cup of coffee, sits by the window, and looks out on to the car park. At 1.35 a car drives slowly past – a familiar car, which turns down the incline into the car park. The automatic arm is raised and the car makes for the furthest corner of the area. The car park is almost full. The man in the buffet puts down his half-finished coffee, lights a cigarette, puts the spent match neatly back into the box, and walks out.

At 2.00 p.m. the young girl in the maroon dress can stand it no longer. The customers, too, though they are only few, have been looking at him queerly. She walks from behind the counter and taps him on the shoulder. He is not much above medium height. 'Excuse me, sir. Bu' have you come in for a coffee, or somethin'?'

'No. I'll have a cup o' tea, please.' He speaks pleasantly, and as he puts down his powerful binoculars she sees that his eyes are a palish shade of blue.

It is just after five when Lewis gets home. He is tired and his feet are like ice.

'Are you horme for the night?'

'Yes, luv, thank goodness! I'm freezing cold.'

'Is that bloody man, Morse, tryin' to give you pneumornia, or somethin'?'

Lewis hears his wife all right, but he is thinking of something else. 'He's a clever bugger, Morse is. Christ, he's clever! Though whether he's *right* or not . . . ' But his wife is no longer listening, and Lewis hears the thrice-blessed clatter of the chip pan in the kitchen.

Chapter Twenty-seven

In the Syndicate building on Wednesday morning, Morse told Bartlett frankly about the virtual certainty of some criminal mal-practice in the administration of the examinations. He mentioned specifically his suspicions about the leakage of question papers to Al-jamara, and passed exhibit No 1 across the table.

3rd March

Dear George,
Greetings to all at Oxford. Many thanks for your
letter and for the Summer examination package.
All Entry Forms and Fees Forms should be ready
for final despatch to the Syndicate by Friday
20th or at the very latest, I'm told, by the 21st.
Admin has improved here, though there's room
for improvement still; just give us all two or three
more years and we'll really show you! Please
don't let these wretched 16+ proposals destroy
your basic O- and A-pattern. Certainly this
sort of change, if implemented immediately,
would bring chaos.
Sincerely yours,

Bartlett frowned deeply as he read the letter, then opened his desk diary and consulted a few entries. 'This is er a load of nonsense – you realize that, don't you? All entry forms had to be in by the first of March this year. We've installed a mini-computer and anything arriving after— '

Morse interrupted him. 'You mean the entry forms from Al-jamara were already in when that letter was written?'

'Oh yes. Otherwise we couldn't have examined their candidates.'

'And you did examine them?'

'Certainly. Then there's this business of the Summer examination package. They couldn't possibly have received that before early April. Half the question papers weren't printed until then. And there's something else wrong, isn't there, Inspector? The 20th March isn't a Friday. Not in my diary, anyway. No, no. I don't think I'd build too much on this letter. I'm sure it can't be from one of our— '

'You don't recognize the signature?'

'Would anybody? It looks more like a coil of barbed wire— '

'Just read down the right-hand side of the letter, sir. The last word on each line, if you see what I mean.'

In a flat voice the Secretary read the words aloud: 'your – package – ready – Friday – 21st – room – three – Please – destroy – this – immediately.' He nodded slowly to himself. 'I see what you mean, Inspector, though I must say I'd never have spotted it myself . . . You mean you think that George Bland was— '

' – was on the fiddle, yes. I'm convinced that this letter told him exactly where and when he could collect the latest instalment of his money.'

Bartlett took a deep breath and consulted his diary once more. 'You may just be on to something, I suppose. He wasn't in the office on Friday 21st.'

'Do you know where he was?'

Bartlett shook his head and passed over the diary, where among the dozen or so brief, neatly-written entries under 21st March Morse read the laconic reminder: 'GB not in office.'

'Can you get in touch with him, sir?'

'Of course. I sent him a telegram only last Wednesday – about Quinn. They'd met when— '

'Did he reply?'

'Hasn't done yet.'

Morse took the plunge. 'Naturally I can't tell you everything, sir, but I think you ought to know that in my view the deaths of both Quinn and Ogleby are directly linked with Bland. I think that Bland was corrupt enough to compromise the integrity of this Syndicate at every point – if there was money in it for him. But I think there's someone *here*, too, not necessarily on the staff, but someone very closely associated with the work of the Syndicate, who's in collaboration with Bland. And I've little doubt that Quinn found out who it was, and got himself murdered for his trouble.'

Bartlett had been listening intently to Morse's words, but he evinced little surprise. 'I thought you might be going to say something like that, Inspector, and I suppose you think that Ogleby found out as well, and was murdered for the same reason.'

'Could be, sir. Though you may be making a false assumption. You see, it may be that the murderer of Nicholas Quinn has already been punished for his crime.'

The little Secretary was genuinely shocked now. His eyebrows shot up an inch, and his frameless lenses settled even lower on his nose, as Morse slowly continued:

'I'm afraid you must face the real possibility, sir, that Quinn's murderer worked here under your very nose; the possibility that he was in fact your own deputy-secretary – *Philip Ogleby*.'

Lewis came in ten minutes later as Morse and Bartlett were arranging the meeting. Bartlett was to phone or write to all the Syndicate members and ask them to attend an extraordinary general meeting on Friday morning at 10 a.m.; he was to insist that it was of the utmost importance that they should cancel all other commitments and attend; after all, two members of the Syndicate had been murdered, hadn't they?

In the corridor outside Lewis whispered briefly to Morse. 'You were right, sir. It rang for two minutes. Noakes confirms it.'

'Excellent. I think it's time to make a move then, Lewis. Car outside?'

'Yes, sir. Do you want me with you?'

'No. You get to the car; we'll be along in a minute.' He walked along the corridor, knocked quietly on the door, and entered. She was sitting at her desk signing letters, but promptly took off her reading glasses, stood up, and smiled sweetly. 'Bit early to take me for a drink, isn't it?'

'No chance, I'm afraid. The car's outside – I think you'd better get your coat.'

The man inside does not go out this same Wednesday morning. The paper boy lingers for a few seconds as he puts *The Times* through the letter box, but no lucrative errand is commissioned this morning; the milkman delivers one pint of milk; the postman brings no letters; there are no visitors. The phone has gone several times earlier, and at twelve o'clock it goes again. Four rings; then, almost immediately it resumes, and mechanically the man counts the number of rings again – twenty-eight, twenty-nine, thirty. The phone stops, and the man smiles to himself. It is a clever system. They have used it several times before.

The man outside is still waiting; but expectantly now, for he thinks that the time of reckoning may be drawing near. At 4.20 p.m. he is conscious of some activity at the back of the house, and a minute later the man inside emerges with a bicycle, rides quickly away up a side turning, and in less than five seconds has completely disappeared. It has been too quick, too unexpected. Constable Dickson swears softly to himself and calls up HQ, where Sergeant Lewis is distinctly unamused.

The car park is again very full today, and Morse is standing by the window in the buffet bar. He wonders what would happen if a heavy snowshower were to smother each of the cars in a thick white blanket; then each of the baffled motorists would need to remember exactly where he had left his car, and go straight to that spot – and find it. Just as Morse finds the spot again through his binoculars. But he can see nothing, and half an hour later, at 5.15 p.m., he can still see nothing. He gives it up, talks to the ticket collector, and learns beyond all reasonable doubt that Roope was not lying when he said he'd passed through the ticket barrier, as if from the 3.05 train from Paddington, on Friday, 21st November.

As he steps out of his front door at 9.30 a.m. the next day, Thursday, 4th December, the man who has been inside is arrested by Sergeant Lewis and Constable Dickson of the Thames Valley Constabulary, CID Branch. He is charged with complicity in the murders of Nicholas Quinn and Philip Ogleby.

Chapter Twenty-eight

The case was over now, or virtually so, and Morse had his feet up on his desk, feeling slightly over-beered and more than slightly self-satisfied, when Lewis came in at 2.30 on Thursday afternoon. 'I found him, sir. Had to drag him out of a class at Cherwell School – but I found him. It was just what you said.'

'Well that's the final nail in the coffin and— ' He suddenly broke off. 'You don't look too happy, Lewis. What's the trouble?'

'I still don't understand what's happening.'

'Lewis! You don't want to ruin my little party-piece in the morning, do you?'

Lewis shrugged a reluctant consent, but he felt like an examinee who has just emerged from the examination room, conscious that he should have done very much better. 'I suppose you think I'm not very bright, sir.'

'Nothing of the sort! It was a very clever crime, Lewis. I was just a bit lucky here and there, that's all.'

'I suppose I missed the obvious clues – as usual.'

'But they *weren't* obvious, my dear old friend. Well, perhaps . . . ' He put his feet down and lit a cigarette. 'Let me tell you what put me on to the track, shall I? Let's see now. First of all, I think, the single most important fact in the whole case was Quinn's deafness. You see Quinn was not only hard of hearing; he was very very deaf. But we learned that he was quite exceptionally proficient in the art of lip-reading; and I'm quite sure that because he could lip-read so brilliantly Quinn discovered the staggering fact that one of his colleagues was crooked. You see the real sin against the Holy Ghost for anyone in charge of public examinations is to divulge the contents of question papers beforehand; and Quinn discovered that one of his colleagues was doing precisely that. *But*, Lewis, I failed to take into account a much more obvious and a much more important implication of Quinn's being deaf. It sounds almost childishly simple when you think of it – in fact an idiot would have spotted it before I did. It's this. Quinn was a marvel at reading from the lips of others – agreed? He might just as well have had ears, really. But he could only, let's say, *hear* what others were saying when he could *see* them. Lip-reading's absolutely useless when you can't see the person who's talking;

when someone stands behind you, say, or when someone in the corridor outside shouts that there's a bomb in the building. Do you see what I mean, Lewis? If someone knocked on Quinn's office door, he couldn't hear anything. But as soon as someone opened the door and *said* something – he was fine. All right? Remember this, then: *Quinn couldn't hear what he didn't see.*'

'Am I supposed to see why all that's important, sir?'

'Oh yes. And you *will* do, Lewis, if only you think back to the Friday when Quinn was murdered.'

'He was definitely murdered on the Friday, then?'

'I think if you pushed me I could tell you to within sixty seconds!' He looked very smug about the whole thing, and Lewis felt torn between the wish to satisfy his own curiosity and a reluctance to gratify the chief's inflated ego even further. Yet he thought he caught a glimpse of the truth at last . . . Yes, of course. Noakes had said . . . He nodded several times, and his curiosity won.

'What about all this business at the cinema, though? Was that all a red herring?'

'Certainly not. It was *meant* to be a red herring, but as things turned out – not too luckily from the murderer's point of view – it presented a series of vital clues. Just think a minute. Everything we began to learn about Quinn's death seemed to take it further and further forward in time: he rang up a school in Bradford at about 12.20; he went to Studio 2 at about half-past one, after leaving a note in his office for his secretary; he came back to the office about a quarter to five, and drove home; he left a note for his cleaning woman and got some shopping in; he's heard on the phone about ten past five; certainly no one except Mrs Evans comes to see him before six-thirty or so, because Mrs Greenaway is keeping an eagle eye on the drive. So? So Quinn must have been murdered later that evening, or even on the following morning. The medical report didn't help us much either way, and we had little option but to follow our noses – which we did. But when you come to add all the evidence up, no one actually *saw* Quinn after midday on Friday. Take the phone call to Bradford. If you're a schoolmaster – and all of the staff at the Syndicate had taught at one point – you know that 12.20 is just about the worst time in the whole day to try to get a member of staff. School lessons may finish earlier in a few schools but the vast majority don't. In other words that call was made with not the least expectation that its purpose would be successful. That is, unless the purpose was to mislead *me* – in which case I'm afraid it was highly successful. Now, take the note Quinn left. We know that Bartlett is a bit of a tartar about most aspects of office routine; and one of his rules is that his assistant secretaries must leave a note when they go out. Now, Quinn had been with the Syndicate for three months, and being a keen young fellow and anxious to please his boss, he must have left dozens of little notes during that time; and anyone, if he or she was so minded, could have taken one, especially if that someone needed one of the notes to further an alibi. And someone did. Then there's the phone call Mrs Greenaway heard. But note once again that she didn't actually *see* him making it. She's nervous and anxious: she thinks the baby's due, and the very last thing she wants to indulge in is a bit of eavesdropping. All she wants is the line to be free! When she hears voices she doesn't want to listen to them – she wants them to *finish*. And if the other person – the one she thinks Quinn is ringing – is doing most of the talking at that point . . . You see what I was getting at with Roope, Lewis? If *Roope* were talking – putting in just the occasional "yes" and "no" and so on – Mrs Greenaway, who says she doesn't hear too well anyway, would automatically assume it was *Quinn*. Both Quinn and Roope came from Bradford, and both spoke with a pretty broad northern accent, and all Mrs Greenaway remembers clearly is that *one* of the voices was a bit cultured and donnish. Now, that doesn't take us much further, I agree. At the most it tells us that the telephone conversation wasn't between Quinn and Roope. But I knew that, Lewis, because I knew that Quinn must have been dead for several hours when someone spoke from Quinn's front room.'

'It was a bit of luck for him that Mrs Greenaway didn't— '

Morse was nodding. 'Yes. But the luck wasn't all on his side. Remember that Mrs Evans— '

'You've explained how that could have happened, sir. It's just this Studio 2 business I can't follow.'

'I'm not surprised. We had everybody telling us lies about it. But let me give you one or two clues. Martin and Monica Height had decided to go to the pictures on Friday afternoon, and yet they stupidly tried to change their alibi – change a good alibi for a lousy alibi. Just ask yourself *why*, Lewis. The only sensible answer that I could think of was that they had *seen* something – or one of them had seen something – which they weren't prepared to talk about. Now, I think that Monica, at least on this point, was prepared to tell me the truth – the literal truth. I asked her whether she had seen someone else going *in*; and she said no.' Morse smiled slowly: 'Do you see what I mean now?'

'No, sir.'

'Keep at it, Lewis! You see, whatever happened in the early afternoon of that Friday, *Martin and Monica stayed to see the film*. Do you understand that? Whatever upset them – or, as I say, upset one of them – it didn't result in their leaving the cinema. Need I go on?'

Need he go on! Huh! Lewis was more lost than ever, but his curiosity would give him no peace. 'What about Ogleby, then?'

'Ah. Now we're coming to it. Ogleby lied to me, Lewis. He told me one or two lies of the first water. *But the great majority of the things Ogleby said were true*. You were there when I questioned him, Lewis, and if you want *some* of the truth, just look back to your notes. You'll find he said some very interesting things. You'll find, for example, that he said he was in the office that Friday afternoon.'

'And you think he was?'

'I know he was. He just *had* to be, you see.'

'Oh,' said Lewis, unseeing. 'And he went to Studio 2 as well, I suppose?'

Morse nodded. 'Later on, yes. And remember that he'd made a careful sketch of another ticket – the ticket that was found in Quinn's pocket. Now. There's a nice little poser for you, Lewis: when and why did Ogleby do that? Well?'

'I don't know, sir. I just get more confused the more I think about it.'

Morse got up and walked across the room. 'It's easy when you think about it, Lewis. Ask yourself just one question: Why didn't he just *take* the ticket? He must have seen it; must have had it in his hands. There's only one answer, isn't there?'

Lewis nodded hopefully and Morse (praise be!) continued:

'Yes. Ogleby wasn't meant to find the ticket. But he did; and he knew that it had been placed wherever it was for a vital purpose, Lewis, *and he knew that he had to leave it exactly where he'd found it.*'

The phone rang and Morse answered it, saying he'd be there

straightaway. 'You'd better come along, Lewis. His lawyer's arrived.' As they walked together down to the cell-block, Morse asked Lewis if he had any idea where the Islets of Langerhans were.

'Sounds vaguely familiar, sir. Baltic Sea, is it?'

'No, it's not. It's in the pancreas – if you know where that is.'

'As a matter of fact, I do, sir. It's a large gland discharging into the duodenum.'

Morse raised his eyebrows in admiration. One up to Lewis.

Chapter Twenty-nine

As Morse looked at the Thursday-evening class with their hearing aids, private or NHS, plugged into their ears, he reminded himself that during the previous weeks of the term Quinn had sat there amongst his fellow-students, sharing the mysteries and the silent manifestations. There were eight of them, sitting in a single row in front of their teacher, and at the back of the room Morse felt that he was watching a TV screen with the sound turned off. The teacher was talking, for her lips moved and she made the natural gestures of speech. But no sound. When Morse had managed to rid himself of the suspicion that *he* had suddenly been struck deaf, he watched the teacher's lips more closely, and tried as hard as he could to read the words. Occasionally one or other of the class would raise a hand and voice a silent question, and then the teacher would write up a word on the blackboard. Frequently, it appeared, the difficult words – the words that the class were puzzled by – began with 'p', or 'b', or 'm'; and to a lesser extent with 't', 'd', or 'n'. Lip-reading was clearly a most sophisticated skill.

At the end of the class, Morse thanked the teacher for allowing him to observe, and spoke to her about Quinn. Here, too, he had been the star pupil, it seemed, and all the class had been deeply upset at the news of his death. Yes, he really had been very deaf indeed – but one wouldn't have guessed; unless, that is, one had experience of these things.

A bell sounded throughout the building. It was 9 p.m. and time for everyone to leave the premises.

'Would he have been able to hear that?' asked Morse.

But the teacher had temporarily turned away to mark the register. The bell was still ringing. 'Would Quinn have been able to hear that?' repeated Morse.

But she still didn't hear him and, belatedly, Morse guessed the truth. When finally she looked up again, he repeated his question once more. 'Could Quinn hear the bell?'

'Could Quinn hear them all, did you say? I'm sorry, I didn't quite catch— '

'H-ear th-e b-e-ll,' mouthed Morse, with ridiculous exaggeration.

'Oh, the *bell*. Is it ringing? I'm afraid that none of us could hear that.'

Thursday was guest-night at Lonsdale College, but after a couple of post-prandial ports the Dean of the Syndicate decided he'd better get back to his rooms. He was decidedly displeased at having to rearrange his Friday morning programme, since one of the few duties he positively enjoyed was that of interviewing prospective entrants. As he walked along the quad he wondered morosely how long the Syndicate meeting would last, and why exactly Tom Bartlett had been so insistent. It was all getting out of hand, anyway. He was getting too old for the post, and he looked forward to his retirement in a year's time. One thing was certain: he just couldn't cope with events like those of the past fortnight.

He looked through the pile of UCCA forms on his desk and read the fulsome praises heaped upon the heads of their pupils by headmasters and headmistresses, so desperately anxious to lift their schools a few places up the table in the Oxbridge League. If only such heads would realise that all their blabber was, if anything, counter-productive! On the first form he read some headmistress's report on a young girl anxious to take up one of the few places at Lonsdale reserved for women. The girl was (naturally!) the most brilliant scholar of her year and had won a whole cupboardful of prizes; and the Dean read the headmistress's comments in the 'Personality' column: 'Not unattractive and certainly a very vivacious girl, with a puckish sense of humour and

a piquant wit.' The Dean smiled slowly. What a sentence! Over
the years he had compiled his own little book of synonyms:

'not unattractive' = 'hideous to behold'
'vivacious'   = 'usually drunk'
'puckish'   = 'batty'
'piquant'   = 'plain rude'

Ah well. Perhaps she wasn't such a bad prospect after all! But
he wouldn't be interviewing her himself. Blast the Syndicate! It
would have been interesting to test his little theory once more.
So often people tried to create the impression of being completely
different from their true selves, and it wasn't all that difficult. A
smiling face, and a heart as hard as a flintstone! The opposite, too:
a face set as hard as a flint and . . . A vague memory stirred in the
Dean's mind. Chief Inspector Morse had mentioned something
similar, hadn't he? But the Dean couldn't quite get hold of it.
Never mind. It couldn't be very important.

Bartlett had received the call from Mrs Martin at eight o'clock.
Did he know where Donald was? Had he got a meeting? She
knew he had to work late some nights, but he had never been
away as long as this. Bartlett tried to make the right noises; said
not to worry; said he would ring her back; said there must be
some easy explanation.

'Oh Christ!' he said, after putting the receiver down.
'What's the matter, Tom?' Mrs Bartlett had come through into
the hall and was looking at him anxiously.

He put his hand gently on hers, and smiled wearily. 'How many
times have I told you? You mustn't listen in to my telephone calls.
You've got enough— '

'I never do. You know that, Tom. But— '

'It's all right. It's not your problem; it's mine. That's what they
pay me for, isn't it? I can't expect a fat salary for nothing, can I?'

Mrs Bartlett put her arm lovingly on his shoulder. 'I don't
know what they pay you, and I don't want to know. If they paid
you a million it wouldn't be too much! But— ' She was worried,
and the little Secretary knew it.

'I know. The world suddenly seems to have gone crazy, doesn't
it? That was Martin's wife. He's not home yet.'

'Oh no!'

'Now, now. Don't start jumping to silly conclusions.'

'You don't think—?'

'You go and sit down and pour yourself a gin. And pour one for me. I shan't be a minute.' He found Monica's number and dialled. And like someone else the day before, he found himself mechanically counting the dialling tones. Ten, twenty, twenty-five. Sally must be out, too. He let it ring a few more times, and then slowly replaced the receiver. The Syndicate seemed to be on the verge of total collapse.

He thought back on the years during which he had worked so hard to build it all up. And somehow, at some point, the foundation had begun to shift and cracks to appear in the edifice above. He could almost put the exact time to it: the time when Roope had been elected on to the Board of the Syndics. Yes. That was when things had started crumbling. Roope! For a few minutes the little Secretary stood indecisively by the phone, and knew that he could willingly murder the man. Instead he rang Morse's number at the Thames Valley HQ, but Morse was out, too. Not that it mattered much. He'd mention it to him in the morning.

Chapter Thirty

Mrs Seth arrived at a quarter to ten and made her way upstairs to the Board Room. She was the first of the Syndics to arrive, and as she sat down her thoughts drifted back . . . back to the last time she had sat there, when she had recalled her father . . . when Roope had spoken . . . when Quinn had been appointed . . . The room was gradually filling up, and she acknowledged a few muted 'good mornings'; but the atmosphere was one of gloom, and the other Syndics sat down silently and let their own thoughts drift back, as she had done. Sometimes one or two of the graduate staff attended Syndics' meetings, but only by invitation; and none was there this morning except Bartlett, whose tired, drawn face did little more than reflect the communal mood. A man was sitting next to Bartlett, but she didn't know him. Must be from the police. Pleasant-looking man: about her own age – mid-, late-forties; going a bit thin on top; nice eyes, though they seemed to look at you and through you at the same time. There was another man, too – probably another policeman; but he was standing diffidently outside the magic circle, with a notebook in his hands.

At two minutes past ten, when all except one of the chairs were occupied, Bartlett stood up and in a sad and disillusioned little speech informed the assembly of the police suspicions – his own, too – that the integrity of their own foreign examinations had been irreparably impaired by the criminal behaviour of one or two people, people in whom the Syndicate had placed complete trust; that it was the view of Chief Inspector Morse ('on my right') that the deaths of Quinn and Ogleby were directly connected with this matter; that, after the clearing-up of the comparatively small Autumn examination, the activities of the Syndicate would necessarily be in abeyance until a complete investigation had been made; that the implications of a possible shut-down were far-reaching, and that the full co-operation of each and every member of the Syndicate would be absolutely essential. But such matters would have to wait; the purpose of their meeting this morning was quite different, as they would see.

The Dean thanked the Secretary and proceeded to add his own lugubrious thoughts on the future of the Syndicate; and as he tediously ummed and ahed his way along, it became clear that the Syndics were getting rather restless. Words were whispered along the tables: 'One or *two*, didn't Bartlett say?' 'Who do you think?' 'Why have we got the police *here*?' 'They *are* the police, aren't they?'

The Dean finished at last, and the whispering finished, too. It was a strange reversal of the natural order, and Mrs Seth thought it had everything to do with the man seated on Bartlett's right, who thus far had sat impassively in his chair, occasionally running the index finger of his left hand along the side of his nose. She saw Bartlett turn towards Morse and look at him quizzically; and in turn she saw Morse nod slightly, before slowly rising to his feet.

'Ladies and gentlemen. I asked the Secretary to call this meeting because I thought it only proper that you should all know something of what we've discovered about the leakage of question papers from this office. Well, you've heard something about that and I think' (he looked vaguely at the Dean and then at Bartlett) 'I think that we may say that officially the meeting is over, and if any of you have commitments that can't wait, you should feel free to go.' He looked around the tables with cold, blue eyes, and the tension in the room perceptibly tautened. No one moved a muscle, and the stillness was profound. 'But perhaps it's proper, too,' resumed Morse, 'that you should know something about the police investigations into the deaths of Mr Quinn and Mr Ogleby, and I'm sure you will all be very glad to know that the case is now complete – or almost complete. Let's put it in the official jargon, ladies and gentlemen, and say that a man has been arrested and is being held for questioning in connection with the murders of Quinn and Ogleby.'

The silence of the room was broken only by the rustle of papers as Lewis turned over a page in his notebook: Morse held the ring and the assembled Syndics hung on his every word. 'You will know, or most of you will, that last Monday one of your own colleagues, Mr Christopher Roope, was detained in connection with Quinn's murder. You will know, too, I think, that he was released shortly afterwards. The evidence against him appeared to us insufficient to warrant further detention, and everything seemed to point to the fact that he had a perfectly valid alibi for the period of time on Friday, 21st November, when in the view of the police Quinn must have been murdered. Yet I must tell you all here and now that without a shadow of doubt Roope was the person responsible for selling the soul of the Syndicate – certainly in Al-jamara, and for all I know in several of your other oversea centres as well.' Some of the Syndics drew in their breaths, some opened their mouths slightly, but never for a second did their eyes leave Morse. '*And*, ladies and gentlemen, in all this his principal lieutenant was your former colleague, Mr George Bland.' Again the mingled surprise and shock around the table; but again the underlying hush and expectation. 'The whole thing was brought to light by the vigilance and integrity of one man – Nicholas Quinn. Now, precisely when Quinn made his discovery we shall perhaps never know for certain; but I should guess it may well have been at the reception given by the Al-jamara officials, when the drink was flowing freely, when some of the guilty were less than discreet, and when Quinn read things on the lips of others so clearly that they might just as well have been shouted through a megaphone.

And it was, I believe, as a direct result of Quinn's deeply disturbing discovery that he was murdered – to stop him talking, and to ensure that those guilty of betraying public confidence should continue to draw their rewards – very considerable rewards, no doubt – from their partners in crime abroad. Furthermore, I think that in addition to telling the guilty party of what he knew, or at least of what he strongly suspected, Quinn told someone else: someone he firmly believed had absolutely nothing to do with the crooked practices that were going on. That someone was Philip Ogleby. There is evidence that Quinn had far too much to drink at the reception, and that Ogleby followed him out as he left. Again I am guessing. But I think it more than likely that Ogleby caught up with Quinn, and told him that he would be a fool to drive himself home in such a drunken condition. He may have offered to drive him home, I don't know. But what is almost certain is that Quinn told Ogleby what he knew. Now, if Ogleby were in the racket himself, many of the things which were so puzzling about Quinn's murder would begin to sort themselves out. Of all Quinn's colleagues, Ogleby was the one person who had no alibi for the key period of Friday afternoon. He went back to the office after lunch, and he was there – or so he said – the rest of the afternoon. Now whoever killed Quinn had to be in the office both in the latter part of the morning, and again between half-past four and five; and if any single person from the office was guilty of murdering Quinn, there was only one genuine suspect – *Ogleby*, the very man in whom Quinn had confided.'

There was a slight murmur around the table and one or two of the Syndics stirred uneasily in their chairs; but Morse resumed, and the effect was that of a conductor tapping his baton on the rostrum.

'Ogleby lied to me when I questioned him about his exact whereabouts that Friday afternoon. I've been able to look back on the evidence he gave, since my Sergeant here' – a few heads turned and Lewis sheepishly acknowledged his moment of glory – 'took full notes at the time, and I can now see where Ogleby lied – where he *had* to lie. For example, he insisted that he was in the office at about 4.30 p.m., when not only Mr Roope but also Mr Noakes, the caretaker, could swear quite categorically that he *wasn't*. Now, this I find very strange. Ogleby lied to me on the one point which seemed to prove his guilt. Why?

Why did he say he was here all that afternoon? Why did he begin to tie the noose round his own neck? It's not an easy question to answer, I agree. But there *is* an answer; a very simple answer: *Ogleby was not lying.* On that point, at least, he was telling the truth. He *was* here, although neither Roope nor Noakes saw him. And when I looked back on his evidence, I began to ask myself whether one or two other things, which on the face of it seemed obvious lies, were in fact nothing of the sort. So it was that I gradually began to understand exactly what had happened that Friday afternoon, and to realize that Ogleby was entirely innocent of the murder of Nicholas Quinn. The fact of the matter is that precisely because Ogleby was in the office on the afternoon of Friday, 21st November, *he knew who had murdered Quinn*; and because of this knowledge, he was himself murdered. Why Ogleby didn't confide his virtually certain suspicions to me, I shall never really know. I think I can guess, but . . . Anyway, we can only be grateful that the murderer has been arrested and is now in custody at Police Headquarters. He has made a full statement.' Morse pointed dramatically to the empty chair. 'That's where he usually sits, I believe. Yes, ladies and gentlemen, your own colleague, *Christopher Roope.*'

A babel of chatter now broke out in the room, and Mrs Seth was weeping silently. Yet even before the general hub-bub had subsided there was a further moment of high drama. After several whispered conversations along the top table, the Vice-Dean requested permission to make a brief statement, and Morse sat down and began doodling aimlessly on the blotter in front of him.

'I hope the Chief Inspector will forgive me, but I wish to clear up one point, if I may. Did I understand him to say that whoever killed Quinn had to be in the Syndicate building both in the morning and also at the end of the afternoon?'

Morse replied at once. 'You understood correctly, sir. I don't wish to go into all the details of the case now; but Quinn was murdered at about twelve noon on Friday – no, let me be more honest with you – at *precisely* twelve noon on Friday 21st, and his dead body was taken from this building, in the boot of his own car, at approximately 4.45 p.m. Does that satisfy you, sir?'

The Vice-Dean coughed awkwardly and managed to look extra-ordinarily uncomfortable. 'Er, no, Chief Inspector. I'm afraid it doesn't. You see I myself went to London that Friday morning and I caught the 3.05 back to Oxford, arriving here about a quarter- , twenty-past four; and the plain truth is that *Roope was on the same train.*'

In the stunned silence which greeted this new evidence, Morse spoke quietly and slowly. 'You travelled back with him, you mean?'

'Er no, not exactly. I er I was walking along the platform and I saw Roope getting into a first-class carriage. I didn't join him because I was travelling second.' The Vice-Dean was glad not to have to elaborate on the truth. Even if he'd had a first-class ticket he would rather have sat in a second-class carriage than share a journey with Roope. He'd always hated Roope. What an ironic twist of fortune that he, the Vice-Dean, should be instrumental in clearing him of murder!

'I wish,' said Morse, 'that you could have told me that earlier, sir – not, of course' (he held up a hand to forestall any misunder-standing) 'that you could have known. But what you say is no surprise, sir. You see, *I knew that Roope caught the 3.05 from Paddington.*'

Several of the Syndics looked at each other; and there was a general air of bewilderment in the room. It was Bartlett himself who tried to put their unspoken questions into words. 'But only a few minutes ago you said— '

'No, sir,' interrupted Morse. 'I know what you're going to say, and you'd be wrong. I said that no one could have murdered Quinn without being in this building at two key periods; and that fact is quite unchallengeable. I repeat, *no single person* could have carried out the devilish and ingenious plan which was put into operation.' He looked slowly round the room and the full implication of his words slowly sunk into the minds of the Syndics. To Mrs Seth his voice seemed very quiet and far away now; yet at the same time heightened and tense as if the final disclosure were imminent at last. She saw Morse nod across and over her head, and she turned slightly to see Sergeant Lewis walk quietly to the door and leave the Board Room. What—? But Morse was talking again, in the same quiet, steely voice.

'As I say, we must accept the undoubted fact that one person, on his or her own, could not have carried through the murder of Quinn. And so, ladies and gentlemen, the inference is inevitable:

we are looking for two people. Two people who must share the same motives; two people for whom the death of Quinn is a vital necessity; two people who have a strangely close relationship; two people who can work and plot together; two people who are well known to you – *very* well known . . . And before Sergeant Lewis comes back, let me just emphasize one further point, because I don't think some of you listened very carefully to what I said. I said that Roope had been arrested and charged with murder. But I did not say *whose* murder. In fact I am absolutely convinced of one thing – *Christopher Roope did not murder Nicholas Quinn.*'

In Quinn's former office Monica Height and Donald Martin had not spoken to each other, although it was now more than half an hour since the two constables had fetched them. Monica felt herself moving through a barren, arid landscape, her thoughts, her emotions, even her fears, now squeezed dry – passionless and empty. During the first few minutes she had noticed one of the constables eyeing her figure; but, for once, she experienced complete indifference. What a fool she'd been to think that Morse wouldn't guess! Little or nothing seemed to escape that beautifully lucid mind . . . Yes, he had guessed the truth, though quite how he had seen through her story she couldn't begin to understand. Funny, really. It hadn't been a big lie, at all. Not like the stupid, stupid lies that she and Donald had told at the beginning. Donald! What a non-man he now seemed, sitting there next to her: sullen, silent, contemptible; as hopeless as she, for there was little chance for him, either. The truth would have to come out – all of it. The courts, the newspapers . . . For a moment she managed to feel a fraction of sympathy for him, for it was her fault really, not his. From the day of his appointment she had known, known instinctively, that she could do with him exactly as she wished . . .

The door opened and Lewis came in. 'Will you please come with me, Miss Height?'

She got to her feet slowly and walked up the wooden stairs. The door of the Board Room was closed and she hesitated a few seconds as Lewis opened it and stood aside for her. The burden on her conscience had become intolerable. Yes, it would be relief at last.

* * *

Mrs Seth turned her head as the door behind her opened. The Inspector had just been talking about Studio 2 in Walton Street; but her mind was growing numb and she had hardly been able to follow him. She heard a man's voice say quietly, 'After you, Miss Height.' Monica Height! Dear God, no! It couldn't be. Monica Height and Martin! She'd heard rumours, of course. Everyone must have heard rumours but . . . Monica was sitting in Roope's seat now. Roope's! Had Morse meant Roope and Monica? *Two* people, he'd said . . . But Morse was speaking again.

'Miss Height. I interviewed you early on in the case, and you claimed you had spent the afternoon of Friday, 21st November, with Mr Martin. Is that correct?'

'Yes.' Her voice was almost inaudible.

'And you said that you had spent the afternoon at your own house?'

'Yes.'

'And subsequently you agreed that this was not the truth?'

'Yes.'

'You said that in fact you had spent the afternoon with Mr Martin at Studio 2 in Walton Street?'

'Yes.'

'When I originally questioned you about this, I asked whether, apart from Mr Martin, you had seen anyone you knew in the cinema. Do you remember?'

'Yes, I remember.'

'And your answer was that you had not?'

'Yes; I told you the truth.'

'I then asked you whether you had seen anyone you knew going into the cinema, did I not?'

'Yes.'

'And you said "no".'

'Yes.'

'And you still stick by what you said?'

'Yes.'

'You saw a film called *The Nymphomaniac*?'

'Yes.'

'And you stayed with Mr Martin until the film was finished?'

'We left just a few minutes before it was due to finish.'

'Am I right, Miss Height, in saying that I could have asked

you a different question? A question which might have had a
vital bearing on the murder of Nicholas Quinn?'

'Yes.'

'And that question would not have been "Who did you see
going *into* the cinema?" but "Who did you see coming *out*?" '

'Yes.'

'And you did see somebody?'

'Yes.'

'Could you recognize the person you saw coming out of Studio 2
that day?'

'Yes.'

'And is that person someone known to you?'

'Yes.'

'Is that someone here, in this room, now?'

'Yes.'

'Will you please indicate to us who that person is?'

Monica Height lifted her arm and pointed. It seemed almost
like a magnetic needle pointing to the pole, gradually settling on
to its true bearing. At first Mrs Seth thought that the arm was pointing directly at Morse himself. But that couldn't be. And then she
followed that accusing finger once more, and she couldn't believe
what she saw. Again she traced the line. Again she found the same
direction. Oh no. It *couldn't* be, surely? For Monica's finger was
pointing directly at one man – *the Secretary of the Syndicate.*

Chapter Thirty-one

Lewis (*mirabile dictu*) had not been kept completely in the
dark. It was Lewis who had taken his turn of guard-duty in
watching Roope's house. It was Lewis who had seen Roope
leave that house and walk slowly to the car park at the railway
station. It was Lewis who had traced the paper boy and who had
discovered the address of the person to whom Roope had written
his brief and urgent note. It was Lewis who had summoned Morse
to the station buffet, and who had shared with him the magnified
view of two men seated in the front of a dark-brown Vanden Plas

at the furthest reach of the railway car park. It was Lewis who had arrested Roope as he had ventured forth, for the last time, the previous morning.

But if Lewis had not been kept in the dark, neither had he exactly been thrown up on to the shores of light; and later the same afternoon he was glad of the opportunity to get a few things clear.

'What really put you on to Bartlett, sir?'

Morse sat back expansively in the black-leather chair and told him. 'We learned fairly early on in the case, Lewis, that there was some animosity between Bartlett and Roope; and I kept asking myself why. And very gradually the light dawned: I'd been asking myself the wrong question – a non-question, in fact. There was *no* antagonism between the two at all, although there had to *appear* to be. The two of them were hand in glove over the Al-jamara business, and whatever happened they were anxious for the outside world never to have the slightest suspicion of any collusion between them. It wasn't too difficult, either. Just a bit of feigned needle here and there; sometimes a bit of a row in front of the other Syndics; and above all they had their superb opportunity when the appointment of a successor to Bland cropped up. They had the whole thing planned. It didn't matter much to either of them *who* was appointed; what mattered was that they should disagree, and disagree publicly and vehemently, about the new appointment. So when Bartlett went one way, Roope went the other. It was as simple as that. If Bartlett had been pro-Quinn, Roope would have been anti-Quinn.' A slight frown furrowed Morse's forehead, but was gone almost immediately. 'And it worked beautifully. The rest of the Syndics were openly embarrassed about the hostility between their young colleague, Roope, and their respected Secretary, Bartlett. But that was just as it was meant to be. No one was going to believe that either of them had the slightest thing in common. No one. At first their carefully-nurtured antagonism was merely meant to serve as a cover for the crooked arrangements they made with the emirate; but later on, when Quinn discovered the truth about them, the arrangement was ideal for the removal of Quinn. You see what I mean?'

'Yes, I do,' said Lewis slowly. 'But why on earth did Bartlett, of all people, agree to— '

'I know what you mean. I'm sure that in the normal course of events he would never have been tempted in the slightest to line his own pockets at the expense of the Syndicate. But he had an only child, Richard; a young man who had started off life with quite brilliant promise; who carried the high hopes of a proud mum and a proud dad. And suddenly the whole world collapses round the Bartletts' ears. Richard's been working too hard, expectations are too high, and everything goes wrong. He has a nervous breakdown, and goes into hospital. And when he comes out it is clear to the Bartletts that they've got a terrible problem on their hands. He's sent to specialist after specialist, consultant after consultant – and always the same answer: with a prolonged period of treatment he *might* get well again. You discovered yourself, Lewis, that within the past five years Richard Bartlett has spent some time in the most advanced and expensive psychiatric clinics in Europe: Geneva, Vienna, London, and God knows where else. And this isn't for *free*, remember. It must have cost Bartlett thousands of pounds, and I don't think he'd got that sort of money. His salary's more than adequate, but— Well, Roope must have known all about this and, however it came about, the two of them struck a pact. Originally it had been Bland and Roope, I should think. But Bland decided to go for even richer pickings, and Roope had to have someone *inside* the Syndicate if the goose was still to lay the golden eggs. I don't know exactly how they worked it between them, but— '

'Do you know exactly how Bartlett murdered Quinn, sir?'

'Well, not exactly. But I've a pretty good idea, because it was the *only* way the deception could have been worked. Just think a minute. You get your dose, a pretty hefty dose, of cyanide. Roope sees to that side of things. Now, from an indecently large dose of cyanide death follows almost immediately, so there's little problem about actually *killing* Quinn. I should think that Bartlett called him into his office and suggested a drink together. He knew that Quinn was very fond of sherry and told him to pour himself one – and probably one for Bartlett at the same time. He must have wiped the sherry bottle and the glasses beforehand so that— '

'But wouldn't Quinn have smelled the cyanide?'

'He might have done, in normal circumstances; but Bartlett had timed his actions almost to the second. Everything that morning had been geared with devilish ingenuity to the next few minutes.'

'The fire drill you mean.'

'Yes. Noakes had been instructed to set off the alarm at twelve noon precisely and he'd been told to wait for the word from the boss. So? What happens? As soon as Quinn is pouring the sherries, Bartlett picks up the phone, probably turning his back on Quinn, and says "OK Noakes". And a second or two later the alarm goes. But this is the point, Lewis. *Quinn can't hear the alarm*. The bell is just inside the entrance hall, and although everybody else can hear it perfectly clearly, Quinn can't; and it gives Bartlett just the little leeway he needs. As soon as Quinn has poured the sherries, and only when the time is *exactly* ripe, does he say something like: "The fire alarm! I'd forgotten about that. Toss that back quickly; we can talk afterwards." Quinn must have drained at least half the small glass at a gulp, and almost immediately he must have known that something was desperately wrong. His respiration becomes jerky and he suffers from violently convulsive seizures. In a minute, or at the outside a couple of minutes, he's dead.'

'Why didn't he shout for help, though. Surely—?'

'Ah! I see you still don't appreciate the infinite subtlety of Bartlett's plan. What's happening outside? A fire drill! As you yourself found out, Noakes had been instructed to let the alarm ring for two minutes. Two minutes! That's a long, long time, Lewis, and during it everybody is chattering and clattering down the stairs and along the corridors. Perhaps Bartlett made quite sure that Quinn didn't shout for help; but even if he had managed to shout, I doubt if anyone would have heard him. And remember! *No one is going into Bartlett's office.* The red light has been turned on outside, and none of the staff is going to disobey the golden rule. And even if *everything* had gone wrong, Lewis, even if someone had come in – though I expect Bartlett had locked the door anyway – Quinn's prints are on the bottle and on the glasses, and police inquiries are going to centre on the fundamental question of who had poisoned Bartlett's sherry – presumably with the intention of poisoning *Bartlett*, not Quinn. Anyway, Quinn is dead and *the building is now completely deserted*. Bartlett puts on a pair of gloves, pours his own sherry and whatever is left of Quinn's down the sink in his private little cloakroom – remember it, Lewis? – and locks away the sherry bottle and Quinn's glass in a briefcase. So far so good. Quinn was a fairly slight man and Bartlett may have carried him over his shoulder, or put him into one of the large plastic containers they use there for rubbish and then dragged him along the polished floor. Probably he carried him, since no scratches or abrasions were found on Quinn's body. But whatever he did, it was only a few yards to the rear entrance, and Quinn's parking place was immediately outside the door. Bartlett, who has already taken Quinn's car-key and house-key from his pocket – or from his anorak – dumps the body and the briefcase in the boot, locks it, and the deed is done.'

'We should have examined the boot, I suppose, sir.'

'But I did. There were no traces of Quinn at all. That's why I think Bartlett may have used a container of some sort.'

'Then he goes out to join the rest of the staff— '

Morse nodded ' – standing meekly outside in the cold, yes. He takes over the list, which by this time has been handed round the thirty or so permanent staff, ticks in himself and Quinn as present, and finally decides that all are accounted for.'

'And it was Bartlett who rang the school in Bradford?'

'Certainly. Doubtless he'd been looking out for anything that could be used to help mislead the inevitable investigation, and he must have seen that particular letter in Quinn's tray in the registry earlier that week. If you remember, it was postmarked Monday, 17th November.'

'Then he went home and had a hearty lunch.'

'I doubt it,' said Morse. 'Bartlett's a very clever man, but basically he's not as ruthless as someone like Roope. Anyway, he's still got a lot on his mind. Certainly the trickier half of the plan is over, but he hasn't finished yet. He must have left home at about ten-past one, telling his wife – perfectly correctly – that he had to call in at the office before going off to his meeting in Banbury. But before he did that— '

'He called in at Studio 2.'

'Yes. Bartlett bought a ticket, had it torn through, asked the usherette where the "Gents" was, waited there a few minutes, and then nipped out when the girl in the ticket office was busy with one or two more clients. But after that things began to go awry. Not that Bartlett saw Monica Height – I'm pretty sure of that. But she saw him, coming *out* of Studio 2. Monica and Donald Martin, remember want to spend the afternoon together. They can't go to her place, because her daughter's home from school; they can't

go to his, because his wife's there all the time; they can go somewhere in the car, but that's hardly a romantic proposition on a
rainy November afternoon. So they decide to go to the pictures.
But they mustn't be seen going in together; so Martin gets there
fairly early, soon after the doors open, and buys a ticket for the
rear lounge and sits there waiting. Monica's due to come a few
minutes later, and he's straining his eyes and watching *everybody*
who comes in. Now get this clear in your mind, Lewis. If Quinn
had gone into Studio 2 that afternoon, Martin would certainly have
seen him. He'd have seen Bartlett, too. And if he'd seen either of
them, *he wouldn't have stayed*. He'd have left immediately, waited
discreetly outside for Monica, and told her the bad news. But he
did no such thing! Now, put yourself in Monica's shoes. When we
questioned her – and Martin – one thing became quite clear: *they'd
seen the film*; and they certainly wouldn't have done that if any
other member of the Syndicate had come *in*. There was only one
explanation: Monica had seen something that, in the light of what
she learned later, troubled her sorely. Yet whatever it was, it had
not prevented her from joining Martin inside the cinema, all right?
We can only draw one conclusion: she saw someone coming *out*.
And that someone was Bartlett! He goes back to the Syndicate and
he's got a ticket. But where is he to leave it? He could leave it
in Quinn's room, because he's got to go in there anyway to leave
the note for Margaret Freeman, and to open the cabinets. Bit careless of Bartlett that, when you come to think of it . . . ' Morse
shook his head as if a fly had alighted on his balding patch. But
whatever was troubling him, he let it go. 'Just remember that all
this had to be planned meticulously in advance, and from this point
onwards things had to be arranged to meet Roope's convenience,
not Bartlett's. Roope has dutifully fixed himself up with a water-
tight alibi until late afternoon, but now he needs some plausible
reason for visiting the Syndicate. He couldn't know – nor could
Bartlett – that not one of the graduate staff would be there; so it's
arranged that he will leave some papers in Bartlett's office. You
see, if anyone else is around, he hasn't got much excuse poking
around in *Quinn's* office. He'll have to go there later, of course,
to get the anorak; but by then he'll have been able to see the lie of
the land and he can play things by ear. So they've decided between
them that the cinema ticket and Quinn's keys are to be left somewhere carefully concealed on Bartlett's desk or in one of his

drawers. Well? What happened then? Roope knocks on Bartlett's door, gets no answer, goes in quickly, leaves his papers, and picks up the ticket and the keys. Easy. Originally the plan must have been for him to hang around somewhere, probably by the trees at the back, until the rest of the graduate staff went home. Then he would only have to nip in the back entrance, pick up the anorak from Quinn's office, and drive off in Quinn's car. But in fact it was easier than he could have hoped. Noakes, it's true, was an unforeseen problem, but as things turned out this helped him enormously. Noakes was able to confirm that *none of the graduate staff was in his office that afternoon.* And when he told Roope that he was off upstairs for a cup of tea, the coast was clear – half an hour or so earlier than he'd expected it to be.'

'And from then onwards it must have gone very much as you said before.'

'Except for one thing. I suggested to Roope when we first brought him in that he'd pocketed the note from Quinn's desk; but I don't think he could have done. Otherwise I can think of no earthly reason why he had to phone Bartlett when he discovered the shattering information that Mrs Evans was going to return. It was the worst moment of the lot, I should think, and Roope almost panicked. The rain was sluicing down outside, and he couldn't just dump the body and run for it. Mrs Greenaway – he must have seen her – was sitting in full view in the room upstairs with the curtains open, and there was only one way for Quinn's body to be carted out, and that was by the front door of the garage. There was nothing to do but to wait; but he couldn't wait *there.* He must have been feeling desperate when he rang up Bartlett; but Bartlett came up with the masterstroke – the note on Quinn's desk! It was a wonderful piece of luck but, my God!, they needed some luck at that stage. Bartlett had only just got back from Banbury, but he drove off again almost immediately, called in at the Syndicate for the note, and met Roope as arranged at the shopping area behind Pinewood Close, where Roope had already bought the groceries. I suppose it must have taken Bartlett at least twenty minutes, but time was still on their side – just. Roope got back to Quinn's, took off his muddy boots, left the note – and went out again. He must have got wet through; but imagine his immense relief, as he watched and waited, first to see Mrs Evans come and go, and then, almost miraculously, an ambulance draw up and take

Mrs Greenaway off to the maternity hospital. The house was in darkness then; no one was about; the street lamp was broken; the curtain could go up on the last act. He carries Quinn's body to the back door and into the house, puts it on the carpet by the chair in the living-room, arranges the sherry bottle and the glass on the coffee table, lights the fire – and Bob's your uncle. He walks over the back field again, and catches a bus down to Oxford.'

Lewis reflected. Yes, that's how it must have happened all right, but one thing still puzzled him mightily: 'What about Ogleby? Where does he fit in?'

'As I've told you, Lewis, a good deal of what Ogleby told us was true, and I think he was virtually certain that Bartlett had killed Quinn long before I ever— '

'Why did he keep it all to himself, though?'

'I dunno. I suppose he must have been trying to prove something to himself before— '

'It doesn't sound very convincing, sir.'

'No, perhaps not.' Morse stared out on to the yard and once again wondered why on earth Ogleby . . . Mm. There were still one or two loose ends that wouldn't quite tie in. Nothing vital, though – and Lewis interrupted his thoughts.

'Ogleby must have been a clever fellow, sir.'

'Oh, I don't know. Remember he had a couple of leagues' start on me.'

'How do you mean, sir?'

'How many times do I have to tell you? *He was in the office that afternoon.*'

'Must have been upstairs, then, because— '

'No. That's where you're wrong. He must have been *downstairs*. And what's more we know exactly where he was and when he was there. He must have realized when he finally got back from lunch that he was the only one of the graduates in the office, and that this was as good a chance as he was going to get to poke around in Bartlett's room. Whether Quinn had told him that he suspected Bartlett *and* Roope, or just Bartlett – we can't know for certain. But he's got cause to suspect Bartlett, and he decides to do a bit of investigation. No one is going to come in, because no one's there. At about 4.30 he hears voices outside – Roope's and Noakes' – and he doesn't want to get caught. Where's the obvious place for him to hide, Lewis? In the small cloakroom just behind Bartlett's desk, where I went the first afternoon we went to the office. Ideal! He just stands inside and waits; and he doesn't have to wait long. But what does Ogleby find when he emerges from the cloakroom? He discovers that the cinema ticket and the keys which he'd found earlier have gone! His thoughts must have been in a complete whirl, and he daren't leave Bartlett's office. He hears Noakes in the corridor outside, and later he hears someone walking about, and a few doors opening and slamming to. And still he has to stay where he is. Anyway, he finally satisfies himself that it's safe to come out, and the first thing he notices is that Quinn's car has gone! Perhaps he looks into Quinn's room, I don't know. Has Quinn come in? And gone out again? I don't know how much of the truth he suspected at that point – not much, perhaps; but he knows that Roope has taken some keys and a mysterious cinema ticket, a ticket which he has carefully copied into his diary. It's his one piece of real evidence, and he does what I did. He rang Studio 2, and tried to find out— '

'But he couldn't. So he went along himself.'

Morse nodded. 'And found nothing, poor blighter, except one thing: that in all probability the ticket he'd found must have been bought *that very afternoon*.'

'Funny, isn't it, sir? They were *all* there that afternoon.'

'All except Quinn,' corrected Morse sombrely. 'Have you got your car here?'

'Where are we going, sir?'

'I think we'd better follow in Ogleby's footsteps, and have a look around in Bartlett's office.'

As Lewis drove him for the last time to the Syndicate building, Morse allowed his mind to come to tentative grips with the one or two slight inconsistencies (very slight, he told himself) that still remained. People did odd things on occasions; you could hardly expect a smoothly logical motive behind *every* action, could you? The machine was in good working order now, there was no doubt of that, the cogs fitting neatly and biting powerfully. Just a bit of grit in the works somewhere. Only a little bit, though . . .

In Cell No 2, the little Secretary sat on the bare bed, his mind, like Yeats's long-legged fly, floating on silence.

WHO?

Chapter Thirty-two

The Syndicate building had been locked up, and all the staff informed to stay away until further notice. Only Noakes was performing his wonted duties, and was on hand to let the two policemen in.

Seated at Bartlett's desk, Morse amused himself by switching the red and green lights on and off. He seemed like a little lad with a new toy, and it was clear to Lewis that as usual he would have to do the donkey-work himself.

It was over half an hour later, after Lewis had methodically gone through the safe (and found nothing of interest) that Morse, who had hitherto been staring vacantly round the room, finally condescended to bestir himself. The top right-hand drawer of Bartlett's desk had little to offer but neatly-stacked piles of office notepaper, and Morse idly abstracted a sheet and surveyed the decimated graduate team:

T. G. Bartlett, PhD, MA Secretary
P. Ogleby, MA Deputy Secretary
G. Bland, MA
Miss M. M. Height, MA
D. J. Martin, BA

Mm. The typists had been instructed to strike through Bland's name, and print in Quinn's at the bottom. But that wouldn't be necessary any longer. Just strike through the top three; much quicker . . . And then there were two . . . Would Miss Height be asked to take over? Advertise for new personnel? Or would the Syndicate just fold up? God knew that Donald Martin wasn't

578

going to make much of a Deputy if it were to carry on. What a wet he was! And God help the young men they might appoint if Monica twitched her bewitching backside at 'em! Morse took out his Parker pen and slowly crossed through the names: Dr Bartlett; Philip Ogleby; George Bland. Yes, just the two of them left – and now they could fornicate for a few months to their hearts' content. A few months! Huh! That's all Quinn had been there; not even long enough to get his name printed on the notepaper. Nicholas Quinn . . . Morse thought back for a few moments to the lip-reading class he'd attended. Would Quinn have been able to cope at the office if his hearing had failed him completely? No, perhaps not. Lip-reading might be a wonderful thing, but even the teacher of the class had made a mistake, hadn't she? When he'd asked her . . .

Morse froze where he sat, and the blood seemed to surge away from his arms and from his shoulders, leaving the top of his body numbed and tingling. Oh God – no! No! Surely not! Oh Christ, oh Blessed Virgin Mary, oh all the Saints and all the Angels – no! His hand was shaking as he wrote out the two names on the notepaper, and he found it impossible to keep his voice steady.

'Lewis! Drop whatever you're doing. Go and stand over by the door and take this notepaper with you.'

A puzzled Lewis did as he was told. 'What now, sir?'

'I want you to read those two names to me – just using your lips. Don't whisper them. Just mouth them, if you know what I mean.'

Lewis did his best.

'Again,' said Morse, and Lewis complied.

'And again . . . and again . . . and again . . . and again.' Morse nodded and nodded and nodded and nodded, and there was a vibrant excitement in his voice as he spoke again. 'Get your coat, Lewis. We've finished here.'

She would say nothing at all for a start, but Morse was merciless. 'Did *you* clean the blood off?' (He'd asked the question a dozen times already.) 'My God, you must be blind if you can't see what's been happening. How many other women has he had? Who was he with last night? Don't you know? Have you never suspected? Did *you* clean the blood off? Did you? Or did he? Don't you understand? – I've got to know. Did *you* clean it off? *I've got to know.*'

Suddenly she broke down completely and burst into bitter, hysterical tears. 'He said – there'd been – an accident. And he – he said he'd – tried – tried to help – until – the ambulance came. It was – it was in – in the Broad – just opposite – opposite Blackwells – and— '

The door opened and a man came in. 'What the *hell*?' His voice had the lash of a whip, and his eyes shone with a primitive, blazing madness. 'What's that fucking man Roope been telling you, you snooping bastard?' He advanced on Morse, and lashed out wildly, whilst Mrs Martin rushed from the room with a piercing scream.

'You should get yourself into better shape, Morse. You're pretty flabby, you know.'

'It's the beer,' mumbled Morse. 'Ouch!'

'That's the last one. See me in a week's time, and we'll take 'em out. You're all right.'

'Bloody good job I had Lewis with me! Otherwise you'd have had another corpse.'

'Good, was he?'

Morse smiled crookedly and nodded. 'Christ, you should have seen him, doc!'

In Morse's office the next morning it was Lewis's turn to grin. 'Must be a bit tricky talking, sir – with all those stitches round your mouth.'

'Mm.'

'Well? Tell me, then.'

'What do you want to know?'

'What finally put you on to Martin?'

'Well, it's what I said before, though I didn't really have a clue what I was talking about. I told you the key to this case lay in the fact that Quinn was deaf. And so it was. But I kept on thinking what a marvel he must have become at lip-reading, and I overlooked the most obvious thing of all: that even the best lip-reader in the world is sometimes going to make a few mistakes; and Quinn did just that. He saw Roope talking to the sheik, and *he read a name wrongly on his lips*. I learned from the lip-reading class that the commonest difficulty for the deaf is between the consonants "p", "b" and "m", and if you mouth the words "Bartlett" and "Martin", there's very little difference on the lips. The "B" and the "M" are absolutely identical, and the second part of each of the names gets swallowed up in the mouth somewhere. But that's not all. It was *Doctor* Bartlett, and *Donald* Martin. Just try them again. *Very* little difference to see; and if you put the two names together, there's every excuse for a deaf person mixing them up. You see, Roope would never have called the Secretary "Tom", would he? He'd never been on Christian name terms with him, and he never would be. He'd have called him "Bartlett" or "*Doctor* Bartlett". And the sheik would almost certainly have given him his full title. But Martin – well, he was one of them; one of the boys. He was *Donald* Martin.'

'Bit of a jump in the dark, if you ask me.'

'No, it wasn't. Not really. There were one or two loose ends that somehow refused to tuck themselves away, and I had an uneasy feeling that I might have got it all wrong. As you yourself said, it was so much out of character. Bartlett's spent so much of his life building up the work of the Syndicate that it's very difficult to see him stooping to the sort of corruption we've got in this case – let alone murder. But I still couldn't see in what other direction the facts were pointing. Not, that is, until I suddenly saw the light as we sat in Bartlett's office, and then all the loose ends seemed to tidy themselves up automatically. Just think. Quinn discovered – or so he believed – that Bartlett was crooked, and he rang him up. Rang him up, Lewis! You can guess how Quinn dreaded ringing *anyone* up. The fact of the matter was that he couldn't face Bartlett with it any other way, because *he just couldn't believe that he was guilty.*'

'Did Quinn tell Bartlett that he suspected Roope as well?'

'I should think so. Quinn must have been a man remarkably free from any deception, and he probably told both Bartlett and Roope everything he suspected.'

'But why didn't Bartlett do something about it?'

'He must have thought that Quinn had got everything cockeyed, mustn't he? Quinn was accusing him – the Secretary! – of swindling the Syndicate; and if Quinn was totally wrong about himself, why should he think that Quinn was right about Roope?'

Lewis shook his head slowly. 'All a bit thin, if you ask me, sir.'

'In itself, yes. But let's turn to Monica Height. How on earth are we to account for the bundle of lies she was prepared to tell? It's fairly easy now to see why Martin must have been happy to agree to the lies they cooked up together after Monica told him she'd seen Bartlett coming out of the cinema. In fact I should think that he almost certainly instigated them himself, because it was going to suit his book very well not to have himself associated with Studio 2 in any way. And later, after Monica learned that Quinn himself might have been in Studio 2 that same afternoon she immediately realized that things would look pretty black for Bartlett if she said anything about seeing him there. And so she continued to conceal the truth. Why, Lewis? For the very same reason that Quinn couldn't face Bartlett: *because she just couldn't believe that he was guilty.*'

Lewis nodded. Perhaps it was all adding up sightly better now.

'And above all,' continued Morse, 'there was Ogleby. He worried me the most, Lewis, and you made the key point yourself: why didn't he tell me what he knew? I think there are two possible reasons. First, that Ogleby was quite prepared to go it alone – he was always a loner, it seems. He knew he hadn't long to live anyway, and it may have added that extra bit of mustard to his life to carry out a single-handed investigation into the quite extraordinary situation he'd stumbled across. It couldn't have mattered much to him that he might be living dangerously – he was living dangerously in any case. But that's as may be. I feel sure there was a second reason, and a much more compelling one. He'd discovered what looked like extremely damning evidence against Bartlett – a man he'd known and worked with for fourteen years – *and he just couldn't believe that he was guilty.* And he was determined to say nothing which could lead us to suspect him – not until he could prove it, anyway.'

'But he didn't get the chance— '

'No,' said Morse quietly. He leaned back in his chair and gently rubbed his swollen lip. 'Anything else while we're at it, my son?'

Lewis thought back over the whole complex case and realized that he hadn't quite got it straight in his mind, even now. 'It was *Martin*, then, who did all the things you accused Bartlett of?'

'Indeed it was. And *more*. Martin killed Quinn at exactly the same time and in almost exactly the same way. The deed was done in Martin's office, and Martin had exactly the same opportunity as Bartlett would have had. Admittedly, he was taking a slightly bigger risk, but he'd planned the whole thing – at least up to this point – with meticulous care. You see, the main plot must have been hatched up immediately after Bartlett had announced the fire drill for Friday. But the Syndicate staff only received that notice on the Monday, and there wasn't *all* that much time; and in the event they had to improvise a bit as the situation developed. On the whole I suppose they made the best of the opportunities that arose, but they tried to be a bit too clever – especially about the Studio 2 business, which landed them both in a hell of a lot of unnecessary trouble.'

'Don't get cross with me, sir, but can you just go over that again. I still— '

'I don't think Studio 2 figured in the original plan at all – though I may be wrong, of course. The original idea must have been to try to persuade any caller at Quinn's office that he was there or thereabouts during that Friday afternoon. It was all a bit clumsy, but just about passable – the note to his typist, the anorak, the filing cabinet, and so on. Now, I'd guess that Martin's nerves must have been pretty near breaking-point after he'd killed Quinn, and he must have breathed a huge sigh of relief when he managed to persuade Monica to spend the afternoon with him: the fewer people in the office that afternoon the better, and being with Monica gave him a reasonable alibi if things didn't go according to plan. As I say, I don't think that at this stage there was the remotest intention of planting the torn half of a cinema ticket on Quinn's body. But remember what happened. Martin and Monica decided to lie about going to the cinema; and Martin himself gradually began to take stock of the situation. He must have realized that the elaborate attempt to convince everyone that Quinn was alive and well at the Syndicate was pretty futile. No one's there to be convinced. Bartlett's not there – he knows that; he himself and Monica are not there, either; Quinn is dead; and Ogleby is out lunching with the OUP people and may not go back to the office at all. So. He gets his brainwave: he'll get Roope to put the cinema ticket in one of Quinn's pockets.'

'But when—?'

'Just a minute. After leaving the cinema – by the way, Martin lied to me there, and I ought to have noticed it earlier. He tried to stretch his alibi by saying he left at a quarter-to four; but as we

know from Monica they both left just before the film was due to
end – at about a quarter-past three. Obviously they'd want to get
out before the general exodus – less risk of being seen. Anyway,
after leaving the cinema, they went their separate ways: Monica
went home; and so did Martin, except that on his way he called
in at the Syndicate, at about 3.20, found no one about – not even
Ogleby – and he left his own cinema ticket in Bartlett's room for
Roope to pick up.'

'But Roope wouldn't have known—?'

'Give me a chance, Lewis. Martin must have written a very
brief note – "Stick this in his pocket", or something like that –
and put it with the ticket and the keys. Then, about ten minutes
later, Ogleby got back, found everyone else out, and decided that
this was as good an opportunity as he'd get of poking around in
Bartlett's room; and he was so puzzled by what he found there
that he copied out the cinema ticket into his diary.'

'And then Martin went home, I suppose.'

Morse nodded. 'And made sure, I should think, that somebody
saw him, especially during the vital period between 4.30 and
5 o'clock, when he knew that Roope was performing *his* part in the
crime. He must have thought he could relax a bit; but then Roope
rang him up from Quinn's house at just after 5 o'clock with the
shattering news that Quinn's charlady— Well, you know the rest.'

Lewis let it all sink in, and he finally seemed to see the whole
pattern clearly. Almost the whole pattern. 'What about the paper
boy? Did Roope send him with a letter to Bartlett just— '

' – just to make things difficult for Bartlett, yes. Roope must
have said he wanted to have an urgent talk with him about police
suspicions – or something like that. Roope knew, of course, that
we were watching him like a hawk, and so he walked slowly down
to the railway station and let us follow him.'

'You haven't talked to Bartlett about that?'

'Not yet. After we'd let him go, I thought we ought to give
him a bit of a breather, poor fellow. He's had a rough time.'

Lewis hesitated. 'There *is* just one more thing, sir.'

'Yes?'

'Bartlett will have *something* to explain away, won't he? I
mean he *did* go to Studio 2.'

Morse smiled as widely as his swollen mouth would allow him.
'I reckon I can answer that one for you. Bartlett's as human as

the rest of us, and perhaps it's a long time since he's seen the likes of Inga Nielsson unbuttoning her blouse. The film started at 1.30, and since he didn't need to leave for Banbury until about 2.30, he decided to be a dirty old man for an hour or so. But don't blame him, Lewis! Do you hear me? Don't blame him. He must have gone in immediately the doors opened, sat there in the rear lounge, and then, as his eyes accustomed themselves to the darkness, *he saw Martin come in*. But Martin didn't see *him*; and Bartlett did what anyone in his position would do – he got out, quick.'

'And that's when Monica saw him?'

'That's it.'

'So he didn't see the film after all?'

Morse shook his head sadly. 'And if you've got any more questions, leave 'em till tomorrow. I've got a treat for you tonight.'

'But I promised the wife— '

Morse pushed the phone over. 'Tell her you'll be a bit late.'

They sat side by side in a fairly crowded gathering, with only the green 'Exit' lights shining up brightly in the gloom. Morse had bought the tickets himself – rear lounge: after all, it was something of a celebration.

'Christ, look at those!' whispered Morse, as the camera moved in on the buxom blonde beauty, her breasts almost toppling out over the low-cut closely-clinging gown.

'Take it off!' shouted a voice from somewhere near the front, and the predominantly male audience sniggered sympathetically, whilst Morse settled himself comfortably in his seat and prepared to gratify his baser instincts. And with only token reluctance, Lewis prepared to do the same.

Epilogue

The Syndicate was forced to close down as soon as the Autumn examination results had been issued, and its oversea centres were parcelled out amongst the other GCE Boards. The building itself has been taken over by a department of HM Inspectorate of Taxes, and today female clerks clack up and down its polished corridors, and talk of girlish things in the rooms where once the little Secretary and his graduate staff administered their examinations.

From her considerable private income, Mrs Bartlett bought a farm in Hampshire, where Richard at last found a life which served to soothe his troubled mind, and where his father's eyes were occasionally seen to blink almost boyishly again behind the rimless spectacles.

Until Sally had completed her undistinguished school career, Miss Height stayed in Oxford, taking on some part-time teaching. Several times in the months that followed the conviction of the Syndicate murderers, she had found her way to the Horse and Trumpet – just for old time's sake, she told herself. How dearly she would have loved to see him again! She owed him a drink, anyway, and she wanted to square the account; to make up for things, as it were. But much as she had willed it, she had never found him there.

More than sufficient evidence was found to justify the immediate disqualification of Master Muhammad Dubal from all his Autumn O-level examinations; and six weeks later his father, the sheik, was listed among the 'missing' after a 'bloodless' coup within the emirate.

George Bland, though reported to have been seen in various eastern capitals, remains unpunished still; yet perhaps no criminal can live without some little share of justice.

No 1 Pinewood Close is tenanted again, both upstairs and down; and Mrs Jardine is thinking of buying herself a new outfit. As she'd expected, it had been no more than a few weeks before the notoriety had died down. Life was like that, as she had known.

Just after Christmas, at a christening in East Oxford, the minister dipped a delicate finger into the font, and in the name of the Holy Trinity enlisted his little charge in the myriad ranks of the great Church Militant. But the water was icy cold and Master Nicholas John Greenaway squawked stentoriously. In the end, the name had been Frank's choice: it had sort of grown on him, he said. But as Joyce took the baby in her arms and lovingly there-thered his raucous cries, her mind ranged back to the day when Nicholas, her son, was born, and when another man called Nicholas had died.